The Long Trail

The Long Trail

Book Three
of
T. H.Bear's Trilogy:

The Owl Hoot Trail

The contents of this book regarding the accuracy of events, people, and places depicted; permissions to use all previously published materials; opinions expressed; all are the sole responsibility of the author, who assumes all liability for the contents of this book and indemnifies the publisher against any claims stemming from publication of this book.

International Standard Book Number 13: 978-1-60452-089-7
International Standard Book Number 10: 1-60452-089-2

Library of Congress Control Number: 2014902027

BluewaterPress LLC
52 Tuscan Way Ste 202-309
Saint Augustine Florida 32092
http://bluewaterpress.com

This book may be purchased online at -
http://bluewaterpress.com/longtrail

This last book of the trilogy I dedicate to Ardis and Joe Clark
Who have spent so much of their personal time
helping me to get this story in print.

Acknowledgements

It would be a foolish thing and an insult to the reader's intelligence to say that this is wholly a piece of fiction, and all the characters are from my imagination. History has given us a Governor Rufus Bullock of Georgia, George Armstrong Custer and his defeat in June of 1876, as well as the War Chief Gall, and the Lakota Medicine Man, Sitting Bull. The scout, Luther Kelly, and the Stage Stop operator, McAndow, as well as Perry W. McAdow who owned both a saloon and a hotel in the early days of Coulson, Montana. I could go on, but the point is, I try to integrate actual history as well as the characters that lived during the times of this story, whenever possible. However, as in Books One and Two of this trilogy, the main characters are purely images cultivated from my imagination, and with the exception of what is recorded above, so are the incidents from my imagination.

Appreciation

Most of the illustrations contained in this book are taken from my personal photos. However, a few are from The State of Wyoming, Division of State Parks and Division of Cultural Resources, State Archives, and it is with a thankful heart I acknowledge these great folks who go out of their way in assisting when called upon.

The photograph on the rear cover I took myself a few years back while doing research for this story. It is of the ridge where Copperopolis once stood, about a mile from the copper mines, a truly beautiful part of our great land.

My appreciation goes out to Jim Gillis in his assistance with the editing of this book, as well as to Agnes Brewer for her sketch of John Tidwell, and to the good folks at the Poplar Bluff Library who copied some of their historical photographs of Butler County from the days after the war, for me to use in this publication.

I have said before and I say again, there is a need to relate something most important in making any novel complete. I believe any work of literature has different purposes to different people. Some read to kill time, a simple means to occupy one's mind for a few hours. Others read to learn and these often hunger for education. Then you find those who read for the pure and genuine pleasure of the tale, my favorite readers.

However, I have also learned as well, there are those whose greatest enjoyment in reading a manuscript is to find fault, usually in spelling and grammar. These people tend to be English majors or masters of the perfect sentence. This last group used to be a thorn in my side but not any longer. I now purposely leave a few words misspelled and a few sentences grammatically incorrect. On occasion, I will even write less than the perfect paragraph, just so these readers will find something gratifying in my work. So, when you come upon a misspelled word or a comma where a period should be, or even that less than perfect paragraph, just smile and continue, knowing it was intentionally left uncorrected to please the Grammar Troopers. This way, I hope all who read my work find something in the story that brings them pleasure.

I do a great deal of research finding what was politically correct at the time and place of the story, and really don't give consideration to what is politically correct today. The jargon of the twenty-first century would have been completely out of place in the Deep South as well as the Western Plains of the 1870's, and that is when and where this story takes place.

Introduction

The reader found in *Gold in the Red Desert*, the first of the trilogy of *The Owl Hoot Trail*, Clifford 'Reb' Brown had fled his home state of Georgia ahead of a warrant for a murder that had actually been committed by a corrupt appointed official.

His travels allowed him to be in the right place at the right time, to witness another murder, also by corrupt men in power, although this killing took place on the great plains of Wyoming Territory in the Year of Our Lord 1869.

During the following year, he is the one person mainly responsible for the righting of this wrong and the returning of stolen property to its rightful owner. There, also he falls in love with a beautiful woman, Nadine, who became his wife.

The second book of the trilogy is entitled *The Withlacoochee Renegades*. It is the story of Cliff's and Nadine's return to Georgia during times many considered more horrible than the war itself, the unholy Reconstruction Period, a time when Corruption overcame Christianity in the Occupational Government.

A telegram had been received telling of the murder of his older brother and the threat of the same to his father and younger brother. Clifford Brown and his bride arrive to find the worst, and not only to his family, but to almost all of 'the home folk'. In short order, he forms a vigilante group that a local newspaper dubs, "The Withlacoochee Renegades", and leads them until most of the corruption is cleaned from the area, and many of those responsible for their cruel deeds are either dead, arrested, or have fled the state. The cost of this cleaning is so great one wonders where a man finds the strength to bear it.

When the very carpetbagger who had falsely accused him of the murder, which caused him to flee Georgia in the first place, kills members of his family before he himself flees the state, we find Reb Brown setting out on an almost impossible journey after this murderer. In the third and final book, *The Long Trail,* we ride with Reb as he experiences many hardships and disappointments. Yet, with a bulldog grip on his responsibility, he endures mile after mile, year after year, in pursuit, missing by shear minutes and at times, yards rather than miles, until he and the carpetbagger finally cross paths resulting in a most unexpected experience.

I want to do something here perhaps better writers will say is unnecessary, but I feel the need. Recently, I was talking with one of my readers discussing his take on *Gold In The Red Desert*, and since this man hailed from Illinois, I made the comment that it is true I am a Johnny Reb myself through and through. He chuckled slightly, but friendly, and admitted he had surmised that.

It is also true this story's hero is a former Confederate soldier who has strong feelings for the cause for which he fought. However, I want you to know that in no way did I write this as a means to wave the Battle Flag. This trilogy is to give the twenty-first century reader a look at the times in the post war days from a southerner's viewpoint.

I have studied hard and long and am convinced the attitudes expressed herein are as close as possible to what one would experience, were he to suddenly find himself in those couple of decades after that awful conflict.

History does reveal, to those who take the time to seek it out, that the Southerner was persecuted deeply in his homelands, as well as having to endure excessive prejudices when he went west.

Do not be deceived, this is not a cry for sympathy, rather a point of fact that I tried to expose in the story.

Many of my closest friends, both male and female, have been Yankees, some quite proud of the fact and others not. We are all Americans, and were so then, as now.

Another area I would like to say a thing or two about is in the spelling or perhaps better expressed, the pronunciation, of certain words. I have, through research and study, as well as my own observations, tried to give the correct jargon of both the time and location where the story takes place.

An example of what I'm getting at is the word 'maybe'. I have learned that this was, as so many words were, and still are, pronounced differently depending on where one learned to talk. Most of the northeast and central US pronounced this as it is correctly spelled. However in the drawl of the Deep South, it would be pronounced as 'mee'be' and yet in the southwest, from Texas on to the Pacific Coast, where the Mexican version of the Spanish language was influential, it was pronounced 'me'bee'. Thus the reader often can tell where the character hails from, by the way they talk. Texans would say 'ootfit' rather than 'outfit' and so on. Sir, verses Sur, and many other words will reveal the background of the speaker. Another thing, in Dixie the title 'Sur' is one of great respect and is always capitalized, where in other areas it is usually offered as a small letter, as in 'sir'.

I hope this little tidbit will be of some use to you, as well as perhaps some humor.

The Owl Hoot Trail

Book III

The Long Trail

Preface

Those of us who have ridden The Owl Hoot Trail with Reb know him well, though he has surprised us at times; nonetheless, he has always been steadfast in determination. A man considered quite charming and handsome by the ladies, however to the men who have crossed his path run deeper considerations, certainly that of respect, perhaps stained with a bit of fear; a complex man for sure and certain.

I, for one, when attempting to expose my inner feelings, find simply I want to convey he is a man I feel deep emotions for and want to admit he has become a true and trusted friend. So it is with admiration, I take pen and paper and attempt to bring to those who are meeting him for the first time, a short history of who he is and the streams of his life that have brought him to us at this time.

It was a frosty February morning only minutes past the midnight hour in The Year of Our Lord 1843, some ten miles north of the Florida state line; Clifford James 'Reb' Brown was born. The second of three sons that blessed the home of Louis and Addie Brown, in a time and place where the Creek Indians out numbered the Euro Americans two to one.

His mother was a hard-shell Campbellite[1] totally devoted to her husband and holding none before him, save her Lord Jesus Christ.

---

1 Campbellite: Followers of Alexander Campbell, who broke away from the Baptist Church claiming to be the restorers of "Primitive Christianity". Campbell was disenchanted with the Baptists introducing instrumental music like the Catholics and Methodist had, as well as other new doctrines.

Louis Brown, a transplanted Kentuckian, was a lumberman by trade, standing some six-foot-three inches and carrying a body as strong as an ox. A hard working, God fearing man, who had without hesitation laid down his axe and lifted his musket to fight with General Scott against the Red Stick Creeks, then again by enlisting in the Navy of those United States when the war with Mexico was thrust upon the citizens. He was the builder and owner of more than one sawmill whose cut cypress were largely responsible for the building of the little burg of Troupville, Georgia and later much of the railroad stop that became known as Valdosta.

It was from within and under the umbrella of such parents, Reb spent his young life. He was privileged to be educated, above what most South Georgia men were, by having the honor to study at Cumberland University in Middle Tennessee. He was bright, determined, and handsome, yet were we to ask what he himself considered his better qualities to be, he would, without hesitation reply honesty, courtesy, and dependability.

When his home state seceded, he never doubted or questioned the why there of, for politics played not in his thoughts. Later, when war broke out, he immediately enlisted, not because he owned slaves for he owned none, not because his father owned slaves for he neither owned any; in fact the subject of slavery never entered his mind, rather his state called for its sons, and Reb Brown was a true son of Georgia.

For almost three years he served in the Army of The Tennessee until finally being captured north of Franklin in the late winter of 1864. He spent the last months of The War for Southern Independence in Maryland's infamous Point Lookout Prison.

Most knew him by Reb, not because he rode with Nathan Bedford Forrest in the Rebel Army, rather because it had been his nickname since childhood.

After returning from that awful war he found everything he owned gone, and everything his family owned in the hands of the invaders. Although penniless, his greatest riches had not been, and could never be taken from him. With this pride, and the fierce loyalty he gave to honesty and honor, he took a job at the very sawmill his father had built, though it was then controlled by a corrupt politician and operated by a Freedman.

Unfortunately, soon thereafter this led to a murder of which Reb was falsely accused. This launched him on The Owl Hoot Trail and eventually onto the high plains of Wyoming's Red Desert during the gold rush.

There he lived for more than a year trying to right a wrong he had witnessed and struggling to fulfill a promise he had made to a dying man.

It was there in South Pass City he found a love that would never slip from his heart for the remainder of his life, and when he returned to Georgia, he brought his beloved Nadine with him.

Their journey south had not been by choice; rather because of a desperate plea from his mother sent those two thousand miles by wire, a beckoning with disturbing news of death and fear.

The newly wed couple arrived to discover the murder of his two brothers, and a father whose mind no longer served him faithfully. Further, the very man who had been responsible for his fleeing to begin with, was now even more powerful, and the very venom of the local corruption.

However, this time Reb Brown refused to be bullied, refused to be a subject, refused to flee, thus soon thereafter he organized a band of homefolk into a cunning and fearful vigilante group that even the occupying forces often found too much to deal with.

Unfortunately, just as victory was within his grip, his old foe stole from him his most precious jewel, and once again he was launched from his homeland in a desperate pursuit of this almost mythical vermin.

We come upon Clifford 'Reb' Brown as he prepares for his mission of finding and putting to death John M. Tidwell, the very man who had taken so much from him, before the New Englander was himself forced to flee South Georgia.

Our final book begins at Estherbrook Stage Stop where we find Reb getting ready for his journey. A mission of determination which will once again take him west in a seven year pursuit filled with adventure, disappointment, loves, and losses.

The Long Trail begins with wonderment and questions as to whether he or the dark one will ultimately win.

Chapter One

The Turning of the Earth

Cliff had done all he could do here. He had buried his wife, made out the necessary paperwork to have his land put into Sam and Esther Brooks' name, and after seeing each of his men had what they would need to defend and feed their families, sold all but a few of the weapons and ammunition back to John Inglis.

He took his old converted Colt, because he felt too much of himself belonged to that assembly of machined steel. He also took his Winchester Yellowboy, the Smith & Wesson he liked to carry in his cross-draw holster while riding and two of the new Open Top Colts for his pommel holsters that Nadine had engaged a local leather-smith to make for him. For some reason he did not understand himself, for he surely did not need them, he took an extra brace of the new Colts and placed them in his saddlebags.

He kept five hundred rounds of 44 Henry cartridges to balance the load and left the remainder with Sam with instructions to ship to him, should he wire for them.

His dear friend Sam Brooks had gone to New Orleans the previous month for the express purpose of purchasing extra draft horses for Estherbrook Stage Stop, while there he had come upon a strange looking stud that was totally unlike any he had ever seen before. The animal was only 16 hands but broad and quite muscular. He had the good lines of every riding animal Sam had ever seen. The big horse was in reality white, he supposed, but may be what some would call a blue roan, at least everywhere except on his rump. There he showed no signs of splattering, rather, on his snow white haunches were large round spots of the same deep blue/gray color as the rest of his coat. He was without question the most beautiful riding animal Sam had ever seen.

Approaching the auctioneer, Sam said, "I have never seen such an animal, is he Arabian?"

"Heavens no, he is an Appaloosa."

"I have never heard of that breed."

The man with a strange twang in his speech replied, "Neither has anyone else in these parts. He comes from Washington State. Only the Nez Perce Indians have the Appaloosa; it's their special breed. They are bred especially for the mountains there. He can climb where no other horse would attempt and will still be going long after your Morgans and Walkers have tuckered out."

"How did you get him if only these Indians have them?" Sam inquired.

"He was a gift from Chief Tooyalakekt to my brother, but he died, and now I own him."

"Is he fer sale?" Sam asked.

"No, not really," the man said looking away.

Sam rubbed the stud's neck, patted his shoulder, and then turned to leave. "Too bad, I know just the man who would appreciate such an animal."

"Of course, everything has a price," the trader said quickly.

Turning, Sam looked this time at the man rather than the animal. "And just what would be his price?"

The stranger looked down and nodded his head, "I sure do admire that brace of Colts you are wearing there. They be the new cartridge model?"

"That they be," Sam replied.

When the train pulled into Madison a week later, he was glad to see Reb waiting there with his wife Esther. After the proper affectionate greeting a man and his wife not only must display, but with these two needed to display, Sam turned to Cliff, "I'm so glad you have come, Reb," he said extending his hand to the younger man. "I have something for you."

"I had to beg and plead to keep him here until you got back," Esther said placing her arm through each of their arms and walking between them.

"I'm really glad you did," her husband said back.

Reb felt the need to say, "On the square, Sam, I really intended to be on the move before now. I don't want this trail to get cold."

"I realize you have a driving force that is building in you to see justice is done to the bastard, and that is precisely why I have brought you this gift," Sam said as they walked back towards the animal car.

Finally, when the railroad workers dropped the ramp and Sam was able to enter the car, the first horse he led out was the big Appaloosa.

"That don't look like any draft animal to me," Esther said admiring the fine piece of horseflesh.

"He's not, he's the best endurance animal in the world, and I want Reb mounted on the best when he goes after that murderer," Sam said, and handing the lead rope to his taller friend he added, "He has an Indian name, but I can't remember it and can't even pronounce it when I do; so you'll have to teach him a new name."

Cliff walked around the stout animal ingesting his beauty while Sam was following his every step, telling him all about the history of the beast.

Cliff felt he should decline the present. He realized the animal had cost Sam a pretty penny, but the more he saw of the horse, the more admiration he felt for him. Not since he had lost Big Red, had any horse captured his heart so. Finally all he could think to say was, "He's beautiful, and I will call him 'Ola' for the Great War Chief, Osceola."

"A wonderful and most appropriate name," Esther said smiling, so thankful they had finally done something for the man who had done so much for them.

Three days later, she looked out the back window and saw Reb walking towards their home. "Sam, Reb's coming, and he is leading Ola."

The long minutes spent saddling the big spotted animal was a sad time for everyone at Estherbrook Stage Stop. He did not want to leave his friends, and not one of them wanted to see him go. Still, they knew as well as he, he would not have peace a single day that

John Mouton Tidwell lived, and spending time here was just allowing the trail to get colder.

"Reb Brown, you take care. I'm gon'a miss you," said the short man wearing the Bobcat pelt hat.

"I too, will miss you, Johnny," he replied to his friend.

"We rode a trail together, didn't we?" Johnny said looking down for a second, fighting eyes that were filling with water.

"That we did," Cliff agreed and nodded his head, "That we did."

Then turning to the older couple who stood on his other side, Cliff smiled faintly. First he looked at Esther and touched the brim of his hat, "I'd be obliged were you to watch over Nadine."

"You know I will Reb," she said with tears building in her eyes, and in broken speech she added, "It could be you are starting out on a long trail that will not be an easy one, ya' know."

"Yeah, I reckon so, but I'll catch 'im in the end, I'll catch 'im just as sure as the turning of the earth. I'll catch 'im, this I promise you," Cliff said. Then he nodded his head, forcefully this time, and simply added his friend's name, "Sam," knowing more words need not be spoken.

The man on the ground returned the nod, and Cliff touched his spurs gently to the side of the big Appaloosa beginning his journey on the long trail that would lead him to faraway lands with never before heard of names.

His stop in Valdosta was short. David Clark, whose wound was healing well, had gotten a job in the town hall. The slot was vacated by one of the appointed officials who disappeared suddenly when it was learned Governor Bullock may flee the state.

Clark helped him search through Tidwell's papers until they found where he had received an invitation to attend a social gathering to be held in Macon on the following Tuesday.

"Well, this might be a bad lead, but at least it is a lead," Cliff said, and shaking hands with his friend, he left for the depot where he arranged transportation for his horse and himself westbound to Thomasville, there they changed to the northbound Central of Georgia Railway train.

'The last time I rode this train,' he remembered, 'was to kill Tidwell. Unfortunately, I failed, and now I must ride it again for the same reason.'

A small girl sitting across from him on the rickety yellow car, pulled on her mother's sleeve, "Mommy, why is that man crying?" she asked.

"I think he must be pretty sad about something. Now don't stare, look out the window at all the trees that are rushing by. We are going so fast. I think we must have traveled twenty miles in the last hour."

The little girl looked out the window for a few moments and then back at the sad man who had a single tear slowly moving down his right cheek.

In the years since the war, Macon had been restored even more so than Valdosta. There were all kinds of new shops, three large mills, and a foundry.

Cliff detrained among a small sized group of departing passengers. The little girl who had wondered about him and her mother were not among them, but there were two other unescorted ladies walking in front of him, struggling with their heavy loads. A man came by pushing a flat, four wheel cart that had several pieces of luggage on it. He passed the group easily as the walkway here was slightly on a down grade, however, suddenly he pulled up and stopped the partially loaded cart. "Misser Johnstone," he said, "I's don' know you be back in town."

"Why yes, Jefferson, I just arrived on the 3:10 from Thomasville."

"Misser Johnstone, please, you puts your bags here, I take dem fors you."

"Thank you, Jefferson, but I am only going to the platform there."

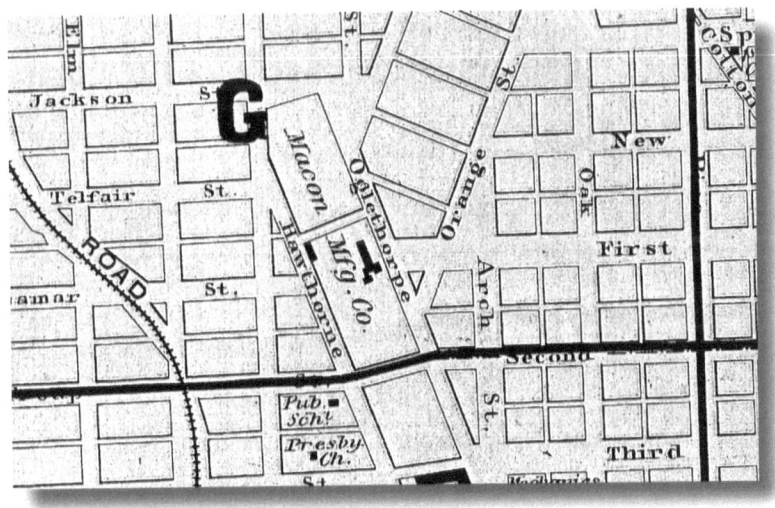

Map of Macon Georgia 1871

"I be pleased to tell my Mam' I don' carried yous' bags," the young man said.

"All right, Jefferson," the man said back and sat his single leather bag on the cart.

Cliff could see there was plenty of room for other luggage also, and it would be no trouble for the porter, so he stepped forward and spoke, "You are a kind man, I know you wouldn't mind if the ladies placed their bags here too, they seem to be having a bit of a strain with them."

The man looked at him with a start and then at the saddle carried over his shoulder and the big bag that was in his other hand.

"White trash kin carry 'deys own."

Cliff raised his head a little and ran his tongue between his lip and his lower teeth, then swallowed. "I'm not askin' fer me, rather for the ladies."

The younger man looked at the two women, who at this time, were at a loss as to what was taking place here.

"White bitches, white trash, be de same t'ing."

"Excuse me ladies," Cliff said as he lowered his saddle from his shoulder to the walkway. Then without looking back, suddenly produced his big 44 Smith & Wesson with which he slapped the train employee across the side of his face, knocking him unconscious; at the same time he knocked his molars from their roots. The man fell without a cry.

"See here, young man," Johnstone quickly said. "I happen to be a member of the Georgia Legislature, and I assure you that assault against a Freedman is a crime here."

Cliff moved with the quickness of a snake as he shoved the muzzle of the revolver into the intruder's nostrils. "That be elected or appointed?" he replied to the man with the unnatural accent.

"Ah, ah, I was appointed by President Grant."

"I have a mind kill you then," Cliff said, as he added pressure to the gun causing the man's nose to twist as it turned upwards even more.

The chubby man began to shake uncontrollably, and then everyone around saw he had lost control of his bladder. When that occurred, he began to sob. "Don't shoot, don't shoot."

Cliff shoved him backward, and then with a disgusted look returned his Smith to the holster under his coat.

He then took the black leather bag and flung it on the sobbing man who now had dropped to his knees.

Reaching for his saddle, he put it on the cart just before he extended his hand to the younger of the two women, "Your bag, Ma'am."

"I, I don't know," the other one said, concern showing in her face.

"Ma'am, I have spent considerable energy teaching these two some manners, you aren't gon'a let their education just go to waste, are you?"

The younger lady looked first at the two men who lay there on the boardwalk, then back at the lanky stranger, and suddenly she smiled and handed him her bag.

Cliff took it, placed it beside his saddle, and then stretched forth his arm for the other bag.

"Charlotte, I think we would be wise ___," the older woman said, looking over at her friend.

"Come on Margaret, that sorry Randal Johnstone has been bothering us both for most of the day; now this man has put him in his place. The least we could do in thanking him is to allow him to assist us."

"I suppose you're right," she said, and handed her large cloth bag to Cliff who placed it beside the other.

He then turned to the people who were standing there in awe of what had just happened and added, "Would the rest of you like to have your bags carried to the awaiting taxis?"

One older man with age in his eyes pushed past a couple of others who were just standing there and said, "You bet Sonny. I'd be obliged."

Suddenly several more followed his lead.

Cliff, satisfied he had all who wanted his help, nudged Johnstone with his boot toe. "Congressman, get up, and pull this here cart on out to the street yonder. These decent folk will be voters again, now that Georgia has begun running out the riffraff."

The man slowly came to his knees and then looked at the small group of people who were standing there staring at him. With disgust in his voice, he spat before he said in a low tone, "You southern trash, I'll never ___," but he failed to finish his statement. Before he could, Cliff stepped forward to a place where the cart of luggage was between them and the others. Hence, no one else was in their view, and from there he spoke just above a whisper, "What were you saying, Congressman?"

Johnstone looked into Cliff's cold eyes, and suddenly a streak of fear shot up his spine only moments before he struggled to his feet. Releasing the wheel brake, he took the cart's tongue and began steering as he struggled to pull the heavy vehicle along the walkway.

When everyone had gotten their bags from the cart, Cliff moved away as if nothing had happened. However, he did not go far, just out of sight. There he stopped and watched Johnstone.

He remembered several other appointed officials were to attend the meeting Tidwell had been invited to. However, he was unsure if there had been a Johnstone listed there. Nonetheless, he figured it was a good bet to follow the man and see where he was staying. *'Perchance others of the same flock will stay there too,'* he thought.

The beaten man took his bag, the last on the cart, and tried to gather his dignity before hailing a carriage.

Cliff whistled to a single horse taxi that was standing close by and told him to follow at a safe distance.

Johnstone's carriage simply made a wide turn and stopped almost straight across Forth Street.

'Just like a pompous Yankee, needing a saloon-carriage to get him across the pike,' Cliff thought, but he also recognized where they were. He had been there before the war, only the hotel was called, *'The Spotswood House'* back then. *'It was quite near 'The Brown House' where father and I stayed.'*

He remembered, as a youth he had suggested that perhaps the owner of this fine old hotel was some distant relation. Louis Brown quickly put a stop to such foolish ideas with a sharp tongue, "None of our people would set on their haunches and run a hotel. We are working men as men should be, not insiders!"

Noting the *'The Spotswood House'* was now shingled, *'The National'*, he realized the old hotel was under the influence of The New South[1] that had swept through Macon like the tide of a mighty blue ocean.

Cliff had his driver stop, and as they waited for Johnstone to alight, he asked his hackie about the hotel.

"It be' one of the finest in Middle Georgia, only those rich in Yankee dollars can pass through 'dos doors."

'A fitting place for a meeting of such scoundrels,' Cliff thought.

---

1 The New South: A term given to those areas which had fallen under the influence of Northern control and ideas, as opposed to The Old South where Southern ideas and values had been in place.

He had the driver take him to 'The Lanier' on Second Street across from the courthouse, which was walking distance from 'The National'. It was there he took a room.

The clerk was ready to stop the man as he walked inside with a saddle over his shoulder, but when Cliff suddenly produced a ten-dollar greenback, he froze momentarily, before returning to his counter and offering Cliff a freshly dipped pen with which to sign the register.

Quickly depositing his saddle and bags in the room, he returned to the waiting taxi and headed to the corral near the Union Depot, where he picked up Ola.

Cliff tied him to the back of the hack and then they rode back to' The Lanier'.

"What 'da I owe ya?"

"Four bits, altogether."

"You have been a good driver," Cliff said to the older man whose old gray kepi was worn and frail. He gave him a new greenback, which had once been destined for the paymaster of the 103rd Mounted Infantry Colored, the occupational troops stationed in Valdosta. "Keep the change, you earned it."

The old man looked at the linen money and rubbed his fingers and thumbs all over it. "You know Mister, I seen a mite a these since the war; never did get to touch one 'afor."

"Spend it well," Cliff said, untying Ola and leading the big horse towards the livery behind the hotel.

"I be a thanking you Sur, ma' name is Ciphers Maynard, ma' brother Horace[2] has some friends what helps too at times, if'n you get my drift."

Cliff wasn't sure he did but stored the offering in his memory just in case.

Next, he went to a tailor's shop just down the street and bought a new, dark gray, double-breasted suit, altered for him while he waited. The tailor protested that he was too far behind to get to it in less than two days, but once again, the sight of greenbacks changed the tune rapidly. The seamstress knew only soldiers, government officials, and thieves had greenbacks, and Cliff Brown did not look like a thief and did not sound like a Yankee soldier, so it stood to reason he was someone who worked for the government.

---

2 Horace Maynard: Leader of the KKK in Bibb County during the early post war years.

Wally Wallace had been a tailor in Saint Louis before the war, and even though he really had sympathies with both governments during the conflict, he had been wise enough to side with the officers who needed union blue uniforms tailored to their needs.

He was good enough at his trade not to be overlooked by Fremont or Schofield when they were in Missouri. In fact, it was Major Schofield's influence that had gotten him this business back in '67, when the original owner lost it for war taxes.[3]

Wally had hoped he would have been able to obtain a sizeable spread of land in Georgia. Schofield had lead him to believe it was there just for the taking, but when he arrived, he found that it had been decided, even before the shooting had stopped, that most of the good land would be divided between the politicians and higher ranking army officers. Eventually, he was glad to get the shop, it being so near the better hotels in Macon.

One day, after he had saved enough money, he would sell out and move to Atlanta or Charleston or maybe even back to Saint Louis. Until that day came, he would do as good a job here as he could and save diligently. 'Yes, a man with greenbacks is surely one to befriend,' he thought.

Cliff had no trouble passing through the front doors of 'The National' dressed as he was and with a five-dollar bill slipped inside Tidwell's folded invitation. Once in, he headed for the smoke-filled bar, where a man could learn a multitude of sins by just listening.

Tidwell had arrived a week ahead of Cliff Brown and had indeed taken a room at 'The National' but under the name, John Mouton. Although, in his haste to leave Valdosta, he had not taken time to go by his office and therefore had no presentable invitation. However, this did not cause him great concern; he knew there would be enough of his colleagues there who knew him on sight, and he really never for one moment thought he would be denied entrance. He had been right.

The first few days had been a series of meetings and strategy planning on the election and how to defeat the Southern Democrat influence that was once again rising in power. Too many incidents of the like that had caused him to flee Lowndes County had arisen

---

3 War Taxes: In the years following the end of hostilities Congress gave power to the new state governments to levy a tax on former Secessionists who owned real property or businesses. It was said it was to repay for the expenses experienced by loyal Union people for their losses during the conflict

throughout Old Dixie, giving these radicals more influence with some of the papers, especially in old Whig areas.

This night, John Mouton was descending the stairs when the curvy shape of a young woman, escorted by a man three times her age, passed him. John smiled at her, and she smiled back. When she and her escort entered the outer room, which comprised W. A. Wylie's Saloon, her man momentarily left her to speak to another gentleman, and Mouton moved toward her with the speed and ease of a bobcat.

The National in Macon 1871

He had almost reached her side when he sensed something was awry, he did not know what, but he knew instinctively that danger was about, and scanning the busy room, he suddenly saw, through a smoky haze, the form of Reb Brown.

'How?' he wondered.

Quickly, using the cover of other people, he slipped out of the saloon.

Reb had also felt the danger, but he simply did not know where it had come from. Finally, he moved back and left the room, reentering the hotel lobby.

For the next twenty minutes, the two old enemies stalked each other. Mouton looking for Brown, Brown looking for he knew not what. Neither found the other for almost an hour, until Mouton espied him again.

Cliff had finally decided whatever was bothering him was strong enough it was real, and he had better move away, and give room. He had experienced the same emotion before, on the banks of the Salem River in Alabama, and when he gave into it and hid, almost immediately, a company of Yankee cavalry descended upon the bridge he had been guarding. Had he waited another two minutes, he would have been caught in the open and if not killed, most surely captured. This night, instead of hiding, he left 'The National' and started for his own hotel.

Mouton quickly spotted the tall sinewy figure as the Georgian walked east and stealthily, gave pursuit.

A block away, as he was crossing Cherry Street, Cliff felt the sharp sting a split second before he heard the report of the pistol.

The conical bullet had entered his left shoulder half an inch below the collar bone and stopped in the skin on the front side of his body. Immediately and swiftly, he moved to the other side of the street and waited in the darkness of an alley between 'The Exchange Bank' and 'The Bell Saloon'. However, he never saw his ambusher and never heard him slip away into the night. Nonetheless, he knew it had been Tidwell; he was as sure of that as he was the sun would rise in the east only a few hours later.

Hastily, he went on to his hotel and up to his room without attracting attention, and only then did he examine his wound.

The bullet was plainly visible under the skin, and he took his boot knife, and cut the flesh removing it. Then he applied generous amounts of whiskey to the front, drenched a white silk cloth in the fiery liquid, forced it into the bullet hole, and with great difficulty pulled it out the backside. Soon after accomplishing this, he passed out from the pain.

The next morning, a colored maid found him lying upon blood-soaked sheets on the bed and summoned Miss Bea Landry. Her husband, Dub, contacted their personal doctor who was cautioned to hurry but without drawing attention.

Cliff had lost a considerable amount of blood after passing out but his cleansing of the bullet hole had kept infection from starting, and Doc Boon was able to dress the wound without much difficulty. However, Cliff would be laid up for at least two weeks while he regained sufficient blood to be considered out of danger.

The next day after reading in the Macon Gazette:

THE MAN SHOT LAST EVENING ON CHERRY STREET WILL MOST LIKELY RECOVER

John Mouton left for Atlanta.

He was 47 years old and had made and lost more fortunes than any ten men he had known in his lifetime. Still, for some reason, he seemed to have always had someone following him, trying to stop him in his endeavors. It had started with his father, then Jewell's father and the son of Diane Coleman, who had pursued him for thirty years. Now, this Reb Brown seems to have taken up his trail, for what reason he did not know. *'Why won't this Cracker let it go? I'm away from his precious Lowndes County forever. Doesn't he realize this? Of course it could be simply a coincidence that Brown was in Macon, at the same hotel I happen to be staying at, but I seriously doubt it. No, this ignorant Copperhead is after me,'* he thought. *'But why am I so important to him?'* Then with a sobering realization, he considered better on his last thoughts. *'This man may be a southern sympathizer but by no means is he ignorant, nor stupid. He organized and led a gang of undisciplined backwoodsmen and soundly defeated two Union companies on a battlefield. He was able to gain sympathy of the local people and newspapers. Ignorant? Never. Cunning and brilliant is a much better description. Perhaps this Brown is the first opponent of equal or near equal abilities I have encountered. This could be an amusing challenge.'*

Mouton's years and experiences had made him into a fine tuned warrior, as well as a far better diplomat than any politician he had ever met. He was six-feet tall and still only 170 pounds, every inch a man and a well-honed man. The gray streaks showing in his hair were earned, and if anything, gave him an appearance of dignity rather than age. He could hold his own with most men twenty years younger in feats of strength, as well as with admiration from the ladies.

Thinking more on it, he concluded, '*Brown is a worthy opponent, but he is too young and too inexperienced to be a real threat. Nonetheless, I must give him a wide berth as one would a deadly snake until the proper time to kill him presents itself. That is, unless I send another to do the killing while I am miles away.*'

Atlanta was the busiest city he had seen for many years. Everything that could be said about Macon, could be said about Atlanta ten times over. The population was now almost 22,000, with half as many attorneys as there were doctors, a sure sign of a growing empire. The Capital location had finally been settled, and only a few loyal to the ideas of 'The Old South' still even thought of returning it to Milledgeville.

There now were ten large lumber mills within Atlanta itself and many more in the surrounding communities. Commerce was at an all time high, now that the railroads were once again in full swing.

John Mouton had to admit, no other non-port city had he ever seen, moving with such gusto, as did Atlanta in the fall of '71.

Rufus Bullock was in a state of nervous hysteria when John arrived. There were newspapers calling for his resignation, others calling for his impeachment. There were rumors that within the state, certain counties were preparing indictments of **Corruption and Conspiracy to Commit Murder** against him.

"John, my friend, what am I to do?" the overweight Governor asked. "Pray I have done nothing, nothing to be arrested for. I have not taken anything anyone else has not taken. I have killed no one; yet they say I am involved in the disappearance of these secessionists. I never gave the order to murder them. Just because I did not stop the military leaders in their ambitions to control these rebels, they say I am a coconspirator."

"You did issue the arrest warrants," Mouton pointed out.

"Yes," he replied, thinking hard. "But only on the advice of men of power, General Ely and others, men like you yourself."

John realized it was true; he had called for the murder warrants for this Clifford Brown and his father and brothers, as well as other trouble makers, in his endeavor to bring a stable government to South Georgia.

"It's this damn Walter Toombs," Bullock continued. "He is heading an army of Democrat attorneys bent on having my head on a chopping block."

The Governor stomped around the room before suddenly rushing to the window, and pulling back the heavy drapes he gazed outside. Satisfied no one was approaching to arrest him, he slammed the drapes back as if they were a huge wooden door and turned to begin his pacing once more.

John Tidwell[4]

"It's that damn Grant, he appointed me to this office. Now he acts as if he has never heard of me. It's not my fault some of his ex-generals have manipulated the Freedman out of their properties. I didn't steal any of their damn property. I did not take one penny

4 John Tidwell: Also known as John Mouton Tidwell, Jean' Mouton, John Mouton, John Martin, John Brown, J. D. Mather, and John Morris.

of their money. It was Grant's big shot army leaders that did these things I am being accused of."

He stopped, and reaching for the brandy decanter, poured himself a stiff drink. "Sure, I over-looked some of what they were doing. Hell, Grant himself sent them here just like he did me! Was I supposed to question the President's own men?"

John listened to this relentless raving for most of the first morning he was in Atlanta and then tactically decided, *'I will keep my room here at the Governor's Mansion, that in itself carries some prestige not found elsewhere;, but I will spend most of my hours at a quieter location.'*

That evening, he dressed in a black suit with satin lapels on his top coat, proper attire for a government gentleman. Upon leaving The Mansion, he advised he was bound for the Opera House on Peachtree Street, where The Ghioni & Sussini Italian Opera were once again giving performances.

He boarded a car of The Atlanta Street & Railway Company and occupied a seat near the rear door. At the next stop, a stately looking gentleman, accompanying a beautiful dark-haired young woman boarded and sat down a few seats ahead of him.

John had not failed to notice the driver giving an unusual welcome to the couple when they stepped aboard, and thereafter the trolley conductor seemed to have a nervous twitch that annoyed him about the neck.

The dark-haired woman was perhaps in her early thirties and her escort at least twice that age.

'She is obviously quite well-kept, considering the dress she is wearing cost more than the wages five men can earn in a year in Georgia in these times. Too, the necklace of small rubies resting above those magnificent breasts is a treasure queens dream of.'

Her hair was done up with a half dozen long curls dangling from the back, a feat that had taken someone with skilled hands an hour or more to accomplish. Her beauty demanded ones almost constant attention, and he found he was annoyed at himself for her having such a captive command of his awareness.

John Mouton knew well a man who hunted, or was hunted, could ill-afford such attention grabbers, if he were to survive long in this world.

He suspected it was this very thing that had caused him not to pay proper notice when the two men dressed in soiled coats and patched trousers, boarded the rear of the car as it crossed Tenth

Street. The sound of a firearm being slowly cocked was his first knowledge they were aboard.

One of the men immediately rushed forward and reaching over her shoulder, grabbed the necklace and snatched it from her neck with one hand, while he slapped the older gentleman hard across the temple with a Spiller and Burr revolver[5].

The second man remained near the door, standing behind John's seat, with his large Remington pointed forward.

The woman screamed at the pain caused by the chain breaking on her flesh, immediately the assaulter turned and rushed towards the rear of the car.

John slipped his boot out into the isle a split second before the thief arrived at that precise location, which caused him to stumble forward into his comrade in crime.

John Tidwell did not make the mistake of allowing them a single moment to recover; instead, he was up and turned with his own revolver in hand before they had fully collapsed onto the trolley's deck.

The astonished look on the accomplice's face was quickly replaced with pain when John fired his 38. Although his second shot followed only a moment later, he had taken the time necessary to move the point of aim from the neck of one robber to the back of the head of the other.

Before the smoke cleared enough for the other passengers to fully realize what had taken place, he was ejecting the two spent cartridges from his converted Navy Colt and replacing them with fresh copper rounds.

Then, almost as if it were part of some prearranged plan, he leaned forward and removed the ruby necklace from the dead man's grip. Lifting it free, he gave it a good once over before turning and saying, "I do believe this belongs to you, Madame."

She just sat there with an expression of total astonishment until the man beside her groaned.

John moved forward to hand the jewels to her, and replacing his revolver beneath his coat, he quickly produced a white handkerchief and began cleaning the cuts to the gentleman's head.

"Uncle Hannibal, are you alright?" she asked.

---

5 Spiller & Burr: The .36 caliber revolver was originally produced in Atlanta, Georgia between 1862 and 1864. The Confederacy ordered 15,000 of such revolvers, only 1451 were ever produced. The Atlanta Company was unable to make delivery and eventually was then moved to the Macon Armory for further production.

John detected an accent local to lands far north of Atlanta when she spoke.

"Yes, child, I am. Whatever did they want?" he replied, still not looking up.

"My necklace."

"That's all? Then we are lucky."

"Pretty lucky Uncle, this gentleman recovered it for me."

"What? How?" the older man now looked up at the Good Samaritan who had been wiping the blood from his head and ear.

"Who are you, sir?"

He almost replied John Tidwell and then thought better of it, "John Mouton, at your service, sir."

"Well, Mr. John Mouton, one Hannibal Kimball is most appreciative, I assure you."

John knew well the name Hannibal Kimball. It was he who had recently built the grandest hotel in all Atlanta and whose Opera House was being used as the state capital building until other arrangements could be made. Hannibal Kimball, was perhaps one of the most influential men in all of Atlanta.

"It is my pleasure to meet you, sir."

"Yes, and this is my step-brother's little girl, Mrs. Cabela," the older man said less enthusiastically than she, "but she will always be Connie, to a tired old man."

"Oh, Uncle Hannibal, are you sure you are all right?"

"I will be, if I can get up off this filthy floor," he said, giving the trolley driver a hateful look.

The car proceeded ahead for two blocks more where Mr. Kimball and his niece departed, at *The Kimball Hotel*. Just prior to stepping to the street, Kimball looked back at John and spoke, "When you are finished with the authorities over this mess, come back and see me. I want to thank you properly."

John did not fail to take notice the moment they started for the hotel entrance, two men suddenly rushed forward to give him assistance.

Atlanta did not have a police force as they were still under Martial Law, so at his first opportunity, the driver hailed a soldier and explained what had happened.

"You had better stay here, sir," the Corporal said to John. "I'll have to get an officer to handle this killing."

When the soldier left, John turned to the driver and handed him a card that indentified himself as the Commander of the Civilian Department of South Georgia. "If anyone wants to speak to me they may call on me at The Governor's Mansion." Then he too, left the streetcar and returned to *The Kimball Hotel* on foot.

Entering the lounge, he took a table in the rear next to the wall; he wanted no part of that damn Reb Brown catching him with his back exposed. However, he feared that little, *'I doubt the rascal will be able to pursue anyone for several months, and besides, I don't think it falls in Mr. Brown's code of justice to shoot a foe in the back.'* Still he was fully aware there could be others who possibly carried a grudge that may not have such standards; therefore, he thought it wise to take no chances.

He ordered baked quail and a bottle of wine for his dinner, and when finished asked the waiter for pen and paper. On that he inscribed a short note to Hannibal Kimball, *As you requested sir, I have come by.* He decided to sign it in his French name *Jean Mouton.*

'John Tidwell is just a little too unpopular right now,' he thought, as he handed the waiter back his feather along with a folded greenback.

"Will you see that Mr. Kimball gets this?"

The waiter raised his eyebrows at the name.

"He is expecting it," Tidwell said, with determination in his voice.

"Very well, sir."

He waited thirty minutes and decided it had been a mistake to have come back so quickly, perhaps at all. Hannibal Kimball was not a man known to socialize with anyone he considered below him. He was about to leave, when a young very black man, dressed in the finest uniform of a bellboy he had seen in America, approached him, "Misser Mouton?"

"Oui?"

"I wus axed to give you 'dis," he said, and stretched forth his arm displaying a small pewter plate on which lay a folded note.

On the note was simply, *Room 600*, written in fine penmanship.

He replaced the note with a quarter and dismissed the bellboy with, "Merci."

The boy looked strangely at him.

"Thank you," John then said in perfect English.

"T'anks you's, Sur," the young man replied, and as soon as he was out of sight he placed the coin between his teeth to see if it would easily bend, when it didn't, he smiled and slipped it in the front pocket of his shell jacket.

Jean Mouton started for the stairs and then remembered *The Kimball* advertised it was the only hotel in The New South providing elevators for its guests.

When he arrived at Room 600, Jean realized it was the entire center tower of the Hotel. There was a stately negro sitting at a desk just as one exited the elevator. He was dressed in a black-tailed coat, a lacy white shirt, with a large red tie.

"Sur?" he questioned.

Jean Mouton handed him the note without speaking.

"One moment, Sur," he said and then entered the large white door.

A few seconds later he returned and nodded his head, "You may enter, Sur," he said as he stepped aside.

Jean went in and the black closed the door behind him.

He was admiring the large room when she appeared, as if from nowhere. "Oh, I am exceedingly glad you were able to come so soon. Uncle Hannibal was not feeling quite as well as he anticipated and has retired I'm afraid, so he won't be able to thank you in person."

"I'm sorry. I should come back another time."

"No. I forbid it. You stay and have a glass of sherry with me. I am so dreadfully lonely here, and I shall not be denied the company of the first gentleman who comes calling."

"Well, I ____."

"This way Mr. Mouton," she said, walking away through an oversized oval entrance into another room even larger and more luxuriously decorated and furnished.

Upon reaching the elegant bar, she slipped behind it, and taking down two tall glasses, she began pouring the deep burgundy liquid from a decanter into each.

"Jean Mouton, I do believe that is a French name," she said taking a sip. Then holding the wine to her lips and staring at him over the edge of the glass added, "You do not speak with a French accent."

"Ah, well what accent do you detect, Mrs. Cabela?"

"I am not quite sure," she said lowering the glass. "I wondered on that, when I read your note."

"My ancestors were from France, but I am American through and through."

"A pretty brave American too, I must add. You could have been killed helping us as you did."

"To have so ruthless a creature rip jewels from so beautiful a neck was more than a man of honor could stand. I acted out of rage, that's all."

Again, she raised the glass to her lips but this time she did not sip, "You certainly control your rage very well, Mr. Mouton. I would have said your actions were more like ice," she paused briefly, "than rage."

"You are too kind," he replied with narrowing eyes as he pondered this lovely young woman.

Finally, he sipped himself and immediately tasted the finest sherry that had ever crossed his buds.

"Tell me, Mrs. Cabela, how could so beautiful a woman as you be lonely? Doesn't Mr. Cabela appreciate what awaits him here?"

"Mr. Cabela is in Kansas City, where he has been for nine months," she shot back bitterly.

"What a pity."

"Yes," she agreed, still with the bitter tone on her voice. She took a long drink from her glass, this time almost choking as the fiery liquid rushed down her throat.

She then walked past him to a round cherry table and retrieved an envelope lying there. "Here, my uncle wanted you to have this, to show his appreciation."

Mouton took the envelope and looking inside, saw five new twenty dollar bills on *The Bank of New York*. He smiled inwardly, *'The old bastard is a little cheap I see.'*

"I couldn't possibly take this or any amount," he lied. "I told you, I was outraged at the assault."

'Had he offered a thousand, perchance I would not be so gracious, but for a hundred perhaps I can become better acquainted with the both of them,' he considered.

"He meant for you to have it," she insisted. "It's not a small amount in these hard times."

"It's a fortune in these times, nonetheless, I want not one penny for doing my duty. The duty any well bred Yankee would do in a dreadful land."

"Yes, Mr. Mouton, it certainly is that," she agreed. Then gently slapping the envelope in the palm of her left hand, she looked away before adding, "Very well sir, if you insist, I will tell Uncle Hannibal of your decision."

He turned and walked back slowly to the door as she walked along side of him.

"Another day perhaps, when Mr. Cabela returns," he said.

"I wonder if Mr. Cabela will ever return," she said, and then looking up at him she asked, "Where are you staying Mr. Mouton?"

He started to tell her but knew he was known there as John Tidwell and didn't want to have to explain the two names. "Oh, downtown," he replied.

"I'm sure my uncle would insist you stay here as our guest," she said. Then without giving him an opportunity to refuse, she opened the door and spoke to the servant there, "Moses, accompany Mr. Mouton to the desk in the lobby, and have the clerk there find him a room on the fifth floor. He is our guest."

"Yas'um, Miss Connie," he said, nodding his head.

"Mr. Mouton, please have breakfast with us in the morning in the east wing, shall we say ten o'clock."

"You are exceedingly kind, Mrs. Cabela," he said, and taking her hand, he lightly kissed it before bowing slightly.

'This may turn out just fine,' he thought, as he descended in the elevator with the black man.

The breakfast date assured him of two facts, Hannibal Kimball was no fool and a reasonably good judge of character, and Mrs. Cabela was a very lonely wife.

Kimball offered him a job as "Protector" while they were in Atlanta. The rewards from Hannibal were less than he would have worried about losing at a good poker table but perhaps priceless considering the niece. He accepted.

A week later, Hannibal Kimball departed on the train for New York. He had encouraged Connie to go along, but she said, "Now that we have such a competent protector, I no longer fear Atlanta."

That night, Jean demonstrated just how well he could provide the services she requested.

Connie Cabela had once, when she was only a girl of twelve or thirteen, overheard a conversation between her mother and her aunt talking about the man courting Aunt Lucy at the time.

Her mother's sister had said quite enthusiastically, "My new beau is almost twice my age, yet so much better at pleasing me in the bedroom than any other man I have ever slept with."

This shocked young Connie; she had never imagined her aunt was allowing men to sleep with her, and she, too, was surprised that her mother had not chastised her on the spot.

Still, the idea that an older man would be better at pleasing a woman had always dwelled in the back of her mind.

'Anyone, surely, would be better than Charles Cabela,' she thought. *'He has only one aim in the bedroom, his own satisfaction.'*

This night her wonders had been answered. *'It appears Aunt Lucy was right after all,'* she thought, after experiencing the first orgasm in her life.

Mrs. Cabela and her protector were seen in and about all of Atlanta's finest restaurants and theaters for the next several weeks. They had become the talk of the upper class, mostly in whispers between condemning and envious wives.

The servants had even begun to discuss what they would say if Mr. Kimball were to ask them about the talk, as well as, what to do were Mr. Cabela to return suddenly.

Norman and Iris Damon had been friends with Charles Cabela before he had married Connie. In fact, Iris had been Charles' first lover years before she tied the knot with Norman.

Charles and she were from the same region in up state New York and had been sweethearts since they were children. His employer, Johnson and Harris, an old and well-established land construction company there in Rome, had been the first to dig in what became known as the Erie Canal.

Some 47 years later, when the war dragged on so long, that Charles became of age; his father had the company send him to the city to work on behalf of the war effort, thereby avoiding conscription[6].

Johnson and Harris had a good size contract with Hannibal Kimball's New York office, and it was through this path he had met the beautiful Miss Constance Barclay, niece and one of the heirs to the Kimball fortune. She was only fifteen at the time and much too skinny for his desires, but her uncle's wealth more than made up for what she lacked in the size of her breasts.

Hannibal did not particularly like Charles Cabela, but he immediately saw the affection his niece had for the young man and tolerated him. When they were married in the summer of sixty-six he offered Charles a job in the railroad division of Kimball Enterprises.

---

6 Conscription: A term used in the nineteenth century meaning the draft.

After several years passed and no children had come, Hannibal was somewhat pleased. He was not sure he wanted any of a draft dodger's seed mixed into his family, even with a step-brother's daughter.

Iris was devastated when Charles married; she had so planned on a continued relationship that ended with the union. Two years after the rejection, she agreed to marry a quondam[7] soldier of the 27th New York Infantry who had also come to work at Johnson & Harris, after he had mustered out of the Army.

He and Charles had become close friends in the days when they both still worked for J & H, as most referred to the company; although Charles sometimes felt a twinge of jealousy when he thought of Norman having sex with his first love.

Once, the two old lovers seized an opportunity when no one else was around, and spent a rushed thirty minutes in sexual bliss in a backroom at the Johnson and Harris office building. They each came away with the knowledge that they were still very much attracted to one other. After that day, Charles found more and more reasons to spend time with the Damons, even when he had to take Connie along.

Hannibal, sensing the bond between Charles and Iris, saw to it he was sent to Kansas City for a few months, to see if the distance between them would cause him to cool off. Also secretly hoping Connie would find she didn't miss him as much as she believed she would.

Until the mysterious Mr. Jean Mouton appeared one night, he had just about given up on the idea of this happening.

Being far more alert to the expressions of others than anyone realized, the old man immediately spotted the twinkle that would suddenly appear in her eyes when Mouton came around. It was for this reason that he had found it necessary to go back to New York for a short period of time.

It wasn't that he in anyway admired Jean Mouton. On the contrary, he rather disliked him in the same manner he did Charles Cabela. However, he was certain given the chance, Mouton would seduce his niece in hopes of gaining entry into the Kimball wealth. A reward Hannibal would see he never received. Nonetheless, this new union would awaken his niece to the knowledge she really was not in love with the detestable husband she had married.

---

7 Quondam: Often used in the nineteenth century instead of the word Former.

Reb Brown had not recovered as the doctor hoped. The wound had become festered and infected six days after he had been summoned, and it was a hit and miss conclusion in the doctor's mind if his patient would pull through. On the Monday of the second week, Cliff was in fact weaker than the days immediately following the shooting incident.

That night, another guest espied an unknown assailant, who apparently slipped into the hotel through the back entrance, attempting to pry open the door to Brown's room with an Arkansas Toothpick. When the lady accompanying the guest screamed at the sight of the stiletto, the felon sliced the forearm of her escort and made good his escape.

In the wee hours, while heavy clouds obstructed the light of the moon, Cliff was moved to the Widow Boland's Boarding House on 4th Street, just east of Elm.

Mrs. Boland's husband marched away from Bibb County in the summer of 1861 with the 27th Georgia Infantry. He didn't have to go, he was 40 years old at the time and beyond the age of conscription in the early years of the war, but he had felt it his duty. Although she hated the very thought, she knew she must be strong for him as he had always been strong for her.

Had he not been sent home during the summer of 1864 to recover from a bad wound to his arm, received during the Battle of Olustee down in Florida, she might never have seen him again.

Unfortunately, his honor to the cause was powerful, and as soon as he could, he returned to the unit. In early 1865, he was one of only 41 killed at Fort Drewry on the James as they stopped the mighty Union flotilla consisting of the ironclads USS Monitor and USS Galena, the screw gunship USS Aroostook, the side-wheeler USS Port Royal, and the twin-screw ironclad USS Naugatuck in their attempt to take Richmond via the James River.

In the early morning hours of Reb's third night of delirium, Liz Boland found Cliff calm and cold and the sight of so sudden a change frightened her into the belief he had passed. Immediately, she summoned Doctor Boon. However, John Boon quickly realized her dead man was only resting in deep sleep; the fever had broken in the preceding hour, and he felt a great weight of burden lift from his shoulders.

Liz Boland did not know this man but had come to like him very much in the weeks he was in her care. During the time after the infection had been overcome, they would carry on conversations together. He was young enough to be her son, and she would at times feel a slight tingle when she saw him smile. 'He is,' she thought, 'the son I never had.'

Another three weeks passed before he was up and around, even more before either of them spoke of his leaving. When that time did arrive, he realized there was still a great deal needed. Especially relearning proper coordination before he would be able to make everything work together, particularly the instructions his mind gave to arm, hand, and fingers.

'I am sure glad this is not my gun hand,' he thought every time he tried to shoot with his left hand.

He had long ago learned a man had a much better chance of staying alive if he could shoot reasonably well with his off hand, and staying alive was one thing he fully intended to do, at least until he saw Tidwell dead. Beyond that, he really did not have many thoughts.

When the day of his reentry into the world of everyday folk arrived, he was surprised and humored to find the bill at Porter's Stable and Livery on 3rd between Plum and Pine Streets, where his Appaloosa had been housed while he was laid up, was greater than his bill with Doctor Boon and Mrs. Boland combined.

After saddling Ola, he rode back by the boarding house to retrieve his poke that Nurse Gladys had brought from his room at the hotel, weeks before.

While securing his saddlebags and tightening the cinch strap, words were not spoken between the two, not even when he mounted his horse. Sitting there atop the big stud like a statue in the center of a city square, Cliff looked down at Mrs. Boland and offered a slight smile before he touched the brim of his hat. She lifted her arm slightly in a farewell wave, and they stared into each other's face for a few moments before he pulled the reins to his left; obediently, Ola turned and walked away.

Cliff did not look back; he did not want to see the tears slipping silently over Miss Liz's puffy cheeks. She knew she would never see him again; he was on a deadly mission, a mission that could very well take his life as easily as it could the man he pursued. She now understood how the mothers had felt when they watched their sons march off to war, especially during those last two years when it had become obvious so many never would return.

The depot in Atlanta did not resemble in the slightest what he had seen the last time he had been there. At that time, it was busy as a beehive with men and boys in their new gray uniforms. Each showing a face of pride and providing, as well as they could muster, a strong shield to hide any sign of fear. There were cannon, limbers, caissons, troops of all branches of the service and a multitude of coloreds, some in gray uniforms also. These black boys would go with the white boys into the very heat of battle.

However, most of the darkeys were moving about, tending to their masters, their friends, before they went away. All, white and black, cursing the hated Yankee. Several of the dark skinned lads had grown up playing side by side with their masters' white children. Now these white boys were going away to fight the hated invaders, hated by the Blacks as much as the Whites.

Now, Cliff looking about realized, with a sour taste building in his mouth, that time was no more at this depot; in truth that depot was no more either. Sherman's shelling had destroyed it some time before the home guard, in a desperate effort to render it as useless as possible to the enemy, finished burning it to the ground.

Where Cliff Brown now stood was a new depot. Completely new; a product of The New South, built with Yankee money.

These Darkeys did not speak with a Georgia accent. It was obvious many had been imported from some faraway land to take the good paying jobs. No longer was the assistance given with affection. Now, when a helping hand was offered, it was not withdrawn until a coin was placed in its palm, a fact that caused Brown to feel a streak of bitterness shoot through his gut. Nonetheless, he controlled it and headed back to the rear of the train where the animal car would be located.

He took a room at *The Peach Tree Hotel* and stabled Ola near by at *Cobb Brother's Livery* on Auburn Street; then he began long hours of surveillance of the Governor's Mansion.

During his third night in Atlanta, he saw a newspaper announcing Governor Bullock apparently had fled the state. It was believed he returned to New York, but that had not been confirmed.

'Shit, if his good buddy Bullock has fled, perhaps Tidwell has also. New York! God I hope not,' he thought. *'I have no desire to go to New York.'*

Returning to his room, Reb felt sick. He was still weak from his bullet wound and the night had been exceptionally damp and cold.

The next morning, folks began the day with fresh air and a clean blanket, compliments of three inches of new snow, the first to stick so far in this New Year.

Cliff was almost to the point of depression. He had always felt if he watched Rufus Bullock's home long enough he would find Tidwell, now that seemed unlikely. It was not that he had been discouraged in his ultimate task, only terribly set back.

Finally, he stopped this line of thought; realizing depression was simply a demon embedding itself into one's mind as a tick does one's skin. *'I do not lack faith in the Lord, and I will not allow you to get a hold on me. My mother has brought me up in the admiration of the Lord, and I with faith cast you out of me.'*

Within seconds, his head was once again thinking clearly. *'I have known from the start this would not be an easy chore. What was it Esther said?'* As he tried to recall, strong lines appeared across his forehead. Remembering her statement, *'You are starting a long trail that will not be an easy one.'* He began to nod his head in agreement, *'She is so right, this is a long trail I'm traveling and I have only just begun.'*

The next morning, he picked up Ola and headed for the depot to get information about the northbound trains. While waiting his turn in line, he overheard two men he assumed were reporters, talking about the richest man in Atlanta coming in on the 10:11 this morning.

'The richest man in Atlanta?' he thought. *'Three months ago I was the richest man in Georgia. Perhaps not in money but with Nadine by my side, I was rich beyond this Yankee's wildest dreams, now she is gone.'*

His thoughts were interrupted suddenly by one of the reporters bumping into him, as the man dashed off toward the arriving train.

Cliff moved on ahead in the line to the ticket seller. After some time, he had the information he needed, and turning to leave, he saw a carriage with a young woman and an older gentleman. The two reporters who had been next to him earlier, along with several others, were now gathered around the carriage listening to the older man speak.

'Well that must be that rich Yankee they were so wanting to interview,' he thought as he started walking toward the exit. Moments before he would have entered the street, the big black carriage, being drawn by a brace of fine gray dapple geldings, passed him. He and several others had to step aside to allow it to pass.

Cliff had always been an admirer of fine horseflesh and these two were as good as he had seen in a long time. When the horses passed, he looked for a moment into the carriage, trying to catch a glimpse of the richest man in Atlanta. The old man was talking to an exceedingly pretty young woman, fully a third his age. She was sitting beside him, holding both tightly and affectionately to his arm. Sitting across from them was another man whose back was to Cliff, offering no reason to pay him interest until he turned his head for a split second, and Reb recognized him. Immediately, his eyes narrowed and his mind came abruptly to attention, *'That's John Tidwell; at least I think it is.'*

However, before he could move forward in the crowd, the well-dressed darkey gave the grays their head, and the carriage moved away swiftly.

Standing there gazing at the big black vehicle as it disappeared around the corner, he was suddenly bumped into by one of the reporters he had seen earlier. Cliff reached out and grasped the man's bicep. He stopped and immediately said, "Hey buddy, un-hand me!"

Cliff did not look at him, rather he continued to stare at the last place he had seen the carriage. "Who was that?"

"Who?"

"In that carriage."

"Unhand me, and I will tell you," the man in the checkered suit replied.

"Oh, sorry," Cliff said, as he looked down at the shorter man. "I am sorry."

"You should be," the reporter said back sternly, as he was smoothing out his coat sleeve.

"Who was that?" again Cliff asked.

"Mr. Kimball."

"And who was with him?"

"His niece, Mrs. Cabela."

"Was that Mr. Cabela with them?" Cliff asked again, looking where he had last seen them.

"No, though it might as well be, from what I hear," the man's friend added.

"Who was it then?"

"I think he calls himself Jean Mouton. Some Frenchman who is said to be employed as their bodyguard, but I heard he does more than guard her body," the man said and snickered. "Why do you want to know?" the shorter man asked.

"Thought I knew him, down Valdosta way," Cliff said, then turning back he looked at the two men. "Can I buy you two a beer?"

An hour later, he knew most of all they could provide concerning Hannibal Kimball, Mrs. Cabela and their bodyguard Mr. Mouton.

The Kimball House in Atlanta 1871

The cost of service at, *The Kimball House*, was three times as expensive as it was at *The Peach Tree* only a few blocks away, but it would be at *The Kimball* he intended to be spending his time and money.

Cliff still had a goodly sum of the money he and Nadine had brought back from the gold fields of Wyoming, and he had recovered some of his expenses used forming and equipping the Renegades, when he sold much of the material he had purchased for them, back to Captain John Inglis. Also, there still were several thousand of the greenbacks they had taken from the paymaster's train, but that money he wanted to be used to help those in need back home, and he hoped he would not have to send for any of it.

Of course, a man could not go on indefinitely spending money like he was making more everyday, but for a time he would drink two-dollar beers and eat five-dollar steaks just to be in Kimball's hotel.

Reb still had not fully recovered the use of his left hand, and living in the city made daily practice difficult. As a result, he had started carrying only his S&W Model Three, in the cross draw holster. There it was easier to conceal than one on his hip, and now that he decided to carry only one, and since the Smith reloaded much faster than his Colts, he reasoned it was the practical one to carry; he would later regret this.

His friend Johnny Gaston had made him the holster so it would lay flat against his waist. The barrel pointed out to his left side, a much better and faster angle than straight down, which was the manner most cross draw holsters held their weapons. The only problem was, Cliff had to really push it down tight into the holster when he rode, or it would want to creep out. He had done this so many times that now it was second nature for him to give the big revolver a second push after he had fully dressed.

In the past, Connie was always glad to see her uncle return, but this time she discovered she was somewhat disappointed.

'Obviously the freedom I have enjoyed with Jean will now be quite restricted.'

Jean Mouton was, on the other hand, grateful for the relief the old man's presence gave him. Trying to keep a woman half his age pleased was beginning to become more of a chore than a pleasure.

He had wanted to go out and do some card playing, but the moment Hannibal awakened he wanted Jean with him, and as soon as he went to sleep, she wanted him to be with her.

Finally, this morning he had slipped out the back door between them and enjoyed a good breakfast at Del Monaco's on Auburn Street. Afterwards, he enjoyed a long walk in the park, which had once been where General Hood's Headquarters stood.

Just as Jean was returning, Hannibal stepped from the elevator, "Ah, I was wondering where you had gotten off to."

"Just out for a breath of fresh air."

"I don't see anything fresh with all the blame coal dust hanging in the air," the older man replied. "Breathing this stuff keeps me with a sore throat most of the winter months."

"I too, have a touch of soreness in my throat," Jean agreed not really knowing what else to say. He realized that ole' Hannibal was far more clever than the ole' devil would lead one to believe. There were times when he thought the old man was just leading him on, trying him in his shrewd ways.

"I need to go to the office this morning, and Connie is sleeping in. I think you should accompany me."

"As you wish, sir," Mouton replied, but his tone was less enthusiastic, a small sign that did not fail to be noticed by Hannibal Kimball.

With an unseen smile in his mind rather than upon his lips, he thought, '*I think perhaps Mr. Jean Mouton is losing his desire to enter the Kimball family.*'

He had indeed read Mouton right. In the early hours of that very morning, after she had returned to her room, he had laid there for a long time unable to sleep and realized he was tiring fast of this woman. Not that she wasn't exceedingly desirable, rather far too demanding.

He also realized before he would enjoy the pleasures of the Kimball wealth, he would have to somehow eliminate Charles Cabela. After that, he would have to wait a respectable length of time before she would be free to marry again. Also, he would have to wait or find a way to arrange Kimball's death, all the while having to respond to her every demand, a task he no longer relished. '*No, I believe I will be moving on before long.*

Perhaps I should spend some time studying how to go about relieving Mr. Kimball of only a small portion of his fortune, say twenty thousand or so.'

Hannibal had been watching Mouton's facial expressions. It was obvious the man was thinking, and when the devious smile suddenly crossed Mouton's face, even for only a moment, the older man knew his mind was playing with schemes more pleasing to Lucifer than Jehovah.

"You know, Mr. Mouton, I have been thinking of sending for Charles. He has been away for some time, and I know Connie must be lonely by now. The problem is, we have so many enemies, and he must travel through a land filled with defeated rebels who hold strong grudges. I fear for his safety on so long a journey."

"Yes sir?" Mouton replied lifting his head and showing an immediate curiosity.

The change was quite obvious, and Hannibal knew he had struck upon a subject which interested Monsieur Jean Mouton.

"I think you should go to Kansas City, and return with him." Hannibal paused before continuing, "Be his companion as you have been to Connie and me."

"As you wish, sir."

"Of course, you will be justly rewarded for your time," Hannibal added.

Immediately he saw, through the cold blue eyes, Mouton's mind go into gear, even though the man's stare revealed a totally blank expression.

"I must warn you, Jean, this trip may not be one of pure pleasure. Charles will be returning with a considerable sum of cash," Hannibal added, deliberately looking away from his companion as he spoke.

"I think I'm up to the job," Mouton quickly replied.

"I'm sure you are the man to accomplish just what I want," Hannibal remarked, slowly turning his head and looking straight into those cold blue eyes.

Mouton suddenly felt as though the old codger was looking into his mind, as he himself had done to so many others, and a slight chill ran up his spine.

Later, when he told Connie of his plans to send Jean Mouton out to Kansas City to escort her husband back, she quite obviously became upset.

"Why don't you just send him a wire, and have him return on his own. He's a grown man you know."

"I know what kind of man he is, and that is exactly why I'm sending Mouton to protect him on the return trip. I plan to close my accounts in Kansas City, and Charles will be traveling with more than thirty thousand in cash. I want to be certain he arrives here with it," Hannibal said sternly.

'That is true of course, Charles is a weak man. He would be easy prey to robbers, and he may just try to lift some of the cash himself. Although, Uncle Hannibal will surely catch him should he try,' she thought, and her reply confirmed it. "Very well, perhaps it is best," she agreed just as she turned and walked from the room.

The moment he heard the door close, Hannibal beckoned Moses to him.

"Yas, Sur?"

"Let me know when she leaves for his room."

"Yas, Sur," the older colored man replied nodding his head.

The next morning she spoke as they were walking to the train, "Jean, I have never noticed you walking with a limp before."

"I have an old wound that acts up sometimes when it is damp like this," he replied.

"Ah, the scars on your legs."

"War wounds."

"And the loss of your fingers, are they war wounds also?"

"Yes, old war wounds, both."

"Really, which war was that?" she asked.

'The war with that damn Reb Brown,' he thought, but replied, "Oh, only a small one that was raging while I was in China." He then quickly changed the subject, "I do hope this rain stops soon."

"I suspect it will turn to snow before you get to Missouri," she said without expression.

"I do hope it clears this awful smoke from the city," Hannibal added, looking out at the dirty cloud of air that always seemed to hang over Atlanta in the winter.

After the W&A coal burner had pulled away, she noticed the rain had indeed turned to pretty light flakes of snow that seemed to dance around in the morning air rather than fall.

She asked if they could have Moses drive them to *Rich's Department Store* where she wanted to do some shopping. Hannibal was not pleased but decided to indulge her, and it would give him an opportunity to read *The Atlanta Constitution* near the potbelly while she entertained herself.

Afterward, they went to the telegraph office where Hannibal handed the telegrapher a previously written script. Then turning to his niece he asked, "Do you wish to send a note to Charles?"

She thought a moment before replying, "No, I suppose not."

Later they rode along Peachtree Street, but when the snow became a nuisance Kimball called to his driver, "Moses, take us back to *The Kimball House*."

Charles Cabela opened the yellow paper and read:

I HAVE SENT ONE JEAN MOUTON TO MEET YOU AND ACCOMPANY YOU BACK TO ATLANTA AS A BODYGUARD DUE TO SEVERAL THREATS RECENTLY MADE BY JEALOUS REBELS STOP

Now I even question his loyalty Stop

Do not have over a few hundred dollars in cash ib you Stop

Do bring my papers on the Missouri River land as well as the car End

'I wonder why he wants me to travel with this Mouton if he doubts his loyalty,' Charles questioned. *'Oh well, I'm rather tired of this dreadful frontier anyway, and it will be good to get back where I can again see Iris.'*

Hannibal Kimball owned several private railroad cars. The oldest, a sleeper of wooden constructed, which he had converted to his personal home on wheels before the war. However, since it was seldom used anymore, he had allowed Charles to take it to Missouri when he had sent him west. Now he wanted it back, and it was in this car, only one ahead of the Iron Mountain caboose, that Jean Mouton slid the thin blade between the lower ribs on Charles Cabela's right side.

Finding no more than eight hundred dollars in the leather satchel Charles had kept so close, drove Mouton into a rage. He began to rip away at the interior of the old car trying to find the $30,000 Connie had mentioned her husband would be bringing back with him.

Finally succumbing to the realization there was no more money; he dumped both Charles and the brakeman, who had caught him with Cabela's nude body on the platform, into the Missouri River as they crossed the Rocheport Bridge.

Jean considered detraining the next time they stopped for water but decided it best not to be anywhere near, if one or both bodies were identified, should they even be found.

There had been a considerable outcry in Saint Louis when it was discovered the brakeman was missing, however when Monsieur Mouton assured them all was well in their car, and considering whose car it was, no one dared to pursue further investigation in there.

"Surely, no one in Mr. Hannibal Kimball's party would have knowledge of the brakeman's disappearance," Jean had overheard someone say outside the car window, and then immediately the investigators moved away.

He wisely waited to detrain when they made the last stop for fuel and water before reaching Cape Girardeau, which was as close to Atlanta as he wanted to ever again be. However, he would have enjoyed seeing the expression on Hannibal Kimball's face when he learned that neither he nor his Charles was aboard. *'Will it be an expression of surprise or satisfaction?'* Mouton wondered.

A day later when Hannibal received a wire from Nashville explaining that both his employees were mysteriously missing from the train and that his private car was a wreck inside, he just smiled and said nothing to his niece.

That same evening, Cliff had stationed himself where he could watch all comings and goings from both the front and side door of *The Kimball House*. If indeed Tidwell was staying there, as he had been told a man meeting his description was, he would have a good chance of spotting him.

Sometime after midnight, a man looking much like his target left by the front door accompanying a slender woman with dark hair, and hailed a taxi.

Cliff had to hurry along after them for two blocks before he, too, was able to secure a hack for the pursuit.

They had almost reached Alabama Street when the driver leaned over and spoke to the gentleman below him, "Sur, I b'levs dey be anotter' hack following us."

The man quickly looked out, and then as they turned the corner onto Pryer, he jumped from the vehicle and hid in a doorway watching the approach of the second taxi.

Cliff saw the flash of the gunshot before he heard the report. Immediately, he reached for his Smith and jerked it out, only to see to his horror the barrel pointing down and the loaded cartridges shooting up and out of the cylinder.

He knew instantly what had happened. When he pushed the revolver into the cross-draw holster, he had pushed too hard, and the locking toggle had been disengaged. When he pulled the big revolver out, the carefully engineered Smith & Wesson had done exactly what it was supposed to do under the circumstances, eject the spent shells; only this time the shells were not spent.

Instead of using the gun to shoot the assailant, Cliff dove at the shadow and used it to club the man down.

As soon as the struggle was over and the taxis had returned, a lamp was brought over, and Cliff could see the man lying on the cold street was not John Tidwell.

"Why did he shoot at me?" he implored the woman.

"He is a gambler and won big back at the tables in *The Kimball House*. He thought you were one of the men he had won from," she sobbed as she tried to stop the blood that was flowing from the man's head wounds.

Cliff reloaded his revolver and had the driver return him to his hotel where he exchanged the Smith for his faithful Colt conversion.

The next day while he ordered lunch, one of the young darkeys who worked at *The Kimball House* told him the Frenchman who had been staying with the Kimballs had gone to Missouri. Cliff slipped him a folded one-dollar red back and thanked him. A week later he was convinced it had been good information, and he saddled Ola and headed northwest.

Chapter Two
MISSOURI

Cliff moved slowly through the thick poplar trying not to make any noise, his right hand resting gently on the stock of his Colt as he eased along.

The sun was setting, and he was having a difficult time keeping his eyes on the movement through the trees.

The horse was moving fast on uneven ground, and he could not understand why anyone would put an animal in such perilous conditions. Then finally what he had expected to happen, happened. The steed stepped in a hole and fell. The sound of the bone snapping could be heard in the still of the evening, and the rider was last seen flying over its head and immediately out of sight, somewhere just over the short ridge.

He waited. Two, three, four minutes passed, and the only sound heard was that of the injured animal as it struggled on its side.

Finally, dropping Ola's reins, he slowly began to move forward. The dirt or clay of this land, he knew not which, was somewhere below the thick blanket of leaves.

'Leaves,' he thought, 'are the worst possible covering for one to try and slip up on someone else.'

Still, with revolver now in hand, he eased up to where the big bay could be clearly seen. There he stopped, crouched behind a bush, and waited again.

Nothing moved, save a woodpecker that cut through the late afternoon air seeking his resting place for the night.

If there was one thing Reb Brown had learned during the war, it was patience. The impatient were very often the first to die. The wait was not as tedious as some may think. He had learned to put his mind into some sort of neutral, not unlike the way an engineer does a train when he wanted plenty of steam but no motion.

His senses were at their peak, and his consciousness was powered with a full head of steam, but his mind was not moving. It was a unique form of self-control he had developed, and he used this talent for more than one need in his life. Time moved on, but he was almost unaware of it.

After a long period, he heard a noise over the ridge, human noise. Still he waited, listening, watching. Finally, he heard it again. It was a groan, a subconscious groan.

'The rider is hurt,' he thought, *'hurt and unconscious.'*

Still he was slow to move. When he did, it was as if he floated between the trees in the dying light of the timber, until finally he could make out the shape of a body laying face down in the thick leaves beside a sizable white rock.

Reb now straightened his frame and moved forward. The only sound made by him was the three loud clicks of the hammer as it slipped on the sears.

The body did not move.

'If the rider had heard those clicks, he would have surely recognized them, and now have no doubt, but a man with a revolving pistol was approaching.'

When Reb arrived at the body, he could see there was blood on the rock.

As September 16, 1872 gave up its last rays of light, Reb placed the long barrel of his Colt in the ear of the man, and with the other hand on his shoulder, rolled him over.

Reb jerked back as if he had suddenly seen a ghost. The rider was not a man, rather a woman, a beautiful woman, with a bad cut on her forehead.

When he tried to move her, she cried out, and he realized she very likely had internal injuries as well.

Looking about, he knew this was no place to help her. The ground was damp from the passing storm two hours earlier, and remembering the dark clouds he had watched slowly moving in from the south, he suspected more showers were in store.

Reb gently laid her on the ground and walked back to where he had drop-reined his horse. There he took his spare union suit and tearing it in half, twisted it around a short branch that he had cut with the long-bladed Bowie whose scabbard was sewn into the stovepipe of his left boot. With a few sprinkles of coal oil from the tin he kept in his saddle bags to prime it and a Lucifer for the necessary energy, he had a torch.

Before leaving the big Appaloosa, he tied the reins to the small strands of a willow bush and then walked to where her horse lay. Now with the light of the torch, he could see she had been riding a sidesaddle.

'It's a pure wonder she was able to stay on that contraption at all the way she was riding, even before the animal broke it's leg,' he thought.

Lowering his revolver he placed the muzzle behind the bay's left ear and squeezed the trigger.

The sound was tremendous in the still of the early evening, and for a minute or more, the forest was silent of its normal sounds.

"Did you hear that?"

"Yes," the strained man replied, looking off into the night. There was only a sliver of a moon and it revealed nothing at a distance greater than twenty feet.

"Can't tell where it come from," the foreman said, as he turned his horse around in a circle. The other men in the group scattered some, giving room.

"No, a single shot at such a distance is untraceable," Will Hickey agreed. "We had better go back, a storm is coming. First light, I want you here, where we last saw her trail," he added looking at Lance Spain.

"Yes sir," the man answered, and pulling on his rein he turned his horse following his boss, as did the remaining cavalcade.

William Telfair Hickey had been born to a family of some quality, near the township Folkestone, along the coast of Kent in southeast England, that fall of 1830. Five years later, his father and uncle left for the Americas to make their own fortune but more so to be free of the commanding authority of their father.

Each having a sizeable amount to invest, they immediately began looking for a business. Erick Junior, Will's father, had always been talented with woodworking. However, his father, Jonathan Erick Senior, Will's grandfather, had forbid such lowly work to be carried on by a Hickey. As a result, young Erick had never had the opportunity to apprentice in England.

Will's Uncle Bartholomew, who liked to be called Bart, had been befriended by a chap who sold him on the idea of untold fortunes that could be made in the unspoiled forest of Canada.

Erick Junior was not so sure but being the younger of the brothers, went with Bart to Vermont where in the dead of winter they crossed the frozen Missisquoi Bay into Quebec.

Chbougmau, some three hundred miles north of Montreal had been the home Will Hickey knew most of his youth. His father and uncle had indeed accomplished everything their dreams had sought. The wealth they accumulated in the timber and sawmill business, exceeded that of Jonathan Erick Hickey Senior, including the fortune he had inherited. The only loss of their accomplishment was Erick Senior died before they could relish their glory upon the older Hickey.

Will had learned two things well living in the wilds of Quebec; he knew the timber business to and fro, and to speak the French language fluently.

In 1858, while he was touring The States, his trip was delayed four days while repairs could be made to the damaged boiler on the steamboat, *Ben Campbell*, at the docks at Cape Girardeau. There he read in the 'Revue Icarienne', a Saint Louis newspaper printed in French, that Butler County was selling 10,000 acres at one dollar an acre, in order to acquire the money to build a new courthouse.

Will made good use of his layover by renting a carriage and a team of two fine chestnuts to make the 60-mile journey in time to purchase the majority of this land. Although most of it was swamp, he soon had a dredging operation in gear and was draining the land so access to the untold millions of trees could be harvested at his will.

With the ending of the rebellion in America some eight years later, he moved into Missouri and began one of the largest timber operations in the state. His sawmills were scattered throughout southeastern Missouri and northern Arkansas.

Hickey Engine Hauling Kent Timber to the Hickey Sawmill

He had a contract to furnish all the ties for the *Iron Mountain Railroad* and even laid his own track spur to bring out his huge logs.

He also owned a sizeable dock facility in Cape Girardeau, from where his lumber was shipped all over America, as well as to foreign ports. As had been with his father, timber was his business, but Will differed in that raising horses, rather than raising a fortune, became his passion.

He had met Honey Brodel while she was singing in a theater in Detroit. She was a lovely little thing with light brown hair and blue eyes. Standing only five- foot-four inches tall made her quite pleasing to the five-foot-six inch Will Hickey.

Her face was breathtakingly beautiful and her skin smooth and flawless save one small mole on her right cheek half an inch below the eye.

She was educated and well mannered, and away from Detroit no one would know of her past.

They were married on her twentieth birthday, and spent a long honeymoon aboard the *Sheboygan* as it sailed to Buffalo. Although this sudden change in her life was more than pleasing, it was simply a miracle and one that titillated her. Unfortunately, she soon learned Will Hickey was not only her new husband; he also was her master. He even forbade her to speak of Michigan or the name Honey ever again.

Her given name was Leslie, and that is what she would be called by those very few who did not know her as Mrs. Hickey. Will himself only referred to her as Mrs. Hickey, even in the bedroom.

Life with Will was less than perfect. The sixteen years between them was always a thorn in the side of the marriage. One would say it was obvious he loved her, to the fault of extreme jealousy, especially of men younger than he who showed even an admiring glance at Mrs. Hickey. She found when this happened he would become angered to the point he often would turn cold and standoffish for weeks at a time.

Eventually, she realized his love for her was little different from his love for his prize Morgans, Arabians, and Thoroughbreds. It was his possessions Will Hickey loved, not the soul that lived within them. Nonetheless, the luxury of wealth, at a time when most white families in Missouri were struggling to make a dollar a week, had its merits.

She had begun to turn to the horses and the huge facility known throughout the area as *The Kent Farm*. More often simply 'Kent', as Will referred to the fifteen thousand acres of land he owned, which comprised a considerable portion of Stoddard and Butler Counties.

Working at Kent was a young man who had a wonderful gift with the large animals. He, in some unknown manner, was able to ride the horses without having to break them. The lad was uneducated and penniless save what he made at Kent, and with that, he supported a very pregnant wife who could no longer work. They lived in what at one time had been a slave shack on the Hogganoff Plantation, which before the war was owned by Colonel Sidney Hogg. Now, in 1872, Hogg's land was a portion of Kent.

Leslie had taken a liking to Wanda and Troy Meyers and on several occasions sent food from Kent's vast stores, sometimes even small amounts of money to help them make it through their hard times.

Wanda Meyers had helped with the tending of the horses before she developed complications, and Leslie had found her to be a most pleasant girl.

Troy now worked harder than ever for Kent. However, Kent's foreman, Lance Spain, had led his boss to believe Troy was staying late around the stables so he could be near Mrs. Hickey, and three nights past, Will walked up to the boy and called out his name.

Troy was trimming a front hoof on Mrs. Hickey's favorite horse, a big bay she called Chesterfield. Immediately, he stopped and gently let the leg down and then wiped his hands on his pant legs before standing straight and walking over to the white fence that separated them.

"Yes Sur?"

Will Hickey without reply, produced a double action Starr revolver and shot the lad three times in the chest, then turned and walked away. Passing the astonished Spain, he said without slowing his pace, "Be sure all of the other men who might have eyes for Mrs. Hickey, see of their fate."

Spain nodded his head and then looked back at the bloody body laying there on the clay. *'I don't need to parade the men past here; the word will spread like wildfire 'afore I could anyhow.'*

When Leslie found out what had happened to Troy Meyers she cleaned out the bedroom safe and took off on Chesterfield.

The fifteen hundred dollars she had taken was not even a dent in the wealth of Will Hickey, but the fact she would defy him in such a manner outraged her husband. He immediately dropped everything and started after her.

Now she lay injured in the Ozark Plateau, near the state line, with a man she neither knew, nor ever wanted to know.

Reb had, with great difficulty, gotten her to a level piece of ground, and stretching his canvas between two saplings, had made a lean-to that would keep out most of the now falling drizzle.

While retrieving her saddle and the leather bag tied to it, he had spotted the large sum of folding money in the bag but had not counted it.

'Her dress is certainly that of wealth. Hellfire, the riding skirt alone may have cost more than most women could afford to spend on their entire wardrobe.

Answers of why she is carrying so much cash or who she was fleeing, will come later; right now I just hope I can keep her alive.'

She was wet through before he was able to get the lean-to up, and in the night, she began to shake from a strong chill.

Reluctantly, he removed her clothes and using the saddle blankets from both horses to cover the damp ground, laid her on them before covering her with his bedroll.

It had been eleven months since his wife was murdered. During that time, he had nothing on his mind save catching up to the man who had killed her.

Once, in Memphis, he had seen a whore whose hair was the same raven black color as his Nadine's. Then after too many whiskeys, he had taken her upstairs but changed his mind when she began to undress.

She was not Nadine, and no one less could take her place. He paid the girl double and left.

Until this night, he had not touched a woman or even looked at one in a manly fashion, but now this one seemed somehow different, and she too, reminded him of his wife.

She in no way looked like Nadine. Her hair was light, and her breasts, though well developed, were not large and round like Nadine's had been. The injured girl was about the same age, though somewhat thinner than Nadine had been. Still, there was something there that made him think of his precious Nadine as no woman had in almost a year. Perhaps because Nadine had been in need of his help, as this girl is, and he could never deny a lady in need.

The rain lasted throughout the night and showed no signs of letting up when the hands on his watch moved to the seventh hour of the day.

Reb had stayed awake keeping the small fire going all night, as she had alternated from chills to burning fever hourly, and he had drenched the remainder of his new union suit wiping the sweat from her body.

When the light of day began to slowly appear, he saw she had developed a large dark bruise on her left side. When he gently pressed there with his fingers, he could feel the break in the rib.

He had no bandage material, but he managed to locate some dry sticks that he sliced flat. With these he made a splint, which he tied tightly around her with the wide leather that had been part of a reata he found on her saddle.

Reb had in his poke a small amount of salt pork and a bag of Arbuckles. Both were now on the fire, and as he sat there pondering the situation, he saw Ola lift his ears and turn quickly looking over the lean-to.

Reb reached for his Colt and tucked it under his shirt, then slowly he stepped forward and stood with sweeping eyes.

The rain was still falling hard, and he knew whatever the horse was interested in was likely danger of some sort. *'If it is human, he better have a good reason to be out in this downpour,'* Cliff thought.

Slowly he moved forward and turned slightly so he could see in the direction his horse was looking; he unbuttoned his fly and began to relieve himself. Although to anyone watching, it appeared he was looking down at his business, in reality his eyes were up and keen, just below the brim of his Stetson.

There was nothing that he could see through the rain so he bent over and took some sanitary paper from his saddle bag and then walked off behind a tree; there he waited, but his patience was not tested for long.

Two men slowly appeared from out of the rain, with one keeping vigilance toward where the man had disappeared, the other moved straight for the lean-to.

"Holy Shit!" the man exclaimed. "Thar be a woman here, Ad."

The sentry turned and looked back.

It was all Reb needed. In only seconds, he had the barrel of his 44 stuck hard against the man's neck, just behind his right ear.

"Ah!" he screamed.

The first man had lifted the blanket so he could take a good look at the naked woman, but he still had his rifle.

"Drop it, or this fellow will have his brains all over your face before you can cock that piece."

"Fer God's sake Horace, do what 'ere he say!"

The man with the musket was down on one knee still holding the blanket with his right hand, and his rifle was indeed un-cocked.

The rain had drenched them, and remembering half an hour before, when he attempted to take a opossum, it had failed to fire. Their predicament he easily recognized; and slowly laid the old rifle down before standing and lifting his hands.

"We don't mean no harm mister."

"Yeah," Reb replied as he shoved the man towards his apologizing pal.

"Me'nm'brother just out tryin' t'get som' breakfast food, when we com' across th' smell a' bacon."

"Remove your coats."

"What fer?"

"I said remove your coats."

They looked at each other and then slowly began to take off their outer garments.

"Fling them here."

They each did as told, and watched as the stranger searched them.

Satisfied they contained no weapons; Reb looked back at the men, "Now slowly turn around."

"You's ain't't gon't shoot us?"

"Only if I have to," Reb replied.

Seeing the knife in the boot of one of the men he added, "You got any knives or other such, get rid a' them, or I'll have you peel buck naked."

Ad reached down and slowly retrieved his knife and pitched it at Reb's feet. "That be all. Like we said, we wus just doin' a little huntin' when we come upon your'n camp."

At that time, the woman groaned loudly, and they both jumped at the unexpected sound. Horace looked at her and then exclaimed, "She be hurt!"

"Your'n woman hurt, Mister?"

"She's hurt. Fell from her hawse."

"This an' tain't no place fer a hurt woman to be, Mister. We need to fetch her t' Granny Vernell. Granny has a heap a healin' stuff t' her house."

Reb thought on this a little while and realized the intruder was right, this was no place for a woman who was hurt, and this one was surely hurt. "How far is this Granny's house?"

"Yonder, cross t'holler an' up t'other side t'hill."

"You boys got horses?"

"Naw, we's don't own none," Ad answered.

"Well, take back your knife, and cut some saplings so we can make a travois for the woman; tie your coats to 'em." Reb said, as he kicked back the large butcher knife.

The two men worked hard and made no threatening moves. Soon they had the woman on the travois and were slowly coming off the ridge.

Cliff was pleased to see the big man walking beside her watching carefully, while the other led Ola. He followed five steps behind.

Two hours later, they came over a small hill, and there in a clearing less than half an acre in size, was a small, high-roofed shack, with a thin trail of smoke pointing skyward from the chimney.

"Thar yonder. I's tol' y' it 'tweren't fer," Horace said, pointing at the structure.

"Granny, Granny Vernell," Ad called out, then he turned back and looked at Reb. "Granny, she be a' mite skittish. Sometimes she shoots a' for she looks."

"That's comforting," Reb said back.

Indeed, a barrel was extended from a cracked door as they approached, but after a lot of talking from the brothers, finally the door was opened fully, and the long black pole was lowered.

The little woman that Reb could now see, stood not an inch over five-feet. Her hair appeared to have been combed last on Christmas day, but he was not sure what year that had been. Strangely, her dress was store-bought, but many years before; it now carried many patches, as well as many tears that needed patching. There were equal stains of tobacco juice that ran from her lower lip to her lower jaw in the creases at each corner of her mouth.

She had little to say that wasn't direct, and when she spoke, the boys jumped as if the sound of her voice brought back memories of many a switching given freely by her old wrinkled hands.

"Who'd you brung this time?"

"It be a lady," Ad offered.

"A flat-land lady," his brother said.

"An' she's hurt," Reb added.

The old woman walked from the door onto the small porch, staying just out of the rain that was pouring from the roof. There she peered at the body on the travois.

"Fetch 'err in heres."

When Reb lifted the woman from the sled's bed into his arms, so she could be moved inside the shack, she groaned loudly.

"Easy thar' boy, she t'ain't no sack a' 'taters," the old woman scolded.

Once inside she pointed, "Yonder, put 'err on t'bed."

Turning and looking about, he thought, *'There is no bed.'* Then he espied a gathering of quilts laying unarranged over some loose straw and weeds in the corner and realized it was there she meant.

Doing as told, as gently as he could, he removed the wet bedroll and covered her with one of the patchwork quilts.

His broad shoulders hid the scene from the two men, who each leaned out to catch a glimpse of the denuded body, before he covered her again.

Granny Vernell slapped each of them when they did, before she implored, "What ails 'err?"

"Fell off her hawse and landed on a rock. She has been out ever since. Bad bump on her forehead and at least one broken rib," Reb replied, removing his soaked hat and slapping it against his leg.

"Who be you?"

"Just passing through," he said and started for the door to tend to his horse.

"She your'n?"

"No," he shook his head and looked over at the pretty face. "Never saw her before I seen her fall."

Reb stopped and looked back at Granny. She was old, true, to him anyway. Her eyes were the color of a rifle barrel that had the bluing worn mostly away but there was kindness in them. Her face, he could visualize, had once been attractive before the skin dried, and the wrinkles took over her expressions. There was a touch of Granny Keeling in her but only a touch. Nonetheless, somehow he suddenly felt a warm cloud sweep over him, and he knew this woman would help the lady, if she could be helped.

Seeing there was no barn or corral, Cliff tied Ola to a low branch of a sapling growing at the rear of the old shack. From his saddlebags he retrieved a small amount of grain. It was mostly damp, but still the big Appaloosa took it gratefully.

Next, he removed the saddle. Then took his Winchester and pommel bags, along with her bag inside.

The shack was a small, one room structure with a stone fireplace at one end and a table in the center on the dirt floor; no other furniture adorned its interior. Several pegs protruded from the walls that served as necessary hangers for various items, from leather goods to rags and cooking utensils. The only light for the moment was what was intruding through the two front windows. The single window on the side behind the chimney had been removed and now was used as a wood box where one could load it from the outside and unload it from the inside; however, he also saw it was empty.

Reb dropped his saddle along the opposite wall and sat on it as he began wiping the dampness from his weapons. First, he took care of the Yellowboy and then his holster pistol[1].

The two boys watched everything he was doing, while Granny brewed something in her pot there in the fireplace.

When he finished with the Colt, he gently laid it on the table before looking up at the boys.

After a few seconds, Horace spoke, "That there, hit's a revolvin' gun, hain't it?"

Cliff nodded his head in agreement.

"I heard tell a' 'em down to the settlement. A man thar say he could shoot nine or ten times a'for he had to reload."

"No such," Ad interrupted. "Six, 'na'more. I count's 'em, when he stuck 'em back in."

"That thar' man did say ten times," Horace argued.

"You are both right," Reb answered.

"See," Horace said back, elbowing his brother in the ribs.

"Yow!"

"Dang it! You two stop a cut's th' fool," Granny said. "You make me spill this an' a' switch you good."

"My Colt holds six. That's why they call it a six-gun, but there is a revolver that holds ten. It's called a LeMat."

"See."

"'em shiny things you put in thar', that be the powder and ball?" Ad asked.

"Yes, they are self-contained, made of copper, sometimes brass," Reb replied, and taking one from his pouch he pitched it to Ad. "It's called a metallic cartridge."

"I heard a' paper cartridges. Pa sa'd they had 'em in the war."

"Same principal, only these can get wet and still fire."

"Sho-nuff?"

The boys looked at the 44 round for some time, passing it back and forth, and then finally Horace handed it back to him.

Reb then removed the other two Colts from the pommel bags and unloading one, he handed it to them.

The boys were mesmerized by the revolver.

Cliff showed them how to open the loading gate and how, when the hammer was placed on half-cock, the cylinder would spin freely

---

1 Holster pistol: Colt had three frame sizes, a large frame referred to as a horse pistol, a small frame called a pocket pistol, and one in between that was worn on a belt and referred to as a belt, or holster pistol.

so as to accommodate loading. After a few minutes, Horace asked, "Why y' got so many?"

"There was a time I needed them," Reb answered.

They both nodded their heads, understanding.

Around three o'clock the rain let up, and slowly the clouds moved north allowing the sun to once again begin it's chore of drying the mountains.

Late in the day, after Granny had served a hot bowl of opossum stew, she called out for the brothers to gather some wood for the night fire, but when no response came to her beckoning, Reb devined[2] both boys and their belongings had suddenly disappeared.

"No wonder, 'em Fleetwing boys are always good for a feeding but blame scarce when it comes time t'do work," she said, as she spit out the door. Then she turned and looked at the tall lean man who was standing there.

Recognizing her expression, Reb nodded his head and asked, "Do you have an axe?"

"Behind the house, can't miss it."

He walked around, and feeling good about being out in the fresh air again, he found the thought of splitting wood as pleasant. That is until he realized how dull the axe was. He had just picked it up and run his finger down the blade, when he heard her call out from inside, "Th'grind'rock's yonder t' th' little house."

Turning, he saw the small structure that served as her outhouse, and there beside it he could just make out what was a grinding stone on a short bench, which served double duty as a shaving horse.

Walking towards it he heard her again call out, "You's hand's stouter'n mine, so split me some splints while you are out there. An' fetch a mite'a red clay an' a bucket a' water from th' well yonder. I need to make a' mixture t'put under th' splints t'her ribs."

Cliff raised his left arm as a reply and continued on to the grinding wheel.

'The stone is a good one,' he thought as he peddled away.

His next thoughts were of the continuing quest of locating Tidwell. 'I'll stay the night, if the old woman allows it, then head out come first light.' Splitting another oak limb, that was there against

---

2 **Devined: Nineteenth century word meaning realized.**

Granny Vernell's Cabin After a Light Snow

the back of the shack, his thoughts continued, *'Take that long for my outfit to dry anyway.'*

Cliff had not come into these hills by accident. He had gotten a lead that a man fitting Tidwell's description was seen two days before. Supposedly, he was traveling on the very trail Reb had beenfollowing when he spotted the woman tearing up the countryside. Now this incident had set him back a day perhaps two. Of course, he knew he would have to have held up somewhere during the storms, but he had rather blame the delay on the woman than the rain.

He also knew that if it was Tidwell whose trail he was now riding, the delay wasn't that bad unless the killer had made it out of these mountains before the rain, he too would have lost the same time, holed up someplace. Nonetheless, a man who has been inconvenienced by an unwelcome guest had rather place the blame there than on the weather. It's in his nature.

Reb split the requested splints, as well as enough wood to last several days. Most of it he dropped into the window box, but he carried the last armful in for her and was about to tell Granny of his intention to leave when she spoke, "T'mornin' you best be going over't th' settlement 'n' fetching some quinine 'n' some bitters. I got most 'erry' thing else."

"Granny, come first light I got 'a be heading out. I ain't nothing to do with this woman."

"You be everything t'do with this woman. You brung 'er 'ear. You stay 'til she can travel on 'er own, or take 'er now, and I'll be done wif' ya' both, now."

He could see she wasn't going to let him go away without a fight, and he wanted nothing to do with fighting with a woman twice his age.

"How far is the settlement?"

"Hain't that far," she replied, cutting him a glance.

He saw the sternness in her expression but also read the laughter in her eyes at her having him back down so easily.

"Moark be yonder over the ridge," she said, pointing south, "but I don't know nutton 'bout them Arkansas folk. Be better you go to Poplar Bluff, that way yonder, a day in t'wagon."

"What's wrong with Arkansas folk?" he asked, remembering General Cleburne was from Arkansas. "Patty Cleburne had some mighty good fighting Arkansas men under his command."

"Ya don't know, won't be me what tells Ya'. You go to Poplar Bluff."

She stopped and almost closed one eyelid while she was thinking strong on something, then she continued, "Be best you say nary a word 'bout her," nodding her head at the sleeping woman.

"It might be best if we find out who she is and get her own people to care for her, with a proper doctor."

"You fetch 'em things I tol' you't an' she be needing no doctor," Granny said placing her hands on her hips and then looking hard at him. "Asides, you tol' me she were a tearin' up the ground when she fell."

"That's right."

"She be runnin' from you?"

"No. I told you I never saw her before."

"Who den' she be runnin' from?"

He thought on it a moment. '*Granny is right,*' he remembered the woman was looking back over her shoulder just before she fell. '*She was running from something or someone.*'

He was nodding his head when she spoke again, "Could be she 'aire runnin, from som'un in Poplar Bluff."

He again nodded his head. '*She's right, but who, why?*'

"Could be who'eber she be runnin' from won't take kindly a' you helping her. Could be, he'll not tak' kindly you being here with her alone. Did'ja think a' that?"

'She is right again.'

"Hey, wait a minute. I ain't alone with her. Not like you're suggesting."

"You brung 'er 'ear buck naked as th' day she wus born."

"You're trying to twist facts, Granny."

"Naw, just want you to move like the fox, when you be fetching t' medicine."

Sunrise found him two miles below Granny's shack once more on the route he had taken into these hills. Half an hour later he came upon a strong trail that cut sharp left. He was sure it was the way to Poplar Bluff; it was exactly as Granny had described it.

The wagon road was still muddy and slippery from the long rain, and he wanted nothing to do with shooting another horse anytime soon. Thus, he cut slightly to the west and began moving down from the taller hills without the benefit of a muddy trail. However, he still was slow walking his horse. An hour later the terrain became hillier and less mountainous, so he once again took to the road.

After he had stolen on a little further he came upon as many cleared fields as forest. Here and there were ponds, now filled with rainwater. On occasion, he could spot the roof of a barn or the thin trail of smoke escaping from a chimney.

It was while he was watching such a smoke trail that he found himself face to face with half a dozen riders, who had suddenly appeared over a hummock in the road. They reined up when they were upon him.

"Who are you?" the lead rider demanded.

It had all happened so quickly, he had not had time to pull his hammer strap clear. Looking at them, he saw most were not carrying a handgun, rather rifles or scatterguns. The lead rider and the man next to him wore belt revolvers, but they too had their guns tied down for hard riding.

Considering he might have to fight his way out of the situation he thought, *'My only real problem will come from the shotguns.'*

Before leaving Memphis, Reb had wired most of his money to himself at *The State Bank* in Springfield. This day, he carried less than eighty dollars in folding money and perhaps fifty in coin. It was the gold that worried him. It would be easy to locate, but he was sure they would not find his Yankee Dollars. A man robbing another will take most everything he has, especially his boots, but no one stole someone else's dirty socks, and Cliff had tied his folding money tightly around his right ankle.

Slowly he leaned forward resting the palms of his hands on the saddle horn. His Open Tops[3] were just inches away under the cover of the pommel bags. He knew he could get to them before the others could untie and draw their revolvers, but he wasn't sure about one of the men with a scattergun. It was the new type with internal hammers, and Cliff had no idea how fast he would be. The other man with a shotgun had not cocked its exposed hammers thus far; still he considered it wise not to reach for his Colts, unless he did so.

"I'm a fellow on the trail of a murderer," Reb replied.

They sat a little straighter suddenly.

The leader narrowed his eyes as he pondered Cliff's last statement, *'If he is trailing a murderer he might be law or a bounty hunter. Either way he would know how to use that revolver he's a toting.'* "You the Law?" he asked.

"Well, sure as hell you ain't," Cliff answered.

"We're looking for a woman what got kidnapped."

"I ain't seen no kidnapped woman, but tell me what she looks like in case I do see her."

The towheaded man who had been asking all the questions looked him over and started to reply but stopped and said nothing; instead he again narrowed his eyes. The man beside him with the scattergun answered, "She's Mrs. Hickey. Will Hickey's wife." When he spoke, he lowered the weapon so the barrels now pointed down.

"Charlie," was all the blond said to silence his companion.

"Must be a sizeable reward on finding her," Cliff suggested.

"Who told you that?"

"I see there are enough of you riding out looking for her. Stands to reason you expect to collect something fer your troubles."

"We work for Mr. Hickey."

Cliff nodded his head and then leaned a little more forward, "You saying then there ain't no reward."

"Lawmen don't get rewards."

"Never said I was a lawman."

---

3 Open Top: The nickname given to the Colt Model 1871-72 revolvers.

"You be bounty hunter then?"

"Bounty hunter," the man with the shotgun said and spit at the ground. "I hate bounty hunters." As he spoke, he began raising the shotgun again, but before he got it up, he was looking down the barrel of a Colt 44.

"Never said I was a bounty hunter, neither," Cliff added. "Now drop the scattergun."

"Charlie, don't drop Mr. Hickey's Parker Brothers."

Cliff cocked the hammer slowly so they all could hear the sears. Immediately the rider tossed the gun forward over his horse's head, where it splattered on the muddy road.

"Charlie, I told you not to do that."

"Well, Spain, that pistol he's got is pointed at me, not you. I reckon you would do the same were it your gut about to get ventilated."

"Charlie, you're fired. When I get back I better not find you or any a' your gear on Kent," Spain said, then turning to Cliff he added, "And you had best be out of Butler County pronto."

"Funny how bullies are always saying that," Cliff replied and then lowered the hammer of his revolver.

The man called Charlie turned his horse out of the group and backed off to the side moments before Spain rode past Cliff, with the other four men following him.

Cliff backed his horse off the opposite side of the road where he could keep an eye on both the riders and Charlie.

When he was sure they were no longer a threat, he looked over at the husky man across from him. "Charlie, get me that shotgun," Reb said, again allowing his revolver to point at the man.

"Well, damn," he said, before dismounting.

Retrieving it, he wiped as much of the mud from the weapon as he could before he handed it up.

Cliff took it, and then gestured with his pistol barrel for the man to back up. He waited until he was satisfied at the distance, before looking down at the weapon. There he saw on the top of the barrels, **Parker Brothers Hammerless Shotgun Meriden, Conn.** The piece was highly engraved and seemed to balance perfectly in his left hand. "You got more shells for this?"

Poplar Bluff Missouri 1872

The man struggled in the pocket of his overalls, produced four green paper shells and stretched forth his hand. Taking them, Cliff asked, "You got more than four?"

"No I ain't. That is all Spain let me have."

Cliff then removed the two from the chambers before saying, "Sorry I cost you your job, didn't mean to do that." He then pitched the shotgun back to the man standing in the road. "Clean this up, and take it back to your boss. It might make a difference on the job."

The man looked up at him and cocked his head a little, as if trying to understand why the stranger had done this act.

"See you around," Cliff said, as he slipped the Colt back into the pommel bag in front of his saddle and heeled his horse on north.

When he got to Poplar Bluff the words on everybody's tongue was in some way concerning Mrs. Hickey.

Most of the talk was about her kidnapping. He heard some talk of a $1000.00 reward for her return, but he learned there was a condition to the reward; she had to return uninjured.

He also heard in *Axtell's General Store*, while he was arranging for a sack of oats for his horse, two women talking on the subject. One spoke of Leslie Hickey as having run off, after her husband killed her lover.

'*That makes the most sense,*' Reb thought. '*She was fleeing something for sure, and I wouldn't be surprised if it weren't Spain and his boys.*'

"It wasn't that handsome Mr. Mouton was it?" the other woman asked.

"Heavens no! It was some common stable boy. Mr. Jean Mouton is a close personal friend of the Hickey family. He would never do something so crass as to seduce a friend's wife. I met him you know, and he is considering having Sunday dinner with us after the services."

"Oh, Rachel, you just have all the luck."

Their conversation meant nothing to him at first until he heard the name. Not only had Tidwell used it in Atlanta, but also Roland Darktower had said the man he was after was called John Mouton, and it turned out he and John Tidwell were one in the same. '*I wonder?*' he thought. '*Mouton is not a common name, not in Dixie anyway.*'

A light snow fell in the high country that evening, and it was near dark when he found Granny Vernell's shack again.

"Thought y' tweren't a comin' back," she said, as he stepped inside and sat the bag on the table.

"You knew better than that," he replied.

"Well, this must be my savior."

Cliff turned and saw the woman, still laying on the pallet but raised on one forearm where she could look at him.

He immediately removed his hat, "Ma'am."

"Yep, that be you'n's hero, sho-nuff'," Granny said, looking at Reb.

"I understand were it not for you, I would most likely be dead by now."

"You did take a nasty fall," he agreed.

"And Chesterfield?"

He narrowed his eyes and wondered if he had heard that name today. No, he was sure he had not. '*Maybe it is her husband's name.*'

Realizing he did not know of whom she meant, she added, "My beautiful bay horse."

"I had to put him down. His leg was broken in two."

Suddenly, he saw tears swell in her eyes. Immediately he remembered how he felt when he lost Red, and his heart went out to her, "I had no choice. The wolves____."

"I know. It's my fault. I was running him too hard."

'*That sure is the blame truth,*' he agreed but did not say it to her.

"I brought what you asked for Granny, and some flour and sugar; and a few cans a' peaches; and five pounds of Arbuckles beans, if you got a grinder." Cliff was talking to change the subject. He had always hated watching a woman cry.

"Tarnation, sounds like you'n's 'specting me t'bake a pie."

"Just though you might need some staples," Cliff replied, without looking at either of the women.

"Well, t'night we be etin' more stew, so get yourself washed up, and while you'n's at it, fetch in Mis' Honey's britches."

He strung a rope across the room from one wall to the other and hung a blanket and a quilt there blocking off the back of the cabin. Soon, with Granny's help, Honey Hickey was dressed and sitting up with her back to the wall. When the old woman moved forward, she removed the fabric wall, and he saw her sitting there with a smile on her face.

"My, but you look so much better," he said.

"I do feel better, I guess. At least I'm awake and ready to take nourishment."

"That be a smil'n sign," Granny said, as she spooned out a hardy portion of her soup in a wooden bowl. "You got 'a wait," she said to him. "Ol' granny ain't got no need fer morn' one bowl."

"I got a couple in my saddlebags," Cliff told her.

"Well, stop a gazing at that thar purty girl, and fetch 'em."

Cliff didn't like the statement. *'I was not gazing at Mrs. Hickey. I was just looking at her for politeness during the conversation we were having.'*

He fed his horse while he was outside and took care of the other necessary chores that need doing before all light was gone. When he returned, he had an armful of split oak for the fire.

"Here Granny," he said, handing her a tin plate and a pewter bowl. He also brought in his two spoons, one large he used for dipping, and the smaller for eating.

They ate, talked and laughed a little. Then Granny rose and picked up the utensils before she said, "I aim t'have me a smoke a'for I turn in." Reaching over the top of the door, she retrieved a pipe from the shelf there, "Be back directly."

Leslie looked off at the flames flickering in the fireplace and said softly, "You think she went out to smoke or to give us time to talk?"

"Probably both," he agreed. Then shifting where he could stretch out one leg, which was beginning to cramp, he said, "I do want to talk to you."

"I thought you would," she said, but when she tried to move some herself, she cried out.

He jumped up and reached to help but stopped before his hands touched her, as he didn't really know what he needed to do to help.

"It's alright. I just have this sharp pain in my side when I move wrong."

"You broke a rib," he said to her.

"Three or four, Granny says."

He nodded without reply.

When she was settled again and seemed to be comfortable as possible, he spoke, "I ran into a man called Spain on my way to Poplar Bluff."

She immediately jumped and gritted at the pain when she did but gave no vocal cry. Then taking a deep breath she asked, "You didn't___?"

"No," he interrupted her shaking his head, "I never let on that I had ever heard of you."

"I should have known that," she replied. "Granny said you were one to ride the river with."

"She did, did she?" he said, turning and looking at the door as if he could see the old woman through it.

"Yes, she did. I think she fancys you, Reb Brown."

"You know my name."

"Yes, she told me."

"Funny, I don't recall telling her," he said again, looking over at the old woman's door. Then turning back and looking straight at the injured girl he said, "And you are Mrs. Hickey."

She lowered her head and twisted the edge of the quilt around her finger before replying, "Yes, I am, or at least I was."

"It was Spain, who you were running from?"

"Yes, Mr. Hickey sent them after me. I'm not sure if it was for the money or for me, but they were after me. I just barely got away from them. Wouldn't have, had I not found that mountain trail."

"You stole that money?"

"Stole! Hell no. It is as much mine as it is his. I took it from the little safe. It is just petty cash for running Kent. I never touched his safe in the house or took any money out of the bank."

"Reb? You were a Confederate," she said.

"Yes, I was and am, but that ain't where I got that name. I was called Reb since I started to school, even before that, I suppose. Everybody used to say I was a rebel in the crib."

She smiled at that. Then with a more serious tone she said, "My father was killed by a rebel."

He gritted his teeth and nodded his head before he asked, "In the war?"

"Yes."

"Where? Do you know?" he was hoping that he would be able to tell her he never was there, so she wouldn't feel hard at him.

"I'm not sure, some river in Tennessee."

'Damn. I fought at nearly every river engagement in Tennessee,' he thought, then an idea came upon him.

"How do you know it were a Reb that killed him?"

"Why, do you think our own men would shoot my father?"

"It happens; things get confused in a battle. Our beloved General Jackson was shot by his own men, mee'be the worst blow of the whole war, for our side."

She raised her head and looked high along the far wall for several seconds, "I never thought of that," she finally said back.

"Your name is Honey?"

"I must have told Granny that while I was delirious. I haven't been called Honey since I married, six years ago. It was my stage name. I was an actress when Mr. Hickey and I met. He deplores the name and insists I be called Mrs. Hickey. He doesn't even call me by my real name."

"Leslie," he injected.

"Why yes. How on earth?"

He just smiled back at her. Then he too took on a more stern tone and asked, "Why did you leave him?"

She twisted her head, and tears came to her eyes. Finally, with broken voice she said, "Because he shot a boy. For no good reason, he just shot him dead."

Cliff now was convinced the story he had heard was true, so he spoke of it no more.

"Well, you are free now. I'll see that you get away when you are well."

Again tears began to flow, but with broken voice she managed, "I will be so grateful."

Later, she had a relapse, and her fever returned. Reb and Granny were up most of the night trying to break it. The next day she was little better, but on the third day she awoke cool and dry.

Granny made her take some more quinine and a little soup, but by ten in the morning she said, "I believe most of her ails be past. If'n she don't go and poke a rib through 'er lung sack."

"I'll try not to," Leslie replied, and smiled. "But this might take longer than I imagined."

Reb noticed she had lost color, and her face was thinner than when he first brought her here, but at least she was awake and talking once more.

Sometime that morning, while they were talking, he mentioned that her husband had posted a reward of a thousand dollars for her safe return.

Granny stood suddenly, "Who all knows 'er this?"

"Most everybody I would suppose," he replied. "It was the talk of the town when I was in Poplar Bluff. I ran into a posse of men looking for her."

"Do the Fleetwing's know 'et?"

"I don't know. If they have gone to town___."

"They never go to town," she said. "No mind, we got'a gat 'er out a' hare', 'em boys a' snitch on thar own Pap fer a thousand dollars."

"But where?"

"Let me ponder," Granny said, and placing her chin in her palm, she began to rub it around as if it helped in the thinking process. Finally, she said, "Thar be a cabin, yonder, cross the hollow, two hills past th' stream. It were Neely's a'for he got 'imself shot dead two year ago. I don't recollect thar being nary a-body what took it up. Neely had no woman you know."

"How will I find it?" Cliff asked.

"I'll be a' leading ya'," Granny said back solidly.

"I can't ride," Leslie pointed out. "Not yet."

"I can make another travois. It worked getting you here," he replied and then added, with a smile, "I'll do a better job this time."

"You must have done a good job the last time," she said, smiling back at him.

"Boy, you go out now an' put that thar travois together. Use my blanket," Granny ordered. "I be a' gatherin' stores you be a' needin'. We's best t'be gone from here come sunup."

Cliff did as she had instructed although he doubted it was as critical as she let on. He hadn't had any trouble handling the brothers before, and he didn't think he would again. Still, considering that the woman might be in danger, he made no protest.

That night he slept restlessly. He didn't really know why, but several times he would awake after a strange dream that made no sense at all. Afterward he would have to struggle to get back to sleep. Once, when he had awakened he checked on Leslie and found her resting. He then went outside to relieve himself and have a look around. When he turned to go back, she spoke, "Can't sleep neither, eh?"

He jumped and reached for the Colt he had stuffed into his waistband before he recognized her voice. "Damn Granny, I nearly shot you."

"Mite jumpy 'er ya?"

"I reckon I am at that," he admitted and leaned back against the front of her shack and raised one leg until he had the sole of his foot against the slabs, and there he stood with all his weight on his other leg.

"How did this here Neely get himself shot?" he asked more as a piece of conversation than in real interest.

"Alsop, Ken Alsop shot 'im. I heared tell."

"What was that over?"

"Ah, 'em Fleetwing's and Alsop's been feuding morn' I been alive, I reckon," she replied. "Some say it ended wid' t' war, but 'tain't so. Hit were Ken alright. I hear tell."

"Why you doing this for her, Granny?" he asked. "It ain't none a' your scrap, could even get you in a mite a' trouble."

"I like that girlie in thar. She be a true shooter, fer a Yankee girl."

The old woman coughed, and then after clearing her throat she spit a long distance into the night air. "Asides, she needs help, and Granny ain't one to turn away 'em what needs help. Kind a' like a young man I know, here'bout."

He struck a Lucifer, and looked at his watch, "Four-twenty," he said.

"Well, be time 'afor you know it," she replied. "Best you go ahead and hitch up that travois. I'll be fetching the stores, and gat'en her ready."

He knew she was right. He just had a bad feeling about the whole affair.

The sun never came into view that morning. Fog began to form before light and lay thick in the hollows all day. Near the ten o'clock hour, they were atop a sizable hill and found themselves clear of the fog, but there was complete cloud cover overhead, and Cliff noticed more dark weather moving in from the south.

"How much longer, Granny?"

"Ar, longer mee'be."

The fog had dispersed some when they arrived at their destination. It was clear on that side of the hill, providing a wonderful view to the east and west, but nothing could be seen over a hundred yards to either the south or the north. That was all right with him.

They arrived at the cabin ten minutes before the rain came, and he had just gotten Leslie inside when the first drops began to fall.

Neely had located his cabin on a bald knoll, which slopped away steeply all around. Anyone approaching would have to climb to get within pistol range.

He had designed it well, too. It was mostly made of heavy hewed log, supported on a large stone foundation. On the front and back sides, he had left a four-foot opening for entrance from both directions. The roof was still in decent shape and only had a couple of leaks.

The corral was built on the back of the cabin with a portion wrapping around to one side. It was still pretty much intact. Here, too, was an opening which allowed one or two animals to get shelter. The opposite wall also had a door that opened to a short porch.

Inside he saw a trapdoor that lead to a root cellar, and also served as a means to go to the underside of the house, which gave access to the wooden windows located down there.

The cabin windows had glass panes, but inside there were strong board coverings that hinged at the top. It was a natural rampart, easily defended from any side.

In the cellar, Granny found a case of canned pears and five pounds of salt that was still good. The flour was full of boll weevils, as was the bag of ground hominy.

She had lugged most of the goods Cliff had bought in the settlement with her, and immediately set about preparing supper.

There was a frame bed, although the straps were mostly rotten, and the bedding had worn through. Cliff repaired that right away, while Leslie rested in one of the two wooden chairs that were at the table.

They found two coal oil lanterns that still had oil in them, and with a blaze going in the fireplace, the little cabin became cozy in no time.

The next day the rain continued, however the opening from the corral allowed his horse to stay out of the weather.

Just before dark, they heard a commotion outside, and Ola began to dance around and display all sorts of unhappy noises. Cliff opened the window to the north side and saw six or seven tall thin hogs milling around where he had pitched the bad flour.

"Em's razorbacks. Good eaten' wid sage'n'blackpepper; shoot 'em," Granny said, just above a whisper.

Cliff took his carbine and squeezed off a shot. The lead slug struck the pig behind the left ear, and he fell over and kicked for several seconds, then lay still. The others scattered at the report but in a few minutes came back, and he killed another one.

The remainder of the day was spent skinning and butchering the wild-hogs.

"Been better if'n you'd sing' 'em an' scald'em. Hit takes awful 'ot t'clean'em til'they'fit't'et yours way. 'Could'a made souse if'n we's' t'boil head a'th'hog. I'm plum silly 'bout souse."

"I'll settle for a nice thick chop," Cliff replied.

"Me too," Leslie agreed.

That night they ate well.

When the sun finally began to shine again, Granny gathered her belongings, and gave her advice, "Y's linger fer a while, an' when you go, follow this trail, don't tell nawy a'body of where you be stayin' or where you been. Shoot all Alsops first, an' ask questions later."

"Granny, I'll take you back on the horse," Reb offered.

"Naw, that thar' rain done washed clean all sign a' us'n a comin'. When Granny goes, she be following t' stream yonder, to a rock-slide an' then work 'er way back to da' path. 'Haint no flatlander eria' gon'a track Granny Vernell."

She stopped at the door and looked back at the tall man standing there and then at the woman who was sitting in the chair, "I come to find feelings deep inside a' me fer you two. That be why I's tell ya' now. Don't never come t'my house again. Hit's best that way."

She took a deep breath, turned and was gone from their sight before either could digest what she had just said.

Reb walked over to the door to watch her leave, but she had vanished, *'Almost like her spirit just whisked her away,'* he thought.

Travel in the hill country of the Ozarks is not easy on foot. It is much harder for a woman who turned sixty-two Christmas past. She slept the first night on a large, flat stone outcropping at the entrance of a small cave. The next day she worked her way to the trail that lead from the Poplar Bluff Road then cut back southwest towards her home.

It was near dark when she arrived to find the Fleetwing brothers there.

"What you a doin' sneakin' round m'house?"

"We come to saw how th' lady were doin'," Ad said.

"She be doin' fine," Granny said. "Now get, 'taint feeding ya' t'night."

"Whar' she be Granny?"

"Gone."

"Whar' she gone, Granny?" Horace asked.

"Arkansas, I reckon."

"Arkansas!" Ad exclaimed. "Hellfire Granny, no sane man travels overt'Arkansas."

"You be som'-on to be a spat in' off 'bout sane men," she shot back. "Now get out a' m'way."

When she rushed passed the brothers heading for the door, she cocked the hammer on her old squirrel rifle, and the boys backed off. Lance Spain however, was not frightened by the scrawny old woman. He and his men suddenly stepped from around the side of her shack, and she stopped cold.

"Granny, we came to get the woman. We know she was here, and you took her off somewhere. I aim to find out where."

When he finished she took notice he had a mean look in his blue-gray eyes, his jaw was locked, and his facial muscles were drawn tight. Sizing him up before she spoke, *'He's not a stout man, not really. He's perhaps half a foot taller than me, an' he shoulders 'aire narrow which causes his head to appear too stout fer his body, an' his hips be wider than his shoulders,'* she thought. *'Reminds a body er' a pinecone.'* However, what she replied just before she spit between his legs was, "Who be you?"

"That thar' is Mr. Spain, Granny," Ad said. "He be from Mr. Hickey, you know da' lady's man-fellow."

"Don't mean nutton ta' me," she said, starting on towards her cabin.

Spain stepped between her and the door. "Granny, we come a long ways to find 'er. 'Er husband is paying a lot a' money fer her, and we're gon'a fetch her back safely. We ain't leaving until we find out where she is."

"I don' tol' whar' she be. They's went to Arkansas."

"Who is the man with her?" Spain asked, reaching and clasping her upper right arm and squeezing tightly.

"One t' likes a' you best not be a' tanglin' with," she replied and tried to twist free. Spain only increased his grip, and the arm began to go numb on her. She knew she had to do something soon or she would be unable.

Twisting her body allowed her to wrench almost free. He lost his grip on her arm but retained a grasp on her sleeve.

It gave her enough room to bring the butt of the rifle up and slam it into his knee.

Spain yelled loudly and staggered back.

She then brought up the rifle and pointed it at him, but Edward Ford saw what was happening and pulling his 58 caliber Harpers Ferry pistol, shot her full in the chest.

The two brothers stepped back with their mouth's open in horror.

"Damn it to hell," Spain yelled. "Now how the shit are we gon'a' find Mrs. Hickey? You idiot."

"She were about to shoot you, Lance!" Ford tried to explain.

"Don't you think the six a' us could have handled a scrawny old woman like that?" he shouted, and turning, he removed his hat and slapped it against his leg. "Damn it to hell!"

Horace looked at Granny laying there in a twisted, grotesque position with a huge black spot on the front of her old dress. The area was still smoldering from where the powder had begun to burn the material. He knew she was dead. He knew she was dead before she ever hit the ground. Still he wanted to somehow help her, but he didn't know what to do. Finally, he slapped his brother, turned and started running from the clearing. Ad followed.

Spain saw this and yelled, "Don't let them get away. We can't have no witnesses to be telling of this."

Several shots immediately filled the air, but neither brother fell.

Horace ran through the trees down the slope until he couldn't move anymore, and then he lay still in a patch of mulberry bushes.

He could hear others moving about. Once a leg came so close he could see it, but he made not the slightest sound or movement.

Finally, after all had been quite for sometime, he slipped on off.

Ad never came home that night. The family found him laying in a huge puddle of dried blood, roughly six rods distance from Granny's shack, with a hole in his upper leg.

"He must a' been hit when we wus trot'n' to gat away," Horace said. "I nary heard no more shots after then."

The Fleetwing clan dragged him and Granny into her shack before setting fire to it. Then they turned and left without looking back.

Horace stayed until it was burned completely through and mostly out, then he walked over to where Granny's rifle lay, exactly where she had dropped it. After picking it up, he followed his kin into the woods to the west.

Sunday morning a week later, when the respectable people of Poplar Bluff began arriving at the Episcopal Church, they were greeted by the dead body of Edward Ford. He had been shot seventeen times and was hung from the 4x4 brace that also supported the church's shingle.

Only those who had been at Granny Vernell's shack, that day, knew why he had been shot and displayed so dramatically. His murder was never solved by the authorities, but it was a sobering thought to them that knew.

Cliff and Leslie knew nothing of it. They stayed there in the cabin for the remainder of the month as her ribs healed. The days were turning cool and the leaves changing their color. It was the most beautiful time of the year in the Ozarks, and the two enjoyed the beauty and serenity of it.

Cliff had remade her bed and built a light structure wall separating a small area of the one room cabin for her privacy. He had built himself a separate bed and set it beside the trapdoor that led below.

Not once, during the time they were there together, had he touched her. She was another man's wife, and his was too soon in the cold dark ground.

She, on the other hand, had fallen hopelessly in love with her White Knight. He had rescued her from Beelzebub and his men, nursed her back to health, and protected her from evil and harm.

He was strong, handsome, and the first true gentleman she had ever met.

Not that Will and his friends did not profess to be the only gentlemen in Butler County, or all of south Missouri for that matter, but professing something and living up to it were two totally different things.

She had not intended to fall in love with this Rebel. She did not even want to be in love with him, for surely when he felt she was well enough, he would take her to some place he considered she would be safe and be gone from her forever. Still she had no control over her heart, and the thought of his leaving brought great pain to her chest. She often exaggerated her condition to prolong their stay there.

There was a new moon on the first of November, and the night was as black as any he had ever seen. Not a star or anything that reflected light could be seen, save the coal oil lanterns in the cabin.

They stood outside together, inches apart, thinking, talking, teasing and laughing lightly. She craved his touch so, but he made no move in that direction. She wanted to reach out and grab him, pull him to her, throw her arms around him and squeeze him as tight as she could. She almost did but stopped.

"You seem to be getting along much better these last few days," he said. "Snows will come before long, and we are almost out of coal oil for fuel."

"I, I don't think I can ride yet. When I try to raise my arms, like I would have to, to get on your horse, I get a sharp pain here," she said, reaching for his hand and guiding it to where her ribs had been broken. "I almost pass out, it is so sharp."

"Well, mee'be I could go get a few supplies. We are getting low on most everything. I just don't want to leave a trail a hound scent could follow."

"Hound scent?" she queried.

"Ah, a good tracker, you know like a hound."

"Oh," she said back, wondering if he considered her ignorant of his ways and language.

"The next time the rains come, you go. I'll wait here. I just don't think I can make it yet."

He knew she was lying, and he understood. At least he thought he did. *'She is scared to death of her husband, and yet she has so much to lose by leaving all that wealth behind her. I understand her wanting to put off the decision on returning or going on someplace else, but winter will make it for her before long.'*

"Alright, we'll stay a few days longer, but we'd die should we try and stay out the winter. If you are not healing right, mee'be we should get you to a proper doctor, and have him see what the reason is."

She quivered at his statement, and he felt it against his arm. "Come on. It's getting cold; better go back inside 'afore you catch your death."

He took her elbow and led her to the door, then opening it, stepped aside allowing her to pass before him.

'*Funny,*' she thought, '*the only time Will does that is when he is trying to impress his friends.*'

Once inside, they each settled into doing the little things people do before retiring for the night. She washed her face and dried her hands on a towel that had once been a curtain when Neely owned the cabin. He sat in a chair and cleaned each of his guns as he did every night before reloading them.

When finished, he spoke to her without looking away from the last Colt he had loaded, "There is a man, Jean Mouton I think is what he is called in Poplar Bluff. Do you know him?"

"Why yes, he is a friend of Will's. I think they knew each other some years back."

"How long has he been around these parts?"

"I don't know. Will brought him to Kent sometime in the late summer. Let me see," she paused and thought a few seconds before continuing, "around the last of August or the first of September, I think."

"Where did he go when he left?"

"I don't know. He was still there when I left. I really detest him, he is always looking at me as if he could see right though my clothes, gives me a slimy feeling," she said and shuddered immediately afterward.

"Do you think he is still there?"

"I don't know, possibly. I try not to think of him."

"Alright, one last question. Describe him for me."

"What is your interest in him?" she suddenly asked, wondering how he would have even known of Mouton.

"The man I'm after has gone by the name of John Mouton in the past. I think Jean is French for John."

"Yes, it is. Is the man you seek a Frenchman?"

"No. He's an American, speaks with a northeastern accent."

"Well, he couldn't be the same man. I have heard Jean Mouton and Will speak, and he only speaks French. It really irritates me, they know I don't know the language and carry on as if I wasn't even there."

"Your husband French?"

"No, but he grew up in Canada, and speaks the language fluently."

"And Mouton couldn't have grown up in New England and speak the French language fluently? Isn't French Canada just across the river from New York?"

"Why yes, it is. I see what you mean," she replied, then pausing added, "No, he's French, he even speaks English with a French accent, what little bit of English he has spoken."

"Is he about forty-five, maybe a little older, six foot tall, graying black hair, cold blue eyes and perhaps walks with a slight limp, missing two fingers on his right hand?"

She stood there with a blank expression on her face. He had described the memory she had of Jean Mouton to a tee. *'Could this be the same man?'* she wondered.

Finally she spoke, "Why, yes. I would say that is an accurate description of him, although I have never seen him without benefit of his leather gloves."

"That's what I thought," he said back, now looking at her.

"Why are you after him?"

He took the Colt and shoved it forcibly into his belt holster before he spoke, "The bastard murdered my wife!" Then Cliff stood, strapped on the belt and adjusted it on his hips, before he reached for his hat. He then went outside without saying another word. She knew not to follow him. She also realized her time with him at this cabin was drawing to a close.

It was a long time before he came back in, and she had already gone to bed. Although she could not see him, she could see the shadow he cast along the top of the far wall as he walked around. Now it seemed to her his back was bent, and his broad shoulders were slumped. She was grateful when he turned down the light. It was an hour before she heard his steady breathing and low snore. Until then, she did not sleep.

When she awoke the next morning, Reb was gone.

It had been some over two weeks since the town had experienced the intense and distressing brutal murder of Edward Ford. Even though the shock was wearing off, it remained the subject on the tongues of most of those who enjoyed the sin of idle palaver.

He stopped by the blacksmith's, next to a livery, to have a shoe repaired, and it was there he heard the story.

No one knew who Eddie had pissed off, but everyone knew whoever it was, was one bad dude.

There Cliff met Ervin Dancer, the Smithy and owner of both businesses, and being satisfied with what he saw, he boarded Ola there

Sternwheeler Docked at Poplar Bluff

for the day. Then he looked for a small horse that would be suitable for both a pack animal and broke to ride. In the corral, he spotted a little sorrel about 14 hands that he liked, it sort a' reminded him of Red when he was a colt.

Next, he rented a room at *The Black River Hotel* and then went to *Deal & Brown's General Store,* where he bought enough supplies to get them through another two weeks or him three weeks on the trail. He also made arrangements to have the boy, who helped out there, take them over to the livery at ten o'clock the following morning. Next, he strolled down the boardwalk to *The Saint Francis Saloon* where he bought a bottle. Easing into a chair at an empty table, he began sipping and listening.

Two hours passed, and he had consumed two shot glasses of the not-so-old whiskey.

There was a working girl there he overheard others call Lilly, who may have been twenty years old. Twice she came over and asked if there was anything she could do for him. He just shook his head, and after the second try, with a disappointed expression, she moved away and began talking to others who seemed to be regulars at the bar.

He realized it was early, and only the wealthy or the old would be there at this time of day, still he wanted to hear what was the talk of the town. Around six, a few young men came in following a fellow about twice their age. They were dressed as lumberjacks, and he assumed they were all from the same squad. They were loud and annoyingly often drowned out the conversation of others; still he waited. Half an hour later, he saw Charlie come in.

The man did not go directly to the bar, rather stood back behind the others and sort of moved into their group. However, they ignored him, and presently he went over to a table where three men were playing a game of cards and stood there for a while. They too failed to offer him acceptance. He then slowly turned and started for the door.

"Charlie."

He stopped and looked over at the lone man sitting against the back wall.

Cliff raised the bottle about a foot off the table and then set it back down again.

Charlie Nash was thirty-two years old. He had been raised in Scott County near Tywappity but had made a bad choice during the war. It was not really his fault. When the war broke out, he was employed as a woodcutter aboard *The Lexington*, a stern-wheeler who worked mostly the Ohio between Cincinnati and Cape Girardeau. Everyone onboard jumped ship in Evansville and joined the Union. Charlie, who was drunk at the time, went along with his buddies, none of which were expecting the conflict to last over the summer.

When he returned home four years later he learned his father, two brothers and three cousins had been killed. He also learned every male of age in his entire family had been in the Confederate Army. Now, they considered him a traitor and banished him from the family.

For the next five years, he had bounced from one town to another, never able to keep a job very long. Finally, on New Years Day, 1870, he was hired by Lance Spain as a stable boy, where he found a life of security at Kent. He had given up hard drink and worked night and day. Finally his accomplishments were noticed by Mrs. Hickey, who had him moved to the tack shop where his talents with leather could be better appreciated.

Charlie never knew it had been on Mrs. Hickey's orders that he was moved to the better position. Spain had told him it had been his idea, but he did notice Spain had always been cold to him after that, and he wondered why. Since he had been fired from Kent, he had been unable to find work and returned to the bottle.

He was in need of a drink and was most appreciative of the offer from the stranger. It wasn't until he had sat down and swallowed the fiery liquid, and just sitting the glass back on the table, hoping for a second, did he recognized the stranger.

"Son-a-Bitch. It's you," he stood and backed off a couple steps.

"Well, looks like returning the shotgun didn't help," Cliff said, again holding the bottle up.

Charlie remembered that the man had done him a good turn by letting him keep Mr. Hickey's Parker Brothers gun. However, it had done him no good. When he returned to Kent, Hickey was gone. Since he didn't want to give it to anyone else, after all only Hickey could save his job, he kept it, hoping to see him the next day. That didn't work out either, and when Spain came back he had to slip away. Finally, he traded the prized shotgun for a bottle in Benton.

"No, it didn't. Got fired anyway," he said, dropping his head.

"Come on, and sit back down. I won't bite you," Cliff said. Then he waited a second or two before adding, "Unless you are afraid Spain might see you drinking with me."

"I ain't a'feared a' nothing Lance Spain does," Charlie snapped back and then twisted his mouth around as if he was settling something with himself before he pulled the chair back and sat down.

The two drank, Cliff actually sipped, as Charlie downed a few rounds while they talked for the next thirty minutes about nothing in particular. Finally, Cliff asked, "How much were you making at Kent?"

"Twenty a month and found," Charlie said back proudly.

"How would you like to work for me?"

Charlie lowered his eyes into a squint and brought a frown to his forehead, "Doing what?"

"Do you remember a Frenchman staying as a guest at Kent?"

"Yeah, I remember him."

"I need to know if he is still there," Cliff said, as he half filled Charlie's glass again before he put a cork in the bottle, a gesture that Charlie did not miss.

"I see'd him the last time I was there."

"I need to know about now. Is he still there now, and if not, where he went."

"What you want to know about a dandy like him fer?"

"Personal."

Charlie again squinted his eyes before replying, "How am I gon'a find that out?"

"Clean up, and go ask for your job back. If you get it, great, if you don't, at least you will be out there where you can have a look-see. It's worth a month's wages."

The Black River

"Mee'be, mee'be I could," he said.

"I will be near the entrance of Kent Farms tomorrow at ten-thirty. If you have my information, you'll get the twenty."

"And the bottle?"

"And the bottle," Cliff agreed.

They left together but separated outside. Cliff headed for the restaurant near the hotel, and Charlie simply disappeared, walking along the grassy slope towards the river.

Cliff ate a plate of good cut beef and enjoyed a side dish of collards, the first he'd had in months. Later, he returned to the tavern but learned nothing new.

He was up with the sun and enjoyed breakfast before the livery opened and had completed the haggling on the sorrel before the boy arrived with the goods.

The trip to Kent took longer than he had estimated. The farm was exceedingly large, and the entrance was five miles from town, still when he arrived, Charlie was not in sight. Finding a live oak two hundred yards away where he could see the big, white fenced entrance, he dismounted and waited.

A little after eleven he was beginning to think he had made a bad deal and was preparing to leave when he saw a man walking up the long lane. Ten minutes later, Charlie came around the fence, and after looking both ways, he started back to town.

Cliff mounted Ola and headed his way. When he caught up with him, Charlie jumped sideways as if something was after him.

"I never seen nor heard you, that there horse must walk on air."

"I try to make it that way," Cliff replied, then asked, "You got anything to tell me?"

"I can tell you I didn't get no job back."

"The Frenchman?"

Charlie shook his head before speaking, "He ain't there."

"How do you know?"

"I asked Stoney, and he said he drove Mr. Hickey and the Frenchman to the depot a week ago. They went som'ers up north."

Cliff took a deep breath and then let it out. Charlie had done what he asked of him so he took a folded twenty and leaning over handed it to him.

"Thank you, Charlie. I might need your services again."

Then he heeled Ola and pulling the sorrel behind, left the man standing in the dirt road. He had gone about a quarter mile when he remembered the bottle, and he stopped and leaning over in the saddle, he sat it in the middle of the road.

Cliff was out of sight when Charlie found it, but he waved a thankful gesture anyway.

Cliff thought it would be raining by now, but even though the sky was hidden by low, fast moving clouds that were dark and heavy, nothing had fallen from them.

He had bought an extra sack of flour for Granny Vernell and decided to go by way of her shack, rather than the trail he had taken coming out. It was near dark when he arrived.

Noticeably shaken, he sat down on the bench where the sharpening stone was attached, and shook his head.

He had been there for an hour and had decided he would just make camp here rather than trying to find his way to Neely's cabin, when he saw a man come out of the woods on the far side of the clearing.

The horses were now behind him scratching for the little grass that grew there, and in this light Cliff blended in with the outhouse enough that the man didn't notice him.

The man walked up to what was left of the burned wood, then suddenly dropped down on his knees and began sobbing.

After a minute and he had not stopped, Cliff stood and eased forward and around the remains of the shack until he was within eight feet of the man.

Suddenly he was sensed, and the man jumped and looked at him and cried out with a frightened voice.

It was then Cliff realized it was Horace.

The man backed up a few steps, and Cliff could see he was ready to cut and run, so he said, "Horace stop. It's me."

Hearing this he settled down some, but Cliff could see he was still unsure of himself.

"What happened here?"

That was all that was needed, and the man burst out in tears again; placing his palms over his face, he howled as if he were in great pain.

"Come on," Cliff said, laying his left arm around Horace's shoulder, "I'll make some coffee."

"I got some grieving to tell ya'," Horace began. An hour later, Cliff had heard the whole story.

"I never meant fer Granny, fer nobody, to spend their last days. I nary meant fer nobody to get hurt none neither. We just wanted that thar' re-ward money. They said it would help the lady to be back with 'er husband man. We be lookin' fer a mite a' smilin' if'n all that money were iron."

"You are the one that killed that fellow in town," Cliff surmised.

"M'kin. He be the one what shot Granny. I nary saw Adam shot. I have no recollection a' who done that."

It was the first time he had heard Horace's brother referred to as anything but Ad.

"My kin will kill 'em all. Just," he paused before he spoke again, "Pa says better not to do too much killin' at once, causes flatlanders to get all upset, you know."

"Yes, I believe your Pa is right about that."

"No mind though. Each 'er them 'as been appointed a Fleetwing to get 'em. Just be a matter 'er time."

"I see. Well, I might help you out on that," Cliff said, thinking of all Granny had done for him and Leslie.

"That be mighty kindly 'er you mister, but we Fleetwing's a' take care 'er it. Granny Vernell be my Ma's sister. She be kin."

Cliff hobbled the horses and then put up his canvas as a lean-to in front of the small fire. "Come on, and eat something. You're hungry ain't you?"

Horace stood there a few seconds as if confused, then said, "You ain't gon'a shoot me or nothing?"

"No Horace, I ain't gon'a bore you."

"You ain't even sore. I brung them flatlanders up here to get your woman?"

"I'm not sore. The lust of money has caused many a man to fall. You are among some pretty famous names Horace, now come on."

They ate fried pork and drank coffee without saying a word for nearly thirty minutes, until Horace broke the silence, "I never meant no harm."

Cliff didn't want him to go back into his crying again so he changed the subject, "Will your folks be wondering where you are this late?"

Horace shook his head and then waited several seconds before saying anything. "I come here every night."

When Cliff awoke the next morning, snow was falling, and Horace was gone. He quickly cleared camp and started off so the snow would hide his trail.

It was noon when he found the cabin, and then he wasn't sure he would have, had he not smelled the smoke.

She was exceedingly glad to see him, and ran out, and hugged his neck before he could get the saddle off Ola. She did it again when he told her the little sorrel was for her.

"What is her name?"

"That's your department," he said unloading the stores from the mare's saddle.

"I think I might call her Dixie."

"Dixie?"

"Yes, Dixie. What better name for a gift given by a Reb," she said, sashaying around him with a big smile on her face.

He decided not to tell her about Granny just yet. She seemed so happy; he just didn't have the heart to break her mood at that time.

That night she did everything she knew short of asking him to sleep with her, but he paid her no attention, other than brotherly kindness.

The next morning after breakfast, he told her about Granny, and she immediately began to sob.

Having never been good around women when they were crying, he wanted to get up and go away. He might have too, had it not been for the eight inches of snow on the ground.

'Traveling in this would leave a trail a man from New York City could follow,' he thought.

Finally, after an hour of her crying, and thinking, and crying more, she came to him, "Reb, when can we leave?"

"This is not a good time. Snow will be deep in the hollows, and there is too much of a chance the horses might slip and fall. In a day or so, when the weather breaks," he said, and then after taking another sip of coffee he added, "I think we can find Horace; he will show us the trail over into Arkansas. You will be safe there."

"No," she said, shaking her head. "I want to go back to Poplar Bluff."

"Are you sure?" he questioned squinting his eyes at her.

"I am dead sure. I want to see the people who killed Granny hang," she said with a determination.

"I wouldn't be worrying about them none. The Fleetwings will take care of them," he said and then told her about what happened to Ford.

"No matter. I also want to see Will hang for the murder of Troy Meyers," she said staring at the fire without seeing it.

"Who is gon'a testify against him?"

"I will," she said back sharply, as if she couldn't believe he had asked.

"You can't. A wife can't testify against her husband."

"What?"

"It's some kind a' new Yankee law. I read about it in *The Commercial Appeal*[4] when I was in Memphis."

"That's ludicrous."

"That's Yankee justice," he said back, forgetting where she had been raised.

"I still want to go back. I will make his life so miserable he will wish he was dead," she said. Then turned and ripped down the curtain wall that separated the room and immediately began packing.

"Not so fast. We may not be able to get out of here for two or three days."

"What difference does it make? You have no desire to look at me anyway. I don't need privacy. Hell, I could walk around here stark naked, and you would never notice."

Cliff reached for his hat and gun belt and went out to the corral to tend to the horses. Shaking his head in wonderment, he took both feedbags, and filled them with oats and slid them over the horses' heads.

"I tell you something Ola. Don't you get to looking too strong at Dixie there. She is a female woman, and a woman will keep you confused the remainder of your life."

Will Hickey and Jean Mouton had enjoyed their trip upriver. *The Robert E. Lee* was considered the finest riverboat on the Mississippi, and the accommodations were superb.

They traveled up The Big Muddy[5] to Saint Louis and then changed to *The River Queen,* a side-wheeler that took them up the Illinois to Chicago.

At Mouton's insistence, they took rooms at *The Day House,* one of Chicago's most luxurious hotels, which contained within its walls the finest brothel in the state. Here Hickey had been enter-

---

4 Commercial Appeal Newspaper: The Memphis Appeal's name was changed to the Commercial Appeal during The War Between the States.
5 'The Big Muddy': Nickname of The Mississippi River.

tained by some of the fairest and most pleasing of fallen ladies in all of Illinois.

Their reason for being there was of a different nature though. Jean Mouton was trying to convince Hickey there was a bonanza of money to be made in the rich grasslands of the government-owned prairies of Wyoming and Montana.

"The army is pushing the northern tribes back daily. Soon these lands will be consumed at a rate so swift, only those who have gotten there first will be in a position to profit. The real money lays in the ownership and sale of land," Jean said, "not in cattle as the majority of speculators believe. Cattle are a valuable crop and much can be made from it until the Indian problem is settled. Once that is accomplished, there will be hordes of families charging westward to occupy those deserts and turn them into farmlands, just as happened here only a few decades ago."

Will listened as he turned his cigar over and over in his hand.

"Only those who invest now will have the land with the water rights. These people will control all the other investors."

"How much are we discussing here, Jean?" Hickey asked, not fully convinced.

"To get started, two million will secure a large portion of Wyoming or Montana, another million for the cattle. Of course, five times that much is needed to lock this thing up."

Will looked at the short buxom girl who was serving his tea and smiled at her. She smiled back. "I'll arrange for a half million to be available, as needed. When you repay that, I will advance you another five."

He couldn't believe he was saying this on such a wild scheme, it was not his nature to do anything half-cocked, but he did enjoy the expression the girl suddenly developed when she heard him say it.

Later that night she asked him about it, and he told her it was only petty cash. Before morning, he had agreed to set her up in her own brothel in Montana.

On November first, Will Hickey was southbound for Missouri and Mouton was westbound for Dakota Territory[6].

To say there was a small stir in the town of Poplar Bluff when the two of them came riding up Main Street, would be a misstatement.

6 Dakota Territory: Became an organized territory on March 2, 1861 and included much of present-day Montana and Wyoming; by 1868, the creation of Wyoming and Montana Territories reduced Dakota Territory to the present boundaries of North and South Dakota.

The story had been she was kidnapped, but after so many weeks passed and she had not been found, a rumor spread that she was dead, killed by her kidnappers.

Dan Nooly turned to the Harviell lad and said, "For a ghost, she sure is in beautiful shape, don't you think Simmy?"

"I wish it had been her husband, 'stead a' her, what wus kidnapped."

"Now boy, a little competition is good for the business, keeps you lumbermen honest."

"I am honest. I can't say that for every lumberman in Butler County," Simmy Harviell replied.

They stopped at *The First Poplar Bank,* and she opened an account in her own name. She then withdrew twenty thousand from their joint account and deposited it in her new account. She placed Clifford Brown as a co-owner in the new account but did not tell him this, a move that would prove to be very wise later on.

Sheriff Bill Percival's office was the next stop she made. "I want to swear out a complaint in the murder of Troy Meyers."

"Now Mrs. Hickey, I was led to believe that was an accident. Young Mr. Meyers shot himself while cleaning his gun."

"You know very well Troy Meyers didn't shoot himself. He didn't even own a gun."

"That's not what Mr. Spain said at the inquest. There were half a dozen witnesses who also swore that was the way of it."

"I am a witness, and I saw him murdered."

"Well now, just who do you want to charge with that murder?"

"My husband. He shot him down, and Troy was not armed," she said. "I saw it, and I want him charged."

"Well, Mrs. Hickey, that just ain't gon'a happen. First off, you can't swear nothing again your husband, 'cause you can't testify again' him."

"Surely even you have enough intelligence to know a man don't accidently shoot himself three times."

"Well now, I never knowed nothin' about him being shot three times, and there be half a dozen men who says it were a accident."

"Alright Sheriff, if you won't take my complaint I will have a paper from you saying I tried to have you take it."

"I don't know about that sort of thing, Ma'am."

"I do. I done a little sheriff' n' myself," Reb said, "and I know you can be charged yourself, civilly, if you fail to acknowledge a complaint."

Percival looked up at the tall stranger, "Just who are you?"

"I'm the man that will see to it you are brought up on charges in state court if you don't at least give her a paper showing she reported a murder to you."

"You some kind a' lawyer or something?"

"The worst kind," Cliff replied.

The sheriff scribbled on a piece of yellow paper:

> Mrs. Hickey made a complaint that Troy
> Meyers had been murdered.

He signed it, then shoved it across his old wooden desk and said, "Thar, now you best be getting out of here."

When they left the sheriff's office, she turned to him and said, "Now, let's go to Kent."

"I think since you already stirred up a hornet's nest there is one more place you need to stop at first."

"Where's that?"

"The newspaper office, show them that and tell them your story."

She thought on that a few seconds, and remembering Ken Horsley had on more than one occasion been caught giving her a longing look, she nodded her head, "Maybe you are right." Smiling she added, "Come on."

Horsley had bought out the paper right after the war was over. Actually, he bought the press and other equipment. The paper had shut down in '64 when Red Legs[7] had resented something that had been printed and set the small building on fire. It was a miracle the press was saved, but Jody Campe, who owned it, decided not to reopen and was grateful Horsley wanted it when he did.

Horsley hailed from McCracken County, Kentucky. He had been a loyal Union Man and based on his war record was able to obtain a loan through a bank in Saint Louis. Horsley, nonetheless, reported facts as he saw them and was not always popular with everyone in

---

7 Redlegs: The infamous Redlegs were originally a band of irregular Calvary from Kansas who began raiding in Missouri in 1857. Redlegs were active in all the central border counties, looting, burning, terrorizing, etc., all under protection of Senator James Lane. He led a like band of guerrillas known as the Kansas Jayhawkers. Capt. Jennison led the Redlegs. They got the name Redlegs after looting a leather shop in Independence, stealing a shipment of red sheepskins, and wearing them as leggings. After the war, Lane committed suicide and Jennison ended up being dishonorably discharged from the Union Army.

Butler County. Mrs. Hickey's tale was just such a story he liked to get his teeth into.

The Kent plantation was north of town something less than an hours ride at a normal pace. Once they turned in from the road where Cliff had waited for Charlie, they still had a half mile ride before the big house could be seen shining somewhat like a ghost through the trees.

Three hundred yards from the house the driveway forked. The left fork went to the stables and other out-buildings, including the quarters of the hired help. Leslie took the right fork and Cliff side-rode her.

The mansion itself was a huge, two-story affair, with four white columns supporting the front roof, which other than cosmetically enhancing the structure, also shaded and protected the front balcony. The entire manor was roofed with a red stone Cliff was not familiar with, and he suspected it had been imported from a distant land.

A perfectly manicured hedge surrounded the home and bordered the long walk from where the driveway circled and where, by necessity, they dismounted. Reb did not want to go inside. He really didn't want to come this far, but she had asked him to escort her home, and he could not respectfully refuse.

Once there, he was glad he had come. Just getting the lay of the land and location of the buildings, was useful information in the event he had to come here to find Mouton. Also, he did not fail to notice the side entrance through a room completely glassed, that somehow appeared to not belong. *'Perhaps a later addition,'* he surmised. *'Nonetheless, a certain breach in the houses' security.'*

When she asked him in, he followed her for the same reason.

She rang the draw bell, and two colored servants came from the kitchen. Both looked quite surprised when they saw who had pulled the bell's ribbon.

"Oh, my sweet Lawd! Mis' Leslie, I don' thought yob' be kilt'," the large woman said.

The tall skinny man just lowered his head as if he had been caught doing something he wasn't suppose to.

"Now, George. What is the matter?" she asked.

The Kent Mansion

"I'se be powerful sorrowful Mam. I'se don' givs' up hope a' you wars livin'. I don' should neber a' don' dat."

"Not to fret George. I had a good protector, or I would have been dead. This is Mr. Brown. He saved my life and took care of me while I was sick and hurt."

The skinny man lowered his head in respect, and the colored woman smiled, "We's be shor' glad you don' dat', Mr. Brown. Mis' Leslie is a fine lady."

"Yes, I believe you are right," Reb agreed and then looked around as if he was trying to find an escape route.

"What the hell is going on down there?" came from the cat-walk above. "You niggers get back to work."

At that moment, Lance Spain's head appeared over the railing. He was shirtless and for what they could tell possibly pantless as well.

"Mr. Spain! What are you doing in my house?" Leslie yelled.

A blank expression came over his face, and he began to stammer, trying to find words to reply to her.

He had received a wire to pick up Will Hickey at the depot at noon the next day and felt sure he had plenty of time to get Nora back home without anyone catching the two of them. He had been sleeping in one of the guest rooms while his boss was away and he certainly never expected to be caught by the woman he had trailed all over southeast Missouri and was unable to find.

"Lance, come on back in here. I want some more peter," was the next thing heard from above.

"Mr. Spain, you get whoever that whore is from one of my bedrooms, and you get out of here immediately. When Mr. Hickey returns you will be lucky if you still have a place to stay in the bunkhouse."

"Ah, Mrs. Hickey. I never ___. I didn't expect ___. I ___."

"You get now!" she screamed.

He immediately disappeared from sight.

"Get dressed!" they heard him yell.

"Why? I want some ____."

They then heard him shout to the woman, "Get dressed now!"

"But why?" came a faint reply.

Spain would have given a month's wages for there to have been an escape route of back steps right then but there wasn't. The two had to walk down the long winding staircase in front of the four viewers below.

Neither had completely dressed. Spain was carrying his boots and shirt in one hand. The woman had her coat under one arm, and he helped her along by the other arm.

Reb couldn't help but give Spain a snickering expression as the man scooted for the door. When their eyes met, he could see the hate in Spain's expression.

As soon as he was sure she would be alright Reb left, half expecting to have trouble on his way back to town, but none appeared.

That night, while he was sitting at a table in *The Black River Tavern* he saw the woman who had been with Spain at Kent. She came from a back room and spoke to the bartender, then returned through the same door.

Half an hour later Charlie came in, and when he saw Reb he wandered over, "Howdy."

Cliff motioned for him to sit and then raised his arm to attract the attention of the bartender.

The big barkeep came over, and looking at the man in the dirty, smelly shirt and bib overalls said, "Damn it Charlie, I told you not to bother the paying customers. Now get out of here."

Charlie started to stand. He had been run out of so many taverns in the last few weeks it was almost a routine.

"Sur, you are wrong this time. I asked Charlie to a have a drink with me. I wasn't trying to get your attention to have you run him out, rather for you bring him a glass and us a bottle," he paused, "of something better than this stuff," Reb said holding up his half-empty glass.

The bartender looked at him in total surprise, then at Charlie, who was now sitting back down, then back at Reb and finally shaking his head he walked away.

Later, when Spain's companion came out once again, Reb asked Charlie, "Who is that woman?"

"Oh, that's Nora, Nora Lee," he said. "You want I should get her to come over? I know her."

"No, I was wondering who she is," Reb said as he watched her pick up another bottle from the bartender. "She is a whore here?"

"No, hell no. She's Nora Percival, the Sheriff's wife. The Sheriff and the boys always have a big poker game on Monday night, yonder in the back room," he said pointing at the door she was headed towards.

Cliff looked her over more closely this time. She was in her early forties, he figured. Not pretty but still attractive. Her body had most likely been quite nice before childbearing, but now she sported hips somewhat too large for her height, and her middle was a little thick. She kept her brown hair parted in the center, as was the fashion of most respectable, married women, but the sashay in her walk revealed she was not so respectable after all.

"I used to be allowed to play back there too, 'afore I got fired," Charlie said, lowering his head. "Now I don't have any money, and they won't let me in no more."

"Do you want to work for me, Charlie?" Cliff asked with a no nonsense expression on his drawn face.

"I did once," Charlie replied looking up at the man in the big gray hat, then quickly back to his glass.

"Yes you did, and you did a good job, too."

"What'll I got to do?" Charlie asked once more looking up at Cliff.

"Stay sober and get cleaned up, to begin with," Cliff said, wondering if he was making a good judgment call with this move.

The night had turned cold, and now in the predawn a wicked wind was blowing from the northwest. Lance Spain pulled his suede coat up so the collar covered his neck and hunched his shoulders over, as he thought hard and long while driving from the bunkhouse to the depot. He had simply failed to come upon a good manner on how he would tell Mr. Hickey about what had happened at Kent the day before.

The heavy rainfall they had received in the last two months flooded most of the low lands south of Poplar Bluff, and now at night, light ice would form in the swamps adding a bite to the air. The depot was located near the Black River and that too added to the humidity and his discomfort.

Mr. Hickey was the first to step from the train, and he immediately, upon sighting Spain, raised his arm.

Lance rushed as fast as he could, without being too obvious to anyone who might be watching the beckoning.

"Good morning, sir. Good trip, I hope," he said, as he took the small satchel from his boss's hand.

"So-so, Mr. Spain, so-so," Will said, and then looking about to make sure no one was close enough to hear his next question, he asked, "Is the bitch dead yet?"

"Ah, Mrs. Hickey?"

"Yes, that is the only person who has disgraced me, the only person to humiliate me, the only person that I have told you to make sure of," he replied without looking at his lesser.

"Well, no sir."

"You haven't found her yet?" he said disgustedly. "Spain, I want her found."

"She's been found."

"What? Where?" Will asked, wondering where she had been found.

"She's at Kent."

"How did you let that happen?" he paused and fumed a moment, "You idiot!"

"She just showed up there, out of nowhere."

"Where has she been all this time? If someone has been hiding her, I'll___."

"George said she told him she has been in the mountains, probably near where we lost her trail. You know I took care of that old witch for you."

"Yes, I heard about that; you killed her. The only lead we had. Sometimes I wonder why I have kept you this long," Hickey hissed.

He then slapped his leather gloves against his tight pants leg and said, "There is no way she could have survived up there this long alone, someone has been helping her out."

"Yes sir, she's been living with a man there," Spain said, then added, "She brung him with her to Kent when she came back."

"The whore!" Will spit out, just above a whisper through gritted teeth.

Leslie's first intention was to attack him the moment she saw him, but the more she thought about it, the more she realized how much more she could torture him by staying there in the same house with him. She knew he was very insecure about her, and that was what led to his insane jealousy. *'No, I'll be the sorrowful wife,'* she thought.

She was standing at the banister on the second floor level when he and Spain came in. "Oh Darling, you've come back safely. Mr. Spain led me to believe you were gone because of some danger."

"Huh?" Spain said.

Hickey looked up at her, and her beauty washed away his anger. "You're safe, that's what is important," he said and then, "and you're home where you belong."

She rushed down the stairs and threw her arms around him, "I've missed you so!"

"And I, you," he said. "Where, how ___?"

"Not now Dear. I'll tell you all about it when we are alone," she said looking straight at Spain.

"Ah yes, Mr. Spain, that will be all for now."

That night she made a point of seducing him and afterward as they lay together he asked, "Where have you been? I was so worried. Why did you leave like that?"

"I was sore at you. You shouldn't have shot that boy."

"I know that now, but I was so jealous. I can't bear the thought of another man touching you."

"He never touched me. He was just a good young man with Chesterfield, and I was worried about his wife, she is pregnant and sickly."

"I am sorry. I'll make it up to you, Darling."

'How are you going to make it up to Wanda Meyers?' she thought but never gave a hint of it.

The next morning he awoke first and after dressing came over to where she lay. Feeling his presence, she opened her eyes and smiled at him, "Good morning, Dear."

"You are such a lovely creature," he said. "I have to give you that."

"That's all you'll give me?" she replied, as she raised her arms and twisted her shoulders, causing her left breast to move, almost exposing it completely from the cover of the sheet. The sight of it caused him to catch his breath for a moment, with the loss of focus on the subject he had in mind when he awoke her.

However, he quickly composed himself and spoke, "Mrs. Hickey, I must ask you about the man Spain told me of, the man you have been living with for the last two months," his tone was certainly stern, but there was not the anger in it he so often displayed.

"Spain. Oh Will, when are you going to realize he uses you. He knows how to pull the trigger that sets you off, and he does it for his own benefit," she said back sharply. Having not yet found the way she would need to talk to him concerning Reb Brown she hoped sincerely she would not be pushed into it so quickly and looked away from him.

"He's probably the one that lied to you about the Meyers boy."

Hickey thought for a moment, *'It was Spain who led me to believe the stable boy and she were having a relationship.'*

"Did he also tell you he brought a whore here while we were gone? Right here in our own house, in our own bedrooms."

"Here? Who told you that?"

"No one told me. I saw them when I finally was able to make it home," she said. "They were up here having a go, in one of our beds. And when I told them to leave she said such vulgar things. Oh, I can't repeat them."

"I'll have to talk to him."

"Talk? You need to fire him."

Hickey thought on that for a moment and realized, *'I can't fire Spain. Spain knows much too much to be fired. Kill him perhaps but never fire him.'*

"Now, tell me about this man you were with," he again asked, however this time it was in a less hostile tone.

"His name is Brown. That is all I know. He is from Arkansas," she said hoping he did not detect her lie. "A handsome man, around thirty, I would guess, and he gives one the impression of being educated, although his speech would never reveal that."

She knew these were thorns that would drive her husband mad. However, she said them in such a manner one listening would never believe she meant harm.

"He found me when I was unconscious and hurt very badly," she said rising from the bed and walking nude before him to where she had hung her long multi layered nearly sheer dishabille[8] made of gossamer fabric. This she wrapped about her while looking away from him. Again, the sight of her nakedness grabbed his breath. Leslie then strolled over to the window and looked out. She could feel his eyes locked on her every move and knew his brain was trying to pry into the emotions that might be revealed in her speech. Continuing, she asked, "Will, did you know I was injured?"

"No. I had no way of knowing."

"I was; several men were chasing me, and I was so afraid they would kill me or worse. That was when poor Chesterfield stepped in a hole and broke his leg."

She knew this news would bring much pain to him. He had paid a great deal of money for the horse and then much more in his training. The loss of Chesterfield was a financial loss but also an emotional one to her husband.

"If only there was some way to find out who those men were, the one's who were after me. They are directly responsible for losing Chesterfield."

She paused a second or two and then continued, "I was thrown clear, but I landed on a rock, hit my head, and broke several ribs. I would have surely died had this Reb Brown not happened upon me," she paused giving him plenty of time to digest what she was saying.

"He took me first to the home of an old woman he knew who had medicine and she kept me alive that first night. Then he took me over into Arkansas to the home of his aunt, somewhere near Corning, I think."

Again, she paused as if she was trying to remember every detail, "It was only last week, when I decided I was well enough to ride, I sent for him to come and bring me back home and to you. He did, too. He is such a gentleman, you know, in the tradition of The Old South."

Will Hickey felt a chill run up his spine when she said that. He detested the very idea that a mongrel, no matter where he may have

---

8 Dishabille: Night gown.

been raised, could be considered a gentleman. *'To be a gentleman is a blood right, not something that one could be taught and especially not in the rural south, certainly not in Arkansas.'*

"Then you did not stay with him?"

"Of course not, he is some sort of leader of men they have down there. I don't understand it, a vigilante group or something. I stayed with his aunt; he was only my rescuer," she paused and then softly but not so softly as he could not hear, "and an exceedingly nice one, too."

"I see. Well, it is too bad he has left the area. I would like to thank him myself."

"Oh, you probably will have that chance. He said he would check on me from time to time, just to see that I'm alright."

"That doesn't sound like something just a passerby would do."

"I think it has to do with that southern chivalry or something, and also he plans to hunt down the men who killed his Granny," she added. "I think some of his men already found one of the murderers."

This time the chill seem to explode when it reached his brain stem, and he felt sudden pain and saw stars for a split second.

"I would hate to be one of those men. I heard the people there in Arkansas talk about Mr. Brown, and most of them fear him greatly, even his own family," she again paused. "I don't understand that, he is such a gentle man."

"We'll see," Will said, and slapped his leather gloves against the palm of his hand just before he left the room.

Leslie turned and watched him disappear down the stairs. She felt good. She had been able to accomplish the return to Kent and at the same time plant the seeds of both confusion and envy in her husband's mind. She also hoped she had created a hot bed, for Lance Spain. *'Yes it has been a good return.'*

Hanna Mae, who had been cleaning the bedroom where Mr. Hickey usually slept, heard every word. She smiled and spoke to herself just above a whisper, "'Dat Mis' Honey, don' took ober 'dis here plantation sho' as God made de' sun an' 'de moon."

Cliff had watched Spain pick up the man at the depot. *'That is not Tidwell, it must be Hickey. So where is the Frenchmen she spoke of?'* he wondered.

That afternoon he instructed Charlie to make a list of every man who had rode on the posse the day he had taken the shotgun away from him, also, all who rode with Spain to Granny Vernell's home.

Charlie wasn't one hundred present sure of the latter bunch, as there had been two new men hired at Kent since he left, but for the most part the same names adorned both lists.

Lance Spain	*John Striker*
Eddie Ford	*Dusty Agar*
Jeremiah Star	*Tyrone Dunn*
Fuzzy Karn	*Windy Burr*

The following Saturday night Cliff found Star, and another man he didn't recognize, walking down River Street after leaving the tavern. Both seemed to have had more to drink than they should have and still be standing. When he stepped from the blackness cast by *Donaldson's Warehouse*, Star stopped to relieve himself and the other man had staggered on a few paces.

"Star."

"Yeah?" the drunk answered and looked at the tall, thin man, who was now some fifteen yards away in the shadows.

"You were in on the killing of Granny Vernell."

"What ___. Who the hell is Granny Vernell?"

"The poor defenseless woman you helped murder before you burned her body and shack."

Star straightened up some. His privates still hung from his un-buttoned fly, but he had forgotten all about his bladder. He was trying desperately to clear his head and focus his eyes.

"Who are you? Do I know you?" he asked, twisting his head slightly trying to focus as well as clear his mind.

The other man, who was now to Cliff's right, started to move. Without looking at him, Cliff spoke sharply, "So far I don't know you Mister, so if you don't make me, I won't kill you, too."

The man froze.

"What do you mean, kill him, too?"

"I'm gon'a kill you Star and every other coward what kilt Granny Vernell. It just happens to be your turn tonight."

Jeremiah Star had been working his hand under his coat to the butt of the big 44 Remington he kept in a belt holster there. He slowly moved the cylinder so the hammer rested over a cap rather than the safety notch and then fully cocked it.

When he drew the pistol, he was a split second faster than Cliff, but his ball went high and struck the wooden planking on the warehouse.

Cliff had taken notice during the war and with his days in Wyoming, as well as his fighting with the Renegades, that most men when frightened, couldn't shoot straight enough to hit their target at a distance greater than fifteen feet, especially on the first shot. For that reason, he had practiced to be deadly at three times that distance, and then some.

His 44 bullet struck Star in the second button below his collar. The bone button splintered into a hundred pieces, most of which were carried along with the heavy lead into Star's pumper.

The report of the two shots was so close together, they sounded as one and echoed loud and long between the quiet buildings. Tyrone Dunn had wet his trousers at the sound. Now he stood there, frozen in his tracks, while the shooter turned towards him.

Genuine fear swept over the drunk, and he sputtered out, "You done said you wouldn't kill me if'n I stayed put."

"Tell the rest of them. There ain't no place on earth I can't find them, and I'm coming after them."

"But, Mister, who are you?"

"Granny's Avenger," Cliff said back strongly. "Now get."

Dunn ran as fast as he could. He didn't really know where he was going, but he wanted to be away from there as soon as he could.

Twenty minutes later, he was saying to Bill Percival, "I don't know who he was. He just suddenly appeared from nowhere. I couldn't see his face; it were too dark. He said he was Granny's Avenger. He aims to come and get each a' us what went up in the mountains after Mrs. Hickey."

Lance Spain walked up and after checking Star's body, turned to Dunn, "It was that Brown, wasn't it?"

"I don't know. It were dark, and I never see'd his face. He was tall, could a' been him."

"Sheriff, get up a posse, and let's go after him," Spain said.

"Not on what this here fellow has said, I ain't," he quickly replied, shaking his head. "Get me a witness that will hold up in court, and I'll go get him."

"Hellfire, Percival, we know it's him. Who else could it be?"

"Could be one of the same who shot Ford," Percival said back.

Spain cursed and walked away.

Dunn, following a few steps behind him called out, "Lance, he said he was gon'a kill us all, everyone what was in on the killing a' that old woman."

"Shet' up, or I'll bore you myself," Spain spat back at him.

Cliff did feel the need to settle the score for Granny. He knew the Fleetwings would eventually get it done. However, he especially wanted Spain for himself. He also figured, as much as he could throw that killing on Hickey and his men, the better off Leslie would be in her endeavors. That, too, was something he wanted to help in.

'Still this is not finding Mouton,' he thought.

"I found him! I found him!" Fuzzy Karn said as he rushed up to Spain. "He took a room at *The Poplar Bluff Hotel*. He has a hoss over at *Dancer's Stables."*

"Well, let's wait for him to come out tonight, and we'll get him then," Lance replied. Then the foreman instructed Striker and Dusty to keep an eye on the hotel.

Spain knew Hickey, and that meant the boss had no use for any man who had been closely acquainted with Mrs. Hickey. Mr. Hickey had not instructed him to kill Brown, but if it was done and done in a manner that would not throw any reflection on Kent, it would please Hickey, and he needed a point or two with him right now.

The Poplar Bluff Hotel was a two story structure, typical for boardinghouses in the post war south. Most of the lower floor was rented out to Sarah Ross as a better than average restaurant, with rooms to let on the top floor. There was a door at the front of the hall upstairs where entrance could be gained to a balcony. Out there, four rocking chairs were sitting, for the use of paying guests.

A body could rest there in the early evening and have a pleasant view of the Black River, only a block away. The floor of the balcony served as a ceiling to the front porch where an equal number of rockers were located on the boardwalk.

Cliff Brown had room 23, the front room on the second floor, to the right of the hall. His only window opened onto the balcony, and through it, he had no view of anything, save the roof of *Axtell's Store* or what might be happening on the balcony itself.

This was all right with him. He had no plans of needing to see more at the time. If need be, he could go out onto the balcony. From there he could see the boat landing to the south and with a little maneuvering of his chair, the train station to the north.

The previous day, he had gone to the depot and inquired about passage to St Louis, with no intention of purchasing a ticket. His purpose was to check the schedules, and he plainly saw the agenda of departures and arrivals, which was printed on a large sign posted on the wall behind the attendant. Later he did the same, with somewhat more difficulty, at the docks. He figured Mouton most likely would return by one or the other.

Shortly after sundown, with no trains or boats scheduled to arrive that evening, he moseyed down to Sarah's dining room.

Sarah Ross was a pleasant looking woman in her mid-thirties with a handsome face and a well-preserved figure. She had a friendly, no-nonsense attitude and served a good meal in a happy atmosphere. She also had Lucy, an exceedingly large and strange-looking dog that followed her every step. Chili, the Mexican helper who cleaned the tables of soiled dishes, told him it was some kind of Chinese dog.

Cliff had planned to have his supper and then wait until around ten before he ventured out.

He checked *The Black River Tavern* nightly, as it seemed to be the place Spain and his crew hung out when they were in town, but he also liked the information he had picked up in *The Saint Francis Saloon* that was several doors to its north.

This night, before he had finished his usual meal of rare beef and potatoes, Charlie came in looking for him.

Cliff was pleased to see Charlie looking ten years younger than he had the last time he had seen him. He was obviously sober, had bathed and was clean-shaven, save his long mustache. His clothes were clean, and he looked almost respectable.

"Mr. Brown."

"Come in and sit with me Charlie. Will you have some supper?"

"Oh no. I don't need nothing. I just wanted to talk to you."

"I just ordered a peach pie, are you sure you won't have a piece with me?"

"Well," Charlie said, looking down at the table.

"Miss Sarah, would you fetch Mr. err, my friend a piece of that pie also?"

"What is your name, Charlie?" he asked after she turned and started towards the kitchen door.

"Nash. I'm Charlie Nash," he said courteously.

"Nash," Cliff said with authority. "Nash is a respectable name."

"Thank you, Sur. My Pa was a good man, 'afor he died."

"I see you have the makings of taking after him, Charlie. You look nice yourself, tonight."

"Thank you, Mr. Brown. You said I should stay sober and clean up and all."

"That's right, and you are doing well, now what do you have for me?"

"I wus a hanging out down to *The Black River Tavern*, only out front, I 'twern't a drinking inside," he pointed out. "Just a sitting out on the porch and watching and listening, like you told me, and I heard Spain tell some a' the boys that they were gon'a get you tonight. They are watching for you to come out a' here."

"Did they see you?"

"Yeah, I guess, but they didn't know who I wus. I had my hat down over my face like I wus asleep."

"Alright, you did good Charlie," he said, laying a small gold coin on the table. "Stay here until I'm gone and then go out the back door."

"Yes, Sur," Charlie said, as he swept the coin from the table and out of sight.

Cliff had only his single Colt conversion in a belt holster with him, and he thought if there were several of them, he might need more. So before leaving the hotel, he went back up to his room and picked up one of his newer Open Tops. He slipped it between his trousers and the small of his back, where it was hidden by his coat. Then he cinched his gunbelt one notch tighter to insure the extra revolver would not slip out when he moved about.

Next, he walked out onto the balcony and looked around at the street below.

He thought he could see someone in the small alley between *Axtell's Store* and the barbershop, but he wasn't sure. Otherwise, he saw nothing out of the ordinary.

When he returned to ground level, he noticed Charlie was gone. He found Sarah and paid her for the supper and then asked if he could use her kitchen door as an exit. She gave him a queer look but nodded her head in agreement.

As soon as he was in the alley behind the hotel, he moved quickly across to an empty building. It had, at one time, been used as a shed to store supplies for the railroad, but many years before, they moved the spur closer to the river. Now it was unused and worse for the lack of attention. At times, river-rats would sleep in it, but it was too early in the night for them to have turned in.

Exiting the backside, he headed down River Road until he came to East Street. Once more, he looked diligently up the dark boulevard from right to left, and after a few minutes, being satisfied, he cut across Main and came up behind *Axtell's Store.*

Again, his ability to use patience would pay off. Now he slowly moved to the rear of the little alley where he thought he had seen someone, and slipping his mind out of gear, he waited.

A man in this state has no realization of time. It might have been two minutes, it might have been twenty, it might have been longer. He knew not, nor did he care. After some period of time, a voice spoke at the other end of the alley, "Damn it, Striker, I'm getting cold."

"Yeah, my left leg is asleep; I've been standing on it so long."

"Yeah, but Spain said wait for him here, and we had better do it. Shit, if'n he weren't where he could see, I'd just ease out a' here and get me a drink down to the Saint Francis."

"Better not Dusty. Spain catch you, and it a' be your job, after he gets done with your ass."

There was more fussing between the two bushwhackers, but their conversation was of no value to him, and thus he did not hear it.

This was a strange ability he had acquired during the war years. Conversations could be heard, but if they had no meaningful purpose to him, he did not ingest them. That is to say, he did not pay enough attention to let them become a part of his thoughts. During this same time, should his name or some other word be said that was of importance to him, he would come alive and suddenly be part of the conversation as if he had been listening all along. This ability helped greatly and became entangled with his patience.

At some point, he recognized Dusty Agar say, "I can't stand it any longer. I'm slipping over to the Saint Francis and get me a nip. You want I should fetch back somum' fer you?"

"I reckon, if you are gon'a go anyways, you could bring me back a stout one."

Cliff moved just far enough away from the alley so his actions would not be heard by Dusty's partner. There he waited and watched, as the man stepped from the darkness of the alley. A dim light was being cast from a window in the rear of a house that backed up to the little street behind the store; this illuminated him slightly as he moved away.

Cliff had intended to take Dusty as he left but decided to wait. It proved to be a good move.

Thirty minutes later when he returned, Cliff saw he carried what looked like a single barrel scattergun in one hand and a dark bottle in the other. A few steps from the alley he kicked a wooden box with the toe of his boot, and it fell over causing quite a clamor in the still of the night. A cat screeched loudly and ran from the overturned box, and Dusty cursed.

"What the hell?"

"It's just me. I tripped on a box," he said back to the other man in the alley.

Cliff let him pass before standing and buffaloing him a hard blow across the back of the neck with the underside of his Colt's barrel. In doing so, he heard a sharp crack.

Cliff was able to catch the bottle before it crashed on the hard clay, but the shotgun fell and also made a noise.

"You trying to wake the dead?"

"Sorry," Cliff said, as he picked up the shotgun and continued on Dusty's trail toward his partner.

When he reached the opposite end of the alley the man said, "Damn, shor' took ya' long enough. I tell ya', I don't think he's coming out tonight."

Cliff tapped him on the forearm with the bottle, and the man laid his double-barrel against the side of the building and took the whiskey. "Thanks."

"My pleasure," Cliff replied, making no attempt to disguise his voice.

"Huh?" the tall man said, lowering the bottle from his lips.

Cliff slipped the long blade of his boot knife under the last rib and jerked upward. There was a high-pitched cry as the sharp blade sliced through organs until the pointed tip punctured the base of the heart.

He released the knife leaving it where it was and used that hand to cover his victim's mouth while his other hand found the butt of the dry-gulcher's revolver. A split second later, he felt a hand cover his, as Striker tried desperately to get to his gun. It was a losing battle.

Cliff held him for almost a minute until he felt the strength slip from his opponent, then he shook off the hand and pulled the old Remington from where it had been stuffed in Striker's waistband. Only then did he let the man slowly crumble to the ground.

Striker was not without a few vocal attempts, but his volume was too low for anyone to recognize them as distress cries. While he was trying to call for help, Cliff retrieved his knife and wiped the blade on the dark coat of the dying man.

Before leaving by the same route he had come, he dipped his finger into the blood that was oozing from the wound and wrote on the whitewashed wall of the store, *Two more for Granny.*

Spain had waited up the street for Brown a long time before he sent Karn for a closer look. When Fuzzy reported he was not to be seen in Sarah's, they moved to where they could cover the rear of the hotel, figuring Dusty and Striker would be able to cover the front of both places.

While they waited in the cold night air, Cliff walked right up Main Street and entered his hotel through the front door as if nothing had happened.

It was almost sunup when Spain finally gave up and admitted he had been fooled, turning to Fuzzy he said, "Go get Dusty and Striker, and let's all get back to Kent where we can thaw out."

Leslie did not know what was happening, but she could tell by the shouting taking place behind the heavy doors of Will's study, that he was not pleased with someone or something.

"I'll tell you one thing Lance Spain, if you expect to remain my foreman you had better put a stop to this Brown chap, and do it soon. I will not tolerate this sort of thing. It is bad enough to have the men of Kent being murdered on the streets of Poplar Bluff, but to have signs and blood writing being left on their bodies, that connect them to the death of that old witch, is unacceptable."

He stomped around his desk and then grabbed a riding quirt and slapped it hard against the leather chair, "This is just unacceptable. Where is he now?"

"He took a room at *The Poplar Bluff Hotel,* but we couldn't find him there," Spain replied.

"Why don't you ask your wife where he is, 'spect she will know," Tyrone Dunn offered.

Will Hickey didn't look at him before he swung his arm in a long and powerful backhand. The end of the quirt struck Dunn in the left temple, and he went down as if he had been hit with a steel hammer.

"Get him off Kent, and see that he stays off, and let it be known, any man who says anything that is derogatory about Mrs. Hickey will receive the same or greater." Then he turned and stormed out of the study and headed for the stairs.

"Misser Hickey, I's wondering 'iffen___," George attempted to ask as his employer charged past. Presently he realized it was the wrong time to ask anything of Will Hickey, so he turned and disappeared into a backroom as quickly as a slow moving servant could negotiate such a task.

Hickey bolted from the top stair and shot into her bedroom only to find it empty. "Mrs. Hickey!" Will shouted upon returning to the top walkway.

She came from one of the other rooms and looked out at him, "I'm down here, Mr. Hickey!" she snapped back and then turned and continued the instruction she had been giving to Hanna Mae.

"I want to talk to you."

"Well, talk if you must, but if you continue shouting, I refuse to hear it."

"You better damn well hear it. I have just had one of my own men say if I wanted to know where to find the man who murdered two of our hands last night I should ask you."

"Sounds like something Spain would say, trying to get you angry at me, to cover up something he, or one of his incompetents did."

"Do you know where he is?" Will shouted.

"Who?" she shouted back.

"Brown. Brown, that's who."

"No, I haven't seen him since he brought me home," Leslie replied in a less confrontational tone. Then she turned to say something more to Hanna Mae, only to find the colored woman gone.

"You had an affair with him, didn't you? Everyone is talking about it. Everyone knows you are in love with him."

"Oh Will, don't be so childish. I did not have an affair with him. More of Spain's dirty talk," she said, and started walking past him.

Still furious, he grabbed her upper arm and grasped it tightly, "I'll kill you! I'll kill the both of you!"

She tried to jerk free, but he held her fast.

Once more, she was unable to control true feelings, and she spat at him, "You may be able to kill a defenseless woman, who is one of the few people on earth that is smaller than you, but you will never kill Reb Brown. Hell, you can't even reach high enough to slap him!"

That was a breaking point for Will Hickey. His insane jealously was enough to drive most men crazy, but when she spoke of his stature in such as demeaning manner, he went berserk and started backhanding her, slapping her back and forth, while he held her arm with his other hand.

Finally, she lost her will to stand and releasing her legs from their task she slumped to the floor of the balcony.

With that motion, he released her arm and slowly began to regain some of his senses. Only then did he focus on the awful beating he had inflicted on her. Turning, he slowly walked away.

Just as he reached the top stair, she spoke, "You are wrong about me and him, but that is because he was too much the gentleman. Love him, oh how I could love him, but he never once touched me."

Down the stairs Will rushed and out into the cold air.

Reb had left town the morning after his encounter with Dusty and Striker. He had made some inquires about where Jean Mouton had gone and one lead carried him to Saint Louis. There he stayed for two weeks, only to find that truly Mouton had been there but only for a short time, and then had left again.

The railroad conductor who had worked the train Mouton had arrived on took the promised fifty dollars, but could only venture a guess that this man Mouton was headed south after getting off the train at Saint Louis. "I overheard him saying to a traveling companion that he had business with Mr. Hickey, and I assumed that meant he headed south."

It had been a long, unfruitful ride, but he knew well, no lead was not worth following.

Cliff obtained a stall on a boat for his horse and headed south on the river as far as Cape Girardeau, from there he once again took to the saddle.

Spain had led his boss and most of the able-bodied men who worked at Kent, all over Butler County for ten days without a trace of Brown. Finally, they assumed he had fled back to Arkansas.

"Spain, I want you to take three men and go over to Corning, and see if you can find out anything about where he is at this time," Hickey finally said before turning his horse back north.

Spain didn't like the order, *'If this Brown is the leader of a vigilante band it could be we'll be riding straight to our deaths,'* he thought, but he was not yet willing to give up his plans for Kent, so he gritted his teeth and headed to the stables.

Ten days passed, and Will had not been home since the morning he had beaten Leslie so badly. Partly because he had been constantly on the trail in Butler County trying to find Brown but mostly because he was ashamed of what he had done.

It was true she had deliberately provoked him, but she had been right about who had made the accusations that had sparked his fury. *'I had no right to have beaten her as badly as I did, and I know it,'* he thought, and he shook his head slightly back and forth, dreading the moment when he must face her again.

Riding his favorite thoroughbred bay through Poplar Bluff, he stopped at the depot to see if there had been any replies to the wires he had sent out. There he saw Jean Mouton stepping from the train. This immediately changed his whole outlook; his thoughts of this Brown fellow vanished and were gladly replenished with news of the business venture Mouton and he were engaging in.

At Kent that evening, she was surprised to see Jean Mouton arriving with Will. She had not seen or heard of him since before she had left, save the conversation she had had with Reb about this Frenchman. Now, he was suddenly once again in her home.

This time she took a special interest in Mr. Mouton, something she had not done before because of her distaste for him, however now she was curious.

'Could this be the man Reb is here after?' she wondered. *'Is this the man who murdered his wife? He is certainly capable of murder, of that I can feel.'*

Later when she had an opportunity to speak to Hanna Mae and George, she asked them to keep their ears out for anything Mouton might say in English, when she was not around.

"Why Mis' Leslie, fer back as I 'members almost ever'thing him allus' sez' be 'merican, when yous' arnt' 'round," George said, looking up with his eyes as wide as he could get them.

Hanna Mae nodded her head in agreement, "Yas'am. I t'ink he be a 'spicable man. He be looking one way and a talking 'tuther."

"I think you might be right," she said. "You let me know if you hear anything, anything at all."

"Yas 'um."

It was quite late when she heard Will come up stairs. He went straight to his bedroom without even looking in on her. This was the first time he had done that since she came back, and she suspected he had consumed too much bourbon.

The next day, as soon as the two left her home, she went looking for her house servants, "Well, what did you hear?"

"I's don' kno' iffen' it be impornut but las' ebenin' I is out gittin' up de goslins when I hears deys sayin' 'bout som'ers called Montanna, 'bout buying land an' a house in Bismay, 'dis goes on fer a long time," George said.

"Bismark," Hanna Mae snapped a correction.

"Bismark," George repeated.

"Anything else?"

"Jus' stuff 'bout hooses and cows, 'dat's all Mis Honey, 'sept dat man be wicked'er den sin."

'I have got to get word to Reb,' she thought, as she twisted the lace handkerchief she held in her hands.

"Hanna Mae, fetch me my riding clothes."

"Whar yawl be gwine?"

"Never you mind, just do as you're told," she said as she dropped her robe to the floor and headed for the armoire.

George immediately turned his head and departed the room.

She was glad to see that Spain was nowhere in sight when she reached the stables.

"Saddle Gray Wind for me," she said to Billy Gallant as he came through the big doors of the white barn.

"Gray Wind?"

"You aren't hard-of-hearing are you?"

"Ah, no Ma'am, ah."

He had heard Spain talking about his keeping an eye on her, but Spain wasn't here, and he knew no way of stopping her. After all, she was the Mistress of Kent, and he dared not defy her without orders from someone to do so.

"Yes Ma'am, Gray Wind."

When she arrived in town, she did not know at first how to go about finding him but finally saw a young boy around ten or twelve who was rolling an iron tire with a stick. "Young man, would you like to make a quarter?"

"Yes 'um."

"I want you to go to all the hotels, and ask if a Mr. Brown is registered there. If you find him come back, and I will give you another one of these," she said, placing the silver coin in his palm. "I'll be in *Miss Thelma's Dress Shop.*"

The boy moved his tire to the side of the street and started off, when she called after him. He stopped and returned to her but slid the quarter up his shirtsleeve. He planned to say he had dropped it, if she had changed her mind.

"Don't let anyone know why you are asking," she said.

His expression changed from worrisome to a big smile, and he quickly turned and dashed away.

Thirty minutes later, he came into the dress shop, "Found two of them."

"I see," she replied, biting her bottom lip slightly. "Where?"

"You said you would give me another coin."

"So I did," she replied opening her snap purse and retrieving the quarter. She held it out just short of his hand and said, "I see you are a good businessman, but I too am a good businesswoman. Tell me what you have learned, and the coin is yours."

He hesitated a moment. Finally, he decided he might as well tell, or she wouldn't give him the quarter. "There is one at *The Poplar Bluff Hotel* and another at *The Black River Hotel.*"

"Did you see either of them?"

"No."

She handed him the quarter, "Want to make another?"

"Sure."

"Take these notes, and give them to the clerk at each of those hotels," she instructed. Then writing out something with a lead pencil on brown paper, she folded each twice.

The notes had Mr. Brown on the outside of each, and inside she had penned *'With Dixie and have information of Jean M.'* and signed each, *Honey.*

Then she returned to where she had left her horse and waited.

An hour passed before she saw Reb walking briskly toward Wilson's Stables. When he had entered, she rode over and followed him inside.

He turned when he heard the horse approaching in the dark shadow of the stable. When he recognized her figure, he lowered his hand from the stock of his Colt and smiled.

"You got my note," she said.

"Yes."

"Good. I wasn't sure where you would be. There is a Brown registered at both *The Poplar Bluff Hotel* as well as *The Black River Hotel*."

"I know. I have a room at each," he replied removing his hat. "Keeps 'um guessing."

She smiled at his ingenuity before she spoke, "Last night Jean Mouton showed up at Kent. He and Will are in some kind of business arrangement. I think in Montana."

"Where in Montana?"

She started to tell him about Bismarck as well, but then figured he would leave as soon as he knew, and be gone from her life forever, "I don't know that yet," she lied.

"Is he still there?" he said anxiously. "At Kent?" he added when she did not respond immediately.

"He and Will left early this morning. I don't know where they have gone."

"They are still in town, though?"

"I don't know. I just thought you would want to know Mouton came back, and he does speak both English and French."

"I am glad you told me," he said realizing she seemed hurt that he had not shown more appreciation for her effort. He knew she had taken a big chance coming to town for him.

"Well, I must get back," she said, holding to the bundle of fabric she had bought from the dress shop as an excuse for being there should she be caught. "I must get back now."

"Thank you, again," he said. "I will be out your way for the next few days keeping an eye out for Mouton."

"Do be careful," she said, before turning and placing her foot in the tapadero[9]. When he placed his hands on her waist to assist her in the mounting, she paused and then placed her foot back on the hard packed earth. Turning, she took a long moment looking into

---

9 Tapadero: Fancy leather hood that covers a stirrup.

his eyes, and then placing her hand on the back of his neck she drew his head down and kissed him softly. "I do mean it when I say, be careful."

"I know you do," was the only thing he could think to say in return.

"If it were not for Will finding out," she paused, "I would stay the night with you, but he is so jealous of any man," she said shaking her head gently. "He would surely kill you or pay someone else to do it."

She then took a deep breath, turned, mounted and was moving away before he could think of a reply to her statement.

She was wearing a corduroy riding skirt the shade of buckskin, with a white Gibson Girl blouse. Her jacket was the same doeskin color as the skirt, and it reminded him of the butternut shell jackets that had been so popular in some units during the war, before uniforms became a thing of the past. Only her jacket did not quite come together where it could be buttoned, rather it was held steady by two gold chains attached to large flat buttons of pearl, giving one a view of the blouse and also allowing the viewer to see her narrow waist and flat stomach.

Instead of a hat, this day she had her light brown hair pulled back to a bun of curls that rested on the left side at the back of her head.

'A lovelier creature would be hard to find. She surely would be a woman to enjoy,' he thought, as the big gray disappeared up the street. 'It's just been so recent that Nadine left me.' He slowly shook his head as he began to gather his gear.

Sunset found him in a grove of white oaks that was spotted here and there with hickory and black walnut. He was lying under the canopy of a big black locust tree along the edge of the woods. From this location, he could see anyone who came into Kent from the road, as they made their way along the long driveway to the main buildings.

The bulk of the little hammock was down in a shallow hollow with a small stream flowing easily along to the north of a large pasture where twenty or so white faced steers were fenced off to graze.

He had hobbled Ola just out of sight in the hollow, then laid out his bedroll around the black locust.

Off in the distance was the faint sound of dogs barking, and he assumed they were near the house. 'Queer dogs,' he thought, listening to their howls, *'not hunting dogs or hounds.'* A bred he surmised to be foreign to this country.

As the sun settled behind the tall trees, a gray squirrel began chattering at the man's intrusion of his territory. Cliff smiled at the little bushy-tail before lifting his arms as if pointing a rifle and saying, "Boom." The critter sat upright on his hindquarters and became very silent for a couple of long seconds. Then scurried away to his nest, near the end of the limb he had been perched on. "You're lucky, or I'd be having you for supper," Cliff said aloud.

Twenty minutes later, darkness fell, and a cold chill began to descend on his little camp, so he built a small fire a little deeper in the forest, under some low hanging branches, so the smoke would be dispelled.

Ensuring there was not a hint of a breeze, he boiled a pot of Arbuckles and fried two thick slices from a pound of sow belly he had picked up from the butcher before he left Poplar Bluff.

The night was clear, and he watched the stars through the bare branches overhead.

Two hours after full dark, the dogs stopped barking, and all was quiet, save the evening noises one finds in the woods on a black night.

Cliff's thoughts fell on Nadine and the way her heavy breathing had sounded beside him that night they had camped beside a creek south of Jackson, Mississippi, on their way home[10]. This was the same night the two men had tried to attack them. It all seemed like only yesterday to him. Affectionately, he remembered it had been Big Red who alerted him then. Only Big Red was now in the cold ground as was his beautiful Nadine.

The horse he now rode was a good horse, better than most found these days, but he was not Big Red, and Cliff was not so sure of Ola's alerting him, the way he had been while sleeping beside Big Red.

Sometime after midnight, the moon came up and bathed the pasture in a silver glow. Ice crystals were forming on the grass, and his feet and hands assured him the temperature was falling well below freezing.

'It is just too blame cold to stay out here more than one night like this,' he thought as he blew his breath into cupped hands. *'Just too cold and damp here in this country.'*

---

10 Night by a creek: See The Owl Hoot Trail Book Two, The Withlacoochee Renegades.

He had spent many nights much colder than this out in the big open of Wyoming, *'But it is so dry out there, a body doesn't feel the cold down deep in his bones like one does here in these eastern woods.'*

He realized his plan to wait out Mouton was bound to fail with this cold snap coming on, *'I will have to chance getting past the dogs and into the house if I'm to find him.'*

Finally, he cleaned up his camp leaving little evidence it had been there and then rode through the trees and pastures toward the house.

Kent was a very large plantation, having a multitude of out-buildings necessary for the equipment and hands that were required to keep it operational. To his benefit, Will Hickey was a man of perfection, and in the fourteen thousand acres, all the fences were painted white, as were all the buildings, save the huge mansion itself, and it was an off-white hue with just a hint of pink.

'Some say all roads lead to Rome, but here they all seem to lead to the main house,' he thought as he followed the fences.

The big house could be seen through the leafless trees, for more than a quarter of a mile, shining like a dull beacon in the moon light.

The only movement he could see was the thick cloud of vapor his horse produced with each breath as they neared the big pink building.

At each entryway, an oil lamp flickered faintly. There was one to each side of the huge doors that opened onto the front veranda. Cliff chose the entrance on the opposite side of the stables and bunkhouse.

He drop reined the Appaloosa fifty yards away under the limbs of a huge white oak. Cliff thought of hobbling him but decided against it in case he needed to make a rapid retreat. *'I just hope he's learned to stay put when drop reined,'* he thought, as he slipped in on foot carrying his faithful Colt conversion in his holster by his right hand and a new Open Top in the small of his back with the long barrel stuck down inside the holster belt.

The Yellowboy had been fully loaded before he left his camp, but he left it in the saddle-sheaf.

Under normal circumstances, he would carry the revolvers with the hammer on an empty cylinder, but tonight he had loaded all six in each gun and lowered the hammer so the firing pin would rest on the cylinder between the cartridge rims. *'I might need all twelve rounds before I can return to where my carbine awaits,'* he reasoned.

The soles of his old brown boots crunched the thin layer of ice that lay over the dead grass, as he eased forward towards the silent house.

He remembered the interior from when he had brought her home, but Leslie had also described the house in detail to him back in the cabin months before. Now he tried to remember every word she had said.

There was a full-size basement, four feet below ground and four feet above, used as a root cellar under the cooking area and a wine cellar under the dining areas and study. The remainder was used for storage.

Will Hickey had his den and study on the main floor on the opposite side of the great room from where he would enter. Behind this was a dining room for entertaining and then a smaller one where the Hickeys took their meals when alone.

Even further back was the cooking area; lastly, three more rooms were at the rear of that side of the house. The larger one used as a pantry and the two smaller ones for Hanna Mae and George's sleeping quarters. Their two together were the same size as the pantry.

A water closet was located across the hallway as was a large walk-in cloakroom. The remainder of the near side of the main floor was occupied by a staircase that wound its way to the top floor, where there were four bedrooms.

He knew from being there previously, her bedroom was the first one at the top of the stairs, it connected to Will's. Then over the dining area were the guest bedrooms. *'It would be in one of these I will find Mouton, if he is in the house.'*

He moved slowly, easing from shadow to shadow and waiting long periods before moving again. The leather soles of his boots made more noise than he wanted on the hardwood floor, but he could not take the risk of removing them. The stairs, too, creaked under his weight as he began his climb, but the soft carpet there hid the sound of his boot soles.

When he reached her door, he almost opened it to look at her, but resisted and eased on around the balcony past the second door. By the time he reached the third door, he had been in the house forty minutes.

The cut glass knob was cold to his fingers as he slowly turned it. True to his belief that Will Hickey would not tolerate a squeaky door, the hinges moved silently on thick grease as he slowly pushed the heavy door open.

Again, he waited for more than two minutes before he darted his head in and quickly returned it behind the wall.

He had seen nothing in the room save a well-made bed and other furniture that belonged there.

When he reached the last door, he had his Colt in hand. The same precaution was employed with the same results. There was no one in the room, and there had not been anyone in there that night.

Thirty minutes later, he was back at his horse, rather disappointed with the nights work.

Just as he pulled Ola around to mount, he heard a noise. A noise made by a man, a man relieving himself on the frozen ground, there to the side of the bunkhouse about half the distance to the outhouse.

'Apparently he couldn't make it that far,' Cliff thought and started off again on foot.

The man finished his business and turned back towards the bunkhouse causing Cliff to hold up, still some fifty yards away. However, once again the stout figure stopped and looked back, before slapping his hands along side his legs. Then he turned once more and headed back and on into the outhouse. It was then he was recognized as Fuzzy Karn.

Easing up to the front of the bunkhouse, Cliff removed the unlit lantern hanging to the side of the door and shook it making sure it contained plenty of oil. Next he walked over to the outhouse and spoke out, "You gon'a be in there all night, Fuzzy?"

"Ah, I'm about done," the voice replied from behind the closed door. "I aught a' charge you fer warming up the seat."

When he opened the door, Cliff struck him hard in the forehead with the butt of his Colt, and the man groaned slightly, then fell backward into the one-holer.

Cliff emptied the coal oil from the lantern, soaking the door before tossing the lamp in with Fuzzy; then he struck the Lucifer.

The fire was a little slow to catch the frozen wood ablaze, but by the time he got back to his horse, the little privy was a torch in the frozen night.

He spurred the Appaloosa and fired off a single shot in the air, as he headed for the front gate.

Spain was the first out of the bunkhouse, followed shortly by two others, "What the hell?"

The next morning driven deep into the middle of the street, in front of the newspaper office, was a pole standing five feet out of the hard ground. On it was nailed a note which read:

*"Another of Granny Vernell's murderers
dies at Kent"*

It was well up in the morning when Sheriff Percival arrived at Kent with the note.

Spain stopped the sheriff before he got his foot on the first step of the Kent mansion. He tried to run interference, but finally realizing there would be no satisfying Percival until he spoke to Mr. Hickey, he reluctantly told the lawman to wait, and he went inside.

When Will stepped out, Spain hurried off towards the bunkhouse.

"I hate to bother you Mr. Hickey, but there been some trouble in town concerning Kent."

"How could there possibly be trouble concerning Kent?"

"Well, there is, and I have to be asking about whether or not someone was killed here, and if so, why hadn't someone from Kent reported it."

"I know nothing of anyone dying here," Will said.

The sheriff noticed Hickey's ears were turning red, and he wondered if it was from the cold or from anger. *'It is obvious the man is pretty irritated about being asked such a question,'* the sheriff thought. *'Or is he irritated about me finding out about it?'*

"Well Mr. Hickey, I have to make an investigation. There was this note nailed to a pole in town, and the paper knows about this note and plans to make a story around it. If someone did die out here, it's only a matter of time before it gets out, and then it would really look bad for Kent."

Hickey took a deep breath, and then without another word, walked toward the paddock area, where several men were hanging around.

"Mister Spain, was someone killed here recently?"

Spain looked at him searching for a sign. Finally, he saw a slight nod in his boss' head, and he replied, "Well, yes sir. Old Fuzzy dropped the lantern in the outhouse last night, after everyone else was asleep and burnt himself up."

"Why wasn't I informed?" Hickey asked.

"Well, it were an accident pure and simple, and weren't no need to disturb you 'afore you had your breakfast. I intended on telling you when I seen you this morning."

"Well Sheriff, I suppose I was mistaken. There you have the straight of it."

"I see," he said, scratching at the mustache on his upper lip. "When did you find him, Lance?" Percival asked.

"This morning when we woke up, an hour or two ago. Why?"

"Anybody leave here since you found him?"

"No, nobody. What has that got to do with it?"

Will Hickey was well aware what was taking place; he just didn't know how to help out his foreman before he got himself in a hole too deep to get out of. Finally he said, "Mr. Spain, there seems to be someone who slipped out early this morning and told the newspaper about it."

Spain suddenly looked a little sick, and the other men were looking around at each other knowing Spain had been caught.

The Sheriff at this time produced the note, "This here note was tacked to a pole driven in the middle of River Street during the night. Took the fellow who done it some time in this frozen dirt, too. Had to be pretty early cause nobody heard 'im digging the hole fer the pole."

Spain looked at Hickey and then back at Percival, "Well, what do it say?"

"It says, and I quote, 'Another of Granny Vernell's murderers dies at Kent'; that's what it says."

"Who the hell is Granny Vernell?" Spain spit out.

"I don't rightly know, but ain't that about the same thing that was pinned to Ford's body and writ on the wall of Axtell's store?"

"Hell, I don't know," Spain spit back, looking away.

"I reckon I best take Fuzzy's body back to town with me."

"What fer? We plan to bury him here among his friends."

"You can do that after Doc Spangler looks him over. Want 'a be sure it were an accident and that he weren't shot first."

"Hell, if he had been shot, we would have heard it," Spain protested.

"Mee'be. Mee'be not," Percival replied. "Load 'im in a wagon, and bring 'im on."

"I'll see he gets there Sheriff," Spain said, obviously irritated, "But I don't see no sense in it."

"I'll just wait, and ride on in with your wagon."

Spain looked at Mr. Hickey who nodded his head, "Alright, get him loaded in a wagon. Windy, you drive him in, and then just as soon as Doc gets finished seeing there ain't no bullet holes in him, fetch him back so we can plant him proper."

As the sheriff was riding away, following the buckboard, Spain turned to Will. "That Bill Percival is getting a mite too big fer his britches, I'd say."

"Possibly. Too early to tell," Will replied. "I want you to take two men, and make sure Mr. Mouton understands this was an accident. I don't want him to think we can't take care of our own laundry."

"He's in town?"

"At my hotel room."

After Reb finished his chore, it was coming on sunup, so he returned to his room at *The Black River Hotel*. He was tuckered out and cold and wanted to catch a little shuteye. Satisfied he had lit a fire that would be burning bright by the time he awoke in a few hours.

Lance Spain located Jean Mouton having a late breakfast in the dining room of *The Black River Hotel*. There he talked to the Frenchman, trying to explain as well as he could what Mr. Hickey had wanted him to.

When Spain turned to leave, Mouton inquired, "You traveling to Kent, Monsieur, non?"

"Yes I am, in a few minutes."

"You take me with you, oui, non?"

"Err, sure I reckon so. I ere, I have to check by Doc Spangler's first."

"I walk with you, non."

"Well, all right," Spain replied not knowing anything else to say.

Cliff walked down the stairs three minutes after Spain and Mouton had left. He entered the dining room, and sitting at a table next to the one with soiled plates, he ordered a beefsteak, "Juicy, and two hen eggs, runny."

When they reached the Doctor's office in the rear of *Hatter's Gun Shop*, Doc Spangler was just leaving with Sheriff Percival.

"I come to get Fuzzy," Spain said.

"Nope, can't have him," the sheriff said back.

"Now Bill, you know Mr. Hickey said fer me to fetch him back to Kent."

"No," Percival said with determination. "Doc here tells me he was dead before he got burnt."

"Now that ain't so. I looked him over, and there weren't no bullet holes in him, no where."

"That is precisely correct, Mr. Spain," the doctor said. "But his forehead was crushed in. He was dead before he hit the ground, and that was before any fire touched him. Besides, he wasn't burned enough to kill him, right off, anyway."

"Bill, you know Mr. Hickey ain't gon'a like this."

"Can't help it, there got 'a be an inquiry. Tell him that."

Spain didn't like this at all. He knew someone had deliberately set fire to the outhouse. *'The moon wus bright enough so Fuzzy didn't need no lantern. Someone fired off that shot what woke me, and now I realized it was fired just fur that purpose.*

Mr. Hickey is worried about the Frenchman finding out too much about the whole affair, which is obviously going to happen now, and this might get me in more bad favor. This has not been a good day, and it's just starting out.'

It got no better when they reached Kent.

Mrs. Hickey was in the dining room with her husband, and Spain knew full well of her dislike of him, and he thought she suspected him of being the leader of the men who had tried to kill her. She was constantly trying to have Mr. Hickey fire him, but he was pretty sure Hickey would never do that; still she was a huge thorn in his side.

He began to explain what had happened in town. Hickey immediately grew a substantial frown across his forehead, an unintentional gesture that had too many times in the past, revealed his growing anger.

Leslie, too, saw the sign; being around Will when he was in this mood was not to her liking. Being in the same room with Spain and Mouton were also not to her liking, so she stood and with a swift statement, left the room, "I see you have business with our incompetent foreman. I will leave you to that task."

Her statement did not ease the already angered Will Hickey.

When Lance had finished his story, Hickey slapped his fist hard on the heavy table, then turning toward Spain, his face growing a deeper red by the second; he shook his head before screaming, "Get out of here!"

Spain replied, "Yes sir," but it was not heard by his boss, nor was his rapid exit even realized.

Mouton did not speak for a full two minutes, when he did, he was handing a glass of brandy to his partner, and speaking in perfect English he said, "It would seem there is someone about that intends to cause you embarrassment."

"Yes," Will agreed as he took a long swallow of the warm liquid. "I think several."

He sat back down, and pushing aside his lunch plate, he stared intensely into the shiny hardwood cherry table. Finally, he took a deep breath and began telling Mouton of the incident that caused the death of the old woman known as Granny Vernell. He did not mention Mrs. Hickey was fleeing him and his men, only that the old woman knew where she was being held and of the blunder of her death, as well as the revenge the Hill People were bringing on him as a result.

Hanna Mae entered the room at that time. She removed the noon meal from the table and was gone as if no more than a silent wisp of wind.

Mouton was no fool when it came to matters of this nature; he had been dealing with people who got in his way for forty years. He certainly would not step aside and have a few Hill People distract Will Hickey from their business agreement. Hickey had already arranged enough money to be transferred to more than one bank in the west, especially *The Bank of Bismarck*. With these funds, he was to begin purchasing the land and water rights in and around the junction of the Tongue and Yellowstone rivers in Montana Territory.

His contacts had suggested trying to obtain all the rights between the Yellowstone and the Milk Rivers, a vast sea of grass that would be perfect for the grazing of hundreds of thousands of beef cattle. This of course was contingent on the army driving the hostiles from the area.

"Will, perhaps I should go with your man Spain and see what I can find out about this pest that is disturbing you."

Without thinking, Hickey agreed, "Would you?"

"Yes, certainly."

"Mis' Leslie," Hanna Mae said just above a whisper, "Mis' Leslie."

"What is it Hanna Mae?"

"Mis' Leslie, yous don' tol' Hanna Mae to keeps 'er ear out on 'dat no account Mouton." When she spoke the name, her voice revealed a distinct disgust.

"Yes, have you found out something?"

"Mis' Leslie, he be down ter 'de dinin' room a talkin' ter Mr. Hickey and he be talkin' plain as you and me."

"What do you mean?"

"He be talkin' 'merican jus lak us'en' do. Jus lak' George 'on me tol's you."

"You mean he had no French accent?"

"Dat's what I's tryin' ter tells you. He ain't no Frenchy."

"Are you sure?"

"Yas 'um."

"Reb needs to know this."

"Mis' Leslie, you be better off furgattin' 'bout 'dat Reb fellow. He's be getting you in tr'ubles."

"I wish I could get him to get me in trouble," she said looking off into another time.

Hanna Mae read her thoughts and shook her head, "You be tinkin' 'bout dangers waters now."

Spain was not too pleased with the information the Frenchman gave him. It sounded much too much like he was being demoted to second in command, and this he did not want. He had to be number one to Hickey in order to inherit Kent when Will Hickey died. *'I must find a way for Mouton to have a grave accident.'*

"Monsieur, you must show me where this man died."

"Come on," Spain said, as he began walking toward the remains of the outhouse.

Several of the men had now gathered and followed a few paces back.

Mouton looked at the burned timbers that were presently little more than a pile of heavy charcoal, and then backed up a few steps where he espied the broken glass that had been the globe on the lantern.

Studying it for a few seconds, he then began looking around on the now thawing clay until he saw the black-ended stick that had been the Lucifer Cliff used to light the fire. There also, he saw a slight mark where a boot had crushed a small ridge of frozen clay, not a foot print, just an indention left there earlier.

He immediately extracted it in his mind from the other footprints made by those who came after the fire had warmed the ground. *'One of the killers made this mark, of that I am sure.'*

Looking around, he placed himself in the situation of the men who had come in the night. *'Were I them, I would have left my horses there,'* he reasoned looking at the tall trees on the opposite side of the fenced driveway. Crossing with Spain and the men following, he found where Cliff had mounted Ola and rode away.

"There was one man only. I see just one horse."

The men were now talking softly among themselves, some to Spain, others not.

Mouton made no move to follow the horse; rather he began looking for the backtrack made by the horse.

Finally, he located the black locust where Cliff had left Ola while he searched for the very man who was now searching for him.

There were very few signs once you left the area of the big tree, but he did find where a boot had crushed a small stone against the frozen ground at the very edge of the tree cover. Looking forward from this stone, he was staring straight at the side door of the house.

Moving ahead towards the house, with the group following, Hickey's two Airedales began to bark with a vengeance from their pen at the rear of the house.

'This man is good,' Mouton thought. *'He made his way to and from the house without awakening the dogs.'*

When he got to the door, he saw there on the threshold, fresh clay and the faint outline of a round toe boot pointing out of the doorway.

Entering, Spain lifted his hand, stopping the men from following.

Once inside, Mouton spotted small debris on the stair carpet, but the trail vanished by the third step; still he continued upward.

Upon reaching the top, Hanna Mae suddenly came out of Leslie's bedroom; when she saw him she screamed.

"What is it, Hanna Mae?" Leslie called.

"Mademoiselle please, no harm, you forgive me, non."

"Shush," Hanna Mae said disgustedly.

Leslie appeared in the doorway with a questioning look on her face.

"Pardon, Madame, I frighten the maid, non."

"I believe you did. Do you wish the men to bring your things to one of the spare bedrooms?"

"Madame is exceedingly kind, but non, I bring nothing with me this day."

Leslie looked at him, and turned her head slightly at an angle, before asking, "Then why are you here?"

"Le rodeur. How do you say? The trail, the prowler. He came this way."

"What do you mean?"

"The killer, he was here," he said, looking hard at her with his cold blue eyes.

"Laud', Laud'," Hanna Mae said, lifting her apron up and covering her mouth with its hem.

"Here, in the house?" Leslie questioned.

"Oui, Madame," he said, nodding his head. "Here at this door."

"Why, that's hard to believe. Why would _____," she stopped, realizing who may have been the intruder.

"Perhaps he wished to harm you."

"Laud', Laud'," Hanna Mae repeated, before she turned and fled into the bedroom.

"I don't see that. Why would anyone want to harm me?"

"Madame is exceedingly beautiful."

"I'd worry more about Spain than some mysterious killer," she said.

At that moment, Will Hickey came out of his study after hearing Hanna's cry. When he saw Mouton at Leslie's bedroom door a streak of jealousy shot through him like a bolt of lightning.

"What are you doing up there?" he shouted.

Mouton was stunned at the display of anger in his question.

Leslie did not fail to seize the moment and replied, "Frightening the daylights out of all of us."

"Jean!" again the voice was loud and threatening.

"Pardon," he said softly. "I have trailed the killer this far. It frightened the Mademoiselle to learn of this."

"In here? Nonsense," Will replied, still thinking Mouton had approached Leslie for personal reasons. "The dogs would have announced his presence long before he could have entered the house."

"Oui, an ordinary man. This man, non."

"Are you sure he was in here?"

"Oui, come I show you here," Mouton moved down to the third step and pointed to the clay.

"That could have been made by anyone."

"Non, it was made early, while the earth was still frozen. Come I show you."

He led Will back out pointing to the trail he had been able to uncover.

Finally looking at the evidence, Hickey turned to Spain, "Why the hell didn't you find this?"

Spain said nothing in reply, only confirming in his mind the Frenchman had to go, and soon.

Before dark, they stood over the traces of Cliff's campfire.

"Qui homme, uh, how you say? One man only here."

"That's hard to believe."

Spain suddenly knew who the intruder had been, but he said nothing. *'This is one I will take care of myself, after I take care of the Frenchman.'*

"I would appreciate it if you would remain here at Kent the remainder of your stay, Jean," Will said. "I'm sure Mrs. Hickey would feel safer."

Spain grunted; turning to his men he nodded and started walking back up the little ridge to where their horses were browsing.

"Spain, send someone to town, and fetch Mr. Mouton's belongings."

"Sir," with a nod, was the only response he gave his boss.

Cliff enjoyed the afternoon; he spent it lounging around town, listening to the gossip. The killing of another Kent hand, with a direct reference to the murder of the old woman in the hills, was what ten out of twelve mouths were speaking of, just what he wanted.

While in *Miss Thelma's Dress Shop*, under the pretense he was looking for a gift for his sweetheart, he overheard two ladies discussing the murder of Fuzzy Karn while they admired several bonnets.

Miss Thelma was a petite woman in her late thirties with a pleasant smile and a deep southern accent, Tennessee he was sure.

"May I show you ladies a bonnet?"

"Well, I don't know."

"This one I ordered special for Mrs. Hickey. It only arrived today on the steamboat. I know everyone appreciates her taste and thus, I ordered two extra."

"Oh, Mrs. Hickey ordered it?"

"Yes, I will send her a note tomorrow that it is in."

"I do hope she is not one of the murderers at Kent," the over-weight woman said back.

"Not Mrs. Hickey," Miss Thelma replied.

"No, not Mrs. Hickey," Cliff agreed, and reaching around the large woman he gently lifted the hat from Miss Thelma's hand.

"And not everybody that works at Kent, only a few of us are murderers."

Looking then at the Tennessean he added, "I will take this to her. The boss would want her to have it right away."

"Oh!" Miss Thelma said, catching her breath.

"Shall I pay you now?" Cliff asked.

"Oh, ah, no; she has an account."

"Please wrap it then, and I will be on my way." Turning back to the two women who were now standing with their mouths open, he touched the brim of his hat and said, "Ladies."

They immediately scurried out the front door.

When she saw the smile ease across his lips, Miss Thelma softly scolded, "That was mean; you intentionally ran off my customers."

"Sorry. However, I think they were more into gossiping than buying."

"I'm afraid you are right Mr.____?"

"Brown," he replied.

"Do you really work for Kent?"

"I work for Mrs. Hickey, kind a' take care of her."

"Oh, I see," she replied, it made sense that Will Hickey would have hired a gunman to protect his wife remembering Leslie's ordeal before. "Then you really do want the bonnet."

"Oh yes, just place her name on a card and slip it into the ribbon," he said, fully planning to add something to the note later.

She started writing, Mrs. Hickey, Mr. Brown ____.

"No! Ah, excuse me, ah, just put Honey on it. That's what Mr. Hickey calls her when they are alone."

"Oh, how sweet."

Walking from the store wondering how he would get it to her, he suddenly spotted Windy Burr loading suitcases in the back of a white Kent buckboard.

'He's the last of Granny's killers, save Spain. This would be a great time to bring the number to one.' Then he remembered the hat, and in-

stead, he walked up to the back of the wagon and slipped the package just out of sight under the soft side of a well-worn carpet bag.

'*Seen too many of them,*' he thought, as Windy dropped the reins on the back of the brace of white horses.

Not once did he consider whose bags were in the wagon.

Cliff rested in his room until seven, then went downstairs to eat supper. He carefully considered his options; if Mouton was not at Kent then he must be in town, if he was still in the area. '*I have checked every hotel register in this burg, and there is no Jean Mouton registered on any of them, all that is except this hotel. I never bothered to check here, I assumed I would see everyone who is staying here. Of course, I don't know for sure if the Jean Mouton is the same man I know as John Tidwell,*' he admitted to himself, '*but he sure is a good excuse for him, if he is not.*'

Cliff cautioned himself not to stray from focusing on his main objective, that of locating and killing John Tidwell, his only real reason for being there.

However, he also knew he had other debts to settle before he could leave Missouri. '*There is Windy Burr and Lance Spain that have to be killed for what they did to Granny Vernell,*' he thought as he cut into his steak. '*Too, I must do something to Will Hickey for what he put Leslie through. Just not sure if I want to kill him. Mee'be I will just ruin his reputation as a gentleman. That would be almost as devastating to him.*

Taking care of Burr and Spain will be no trouble; probably will just come naturally in the course of my time spent here. What to do to Hickey? That will be something I have to ponder on. Right now, I need to find out if Mouton has a room here in this hotel.'

The hotel had two men employed as clerks, Larry McElhose, who made sure everyone knew he had served with the Kansas Redlegs and a scrawny little guy named Heath Best. Long before Heath became a man, friends and those who were not friends, had shortened his name to He-Best, and that is what everybody who now knew him, called him.

He-Best had a terrible memory and often would forget who a person was, even after he had been registered for several days. He also was forgetful of the items that the management wanted available to its customers. One such item was good cigars, and when McElhose was on duty, a box was always open for the pleasure of the gentlemen guests. This day there was no such box.

"He-Best."

"Yes, sir."

"Are there any cigars?"

"The cigars are only for the registered guests, sir."

"I know. I happen to be a registered guest."

"You are? What's your name?" he replied, lifting the hardback book to the countertop.

"Here," Cliff took the book and turning it so the man could read it, "I'm Brown, in room 22. See."

He-Best looked through his wire-rimed spectacles down the page until he found the name Brown. "Oh yes, Mr. Brown in Room 22."

"That's me," Cliff agreed. "Now how about a cigar?"

"Right there," he said, pointing to the edge of the counter, only to see they were not there.

"Gee, I must have forgotten to bring out a new box. I'll be right back."

While he was gone, Cliff scanned the book and found who was registered in each occupied room except Room 20, which, like his room, overlooked the front balcony.

There was no Mouton on the books. *'Could he be in 20 and for some reason not registered?'*

When He-Best returned with the box of cigars, he sat them on the counter unopened. "Can I help you sir?"

"He-Best, you got the cigars for me."

"Oh yes, I remember. Here they are."

"Tell me He-Best, who is in Room 20?"

"Room 20?"

"Yes Room 20," Cliff replied, looking hard at the small man.

"Why, that's Mr. Will Hickey's room. He owns *The Black River Hotel*, you know."

"Oh yes, I forgot," Cliff said, without opening the box of cigars.

"I understand," Heath called out to him as Cliff walked out the door, "I sometimes forget things myself."

A south wind had come up late in the day, and the temperature was actually warmer at sundown than at noon.

Cliff thought about returning to Kent but decided against it. He was convinced Mouton was staying in Room 20, and all he would have to do was wait for him.

That night he did just that, all night long.

Leslie could not find an excuse to go to town where she could get word to Reb about Mouton not being French after all. Every plan she thought of had a flaw in it. Finally, just before dark, she decided she would go to the Meyers cabin and see if Wanda would take him a message. Unfortunately, when she got there the house was empty. No one had lived there for some time.

She now felt pretty guilty for not coming sooner, *'Perhaps Mrs. Meyers needed me. Where has she gone?'*

Walking out of the house, a sudden clap of thunder and a bright flash from the heavens startled her horse, and the mare charged away, back for the safety of Kent's paddock.

'Now what shall I do?'

The Meyers shack was out almost to the Hillard Road, two miles north of the main entrance. It would be a five-mile walk by the trail and road but something less than four across a big pasture to the house.

Rain started falling before she had gone two hundred yards up the trail.

'Will, will be furious when he finds I'm not home by dark,' she thought. *'If he were to find out I have come here, he would want an explanation, and I have none.'*

She could not stay at the Meyers house and saw no other choice. *'I have to walk on in the rain,'* she thought and considering her options decided, *'The pasture does look the best route.'* So she began the journey hoping to make it before he returned home.

Mouton had considered the possibility that the intruder would return, especially since the weather had turned off warmer, and had dispersed Spain and his seven men strategically in an uneven circle of about two miles out from the main house. He himself, moved amongst them making sure they stayed awake and did not leave their post.

Spain considered it beneath him to sit on a post, and took it upon himself to follow Mouton at a distance. Jean spotted him within the first hour but waited to catch the foreman in an embarrassing situation, before exposing him to be the unskilled man-hunter he was.

When the sudden storm blew in, Mouton was moving through the same large pasture Leslie was now struggling in the mud to cross.

He watched her for several minutes before he approached from her backtrack.

She did not hear his horse in the downpour and knew nothing of his presence until he spoke. "Madame, you do seem to be in a bad way."

She whirled around at the sound of his voice, suddenly terrified. "Oh my God! You scared me to death," she gasped.

"Pardon, Madame."

The rain now intensified, and the wind picked up. Lightning began to streak across the sky, sending claps of thunder in an unending roar. A bolt struck a lonesome pine close ahead and sent sparks and needlelike splinters out for fifty feet in every direction.

"I do believe we should seek shelter, non?"

"There is a shack back about a mile," she said, pointing behind her.

Leslie did not want to be alone with this man, but the storm was now so severe she was more afraid of being out in it. When he offered his hand, she clasped it and allowed him to pull her up where she sat on the front of the saddle. Her backside pushed tightly against his crotch, which she could feel stirring some. She had no choice. The shape of the saddle and the horn prevented her from moving forward, and he had both of his powerful arms around her holding to the reins.

She was grateful when they arrived at the Meyers cabin, and as soon as she was on the ground, she ran inside.

In the brightness of the lightning, she located an oil lamp but had no source of flame.

Moments later, he brought the horse inside and led him into the backroom, which had served so well as a bedroom for Tony and Wanda.

"Pardon Madame, but to leave him out in this storm might cause us to both be without a ride home."

She nodded her head in approval. In-fact, she was glad that there was some other living creature there with them. "I found a lamp, but I have no match."

"I have a few, if perhaps we find one dry enough to strike," he said, reaching inside his coat.

In a few seconds, he produced a Lucifer and gave it a sharp run across the buckle of his gunbelt. When it burst to life, he shaded it from the wind which was slipping in through cracks in the walls, and lit the lamp.

She was wet through to the skin, but she had no intention of shedding any of her garments around Jean Mouton.

He, on the other hand, removed his coat and shirt and wrung them out.

The sight of his naked chest brought a cold chill to her spine, but she did secretly relish the sight of the gray that dominated the hair on his chest. *'It would seem Mr. Jean Mouton is rather gray. I wonder what he uses to hide that fact with what is displayed on his head?'* she thought.

Spain had been half-a-mile behind Mouton when the storm struck, and he gave up the pursuit in exchange for the shelter of a small patch of evergreens he saw at the edge of the pasture.

There he stayed until the sound of a steam train came rushing at him, and kicking his horse, dashed away just as the small twister ripped away the very trees he had been hiding under. This caused the horse to spook and dash off into the black air, lit now and then only by flashes of lightning. When he finally got the beast slowed, and again under control, he, too, remembered the Meyers cabin.

He had not been over there but once since Will Hickey had shot the Meyers kid, but he remembered the young wife and thought she might be just the ticket with which to wait out the storm. Smiling, he also laid his hand back on his saddlebag and felt the hard bottle he had placed there before leaving that morning.

'Yes, me and Wanda Meyers and this here bottle might just have to have ourselves a little party,' he thought as he turned his horse towards the cabin.

When he spotted the light from the lamp, he tied his horse tightly to a small sycamore before retrieving the bottle. Then he headed straight for the lighted window.

By the time he reached the cabin, the wind had let off a little, and the rain seemed to be somewhat less intense than before. Suddenly, Spain stopped in his tracks seeing a man cross the room through the dirty glass.

'Damn, never thought Wanda would have a man out here so soon after her husband was shot.'

Creeping closer, he looked in and saw it was the Frenchman. "Son-a'-bitch," he said aloud, but no one heard him.

Now he suddenly was exceedingly cautious as he eased up to the window where he could get a good look inside. There he saw a woman, sitting with her back to him watching the tall man pace around the room. Even being unable to see her face, he knew without question it was Leslie Hickey there with Mouton.

Spain now backed off some, so as not to be seen should either of them look out the window, and he waited. *'This is too good to be true. Rain or no rain, I'm going to wait them out, and see if there is something going on.'*

Three quarters of an hour later the storm had moved on into Wayne County, and the night was now dark with a heavy overcast.

Lance Spain was now at his horse. He had seen enough to know there was nothing happening between the two in the cabin; nonetheless, he was pleased beyond dreams of his new knowledge. *'I must now slip away ahead of them and get back to the house, where Mr. Hickey will surely be in a rage wondering about his dear wife.'*

Mounting, he turned his horse in the general direction and laid the reins across the saddle horn. *'She can find her way home in this blackness better than I,'* he thought as he took a long draw from the bottle.

As suspected, Will Hickey was in a rage, shouting and screaming orders at anyone he saw.

"Where the hell have you been?"

"Following the orders of your Frenchman, just like you told me to do," Spain replied, as he walked up the steps to the front veranda.

"Well, where the hell is Mouton?"

"The last I saw of him, he was walking around half-naked in the Meyers cabin."

"The Meyers cabin, how the hell did he know about that?"

"I think maybe someone told him about it," Lance said, removing his hat and shaking some of the water from it.

"Do you know where Mrs. Hickey is?"

"I'm sure she is alright. My guess, she will be home in no time."

"Just what is that supposed to mean?" Will shouted.

"Mr. Hickey, if you don't stop shouting at me, I might just up and leave you. Then you would have no one to protect you from them what are deceiving you."

"What the hell do you mean by that?"

Before Spain could say more, the image of a horse appeared from the darkness.

Suddenly seeing the horse, Will Hickey looked sharply at the riders.

With Mouton's assistance, Leslie dismounted. Her blouse was soaked through to the point it might as well have not been there, the perfect outline of her well-shaped breasts were displayed for anyone to see, as were the dark hard nipples that poked forcibly at the now transparent material.

She said not a word to the two men on the porch as she walked inside, knowing full well that her upper garments no longer gave her protection from anyone's sight.

"Hanna Mae," they heard her call out. "Pour me a hot bath."

"Yas 'um."

"You have been with my wife."

"Oui, I found her wandering a-foot in the storm."

"Wandering about in the storm? Not at the Meyers cabin I don't suppose."

"Oui. We did find shelter in an abandoned shack."

Will looked at Spain, who gave him one of those I-told-you-so looks and then back at Mouton.

"Come inside, and get into some dry clothes," he said very calmly, as if all his anger had suddenly left him.

Spain had seen him change from furious to dead calm before. One who did not know better would think he had forgotten all about his anger and was now peaceful once again. However, Spain knew better. Perhaps he knew Will Hickey better than the man knew himself.

Once before he had seen Will Hickey exhibit this same character metamorphosis. He had gone from a frightened husband, to dead calm, and then shot a young man at point-blank range, before calmly walking off as if nothing had happened.

Inside, and away from Spain's hearing, Jean said, "Will, I too would love to have a bath. Will your boy draw me some hot water?"

"George, heat some water for Mr. Mouton. He will bathe in the rear bath."

"Yas Sur," the old colored man replied, nodding his head as he headed for the kitchen.

"Merci, Will," Jean said as he removed his hat and coat.

"George, get Mr. Mouton some dry clothes from his room."

"Yas Sur."

"Oh, that will not be necessary, I can get them."

"No!" Hickey shot back suddenly and then again calmly added, "That is what we have servants for."

"Very well."

Hickey knew Leslie would by now be naked in her bath, and he wanted no man near her.

"Come, while we are waiting on the hot water, I will prepare for you a stiff bourbon."

"Perfect. Just what I need," Mouton said, removing the gunbelt that housed the short-barreled '61 Navy.

It had been converted to shoot the new 38 Colt cartridge and had been the first purchase he made after leaving the battlefield of South Georgia. Percussion caps failing to fire in the damp weather had saved his life when that big brute had tried to kill him with Dragoons[11], and he immediately realized the importance of protected powder that only a sealed cartridge could give.

George moved from the stove to the brass tub, filling it with steaming water. Then, in his slow lazy manner, he strolled upstairs to the second guest room, where he had left Mr. Mouton's luggage earlier.

He hefted one of the bags to the top of the cedar chest at the foot of the bed and opened it. Finding no shirts in this one, he then reached for the second bag and in doing so, knocked over the old carpetbag, as well as the package from Miss Thelma's shop. The new bonnet fell out on the floor. Seeing it, and figuring it belonged to Miss Leslie, he lifted it carefully and laid it on top of the small sewing chest behind the open door. Then he returned and opened the second leather bag and removed a silk shirt.

When she finished her bath, Leslie decided not to go back downstairs and had Hanna Mae bring her some soup made from the broth of a roasted beef shoulder. Hanna had added some carrots and two onions from the root cellar. The broth was perfect, and she soon fell asleep.

Will never again mentioned the Meyers cabin; instead, he waited to see if either would give themselves away.

'The story Mouton told did make sense. That all could have happened. Her mare did come home just after the storm broke. If so, how then did Spain know where they were, and why was he nearly naked when Spain apparently saw them together?'

Hickey unknowingly allowed his jealousy to continue to boil in his thoughts, *'I will wait, and let one of them condemn themselves. Then I will kill Mouton and give her a whipping she will not presently forget. I should kill her too, but there has been too much bad publicity already surrounding Kent, with her disappearance and then unexpected return.'* He stopped for a moment, still deep in thought, *'No, I cannot kill her,*

---

11 Big Brute: See Chapter 15 of The Withlacoochee Renegades for Coleman Darktower's death.

not now, but Mouton most surely, should he give himself away. I'll kill him and tell Bill Percival he was the one who crushed the wranglers head and set him afire. It will make me look good in the eyes of the business-men in town.' He paused, then continued his thoughts, *'I could even have Spain say he had found out this man was the leader of those who had killed the old woman in the Ozarks. Yes, that would clean Kent's name in the whole area. Now, I only have to play the perfect host and wait until he gives himself away.'*

The warm front had sent a squall line from the gulf coast into southern Illinois in a matter of some twenty hours. Twisters had dropped from its angry clouds leaving a path of destruction for hundreds of miles through several states, and Cliff was glad he had chosen to stay in town that night.

The following day and night he had watched Room 20 without interruption, save feeding and complying with nature's calls.

Nothing had happened. No one entered the room.

On the third day of his stakeout, he saw the maid enter Room 20. It was the opportunity he had needed and while she was inside, he stepped in and asked for some soap. The few moments he was there, told him no one was staying in the room and had not in several days.

'Where could he be?'

Suddenly he remembered, Burr was loading suitcases, and that old carpetbag in the buckboard, in front of this very hotel.

"Miss could you tell me when Mr. Mouton is expected back?"

"I don't know. He left rather suddenly Monday."

"Thank you."

"Do you need him?"

"Well, I have something for him."

"I will tell him you are looking for him."

"No. Don't do that, he doesn't know I'm in town, and I want to surprise him."

"Oh, you are an old friend," she smiled, showing crooked teeth, marring an otherwise comely face.

"We used to live in the same town," he replied and gave her a knowing wink.

"I hope he isn't away long."

"As do I. Thank you," he said and left.

'It had been Monday when Burr was loading the wagon. Son-of-a-bitch we have been just missing each other.'

Will Hickey had entered the guest room Jean Mouton was occupying, with intent of finding some note or map she had written that would show how to find the Meyers Cabin. He found nothing of the kind, but he did find her new bonnet with the note, *For Honey*.

"Son-of-a-Bitch!" he said, as he gritted his teeth. Suddenly he began trying to remember, *'Just when was it Mouton said he was in Detroit? He must have known her there. How else would he have known she went by Honey in her whoring days?'*

"I'll kill the bastard," he said and flung the bonnet against the wall, but the note he crushed with his fist before he stuffed it in his pocket.

Two nights later, Cliff again went to Kent.

He had set a snare along the bank of the river and caught a young 'coon; this he placed in a croaker sack[12]. Taking a Hondo[13] from his saddle, he twisted it straight and used it to tightly bind the sack's top.

Arriving an hour after full dark, he watched the buildings from afar.

Finally, when satisfied all the wranglers were in the bunkhouse, he moved in on foot, carrying the sack. Approaching the dog pen, he slapped the sack easily against the pen, and when the two dogs were fully angered and howling at the top of their ability, he pulled the Hondo free and dropped the sack just in front of the pen door before releasing the latch. The raccoon took off for the Black River at speeds too quick for the eye, with both dogs hot on his trail.

George came out the back door and hollered at them, but they never heard a word he said. Cliff could hear him talking to himself as he returned inside, but from where he was hiding, he was unable to understand what the old man was saying.

There was only a faint light downstairs in the rear of the house where the small kitchen was located and one upstairs in her bedroom. Otherwise, the house was dark, save of course, the outside lanterns by each entrance.

---

12 Croaker Sack: Burlap bag often used to place freshly caught frogs, thus the croaking of the frogs gave the sack it's name.
13 Hondo: Usually a metal, but sometimes a rope or rawhide ring, through which a rope slides to make a loop.

Hickey had instructed Spain to stop the night vigil, as he now believed it had been Mouton himself who had been the prowler that entered the house. *'How else could he have known just where to look for that tiny bit of clay?'* Will reasoned, *'He undoubtedly had come here to her room in the night, and upon leaving, Fuzzy had seen him. Then Jean killed the ignorant peasant for his blunder.'*

Mouton in turn, had been surprised at Hickey's sudden lack of concern about the security around the place and had decided to lay in wait near where they had found the camp before. Since they had not disturbed the scene, it was logical the intruder would use it again, and he was now determined to catch the man to show Hickey he had been correct in his assumption.

'If Hickey were to lose confidence in me, he may not come through with the remainder of the money, and that would present grave problems.'

Hickey and Spain had watched Mouton ride off and followed at a good distance. As soon as Spain realized where he was going, they stopped and waited.

"He's probably building another campfire to make it look like someone else is coming around," Will said.

Lance gave him a, "Yep," in answer, but he knew in his heart it was Brown who had been the one there before. *'Still, as long as Hickey suspects the Frenchman, it will work just as well for me. Besides, I can get Brown any time.'*

When Cliff saw all the lamps downstairs go out, he waited for fifteen minutes, and checking her window at the back of the house he saw her silhouette pass.

After blowing out the lanterns, he entered the house through the same entrance as before.

Going up the stairs this time, he moved quickly on as light of feet as he could manage.

He first checked each of the other three rooms, satisfying himself they were empty, before he entered Will's room. There he waited a full three minutes making no sound. When satisfied no one had detected his presence, he eased forward where he could see her room. Finally, content she was alone; he slipped back out onto the balcony and to her door, where he knocked softly.

"Who is it?" she inquired, with a voice full of concern.

He gently pushed open the door where she could see him.

"Oh my God! Reb!" she said, fully relieved and surprised at the same time. "How on earth did you get in here?"

"Came in through the door."

She rushed to him, threw her arms around him and held him tightly. "Oh, I have missed you so."

Now, being here with her, he had to admit to himself he had missed her too, far more than he had realized.

They talked until nearly four in the morning, and then he rose, "I had better be going before I get trapped in here."

"No, don't go. Both Will and Mouton have gone to town. They won't be back until up in the day," she again clung to him tightly, and this time when she looked up he leaned over and kissed her.

It was the first time he had made any move toward her, of a personal manner, in the long months since he had saved her life in the mountains.

During the next hour, their passion was spent and renewed three times. Once she had become so loud, he was afraid she would awaken the servants, but he did nothing to stop her from fully enjoying the coupling.

Hanna Mae had recognized the sounds right off and slipped upstairs to make sure the encounter was one wanted by her mistress. Satisfied with her discovery, she waited outside on the balcony as an unknown lookout and remained there until she was sure they were finished.

When she came back to her room, George was just getting up and heading for the outhouse in the rear and was surprised to find her there in the back hall. "What you be duin' har' woman?"

"I'es a watching over Mis' Leslie," she said back, quite pleased with her recent accomplishment.

"Watching over Mis' Leslie? She be asleep com' 'dis hour, seed dat tere yaller moon way up yonder."

"Jist de same, 'dat's what I'es be doin'. 'Dat Mis' Leslie, when she goes and picks 'er a man, she sho' do pick 'er a man."

"What be 'da matter wi've you woman, you be talkin' crazy."

"Dats wha' yoe' t'inks', heh, heh, heh," she chuckled, as she entered her room.

Cliff slipped out the side door minutes after George came back in. He was on his horse moving away, when he spotted Mouton riding to the paddock area. He wanted to get closer, so he could make a positive identification of his old enemy, and he eased nearer. Suddenly through the timber, he spotted the trailers also approaching, and he held Ola up, waiting and watching as Spain and Hickey followed some distance behind Mouton.

"We'll wait and give him time to get inside," Will said, as they watched Mouton walking from the large barn towards the house. After he entered, they approached the back side of the house.

Leslie, being filled with joy of what she had experienced during the early hours of the morning, was still awake. When she heard someone on the hardwood floor below, suddenly she realized that the whole room smelled of their sex. She hurried to the window, opening it to allow some fresh air inside.

It was then she spotted her husband at the dog pens below. Immediately, she jumped back from the exposure of the window and waited a few moments before chancing another glimpse. She watched as Will turned to his companion and say something, and Spain then reached for the reins of his horse and led him around the house disappearing from her sight, leaving Will's big bay thoroughbred where he had drop reined it. The moment Spain was out of sight, she looked back just in time to see Will head for the back entrance.

She now realized it must have been Mouton who had come in the front, several minutes before. Opening the door, she spotted him exiting Will's study with a tall glass in one hand and a decanter in the other. He placed the crystal container on the highly polished table. Then he removed his gunbelt and hung it over one of the chairs that sided the table, before he refilled his glass a second time.

'Stealing my husband's bourbon are you? You Bastard.'

Realizing she still was nude, save the thin almost transparent gown she had slipped on to take away the early morning chill, suddenly a plan blossomed in her mind. *'He is unarmed, Will is not. Reb will have the murderer of his wife, and Will will do it for him.'*

Grabbing the thin material, she ripped it mostly away; then leaving her door ajar, she returned to her bed.

Upon hearing footsteps on the landing outside her room, she called out softly, "Mr. Mouton."

He pushed the door open and stood there with the glass of bourbon in his hand.

"Is my husband with you?"

"Non Madam, last night, he go to town, I heard him say."

She slowly pulled the comforter from her with one hand, revealing her near naked body, and then said in the sultry voice she had not used since she worked in Detroit, "I keep remembering your hairy chest."

He looked at her lying there. Slowly she moved her legs slightly apart where he would have a full view of the treasure she had for him. He chuckled, and walked in, closing the door behind him. She now looked down at her breasts and gently took each of her nipples and pinched them until they hurt.

Leslie was aware he was undressing, but she did not again look his direction. She was afraid her disgust for him might show if their eyes met. Instead, she let one hand fall to her triangle, and slowly she began to move her fingers through the silky hair there. She could still feel some stickiness from her earlier encounter, but she did not think he would notice.

Suddenly he was upon her, and at the same moment, she once again heard footsteps outside on the balcony.

"No stop! You can't do this!" she yelled out, just before she screamed and began scratching his face and kicking at him.

Totally surprised, he was taken off-guard by her sudden change, and he raised his arm to backhand her for scratching him; at that moment, the door burst open and Will Hickey was there with revolver in hand.

"Oh, thank God!" she ejaculated[14].

"What the hell?" Mouton yelled back, a split-second before he saw the cylinder turn on Hickey's gun.

He indeed had removed his gunbelt and left it on a chair, but when he started up the stairs, he had slipped the Navy into the small of his back with the short barrel resting between his cheeks. She had failed to see it when he undressed as she had chosen not to look at him again. The 38 now lay atop the pile of hastily discarded clothes he had dropped beside her bed.

The ball of Will's Remington Police Revolver passed through his right calf before puncturing her mattress, causing feathers to fly everywhere. Before Hickey realized his shot had not been fatal, Mouton was cocking his Colt. The first bullet entered Will Hickey's chest, only a split second ahead of the next.

---

14 Ejaculated: A nineteenth century expression often used in place of exclaimed.

The short man staggered backward and then just before he collapsed, he said, "Leslie!" It was the only time in years she had heard him call her anything other than Mrs. Hickey.

She suddenly began screaming uncontrollably.

Mouton now realized he had been hit and was bleeding from the leg wound. He suddenly thought, *'She orchestrated the whole thing. She has ruined the source of millions of dollars for my Montana project. She must die.'*

Turning the barrel of his revolver at her, he squinted his cold blue eyes as he cocked it for another shot.

"Mis'Leslie! Mis' Leslie!" the colored woman was screaming as she burst through the open doorway and bumped Jean hard, as she hurried past him to her mistress.

Mouton looked at the huge back of the Nigress. Then moving to his side, he saw he still had a shot at the Hickey woman, a thin shot, but he was a top marksman, and he squeezed the trigger.

Suddenly his arm flew up, discharging the round into the high ceiling, as George bumped him, when he too rushed past trying to find out what all the screaming was about.

Mouton then shook his head and reached for his clothes, and within a few seconds, he was rushing to his room to dress and gather his other belongings.

He was just arriving at the back door when Spain and several of the ranch hands came in the front.

In trying to get out through the narrow back door in such a rush, he dropped his old carpetbag, but Hanna Mae was yelling to the men, "Stop him. He dun' kil't Mr. Hickey." As a result, he did not take the time to pick it up.

Seeing Hickey's bay horse where he had been left, Mouton was on it and making tracks for Saint Louis by the time the men got out the back door.

Spain, who had gone upstairs, watched through the open bedroom window and fired off two shots at the fleeing horseman, but Mouton never heard them strike anything near him.

Finally, Leslie gathering enough wits about her yelled, "Get out of my bedroom Spain, and send for the sheriff!"

Lance Spain looked at the hate in her eyes as she ordered him out and then at the blood-soaked body that had been Will Hickey before nodding his head.

Arriving at the bunkhouse, he entered the foreman's private room and packed all the things he could carry. Then taking one of the better horses, he headed for Poplar Bluff.

Going straight to Bill Percival's house, he told the Sheriff what had happened. He mostly used the story he and Will had thought up, about Mouton being caught as the leader of the gang who had killed the old woman in the Ozarks. He also added Hickey's belief the Frenchman had been killing off members of the Kent workforce, trying to shift the blame of the old woman's murder on them.

"I believe Mrs. Hickey was in on it, with the Frenchman. When Mr. Hickey found them in bed together, Mouton shot him."

"I see. We had better get right out there," Percival replied, reaching for his gunbelt.

On the front porch, Spain stopped him and said, "Sheriff, I had better not go back with you. Mrs. Hickey done up and fired me. She has had it in fer me fer some time, you know."

The truth was, she in fact had not fired him, but he was sure she only waited to do so in front of the men, where she could cause him as much embarrassment as possible.

"Well, all right, stay here until I get back. I'll be wanting to talk to you some more."

"Sure, Bill. I'll be right here," Spain said, wiping his mouth with the back of his hand.

Cliff was eating at Miss Sarah's when the sheriff came in, "Need some men for a posse. That damn Frenchman done up and killed Mr. Hickey out at Kent."

Cliff stood suddenly. "Mrs. Hickey, she alright?" he inquired.

"As far as I know. You want to come along, get mounted," the sheriff said, before turning and heading outside.

There were two other men in the dining room, one shook his head, but a tall slim young man about Cliff's age, who had been eating with the other man said, "I'll go with you, Mister. Mrs. Hickey was kind to me more than once, and she helped my sister Wanda, before her husband was shot."

Cliff nodded his head in approval.

Lance Spain watched Bill Percival come out of *The Black River Hotel* and head north toward the stables. Then he opened the door and went back inside.

"Nora, I have to leave. I been fired, and I suspect that Brown fellow will be gunning fer me, especially now that I ain't got the boys from Kent with me no more."

"No. You can't leave. I love you, Lance."

"I got to. Come with me Nora, we can have a good life. I got several hundred dollars in the bank. We can draw it out and be on the steamer before your husband gets back."

She looked strongly at him. She knew she loved him; at least she thought she did. Lance made her feel like Bill had ten years before, before he had gotten so fat and useless as a husband. She didn't think she could stand not having Lance coming around when Bill was working at night.

Still, could she just up and go? Leave all she had worked for, for so long. Leave her house, and all her dishes, and most of her clothes?

"I don't know Lance, can't you get another job around here, everybody knows you are a top hand."

"No. That damn Brown is out to kill everybody what was up at the old woman's shack."

"You killed that old woman?"

"No, it were Eddie Ford what killed her," he replied shaking his head. "It was an accident anyway. Now get packed," he ordered, reaching for the old brown suitcase he knew was on the shelf in her closet.

She stood there for close to a minute and then shook her head, "I can't go with you Lance, I just can't." She started sobbing, "You don't have to go; Bill will jail that Brown fellow. I'll tell him to. He does what I tell him to do."

"No! You don't understand, I got 'a go. Come on, and go with me, hurry now."

She shook her head as she ran to him, clinging to him and then started kissing him madly.

Neither heard the door open. They were deep in passion, when Bill Percival walked back into the house. The rapid squeaking of bedsprings left little doubt as to what was going on in his bedroom. He had heard the same squeaking springs for almost ten years. With his left palm, he cocked both rabbit ears of the Barker before slowly pushing the door open. From his viewpoint he couldn't tell who was poking his wife, but he could see her face, and read the lust in it, even though her eyes were closed.

Cliff heard the report that could only be a double shotgun firing both barrels almost at once. He turned, as did most of the men who were waiting outside for the sheriff to get his long gun, before they headed out for Kent.

Cliff was off Ola in a moment. With revolver drawn, he cautiously entered the front door. There he heard the sobbing of a woman coming from the bedroom.

Suddenly the pale and blank face of Bill Percival appeared in the doorway. Blood was splattered on his shirt and cheeks, and he held the gun loosely in his right hand. Looking up and seeing Cliff, he spoke, "Better get Doc Spangler. Nora was hit too, and she's bleeding pretty bad." He twisted his shoulder back towards the bedroom as he spoke, and then he went out and poured himself a cup of coffee. Laying the empty gun across the table, he sat down on a straight wooden chair and looked out the window, but he saw nothing. Nothing of this January 30, 1873. What he saw was his beautiful Nora beside the river in that yellow dress with her picnic basket, the day she had agreed to marry him so many years ago.

Entering the bedroom, Cliff saw the naked body of Lance Spain on the floor beside the bed. The torso had almost been cut in two, and it was obvious he never knew he was in trouble before the lights went out.

Nora Percival also was naked, but still on the bed, and she was sobbing. Not hysterically, but steadily. One of the balls that missed Spain had hit her in the right calf, passing completely through; another had struck her in her left hand. It too had passed through taking most of the bones in that hand with it. Two of the 36 caliber balls had passed completely through Spain and were in her lower chest, but Cliff could see they had been spent by the time they reached her and had been stopped by her ribs, before hitting vital organs.

He took one of the pillows that had very little blood on it and placed it on her, to cover her nakedness to some degree. The other he found where it apparently had been knocked before the shooting. From this, he shook out the feather bag from its covering and began tearing the case into strips, for bandages.

When Doc Spangler rushed in the front door, Bill looked at him and pointed with his fist and upturned thumb at the bedroom door. Cliff had most of the bleeding stopped by the time the doctor got there.

"What do you think they will do with Bill Percival?" Leslie asked him.

"I doubt much. Most juries believe a man has a right to defend his bedroom."

"You mean Will would have gotten away with killing Mouton and me?"

"Well, a jury might not have hung him, but he wouldn't have gotten away with hurting you," Cliff said.

"You know, I know that is true. Just as I know the sun will rise in the east come morning," she said, pulling on his arm. "Come on now, we have some times to catch up on ourselves, without the fear of anyone, except maybe Hanna Mae, catching us."

His stay at Kent was never far from her, and while there, he suggested she hire Charlie Nash as her new foreman. He also advised her to retain the remaining hands that had worked for Spain, save Windy Burr who had been found tied to the same black locust Cliff had waited under near where he made his camp. Burr had a gag tied around his mouth to muffle his screams, and in the stomach area a single blood-stained hole could be seen, and it was obvious it had taken him a long time to die. Pinned to his naked body was a sign:

"The Last of Granny's Killers."

Clifford had to admit he enjoyed the time he spent with her these last few days. He would stay, until the inquiry was over and make sure she was not harmed by anyone. However, they both knew Mouton had escaped once more and the trail was getting colder everyday. Also, it was only a matter of time before Reb Brown would be once again heading out on the long trail that could not end, until he saw John Mouton Tidwell's body cold and stiff or his own.

That night, while they were relaxing after loving each other, she asked, "Will you come back when it's over?"

"I was thinking I would," he replied.

Chapter Three
Buffalo City

It was late spring of 1873 when he arrived at Fort Dodge. He had gone to Saint Louis from Butler County and then worked his way west across Missouri. While stopping in Columbia, he had made a sizable profit one night at a poker table and decided that it would be a good means to supplement his bankroll until he was able to locate the money Hickey had sent ahead for their venture.

Jean was confident the accounts would still be there awaiting him, for there was not way Will Hickey would have discussed any subject of business with his wife. Therefore, no one, save himself would know of their existence.

Hickey's Thoroughbred had turned up lame during his dash from Kent, and although he had tried several times to sell him, no one would buy a horse in that condition. John Mouton knew well the value of this fine animal, and his greed was just too great to abandon him. Thus he led him on, without riding the stud, securing an animal car when traveling by train and when by coach, tied him on behind. Without the weight of a rider, the big stallion could keep up with the stage, but he often limped worse after a long trip.

The ride in the Concord was one of the more miserable experiences John Moulton would remember. He had intended to use the train as far west as possible. However, he had a minor mishap in Newton with a former Confederate soldier who had made some ungainly comment about his New England accent. He had taken the time to send the Texas fellow back home, wrapped in salt saturated cheesecloth. This incident created the need to make a hasty exit of the township, and the Wells & Fargo Company offered the only vehicle available at the moment.

Several extra bags of mail were picked up at the station in Larned, since the previous two westbound stages had been halted due to trouble with marauding bands of the Southern Cheyenne. Of the nine people who were in the coach, three were forced to get off in Larned and await a later stage, as the mail had the right of first travel or so the coach officer said.

The officer had ordered him off. However, John was able to persuade the man it would be better for him and all concerned, if someone else were to have to wait. As a result, a tin drummer was put off, instead of Mouton.

There were times along the way that he had wished he had waited himself and caught the train.

The extra bags of mail were stacked on the floor where the middle bench had been, and now there was no area to place one's feet that was below the level of one's hips.

Early on, the trip had been much more pleasant, if anyone could envision a rolling, bouncing, tumbling ride in any way or form a pleasant experience. The most enjoyable stretch had been east of Larned, where not only were they not required to contend with the extra bags of mail, but there had been a spring snow a day before, and the road and terrain was still mostly damp.

The land west of Larned had escaped the sudden storm and as a result was as dry as one imagines a camel's back might be. Now, the dust was so thick he thought they must be having a strong east wind. When he exited the vehicle at Fort Dodge, he soon learned the very opposite was the case.

The dust stirred up by the twenty-four hooves, as well as the front wheels of the coach had been so great, that every pore on his body covered or otherwise, was filled with the white powder.

As soon as they arrived, the other men went straight to the sutler's store for a drink of whiskey. However, John wisely headed for the livery to secure feed and water for the stallion and then for himself, a bath, while the driver and officer filled out the reports for the military, sent off the necessary telegrams and changed the team.

It was more than an hour before the call was given to depart for the last five miles into Buffalo City.

They arrived some two hours after dark, and he immediately took a room at *The Great Western Hotel*, which had only opened two weeks before his arrival.

He registered as J. D. Mather, having given much thought to the matter as they traveled from Fort Dodge. It was not impossible for Hannibal Kimball to have posted rewards on behalf of the death of his niece's husband, and if so, the authorities would be looking for a Frenchman using the name of Jean Mouton. Thus, he returned to his American heritage and made no appearance of having French blood anywhere in his background.

He had considered going back to John Tidwell, so no one would be able to compare the John Mouton and the Jean Mouton, but he thought better of it and chose a new alias altogether. *'That damn Reb Brown surely is still somewhere out there looking for me, and I dare not use Tidwell again.'*

After his stage ordeal, sleeping late the following morning was a pleasant experience, and it was near the eleven o'clock hour before he went down to breakfast. There he immediately was confronted by the most awful smell he had experienced since his time at sea.

The waiter was a man near his own age who had now lost most of the hair on the top of his head. He was dressed in dark trousers and a clean white shirt. *'A pleasant surprise here so far into the frontier.'*

"Sir, I pray, whatever is that smell?"

The waiter turned and looked to the front door and then smiled, "You must be new to the plains."

"I am surely new to that awful, breathtaking odor."

"It's them buffalo hides," the man said. "They stack them over yonder across the deadline[1] awaiting the AT&S to pick them up, fer shipping back east," he said.

"The AT&S?"

"Yeah, the Atchison, Topeka, and Santa Fe Railroad," he replied, and as he was pouring a cup of Arbuckles for Mather he added, "After a while you don't even notice them no more."

"I find that hard to believe," John replied.

"Oh yes you will, if you stay here that is. Give it a couple weeks, and you won't even notice the smell at all." He then turned, and walked over and began serving the coffee to another man who was sitting at a nearby table.

---

1 Deadline: The imaginary line along the railroad tracks, which separated the respectable part of town from the not so respectable.

John overheard him saying to the man, "I don't know, it's his first day in here." He was sure the waiter was referring to him, and it made him uneasy.

From where John was sitting, he could not see the other diner, except for a light reflection in one of the front windows. He seemed to be a tall, lean man. He wore high black boots that came slightly above his knees in the front, and he was dressed in a vested suit. John espied a black Fedora hanging on the hat rack nearby and suspected it completed the inquirer's attire.

After finishing his coffee, John decided to forgo breakfast and wait for an early lunch. Just as he stepped from the room, he turned and took a quick but thorough glance at the man.

Upon stepping outside on the boardwalk, he slowly and deliberately looked both directions, before moving away from the hotel door. To his left was a livery, and to his right, beyond a small alley that separated the clapboard buildings, was *The Saint James Saloon*. He turned left and went to the stables behind the livery.

There were more than a dozen horses in the small confines of the corral. Most seemed to be draft or mustangs. However, there was a Chestnut gelding that showed definite signs of having close relatives of the Morgan line, and John liked him very much.

Although owning another horse was not a necessity for transportation, as he planned to leave by train, there was always the possibility of the need to make a rapid exit at any moment, and in no way was Hickey's big horse ready for such a dash.

He also was well aware that in these parts, a man could get himself hung much quicker for horse stealing than he could for sending a fellow to the Promised Land. Thus, John decided he needed an extra mount just in case.

Turning, he entered the livery through the rear door and saw the hostler forking hay into one of the stalls, where a large black was housed.

"Good Morning, sir."

The man turned slowly, as if he was unsure of who would be approaching from the rear. When he finally got in a position to look at Mather, he pushed the tines of the fork into the clay and leaned on it slightly. "Howdy."

"I am in the market for a good riding horse. Would you, by chance, have any to sell?"

The stablekeeper looked over at the big bay the stranger had brought in the night before, having already spotted he was lame. He then looked back at the dude, giving him a good onceover before he spat a full stream of dark tobacco juice on the ground between the two. With his right hand, he pushed the handle of the fork forward, where it would lean against the planking of the stall. With his left, he pushed the brim of his old hat up and back, revealing an exceedingly wrinkled and very white forehead. Quite the contrary to the remainder of his sun and wind-burned face, that is, the portion of his face not covered with unkempt and thick whiskers.

"Thar be a few in the corral to the back," he said, and started walking in that direction. "Good hoss' run high in these parts," he said, not looking at Mather as he passed. "A good hoss is a prize and apt to save a man's life at times."

"That's precisely why I want a good one," John replied, as he followed from the shade, into the bright Kansas sun.

The older man placed one boot on the lower rung of the corral fence and his elbows on the top. "That there pinto is a good one. Cost ya twenty cash."

"Too nervous."

The man ran his tongue over the outside of his teeth and readjusted his wad to the left cheek. "I'll take twenty fer the buckskin."

"No, too old."

The hostler spit again into the dirt inside the fence. "That thar bay, it'll run you twenty-five."

"I like the chestnut."

The old man now wondered, *'Does this dude know horses, or is he struck with an eye fer beauty.'*

"That chestnut is a Tennessee Walker; he'll fetch forty-five, mee'be fifty anywhere."

"No sir, he's a Morgan, or at least his pa-pa was, and I'll give you thirty."

"No damn way," the old man said shaking his head.

"I'll pay thirty-five, and you can stall him with my Thoroughbred."

"You be crazy mister, forty dollars an' not a penny less."

John turned and started off without saying another word.

When he had gone far enough that it was obvious he wasn't turning back, the man called out, "Be another dollar a day to keep him here."

John stopped walking but did not turn around, "In a separate stall, inside."

"In a separate stall, inside," unenthusiastically, the man agreed, then added for his own benefit, "Damn."

From his leather folding wallet John removed two greenbacks, but before he handed them over he demanded a bill of sale.

"Can't read, can't write. You have to come back later to get it, when a body comes in what can."

John handed him a ten-dollar bill that he had brought from Georgia, "You'll get the rest when I get the bill of sale."

The old man nodded his head and softly cursed just above a whisper.

Walking back up the street John continued past the hotel, as well as *The Saint James Saloon* and went directly to the dry goods and clothing store.

J.G. McDonald stopped tallying on his note pad when the bell, which was attached on the frame just above the front entrance, rang as the door touched it when the tall stranger walked in. "Good morning," he said.

"Good morning," John replied.

"What can I do for you, sir?" the storekeeper asked.

"I need a new satchel, lost mine a while back."

"Yes sir, we have some fine leather cases here with brass snaps. They are called Doctor Bags."

"No, I want something a little larger," John said, walking around looking over the layers of stacked dry goods and boots and then to the hats that were suspended from the ceiling.

"I have a pretty nice bag here, made from the hide of a Florida alligator."

John turned at that note. He had admired just such a bag that Ozzie Scott[2] had brought with him from Florida. Walking back, he reached for the bag and rubbed his thumbs over the uneven hide for a few seconds before saying, "Yes, I like this one. I'll take it."

"That will be eight dollars, pretty hard to find such, way out here."

John paid no attention to the store-keep's sales pitch. "I'll also need a new hat, one with a large brim. There, I like the one with the flat crown."

McDonald took a long pole with a dull iron hook on its end and retrieved the Stetson.

2 Major O.C. Scott: See The Withlacoochee Renegades Chapter 15.

John tried it on, but it was too small. "No, this one's too tight."

"You could have your hair cut, we have an excellent tonsorial in *Hoovers Saloon*, just next door."

"No, get me another, larger."

J.G. McDonald searched several hats but found no other in the style of his customer's choice, large enough.

John had tried on a flat crown hat with only a four inch brim that fit him nicely, but he preferred the larger brim so many of the Texicans were wearing. Not that he wanted to copy anything from Texas, rather he knew the look was well-accepted here, and he wanted to attract as little attention as possible.

Finally deciding there was no hope for the other hat, he took a Boss of the Plains[3] that fit him and paid again in greenbacks.

When J.G. saw the folding money, he thought, *'Only soldiers are paid in greenbacks. Wonder where this dude came by them?'*

McDonald's store shared a common wall with *Hoovers Saloon*, and there was a door allowing entrance from one to the other. At that moment, the door opened, and a man in a white shirt with bright green vertical stripes, entered from the saloon.

Stetson's 'Boss of the Plains'

3 Boss of the Plains: The original Stetson style.

He was palming a wooden tray on which was a sandwich and a large schooner of beer. "Here is your lunch, J.G."

John had to admit the food looked quite inviting.

"Thanks Ben, just lay her yonder, on the counter."

It was then the man, who had been watching him earlier at the hotel, walked up out front and casually glanced in through the large front window.

John placed his new hat upon his head, picked up his new bag and started for the door; then he stopped.

The trailer was now standing on the street, leaning on the hitching post, with his back to the storefront.

"Tell me sir, that man there in front, do you know him?"

John G. McDonald moved around the counter so he could gaze through his large window, "Yes, he's a no account buffalo hunter that came in here last November, near froze to death and has been here ever since. He goes by the name of Nixon, but who knows about trash like that."

"A buffalo hunter should be out of money by now," John replied, deciding the man was following him just waiting for a chance to mug him.

"Oh, he ran out a' money right away, at the faro table over to *The Saint James Saloon,* but he is quick with the fist, and the town fathers gave him the job as Town Marshal," McDonald said in disgust. "He couldn't make it out on the plains on account of the cold, so now he makes his living bullying others around."

"Can't be much of a living."

"He gets four bits on every soul he throws in the well. That's cause the town gets five dollars fine from them before they let them get out."

"The well?"

"Yes, the well, yonder," he said pointing outside. "It's the first well dug here, went dry right away. No wonder, weren't more'n fifteen foot deep. Now Nixon uses it fer his prisoners. 'Taint no calaboose been built yet."

"Sounds like you don't care much for Mr. Nixon," John added.

"You got that right mister, trash, pure trash and nothing more."

"I think I will go next door and have what you are having," John said, nodding at the lunch plate.

"Good idea. George has a Meskin cook over there what can sure make them buff steaks melt in your mouth."

J. D. Mather entered the saloon and moved silently to a rear table, where he sat down facing the door.

Soon a short, attractive woman with black hair parted in the middle approached him, "You're new in town."

"Is it that obvious?"

"Oh no. It's just we get most everybody in here sooner or later, and I haven't seen you before."

"Well then, Miss, I do believe I will have one of those steak sandwiches, like the one sent next door and a mug of cool beer," he said, as he admired her good looks.

When she brought him a mug of Anheuser he asked, "What is your name?"

"Cornelia," she said back with a smile, pleased that he would take the time to ask, it being so early in the day.

When she worked nights, the later it got, the more the men began to notice her, but now that she was working in the daytime, she seldom attracted personal attention.

Cornelia Harris had worked at *The Hoover Saloon* for seven months. George Hoover had been the first to erect a structure at end of track the past June. It was a two-story sod building that served as the first saloon and boarding house. As soon as lumber became available, he sold the soddy and built a clapboard structure with a false front and a good roof.

Business was so good, two months later he installed a plank floor and kitchen in the back. When McDonald came and began talking about moving his store from Wichita, George enlarged his building, adding the store for McDonald.

Buffalo City would not be a year old for several months yet, and already there were over a dozen businesses, not counting the six saloons.

John could hear the faint sound of music, and when she brought him the sandwich, he asked about it.

"Oh, that's coming from *The Long Branch* next door," she said. "Chalk Beeson done had a piano brung in all the way from Saint Louie, and he hired a red-headed woman who can play it too. She even sings," Cornelia said, rolling her shoulders around as she talked. "I wus going to go to work over there, but George moved me to days and put me on two-dollar a day salary, so I don't have to whore no more."

John had to admit he was attracted to this young girl. She of course was not refined as was Connie Cabela. However, it had been several months since he had enjoyed the pleasures of a woman, and he thought Cornelia might just be what he needed at this time.

"Tell me, Cornelia, what time do you get off tonight?"

"Why?" she asked coyly.

"Because I was thinking it would be nice to have dinner with a refined lady like yourself and was hoping you would accompany me."

"Gee, that would be nice," she replied, as she touched the back of her head as if to reprimand any errant strand of hair. "Timberline comes in at seven and Lottie around ten. I guess I could go at seven. I'll ask George."

"Good. I'll be back at seven," he said smiling.

"No, not here, I have a room at Miss Butler's boarding house. You may call for me there, around eight if you would like," she replied, with her eyes as wide open as possible.

"Until eight then," he said. After she walked away, he returned to his meal.

When leaving, he exited by the back door and moved down several buildings before returning to Front Street. Once there, he took note that Nixon was no longer in sight.

By half-past seven, he had bathed, dressed and gone downstairs for a quick beer in the hotel bar. As he drank the cool dark liquid suddenly a great commotion came from several people who were seated near the front window.

Someone yelled out, "I'll be! If it ain't Brick Bond's Ox Train."

John walked over to the door and peered out; coming from the south was a wagon train consisting of nearly a dozen freight wagons. They were of the Murphy[4] design, each pulled by six huge oxen. These wagons were not less than fifteen feet tall. Each was loaded to the top and then some, with buffalo hides, save one that was equally loaded with stores of every nature.

Bond drove right past the toll bridge, which offered dry passage to the traveler. Each vehicle slid down the long bank and forded the Arkansas River as if it were a mere stream, then on to Charlie Rath's Store. There the teamsters stopped to unload their goods. These new hides just added to the already strong stench of Front Street.

---

4 Murphy Wagon: Murphy built these huge wagons in Saint Louis originally for freighting on the Santa Fe Trail.

Cornelia was wearing a light blue dress that sported a dark vertical stripe of a deep blue ribbon-like material on either side of the equally dark blue buttons.

"You do look exceptionally lovely in such a pretty dress," he said, and immediately saw her face flush. "Where do you recommend for an evening dinner?"

"Well, *The Dodge House* has a parlor, and there's always *Delmonico's* but I rather fancy *Beatty and Kelley's* restaurant," she said.

"Then it is *Beatty and Kelley's*," he replied and stretched forth his arm for her to rest her hand upon.

Some time after midnight, when he slipped out the back door of Miss Butler's, he felt something cold and hard strike him across the back of the neck, almost knocking him unconscious. He shot to the ground like a fallen rock and hit hard on his nose. Slowly, he lifted himself to his elbows and shook his head.

Suddenly a cold voice out of the darkness spoke, "I aim to marry Miss Cornelia and best you not come around her no more."

Before he could regain the strength to defend himself, he felt the sting of an exceedingly sharp blade slide gently across his throat. "I let you live this time. Next time I won't," the voice added, and then the lights went out.

Sometime in the pre-dawn hours, a light snow began to fall, awakening him. John didn't know how long he had laid there, and with great effort raised his body to his knees and then finally to his feet.

Prior to going to bed, he checked his throat in the mirror that was sitting on the small clothes cabinet, the only piece of furniture in the room, save the bed. The knife had indeed cut him from just below one ear to just below the other. The depth of the cut was perhaps a sixteenth of an inch.

'*The man knows how to sharpen a knife,*' John thought, as he softly ran his finger across the red line. '*A tad more pressure, and they would be burying me up there on the hill in a few hours.*'

He had no idea who his attacker had been, but he certainly intended to find out and would be exceedingly cautious until he did.

Cliff had followed the tracks across the field until they struck a road, and there they turned northeast. It was here, once they had reached the road, he was able to see the shoe on the right hind hoof had thrown a nail and thereby made a clear track every so often.

The trail led straight to Cape Girardeau, and it was at *The Illinois & Missouri Steam Company* ticket office he found someone who remembered his prey.

It did not take him long to find out Tidwell, or Mouton, had taken a steamer north to Saint Louis. However, instead of giving immediate pursuit, he sent several appropriate wires before returning to Kent. As much as he wanted to catch his old enemy, he also realized Leslie would need him to testify on her behalf at the inquiry concerning her husband's killing.

However, within two weeks, he was himself aboard the steamer *Natchez* northbound once again on the trail of John Tidwell.

He spent three weeks in Saint Louis, finally locating a bank clerk who remembered such a man inquiring about a bank account in the names of, Mouton and Hickey. They finally located one in Kansas City.

After several days of wires and hours spent with the local authorities, Cliff was able to have a hold placed on the funds at the KC bank, but it was too late. The account had already been closed, and he had to assume Tidwell had Hickey's money, how much, he did not know.

Cape Girardeau Docks about 1870

Immediately he wired Leslie to put a hold on all of her husband's known accounts. The question was, did he have accounts she had no knowledge of and little means of finding information about.

Hanna Mae had overheard Mr. Hickey and Mouton talking about some dealings in Montana Territory, but when Cliff questioned them, neither she nor George could remember the name of a town or city. However, since Montana was such a frontier, there were few cities and almost no banks. They quickly dispatched word to the bank in Bannock but had heard nothing in return by the time he left for Kansas City.

Cliff, quite by accident, stumbled onto the information that a man with a strong French accent had robbed a couple of their savings, as they left a bank in Columbia, Missouri. The description matched Tidwell, but he had no sketches of the murdered, so positive identification could not be made. Still, the Sheriff there was alarmed enough to send the description on to the Kansas City authorities.

That was where the trail ran cold. *'From Kansas City the bastard could have gone in so many different directions; it is like picking the correct spoke on a wagon wheel,'* Cliff thought.

After the second day and no one had seen him leave his room, J. D. Mather was awakened by George Cox and his wife. It was obvious to both of them Mather was quite ill.

Doctor T. L. McCarty's office was in the rear of *Fringer's Drug Store* some distance from the hotel, and it was quite plain to them the injured man was not going to walk anywhere soon. Cox turned to his wife and said, "Ann, go get Doc Mac, this man is nigh on death."

Titus McCarty examined the fevered man for several minutes and then slowly removed the wire-rimmed glasses he wore, and folding their arms, he tucked them into the pocket of his vest.

He turned to the two people who were standing there waiting for him to inform them. Slowly and deliberately, he opened his right hand and rubbed its palm across his mouth, as if he needed to clean the area before he spoke, "Better get Marshal Nixon. This man has been assaulted."

"Is he gon'a be alright Doc?" she asked. "What's the matter with him?"

"Go get Asa, I don't want to have to tell this twice," he said, and then reaching into his black leather bag he removed a small corked bottle.

"Go ahead Ann, and fetch Nixon," bid her husband.

As soon as she had left the room, the doctor removed the cork and took a long draw emptying half its contents.

Asa Nixon had been born a twin near East Saint Louis some twenty-four years earlier, to a father who practiced law and a mother who lead the singing at the local church.

As a boy of fifteen, he and his brother had been caught in a severe snowstorm. Both received light frostbite to their legs and feet causing Asa's twin to walk with a slight limp. Asa's injury was much greater than his brother's and caused him much pain in the winters thereafter. This also kept him from doing many of the activities other boys did. After completing superior school, his brother went off to study law in Springfield, but Asa wanted to show that as a man, he could make a living despite his injury. In 1870, he struck out for the Wild West to make his mark.

Being above average with both long gun and pistol, he found buffalo hunting a trade that seemed cut out just for him. That was until the winter of '72, when an early snowstorm again pinned him down, and nearly cost him his life.

He struggled into the five-month-old village west of Fort Dodge, sold his hides to Rath, and took a room in which to thaw out.

There were no banks in Buffalo City at the time. However, McDonald's store would take in money and give a man a line of credit for that amount. It was a fair way to keep one's cash in a safe place, and Asa did just that with most of the eight hundred dollars he received from the sale of his hides. The following night someone broke into the store and stole the money from where it was hidden.

McDonald swore that the only man other than himself who knew where the money had been hidden was Asa Nixon and refused to honor the credit agreement. Nixon claimed McDonald had faked the break in and stole the money himself.

George Hoover, Bobby Wright and Charlie Rath, the first people to settle Buffalo City, all liked Asa, and asked him to stay around as Town Marshal until the city could officially be incorporated, or a local sheriff could be elected. However, there was one stipulation; he had to stay clear of McDonald.

It had been a good way for him to spend the winter months, and he admitted he preferred town life to that of the lonely plains.

Buffaloing[5] a few drunks and dropping them in the well, until they sobered up, was about all he had to do. Most people seemed grateful to have him on the job.

"Well, what is it Doc?" Nixon asked, walking into the room.

"This man has been struck hard with a metal object; probably Buffaloed with the butt of a gun or the shank of a large knife. Someone used a knife on his throat, then clubbed him and left him to think about it. Trouble is, he must have been out in that snow we had a couple nights ago, and now he not only has a bad concussion but also pneumonia."

"Will he live?" the Marshal asked.

"I don't know. His fever is pretty high, and that is bad for the concussion. I just don't know," the doctor replied shaking his head, "but I thought you should know, Marshal.

Too, he still has near a hundred dollars in his pants pocket yonder," the older man added, turning his head to the dark trousers hanging over the chair. "Would seem to me whoever did this wasn't bent on robbery. I'd say it was done as a warning, or grudge, or something of the kind."

"Oh dear!" Ann Cox exclaimed, placing both her hands over her mouth and nose.

"Anything in his wallet to tell us anything about him?" the Marshal asked.

"Not really. He must have a bank account in Kansas City; bank receipts from there. I didn't look in the satchel."

Nixon opened the dark bag and removed several papers, then the very nicely made belt and holster, which housed a Navy Colt conversion with a shortened barrel. He checked it and saw it was loaded with five cartridges. He had to admire the weapon, and even the man to whom it belonged. He had only seen one other revolver that used the fixed cartridges and that was a big 44 over at Zimmerman's store, at a price his income would not permit.

'The dude knows his guns,' he thought, and being so intrigued with the weapon he failed to look at the papers.

In April, the town's people received notice from Governor Osborn that indeed their community was commissioned as an incorporated Township and the County Seat of the newly formed

---

5 Buffaloing: A term used by Law Men when they employed a revolver as a club, rather than a shooter.

Ford County. This came with a name change from Buffalo City to Dodge City. Further, they were advised that, Charles Rath, J. G. McDonald, and James Hanrahan, would be the city's first commissioners.

On the fifth of June, the Commission met and elected Charles Rath, F. C. Zimmerman, and A. C. Myers as County Commissioners, and Charles Basset as Sheriff, George Cox as Probate Judge, and Asa Nixon and Paul Bowen as Justices of the Peace.

It was not until this same week that J. D. Mather was able to leave the confines of *The Great Western*. Not that he was in bed all that time, on the contrary, he seldom was found in bed at sunrise.

However, his concussion had proven far more dangerous than the pneumonia. His strength was simply so short-lived that he could muster enough energy to go downstairs and have his breakfast and a short trip to the little house out back, but that would be all, then he would have to struggle back upstairs for a two-hour nap.

It didn't seem so much the hours awake, as much as the effort to move about, that tired him so. Each night he would be found staying up late at the gambling tables in the saloon side of the hotel.

It was at one of these tables he ran into Steve Boron and Sydney Coey who preferred to be called Muley.

Boron was from Vermont and Coey from Ohio originally, however they met in the Nations[6], having both been chased there by the law on separate trails from Arkansas. Boron for shooting a milk cow that belonged to an older woman who had used her broom on him, when he was found stealing eggs from her hen house. Coey for the theft of several army mules in Fort Smith.

Neither was what one would call the most respectable men a community might want to have settle among them. However, the people of Dodge would count them among their residents for the next several months.

J. D., as Mather was called about town, liked Boron. They seemed to share a heritage from the northeast, and both had grandparents who were French. He had less tolerance for Muley, but the two were a package, and Mather took them as such.

During the final month he was regaining his strength, the three had perfected a conspiracy that had just about cleaned out every honest gambler in *The Great Western*.

---

6 The Nations: The Indian Nations, Indian Territory, now Oklahoma.

Cox had seen a fairly reliable group of nightly customers dwindle to almost none and would have put a stop to the trio, had not Ann felt sorry for, Poor Mr. Mather.

On the fourth of June, Mather left the hotel and walked to *The Saint James Saloon,* and George gave a sigh of relief. That night when the three returned, he told them they would have to ply their trade elsewhere from then on. Boron gave him a cold look that sent a chill up his spine, but he held his ground.

John Mather spoke up and broke the tension, "He's right, boys; we have cleaned out all the losers who frequent this fine hotel. It's time to move on and find another bunch of poor players. After all, was it not for the kindness of these good people, I might be up there on Boot Hill right now, with the drunks and whores."

The three entered Rath's store where J. D. wanted to pick up a box of 38 Colt cartridges. While there, a buffalo hunter came in who had been slaughtering the last of the stragglers that had not migrated north at this late date, and he had news for Mr. Rath.

"What is it Andy?"

"I figured you might want to be the first to know. We seen a herd of Texas beeves some ninety miles south, headed north. Were there loading pens, I reckon they would ship from here."

"You know, Andy, you might have a real good idea there. Steers could be bought fer maybe ten dollars a head here and shipped back east where we could get perhaps trice that much, but," he paused and looked keenly at his friend, "what makes you think they will come this way?"

"I talked to them, and they is headed to Ellsworth, but when I told them that there was now tracks here, they wus interested. It would save 'em more'n a hundred miles, you know."

"Andy Johnson, sometimes I think were it not fer you, I would still be a hunter myself," Charlie said, to his old friend slapping him on his back.

Andy smiled at the compliment and asked, "Thet thar news good enough fer a drink?"

"You blame right it is, let's go to Hoover's," Rath said back, then asked, "Where is the train?"

"I left 'em and come a running to bring you the news. They is mee'be this side a' the Washita 'bout now."

Mather looked at Boron and then motioned with his head for him to follow. Boron in turn, slapped Coey with the fingers of his hand on the arm and did likewise.

They walked past *Zimmerman's Hardware Store* and on down the street to a place where no one could hear their conversation. "Do you think you could find thirty men who would follow orders for a nice sack of money?" J. D. asked Steve Boron.

"Well, they is plenty a' men on the dodge in the Territories what is always looking fer a good thing."

"I want only men that will follow my orders and men that can be trusted to keep their mouths shut afterward."

"Yeah," he said, nodding his head. "I think we could come up with that many if we were of a need." Steve began, rubbing his chin with a dirty palm, "What 'ja got in mind?"

"I want you and Muley to head out tonight. We got more than two thousand we took from these incompetent local gamblers, take half, and get us the men. We'll meet south of here someplace."

"I know a place north of the Canadian, right off the Cimarron. King Fisher's got a cabin 'ere. We stayed over one night with him, while we waited out a Federal Marshal what wus on our trail."

"Good, how do I find this place?"

"You sure you're up to riding that far?" Steve asked.

"For the kind of money we're talking about, I could ride to hell and back," J. D. said and then smiled. His two confederates smiled back.

The plains south of Dodge are mostly rolling or flat with short grass. The only trees are the ones that could struggle through the dry months along a riverbank, except on occasion, where snow would drift because of an unusual outcropping in some form that Mother Nature had stuck there. It was just such a place Steve Boron had sent Mather.

There on the otherwise barren prairie, in a slight depression, was a rock perhaps thirty feet across and nearly the same height. On the northeast side stood a twin-trunked cottonwood that had found enough snow year after year to take root and become tall and stalwart. A lonesome looking thing there on the plains in the middle of nowhere.

Beneath the rock, John Fisher had made a sizeable dugout. Later after the thaw of '71, he found the Cimarron blocked with logs and

Fisher's Cottonwood

other debris it had brought with it from afar. Using these timbers, he added a log front to his dugout and had himself a good cabin.

Even though the cottonwood could be seen from a considerable distance, the log front could not be detected until one came up on the little rise some two hundred feet to the north. From all other angles, the tree and surrounding earth hid it from view. It was a perfect hideout, and few white men knew of its existence. King called it his 'border outpost' because of its close proximity to Kansas' southern border.

King Fisher was a lad no more than nineteen when J.D. Mather rode up to his hideout. The boy, standing some four inches shorter than John and only weighing 125 pounds, did not terribly impress Mather. Nonetheless, he knew Fisher was a friend of Steve's, and he treated him as such.

The men began arriving just after sunrise the following day.

"I wus only able to fetch fifteen with your requirements," Boron said to him, as he stepped from his horse. "Started out with more, but we had a dispute, and about eight pulled out not wanting to take orders."

"You did alright. These will do, I suspect," JD said and then asked if he thought Muley would be up to another ride after a few hours sleep.

"I reckon so. What's up?"

"Come on. I'll tell you."

"You guys hobble your horses down yonder in that little gully thar and then come on up, and get some breakfast," Steve said to the men, and then he motioned for Muley to follow.

When they had walked up on top of the rock, Steve leaned against the split trunk of the tree and looked over as JD began, "Muley, I want you to get some sleep, and then late in the day, take two mounts and head out. Find that herd of cattle those Texans are moving up this way. I want to know how many men they have and how close they are to the Cimarron."

He then looked to Steve, "We will split into two groups and cut into them the morning after they cross the river. We will then drive the cattle on to Ellsworth and sell them ourselves."

"Sounds almost too easy," Muley said.

"There is one thing. We can not leave any witnesses that can identify us."

Both men nodded, but he could tell their moods suddenly had turned solemn.

Charlie Rath worked hard, and with a considerable investment built holding pens and loading ramps down next to the AT&S tracks, to be ready for that first herd into Dodge. He had sent Andy Johnson back to join his ox-train coming with the hides and also with the mission to take a letter and make sure these Texicans knew of the shipping pens in Dodge City.

Andy had intended to go on and find the herd himself, but when he reached the ox-train he was so worn out he asked Billy Rosa to go in his place and deliver the letter to the trail boss. Billy caught up with the herd a few hours later.

Morris Nash gathered most of his boys in around the fire right after chuck. "Boys hev' hyar a letter from a Mr. Rath. He claims there is not only a railroad in this town called Dodge City but loading pens and all. I call ya hyar cause, erra' one a ya got steers in this herd. I me'bee the ramrod but I aim ta give you your say a'for we up and fared forth a change in our plans."

"I ain't never heahed a' no Dodge City a'for," Bobby Beckwith said.

"Hell, you never heahed a' Kansas 'afore we started out," one of the others yelled out, teasing him.

"Tell us Mr. Nash, what'll it gain us to change our'n plans?"

"Save more'n a hundred miles, me'bee as much as ten whole days."

"I got me a bee in my bonnet fer this hyar Dodge, iffen' they got whores," Leroy Kimmer offered.

"Hellfire, Leroy, all towns got saloons, and all saloons got whores, no matter though, hoodlums[7] hyar pert-near too young to get a boner up fer whores anyways."

And with that display of cowboy jawboning they all laughed.

"We be gat'n' the same money in Dodge as Ellsworth?"

"This hyar paper says this Mr. Rath will take on the whole herd at fifteen Yankee dollars a head sight unseen, and I take it to be straight from the hoss' mouth."

"Hellfire, let's skedaddle on to this hyar' Dodge," someone yelled out, and then there was a general commotion as everyone joined in with approving "Yippies!"

The next morning just as they were moving the herd out with Billy Rosa on the point, a lone rider came up to the chuck wagon.

"That be mighty fine looking Mizzourye' Mule you be a leadin' Mister," commented the older man with a white cotton apron around his waist.

"I'd be obliged fer your good sense sir and also fer some a' your Java, iffen you can spare it."

"I reckon so. I'us just about to dump what be left anyhow; might hev' some dredge in it."

"Be fine. I done rid' all night and ain't had nothing since yesterdee morning."

"Where you bound? Iffen ya' ain't offended, me askin'?" the cook queried.

"Over to Santa Fe. I gat' me a job with a rich Meskin what owns a sizable spread there," Muley said, as he took a draw from the tin cup. Then with sweeping eyes he took notice that most of the punchers wore no guns at all, and them that did had no saddle-sheaths on their horses.

"How many head you boys got in this bundle?"

7 Hoodlums: Cooks helper, also often called The Little Mary.

The cook looked out over the slow moving longhorns and said, "We started out with six thousand, lost some crossing the Big Red, and some Injuns took a few in the badlands, but I reckon we still are pushing five thousand, more or less."

"That many?" Muley said, looking beyond the cook, at the mostly white beeves. "Where you headed?"

The cook walked around the mule with eyes of admiration as he examined the stranger's animal. "Some new burg called Dodge City, you ever hear'd a' it?"

"Yeah, been there."

"Nice town?" the cook asked and then added before Muley could answer, "They got a railroad there?"

"Yep. On both accounts."

"I got me two fine mules myself," the cook said looking at the tall red critter the stranger was leading when he rode in.

"Ain't no horse what got the stamina of a good mule," Muley agreed.

"We wus headed fer Ellsworth, but just been told a' this Dodge, and the boss turned them that a way."

"They got saloons and whores in Dodge?" The Little Mary asked.

"Hush up you little pip squeak," Cookey said, to the fourteen-year-old boy. "You wouldn't know what to do to a whore if you caught one."

"Yeah, they got a dozen saloons in Dodge, and every one has a whore or two, I 'spect. Don't you worry none boy, what you don't know, them whores will teach you if'n you got the money," Muley said back to the lad.

"How much do they cost?" Leroy asked.

"Oh, there is some what charge upwards five dollars and some what charge only one. Depends what you want."

"I want five a' them one dollar ones," the boy said laughing, as he put the last of the cast iron pots back in the chuck wagon.

"Boy's got his brain set on poking he'self to death," Muley said laughing.

"Hellfire, he ain't talked a' nothing else since we left San'tone'."

"Well, I reckon I best be pushing on if'n I ever gon'a get to Santa Fe," Muley said and dumped the last of his coffee into the embers of the cookfire, without looking back at either of them. Then changing his saddle from the buckskin over to the mule, he added, "Reckon I'll just ride Rosie fer a spell."

Dodge's Front Street Facing the Deadline

Watching the chuck wagon move on following the herd, Muley waved an adieu before heading out to the west.

After traveling less than two miles, he came to a little draw that gave him cover from those riding drag on the beeves. There he let go of the rope he had used to lead the horse; then quickly cut back to the east and on up towards Fisher's cabin.

"They ain't got morn' fifteen riders that I could see. Most a' them ain't packing iron, and there weren't no long gun on any of the rigs, leastwise I nary seed none," he told Mather and Boron. "I did spy several muskets in the chuck wagon, but that wus all. No repeaters."

Mather looked at Boron, and when Steve smiled, he said, "Get the men ready. We'll move out tonight and hit them just as they head out tomorrow morning."

He went inside and gave King Fisher twenty gold eagles, for letting them rendezvous at his cabin.

"That's a mite a' money," Fisher said holding the coins.

"I want you to know I am your friend," JD said to the youngster.

"You will always be welcome here, Mr. Mather," King Fisher replied, with a big smile.

John had learned the boy's father and brother both were cattle ranchers in Texas, and some of these men on the drives might be friends of his family. As a result, he cautioned his riders not to be talking about their plans in front of Fisher.

Beeves never like to cross a river. The larger the river the less they liked it and often would scatter and drift while doing so. The Mesquite River boys had by now become pretty good at keeping them together, having already crossed several rivers before getting this far.

The cowboys camped for the night and waited until first light before pushing them into the muddy Cimarron, whose bank at this location was quite steep on both sides. This created quite a chore getting them up the north side. Once all were across, they stopped and rested; the steers were tired from the battle with the current, and the men were tired from the battle of keeping them from scattering.

JD watched as they finally got the herd moving again, when satisfied he said, "Muley, ease up to the chuck wagon and deny them the use of their rifles."

The bent man with a dirty red shirt smiled and replied, "Bet I can."

Then turning to their other partner Mather added, "Steve, take half the men around to the far side of the herd and be ready. I'll give you an hour. I'll take the rest and move in from this side and the rear."

JD watched Steve move out with seven men, and once they were out of sight, he motioned for the others to follow him.

They slipped around behind the slow walking cattle and eased up in the dust cloud stirred by twenty thousand hooves striking the dry earth. Moving forward in the thick, brown air they finally saw forms of two drag riders. Actually, John had heard them whistling to the steers two minutes before they materialized in the haze.

Mather rode up to within twenty feet of the man and from there he threw his thin-bladed knife, sticking the rider just to the right of his spinal cord. The cowboy threw both arms up in the air and then slipped off his pony; if he made any cry it was lost to the sounds of thousands of hooves pounding on the hard prairie floor.

Stopping to retrieve his knife, John motioned for one of his men to move up and take the downed rider's place. When he pulled the blade free, the man rolled over and pulling the neckerchief from his face pleaded, "Help me, Mister?"

J.D. Mather was surprised to see he was so young, not yet having begun to shave his tender face. He wiped the blood from his blade on the boy's pant leg and then said, "It won't be long now, best not fight it."

Muley rode up beside the chuck wagon without either of its occupants realizing he was there. When Leroy saw him, he jumped and grabbed for the cook's arm.

"What the tarnation?"

The boy pointed at the man now riding just short of the wagon seat.

"Thought you wus headed to Santa Fee," he said.

"Change in plans," Muley said back.

"You lose your lead hoss?"

"Naw, he's back thar," Muley said. "Cut his leg som'um bad. Could you spare some grease?"

"Shor'," the cook said. "Whoa, whoa, hold up there Sallie, whoa Sam."

When the mules slowed and finally came to a stop, the old man wrapped the leads around the brake handle, and then stepping on the hub, he jumped on down to the hard ground.

"Got some right here," he said, as he headed for the back of the wagon, but he never reached it. Suddenly shots rang out from the west side of the herd, and then several mounted men, who he had not seen before, rode past the wagon at a gallop.

"Som'bitch!" the cook yelled and grabbed for the long barrel shotgun that he kept handy to take a grouse or rabbit that might present itself along the way.

Muley shot him in the back. The ball entered his right shoulder, and the cook simply withered to the ground slowly, as if he had been filled with air and had suddenly started losing it.

Leroy Kimmer looked at the old man laying there in disbelief. Muley had been so close when he shot him, that much of the burning powder entered with the ball and started his shirt afire. The boy then raised his head and looked at the man who had shot Cookey with the biggest eyes Muley could remember ever seeing.

"Well boy, I am going to save you from the sin a' whoring around." Then he shot the lad in the face. The impact of the heavy 44 lead ball striking the skull knocked the boy from the wagon seat onto the dusty brown grass.

Then the killer dismounted and tying his mule to the rear of the wagon, climbed into the seat. "Come on Sallie, get up Sam," he said, offering a nod of appreciation to the cook for letting him know the mule's names before he died.

Mather and his men rode through the herd and shot every one of the riders from their mounts before they even knew what was happening.

Morris Nash was struck in the left leg with a pistol ball, and he fell from his horse. Nonetheless, he was able to clear leather and gun two of the rustlers before he was hit again, this time in the upper chest, which put him down for good.

When the first shots were heard, the inexperienced outriders to the east had moved in closer, trying to see what was happening. In doing so, they rode straight into the guns of Mather's men.

Billy Rosa was the last to realize where the trouble was coming from. He had heard the shots that had taken the outriders on the west side and had turned that direction expecting to see a small band of Comanche, not realizing his danger to be inside the herd.

The shot that dropped him passed through his lower left side and struck his horse in the back of the head killing it instantly. When the big animal fell forward, it took the rider with him and then lay still with Billy's leg pinned under it.

He had lost his revolver in the fall and had no way to defend himself, and that is what saved his life. When the slow-moving cattle and their new drovers passed by, he laid close to the bloody carcass and was missed by the thousands of hooves and assumed dead by the rustlers.

Muley pulled up the chuck wagon only a few yards from where Rosa lay and waited as he saw Mather approaching.

"How did it go with you?"

"No trouble at all," Muley said, and then asked, "Did we lose anybody?"

"I saw a couple of our men go down, but I don't know who they were," Mather replied.

"As soon as Steve gets here, tell him to round up as many of the scattered beeves as he can, then follow us. We're going on now, you will catch up with us when we stop for the night, be sure to stay clear of The Border."

Muley raised his hand as an answer and then stepped from the wagon to examine the mules.

It was then Rosa took the chance to raise his head and look at the wagon stopped no more that fifty feet away. Immediately, he recognized the man as being one he had seen in Dodge the last time he was there, but he didn't know his name.

When the other riders approached, he dropped his head again so his face was covered by his big Stetson.

"JD said to gather as many of them what scattered in the ruckus as you can, and follow on. He's taking the herd on north."

"Will do," Steve answered, before asking, "How ja' do?"

"Lost two I think; how 'bout you?"

"Not a one. Them dumb Texans let us ride up right on 'em. It were like shooting ducks in a muddy pond."

"Good, this bunch will fetch a pretty penny at the railhead."

Steve then motioned with his arm, and his men followed him after the strayed cattle.

Billy, hearing the man climb back onto the chuck wagon and call to the mules, waited for several minutes before he raised his head again. When he did, he could just see a faint image of the wagon before it disappeared into the dust cloud.

It took him almost an hour to wiggle his foot from beneath the dead horse, but when he did, he took his saddlebags and found the bottle of whisky he carried there. Miraculously, it had not broken in the tumble.

Pouring some of the alcohol onto his neckerchief, he stuck it in the hole in his side and probed it with his fingers until he had pushed it through. The pain had been so intense he almost fainted twice, but finally he got it through so each end was sticking out. Having not felt any ragged pieces while probing, he hoped that meant the lead had not torn anything vital as it bored its nasty hole. He had been leaning to his left when hit and assumed that had been some help.

After resting for several minutes, he began searching for the revolver he lost in the fall. Upon finding it, he looked all around until spotting a horse standing off half a mile. Then he started slowly walking back towards it.

The horse actually turned out not to be a horse at all, rather Rosie, that Muley had tied to the back of the chuck wagon, but in his haste he had made a poor knot, and when the wagon started off, the stubborn animal refused to move, and the knot pulled lose.

The mule would have wandered away had it not been for the two bodies lying close by. Something in his nature about not wanting to be alone, and the fact he had been trained to stand when the reins were to the ground, had kept him there.

Billy also found the shotgun where the cook had dropped it, and seeing the mule was ground-reined, he went over and checked the two bodies. Both were dead, but he had no way of burying them and was grateful simply for a means of getting away from this scene of blood and death and perhaps getting help for himself.

It was early the next day when King Fisher noticed the animal standing there alone on the prairie. He watched for quite some time before mounting his own horse and riding out to where the creature stood. He was almost upon him before he saw the body lying beside the tall mule, immediately recognizing it as the one Muley had left with.

Billy Rosa had lost a great deal of blood, but he had kept pouring the whiskey on both ends of the kerchief and riding on. Sometime during the night he passed out, but the instinct of so many years in a saddle had kept his legs tight. The mule was left to go as he wished, and he went to the last place he had been fed a bag of grain.

Billy finally fell a quarter mile short of the lonesome cottonwood, and the faithful mule stopped and waited for him.

It was late the next day before he awoke to tell his story to King Fisher.

Fisher had himself thrown a wide loop from time to time in the three short years since he had left home, but he had killed no one except two Reddies who had tried to steal his horse.

However, he realized immediately who had been the rustlers, and when he found out the dead were from The Mesquite River outfit, he was suddenly sick over his involvement. He did not know the riders of *The Mesquite River Ranch* personally, but he had heard his father talk of them fondly, and he hoped none of the boys he did know back home had ridden with them on this drive.

As soon as Rosa was able, Fisher rigged a travois for him to lie on and led the mule to Dodge City where Billy would get proper doctoring and the incident be reported.

The day he knew Billy Rosa would recover; King Fisher used some of the gold eagles and bought enough supplies from Rath's store for a long journey before heading back to Texas. He wasn't sure how his father would take his Prodigal Son, but for the time being he wanted no more of the Owl Hoot Trail.

At the very time Doc Mac was tending to Billy Rosa in his office behind the drug store, the men who had pushed the stolen herd on were easing out of Ellsworth, headed for the Nations, all that is except J.D. Mather and his two partners.

The final count had been four thousand, eight hundred, and sixteen. Mather sold them quickly for thirteen dollars a head.

He paid each of the men two thousand dollars with the understanding they would be available again for another such venture. He then gave Muley five thousand and seven to Steve. The next morning he opened an account under the name of Jonathan David Mather at *The Ellsworth State Bank* with a twenty thousand dollar deposit.

'This could be easier than finding Will Hickey's hidden bank accounts,' he thought.

The trio took rooms at *The Drover's Cottage* across from the rails of *The Kansas Pacific Railroad* and set out to enjoy spending some of their newfound money.

While there in Ellsworth, JD bought another Navy Colt that had been converted to shoot the 38 cartridge; this one was an 1851 Model and was essentially the same as the '61 except it sported an octagon barrel. He liked the brace and wore them unhidden under his coat.

At the end of the week, another herd arrived, and the Marshal stopped them before they reached the tracks.

"What's it all aboot, Marshal?" Brad Leach asked.

"I want to see some proof these beeves is yours," Hickok said.

"What fer?"

"Just show me some proof, and that will end the matter."

"Hell, Marshal, we done trailed them all the way from Waco. I don't reckon we got no bettern' proof than that."

"That ain't good enough," the lawman said, pulling back his coat allowing the butts of his own Navy's to be seen.

"Wal that's tuff, I say," Leach replied, as several of his men rode up beside him.

Hickok was no fool, even with his cool hand he might get two, maybe three of them, but in the end, he would be laying in the dust with his victims. "You can come into town, but none of your outfit can, and none of your beeves will be sold until you show proof," Hickok said and then quickly turned his white horse and rode back towards Ellsworth.

"What wus that all aboot?" Sandy Crile asked.

Brad Leach just twisted his head indicating he had no idea, "Me'bee more Yankee justice."

The next morning, after seeing to it all the steers were circled, Leach headed into Ellsworth going straight to the telegraph office to send a wire. He addressed it to Mr. H. C. Goodnight, Waco, Texas and then returned to his herd.

The following day when he came into town, he found a reply to his wire. Upon reading it, he headed out looking for the Town Marshal.

"Hickok!" Leach yelled at the man across the street.

The lawman whirled around and threw both his hands inside his plaid cape.

Leach had no doubt where his palms were resting, but his only reaction was yelling, "This hyar proof enough?" as he tossed the folded yellow paper at the lawman.

James reached down and picked up the wire. It read:

To whom it may concern Stop

Brad Leach left Waco on March One this year with six-thousand head of fine Texas cattle sporting the Loving/Goodnight brand Stop

Anyone doubting that brand is too ignorant to call himself a lawman End

Hickok read the wire twice to be sure he had read it right. Few men could say something like that about him and not worry about later reprisals; Charles Goodnight was an exception. His outfit blazed the first trail from Texas to Colorado, and he was known in every cow town in the west, as one of the straightest men in the business.

"I'm gon'a tell you something Leach. I don't like Texicans. I don't like any copperhead. I spent four years of my life trying to kill as many of you as I could. Now fetch your beeves in and sell them and then be gone. If just one of you dumb cowboys makes any trouble at all, I'll jail every one of you, and you'll be the first," he said to Leach and then spat a long stream of tobacco juice into the street between the trail boss' feet. "And I'd like you to resist."

"Jest so you know Mr. Big Bug Marshal, you weren't the only one in thet thar war. I spent a few years killing Bluebellies myself, and I did it in Tennessee and Georgia, not hiding oot west as a' Army Scout."

Hickok straightened up fast, and the anger grew rapidly in his narrow blue eyes. The affront had been sharp, but true, and he immediately realized that if Leach knew his war record, perhaps so did many other men like him.

Brad Leach then turned and walked away from the steaming Marshal. That night he and his men were drinking at *The Drover's Cottage* when the talk settled around his confrontation with the infamous Wild Bill.

Mather did not fail to pick up on the reason the dispute had begun in the first place.

Word was out somehow about a herd being stolen. He was sure they had left no survivors, yet somehow word was out. He decided it was time for the three of them to move on.

Thirty miles south, they stopped for the night and made camp under a cottonwood tree along a small creek; there, while enjoying a cup of Arbuckles, JD told them of his next plan.

"I don't know how it happened, but word has gotten out about us taking that herd. It may be best for us to lay low for a spell. However, the money is so good, and we have, at this time, a good group of men who will follow orders for a fair share in the profit. That is good; however with word being out the next bunch will not be so easy.

These last boys were not expecting any trouble other than perhaps some savages, trying to run off a few head for food. As a result, they were not well armed; the next outfit will be better prepared. I want to attack them differently," John said.

He then stopped and looked directly at the ignorant man, "Muley, I want you to head south into Texas and hang around Waco or Fort Worth and watch for a good-size herd headed north. Wire me when you do. I'll be in Dodge. Send this message." He handed a folded piece of paper to Coey.

"I can't read, nor write," Muley said.

"That's why I'm giving you this paper. Don't lose it. All you have to do is take it to the telegraph office and hand it to the telegrapher and ask him to send it," Mather told him. "And be sure you get it back. I don't want to leave any evidence around with my writing on it."

"Yes sir," Muley said.

"After sending the message, go straight to Fisher's cabin."

Muley nodded his head displaying his understanding of the orders.

"Steve, you go to Wichita and hang around listening to the cattle buyers. Find out what they are paying, and if they are requiring proof of ownership of the beeves."

Steve nodded his head, thankful he had been spared the long ride to Texas and back.

"As quickly as you get there let me know where you are staying, and as soon as you have the information, wire me and wait. I'll let you know when to come." John tossed the last of his coffee aside as he spoke.

"I think it is best we are not seen together before we move again. And Muley, on your way back, swing by and pick up the boys in The Nations."

Again Muley nodded his head.

JD Mather left the next morning en route for Dodge City while his two confederates moved out in the directions of their assignments.

This time when he arrived in town, he took a room at *The Dodge House*, figuring he might not be welcome at Mr. Cox's hotel after their gambling spree a month before.

There was still much talk about town of The Border Raiders, as the gang of rustlers was being called.

He also saw Billy Rosa, who was quite the local hero now. Everyone praised him for his savvy in fooling the raiders into thinking he was dead.

JD never asked Rosa any questions about the raid but did buy Billy a couple drinks at *The Long Branch* and listened closely when others questioned him. John would learn well from his mistakes.

The first day of August, a boy brought a wire to the hotel. JD was in the bar at the time having a friendly game of Faro with a pretty whore named Alice, who ran the table. He had learned, never to be a big winner, unless he intended to be The Big Winner and take everything. For that type game, he needed Steve and Muley.

He thanked the boy with a dime and excused himself from the game for a moment.

The telegram read:

MR. MATHER THE NEW HOLSTERS YOU ORDERED ARE READY STOP

SHOULD ARRIVE IN A FEW DAYS END

Noticing it was sent from Fort Worth he inwardly smiled. Steve had already sent him news of the selling prospects in Wichita and was ready to leave upon receiving his wire. He went straight to the telegraph office and sent this to Mr. Boron at *The Douglas Belle Hotel*, Wichita, Kansas:

FIND A BUYER FOR OUR STOCK STOP

YOUR BROTHERS WANT TO DO SOME KING FISHING AT THE BIG ROCK WITH YOU STOP

COME SOON END

The following morning Mather tied his horse behind a rented wagon filled with the necessary supplies for the intended raid and set out for King Fisher's cabin.

Cliff Brown had spent eight months trying to pick up the trail. It seemed as if Tidwell had vanished off the face of the earth. Most men would have used the good sense God gave them and realized the man he sought may have been killed somewhere, and no one even knew his name. Then again, he could have doubled back and was now in New York with his friend Rufus Bullock.

Reb Brown, however, was not one to give up easily. He knew he would not rest a night through until the man who murdered his wife was in hell, and he dearly intended to be the one to send him to that very place.

Arriving on the Missouri side of the river, he spent a week in Kansas City, hanging around the saloons and billiard parlors before he crossed into Kansas.

It was strange to see the difference a body of water made in the attitudes of people. As soon as he stepped off *Moses Grinter's Ferry* he was met with a strong case of unfriendliness.

In Kansas City, Missouri, he was among folk. People he had never seen before nodded their heads at him, and he had half a dozen men offer to buy him drinks in the saloons. As soon as he arrived in Wyandot City[8], Kansas, he was immediately pegged a copperhead. The people were obviously anti-south, even more than they were pro-union. He was now a Rebel in Yankee Territory. This attitude

8 Wyandot City: Now Kansas City, Kansas.

was more predominant than he had experienced in any other place he had been since the war.

The Sheriff's Office was located in a small building made of hewn logs, it consisted of a front room, and another in the rear, where two cells were located. Cliff entered and looked swiftly at the three men there. Quickly identifying, and aiming in on the one he wanted, before introducing himself. After describing John Tidwell, he explained why he was after him.

The Deputy was a lean sort of fellow, perhaps five years older than Cliff and about six inches shorter. His head was already clearly showing signs of balding, especially so, when he leaned forward in his tall chair and placed his palms flat on the counter that cut the small room almost in two.

"You say this man has a New England accent when he isn't pretending to be a Frenchman?"

"That's right," Cliff confirmed.

"There are a thousand people in Kansas with a New England accent. Kansas was settled by people from the northeast. We were a slave free state, you know," he said, with a bitter tone in his voice. "I'm from Rhode Island myself, and from your drawl I think we can reasonably assume you are not from New England," he added.

"Naw, I'm from Georgia."

"I had a brother in Lawrence, Kansas, when you Copperheads burned most of the town to the ground. They left him dying in the street as they rode off."

"I lost a couple a brothers to Bluebellies myself, it were a big war, Mister, long over," Cliff said. Then, taking a deep breath, he finished, "Right now I'm trailing a man who murders women without regret."

"Listen, Johnny Reb; don't come in here talking about murdering people. I ain't one who forgets so easy. It were your kind what rode with Quantrill and burned damn near the whole blame town 'a Lawrence, just down the road there a ways!" The deputy was almost shouting by this time.

"Mister, I ain't never been to this Lawrence," Cliff said, nodding his head as confirmation. "I did read about the incident and don't hold with burning folks' homes, but I ain't one a them who burned this here Lawrence. Hell, I don't rightly even know whar it's at. There is one thing I do know, it's a narrow-minded son-of-a-bitch who remembers a town being burned during a war and can't remember a whole state what got damn-near burned out. You are so big to condemn this Quantrill fellow for burning your town and then with the same breath you praise a scrawny little General who scorched the whole state a' Georgia!"

Cliff's face was becoming redder and redder as he spoke. "Now get off your high hawse, and do your job as a lawman. Being the avenging angel don't suit your character."

"I'll tell you what I'll do as a lawman; I'll see you hang if you bother one decent man in Wyandot City. That's what I'll do as a lawman."

Cliff slapped his hat on his leg and stomped out of the front door. *'It is obvious I ain't gon'a get any information from the Sheriff's Office, if'n the other deputies are of the same mind as that fellow.'*

"Pardon me, Sur," a strong Texas voice called out to him as he reached the boardwalk. Turning quickly, still in a rage, Cliff's hand dropped to the stock of his old Colt, but it was not needed. There in the sunlight he saw a tall man in a wide- brimmed hat also coming through the doors he had just slammed and then he remembered him as one of the three inside.

The man's drawl immediately presented him as more likely friend than foe, so Cliff took a deep breath to calm his emotions before nodding his head to the gent in the double-breasted suit.

"I do apologize for coming to you uninvited, Sur, but I couldn't help overhearing your discussion with Deputy Brady," the stranger said as he approached closely to where Cliff now stood on the boardwalk.

"I had a similar experience with him myself only a few days ago. Bitter man. I understand he wasn't even in the war himself, stayed home and sold groceries."

Cliff could feel the tension lifting as the man spoke. He knew rancor never accomplished what a cool head could, but the skinny little fellow had rubbed him wrong. Finally, he asked, "What can I do fer you?"

"Mr. Brown? I think I heard y'u say," the man stated, as he stretched forth his hand.

"Brown it is, Clifford Brown, but my friends call me Reb, and you are the friendliest man I've met west of the Missouri," he said back, shaking the Texan's hand before he added, "this time, anyways."

"Thet's a compliment and I thank yu, Sur. Rumans, John Rumans is the name."

"What can I do fer you, Mr. Rumans?" Cliff asked.

"Wal', Mr. Brown, I represent a Texas Cattle Company an' we're hev'in' a passel a' trouble with rustlers jumping our herds after they cross the Red River. We've lost two whole herds, my third ootfit got shot up bad, an' it warr a close shave on some of them what made it. Had nigh on two thirds a' my beeves stole."

"I see," Cliff replied looking slowly to his right and then to his left. "Just how does that bring you to me?"

"I came hyar to Kansas looking fer help from Johnny Law and purty pronto bumped into what y'u jest did. These hyar Red Legs don't cotton much to us Southern boys. Although I will say, Mr. Cornell, the High Sheriff, is a decent man. I don't 'spect he's in ca-hoots with th' Jayhawkers, or as they call them theses days, Border Raiders."

Rumans stopped and took a deep breath before continuing, "Same as Jayhawkers wus, ten year ago. Still, Cornell 'as done nothing fer me. I made an appointment imploring fer a' interview with the Governor an' got no results, an' then to the army with purty much the same.

Seems the army is only interested if it be Reddies what stol' my beeves. I was making one last try with the law here, when I observed yore' fight with Deputy Brady."

"Yeah, he does have bitter feelings fer this Quantrill fellow."

"Funny, Quantrill was not a Southerner at all."

"He weren't?" Cliff questioned raising his eyebrows.

"Naw, he weren't. He hailed from Ohio som'ers. He an' his brother were party to a wagon train headed further west when some Kansas Jayhawkers attacked the train. During the fight, Quantrill was shot and left for daid and his brother was kilt, Bill Quantrill claimed he wus outright murdered. Anyway, after thet, he turned against Kansas with a vengeance, an' since Kansas fought fer the Union, he fought again' the Union."

Cliff shook his head before saying, "I still don't see what all this has to do with me."

"Come with me, Mr. Brown, an' let me buy you a drink. I hev' a hankerin' to talk to you about this idea I hev'."

"I really don't have time," Cliff said back not wanting to get mixed up in another problem. '*Hell, I have enough of my own,*' he thought, but suddenly the old up-bringing of his father eased its way into his thoughts, and he finally said, "but beings you are the only friendly man in Kansas, how can I turn you down."

They went to *The Rosedale Saloon* on Turkey Creek. There John Rumans laid out what he had concluded was his only hope in this matter.

"I've been a' dwellin' on this with powerful consideration." He stopped and with narrowing eyes looked straight at Cliff. "You see, Mr. Brown, we are trailing from three to seven thousand head a' beeves when we leave Texas.

A steer hyar fetches som'ers between ten and sixteen Yankee dollars. Now everyone knows yu're gon'a lose some along the trail, but to lose the whole blame herd is a sizeable chunk a' change, to say nothing of the boys laying daid oot there on the plains.

I figger," he said, nodding his head again, "I figger to get up twenty or so men, good men. Men who were in the war and know what fighting is all about; men who won't be scared oot a' thar johns when the shooting starts and hev' 'em ride along with the herd." He paused a moment and took a deep breath as if he had exhausted all the good air in his lungs with his speechmaking and needed a fresh supply. "Looking like ordinary drovers, only they won't be drovers. When this bunch a' Jayhawkers hit us, we'll be ready fer 'um and then the fun will commence."

"Well, Mr. Rumans, I see that might work, but I think you are talking to the wrong man. I got a trail, admittedly a cold trail, but still a trail a' my own that will only get colder were I to side with you. This here man I'm after, he killed my wife, and I can't let nothing more interfere with me finding him."

Rumans took a couple of quick moments to study back on what he overheard in Dudley Cornell's office. When satisfied he was remembering it correctly at least mostly so, he spoke, "Wal, thet's jest it, Mr. Brown, the only name we hev' on any of these cutthroats is Tidwell."

Immediately Cliff came up in his chair, "What do you know about him?"

"Nothing, 'cept he speaks some French, and he's called Tidwell."

"What do you need from me?" Cliff asked without further argument.

"Wal, Mr. Brown, I think from what I see in your character, what I need is for you to ramrod this ootfit."

Cliff thought hard on this new endeavor being presented to him and decided, '*It will not likely to be more trouble than organizing The*

Renegades had been. At least there won't be womenfolk to tend to their safety on a cattle drive.'

"First thing I need, is fer you to start calling me Reb."

"Then we hav' a deal?" John replied.

"I'll lead your gunmen, but you might as well know now I ain't much of a cowpuncher."

"I don't," Rumans paused, wetting his gums with his tongue before continuing, "I don't aim nor want you to be punching. I want you to come with me to Texas, pronto. We'll get the men there. That way we can trust 'em. I want you to organize 'em into a fighting unit, so when we need 'em, they will be ready."

Rumans was getting excited now. He wasn't sure how he would explain to Brown that he had lied about this Tidwell fellow, but he would worry about that when the time came.

"The herd departed Waco two weeks past. We hev' some time left to get the men and ootfit them before those steers swim The Big Red."

"Alright, Mr. Rumans, I'll lead your men if it be true that John Tidwell is among this bunch of raiders."

"Oh, it's true. It's true, sure enough," he lied. Then adding, "And Reb, it's John. Let's drop the Mister."

Cliff nodded his head and then downed his beer. He was not so sure about Rumans' story. It just didn't seem like the kind of work John Tidwell would be mixed up in. 'He is more likely to be conning some banker into taking him in as a partner, than lowering himself dragging a herd a' beeves, but it is a lead. The only one I've crossed in several months. It is worth a try,' he thought.

Tom Smith had, with much sorrow, watched his Pa and two brothers ride off with The Red River Dragoons in the fall of '63. He was then the only man on the place, and although there were two sisters older than he and another younger, his Pa told them all, "Tom is the man of the house until I return." Something he never did.

Being the only male in a small house with four females was in itself a chore, to say nothing of the hours of manual labor the fourteen year old faced.

Face it he did. Hours and hours of it. From before the light of the sun, until long after the stars were out, he labored about the little 200-acre farm.

His mother was exceedingly proud of her youngest son and often told him how she was reporting his hard work in her letters to his father.

Once, near Christmas time, a letter came from Third Sergeant Henry Smith and their mother read to them. It had been written the previous June. She made a point of calling special attention, by raising her voice, when she came to the part concerning what Henry had said about how proud he was to hear of Tom being such a good worker. He ended by saying he knew he had done the right thing by placing him in charge.

It made Tom mighty proud, so much he felt tears building, and he rushed outside into the cold night before anyone saw them.

That was the same letter in which they learned Joey would not be coming home. Henry Smith had said he buried his boy in a field near a big hickory tree on a Mr. Kolb's farm, which was located in the hill country, somewhere south of Chattanooga.

'The worst thing about thet letter is thet it was the last one Pa ever wrote,' Tom thought from time to time.

They received the news of his death by Mr. Billington, the mail carrier from down in Paris, but nothing ever came about Charles. When the war was over, they all waited for Charles' return.

Of *The Red River Dragoons* who made it back, none knew what had happened to him. Tyrell Johnson told them he had eaten some goobers[9] with Charles one night in front of a small log house he said belonged to some woman called Granny White, north of Franklin, Tennessee, but they never saw her. He also said, "After the battle the next day, Charles was jest gone. I thought me'bee he wus captured by some of Schofield's men, and he surely would be home from the prison camps soon." However, Charles never showed up, and no one ever heard of him again.

That same year, the Comanches came through late one afternoon and stole all their horses. Everyone was able to make it into the root cellar before the savages fired the house.

The next morning when the frightened family came out, no one was around except a lone pony, which had the outline of an outstretched hand painted on his neck, in red. Tom was able to catch him and eventually train him as a good riding pony, but he would never give in to the plow.

---

9 Goobers: Goober Peas, known in some areas as peanuts.

The little family had built a shack with what they could salvage from their burned house and with some wood Tom found floating in The Big Red. It gave them shelter, if not comfort.

Tom named the pony Comanch', using him to gather a small herd of about forty wild longhorns the following year.

In the fall of '68 the Texas State Police[10] came and took them, claiming they were being confiscated for back taxes, and the Smith family was left with only the Indian pony once again.

That Christmas, Tyrell married Tom's oldest sister Josie. He took her down almost to Paris, where he was working his own Pa's old place.

The following spring, *The Fort Worth Stage Line* set them up as a stop on their route to Fort Smith. This gave them enough money to put an addition on the front of the ol' shack, as an eating room. Soon it was known by all the Jehus[11], his mother, and April set a good table for them and what paying passengers there were.

Two years later, April took the northbound herself, hoping for something better than a dirt floor on the banks of Piney Creek in Lamar County, Texas.

If there was anything Tom Smith had learned well in the past ten years, it was how to ride a horse and how to use a revolver, and he did both much better than men half-again his age.

Once he watched a Comanche remove the empty cylinder of an old Colt Dragoon and replace it with one loaded, in a matter of seconds, while Tom was shooting at him. The Indian had never lost his balance on the fast moving pony as he swept by the front of the house during the raid back in '64, and Tom never forgot the savages' skill.

When Tyrell started sparking Josie, he gave Tom a Colt Army Model. Tyrell said he took it off the body of a Yankee Captain som'ers' near Columbia, back in December of '64, when they were retreating from the fighting near Nashville.

Tom realized it was sort of a bribe to get him indebted, so he would not raise a scrap about Tyrell seeing Josie, but Tom didn't

---

10 Texas State Police: Not the Texas Rangers who had been disbanded. The Texas State Police were appointed by the Carpetbag Government of the Reconstruction Period during Grant's administration.

11 Jehu: A stagecoach driver, taken from the name of a Biblical character that drove fast and furiously.

care. He would be glad for them both, although he sort a' felt sorry for Tyrell, knowing Josie as he did.

The 44 gave him exactly what he wanted most, and he practiced over and over, trying to reload while riding at a full gallop. He finally realized the secret was in having the barrel pin screw only tight enough to keep the pin from falling out.

He eventually was able to duplicate the skill of the savage by slamming the pin against the horn on his saddle to drive it home. Now he never went away from his house without an extra loaded cylinder for his revolver. Tom felt he had the firepower of two guns carrying half the weight.

Speed-loading was not the only skill he had learned with that Colt. He could pull it from his sash as fast as most could from a holster and faster than many. Out to a hundred feet or so, he was as accurate as any man with a long gun, providing each was shooting fast.

John Rumans and Reb Brown were eating a tasty bowl of antelope stew at the table in Mary Smith's front room, when the first shots were heard. Immediately, Cliff and the other men were rushing outside to answer the challenge.

Twelve hostiles were riding a small circle around the stage stop, shooting their guns and yelping like a pack of dogs that had run into a bear bigger than they had anticipated.

The whip[12], who had been helping Tom hitch up a new team of horses, took a flaming arrow in the back, just below his right collarbone, but Tom had slapped the fire out before the Jehu was burned too badly.

Cliff saw the boy help the wounded driver under the coach, and all the while he was firing his revolver at the fast moving targets. The boy hit two of them during this time. Then, changing cylinders faster than Cliff could reload his cartridge-gun; he was back shooting once more. This time he took out the one who had dismounted and was sending in the fire arrows from behind a tall bed of Spanish bayonets.

Suddenly the little fight was over, but when checking, they found the round rafters in the roof of the house had begun to burn. The greatest loss though was found next to the cooking stove, where Mary Smith had taken a rifle ball just forward of her right ear.

---

12 Whip: Another slang word for stage driver.

Tom then walked out to the bodies of the Indians and deliberately fired another ball into each one's head.

"Kiowas," he said. Then he just sat down and gazed out onto the lonely prairie, while pondering on his mother's death.

It was Tom who drove the stage on to Paris. He had simply looked around after burying his mother and said, "I got no reason to stay hyar no longer."

Cliff rode as shotgun messenger for him as they made their way down that dusty road, and by the time they reached the county seat, Tom was on Rumans' payroll. Cliff knew the lad had not fought in the war, but he saw him do his cylinder swap and watched his coolness under fire. He was convinced the boy would be all right. Tom Smith was the first man hired after Cliff arrived in Texas.

Tom was able to locate four other Lamar County boys who jumped at a chance to work their way to Dodge without having to ride drag behind a thousand steers. Cliff liked them and took them along too.

John Rumans decided there were now too many to bring with them to Fort Worth. He gave each a gold eagle with the promise of more to come if they were at Cowtown[13], well mounted and ready to ride north on the twelfth of the month. Tom was allowed to continue with Cliff and John.

Tom Smith was a lad of twenty-four when they arrived in Fort Worth. Although not as tall as Reb, he was wiry like his older boss and had a good sense of humor. He never shucked work and could sing as pretty a tune as a lonesome coyote on a bright moonlit night.

Cliff had liked him right off, admiring something about his mannerisms and the way he would laugh at his own mistakes. This also caused others to cater to his presence.

It was the first time the boy had been further from Piney Creek than Paris in his life. The sight of the gaslights along side of the buildings amazed him so he had a hard time looking at anything else at first.

The stage pulled up to the station just after the eight o'clock hour, and Cliff could see Tom was in a state of excitement. He looked one way and then another, and his eyes were as big as they had been in his whole life.

They took two rooms at *Molly Bee's Hotel*, one for Mr. Rumans and the other shared by Reb and Tom.

---

13 Cowtown: Nickname of Forth Worth.

Cliff said as soon as they had settled in, he wanted to take a bath and then get a drink or two before turning in for the night. Tom saw no need to waste the time and wanted to head straight to the saloons.

"Jest hold your hosses, young fellow," John Rumans said. "I give you thet ten-dollar gold piece so you would hev' some money to eat on until the herd arrives, not to go blowing it on a bunch a saloon wimmin', the first night in town."

Tom lowered his head and replied, "Yas, Sur."

"Come on Tom, let's see if we can get some hot water brought up to the tub down the hall yonder," Cliff suggested, seeing the wind had just been knocked out of the lad's sail.

"Sure Reb, what ere' you say," he replied, but it was not an enthusiastic reply.

They enjoyed a couple of beers and a steak in the small saloon to the side of Molly Bee's. There they listened to the sounds coming from down Main Street, at the more lively locations. However, they traveled no further after supper than to the front porch. Here Tom got a breath of fresh air, and Cliff enjoyed a quirley.

"Don't fret, Tom," Cliff said, placing an arm around the boy's shoulders and steering him back inside. "There will be other nights, when we're better rested."

Cliff had a near sleepless night. Every time something happened outside, that made enough noise to drift in their slightly opened window, Tom would be up looking out.

The next morning at breakfast the boy asked the waiter, "When are we gon'a see Miss Molly Bee?"

"Doe' no, ain't never seen her myself," he replied.

"Huh?"

"Wal, it seems Mr. Bartholomew B. Clark come here from San'tone and built this hotel three, four year back. Most say he were in love with a whore down there, and he named the hotel after her, 'cause he thought she would come up here and marry him. She never did, and he ended up getting himself shot daid over a poker game the next year. Now a Mr. Pevy owns her, so I don't reckon none a' us will ever get to see Miss Molly Bee."

When the waiter returned to the kitchen area, Tom spoke, "Can't imagine no one marrying a whore."

"That so?" John asked.

"Yeah, no decent man would want a wife what done slept with a hundred others," the boy said, as he slopped a piece of beef in his runny egg yolk.

"Well, sure beats having to teach them how ta' screw," Reb said, as he reached for his Stetson and stood, stretching. "Come on, let's see what kind a' holding pens they got yonder to the stockyards," he added as he started for the front door.

"Hey, wait up," Tom called, trying to clean his plate as he stood.

The army pulled out of Camp Worth back in '53, and not much was stirring in the little burg that had risen around it, until the war. Then in '65, Union Troops again came. During the Reconstruction Period, the Texas State Police had a small post there, but since politics was beginning to turn and the Rangers were reinstated that bunch of carpetbaggers' henchmen had been replaced and Fort Worth was becoming quite a cow town.

The stockyards were now located just beyond the dancehalls, cheap saloons, and outright brothels.

The city fathers of Fort Worth had for years tried to get the railroads to direct a spur down their way but to no avail.

The little community had instead become the last oasis where one could get the supplies necessary for a long drive through Indian Territory to Kansas. It was the jumping off point, the Plymouth of the cattle drives.

Large holding pens were constructed to contain the wild steers until enough were bunched to make a drive profitable. Very likely, she was the last town of any size the drovers would see for months. As a result, Fort Worth also provided these men with every vice a lonely fellow would want before starting out on such a voyage across the endless sea of prairie grass.

It was in just such a place Tom Smith first experienced the pleasures only a woman can give to a man. Ten days later, he rode north with the bunch, penniless and in love with a dark-haired whore, who used the name Ginger when she was working the floors. Unbeknown to Tom, the remainder of the year she was a village pedagogue[14] near Louisville, Kentucky and betrothed to a son of the High Sheriff.

In addition to the twelve drovers that had brought the beeves north to Fort Worth, they rode towards The Big Red with fourteen well-

14 The village pedagogue: Nineteenth century expression for schoolteacher.

armed riders, besides Tom and Reb. Not as many as John Rumans had wanted, but Reb figured they would be enough to get the job done once they were ready, and he would see they were ready by the time of the Red River crossing.

Reb's recruiting had gone something like this: "What do you want to be known by? What outfit did you ride with during the war? Where did you take your oath to the US? Where do you want us to send your possibles, should you not make it to Dodge?"

He had interviewed thirty-two men who heard of the double pay for this drive, but most had failed to give the answers Cliff wanted to hear. Anyone who had not been in a cavalry unit during the war was not signed on, and anyone who admitted they had sworn an oath to the Union, was also not chosen.

Of course, he did not let on that these were the reasons they had failed in his eyes. Everyman was required to show his skill in the saddle, as well as with both rifle and six-gun.

Cliff had little doubt they could ride and shoot well after serving as one of Hood's or Shelby's Dragoons[15]. He indicated being rusty in these skills was the reason the men who were not chosen had failed.

Among those selected was Billie Ellis who had been a Sergeant under Captain Wingfield when they rode to Tennessee as *The Beaver Creek Rifles* and also later when Wingfield was promoted Colonel and took over *The Third Louisiana Rangers*. Billie lost his right eye at Shiloh and was carried from the hornets nest by Johnny McGee who still side-rode him.

There was also Pete MacSlade, who lost his left arm at Fredericksburg, Virginia, when a Napoleon shell exploded under his faithful bay gelding while serving with *Davie's Second Arkansas Mounted Rifles*. Pete demonstrated he allowed the loss of an arm to be no disadvantage when in the saddle. He carried two LeMat's in a yellow sash about his waist, and with the reins in his teeth, he could shoot them both empty at a gallop, hitting more prickly pear than he missed.

Little J. J. Carlson had ridden with *Colonel Herbert's Battalion* east from Tucson in 1862 and never returned to his home in Arizona.

Next came Tommy Walker who had arrived a day late at Gettysburg along with J. E. B. Stuart. His father, Captain John Walker had led *The Maryland Zouaves* as Stuart's point unit in their clash

---

15 Dragoon: A French term used during and after the war. It later was totally replaced with the English term Cavalry.

with Custer's *Ninth Michigan Cavalry,* who had just received their new Spencers. Unfortunately, Captain Walker never returned to southern soil. Tommy had seen his father fall, but his body was soon trampled by the hooves of Custer's horses and lost from his sight forever but not his memory.

The remainder were Texicans: Frances Archer who had served as a Corporal with *Gurley's Rangers*; Ethan and his twin brother Shep Adams, who were with *Colonel Lane's Lancers* in Missouri and Arkansas; Billy Anderson who had been a Sergeant with *Buford's 19th Regiment*; and the four men from *The Red River Dragoons* that Tom had recruited in Paris; his brother-in-law Tyrell Johnson; Tyrell's cousin Nathan Denver; Tom Dawson; Jubal Currie; and then there was Cyrus Cox, who came out and met them some fifty miles north of Fort Worth. He had heard of the outfit from his uncle Chet, who was Tom Dawson's father and persuaded Cliff not only could he qualify but really needed the money.

For the next week, the only time the drovers saw this bunch was during chuck and a few nights. Reb had them out riding and shooting daily.

Cliff had seen to it Rumans bought all the repeating weapons in Fort Worth and two long-range buffalo rifles, one a Sharps that had been converted from percussion to cartridge, and a Remington Rolling Block. Both of these used the 50-110 self-contained cartridge.

He had purchased nine Henrys, three Spencers, and three Winchesters. The two single-shot buffalo guns he gave to the Adams brothers, as they had demonstrated a keen eye for long range shooting and were always in competition with one another. Ethan had been a Sharpshooter during the war and knew well what his job entailed. He also was familiar with the Sharps, although he had carried a Whitworth in battle, which he preferred. His Union opponents had been armed with the 50 Sharps, and he had great respect for the piece.

They had only been able to find three of Colt's Model 71-72 Open Tops in the Henry caliber and two of Smith & Wesson's Model Three. Cliff was quick to point out the danger of carrying the Smiths in holsters and issued them to Cyrus who wore a sash instead. He let Tom continue carrying the percussion Colt because of his extraordinary ability to reload with speed.

They were riding and shooting and riding some more, from breakfast to supper and then out again until well after full dark.

"You never know when this bunch of Border Raiders will hit the herd, and it's as good a chance it will come after dark as before. Mee'be even more likely," he said to them. "I want you to know how to shoot again in full dark. Get used to the bright flashes of your revolvers, and remember to lean over or off to one side after firing. The other fellows will be shooting at your muzzle flashes, so don't be behind them."

All these men, except Tom Smith, had learned these tactics long before. Now each was surprised at how rusty they had become and how much they had forgotten in the short years since the collapse of the Confederacy.

Leaving Texas behind, they crossed *The Big Red* thirteen days out of Fort Worth with four thousand head. Never before had a trail herd been driven by such a group of men, a band of proud men, proud of what they had become in the previous weeks and how keen and alert they were, each itching for the rustlers to try them.

Little Jimmy Langworthy earned the name Dancer after he had stepped on a baby rattler the first day out. He had danced a jig around the small snake while it was striking at his brogans. John Rumans felt sorry for him and gave him the job of Little Mary to the cook. Dancer was a runty little guy of twelve, even though he claimed to be fourteen.

The boy worked hard and seemed happy as a Jay to be with the other cowboys, although he kept his distance from the men who rode with Reb Brown. Once, when Cookey mentioned this, he had replied, "Thar be som-pin' about 'em, jest seems a mite too daidly fer my likin'."

Late one afternoon, a stranger rode in from the east seeking work. He was a short, bent man who wore a red-checkered shirt. Someone had sewn to the seat and inside legs of his striped trousers what appeared to be canvas from an army tent. There on the inside of one of the legs, just above the black stovepipe boot, Dancer spied some faded letters. Immediately, he remembered seeing this before.

Buck Taylor was the handle the stranger gave Rumans, and he requested a job wrangling, claiming to be an expert with horses. When he was turned down, he then asked to be put on as a drover. He even volunteered to ride drag.

Rumans did not like his look, or his accent and refused to hire him. Nonetheless, he was offered some chuck and a place to throw his bedroll, near the fire for the night. This he accepted.

Dancer was exceedingly nervous around Taylor and spilled some Arbuckles when he was refilling the man's cup. This caused Taylor to jump back and curse the boy as he reached for the long knife protruding from his boot.

Suddenly remembering where he was, Taylor moved his hand away quickly from the knife's tang and shook it as if some of the spilled Java was burning him. Cookey knew better and told Larry Lansbery, one of the drovers who had slipped into camp for a little joe himself, to go and fetch back Mr. Rumans as soon as he could.

When Rumans arrived, Cookey told him about the incident, and at that time, Dancer spilled the beans of having seen Taylor before.

Although Rumans knew his mother and older sister, he had first seen Dancer when the lad was cleaning the jail in Buchanan.

Knowing the boy's father had been killed fighting Comanches, as a member of *The Twentieth Brigade of the Texas Frontier Scouts*, when the boy was not yet weaned, he felt sorry for the family. This had been the main reason he had hired Jimmy.

"Mr. Rumans, I knowed thet' man thar, and he ain't who he claims to be," Dancer said.

"Wait a minute," Taylor scoffed at the accusation. He jumped up, grabbing for the old Remington he was carrying in a cut-down army holster, but before he could get a grip on it, Lansbery had him covered with a shortened 58 caliber musket.

"Don't be a' trying that Mister," Larry said, cocking the heavy hammer.

The sound of the sears connecting behind his back, caused Taylor to immediately spread his hands wide to his sides, with his palms down and all fingers scattered.

"Who do you think he is, Dancer?" Rumans asked.

"I don't remember what he said his name wus then, but he claimed to be a brother to a hoss thief what was in jail in Buchanan. A man named Duncan, a Ken Duncan.

Sheriff Abuck let him talk to his brother, and then the next day, Duncan broke oot a jail with a little four-barrel gun. Sheriff Abuck said thet he reckoned Duncan's brother somehow slipped it to him."

"Ain't no such. I ain't never been to no Buchanan, Texas, and I ain't got no brother. The kids lying."

"I ain't, neither."

The cook spoke up then, "I knowd this boy some time now, and I never caught him in no lie. Even when it would a' been to his better'n fer him to deny a mistake."

"Well, he's mistaken then."

"I ain't neither. I know'd I had seen him 'afore when he first come riding in hare, but I couldn't remember whar until I seed the writing on his pants."

"What? I got no writing on my pants."

"He do too, there on his leg jest above the boot. Look, you'll see a U and a S. I seed the same on him when he came into the jailhouse in Buchanan. I wus scrubbing the wood floor, and he walked right up and stopped beside my bucket and I seed the letters on his pant leg jest above he's boot top."

Rumans walked forward and lifted the revolver from the stranger's holster before nodding, "Cookey, check his pant legs."

"Yep, Dancer's right. There be a U and a S there. Almost faded away, but it be there."

"See, I told you."

"Alright Mister, what's your game?" Lansbery asked, poking him in the back with the barrel of the old rifle.

"Wal, ah, uh, I did go see my brother in jail, but I had nothing to do with his breaking out. I wus clean up in Fort Worth when I heard about it."

"What are you doing here?" Larry demanded.

"I told you. I be looking to get some work. I'm nearly broke, and I need some dinero to get through the winter with."

"Wal, that's probably the first thing on the square you said tonight," Rumans agreed and then turning to Cookey added, "Tie him up good and put him in the spring wagon." Suddenly he wondered, "Has Reb and the boys been in for supper yet?"

"Yep, they hadn't been gone long when this jasper rode up."

"Larry, go see if you can find them, and tell Reb I need him here, pronto."

"Yas Sur, Mr. Rumans," the cowboy replied, and sliding his cutdown musket into a leather scabbard, he mounted and rode off to the southwest following the tracks left by several horses.

It was nigh on an hour before they saw the three riders coming up behind them at a fast trot.

Rumans explained to Reb what had happened, and Dancer watched as the tall man walk slowly over to the wagon.

Taking an oil lantern and holding it high so he could look the tied man up and down carefully, he asked the others standing around behind him, "Any one go through his stuff yet?"

"Naw, we waited on you," Cookey said.

"Well, let's look," Reb replied turning and walking towards the tall mule.

In the old brown saddlebags they found two more Remingtons and eight hundred dollars, mostly in folding money on *The Bank of Wichita*.

John Rumans took a handful of the money and walked back to the spring wagon. "Broke and needing a job to get you through the winter, eh'!" he shouted and then backhanded the intruder across the face. "You come to rob us, didn't you?"

Muley knew he was in deep trouble, but he dared not speak. Without question, JD Mather would kill him if he was to say a word. He remembered the last time they had raided a herd. They had taken three cowboys alive and Mather just walked up and smiled while he shot each of them in the face. *'No, these here cowboys just think they caught someone who aimed to steal from them. They ain't more 'n a thorn in my side as long as I keep my mouth shet,'* he thought. *'The outfit will be hitting them soon and I'll get free then, and Mather will see I ain't told them nothing, and he won't be sore at me.'*

"Get him out of there, and put him on his hawse," Reb said.

"He come on a tall black mule, a good one that we could use," Cookey said.

Cliff looked around and then said, "All right, cut out a mount from the remuda, a spirited one."

Larry brought a little line-back dun and placed Muley's saddle on him. The pony was dancing around, and everyone could see he was barely more than green broke and subject to go to bucking at any moment.

Reb then took a rough haired rope and tied a thirteen-loop knot in it before slipping it around Muley's neck. "Put him on the dun."

"Hey, you ain't gon'a make me ride that wild mustang with a noose around my neck?"

"You better believe I am," Reb said back. "Unless you want to tell us where your buddies aim to jump the herd."

"What?" Muley said surprised, looking at Cliff with wide open eyes. "I, I don't know nothing about nobody jumping you."

"Tom, take the end of the lariat and slip-tie it to your horn, and let's see if he remembers before that pony throws him."

The boy did as told and then Cliff yelled loudly and slapped the dun with his hat, and the three took off across the prairie at a fast gallop, soon disappearing over a small rise to the southwest.

Cookey looked at his Little Mary and said, "Dancer, don't be expecting to see that jasper again." Then he secured the new mule to the rear of the chuck-wagon and walked back to the front, mounted the vehicle and began looking inside for something.

John Rumans stared off into the dark night as he nodded his head, *'I now know without doubt, I hired the right man for this job.'*

Two hours later, they spied Reb's men moving in through the herd. Tom Smith was leading the dun, but now it was by a rope around its neck, and there was no rider on its back.

Reb stopped beside Rumans and nodded his head, "Morning, as soon as we cross the river."

"What's your plan?"

"We'll put the Adams brothers in the spring wagon with their long-range rifles, and Tyrell Johnson and Tommy Walker will slip in with the other wranglers here with you. I'll take the rest of the boys with me and circle around and try to get in behind them."

"That sounds good. We'll be crossing soon, sun 'ill be up within the hour."

"We'll have plenty of time. They won't want to lose any steers in the river and I figure they know your men are better at crossing them than they would be. You'll be alright 'til the herd is across," Cliff said, and then looking straight at his employer he added, "Be sure both Tyrell and Tommy are some of the first to cross."

John Rumans nodded his head, showing understanding and watched as Cliff led the other riders off to the west. Then he told his two Rangers what Reb had said and added, "Ease along and let the boys know to be ready once we cross the river."

They nodded without a word, and each immediately began checking their weapons and loading the sixth cylinder in their revolvers, before one headed out to the west of the herd and the other to the east, to join the outriders.

Rumans soon lost sight of them in the pre-dawn but knew they were doing exactly as instructed. *'After all, they are Reb Brown trained,'* was his final thought on the subject.

This business had been some of the most rewarding Tidwell had ventured into since returning to America. They had stolen six whole herds during the year of '73, earning him an average of some twenty thousand dollars per herd. He knew they could have held out for more and gotten it. However, after finding a couple of buyers, who ask no questions concerning ownership, he settled on a continuing price of twelve dollars a head. With this arrangement he knew he would always have them sold before they reached the loading pens of whichever town they agreed upon.

Realizing it took a herd some six or more months to walk from Texas to Kansas, he knew for the same trail boss to arrive too soon after he left, would bring unnecessary suspicion.

Word was out about Border Gangs attacking herds between the Canadian and the Cimarron rivers. Now he had the men also hit a half-a-dozen outfits and only take a few steers at a time. This kept the idea of taking a whole herd out of the minds of Johnny Law, as well as the owners. With as many herds as were coming north these days, it would be hard to pinpoint any one whole herd as stolen.

They would use Ellsworth, and then Dodge, and Wichita, and then Salina, before coming back to Ellsworth. It was a good plan, but JD Mather realized too, it was only a matter of time before the law would put it all together and come after them.

That morning after he had sent Muley out, he had told Steve that he had plans working on something really big that needed his attention in Dodge City and could not lead them this time. He left Steve in charge with instructions to take the herd to Ellsworth and meet a buyer there by the name of Jeff Graham, pay off the men and deposit the remaining loot in the bank there. Then strike out for Dodge with the bank receipt. There they would divide up the profits between the three of them.

When last in Wichita, he had sent a wire to Kansas City and had his account there closed and the money wired on to him. He simply had to establish an account in Wichita under the name of John Mouton, to transfer the money and then extract it later as cash, and this he did before leaving for Dodge.

John had decided he would be leaving Kansas soon, but before he did, there was a little matter he had to clear up.

As soon as he reached Front Street he began inquiring about her and found she was working the floors again but now for Chalk Beeson. *The Long Branch* was considered the best saloon in Dodge, with a good plank floor and equally good ceiling. There were five rooms upstairs for the girls to rent and a long bar that was as good as any in Kansas. Beeson started out buying local whisky but now had Rath and Cox freight in several barrels from Kansas City every time their regular supplies were brought in.

Cornelia was surprised to see him walk through the swinging doors. Immediately, he took a table and began buying her drinks. Although he knew her's were watered down, after half-a-dozen she was beginning to show the effects of the lethal liquid, and he asked her to take him upstairs for a poke.

"I have to charge you JD," she said in a voice that was surely apologetic. "Chalk takes a dollar out a' my money every time I take someone upstairs, and if he found out I wus doing it fer nothing, he would run me off," she said. "Believe me I do. I even have to charge Asa."

"I don't mind paying for a woman as good as you," he said, helping her to her feet, "and please stop calling me JD someone as special as you should call me Dave."

After enjoying her body, he rose and dropped two coins in the large-mouthed, rose-colored vase there on the table. When dressed and ready to leave, he hesitated before opening the door and looked back, "That was real good Cornelia, I think I could love you."

"Oh my!" she exclaimed in her intoxicated state, "I never."

"By the way, who's Asa?"

"Oh, Asa Nixon. He says he wants me to tie the knot with him, but I don't know."

"Is this something new, since I've been gone?"

"Oh no, he's been saying he wus going to marry me ever since I hit town, a year or so back."

"I see, never knew the Marshal's first name before."

"Oh, he ain't the Town Marshal no more, he's a J.P. now."

"Justice of the Peace, sounds fitting," was John's only other reply before he put on his black, flat-topped hat and left the room.

Steve Boron had twenty good men riding with him this time. Most had been in on one or more of the raids and many had been Kansas Jayhawkers during the war, so none had any squeamishness about what had to be done.

Muley had sent a wire from Forth Worth the day the herd moved out and had not gotten back in touch with them before they left

Ellsworth. Steve felt pretty good that everything was on schedule, right up to the day the herd started crossing the Canadian.

When Muley had not arrived on time, he sent Rowdy and Elgin ahead to scout for the herd. They reported back the night before, but there was still no sign of Muley, and Steve began to wonder if maybe Indians had gotten him. *'Well, no time to ponder on that. We have to be ready come morning,'* he thought, before he gathered the men and gave them their instructions.

As always, Steve divided the men into three groups, one six-men strong, whose job would be to ease up from the rear and the other two to flank the outriders and move in as soon as they heard the shooting begin. He planned to take JD's place and wait ahead and be ready to pickoff any of the cowboys that got by his men.

The plan had worked flawlessly six times before, and he had no reason to think it would not work this day.

Steve lay in the short brown grass atop a knoll, a mile or so north of the Canadian, watching the last of the beeves, and the two wagons drop out of sight behind the riverbank.

Several thousand head had already climbed the north bank and were milling around chopping the wild prairie grass, waiting for someone or something to tell them what to do next.

Suddenly, drifting in on the wind, he heard the faint sounds of gunfire, and looking to the southwest he saw seven riders move towards the river at a fast gallop. Little puffs of white smoke assured him his men had found targets and were engaging the outriders from his right. He knew the same was happening to his left, but there was so much dust now being stirred by the frightened cattle he could not see them.

The first sign of trouble came while the spring wagon was just climbing from the muddy water. Cookey and little Dancer were still mid-stream when the strange men rode up beside them. Masa Fulton brought his horse up along the left side of the wagon expecting Muley to be in the teamster's seat. When he saw Cookey instead, he pulled his revolver, but before he could fire, Dancer blew him from the saddle with a cutoff single-barrel shotgun Cookey had given him.

The other five men behind Fulton now rushed into the swift water to get to the chuck-wagon.

Ethan, hearing the shot slipped off the left side of the spring wagon and leveled his Sharps at the rider who had almost overtaken Cookey and touched off a round. The big fifty lifted the man from his saddle and dropped him into the water, as if he had been bucked there by his horse.

By now, his brother had the team stopped and the brakes set and was just lining his Remington on another man who was firing into the back of the cook's wagon.

In less than a minute, four of the six raiders lay dead in the Canadian River, and the other two realized they were in deep trouble. Turning their mounts, they spurred hard, trying to get up the south bank.

The Adams brother's rifles reported at the same time as one, and a second later, two heavy shells struck Andy Thompson in the back, almost simultaneously. The brothers looked at the other man whose horse was getting a foothold on the top of the bank and then at each other realizing they both had aimed at the same bandit. Ethan quickly reloaded and climbed back into the wagon bed where he took careful aim and blew the fleeing man's head off in a spray of red fog.

Billie Ellis and his faithful friend Johnny McGee rode with J. J., and Tommy Walker, all being lead by Tyrell, were ready on the west flank when the raiders appeared. The five Texans cut into them with a fury none had expected.

Reb led the men on the east side, and as soon as the out-riding drovers came rushing back into the herd, as they had been ordered to do, Reb charged the rustlers coming to engage them.

Pete MacSlade had his reins in his teeth and a revolver in his only hand, Tom Smith seeing this, likewise placed his reins in his teeth and pulled his second revolver.

Tom Dawson, Nathan Denver, Billy Anderson, and Cyrus Cox followed these two into the smoke and dust cloud.

Charging headlong into a battle with revolvers blazing was the type of warfare these former Confederate cavalrymen had done for years, thus the fighting was fast and furious. The outlaws were taken totally by surprise and to a man, dropped from their saddles in less than a minute.

From where Steve lay, he could hear the distant reports and was surprised at the number. However, he had no reason to think that the riders who emerged and began moving back into the herd were not his men. He was pleased no one had been able to escape to the north but had his new yellow Winchester ready, just in case.

Returning the long-barreled rifle to the saddle scabbard, he mounted and began heading south to meet the herd.

Cliff spotted him first and called out to the Adams brothers, "See that rider yonder?"

They both looked and then nodded their heads.

"Keep an eye on him; my guess, as soon as he sees who we are, he will cut and run," Cliff added.

Steve looked for Muley's new black mule and seeing it tied to the chuck-wagon felt better, even though he had already figured out how much more his cut would be without his old compadre there to take his sizeable share.

It was the absence of Rowdy's pinto that disturbed him, as well as the strange way the men were milling around. *'What are they all doing?'* he wondered, then for a moment the idea that they were planning on taking the herd for themselves crossed his mind, but he dropped that thought when he remembered Muley being there.

He was less than an eighth mile from the lead riders when he pulled up.

"Those aren't my men!" he suddenly shouted. Unbelieving, he sat there a few more seconds before he turned his horse's head and spurred him hard.

"Ethan," was all Cliff said, and seconds later, the fifty roared.

The big lead slug struck the horse three inches to the right of the saddle fender and exited through his left front shoulder.

The animal did a somersault and threw Steve Boron head-over-heels himself, breaking the collarbone on his right shoulder.

"I'm sorry, Mr. Brown," Ethan said. "I'd never missed him iffen I had my ol' Whitworth."

"You did all right. We can use someone to tell us about the rest of this outfit," Cliff assured him. "Besides if that's who I think it is, I reserve the right to kill him."

Steve was trying to crawl off when Cliff and Tom rode up beside him, and immediately realizing it was not Tidwell, and a burn began in his gut.

"Well, get him up and let's see if he wants to talk or die right here."

Tom dismounted and removed the revolver from Boron's holster, and then placing a boot toe under his belly, kicked him over. Steve screamed as the pain shot through his broken shoulder.

Soon several others of the outfit arrived and gathered around the man lying on the dusty prairie.

"We lose anybody?" Cliff asked Cookey, when the chuck-wagon arrived.

"Johnny McGee was hit in the chest, and I don't think he'll make it. Billy's with him now. Little J. J. got a hole in his leg, but I don't reckon it hit the bone. They both are in the spring wagon."

"Alright, bring me the board we used on the other one, and some a' you scatter out and find me another rattler," then looking back at Tom and he said, "Strip him naked."

"What?" Steve yelled.

Soon they brought forward a twelve inch plank with a knothole in it; approximately halfway down its length.

The boys tied the rustler face down so his head was off one end, and his privates were hanging down though the hole in the rough plank.

"What the hell you guys doing?" Steve asked again, obviously frightened.

Within half an hour, Cyrus came back with a croaker sack, and dumped its contents out on the ground. A three-foot prairie rattler fell out and began immediately buzzing away as he coiled tightly.

"What the ___?" Steve uttered. "What you gon'a do with that thing?"

Cliff looked over at a couple of his men, and then they lifted the plank and carried it to where it was hovering above the snake.

Slowly, they began lowering the board.

Steve had his head down over the end and as he watched the nasty reptile flick its terrifying split tongue out at his dick and balls, which the boys had positioned directly over the rattler.

"No!" he screamed, when he realized what they had in mind.

"I'm gon'a ask you some questions. If I like the answers, I'll tell my boys to lift the board. If I don't like 'em, I'll tell them to lower it," Cliff said. Then added, "Savvy?"

"Yeah. Yeah, yeah I'll tell you anything you want to know."

"How many herds you stole?"

"Ah, six I think, yeah this wus the seventh."

"Who else is involved?"

"I don't know. I'm just a little man in the outfit."

Cliff nodded for Denver and Dawson to lower the plank some. The snake really began to buzz when they did, and Steve shot his head down so he could look back at the distance between his most precious body parts and the ugly creature. "Oh my God!" he screamed.

Tom looked at him and replied, "You better call somebody who knows you, mister."

Cliff nodded again, and they lowered the board a couple more inches.

The snake now drew back its ugly head ready to strike the instant it perceived the target was within the distance required for a sure hit.

"No! No! No!" Steve screamed. "I'll tell you," he gasped. "There is no more men other than those who came today with me, except Muley. I don't know what happened to him. He should have made contact with you yesterday."

"He did," Reb replied.

Then Steve remembered the mule tied to the wagon. "Whar you got him?"

"He was the first to ride this here board, but he waited too long to talk," Cliff said.

"Course, he talked a plenty after that ol' rattler struck his cod sack the first time," Nathan added, before he laughed out disgustingly.

"Oh my God!"

"There you go again," Tom said. "A calling someone what don't know you."

"Yeah, that Muley fellow, he told us a plenty after that snake hit him, but his cods swoll' up so bad late last night, he screamed he'self to death," Cyrus added.

"I'll tell ya' anything you want to know," Steve screamed.

"Who is the brains with this bunch?" Cliff asked.

"Oh God, he'll kill me."

"Go ahead, and let the snake hit him a couple a' times," Cliff said. "Then he'll talk, or we'll leave him with the tail a' that rattler tied to his pecker."

The boys lowered the board again and this time jerked it back quickly, and the snake struck, but they had it just high enough that he missed and fell back and immediately coiled again for another try.

"Auuuuggghhh!" Steve screamed. "Alright, alright, his name is J.D. Mather. I'm supposed to meet him in Ellsworth, and he'll divide up the money there."

"That J is for John, what's the D stand for?"

"I don't know."

Cliff felt this was probably the truth. "Who were you going to sell the herd to?"

"A man named Jeff Graham in Wichita. He buys all our stock, I think."

"What does he look like?"

"I don't know. Usually Mr. Mather does the dealing. Graham is supposed to contact me when we get in."

"Tell me about John Mather," Cliff said.

"He's a man about six-foot or so, thin, maybe fifty, maybe less, I don't know. I met him in Dodge last summer."

"Where's he from?"

"I don't know, some where's back east."

"I don't like that answer lower him back down."

"No! New York. He's from New York, upstate somewhere. I swear I don't know anymore than that."

"Is he French?"

"No. I don't think so. New York, that's where he's from, I swear it."

"What about Tidwell?"

"I don't know no Tidwell," Steve said, in a convincing voice.

At this time the snake started to unwind and try to crawl away, and Steve let out a sigh of relief, but Cyrus booted him back under the board, and Steve screamed again.

"Alright, let him up for now but keep him tied naked to that board," Cliff ordered, and then before he moved away he glanced back at Steve and added, "and keep the snake."

Dancer had never seen anything like what had just taken place right before his eyes. His killing the robber had not matured him as much as his witnessing the interrogation of Steve Boron. Cookey's Little Mary became a man that day.

That afternoon, after they buried Johnny McGee, Billy Ellis made the naked Steve Boron walk all over the place and bring back rocks until he had enough to cover the small hill. This was a task that soon proved pretty painful as the thorns drove themselves deep into Steve's bare feet, and the sun burned his formerly white body a bright pink.

John Rumans suggested the herd should go on to Wichita. He would register at one of the better hotels as Steve Boron, in hopes the mysterious Jeff Graham would show himself.

Cliff agreed, "I'm headed on to Ellsworth in hopes of finding Mather before he gets suspicious and disappears. There is just a chance he is John Tidwell."

Rumans nodded his head, not having the courage to tell Reb he had made up the story about Tidwell being with the outlaws.

Tom Smith rode north with Cliff, and the remainder of the boys stayed with Rumans just in case more trouble developed.

As soon as they reached the township of Ellsworth, Cliff headed towards the little hole-in-the-wall next to Carter's Store, displaying a small shingle reading Marshal's Office over the door.

Cliff told the tall man what had happened and who he suspected. He also asked the lawman to seize any funds Mather may have in *The Bank of Ellsworth*.

"First off, I don't know you from any of the other Texas Cowboys that drift in here," Hickok said. "And second, I don't know for sure, nor do you, that this man John Mather even exists. You just got some Son-a'-a-bitch's say so, if you are telling the truth yourself. I can't go around looking fer nobody on them grounds."

"At least put a stop on his money, if he has any."

"I ain't about to do no such thing. Now get the hell out of here, and go back where you come from. We got enough a' you Copper-heads coming around as it is, when the herds get to town."

Cliff slapped his gloves on his leg and stomped out of the office.

"Ah damn him," Tom said. "He's got the nerve."

"There is something you might as well learn boy. You ain't in Texas no more, and these here Yankee towns have a hate on for anything that hints of Gray."

Cliff did find out a JD Mather kept a room at *The Drovers Cottage*, but he hadn't been seen there in over a month.

When they approached the bank, they saw Hickok leaving the building. Upon inquiring about a John Mather, the teller explained, "Marshal Hickok just ordered the bank president to hold all Mr. Mather's funds as evidence."

"Well that dirty liar!" Tom exclaimed.

That night they spent over an hour in *The Cottage Saloon*, which was located next to the hotel. There they learned that indeed a dude from the east, that called himself Mather, had been there. Poker Nell remembered him saying something about going to Dodge, just before he stopped coming around.

They took a room at *The Drovers Cottage* for the night, but the morning sun found the two headed into a strong, cold wind blowing from the southwest.

John Mather had indeed left for Dodge long before his pursuers arrived in Ellsworth. When the expected telegram had not arrived from Steve, and no information had come from Wichita, he reasoned something quite wrong was up. He decided rather than go to Wichita, he would head to Dodge City and learn what he could from there.

As soon as he hit town he found Cornelia. After telling her of his desire to have a personal relationship with her, she reminded him they had to be careful because Asa Nixon had asked her to marry him again, just the night before. Even though she had not yet agreed, she had not turned him down either, and he was getting pretty jealous with any of her customers.

John had not been there long before he heard the news that was on everybody's lips, about the destruction of The Border Raiders down on the Canadian. He was very pleased he had wisely decided to stay away during the actual raid; however, there was a twinge of arrogance that kept whispering to him, *'Had I been leading them, this would never have happened.'*

He too was exceedingly pleased that he had taken the alias of J.D. Mather, when he learned that a Reb Brown had been in on the trap that finished his cattle business in Kansas.

While these thoughts were rushing around in his mind, she spoke, "Do you know there is a man here that looks so much like you?"

"Really?" he replied, returning his thoughts to the present. "He must be a handsome fellow."

"Oh, he is," she giggled and slapped him on his forearm. "Only he is a cowman from New Mexico, not a gambler from New York."

"The only real gambling I have done is leave you alone so that Asa Nixon can come around pestering you," he said, trying not to show his interest in the cowman from New Mexico. "Come on, let's go up stairs. I want to see you without this blue skirt on."

"Oh, you are so bad," she said, giggling again as she stood and ran her arm through his bent sleeve. "I can only be gone for a few minutes. Asa checks in on me every hour or so."

"I would think Chalk would find him a touch bad for his business."

"Yeah, he does," she admitted. "I'm afraid he is going to toss Asa out, or me maybe."

After they had enjoyed each other, John stood and dressed. He laid a folded ten dollar bill in the valley between her breasts and said, "Here, a little extra to keep Asa Nixon off your mind."

She unfolded the bill and opened her eyes wide, "You must a' been in real need of relief."

"No, just when I'm in town I want you to know who the man is that really appreciates you and who the man is who only wants you to wash his johns and mend his socks."

"I think you and Asa are bound for a head-on collision just like what happened to them steam locomotives up to Newton last month," she added. Gazing at the greenback, she opened it fully before she kissed it. Then Cornelia rolled over and slid it in the small drawer of the night table beside the bed.

"When did you see this good-looking gentleman from New Mexico last?" he asked casually.

"Oh, a day or so ago. He comes in around nine and takes advantage of the belly timber[16] Chalk puts out fer the drinkers. Why, you want to meet him?"

"No," he replied. Then paused before adding, "I heard a wise man once say the only thing wrong with New Mexico Territory is all of the New Mexicans there."

She looked up at him at sea[17] at first and then she laughed and said, "Hey, that's a good one."

She was still getting dressed when he left the room. Walking out onto the balcony, he saw Asa Nixon in the barroom below.

The idea that struck him was just too strong to resist, so he stepped back and opened her door again and spoke loud enough he was sure those below could hear, "Cornelia, you sure got the sweetest piece of ass in all of Kansas."

Almost immediately, she stepped out wearing nothing but her bloomers and hushed at him. Several below were looking up and saw she still was half-naked, a feature Asa did not fail to see.

Immediately his eyes turned and were glued to Mather as the tall man descended to the main floor, and hate was building within the JP, with each step taken.

---

16 **Belly Timber**: Snacks and sandwiches saloons often offered free to keep their customers from leaving for a meal elsewhere.
17 At Sea: Not Understanding.

When JD approached the long bar, he lifted one shiny black boot to the brass rail. He did so with an elegance he knew Asa Nixon would never possess and a flair of arrogance he himself could not hide.

"Chalk, I must hand it to you," he said, nodding for the shot glass the barkeep was holding up. "You have done wonders for *The Long Branch* since you bought it," nodding his head again, agreeing with his own statement before adding, "Yes sir, you have imported fine Kentucky Bourbon and real classy whores."

Nixon jumped straight up when JD so strongly emphasized the term whore. Moving rapidly to face Mather he said almost in a shout, "I'll have you showing a little more respect for Cornelia. I happen to be planning on making her Mrs. Nixon."

John looked him straight in the eye, and the hate expressed by each seemed equal to the small bunch of men who watched close by. "Yes, I believe you told me that once before."

The statement hit Asa like a gust of strong hot wind. He knew the only time he had said that to Mather before was the night he had mugged him in tin pan alley. Only he didn't, until that moment, realize Mather knew who his assailant had been.

Slowly he backed down. Even though he was still making threats and giving orders to Mather about staying away from Cornelia, it was obvious to all, Asa suddenly had lost the spark to ignite his fuse this night.

John turned and taking a swallow of the bourbon, started talking to Chalk Beeson, completely ignoring Nixon.

Charlie Basset walked in at that moment and immediately recognized the tension in the room. Seeing the strained, clinched right hand of the J.P., he walked over to him. Placing an arm around his shoulder he said, "Asa Nixon, you're the very man I was looking for. I need a warrant on a breed that Jane Taylor says stole her milk cow, can you issue it tonight? I know where he is holed up, yonder across the deadline." The Sheriff paused before continuing, "Might be hard to find tomorrow."

Asa took a deep breath and said, "Just you remember, Mather, you stay away." Then he turned and walked out with Basset.

As soon as he was sure the two had truly left the area, John finished his drink. Tapping a quick salute with his two fingers at his forehead to Chalk, he turned and started for the front doors.

In the long mirror behind the bar, he saw her step from the room and start to the stairs, now fully dressed in the flashy red outfit she wore at night. He did not turn to look at her, however he did stop on the boardwalk out front and for a moment glance back in through the window just in time to see her hand Chalk a single dollar, his half of her upstairs earnings. John D. Mather smiled at the act, thinking how she had beat the bar owner out of four dollars.

Checking his watch and seeing it was only six, he headed for Delmonico's for dinner.

Chalkley Beeson

At eight-fifteen, John returned to *The Long Branch*. There he pulled up a chair out front and waited. He was just finishing a cigar when he spotted a man about his size, approaching from across the street. The stranger was wearing a big-brimmed hat and a canvas vest, and his boots were outside his striped trousers. Even though John thought, *'He doesn't look very much like me, but I'm sure this is the man Cornelia was referring to.'* Still, he waited as his quarry went through the swinging doors.

JD would approach him inside if he had to but would rather do it away from remembering eyes. His wait however was not too long. Shortly after nine, the man exited *The Long Branch* and started across Front Street towards the deadline.

John rose and moved after him. Just before they reached the tracks, he spoke, "Excuse me sir, but didn't I see you in Santa Fe last summer?"

The cowman stopped, turned around and looked back as John walked towards him. Finally, when they were not more than six feet apart, and he determined the stranger approaching did not appear to be a mugger, he answered, "Naw, not last summer, but I've been there numerous times. I'm from Cimarron, New Mexico."

John suddenly remembered overhearing one of the Bull Train drivers saying something about a hotel in Cimarron. "Well, that's right, come to think of it; I think we played cards in *The Saint James Hotel* there."

"Now that might be. I've lost more money playing there than anywhere I can remember," he replied, with a quick chuckle. Then he stopped and looking through squinted eyes, tried to recognize the stranger in the moonlight. "Is there something I can do for you?"

"Oh, no," John replied. "I just saw you in *The Long Branch* and was sure I had met you before." He paused and then added, "Can I buy you a drink?"

The other man, still trying to see him well enough, thought the stranger did remind him of someone, but he couldn't recall the place where he had seen him before.

"Dodge doesn't have a Saint James Hotel, but it does have a Saint James Saloon," Mather said smiling broadly. "Come on, let's go there and down a few."

When it appeared the man was about to decline his offer he quickly added; "You know they have a little Mexican Senorita in there with melons on her chest; I think her name is Maria."

"That I would like to see," the cowman replied. Then, assessing his finances, agreed to the offer.

"By the way, I'm J. D. Mather, perchance you remember," he said extending his hand.

The cowman accepted his shake and replied, "I'm Chad Cheltenham, seems like I do."

After the short walk to the saloon, they soon were sharing a table on which sat a full bottle of bourbon.

John had to admit, when they were in better light, the resemblance was strong. *'Perhaps I'm a few years older, with maybe a little more gray around the temples, but the facial features and general size are close enough.'*

It didn't take long to learn Cheltenham was down on his luck and almost out of money. He had already sold his horse and was waiting for word about his brother sending him enough money to get back to Cimarron.

"Come on, I have a room at *The Dodge House,* and it is plenty large enough for you to bunk in there with me for the night."

Chad hesitated.

"I'll even pitch in for a hot bath."

"That is just too much to refuse," the man said, shaking his head. "I've been sleeping in the back of the livery ever since I sold my hoss. I ain't had a bath since I hit town."

"Yes, well come on. We will have one tonight."

John directed their path to arrive at the back stairs and soon they were in room 22. "I'll just run down and order the hot water; you make yourself at home."

Upon reaching the lobby, he rang the bell several times before the sleepy-eyed clerk came from a back room. "Yes sir, Mr. Mather?"

"Benny, I need a hot bath."

"This hour?" the skinny man suddenly replied, looking up sharply.

"Yes, this hour. A drunk lost his stomach, and I happened to be in the way. I must clean myself before I retire."

"Well, alright, but it will cost extra."

"I happen to have, five silver dollars here in my hand."

"Five dollars! Yes sir. I'll get the stove heated up right away."

The bathroom at *The Dodge House* was room 21 and somewhat narrower than the sleeping rooms.

The tub was a deep apparatus with corrugated sides and higher on one end where a body could lean back and relax. This basin also sported brass railings to support one's weight while entering and exiting. It had been imported all the way from Saint Louis at considerable expense, and a charge of two dollars, the same fee as a room for the night, was not considered extravagant to those who found such comforts pleasing and necessary.

Benny Brady had migrated from Ohio to Iowa, then to Nebraska, and finally down to Kansas where his brother was a deputy. Unfortunately, soon after arriving in Wyandot City, he and his brother Terry had a knock down, name-calling, ass-cussing argument, and Benny took the westbound train the next morning to end of track, which at the time was Buffalo City. He had remained there ever since.

Benny was much like his brother, both being wormy sort of fellows with premature balding taking place before they were twenty-five years old.

Benny fancied himself a gun-hawk or maybe a United States Marshal. In reality he was viewed by most who knew him as a whiny little guy that few wanted to have around.

It was not that he was below average in intelligence that caused the people to dislike him. Rather the fact, soon after arriving in town, he had written a complaint letter to the post commander at Fort Dodge. He reported a couple of Troopers who had supposedly committed a minor infraction. Everyone realized this was done only in an attempt to have their careers damaged.

This was not the only reason folks disliked him. There, too, was his hugely, overweight Mexican wife, who constantly was accusing him of running around with other women, women who would never have given him a second look. In most of the cases, her accusations were of some imagined romance with respectable married women.

Still he had been given the job of night clerk at *The Dodge House,* largely because he was dependable for being at work on time and had a knack for keeping good books. His wages consisted of two-dollars a day and his meals while on duty.

This night, the idea of a three-dollar tip for Mr. Mather's bathwater would be a welcome addition to his secret bank account, a small account that he kept hidden from Juanita.

Every night he would study the small black book that contained the record of his treasure, all thirty-six dollars and forty-two cents. When the account reached a fat sum of one hundred dollars, he intended to leave for work one evening and board the AT&S bound for his brother's in Wyandot City, never to have to put up with Juanita and her two breeds again.

"I thank you very much," Chad said, as the man poured the second bucket of almost boiling water into the occupied tub.

"You are very welcome, Mr. Mather," Brady replied.

Chad thought it funny that the clerk had mistaken him for his host. *'However, Mather did exchange my dirty trail clothes for some fine clean pieces of his own. It is a reasonable mistake in this light I suppose,'* he thought to himself.

Later, John told Chad he would take his clothes to the Chinese laundry on the south side and have them cleaned and for him to continue to wear what he had given him.

Back Bar in the Long Branch

The next day, Chad went down for breakfast, but John told him he thought he would stay in today, as he didn't feel well. When Chad returned later, he told John, "I felt funny, everyone I saw mistook me for you. I guess we really do look a lot alike."

"Perhaps, I never noticed it but maybe," John lied.

When Chad sat down on the bed to remove a boot, John struck him hard across the back of the neck with the stock of his scattergun. The blow did not kill him but did knock him unconscious long enough for John to tie and gag him well before he went downstairs.

He carefully ate at Delmonico's rather than *The Dodge House,* as he knew Chad had done, and after breakfast made himself seen in as many of his old haunts as possible.

He spent an hour with Cornelia at a time he knew Nixon would be coming around, and when he went back downstairs, he intentionally got into an argument with the Justice of the Peace.

That night, after dressing in Cheltenham's ragamuffin outfit, he took the steel butt-plate of the old Barker Shotgun and smashed it into Chad's forehead, causing a huge bump as well as torn tissue. Then after cleaning the wound of blood, he carried the man over his shoulder down the back stairs. He placed him in a buckboard belonging to one Tony Sheffield, a tall Georgian, who shared Room 23 with a beautiful dark-haired woman.

Slipping up into the spring-seat, he drove the wagon out onto Front Street and waited.

A little after eleven he saw Cornelia and Asa walk out onto the boardwalk in front of *The Long Branch.*

John eased around, lifted Chad's body and with much effort leaned it beside the wagon that he now laid in. Then as he held Cheltenham with his left hand, he called out, "Alright Nixon, I've had it with you!" only a moment before he fired a shot in their general direction.

Immediately Asa returned fire.

John's next shot hit the water trough to their right, and Cornelia screamed. Asa fired again, this time two quick rounds, before pushing Cornelia into the alley beside the saloon. Then he dove to the dirt street, where he could get a better aim. One of these shots had hit Cheltenham in the right leg, but he never felt it. It did cause him to fall though, as John lost his grip on the back of Chad's shirt. When the man from New Mexico fell, he rolled over onto his back. Immediately, John fired once more at Asa, this time coming pretty close, and then he placed a 38 slug in Cheltenham's forehead, where the shotgun butt-plate had struck before. Then, stealthily as an Indian, he slipped from the tailgate of the wagon and into the alley where he disappeared.

Asa continued firing until his revolver was empty, only then did he stand.

The wind was blowing cold directly in their faces, when the two weary riders first saw the twinkle of lights ahead on the dark prairie.

"You reckon thet's Dodge City?" Tom Smith asked.

"Got to be," Reb answered. "Nothing else out here with that many lights."

"How far you reckon?"

"Two hours, mee'be more."

"Damn, I'm cold," the lad said, not so much for his friend's knowledge, more because he felt like saying it, again.

"We'll sleep warm tonight," Reb assured him.

"What do you reckon thet awful smell is?"

"Hides."

"Hides?"

"Yep, Buff hides, piled high waiting to be shipped back east. Brown gold some call 'um."

"I call 'um stinkin'," Smith replied, showing much displeasure in his voice.

"You get used to the smell in a day or two," Reb promised him.

The shooting spree was over, the body removed, and all concerned gone, an hour before they rode into town.

The first place they stopped was *Yates Livery* where they awoke the hostler to get stalls and grain for their tuckered out animals. Then they walked to the nearest hotel, *The Great Western*, where they took a room for the night.

Before the sun was up, John Mouton, dressed in Chad Cheltenham's outfit, awakened the hostler for a second time in a few hours.

He bought back Chad's fine dun for riding and a strong, large-chested pinto he intended to use as a pack animal before following the tracks towards New Mexico. He made no mention of the chestnut he had purchased soon after his arrival in Dodge or the big bay he had brought with him.

Chester Yates watched him ride away for a time and then returned to the last stall where he had a warm cot and went back to sleep.

The boys were late getting up that morning. It had been so cold in the early half of the night and so nice under the quilts after midnight, that fatigue over-powered the urge to pursue.

Just before dawn Cliff did arise but after using the pee-pot, returned to the warm bed and went back to sleep.

It was almost ten o'clock when he finally gave in to the pain the bed was creating in his back, and he began to stir.

They took their noon meal in the hotel dining room and were on their third cup of boiled Arbuckles when he heard the name Mather spoken from another table across the room.

Tom was talking away, but Cliff raised his hand and stopped him in the middle of a sentence, to hear better what was being said about Mather. Unfortunately, he did not hear the name again and was not sure who had spoken it.

Finally, when the Mexican boy, with the coffee pot, came around again, Cliff asked him, "You speak American, boy?"

"Si' som', muy poco."

"Do you know a man named Mather?"

The lad looked at him strangely and said nothing in return.

"Mather, a John Mather," Cliff said. "A man about so high, older."

"No, Señor."

"Alright. Thanks anyway."

"I know J. D. Mather," the man who had been sitting with his back to their table said, turning. "Are you a friend of his?"

"Mee'be, not sure," Cliff replied, looking the big man over, before adding, "If you know where I can find him, I'd be obliged."

"I know where you can find him alright, but I would like to know why you are looking for him."

"Well, you got me there Mister. I normally wouldn't see it was any of your business, but right now you got information I need," Cliff replied.

"Mee'be it's my business, and mee'be it's not," Charlie said. "But seeing as I'm the Sheriff of Ford County, I'll be the one to decide that."

"Well, I reckon then you do have that right," Cliff replied. "I had rather tell you about it somewhere it's a mite more private on one hand, and then on the other, I would sure hate to see him slip away while I was jawin' with you."

"Oh, I'll assure you, he ain't gon'a be a slipping no whar."

"He's mighty slippery, he's eased away from my grasp morn' once," Cliff replied showing some doubt.

"He ain't going no place soon. I'll bet my badge on it," Charlie assured him. "Come on over to my brand new office the county just give me, and we'll hear your tale."

In the rear of *Baxter's Feed Store*, was the new office, a two-room affair. In the outer section was a small stove and a desk with two chairs.

It took Cliff almost half an hour to tell his story and convince Sheriff Basset of the truth in it.

"You think this J. D. Mather is your John Tidwell, do you?"

"I of course can't be sure till I see him, but it does seem like it is a good chance, with what I've been told.

Tidwell is about six-foot, he's in his forties, late forties, lean but in good physical condition, hair dark with some graying on the sides, missing two fingers on his right hand. He is from New York with English and French Canadian parents; he speaks both languages flawlessly, as well as some others, quite well-educated."

"Some of that fits, some don't," Charlie said and pausing, then finished, "I guess you ain't gon'a be satisfied 'til you see him fer yourself though, so come on."

"He'll be quick, if it's him, so be ready," Cliff warned.

Charley just huffed a little and reached for his buffalo coat.

The body had been laid out in the rear section of *Oliver and Scearcy's Meat Market*, which was located between *The Occident Saloon* and *York, Hadder & Draper's Store*, waiting to be salted down. There it would stay until the spring thaw came so they could plant him in Boot Hill Cemetery.

Cliff approached the meat market with utmost caution and had very little respect with the laid-back attitude of the sheriff. *'If this is Tidwell, that dumb sheriff will be the first one dead,'* Cliff thought as the lawman opened the door and walked in.

Seeing neither Scearcy nor Oliver, the sheriff spoke to the hired butcher who looked up with a heavy cleaver in his hand, "Need to take these fellows to the back, Costas."

The butcher replied with a strong Greek accent, "Sh'ure Sheriff."

When they were all back in the rear room, Charlie removed the blanket from the body.

"Jesus!" Tom said when he saw the top of the man's head had been blown open.

"This your Tidwell?"

Cliff came closer. *'It does favor him alright, but this man is younger by some ten years.'* "No, that's not him. Looks like him some, but that ain't him."

Cliff suddenly felt exhausted. He had been on this very trail for several months without let up, and now to find he had been after the wrong man, he felt as though a huge arm had struck him across the shoulders knocking him to the ground.

'The trail ended in Missouri a year ago. I reckon I'll have to go back there and do a better job following sign,' he thought.

They stayed over another couple of days, and on the third morning, Cliff was up an hour before the sun, rolling his poke with a sober expression.

"What ya' doing up so early, Reb?" Tom asked, as he pulled the thin blanket over his eyes blocking the flickering yellow glare of the coal oil lamp.

"I aim to go back to Missouri and get started over again," he said without stopping in his packing.

"This time a' morning?"

"Can't sleep anyway," Cliff said and then added as he emptied the chamber under the hammer of his Colt, "Be sunup soon, and I need to make sure the eastbound has a' animal car for my hawse."

"You mean our hosses."

"Tom, this ain't your affair. You are a fine boy and a good pard, but I may be after this jasper for years. You got your own life to live."

"You don't want me?"

"Ain't that," Cliff said, stopping what he was doing and looking at the young man. "I can't see you a wasting your life on my pursuit. Get yourself a job, and get a good trade that you can fall back on when the right woman comes around. That's what I want for you."

Then swinging his rifle and poke over his shoulder, he pointed to the rawhide pouch on the chest-of-draws and added, "I left you a small amount a' cash there in the bag. If you will, pay our bill so I won't have to wake the clerk up."

Tom nodded his head looking over at the small bag, then back to his friend, "That ain't necessary. I got plenty from my share with Mr. Rumans."

"It ain't much," Cliff said. Then just before he left the room, he stopped and looked back at his young friend, "Send some of it back to Texas to help pay off your place."

Tom slowly got to his feet, and after stretching, he walked over to the little bag, and pulling the rawhide strings that were tied at the top, he shook it, but nothing fell out. Then he turned it over and looked in. There inside was a large roll of paper money. He took it out and counted out an even thousand dollars, and then he whistled.

Cliff decided he would forgo breakfast and move on. He wanted to get Ola loaded before Tom got up, figuring he would come after him, when the lad found out how much money he had left.

It was just sunup when he opened the large front doors, and the light flooded into the dark livery stable. He could hear the hostler snoring in the back and he intended to be as quiet as he could, but suddenly, he saw him! He was sure before he even looked at the small H brand in the horse's left ear. *'I would know that big bay anywhere.'*

"Hey, get up. Get up," he yelled at the man sleeping in the back stall.

"What the hell?"

"Get up. Come here," Cliff ordered.

"What do you want?" the old man was still in his long johns and looking about first one direction and then the other, trying to see what was causing this man to act so strangely.

Cliff grabbed his arm and pulled him out and over to the stall. "This bay horse, who brung him here?"

"Why, Mr. Mather. He had him ever since he come here, nigh on a year ago, th' hoss is lame."

"Mather? You sure? When did you see him last?"

"I don't know, a day or so, when he come back from Ellsworth," the old man said.

Cliff slapped his fist into his other palm.

"Where's he staying?"

"I ain't sure, mee'be *The Dodge House.*"

Cliff left his gear in Ola's stall and headed straight for *The Dodge House.*

The dining room was beginning to come alive, but it was early for most town dwellers.

He slapped on the clerk's bell for several times before a man finally came from the dining room and asked what he needed.

"I need to find out which room Mather is staying in."

"Mr. Mather was killed the other night, I'm afraid to report."

"No, that weren't him, someone what looks like him, but it ain't him."

"Sir, I assure you it is him alright. That man yonder is Asa Nixon; he's the one what killed him. It was self defense; I assure you."

"No, that ain't Mather," Cliff said, before turning and heading for the Sheriff's office.

Charlie Basset was still asleep in the single cell in the back of his new office when Cliff arrived.

"Sheriff, get up. Get up!" he shouted.

"What in tarnation?"

"Get up!" Cliff shouted once more. "That man in the butcher shop ain't Mather."

"You crazy, boy? We all knew JD, that's him."

"No it ain't, now come on, and I'll prove it to you."

Charlie slowly got up and started out following Cliff, who was by then pounding on the front door of the butcher shop.

"What you want?"

"Open up, important!" Cliff shouted back.

Costas saw the Sheriff coming and slowly began to get dressed enough to come downstairs.

"What is it, Sheriff?"

"We need to see the body again. You salt him yet?"

"No, no need. He's frozen stiff."

Entering the back room, Cliff pointed to a boot, "See one of his boots is only half on."

"So?"

"Did that bullet in the head knock his boot off? No, he was getting dressed or undressed when he was killed!" Cliff said, just short of a shout.

"That's the proof you dragged me down here fer?"

"No. There's more, but I remembered seeing that boot the other day, and it didn't set well with me then."

"Alright, it didn't set well with you, what other proof you got?"

"John Tidwell has a bullet scar in both legs. Get these pants off him, and I bet there ain't no such scars."

"You done said this ain't your Tidwell. There ain't suppose to be bullet wounds in Mather's legs, 'cept fer the one he got t'other night."

"The man claiming to be Mather rode into town with Will Hickey's Thoroughbred bay horse. It's in the livery now. The hostler will show you which one he is. Look in his left ear, and you will find a small H brand there."

Cliff paused and took a breath, "The man who calls himself Mather is John Tidwell. He stole that horse from the Kent Plantation near Poplar Bluff, Missouri. The horse is worth thousands of dollars, and there is a reward for his return."

Cliff saw he had just spoke the magic word. The Sheriff's expression suddenly changed when he heard "reward".

"How much reward?"

"Substantial," was all he could think of at the moment.

"Somehow Tidwell found this poor fellow who looks like him, pulled a switch and left this here dead man in his clothes to fool anyone into stop looking for him," Cliff added.

"Alright Costas, pull his pants off," Charlie said.

"How I gon'a do that? They frozen to he legs."

Cliff pulled his long bladed Bowie from his left boot and cut a slice down the expensive pant leg and then pealed it back. "See, no old bullet wound," he said.

The sheriff and the butcher looked, and seeing nothing there, both nodded their heads unconsciously.

"And this man is too young to be Tidwell, or Mather as you thought, see no gray around the ears, and here, see his forehead, there are powder burns there, he weren't shot from across the street. Tidwell also is missing a couple of fingers on his right hand. I know, I shot them off. This man has all his fingers."

"That don't prove nothing. This man had a wallet on him with Mather's letters in it."

"Sure, planted there by the real Mather."

"This is too thin."

Cliff thought a moment while he paced about, then suddenly he knew the answer.

"Tidwell is a ladies man. He always has one or more women who he shares company with. They would know about the old wounds."

Charlie had to agree. "This here fight was over a woman," he admitted.

"Get her over here, and let her say if this is J. D. Mather."

"Well, I hate to bring Miss Cornelia in here."

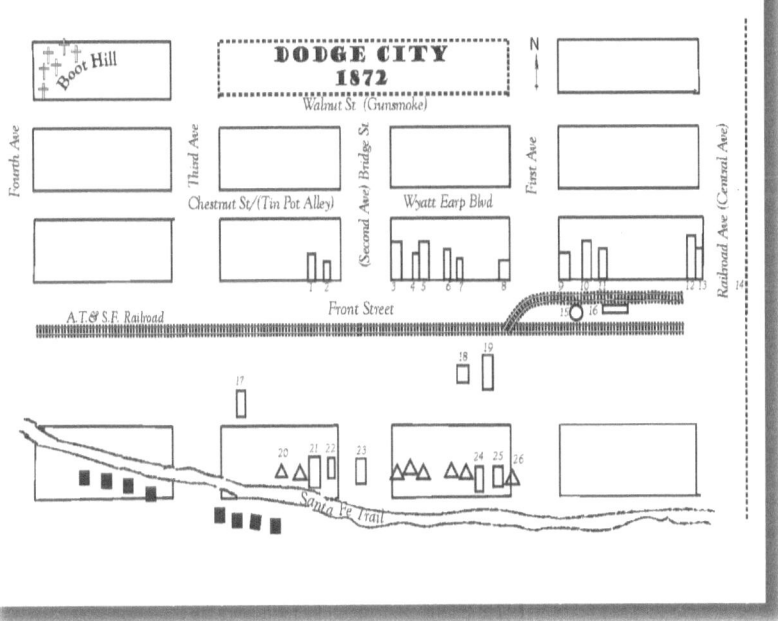

Map of Dodge City 1873

"You ain't never gon'a collect that reward if you don't," Cliff reminded him.

"Alright," he turned to Costas and said, "Go get Mr. Nixon, and tell him we need Miss Cornelia over here."

"But Sheriff, I am the butcher. I don't do errands for the sheriff's office," the Greek reminded him.

"You do as I say, or I'll slap a closed sign on this place that you won't get off for a week. Then Scearcy and Oliver will be looking for a new butcher."

"Alright all ready, I go," Costas said, shaking his head.

Ten minutes later, Asa Nixon came in. "What is all this, Charlie?" he asked rather loudly.

"Asa, there is some pause about this being J. D. Mather," he said, shaking his head.

"What the hell do you mean? It's Mather all right. I should know, I kilt him didn't I?"

"Yes you did, but it might be you killed the wrong man."

"The hell you say. He were shooting at me."

"In the dark, across a wide street?" Cliff questioned.

"So? Who the hell are you, anyway?"

"Just go get Miss Cornelia, and let her decide fer us."

"This is crazy."

"Asa, go get her. I'm getting cold here waiting."

Twenty more minutes passed before Asa returned with the woman. "This better be good Charlie," he yelled as he followed her into the shop.

"How-do, Miss Cornelia," the Sheriff said, removing his hat as she came in.

Cliff too touched the front brim of his Stetson.

"There is some pause as to whether or not this is really J. D. Mather, and we thought you probably knew him best of anybody in town seeing as ___, well you know."

"Sure it's him. I heard him call out at Asa that night in the street, before he started shooting. I recognized his voice," she said.

Cliff stepped around the sheriff and spoke, "Ma'am, you ever sleep with Mather?"

"Wait a damn minute!" Asa yelled.

"Hell, everybody what has been in *The Long Branch* lately knows I did a few times. Ain't no denying that," she said, lifting her head showing she was not going to be whipped by the way she made her living.

"Think back, Mather has been shot in each leg. You remember the scars?"

"Yeah, he had scars that could have been made by bullets," she agreed.

"Well, this here fellow don't, and besides he is too young to be Mather. Look, no gray hair around his ears. Also, the real Mather was missing two of his fingers on his right hand. This fellow ain't." Cliff pointed out.

She thought a moment then replied, "I can't say. He never would remove his gloves. He had a fine pair of black leather ones that he always wore."

"No black gloves here," Cliff pointed out.

She then stepped forward and looked at his exposed leg and seeing there was no scar, then she looked up at what was left of his face. Shaking her head, she stepped back and asked, "Can you remove his trousers?"

Cliff reached over with his knife and cut the other leg, but she stopped him and said, "Remove the whole front."

Cliff suddenly knew what she wanted to see now and cut out the crotch area.

She took one look and said, "You're right. That ain't J. D. Mather. It's that cowman from New Mexico."

"Are you sure?" Charlie questioned.

"Hell no, she's wrong," Asa said sternly.

"No, I ain't Asa. I done had both a' them for a poke, and JD had a cock twice as big as this poor fellow."

"Shit," Asa Nixon said disgustedly.

"I know it were him that shouted at us before the shooting, but this ain't him," she said, nodding her head as she stared at the stiff body.

Cliff looked at Nixon and at the side-arm he was wearing. "That Remington you got there, that what you shot him with?"

"Yeah, so?"

Cliff then walked into the outer shop and returned with the big cleaver.

"What you gon'a do with that?" the Sheriff asked.

Before they could say no, he came down hard across the man's forehead where the bullet had entered. The big knife cut deep into the frozen bone and tissue.

"Jesus!" Charlie yelled.

Cliff then removed the cleaver, and there was the conical bullet stuck to the sharp blade.

"You shoot a round ball, 44 caliber?" he asked Asa.

The man nodded his head as he looked at the smaller bullet.

"You didn't kill this man, Tidwell, or Mather as you folks know him, did."

Then just as suddenly, he chopped at the dark hole in the right leg, and this time when he removed the cleaver, they could see the round ball still in the sliced open wound.

"You hit him in the leg, but my guess is he was already dead, or he would have bled more."

"I done it," she said, lowering her head. "I killed this poor bastard."

"What you talking about, Cornelia?" Charlie asked.

"It were me. I told JD about this here fellow what looked like him being in town. I never thought ___," she didn't finish before she started sobbing, and Asa took her away.

"Well, my guess he's gone by now; this was a clever escape that would have worked, had I not seen Hickey's bay," Cliff said, then added, "Just in case, Sheriff, will you check with the bank, and see if he has any money deposited there?"

"We ain't got no bank yet, but it should be finished come spring."

Cliff walked back to the hotel, and seeing Tom Smith there eating, he joined him.

"Thought you'd be gone by now. I heard the train pull out."

"We may be on that train tomorrow, but today we got some more looking to do," Cliff said, as he reached over for the boy's cup of coffee and took a long sip from it.

And looking they did, before noon they had gotten back to the hostler and learned Mr. Chad Cheltenham had come by early the morning after they arrived in Dodge and bought back his horse and a fine Pinto to use as a pack animal. The old man assured them he had stood at the front of the livery and watched him follow the Santa Fe Trail west out of town.

"It's a cold trail, but not near as cold as it were this time yesterday," Reb said.

Chapter Four
The Dale

Our nation was less than 50 years old when Ben Holliday was born in Kentucky to a pathfinder turned freighter. Even as a youth, Ben spent his childhood riding on the haulers traversing the Cumberland Gap, wagons often filled with whiskey barrels. As Ben matured, the young man displayed a level head and good eye for business. He was quick to see the profit in transportation.

In 1857, thirty-eight year old Holliday acquired control of *The Butterfield Overland Express Company*. He soon established a route known as The Oxbow that ran through Texas, New Mexico, and Death Valley in California, then up the coast to San Francisco.

In the spring of 1860, he allowed a small enterprising idea of Bill Russell's[1] to become a subsidiary of his vast and rapidly growing business interest, a move that soon would lead to both financial loss and substantial profit.

Long before the first Pony Express rider left St. Joe, Missouri, in April of 1860, Ben had several mail contracts and knew well the mail business. The Pony Express, he realized from the start, was doomed to become a financial failure.

It was never more than a stopgap that would not last beyond the completion of the telegraph, and that was expected by 1862. Most businessmen of the day never understood Ben Holliday's reason-

[1] Bill Russell: Whose idea, organization, and implementation, resulted in The Pony Express.

ing for investing in the project, but Ben knew, and it turned out he was right.

The Pacific Telegraph Company actually completed its lines into San Francisco early. On November 21st, 1861 a few witnessed the last run of the Pony Express end in Sacramento, a short distance from the site of the new State Capital Building then under construction.

Russell and most of his other investors went broke and soon were filing bankruptcy. Ben Holliday also took a large loss, but as he intended from the start, he was able to keep possession of the old stations in exchange for some of his money losses.

The War of Northern Aggression was about to enter its second year. Arizona and New Mexico were showing the same strong allegiance to The Confederacy that Texas had already joined.

It appeared The Oxbow Route of United States Mail, was soon to be behind enemy lines. A more northern course had to be found and found quickly. Ben Holliday had such a route, complete with stations. Once more, he received the lucrative mail contract.

However, there turned out to be a hitch in his plan. Of the many Indian Nations who made some claim to the northern plains, three of the fiercest and most warring formed a union of their own, a combined effort to drive the white eyes from their land once and for all.

The Northern Cheyenne, the Arapahoe, and the Lakota, which the white man called the Sioux, bonded into close allies. Soon both the Bozeman Trail into the gold fields of Montana and the North Platte Route of The Oregon Trail, simply were too dangerous to be called a reliable avenue of travel.

Ben had to do something to save his mail contract. His first move was to change the route to follow the South Platte River for some distance and then along the borders of Colorado and Wyoming, until he was paralleling what would become *The Union Pacific Rail Road* into Fort Bridger.

The first Home Station north of Denver was assigned to Division Manager, Joseph A. Slade and his wife, Virginia.

Ben Holliday's Overland Stage enterprise located stage stops or swing stops, as they were sometimes referred to, every 10 to 20 miles, depending on terrain, water locations and other essential necessities, with 15 miles being the average.

These stage stops were small, consisting usually of one-room shacks for the hostlers. At some locations these were simple soddies, a barn with a sizeable granary and stables capable of holding 50 or more horses. Their sole purpose was to have fresh horses ready for a quick change when the stage arrived. Should passengers need the use of the outhouse, they had better hurry or find themselves waiting a day or two for the next coach.

Home Stations were usually 50 or so miles apart and were larger. They were designed for repair to the coach, overnight stays when necessary and always provided meals for the passengers.

Division managers would run the Home Station, occasionally two Home Stations and all the stage stops in between.

Jack Slade was the first such Division Manager on the new route, and he decided to build his Home Station at an altitude of 7000 feet, where grass stayed green longer and park-like scenery was enjoyed. He also intended it to be the best stop along the long route. He began this task by having strong Ponderosa Pine cut high in the mountains and hauled down where they could be hewn into sizeable timbers for the walls of his house.

He constructed this long main building mortise and tenon fashion, which made it not only a strong structure but a long lasting one as well. It was a three-part building with clapboard dividers inside. The roof shingles, he freighted in from the east, at a cost of $1.50 per pound.

He also built a large barn, a blacksmith shop, a root cellar and a much larger than average corral. In 1862, when completed, he named it *The Virginia Dale Station*, in honor of his wife.

Virginia Dale was talked about from Missouri to California in the days before the railroad's completion. It was always referred to as the best and most enjoyable of any of the long journey's overnight stays.

Virginia Slade, a large-boned woman who stood un-shod at just under six- foot, was always spoken of as being both striking and gracious. That is, save were one to view her for the first time, after she allowed the Devil's Brew to overpower her better judgment. Should that happen, she became the Lord of the Manor, and no mere man wanted to bring her to rancor twice.

She played the piano and loved to throw parties monthly, weather permitting. Many a skirt was twirled to the music of Virginia's piano and the fiddles of a couple of talented stage drivers. Often the Table Mountain Boys[2] attended these all night dances.

2 The Table Mountain Boys: Rebel Raiders working behind enemy lines.

Virginia Dale is located less than two miles south of the border of Wyoming Territory in the foothills of the Rockies, some sixty miles northwest of Denver, at an elevation of slightly over 7000 feet.

Close by in the same foothills, at a place known as Table Mountain, was a band of fugitives who used The Dale as a source of supplies and entertainment. Jack saw the color of their money neither tainted nor tarnished, and as a result, a sort of relationship was born, neither friendly nor hostile.

The Bandits, as they were referred to by locals, were in reality irregular troops of the Confederate Army. Their orders were to relieve gold, animals, and supplies from the near by Union Army Forts and outposts.

A good mule would bring three hundred and fifty Yankee dollars, at a time when the average wage was two dollars a day. The men would steal numerous animals and then sell them back to the army, or to locals who could pay the price. The money was then smuggled back to Richmond and into the Confederate treasury.

Late in 1864, a shipment of $60,000 in government gold was moving east from Virginia City, Montana, to Washington, by the Overland Stage. The knowledge of this shipment was a closely guarded secret, and only the Division Managers, who had to have extra horses placed along their routes, were supposed to have knowledge of it.

Less than a mile from Virginia Dale, the stage was held-up and the gold stolen. A cavalry unit that was sent to escort the stage had been ambushed some ten miles west by a few Rebels portraying themselves as Indians. The attack was not intended to stop the cavalry, rather to separate them from the gold-heavy stage.

Unfortunately, the raiders failed to detain the troopers long enough, and at the time of the robbery, they were close behind and almost immediately gave pursuit. A firefight broke out, and it was thought that all the bandits had been killed, however only the empty strong box was ever found. The gold had vanished.

Because of his previous knowledge of the shipment, Jack Slade became the number-one suspect. However, no evidence was ever found to connect him to the robbery. Nonetheless, the company fired him.

Later, other Dale employees often told fondly of how Virginia mounted Billy Boy, her black stallion and turning to her husband said, "Come on Jack, get up on old Copperbelly, and let's shuck these jaspers for better folk."

A few months later, they turned up in Virginia City, Montana, a place known as a Rebel Town in Union Territory.

About a Mile From The Dale, where the Stage was Held-Up

When the Radical Republicans, disguised as vigilantes, decided to clean the Democrats from the gold fields, Jack Slade was one of the first they hung.

The Virginia Dale Home Station continued to serve the Overland Stage route after the Slades were gone. In 1866, when Ben Holliday sold his vast stage holdings to the California firm, *Wells, Fargo, and Company*, new life was fed into The Dale.

However, with the completion of *The Trans-Continental Railroad* four years later, the old home station was abandoned but not deserted. The location was just too good and the buildings too strong. The surrounding meadows of good grazing grass were spotted by many a cattle minded traveler and several ranches sprang up.

It was the uprising of the Northern Plains Indian tribes in the sixties, which caused the government to close the Bozeman Trail once more. Then, only by Holliday's old route from Julesburg through

Virginia Dale, Colorado, to Fort Bridger in western Wyoming, were the emigrants allowed to travel.

The first coach of *The Cheyenne-Denver Stage* as the line was locally referred to, rolled out of Cheyenne on May 18, 1868. This link connected the city of Denver, via The Dale, with *The Union Pacific* rails at Cheyenne.

Now once again, her walls of were filled with voices and laughter for many a happy hour. Though they would never again attend one of her grand parties or hear The Virginia Reel and other tunes pounded out on the old piano by Virginia Slade herself. Still, four years after she left, smaller and less spectacular barn dances were enjoyed by many a cowboy and the local girls, who came from miles around, for the occasions at The Dale.

John Mouton had indeed followed the AT&S railroad west from Dodge City until end of track at Booneville. There he sold his horses and boarded the stage bound for Denver. However, due to an unusually heavy and wet spring snow he was forced to stay over at a home station some seventy miles shy of his destination. This station was located at the crossroads of The Cheyenne to Santa Fe Road and the southern route of *The Smoky Hills Stage Line*.

Before the infestation of the Whiteman, this intersection had been an Indian crossroads, a natural boundary between the Lakota, Arapaho, and Cheyenne Confederation, and their historic enemy, the Utes, of the nearby mountains. By 1874, this little burg was simply known as Colorado City[3].

A man known only as York had ridden into Colorado City during the same snowstorm, on a worn out cayuse, with saddle bags full of gold coin.

For a while, York was interested in only finding out which of the twenty-one saloons had the best sporting girls. Late one evening he managed to enter *The Nugget Hill Saloon*, just down from *The Denver & Colorado City Stage Line* station. There he engaged in a friendly game of stud poker with a foursome of locals and a smartly dressed dude.

In the days to follow, John Mouton slowly began taking more gold from him in friendly games of poker, and a relationship began between the two that no one would call a friendship; rather more on

---

3 Colorado City: Now a section of Colorado Springs.

the order of respectful companionship. They each saved the others' life by quickly doing away with an assailant on separate occasions.

Days later, when the weather cooperated, and the stage line was reopened, York was easily talked into taking the coach on north, believing he could win back his money. They arrived at *The Cherry Creek Station* in Denver in the early evening of the following day.

After giving himself something short of a week of familiarization with the once boomtown, John began trying to locate any accounts Will Hickey might have established in the banks there.

In order for the letter Hickey had written introducing him to the bank president in Chicago to have some creditability here, the necessity to revert back to his French name was apparent. After finding no luck at the first two banks, Jean Mouton entered *The Bank of Denver*. There he was pleasantly surprised to find just what he was looking for.

Realizing it would take him a couple of weeks to begin the withdrawal and transfer of the money without undue suspicion, he took a room at *The Boutique*; Denver's most luxurious hotel, according to *The Rocky Mountain News*.

A few weeks later, after having transferred close to fifteen thousand dollars to his newly established account, Hickey, Mouton and Associates, he began thinking about moving north. There, he could open an account at *The Cheyenne National and Trust*.

By careful planning, he would soon have the whole forty thousand Will Hickey had sent to Denver to begin their land acquisition venture. He spent much of the evening hours enjoying the nightlife when not engaged in relieving more gold coins from York's possession.

It was on Friday night, his third week in Denver, Jean Mouton happened upon *Miss Lola's Parlor House*, an establishment much more to his taste than any others he had found west of Saint Louis.

There, he spent freely for fine wine, Kentucky Bourbon and reveling in the environment, especially after he made friends with Sir Jonathan and convinced him to play Bach and Beethoven on the ivory keys, rather than what Jean considered only an imitation of music, so often found in the west.

He had twice offered Miss Lola, *her price*, but both times she refused, and he was not one to be turned down trois.

A lady once or twice a week was plenty to satisfy his sexual drive at the age of forty-nine. Besides, he was willing to pay her extravagant prices just for the pleasure of lounging in so luxurious a parlor with so many beautiful young ladies.

It was the night of March 13, 1874, when Jean Mouton Tidwell, spotted Reb Brown. His old foe was entering *The Cherry Creek Saloon*, followed by a youthful lad, who as clearly as if he were wearing a brightly painted sign, had Texas oozing from his very pores.

"Come on, York, I think it's time we move on to Cheyenne."

"What fer?"

"I have business there. We'll take the train up. Then buy a couple of horses, and on our way back, you can show me that Cache La Poudre River country you have been bragging so much about."

It was not that Jean Mouton was afraid of Reb Brown. However, he was well-aware of the tenaciousness of the man. Until he had transferred all of Hickey's Colorado money into a join account, he wanted no attention drawn to him or York.

With clever use of the letter Hickey had written and by forgery, a talent he had long before mastered, Jean Mouton soon transferred into his own account, a good deal of Hickey's Bank of Denver money.

Mr. Webster, the bank's President, had shown some suspicion. He even questioned as to why William Hickey, a man of such known stature in the financial world, would have what appeared to be a common gambler as an investor. However, suspicion was all the evidence he possessed, so the letters of introduction Mouton presented had to be honored.

Now suddenly, the need to use his French identity to make his letter believable became an obstacle. *'Certainly Reb Brown will zero in on the name Jean Mouton as sure as a bear does to a honey tree.'*

He pondered strongly over killing Brown, however remembrance gave him pause. *'Times past have revealed this Cracker is not an easy man to kill. Should an attempt turn out unsuccessful, as it did in Macon, Brown would immediately realize I am in Denver and very likely raise enough interest I will be denied further access to Hickey's money and possibly even my own.*

No, 'tis best to move on this time. I can access the account by wire if need be, and Mr. Brown can be taken care of later.'

Tom Smith had been amazed at Fort Worth and later Dodge City, Ellsworth, and Abilene, but he had no previous comprehension of the wonders he would see in Denver.

The other towns that had opened his eyes to the world outside Lamar County, Texas, grand as they were, still had been built on trade, buffalo trade, and cattle trade. Denver had been built on gold, and for a much richer crowd were its saloons and brothels aimed.

It was Holliday Street itself, which was lined with the best saloons and brothels to be found between Saint Louis and San Francisco.

Of course, one with lesser means could also find relief for a price, in the cribs that were available nearby.

Tennessee was the last child and only girl born to the union of Pierre and Yeola Lobell. They were traveling west to Texas in the summer of 1856 when Tennessee chose to be born at the little crossroads where Lou Jennings had a store in southwestern Louisiana.

Pierre unloaded his wagon and started planting rice along the banks of a bayou, so his weak wife could rest up and recover from a troublesome birthing. He intended to stay no longer than necessary for a good crop to be harvested so their dwindling poke could be replenished, but he never left; that is until his state needed him some six years later.

Tenn, as the little girl was mostly called, would always remember waving to her father as he carried his long rifle and walked away with several others from the area. He never returned, as was also the case of Pookie, Yeola's first-born.

When Tenn was eleven, her mother, a spicy Cajun woman, married a man who had come to the bayou country after the war.

Tenn did not like her stepfather from the beginning. He was always walking in when she was bathing and often would seem to relish the opportunity to spank her, an act he insisted she be bare-bottomed before he performed. She detested the way he would rub her fiery red cheeks after he had slapped her several times.

It was in the summer of 1870 when she seemed to suddenly blossom. Her former flat nipples, had in a matter of months, began to ride proudly atop bouncing pear-sized breasts. All too often, they seemed to be with a mind of their own and became hard as stone, much to her embarrassment. Her triangle now was covered by smooth, thin black hair, all of which added to the pleasure of Charlevoix Kacoos.

Yeola seemed to always laugh it off when Tenn would complain to her mother of the way her stepfather touched her.

"Let me tol' you r'at now. T'ank goodness for dat. Men no like you, w'at did wit' do then. An' it a shame to put 'dese on your mother. Be thankful child."

Two years later Charlevoix caught Tenn returning from the bayou with a sack full of crawfish for their evening supper, and raped her among the cypress knees in the mud.

Finished with his pleasure, he left her there and staggered back to where he had dropped his jug.

Tenn eased back into the muddy water and washed herself as good as she could; then climbed into her dugout and pushed off, never to return.

Her first job was cooking in a small restaurant in Charleston[4], but once again, her exceptional beauty and striking figure, which no amount of clothes could hide, brought on unwelcomed assaults from the owner.

She did find a friendly boy who promised to take her away if she would marry him. Finally, she agreed, at least in part. She left with him, but the thought of marriage was not to be found in her mind. She had seen too much of men who owned their women, and she was determined not to let that happen to her. Although Tenn allowed Ralph to have his way with her as they traveled, and she had to admit to herself it was not all bad with him, nothing like it had been with her stepfather, she refused the marriage.

After arriving on Galveston Island, she met a newly inspired bible-beater who called himself Pastor Seagraves. He explained to her, God had sent him a sign instructing him to make a pilgrimage to the sinful city of Denver and there open a parish. She gladly took the baptism in exchange for a place among the five wagons headed north. That same night she slipped off, leaving Ralph asleep.

Tenn soon learned that despite the lack of any intended effort on her part, her appealing looks would be a thorn in her side for some time to come. There wasn't a woman on the train, over the age of fifteen, that didn't feel an immense threat when she was around.

She moved differently than they did, and her very steps attracted the looks of the men-folk. Even Sarah James, who had turned fifteen two days before they reached Crocket, Texas, hated her, mainly because Sarah's sixteen year old brother could talk of nothing else around the fire of an evening.

---

4 Charleston: Now Lake Charles, Louisiana.

Finally one night as they camped in a little grove of cottonwoods on the North Fork of the Cimarron, a herd of Texas longhorns shared the local grass with the wagon train stock. It was Pastor Seagraves himself, who convinced her to hide in the spring-wagon belonging to the cowboys, until they had parted company.

He assured her it was her Christian duty to stay away from married men. He said, "Surely Lucifer himself has entered your body. That's what has made you, as innocent as you try to be, a terrible temptation to the blood of married men."

Tenn knew she had behaved herself while on the long journey and had tried not to be a temptation to married or single men. However, she had just about had all she was going to put up with from the women of that train. Thus, she decided it would be best if she did as Pastor Seagraves suggested, and hide in the Bar B 20's spring-wagon at least until she became too hungry or too cold.

Harvey Wilson, the trail boss, was none too happy when she was discovered the following day, but he was too short on drovers to spare one long enough to take her back.

His problem would cease three days later when the herd crossed the tracks of *The Atchison, Topeka & Santa Fe* just as a train was coming west. The long herd of steers stopped the locomotive, and in the wait, Tenn was put aboard the train.

Her ride to Booneville was swift and enjoyable as this was a supply train headed to end of track, and she found herself the only woman aboard among twenty grateful men.

From Booneville, she took the stage north to Denver, arriving two weeks ahead of Pastor Seagraves and his wagons filled with happy wives.

Tenn, by now eighteen and a full blossom of a woman, found the same trouble in Denver as she had experienced elsewhere.

In time, she came to have a mind that her only recourse in life was to use what God had given her to the best of her ability. By the time Reb Brown and Tom Smith arrived in the golden city, she was working in *Lola Rodges' Parlor House*, on the street named after The King of Stage Coaches, Ben Holliday.

Miss Lola, as she was known to most, was exceedingly beautiful herself and ran one of the best Parlor Houses in Denver, and only Mattie Silks' could compare.

Miss Lola took Tenn under her wing and taught her the ways to please the customer without getting herself in trouble and assured her she would never have to put up with humiliation or pain while she worked there.

Parlor Houses were as different from a crib as was a Thoroughbred, who had just won The Kentucky Derby, from a wild mustang not yet caught by a digger Indian.

Tenn was the first inexperienced working girl Miss Lola had ever accepted. She expected her girls to be the best, look the best, and provide the best in all Denver. She ran her house as a home and the girls who roomed there as her daughters. She had, at the time Tenn became a border, sixteen girls in all, each very talented in the ways to please a man and on rare occasions, a woman.

When a lady would request to spend the night, she was allowed in through Miss Lola's private entrance; often entertained by Miss Lola herself, a service she never offered to a gentleman.

Miss Lola ran the twenty-room house, and in addition to her daughters, she had two maids, Femalie and Millie, both colored.

The Parlor House provided musical entertainment for the guests in the form of a British piano player, Sir Jonathan Wesley Brooke, as he preferred to be called. Brooke claimed to have once played for Queen Victoria herself.

She also had two other workers, a Chinese cook, who said his name was Quai Toi, so she chose to call him Toy, and a cook's helper, Yancy, who was an elderly colored man.

Chinatown in Denver was small in comparison to that of San Francisco or Sacramento, having a population of less that 300, mostly men who had worked on the construction gangs for *The Central Pacific Railroad*.

After the joining of the CP and the UP, these workers suddenly found themselves jobless and often drifted into the gold fields working old digs that had been abandoned by the white miners. The area around Denver had an abundance of such.

On one of the many days the cook went to Chinatown to buy special spices, which he claimed he could not get in the white area of town, he returned with a small half-Chinese about the age of twelve, perhaps less, whose white father was not known. Stating simply, "He follow me home."

Miss Lola felt sorry for the little guy and fixed a bed for him in Toy's room. He never would provide his name, so she called him Little Toy, and in a short period of time, he became the best gopher on Holliday Street.

A week before she brought Tenn home she had hired a house guard, Efrain Dechant. She was not keen on having young men around her daughters and rarely had a house guard. However, a few nights prior, a member of the local government had become unruly, and she had to resort to violence to protect one of her girls.

She experienced considerable anxiety during the time it took to load the body in a wagon, as well as during the two hours Toy was gone delivering it to the rear of a crib of poor Chinese girls belonging to a notorious gambler, a man for which Miss Lola had no use.

The headlines in *The Denver Daily Times* read:

LAWMAN FOUND SHOT TO DEATH

HIS BODY FOUND IN ALLEY DIRECTLY BEHIND

CHINESE HOUSE OF PROSTITUTION.

Police are questioning a gambler named Chicago Jim,
who is suspected of owning the crib.

Efrain was a tall, towheaded man of German decent, standing some over six-feet, with broad shoulders and a well-developed muscular frame.

He was totally without formal education, having no ability or desire to read or write. However, he had become well-educated in discipline and in carrying out orders. A degree he had earned serving in Bismarck's navy from the time he was eleven years old, until he jumped ship in San Francisco the previous summer.

Miss Lola hired him and gave him a contract to protect her and her employees with his life, in return he would receive a dollar-a-day and have room and keep in her house. Too, he received the pleasure of one hour a week with one of her girls. She would do the selecting of which girl and which night.

In addition, once a month, she would pay his way for a night at Mattie Silks. In return, he would keep her informed on anything new her biggest competitor may be providing. He was most pleased with his new job and served her as loyally as he had the Captain of his ship.

Efrain spoke very little English and other than when called upon to assist in removing a gentleman who had overstayed his welcome, was rarely seen by the girls or customers.

It was thus that Tenn entered the world of professional prostitution, and she found it not to be a degrading situation. She explained to Miss Lola, she had been giving it away in exchange for something ever since she fled Louisiana. "Why not get paid something worthwhile for a change."

Miss Lola had found the name Tenn not to her liking, and thinking the girl needed something more erotic, she changed it to Porsche. Her second move in recreating this beautiful child into an irresistible woman was to allow Sir John to be the first guinea pig to enjoy Porsche's training.

However, his worsening cough worried Miss Lola that perhaps he was becoming the victim of consumption, and he was replaced. Porsche's second lesson was with Efrain and the third with Miss Lola alone.

By the end of the first week, she was allowed to entertain a gentleman on her own. Even though, unknown to Porsche or the customer, Miss Lola oversaw the experience through her private corridor, a narrow passageway which allowed her to spy on all the rooms. She was well-pleased with her new Porsche.

A month later, she received a wire from her friend Jewell Allen, who ran a Parlor House in Cheyenne:

> Lola Please help me Stop
>
> Have several   U P Officials arriving April Twenty for hunting trip Stop
>
> Can you send five or six helpers Stop
>
> Good returns on investment End
>
> Signed Jewell

It was not uncommon for her to loan a few girls out on a vacation trip, especially if there would be a big enough profit to make up for the loss of revenue at home. She thought about it for a few minutes and considering she had never lost on these vacations, and she owed Jewell one anyway, she decided to dispatch five girls. *'Now which ones should I send?'*

On April the 19, she had Efrain and Toy take the girls to Union Station. Efrain would escort the ladies on to Cheyenne, and Toy was to bring the surrey back.

It was that very day Cliff had received word, a Frenchman, who called himself Jean something, could often be found socializing at *Miss Lola's Parlor House* on Holliday Street.

He and Tom arrived just in time to see the northbound girls board the surrey. Immediately, Tom was stricken by the beauty of the young black-haired girl with the dancing eyes. He simply could not take his own eyes off her and was still standing there gazing when the vehicle rolled away.

Reb elbowed him in the ribs, "We are supposed to watch the place and not attract attention to ourselves, remember."

"I wus jest lookin'. Did you descry thet girl? Jest the sight a' her made melody in my heart."

"I saw a whole wagon full of girls," Cliff replied, as he walked on past looking for a good place where they could observe without being seen.

"No, I mean the one with the hair."

"Yeah," Reb replied as he gave his young friend a worried glance. "I saw the one with the hair." When Tom didn't seem to understand his mistake, Cliff added, "They all had hair."

"Oh, but not like the one with the coal-black hair."

Suddenly, Cliff was no longer in Denver; he saw neither Holliday Street nor the fine buildings there, rather dusty South Pass Avenue and Morris' Saloon. It was as if he was transformed some five years into the past, and just as suddenly he saw a beautiful whore who had the blackest and shiniest hair he had ever seen in his life. Her beauty was so, it caught his breath; and his eyes sparkled for a moment then clouded over as tears began to form.

Just as suddenly, he was once again back to the present and had to turn his head and walk on before his young friend saw the results of his emotion. This was not the first time he had experienced such, and he knew it was more than a simple memory; he was there, even if for only a few seconds, he was there.

They watched the parlor house for two days and nights, and finally on the third morning, Miss Lola sent Little Toy to fetch them.

Sheepishly, the two exhausted men walked in her front door following the small boy.

Tom had never been in a room so elegantly decorated before, and he could not stop looking first here and then there, taking long stops, gazing at the beautifully painted nude women whose pictures adorned the red walls.

A tall, very gaunt, colored man in a black suit came from behind a door opening covered only by long strings of what appeared to be ruby and emerald beads.

"Her' be sum' wine fer 'wouns gentleman's to relish. Mis' Lola be a-coming dereckly," Yancy said, lifting and extending his right hand, which held a tray with two wine goblets.

They each took one, and the colored man nodded his head before turning and disappearing through where he had entered.

Tom immediately began drinking his, but Cliff only held his glass in his left hand and continued to slowly take in the room. *'There are a dozen places a man could hide in here and ambush you,'* he thought.

After several minutes, she could see the older man was becoming restless and probably was about to leave. *'I should just let them leave. They have been exposed and know their spying will be in vain in the future,'* she thought, but her curiosity over took her judgment, and she opened the door. Stepping out on the balcony, which overlooked the parlor, she spoke, "Gentlemen."

Cliff immediately sat the glass down on a highly polished end table and removed his hat. Seeing this, Tom followed his lead.

"Ma'am," Cliff replied as he tried to size the woman up. Her face was beautiful, older, but she had aged well, *'Much better than most whores,'* he thought.

"I have been watching you for a few days and nights. You are persistent, I give you that."

Cliff digested her voice, *'Strong and confident, yet feminine and sultry, almost alluring.'*

Tom started to speak, but when he saw Reb was not going to, he waited silently.

"I should have sent for the police, but I am curious. I would like to know who sent you to spy on me."

"Weren't spying on you," Cliff finally spoke.

"Well, you certainly were doing a great job, at something you weren't doing," she spat back.

"With apologies, we'll take our leave Ma'am," Cliff said, replacing his hat on his head he touched its big brim and nodded to the woman before turning towards the front door.

'I should let them go and have Toy follow them. I bet they head right back to Mattie Silks,' she thought but seized with uncontrollable curiosity, just as Cliff opened the door, she spoke again, "Gentleman, I would like to buy you breakfast."

"Best be going on," Cliff replied unemotionally.

"I know you must be hungry. I have either been watching you myself or had one of my people watch you all night, and you haven't eaten anything since yesterday afternoon."

Cliff now realized just how foolish he had been trying to watch a place like this, in this kind of neighborhood, and she was surely right; they were powerful hungry. "Why would you want to do that?" he asked.

"I don't know, curious I supposed," she said, stepping forward exposing a naked leg almost to her privates as she started towards the stairs.

Cliff waited as she descended to their level. She was considerably shorter than she seemed when she was above them on the landing. Although not his type, she had a certain business-like beauty about her that her shrewd, attention-grabbing eyes almost hid.

She paraded past with such grace, Tom thought she seemed to float rather than walk. She didn't give the slightest hint of looking at either man until she reached a long silk pull. After two short, firm jerks, she turned back and said, still without looking at them, "Gentlemen, please have a seat."

Almost immediately, the older colored man reappeared, "Yas 'um?"

"Have Toy prepare breakfast for three. Steak and eggs should be about right," she said, after finally looking at Cliff and then quickly away again.

"Yas 'um," the servant replied and without making another sound, he turned and was gone.

"What do you think of my home?" she asked.

"Oh, it's magnificent," Tom replied. Hoping that was the right word to use and that he had pronounced it correctly.

"Thank you," she said to him without looking in his direction, rather staring at Cliff. "And you sir? Do you too think it's magnificent?"

"Yes ma'am, you've got yourself one first class whorehouse here," he replied.

She felt the sting in his answer and used it in trying to size him up. "You sound as if you don't approve of whores, sir." Her voice purposely being the same level of sternness as his had been.

"Ma'am you have no idea what I think of whores," he replied, and then reaching again for the hat he had set upside down on the table, he added, "I'll be taking my leave, Ma'am. You up and caught us rightfully, and I give that to you, but that is all you will be getting from me."

Tom looked at Reb in wonderment. *'The woman just offered us a steak, and I'm powerful hungry. I'm sitting in the finest house I ever seen in my whole life, with a beautiful, older me'bee, but beautiful woman that keeps showing me more leg than Ginger did when she sold me my first peace of ass. I don't savvy us a goin' at all.'* Nonetheless, slowly he rose from the deep red chair he had sat down in to wait on the breakfast and followed the Georgian.

"I'm Miss Lola," she offered. "Surely, you won't leave without giving me the courtesy of knowing who has been my guest, even for so short a time."

Cliff didn't know why she was trying to keep them there. *'Perhaps she has sent for the police and is going to come up with some trumped-up charge. Mee'be Tidwell is using this time to escape; mee'be Tidwell is using the time to get in position to take a shot at us.'*

He wasn't sure the why of it, but he was sure of one thing, she was powerfully strong on keeping them there for something.

"I'm Tom, Tom Smith. I hail from Texas," the boy said holding out his hand to offer a shake.

"Yes, I believe you do," she agreed, but did not look at him, nor did she accept his hand. "And you, sir?"

Cliff stopped, veered, and took one last cautious look around the room.

"Ma'am," Cliff said, and seeing no one else, he turned once again and disappeared through the front door.

"Well, I had better be going too," Tom said, putting on his big Stetson and smiling at the lady before he, too, followed his friend.

She stopped him by placing her palm on his wrist then she stepped in front and led him to the door. When satisfied he was close behind she stopped and turned suddenly allowing her right breast to rub against his elbow, and seeing it had achieved her goal, she spoke, "Your friend doesn't have much to say does he, Tom Smith."

"Naw, Reb ain't much fer jawin'."

"His name is Reb?"

"Oh, yes Ma'am, he's Reb Brown."

"Tell me one more thing, Tom Smith."

"Yas Ma'am."

"Was it Mattie Silks that sent you?"

Tom looked back at her and frowned then in a voice as truthful as she had ever heard, he asked, "Who's Mattie Silks?"

"She owns a brothel down the street."

"No Ma'am, we 'aire looking for a killer," he replied. "A real bad hombre what murdered Reb's wife." Then looking down into her blue eyes he took a hard swallow and nervously added, "I'd better skedaddle iffen I'm gon'a catch up to him." Immediately, the lad turned and hurried down the front steps.

Upon reaching his older partner he asked, "Reb, did you take notice thet whole blame place wus odorous of roses?"

Two days later, Toy approached them as they were leaving *The Miner's House*, "Missy Lola ass' you come back please."

"What for?" Cliff asked.

"I no know. She no tell. She say, find Mistla' Reb Brown, ass' him come back please."

Cliff took a deep breath and studied on it a few moments. *'It is true the only real lead I have to Tidwell, to Mouton, to whatever he's calling himself this month, is her place.'* Finally, he looked down at the smaller man and said, "Alright. We'll go now."

He figured if it was an ambush, Tidwell would be less likely to be ready than if he had offered the Chinaman a later time for their return.

Following a few steps behind, as the oriental pattered away up the street, Reb whispered to Tom, "I wonder how she learned my name, unless," he paused and thought hard on the subject. "Could be Tidwell spotted us and told her."

Tom suddenly remembered he had been the one who had spilled the beans. Now realizing it was not Reb's wishes, or he would have told her himself, Tom did not reply.

Once more when they entered the large house on Holliday Street, they were escorted to the parlor and there abandoned.

Tom as before, began moving about the room, trying to absorb as much of its strangeness as he could.

Everything there was red, or ivory, or a shade there of. All the furniture pieces were upholstered in a deep red cloth. There were several throw rugs about the hardwood floors. In each, though they had multiple colors, the dominant hue was red. Even the wallpaper, which traversed from the three-foot high stained oak wall, all the way to the ceiling, was ivory with a predominance of a red floral design. When Tom rubbed his palm over it, he realized it was not simply paper, rather some sort of linen that gave a rise to the red design.

Turning back towards Reb, he realized for the first time that even the shades on the lamps were of red glass. Unknowingly to him, from this moment on, when he saw deep red on anything, he would subconsciously associate it with a brothel in some way.

Cliff moved over to the front window and ever so slightly pulled the heavy, burgundy drape back so he could look out, *'There appears to be no one on the street,'* he thought, before easing his back to the wall. There he waited with his hand resting atop the grip of his Colt. His eyes kept sharp in the dim light, and his muscles were as taut as a diamondback ready to strike.

Their wait was not long. This time what emerged through the strings of beads was a lovely girl of perhaps twenty-five years, whose light brown hair was loosely tied in a ball atop her head. She was wearing white cotton socks that disappeared above her knees. Tom knew this, as he had his eyes glued to the legs they were covering, as they emerged through the opening in her loosely tied robe.

Upon seeing them standing there, she suddenly hesitated and drew the robe together, before tying the knot tightly. Then she spoke, "My goodness, you two are here a mite early." She paused a moment before adding, "Or are you leftovers from last night?"

"Hi, my name's Tom."

"Hi," she said back, still not sure of the situation. "I'm Jennifer."

"Nice to know you, Jennifer."

The lovely young girl frowned and then in almost a pleading tone said, "Look fellows, I'd like to help you, but I'm really tuckered out. I had to do the Under Sheriff last night, and he always stays till morning. I got to get some sleep."

"That's alright, Jennifer," a sultry voice suddenly said, "I think these men are here to see me."

At this moment, they all looked over at the woman who had entered the room.

"Oh, Miss Lola. I didn't know you were up," the girl said, a little concerned her boss would reprimand her for telling the men no.

"Go ahead, and get some sleep Jennifer. You have some big nights ahead of you for a few days. I think I can handle these two all by myself."

The young girl looked around again at her boss, with a rather surprised expression on her face, thinking, *'My, I never heard Miss Lola indicate she ever took care of customers herself, not men customers anyway.'* However, what she answered was, "Yes Ma'am," before starting up the long, winding staircase that led to the second floor. Just before she reached the top, she stopped and looked back, still disbelieving. There she saw Tom watching her with a huge smile on his face.

The lady waited until the sound of the door closing above was heard, before she spoke, "Mr. Brown. I have asked a few friends about you, and I do think I owe you an apology. You see, I and," she paused, "let us say, one or more of the other Mothers along Holliday Street are somewhat competitive with one another. The ability to offer new and more exciting entertainment can at times, cause steady customers to change their regular houses of enjoyment." Once more she paused before clasping her hands, "The other day, I thought you had been hired to identify who my regular customers were, so my competition could in some way lure them away."

Cliff shook his head, not quite sure whether to believe her.

"As Jennifer informed you," Lola said with distaste in her statement, "I have certain, let us say, connections, with the local law enforcement. Although I have never seen Sheriff Nelson himself enter my doors, some of his men do relax here from time to time. I have inquired of them about you and am informed that indeed you are searching for the murderer of your wife," she stopped and let that fall hard.

"That, Ma'am, is correct," Cliff replied to her, without relaxing his alertness.

"I may be of some help to you. I feel somehow, even though I'm not sure why, I owe you something."

At that moment the old colored man spoke, "Mis' Lola?" Only Cliff knew he had entered the room.

"Yes Yancy."

"Da' beeves-steaks be done."

"Thank you Yancy," she replied, without looking in his direction. He nodded and was gone as silently as he arrived.

"Gentlemen, please do not flee this time, stay and have breakfast with me."

Tom nodded his head a few short times and then looked at Reb.

Slowly Cliff reached up and removed his hat, and after taking a deep breath he answered, "That would be a pure pleasure, Ma'am."

She turned and led the way to the dining room. There they saw a long, hardwood table in the middle of the room; twelve chairs were perfectly positioned on either side with one at the head. To the right along the wall was another much smaller table with three chairs, and Cliff assumed it was there for the servants to use.

Even in this room the drapes were heavy-hued in deep red and hung some eight feet, stealing away most of the sunlight. The semi-darkness required the use of ceiling lights in the form of two quite large chandeliers, each sporting a dozen oil lamps, only half of which were lit at this hour.

There were three plates set, one at the head of the table and two to the left side.

Cliff pulled out her chair and waited.

"I do believe you are a gentleman after all, Mr. Brown," she said, and then seeing the young man reaching for the first chair, she rested her palm on its top and added, "Come sit here, so we can talk about your endeavor."

Tom stopped short and looked up at Cliff. His older friend twisted his head quickly, indicating for him to move over one place, as he slipped her chair in while she sat down.

When he turned, he spotted a hat stand along the back wall and nodding to it, handed his Stetson to Tom. The lad immediately understood and quickly hung both their covers on it, before he came back to the table.

"I hope the beef is prepared to your satisfaction," she said, not as a question but rather a statement.

"As long as it's not burnt, it will be fine," Cliff replied, as he cut into the dark meat with the knife left there for that purpose. '*I wonder how she knew*,' he asked himself as the red juice began to flow from the slice.

Atop the large beefsteak were three sunnyside-up eggs, exactly as he would have prepared them had he cooked them himself. Looking first at her plate and then at Tom's he noticed in both cases, the eggs had been turned over and cooked more thoroughly. Again, he wondered how she could have known his preference on the cooking of beef and eggs.

She made small talk as they ate. Even though she only consumed perhaps a third of her meat, she did so at a pace that resulted in them all finishing about the same time.

"That shor' wus a superb breakfast, Ma'am," Tom said, pushing his plate back.

"Breakfast is the most important meal of the day," she said and then added, "No matter what time of the day one awakes."

Suddenly, as if beckoned, the colored man arrived with three cups and a large glass pot filled with steaming coffee. Also on this tray was a small server containing rich cream and a bowl of sugar.

Tom had never added anything to his coffee before and was surprised to see her do it.

Cliff took a small sip of the black liquid and inhaled its wonderful aroma. The smell of Java had always pleasured him more than the taste. However, he had to admit the ground peanut hulls they had used during the last years of the war, were neither tasty nor did they make a pleasant smelling brew.

"I see you appreciate good coffee," she said with a slight smile on her lips.

"Ma'am," he replied with a pause, "after drinking boiled goober hulls for nigh on three years, all the while listening to the cooks tell us to be grateful for them, this is truly wonderful coffee."

"I'm glad you appreciate it. I have it imported from Louisiana's bayou country," she said. Then changing the subject she asked, "Mr. Brown, what makes you think the murderer of your wife frequents my home?"

Cliff pushed his chair back from the table a few inches; first staring at the dark liquid in his cup, and then looking straight into her eyes he said, "I have been informed this man spends many hours here at your home."

"Is that so? Do you know his name?"

"I don't think anyone this side of the Almighty, save perhaps Lucifer himself, knows his real name. I knew him as John Tidwell," Reb paused as an unknowing expression showed on her face. Then he continued, "I understand he has used the alias of Jean Mouton here." Immediately her expression changed, and he knew, she knew whom he was referring to.

"What makes you think Jean Mouton is the murderer of your wife?"

"I have been on his trail since nigh on the day he shot her. I almost had him in Macon, Georgia, and again in Atlanta. I was within an hour of him in eastern Missouri, where he pretended to be the Frenchman, Jean Mouton. We both were in Dodge City at the same time, but I didn't know it. His trail leads to Denver, and I have been told he fancy's your," he paused then finished, "home."

"I see. Can you describe him?"

"He is just shy a' six feet, well built but not overly large. Somewhere in his late forties, mee'be older, but if so, doesn't look it. His hair is dark with streaks of gray around the ears. He speaks English, French, Spanish, and other languages as if they were his own, perhaps Chinese as well. He had Chinese servants while he lived in Georgia and supposedly lived over there for a few years."

"And his eyes?" she asked.

"Blue, I would say cold blue," Cliff replied and watched as a confirmation swept across her face. "Also, he is missing a portion of two of his fingers on his right hand."

She suddenly reached for the untouched glass of water that was before her. After taking a sip, she sat it back down a little harder than one would expect from her. Within moments, the colored man appeared, and walking over to her, he bent where she could speak softly to him. When she finished he nodded his head and left the room.

Cliff watched her facial expression intensely, trying to read a sign. She waited several moments before standing as she spoke, "I would like to walk out into the garden. It's so seldom I get to enjoy it this time of day."

Leading them back into the parlor and then down a long hall, she stopped at a door and gave some orders to the two maids, who were folding white sheets, before she veered again to the back door.

Suddenly, a girl who obviously had only recently been awakened appeared behind them and asked, "Miss Lola, you wanted me?"

"Yes, Claudia, will you entertain Mr. Smith, as I show his friend my beautiful garden," she directed.

"Sure," the girl replied, a little confused.

"I will take care of you later," Lola Rodgers replied to the young girl.

"Sure Miss Lola."

When they were alone, she walked a few steps ahead, and without looking at him she began, "Perhaps there is such a man that, at times, has entered my doors, not that I'm saying there is."

"Ma'am, we both know he has been here. What I want to know is, where is he now, or when will he return."

"Mr. Brown, were it to become known about this town, that I informed on a customer, I would be jailed and possibly lynched within a matter of days, perhaps hours."

Cliff realized what she said was true, but he sensed he had her feeling an obligation to him, and he needed more. He needed her to feel camaraderie, and for that he replied, "Ma'am, I loved my wife more than life itself, and before I married her I was fully aware she was a working girl, not in an elegant palace as this, but in saloons, in dirty mining towns, west of here. My love for her is so deep, there is not a day goes by, that I don't fight back a strong force that wants me to give in to tears. I will find the man who killed her, with or without your help, but it would be of great assistance to me if you would tell me all you can about his business here and where he is now."

She suddenly stopped and turned, looking deep into his eyes, as if searching for the truth in what he had just said.

"He was here a week ago. It is true he likes my place, not so much for the girls, although he does relish them from time to time, but it appears he likes the atmosphere he finds here even more.

I have not seen him in several days. He always comes alone, although Sir John said he mentioned having a partner who would not know how to appreciate a place like this. This is all I can tell you."

Cliff absorbed what she said, and taking a deep breath before letting it slowly slide out, he asked, "Can I speak to this Sir John?"

She then took a deep breath and said, "I'd rather you did not. Employees are not as loyal as some might think. I will ask him tonight if he knows more of your Jean Mouton and will send you a note," she said before she turned and walked towards the large doors. Just before she started up the stairs she added without looking back at him, "I believe my debt to you will be paid when you receive my note, so the next time you come here, come to see one of my girls."

Cliff nodded his head, without her seeing it and gave no other reply.

He waited outside, adjusting the cinch on his saddle several times, until Tom came out the front door, his gunbelt over his shoulder. He was pushing his shirttail in the back of his trousers as he descended the steps.

An approaching rider who had been watching Cliff, gave a silent laugh when he saw Tom's exit. He said as he passed, "You cowboys don't ever get enough do you?"

Looking up at him, Cliff nodded and touched the brim of his hat as a reply, after spotting the star pined to the shirt, almost hidden by the vest.

"Boy, she was something else," Tom said loudly, "and she didn't charge me nothing. I think she likes me."

"Don't fall in love too easy. Remember, you're the one who can't fancy anybody in his right mind marrying a whore," Cliff reminded him of his earlier statement.

"I didn't say I wus gon'a marry her," Tom replied as he mounted.

The next morning, just as the sun was breaking over the lone prairie, a soft knock was heard at their door. Reaching for his Colt and motioning for Tom to do the same, Cliff moved over to the wall and with his left hand twisted the key and then the doorknob. Slowly the door was pushed in more and more until they saw Little Toy standing there.

"Oh, hi," Tom said, smiling broadly.

"You take," the boy said, extending his hand and opening his palm, revealing a folded piece of paper.

Cliff took it and read it, then reaching in his pocket for a coin he said, "Here."

"No. I no take." Then the boy turned and ran away down the hall, his bare feet softly padding the wood floor until he disappeared down the back stairs.

"What does it say?" Tom asked, "It from her?"

"Well, it ain't Claudia askin' fer your body back," Cliff replied with a slight chuckle.

After reading the elegant penmanship once more, he gave a long sigh, "It says Tidwell skipped town two weeks ago. He is traveling with a man called York, and they left on the train to Cheyenne."

John, accompanied by York, detrained and walked straight to Barney Ford's *Inter-Ocean Hotel* where they obtained rooms.

The next day he established an account with *The First National Bank of Cheyenne*, in the name of Jean Mouton. Then wired Denver, requesting most of his funds be transferred to the new account.

During the next couple of weeks, the two moved from saloon to saloon, checking out where the sharp dealers were and where an easy mark could be found.

Even though gambling was a sport to John, and he really did not need the cash, it gave him pleasure to take it from others. It also kept them in spending money, so he did not have to touch his bank cache.

On the night Jewell Allen's additional help arrived from Denver, the two gamblers were in *McDaniel's Theater* on Pioneer Ave. Mouton at the faro table and York in a six-chair game of stud poker.

Mouton had chosen the Theater only to get a better view of one Israel Godfrey who, it was said, owned a sizeable cattle spread near the old Stage Station at Virginia Dale.

York had informed him of the rich grazing land in the area, as well as the abundance of money that traveled the old trail, even these three years after the Union Pacific had taken over most of the transportation business from the stage line.

Still he believed, as he had informed Will Hickey, the big business in the west would be cattle. To get the gold found in cattle, it would require owning the water and grazing rights on what was at this time, either government or Indian lands.

York had also told him about his friend Abe Loomis, who had ridden with Larney Musgrove's gang. He was one of the informers who set the gang leader up for a fall which took him straight to the gallows over on Cherry Creek, in Denver.

Loomis had also been one of the irregulars who had worked the gold shipments for the south during the war. He had missed the robbery which had cost Jack Slade his job, by being en route to Richmond with newly acquired Yankee dollars at the time.

Upon learning of the deaths of most of the other men in and after the stage robbery, he remained in Virginia until after the war. Then being unable to acquire work and due to the loss of his family's land to carpetbaggers, he drifted back west.

In Owensboro, Kentucky, he bumped into a couple of old Colorado allies. Soon they formed a new union to do what they had been trained for, to do what they knew best.

Only this time when they stole from the Yankee Government, they would keep the spoils, rather than turn it over to the Confederacy. Almost immediately, they headed back to the Cache la

Poudre valley and surrounding mountains to work on an exceedingly profitable business of stealing horses and mules, much as they had done during the war.

With Musgrove out of the way, York's friend Abe Loomis was in charge. Business at hand continued as before, only Loomis was far more ruthless than Musgrove had been on his victims. He was however, wise enough to leave the locals alone and only hassled the government and travelers.

The Inter Ocean Hotel Cheyenne

Even at this late date, due to the hostiles to the north, all emigrants not traveling by rail were forced to use the old trail through Virginia Dale. There still were those who journeyed by coach as well as numerous wagon trains heading west. However, woe be unto the straggler, for surely he would be seen by one of Loomis' many spies and become prey to the gang.

John Mouton wanted to infiltrate the gang and learn as much of their operations as possible, before he removed Abe Loomis and took over himself.

He was not interested in robbing the travelers but rather rustling stock from the local ranchers until they collapsed. He could then take over their land and water rights. He would have the money in Hickey's accounts to buy them, but these had not yet been secured. Besides, he reasoned, that he might need those funds next year when he moved north into Wyoming and Montana. *'If only the army will keep the savages in check.'*

This night however, York won a large hand from a gambler who could ill afford the loss, and the man called him a cheat. York drew his revolver at the loser. Unfortunately, the muzzle of his long barrel pistol struck the edge of the table, and his shot went into the floor.

York's opponent was slower, but steadier, and in a split-second John's mind went into slow motion. He could see his only opportunity of being introduced to Abe Loomis about to meet Ol' Lucifer himself. Without thinking of his own consequences, John threw his Arkansas Toothpick, hard and true, into the man's back.

Both he and York had to make a quick disappearance before the dead man's companion could summon enough help to right what he saw as a wrong.

Gathering their belongings from the hotel, the two were southbound on horseback before they were identified to the law.

Jean Mouton twisted his head in silent thought, *'This is not the reputation I wanted to leave in Cheyenne.'*

Miss Allen put the girls up in *The Railroad Hotel*. It was where the members of the *hunting party* were scheduled to stay. She reserved the entire top floor for the men and her ladies. Each railroad official was paying two hundred dollars a night directly to Miss Allen. For this, they would receive a bottle of chilled wine, delivered to their private room before dinner and the company of at least one lady for the night. At their request, the lady would accompany them to dinner, stand by them at any game of chance they might wish to pursue and pleasure them later, should the gentleman be so inclined.

Jewell Allen paid each girl twenty-five dollars a night and allowed them to keep any personal tips offered by the gentlemen. She also shared sixty dollars with Miss Lola for each of her girls.

Porsche was most happy with the arrangement. In the week she was there she made over three hundred dollars and was treated to superb dining every night. Her obvious youth and beauty kept her in constant demand.

The day the *hunting party* headed back to Omaha without bagging a single head of game, word was received that the trestle over

Lone Tree Creek had collapsed. Two of the men aboard the train had been killed when the boiler exploded upon crashing into the deep gorge, sending scalding steam gushing high into the air.

The Virginia Dale Stage Station and Bunkhouse

The girls would have to wait for several days or take the stage back to Denver. Everyone chose the stage. Cheyenne had been a great place to clear a quick bundle but was no place to hang around after you were no longer needed.

That night they arrived at Virginia Dale an hour after Reb Brown and Tom Smith had stabled their horses in the old livery barn.

Chester Lords had run the swing station, some thirty miles east, for Ben Holliday, back in the heyday of the Overland Express. Now Spuds Lords, his oldest son, was the keeper of Virginia Dale.

Spuds, his wife Sarah and their three-year-old daughter, lived in the main house, along with an old Indian woman who helped Mrs. Lords.

Six other employees, hired by Lords to keep the operation rolling, slept in the bunkhouse which was located immediately to the north of the main lodge.

Unlike the old days when everyone worked for Mr. Holliday, now Lords owned the station and charged the line for his services.

One of his employees was Chigger Morgan, who was considered by many to be the best blacksmith in the area. He was a talented wheelwright as well. Chigger also displayed considerable knowledge about doctoring horses, having learned such serving a hitch in the Sixth US Cavalry while they were at Fort Hayes, Kansas, protecting the Smoky Hill Trail.

Lords also employed two wranglers: a young breed that was called Crazy Boy by the other Arapahoe, because he had refused to listen to the wisdom of his parents, and a hunter, Alex Culpepper.

The elderly Indian woman, who did not seem to answer to any name but Old Woman, spent most of her time helping Sarah prepare the meals and watching over little Sissy Lords.

Unknown to anyone except Spuds and Sarah, Old Woman actually was family. Sarah was the daughter of George Pingree and White Clay, the result of a single winter's union of the Gros Ventres woman and the old trapper.

Sarah had taken on the genes of her father to a much greater extent than that of her mother. Her face was not round and her skin only slightly darker than a full-blooded Euro-American, certainly no darker than any other white woman who worked out in the sun, as almost all pioneer women did. Unless one saw her bathing and realized the tan covered her whole body, no one would have any idea she was the daughter of Old Woman.

The stage arrived half an hour before sundown, and Tom was overjoyed to see the dark-haired beauty he had drooled over in Denver step from it.

Unfortunately, the mood was not enjoyed for long. Shortly before supper was served, Alex appeared with the body of a dead man strapped over his saddle. The man had been shot and his scalp taken. The wrangler explained he had found the hombre face down in a creek only a few miles away. The man had no identification on him and was apparently without a horse.

Everyone, except Old Woman, became quite concerned over his being scalped, anticipating Indian trouble. She told Sarah and Sarah the others, it was not the deed of Indians, but none really believed her.

An hour later, two line riders from Israel Godfrey's Ranch rushed into the Dale with a tale of being chased by a party of twenty or more hostiles, yelping and yelling as they pursued them.

Everyone slept with a firearm close at hand that night. Tom stayed outside crouched under the window of the room where Porsche slept, his rifle in hand and covered only by a horse blanket and his bedroll. Early the next morning, when she rose to use the pot, she heard his heavy breathing and upon looking out, was quite touched to see him there.

For a man to pay for her services was good for her fortune, but for a man to risk his own life and forgo the comfort of a warm room to protect her, was quite new to the young girl and something else again.

Sunrise brought more riders from Godfrey's ranch, located just across the line in Wyoming Territory. They were looking for the two missing wranglers.

A low glow on the distant horizon the night before had given old Israel concern, and he had sent these hands out looking for its cause.

They had found the south line shack burned to the ground and these two missing. Also, tracks of unshod ponies were seen following their two horses. The truth be told, the searchers had expected to find two bodies looking like porcupines from the arrows sticking out of them.

That morning the northbound arrived just as the Denver Stage was loading. However, she was empty of driver and passengers. Two arrows were spotted, one sticking from the leather boot at the rear of the coach and another stuck deeply in the right door. Blood covered the interior, as it did the Jehu's seat. The horses were nearly exhausted, appearing to have been running for a long time.

Spuds recommended the southbound not to travel, until they had escort.

When he attempted to wire Camp Collins[5] they all realized the lines were down. It certainly seemed to the frightened travelers; a major Indian uprising was upon them.

Finally, on the second day after their arrival, with nothing more occurring, the cowboys from Godfrey's outfit struck a trot for the ranch. Cliff and Spuds tried to stop them, explaining that they would have a much better chance here, than to be caught out in the open. Harvey Lathrop, the oldest of the bunch, insisted if there was real Injun trouble, their responsibility was to Mr. Godfrey and his ranch, not Virginia Dale.

Cliff appreciated their loyalty to the brand, and fully realizing he was not in charge, after all this was Spuds Lords' place and responsibility. Nonetheless, he couldn't halt his past military experience and natural leadership from analyzing their situation. They had

---

5 Camp Collins: Later Fort Collins.

only seven fighting men, counting Yazoo Lulkin, the southbound teamster, and a half-breed Arapahoe called Crazy Boy. *'We are far too few to defend six young and exceedingly desirable women, a child, and an old woman from who knows how many hostiles and for who knows how long,'* he thought.

The Dale was, in itself, as good as most forts of the west, better than some. Although there was no outer wall, the buildings were close enough together to be fortifiable. They had enough provisions to last a month, and were lucky to have the deep well Jack Slade had finished just before he departed for Montana; so water would be no problem. However, Cliff had no knowledge of the others' guns, ammunition or abilities.

Approaching Lords in as hospitable a manner as he could muster, Cliff asked, "Spuds, how are we fixed for rifles and rounds? This could be a long siege."

"I don't think so," the younger man replied. "When the stages don't get to the next stations," he paused and gestured both north and south; "someone will realize we need help, especially when they can't get through on the wire. Every home station on old Ben Holliday's route has a telegraph register located there. That is one of Chigger's duties."

"Still, better prepared than mistaken. Can we gather everyone in the main house, it's the strongest by far, and there we can assess our firearms and ammunition situation," Cliff suggested.

"I don't think we have anything to worry about. The Arapahoe have always been our friends, they water their horses here, and we give them grain in the winter. Old Woman would have told us if there was danger. Besides, pulling everyone in a single building will stop the operation of this station. I can't do that unless we know for sure we are going to be attacked," he replied and started walking off.

"Look Lords, we have eight women here, if there are as many Indians on the prod as there seems to be, don't you think they know about the women? You know what they do to white women when they have their blood stirred up."

"They are not all white."

"You think that will make any difference?"

The station owner stopped and without turning back to look at Cliff replied, "Alright, get everyone in the house except Chigger.

He and I are going to make the necessary repairs to the northbound, so it will be ready to roll when the time comes."

Cliff instructed Tom to get the people in the building so they could have a talk, and the lad immediately headed for Porsche.

Within ten minutes, all save Spuds and Chigger were inside the main house standing around looking at each other, questioning what was happening. Finally, Cliff raised his hands high and called for silence. He would have liked for Lords to have been there, but the man seemed not to be concerned, and he definitely was.

"Spuds thinks we have nothing to fear, and I think he is right. However, I also think any time there is a chance of danger, it is far better to be prepared than sorry later, should our assessment be wrong," he paused to let what he had said sink in before continuing. "I would like all the men to get your weapons and all the ammunition you have, and bring it here, and let us look it over." Again he paused, "Ladies, should we be attacked, there is likely to be the need for bandages. Please bring anything you may have that could serve in that capacity and have it in close neighborhood. No need to be tearing up good stuff yet but have it ready should the need be."

He looked at Tom, and the boy saw the concern in Cliff's eyes. Slowly he left the girl's side and moseyed over close to his older friend. When he was sure no one else would hear he spoke, "You think we are in fer it don't you?"

"Could be," Cliff replied without looking at him.

"What should I do?"

"Be alert. When it comes," he stopped. Realizing what he had just said, then correcting he continued, "if it comes, it will be a total surprise and quick."

Cliff pulled his faithful old Richards Conversion from its holster. He kept one chamber under the hammer empty when traveling, but now he loaded the sixth cartridge and set the firing pin between two cartridge rims to keep the cylinder from turning. Satisfied with this, he went to get his saddle and other possibles, which included the carbine Nadine had loved so much.

Years before, he had sent his 1860 Colt back to the factory to have the conversion done. He had specified that it be chambered for the rimfire Henry cartridge, rather than Colt's new 44 centerfire, as most of them were converted to use. Having the Winchester and the revolver both firing the same ammunition, had proven wise on several occasions, and he was not sorry one bit for his original decision.

Upon reaching the livery, he made sure Ola and Tom's horse were fed and watered. While there, he also forked extra hay into all the stalls. Then he opened his saddlebags and took out an old, well worn, yellow sash. He removed his gunbelt and hung it over a gatepost, then slowly wrapped the sash around his middle. When satisfied it was tight enough, he again buckled on his cartridge belt, this time over the sash.

Next, he removed a second revolver from the saddle pommel holster and stuck it into the sash on his left side, butt forward. After swinging the saddlebags over his shoulder, he retrieved the Winchester from its saddle-sheath then headed back to the house. All of this had been done slowly and methodically, as if he were a dancer, preparing her attire before a grand performance.

Cliff had a feeling, an old and not so friendly feeling, burning in his gut. He had first experienced it as a child when his father found out about some of his misdeeds, and Cliff would somehow know he was coming with that wide strap. He experienced it again many times riding under Forrest. In fact, he had honed it into a sharp edge before they headed back towards Nashville in the late fall of 1864. When the war ended, he thought it would be a part of the past, a part he wanted to forget, but this had not been the case. It had been with him in Wyoming and again in Georgia, even in the Ozarks not too long past. He knew the feeling and knew it carried death in its bowels.

'I know Spuds Lords is working on his knowledge of the Arapahoe he has befriended here in recent years, but he is wrong. They will come, and there will be men to bury. I just hope it will only be men,' he thought as he slowly left the barn.

Looking to the surrounding horizons as he walked, he faintly saw just a small cloud of dust rise above the hill to the northeast, and that was all Reb Brown needed. Cocking the hammer on the Winchester, he fired the round high in the air to attract the attention of everyone at The Dale.

"What the ___?" Spuds shouted, looking in the direction of the report. Instantly he saw the man in buckskins start on a run for the house. Only seconds later lead began to rain around him, and he watched Chigger, still holding onto the wheel he had just removed from the stage, fall forward into the hot coals of the blacksmith's oven. His old friend made no cry or attempt to get away from the intense heat, and Spuds realized he was dead.

Now looking towards the house, he saw Brown make it inside but knew he would never survive the run across that open ground, and this place was a poor barricade. Turning to his left, he spotted the root cellar, some fifteen yards away. The door was heavy and the only entrance, or escape route, but as long as it stayed closed, he knew he would be safe, and made a dash for it.

'Ol' Chigger would be alive now if only I had listened to that Easterner,' he thought as he spit, and then speaking aloud while running full out, "Too late Spuds, you was too late a' waking up."

York had led him over some of the best grazing land west of the Mississippi, and he was well-pleased with most everything he saw. Water was there, though not plentiful, and to Jean it was obvious that whoever owned the water controlled the grazing.

This trail meandered through a pleasant valley, rich in grass and walled by tall hills on either side. Boulders were as plentiful on the hills as fleas on a dog's back, but the valley was mostly clean of them; and Jean Moulton could not help but repeat if to no one but himself, "This is beautiful country."

The stage route had been changed some three miles over to the banks of Park Creek, after the Bonner Springs Station had been abandoned back in '63.

Musgrove had found the old swing station to be a good location to camp and hide out, when in the area. Loomis now chose it as his main camp. It was just far enough from the new stage road no travelers would notice any activity there. Yet close enough where one could spy on any activity taking place over the road. Also, there was sweet water, right at the station, flowing from the springs. Although small and the altitude high, old Bonner Springs' buildings were not bad shelter from the cold mountain winds that would come sweeping down upon them at times, and it was there the duo found Loomis' camp.

Loomis was not especially pleased to see the two men ride in. He had been planning on this heist for a long time and needed no interference caused by strangers or late comers. However, upon recognizing York and knowing him to be dependable to do as told, and seeing the eastern dude had the look of a killer in his eyes he thought they might be of some use after all. Furthermore, he realized he needed no trouble at this time, so reluctantly he allowed them in on his plan.

"The train has carried gold from the Boulder mines to Cheyenne and then east on the U. P. several times this year. I got a way a' knowing when it is being moved," he said without looking up. "Trouble is the train is too blame hard to deal with." And then looking up from the crudely drawn map, he stared hard at the dude who seemed only slightly interested, a gesture Loomis did not like.

"We removed the spikes to the rails at Lone Pine, and this ended the train travel for a week, mee'be two. I know they gotta get this shipment to Omaha right away, so we waited and struck the stage just before it got to Virginia Dale, only we found no gold. That is we didn't find none while we had the coach, but," looking up again and giving Wilson Ross a dirty look, he continued, "some dumb son-a-bitch spooked the horses, and they charged off to the station before we could stop 'em."

This time when he ceased talking, he drew himself up straight as a carpenter's rule and looked around at the little group of men encircling him before he continued, "Now we find out that stage has a false floor in it, and that's where the two hundred thousand in gold is hid."

"Won't a robbery of that size bring on a passel a' law?" York asked.

"Would alright 'cept we got nigh on two dozen Utes with us. They are raiding the ranches around, and the law is blaming all this on Injun troubles. We just gotta get that coach from Virginia Dale before the army gets up here."

Later that night, York got Bud Casin off to the side and asked him about where Abe was getting his information. Casin replied, "He got a man working fer the mining company what knows such."

"But how does he know about the false bottom on the stage, the mining company wouldn't know stage business."

"Yep, but we caught up with a stage man 'touther day what had a letter on his body. It said such, thar in the letter."

"You kilt him?"

"Not only kilt him but scalped him too, wanted to make it look like 'em Injuns done it. Then we throwed him in the creek, so his blood would run on down across the trail, so anybody with eyes could see it."

"You think he'll bleed long enough for someone to see it?" York questioned.

"Done already been seen. Man from The Dale found him not half a' hour after I scalped 'im. Want 'a see the hair?" he asked pulling the scalp around on his holster belt where he had it tied.

"Not now," Jean said as he placed his palm on York's shoulder and stood.

York also rose.

The two walked away a few steps and there he spoke, "This is working out better than I thought." Looking around in the dark night air, making sure no one had strolled up close enough to hear, he added, "If we can keep the savages hitting the ranches while we get the gold, this will be a nice round."

"You talk like Ol' Abe is just gon'a hand that gold over to us."

"I'll worry about Ol' Abe. See if you can find out what they are using to keep the savages raiding."

Cliff had not been in many Indian fights, but he had heard many men talk about them. They almost always came running in, yelling and yelping like a bunch a' hounds hot on a whitetail down deep in a swamp. Least wise, that's the way it had been told to him. He was studying on this when Tom approached and asked, "Ya got a pointer on what we should do?"

Cliff then veered around and suddenly realized everyone in the room was looking at him. The men obviously waiting to be told what to do and the women looking like they might burst out screaming at any second.

"Miss," he said to Porsche, "you are in charge of the women, divide them into two groups. Half to cut strips for bandages and the other half get ready to reload guns as we need them. Be sure to caution them, sometimes the barrels get plenty hot. Don't need ya'll to burn your hands and not be able to load."

Porsche swelled with pride that he had chosen her to command the other women, and she immediately took to her rank and began dividing them as she had been told.

Reb turned to their hostess and said, "Mrs. Lords, I think you should be keeping a fire going and keep a poker in the coals at all times, just might be needed."

She nodded her head realizing what he meant. *'I never would have thought of that. Thank you God for providing this man when we need him, and Lord look over my Spuds and keep him safe,'* she thought realizing they had seen nor heard nothing from the blacksmith shop since the first shots rang out, and then aloud she added, "Amen."

Old Woman took Sissy by the hand and moved over near a corner, out of the way and began to play with her grandchild. When Sarah passed close enough, she spoke softly in her native tongue. Sarah looked questioningly at her and then nodded her head.

As soon as she could, she went to Cliff. "Mr. Brown, my, err, the Old Woman says these men who are attacking us are not red men."

Cliff stopped what he was doing and glanced up, not focusing on anything with his eyes but kicking his mind into gear on the subject. He paused a few moments before replying, "Do you believe her?"

"I believe she is pretty wise, and she would die before she would lie to me."

"I think she is probably right," he said, nodding his head in an agreeing gesture. "Go back and tell her so, and ask if she has a reason to believe this."

The young woman showed pleasure in her expression when he believed her mother, and she very softly touched his wrist with the open palm of her hand and said, "You are a pretty wise man yourself. We will be alright with you leading us."

"I hope you are right," he replied and then said, "Now go talk to her."

Sarah nodded her head and swiftly moved to the old Indian.

Cliff thought about what he had just been told and again looking out at the puffs of white smoke coming from the hill, he now was convinced that indeed this attack was being made by white men. Military trained white men.

Loomis, seeing there was no return fire coming from the blacksmith shop, sent Fargo, Pike, and Rome down to hitch up a team and get the stage out of there. They had no wagon in which to transport that much gold and needed the coach.

Jack Slade, while building The Dale, had glass-paned windows freighted in along with his roof shingles. Wisely, he also made strong, heavy wood window coverings in which he had carved Christian crosses. These were hinged at the top, thus when lowered, served as gun ports. They were well thought out, giving the shooter a good view of the area in front of the window and almost none from the outside looking in, unless a body was fool enough to place his eye to one.

'Ol' Slade must a' had the forethought of just such a siege as we're experiencing right now,' Cliff thought as he studied the gun ports.

It was from one of these crosses Tom spotted something slipping along through some high grass, this side of the slope. They were some two hundred yards away and mostly crawling, making a pretty small target. He started to sling a round at them but decided to wait and see if they presented a better shot. Finally, he called Reb over, "Two a' them, yonder crawling this way."

Cliff watched awhile, then he, too, took aim but also chose not to fire. Instead, he looked over at Culpepper who was watching the far ridge where the shots were coming from. In his hands was a long barrel Sharps 52.

Taking careful aim, the old man squeezed off a shot. The big gun roared loudly, and Cliff thought he saw a hat fly up at the top of the ridge.

The man then slowly lowered the big gun and blew heartily into its bore, until blue smoke came pouring out the nipple. Then he took his brass cup and with care, measured out a precise amount of powder before pouring it down the bore. At that point, he looked up. Seeing Cliff was watching him, he said, "Don't got no more paper cartridges, them is all out thar in my possibles bag, yonder in the barn."

Cliff nodded his head and then said, more as a statement than a question, "You was a Sharpshooter, during the war."

"Berdan's Sharpshooters," he replied proudly and then added as if it was necessary, "Second Regiment."

"Yeah, heard a' you, and I'm a mite glad we never came up again you. You look like you know how to shoot that thing."

"I take that as a compliment from a former adversary."

Cliff nodded his head and replied, "Army of The Tennessee, Forrest's Cavalry."

"Heard a' you too. I think I'm equally glad," Culpepper said, nodding his head confirming his statement.

"Come over here, I want to show you something," Cliff said, and walking back to the rear of the building he pointed through the slit in the window. "Yonder, two for sure, maybe three jaspers crawling towards the blacksmith shop."

Culpepper squinted his eyes for a moment before saying, "Got 'um."

He finished loading the big gun and then stuck the long barrel out through the slit and cocked the hammer.

Cliff watched as the man slowly moved the Sharps along, steadily squeezing the trigger tighter and tighter. Suddenly it seemed to explode, and the barrel jumped high enough to hit the top of the slit and bounce back. A split-second later he saw a man rise up on his knees and throw his hands to his neck. There he sat for what seemed like a long time but probably was no more than a couple of seconds, before he fell forward.

The man who was crawling behind him did not move again as long as Cliff watched.

Finally, Cliff turned to Culpepper and softly patted him on the upper arm as he said, "Nice shot; see if you can get the other one."

"Thank you, Capt'n."

Eventually, firing became slow but general from The Dale when a target would expose itself on the distant hill. No one expected to score a hit at this distance, but it did keep them at bay, and it also gave a feeling of confidence to those inside. However, every time a gun roared, Frenchy would squeal like she was being pinched. It had been a little funny at first but eventually became irritating. Finally, Cliff turned to Porsche and instructed, "We need someone to go out and get a bucket of water. Can't spare a shooter; send one of the ladies out to fetch it."

She looked at him as if the order was a death sentence, as they could hear glass from the double windows being broken and lead popping against the outer wall steadily.

Then he added, "Send the little skinny one there, that way we'll hear her squealing, if she gets hit." A moment later, he winked at Porsche so she knew he was not serious.

Frenchy never made another sound.

Cliff had seen the man Alex hit well enough; he was now convinced their attackers were not Indians. *'Who they are or why they're attacking us I can't figure, but they ain't Indians.'*

Pike waited a long time before he moved ahead again. He could not pass Fargo without crawling through the large pool of blood that had escaped from the massive holes in his neck. It almost made him sick as he placed a hand in the warm blood, but to have done otherwise would have exposed him to the same shooter, and he wanted no part of that.

He heard Rome groan when the last of the trio likewise reached Fargo's lifeless body. Still, Pike did not expose the slightest portion of his head to look back. In another three yards there was a small cut in the hillside, made long before by a heavy rain. *'If I can make it thar, I'll be safe. At least for the moment,'* he thought.

Alex Culpepper watched closely, and even though at times he could see movement, there was never again a target. Still faithfully he studied the distant hill, as he had been instructed. *'Sooner or later I'll get another shot. I gotta be ready,'* he reasoned.

Pike and Rome finally made it to the blacksmith's shop unseen but were gagging at the smell of Chigger Morgan roasting in the coals. The wagon wheel he was moving at the time he was shot had fallen under him and was burned almost completely up.

Pike saw the three-wheel coach resting on the jack and looking around realized there were no spares. *'We gon'a have to transfer the heavy gold to the other coach or borrow a wheel from it. Shit, it's in front of the Stage Station. Shit, shit, shit!'*

At that moment, after hearing nothing for some time, Spuds opened the cellar door and looked out. He was ready with a good 44 Remington in hand and cocked. He saw Pike at the same moment the outlaw saw him, and they both jumped with fright. Spuds fired while Pike was trying to get his pistol from its holster, and the ball struck him just above the belt. He made a low grunt a second before dark red blood began spurting from the front of his canvas trousers.

Rome returned fire at Spuds, but the round went high and splintered the top board on the cellar doorframe, a piece of which shot forward and stuck in Spuds' scalp, just above the hair line.

He returned fire but knew he had missed and quickly ducked back inside the cellar and latched the door.

Rome looked at Pike, who was now sitting with his back against the wall. Slowly he shook his head, *'He are a dead man. It might take an hour, it might take a day, but thar ain't no saving him,'* he thought, but what he said was, "Pike, I'll go and get some of the fellows, and we'll be back to get ya'. Need to get ya' to a doctor as soon as possible."

"Yeah, go get me a doctor," the wounded man replied, gazing through glassy eyes.

Rome started back, but just before he left he called to Pike, "See if you can keep that shooter down while I go for help."

"I'll try, but you hurry."

"I'll be back as soon as I can, but you remember if that sharp-shooter gets me, you ain't never gon'a make it."

"I'll keep him busy. Just go," Pike said, as he crawled over where he could get a shot off at the window Culpepper was firing through.

Cliff had heard the shots being exchanged at the blacksmith shop, but he couldn't see anybody and was not sure who or how many were there. He knew two of their men had gone there, and now all was silent. Sarah knew it too.

It took Rome almost an hour to get back to the ridge where Loomis was. When he explained the situation of the coach's wheel to him, the old Rebel slammed his foot hard against a saddle one of the men had dropped on the ground while resting their horses.

"This means we have to kill them all!"

"I can't see any other way," Rome agreed.

"Where are Pike and Fargo?" he asked, and then without waiting for a reply he added, "Can we expect any help from them?"

"Fargo was shot dead before he got to the shop. They have some men hid out in the cellar near there, and when Pike and I got to the coach they burst out and shot Pike."

"How bad is he hit?"

"Gut shot. I'd be surprised if he were still a kickin' right now," Rome replied.

Loomis looked about and squinted his eyes as he thought before he said, "Sounds like they knowed we wus coming."

"I don't see how," Rome said back.

But the bandit leader just shook his head and slapped his gauntlets against the palm of his left hand.

"If I may offer a suggestion?"

Loomis and Rome looked up at the easterner with an air just short of disgust.

"Why not have the savages do a frontal charge on the place while you and your men rope that other stage and pull it out of the way. You can get to a wheel off of it to replace the damaged one."

"That's crazy," Rome said, but Loomis said nothing, instead he thought on it heavily.

"Knowing them Injuns will fight to the death for the new repeating guns I told Sky Warrior wus at Godfrey's ranch, but how can I now turn him from the ranch to the stage station?" he said, more to himself than to anyone else.

"Whiskey," Jean Mouton said, in perfect English which surprised York who had always heard him speak with a strong French accent.

"What?" Loomis asked.

"Tell them there is whiskey in the stage station."

"Hell, there ain't no more than a keg of whiskey in thar."

"They do not know that, Monsieur," Jean replied, once more with a French accent.

"They will when he takes the place."

"They'll never take that place, besides once you have the coach moving away what do you care what happens to them?"

'*Damn easterner makes sense,*' Loomis thought. Turning he yelled, "Casin."

The scrawny ol' mountain man slipped over, taking care not to expose his head above the small rise that protected them from the sharpshooter in The Dale.

Jean could smell him as he approached, and he raised his eyebrows.

"You call me, Loomis?"

"Yeah, I want you to go over ta' the Godfrey spread and find Sky Warrior. Explain that he needs to attack the Stage Station now and let the ranch rest."

"Why should he listen to me?"

"Because he knows you and will believe you when you tell him, there is many barrels of whiskey stored inside the main building there."

The man looked at Loomis a moment or two. It was obvious he did not like his new orders, but he also knew they were nowhere nearer the gold than they were before the siege began, finally he nodded his head. "Take me a' hour or so."

"We can spare you that long," Abe replied. "Now get on with it a'for the army or some'un else comes along."

As Sarah was passing out some hot peppers she had put up in a sweet sauce, she was thinking, actually wishing, that when the station had been built, they had completed the tunnel. The design of most of the Home Stations was to have a tunnel from the main house to the barn to use as a means of escape should the need be.

She knew a few of the them had done that, however here it had been completed about halfway to the barn, but there had been a cave-in, and the project was halted temporarily do to a sudden snowstorm. After Slade left, no one ever got around to putting its completion back on a front burner. *'Had this been accomplished, Spuds might have a way to get back,'* she thought.

The tunnel entrance was off the root cellar under the house and completed almost to where Spuds was now holed up in what had become a second, and much larger cellar which was used to cure game. His hiding place was only some fifteen yards from the black-smith's side of the barn. During the deep winter, Spuds would cut ice blocks from the little stream out back and place them in this larger cellar. This would allow animal meat to be kept cool for many days without spoilage, during the warmer months.

Unfortunately, the cave-in was closer to the house than to the barn. One could enter the cellar, either through a trapdoor Spuds had cut under their bed or through heavy twin doors on the front side of the house, but he wisely had means to keep these bolted from the inside.

They seldom used the trapdoor under the bed, except when the puppy had to go out in the night. Spuds had taught the cute little critter to use the trapdoor to enter the tunnel via a short board. Once there he would go on out into the yard by means of the small hole, located where the cave-in had occurred.

Little Sissy just loved that pup and wanted to keep it with her all the time. The little cur slept with the child most nights as well as during her afternoon naps.

This day, while Sissy was sleeping, Old Woman had gone into the main room to get something to eat. While she was away, the puppy had slipped down the trapdoor and headed out, as he often did. Sissy awoke just as her dog was squeezing through the trapdoor in the floor, and the child followed. When Old Woman returned and found the baby missing, she screamed loudly.

Tom followed as Porsche ran into the room to see what had frightened her so. She only said one word, "Gone," and then pointed to the small cross in the window covering. Porsche looked out and there, less than a hundred feet from the house, was the child following the little brown dog.

It was at this moment Sky Warrior's Utes came charging up from the creek and into the yard. One rode his pony within a few feet of the child as he tried to spear the little dog. Little Sissy suddenly became frightened, sat down and started crying.

Porsche screamed at the sight of the little girl sitting there with all the horses dancing around her and the wild Indians yelping and shooting.

Cellar Door in front of The Dale

Tom too saw the danger, and without thought, he opened the door and rushed out with a revolver blasting at the mounted men, dropping two from their horses.

The Utes were so surprised at this sudden charge, that for the moment, they kicked their cayuses and hurried back around the house, out of the line of fire of this crazy Whiteman.

Tom grabbed the child, turned, and ran back towards the door. He saw Porsche standing in the opening; her face was frightened, yet showed a sign of how proud she seemed to be of his act. This gave him faith and strength and he felt he might just make it, and he almost did.

He was only ten feet from safety when a warrior on a coal black pony, leading three other men with frightening paint on their faces, came around the house from the opposite side. Spotting the exposed Whiteman he fired at Tom's back. Porsche screamed when she saw the smoke erupt from the muzzle of his rifle.

The small lead ball hit him an inch to the right of his spinal column and traveled on past his armpit, stopping in the hard muscle of his right bicep. Tom dropped his heavy Colt but not the baby; he tucked her up under him protecting the child with his own body.

The riders continued on around the building, and as soon as they passed, Porsche rushed out to him, but the man riding the black looked back to make sure his victim was not able to get up; upon seeing her, he immediately wheeled around, heeling his pony hard, and he was upon her in seconds. Leaning over, he easily swept Porsche up and was galloping away when Cliff reached the door. There was no opportunity for a shot.

Cliff fired at the one following the man with the girl, and the brown and white paint continued up the hill, rider-less. He then slid the revolver into his slash and grabbed for the young Texican, who had gotten to his knees, still clutching the child.

Tom's wound was serious. The 36 caliber ball had traveled along the back side of his right lung, tearing away tissue as it went. Reb was well aware they had to get the lead out as soon as there was a lull in the fighting. The bleeding was not his biggest concern, he knew if a man doesn't die soon after being shot, the greatest threat would be from infection. He also guessed the Indians had used any and all sorts of fat to ease in ramming the lead down their barrels, and this was usually what caused the infection.

Sarah soon had Tom laying face down on a blanket. Every time he would attempt to get up to help, she would lash into him with a tongue-thrashing like he had not had since he left home. He would then lie back down. Finally, Eve and Faye were summoned to help keep him in line. They were not needed long, as Tom began to feel faint and stopped attempting to get up.

Sarah had gotten the bleeding stopped, leastwise the bleeding on the outside. She made a pillow of sheets over a hay-filled burlap sack, for his head.

Lone Fox rode over to the hill where Sky Warrior was watching his braves' actions and there dropped the girl to the ground. "Look," he said, proud of his prize.

The older man was not so pleased, "We take no hostages," the chief said back sternly.

"I took her. I will keep her."

"If she slows us down, I will have you both killed," Sky Warrior said before turning and riding away.

Loomis had seen the kidnapping from his perch on the opposite side of Virginia Dale and laughed. However, Jean Mouton had seen it entirely differently. *'Here is something we can use to trade for a coach with four wheels,'* he thought. *'First I must enlighten this fool and then convince the Indians, but we finally have a chance at the gold.'*

"Loomis, that girl captive there, we could trade her for a good wagon wheel."

"I have a better way working right now. We don't need to interfere with Indian business."

Cliff was shooting from the rear of the house when he heard Culpepper call out loudly, "Reb, better come see this."

He turned and looked at the big man who had stopped firing and was staring at something through the window slits.

Cliff rushed up to him and asked, "What is it?"

"Look, yonder at the cut in the bank, behind the coach."

Cliff focused where Culpepper had indicated. "I don't see nothing."

"Watch a moment," he was told. "Two white men with ropes."

At that very moment, Casin and Oiley Wick gathered enough courage to jump from their cover and run to the stage.

"See?"

"I see them," Cliff answered.

"What you reckon theys' up to?"

"Not sure, but we need to keep an eye on them."

Casin stopped with his back to the coach door. The combination of the run from the cut to the cover, and the fear of what they were engaged in, had caused him to sweat. Even on this frosty day, his old fringed shirt was soaked through. Now the deep red paint of the stage was rubbing off and staining his shirt back. At first, when he dropped down to his knees, Oiley thought he had been hit in the back.

Oiley was a tall fellow. At least he appeared tall. Actually, he was not as tall as he was thin. He had never found store-bought trousers small enough in the waist, save those made for boys, and then the legs were too short. It was the combination of his skinny frame, and his pants not quite covering his boot tops, gave one the impression he was tall.

Bud Casin tied his rope end to the stage tongue, and then trading places with Oiley, said, "See you can lassoo the tongue out yonder, near the end."

From the slits where Cliff watched, he could see through the windows of the coach, and he saw the men as they changed positions.

"Culpepper, you see that rear window on this side of the coach?"

"Uh' hu'."

"Look straight through it and out the front window, 'touther side."

The big, bearded man moved where he could get the angle right to see as he had been told and then replied, "Don't see nothing."

"Watch there a spell. One of them is crouched just below that window."

Culpepper did not answer but did concentrate his gaze at the windows and waited. Half a minute later, he saw the man rise just for a second and then go back down. That was enough; the old Yankee sniper took aim through the stage window at the inside wall of the coach.

Oiley had managed, on the second try, to throw his loop over the end of the tongue. Turning to Casin, he smiled a split-second before Culpepper's heavy slug tore through the thin wood of the coach and plowed on through his comrade's body, barely losing any speed.

Bud Casin shot forward as if hit in the back by an ox on the run, then rolled over and ended up sitting on his haunches with his boots pointed back at the stage. He looked at Oiley with wide eyes just before blood began flowing from his open mouth. Then his head fell forward with his chin resting on his chest, and he moved no more.

Oiley suddenly realized his plight. The stagecoach he was hiding behind was no cover at all, not from a 52 Sharps, and he began to scream.

The pair of Utes, who had been waiting for the ropes to be tied, heard his cries as their signal and charged forward. Leaning low from their ponies, they grabbed the ropes and started off, pulling the coach behind them.

Cliff first shot Oiley Wick, who was suddenly totally exposed, and then he dropped the lead Indian.

The second Ute, now having the full weight of the coach alone, had to drop his rope and continue off, lying to one side of his cayuse. Alex sent a slug into the right flank of the spotted pony, causing it to stumble and fall, kicking relentlessly before it died. However, before a second shot could be rendered, the warrior scrambled behind cover.

"What you reckon they want that coach fer?" Culpepper asked.

"Doe-no," Cliff replied.

"You reckon they aim to fire it and run it onto us?"

"No, doubt it. We're up hill from most everything around close. They would never get it going fast enough to get it here without a full team. It's something else," Cliff said back, studying on it.

The first Ute had dropped his lead early enough that the stage had traveled over it, and it was now trailing behind the coach. Seeing this, Cliff decided he would deny them the stage for whatever purpose they wanted it.

After loading both his Colts fully, he yelled, "Cover me!" a second before he rushed out the front door headed straight for the stage. Dropping at its rear wheel, he waited. No shots hit in the neighborhood of the coach, so he crawled under and grabbed the rope that was lying there. Taking a deep breath, he then crawled out from under the stage, and with the hemp in hand, he ran for the well that was some fifteen feet away. There was a hitching post beside the well and then a long water trough made from a split ponderosa, where tied horses could drink.

He slipped the rope around the bottom of one of the hitching post legs and then around the end of the water trough and tied it off fast. Anyone wanting to take that stage off would have to cut this rope first and its entire length was in sight of the station. *'It will be near suicide to attempt such,'* Cliff thought, being well satisfied with his work. He then turned and ran back for the house through a hail of both bullets and arrows.

Abe Loomis stood alone, watching from his perch on the south ridge, at what had happened to his plan. "Som'-Bitch, without a wheel from that coach we will never get the gold out of here," he cursed. Then looking around he began to realize over half of his men lay either dead or wounded, and there were several Ute bodies scattered about around the big house. Shaking his head at the fiasco that had taken place, he wondered how much longer Sky Warrior would continue to send in his braves.

Turning, he saw York and the easterner, *'Neither a' them has done a blame thing to contribute to the success of the day,'* he thought, and it suddenly angered him. "York, you and your Dude go down thar and cut that rope. We gotta get that stage over to that little cut where we can take off a rear wheel."

York looked at the stagecoach and the line of fire that was coming from the house. "We can't get to that coach. Hell, nobody can! Nobody in his right mind, that is."

Abe Loomis became furious and drew his old Dance Brothers 44 and was cocking the hammer as he brought it up towards York's chest. Suddenly, with the swiftness of a snake, Jean Mouton reached behind his neck, brought forth his double-edged knife and sent it deep into the old Rebel's heart.

The man slowly released the half-cocked revolver. It fell from his hand as he sank to his knees. An expression of disbelief was frozen to his ugly face as he stared into the eyes of the man that had just sent his soul to hell. He tried to speak, but the words never came forth, and then he fell forward bleeding profusely.

Mouton walked up and with a boot toe, turned the body over, pulled his knife free, then wiped it clean on the shirt of the dying man. Then, with care, he placed it once again back where he carried it.

Standing, he looked around. *'This is a lost cause. The defenders are too well protected in that house, that fortress,'* he thought, before turning and starting for his horse. "Our only chance is to trade that girl. Come on."

York followed, but the enthusiasm was gone from him; he too believed it was a lost cause.

They rode around the hill, out of sight of Virginia Dale, to the far rise where Sky Warrior was sitting atop a strong pinto. The older man had his attention set on the fight below. Mouton could see from his expressions, he was not pleased with how the battle was taking shape.

A huge Indian standing beside him touched a bow tip to the chief's arm and pointed at the two riders approaching.

Sky Warrior did not know Mouton, but he had seen York before with Loomis.

Jean tried to speak to him first in English, and then French, but he showed he did not understand either.

York, who knew a little plains sign, acknowledged him, and turning to his friend he said, "He wants to know why we are here."

"Tell him we must exchange the captive girl for a good wheel."

York made signs with his hand and arm motions, and the Chief nodded his head, indicating he understood but then asked where Loomis was.

York told Mouton what he had asked.

"Tell him Loomis sent us here to deliver that request to him."

Again, York made sign, but suddenly Lone Fox started screaming at Sky Warrior. Neither Mouton nor York could understand the words, but both understood his argument. The woman was his captive and he wasn't about to let her be traded.

Sky Warrior finally spoke something in a strong and harsh tone, and although much larger in size, the young warrior quieted down but did not lose his anger.

Jean Mouton thought he could see the wishes of the old Chief. If he was right, the problem would be settled. However, should he be wrong he might be just making it worse, and that could be very dangerous. Turning to York he spoke, "Tell him I will fight the foolish one for the woman."

"You crazy?" York said back, looking at his companion. "That buck is half your age and looks like he picks his teeth with a lodge pole."

"Tell him."

Reluctantly, York made the sign.

Lone Fox suddenly produced a wide smile. He turned and waved his rifle high in the air, to the pleasure of a few of his cheering friends.

When he turned back, his new foe was standing there in a crouched stance. The Indian lowered his rifle to his waist, preparing to hand it to another. Mouton did not give him a chance. With lighting speed, Jean drew a revolver as soon as the rifle was pointed in his general direction and sent a conical bullet two inches above and slightly to the left of Lone Fox's heart.

The shot surprised everyone, Lone Fox more than the others. He looked at the Whiteman as if to say, "Wait, I wasn't ready, that's not how we do this." However, no sound came from his open mouth. Slowly his knees failed him, and he fell into a twisted heap, with blood spurting from the hole in his chest for several seconds, before it stopped and all was still about the body.

Suddenly, upon realizing their friend was dead, the two Utes who had ridden up with Lone Fox when he brought the woman, began to scream at Mouton. York quickly signed that Lone Fox had pointed his rifle at Mouton, and Jean saw it as a challenge.

Sky Warrior saw it as the relief to his problem and quieted the two braves sending one of them to bring Porsche.

She was frightened, this was obvious to Jean when he looked at her face, but he also saw she recognized him. 'Not good.' Now he realized she would have to be done away with before they could leave.

"Miss Porsche, I have been able to convince the bandits and these savages here, to exchange you for a good wheel from that coach down there," he said, once more in a strong French accent, nodding his head at the stage tied fast to the water trough.

"What?" she asked, "Why would they want a wheel, Mr. Mouton?"

"My lovely child, I did not ask them what they wanted with it, only what could I give them in exchange for you," he said, placing both palms gently under her jaws and slightly lifting her face up so she was looking into his eyes.

A cold chill ran up her spine when he did, but she didn't understand why.

"How did you even get here?"

"Not to worry about such now. I will explain everything later," he paused, "when we get you safely back with your friends. Now may we have a bit of your petticoat, to make the white flag?"

Turning to York he said, "Go tell them that we will exchange the girl for a good rear wheel from that coach."

York did not like the assignment at all. 'Why don't you go?' he thought, but he did not argue. Jean Mouton had saved his life less that an hour before, and he knew he was in his debt.

"Come here, Miss Porsche," Jean said. "Stand here, it is important for them to see you are alright."

York took the white material and tied it to the barrel of his Winchester. Then he waved it back and forth several times.

Almost immediately all firing ceased from the stage stop.

He then started down the long hill. He would be out of sight of The Dale for several minutes, and then when he topped a small rise, he suddenly was just across the creek, less than a hundred feet from the rear of the building.

"Halloo' the house," he called.

"What do you want?"

"The Injuns have the girl."

"We know that," Cliff yelled back.

Now, despite his wound, Tom struggled to his feet and against their protest made it to where he could see outside.

"We want a' trade."

"What kind of trade?" Cliff questioned.

"We need that stage yonder," he said, pointing at the coach by the blacksmith's hut, "but it has a bad wheel."

"So, we'll give you this one for the girl," Cliff replied.

"No, that won't do, we want that one."

"You want to take off a wheel from this coach in exchange for the girl?"

"Yeah, as soon as we have the wheel on the other stage, you can have the girl."

"We have to think on it," Cliff replied.

Turning to Sarah he asked, "What is so important about that stage yonder?"

She shook her head, "I don't know, unless it is carrying gold or something."

At this time, Yazoo spoke up, "I don't know how they found out about it, but my coach does have a false bottom in it. I am carrying a large shipment."

Now understanding what the whole affair had been about, Cliff nodded his head.

"Why didn't you tell us?" Eve screamed at him.

"Company policy, Ma'am. I ain't supposed to tell nobody about it."

"That's true," Sarah spoke up in his defense.

"We shore gotta do it," Tom said, looking at Reb. "We'll do it, but my way," Cliff answered back, then looking at Alex he asked, "Do you think you could hit one of them atop that north ridge?"

"I don't know, that's nigh on six, maybe seven hundred yards."

"Well, be ready to give it a try if we need to," Cliff replied then he returned his attention to the man waiting outside.

The hill from which Sky Warrior viewed the siege

"What assurance will we have you will release the girl if we leave you what you want?"

"Oh, we'll do it. Jean said so."

Suddenly, Cliff Brown stood up straight, "Jean who?"

"My partner, Jean. He has gotten the Reddies to agree to let her go."

"Where is your partner now?"

"Yonder," he said, turning and pointing to the far hill. "That's him standing by the girl."

"What's his last name?"

"Look, I've said enough, you gon'a trade or not?"

"We'll trade, but only if you bring her down here. That's too far away. I don't trust you."

"I'll go tell him."

"Tell him to bring her himself."

"Yeah, I wish."

When York reached the top of the hill where Mouton was standing with the girl, he saw the remainder of Loomis' gang there also, which did not set well with him. After he explained to Mouton what had been agreed upon, he moved back, keeping an eye on the band of owl hoots.

Jean thought on it a while and finally said, "You men go to the blacksmith's shop, and get the tools you need to take that wheel off, and then come back here."

Rome looked at him and with a bitter voice asked, "Who made you King?" Turning, he looked back at the far hill on the other side of The Dale, where he had found Loomis' body. Then with squinted eyes he added, "It were you what knifed Abe."

"Right now, what we need is a good wheel on that coach down there," Mouton said back to the man. "Are you going to help with that project, or should I show you how easy it was to do away with that fool you have been following?"

Rome knew Loomis was a back-stabber and untrustworthy, even to his own men, but he would not have been easy to knife. Taking a deep breath he replied, "I'll get the tools, but remember them sod busters what are hid in the cellar done killed Pike. I'll need someon's to help me."

"Take whoever you need but be quick about it."

Rome looked over at Micah and motioned with a quick nod of his head. The two then mounted and started off.

Mouton took York aside where Porsche could not hear and told him, "I don't want to be seen by those in the house. They already have seen you, but none of them knows you. There might be some in there," he paused, "that know me, so you will have to take her down. Don't let her go until you see the other stage pull out, then release her and high tail it back to that little cut where you can have cover, but before she gets inside, plug her."

"You mean you want me to kill her?"

"Can't afford to let her go back and identify us. Once they get to talking inside they will convince her we were not sent by them to negotiate her release, and then she will identify us, and the law will be on our trails."

"Gosh, I ain't never kilt no woman 'afore, 'cept squaws a' course."

"Pretend she's a squaw, otherwise she might just be the one who sends you to the gallows."

"Yeah," York replied, looking down at the red earth, not really wanting to think about it.

Jean Mouton walked up beside the small, dark-haired woman, "Miss Porsche, I must remain here. How do you say, the Chief is holding me until the exchange is final. Pardon, but please do not do anything that will interfere with this. My life depends on everything going as planned, oui?"

"Oh, Mr. Mouton, I am so sorry you got yourself in such a terrible spot on my behalf."

"Not to worry my dear. As long as everything goes as planned, I will be safe," he assured her. "Now be quick, and go with Mr. York, he will look after you."

York led her down the long slope into the protection of the cut, and there they waited. Finally, seeing Rome and Micah coming with the jack and other tools, he took her on to the stagecoach.

Cliff and Tom could see her clearly, standing there watching the men working on the removal of the wheel.

"If she would only drop down we could take all of them where they stand," Tom said.

Cliff watched closely for a few minutes and then said, "She sure seems like she doesn't mean to try and run. I hope she has reason to trust them, I sure as hell don't."

After a few minutes longer, the wheel was free, and the two bandits began to roll it towards the blacksmith's shop, while Porsche and her guard stayed behind the three-legged coach.

Alex had studied the range for nigh on an hour. He checked and rechecked his sights. He felt as though he could come close, but without a clearing shot first, to check the range, a direct hit was a maybe at best. The Indian on the horse had turned sideways, and he had the bead on him and pressure against the trigger. All he had to do was squeeze just a tad and the big gun would fire. It was in this position he awaited Cliff's order.

York was watching Rome and Micah as they reached the shop, when he saw the movement it was only a blur, and only a second before the flash.

Spuds Lords had watched the two men as they rolled the big wheel down the long grade. There had been no firing from his house all the while these men removed the wheel. He reasoned the only way that was possible was everyone inside had to be dead. Therefore everyone that made up his reason for living was gone, there just wasn't much left in his life at that moment.

When the men with the wheel were quite close, he shouldered open the heavy door and came out on the run; he headed straight at the two startled men, firing his revolver as he ran. His first shot dropped Rome, and without his assistance, the heavy wheel fell over against Micah, preventing him from drawing his handgun, and he was trapped for a couple of seconds. Finally, he got loose of the weight and reached for his gun, but Spuds was not six feet away, and he emptied his last three balls into Micah's chest.

The sounds of the firing caused Alex to flinch, and his finger touched off the Sharps. Near a second later, the big lead bullet entered the left ear of the pinto and he bucked once, before collapsing on his side where he began kicking his hind legs. Sky Warrior was thrown over his pony's head and rolled free of the dying animal. The startled Mouton suddenly realized the whole affair was up, and he motioned for York to come on back.

Tom opened the front door, and yelled for Porsche to run.

York whirled and started for the cover of the cut behind him, and then just before he got there he stopped, remembering what he had been ordered to do. Turning back, he saw the girl almost to the front door, but she too had stopped and was looking up on the hill where Mouton stood. It was all the opportunity he needed, and York took careful aim and squeezed his own trigger.

At that precise moment, she looked back at York. Seeing what he was doing, she suddenly realized his intention, but it was too late for her to avoid it. Just as she saw the flash from his pistol barrel, she felt the hard strike and was knocked forward to the ground.

Tom too had seen York, and realizing what was happening, lunged forward at Porsche.

A loud scream drowned out the general firing that suddenly erupted all around her, and only then did she realize she had been hit in the back and not by York's ball.

Unknown to her at that time, it had been his scream that she had heard and his lunging at her back that had saved her life. The ball meant for her had hit Tom in the left shoulder, breaking his collarbone and exiting just beyond.

Alex turned to Cliff and said, "Sorry Capt'm, I didn't allow enough for the wind."

"I think you did just fine," Cliff replied and then he went outside and helped the girl with Tom.

Spuds seeing what was happening at his home ran up the rise as fast as he could to the waiting arms of Sarah.

As soon as they were safe inside, Porsche turned and looked up on the far hill, but there was no one to be seen. "Poor Mr. Mouton," she said.

"Mouton?" Cliff asked, almost in a shout.

"Yes, he sacrificed himself for me."

"Jean Mouton?" Cliff again asked, this time taking both hands and placing them on her upper arms as he did.

"Why yes. Mr. Jean Mouton!" she said, startled at his actions.

"I thought so, Son-of-a-Bitch!" Cliff replied and ran from the house towards the livery and Ola.

"I'm heading north," Mouton said.

"Too bad. A lot a' gold down there," York added.

Mouton did not answer him, rather he mounted and headed for the Godfrey Ranch. *'Perhaps the savages burned it and killed them all before they came back. It's worth a try,'* he thought.

Mounted on Ola, Cliff raced up the long grade and over the hill, but no one was in sight.

The tracks of many unshod ponies were everywhere, and he also saw where six horses wearing shoes had been. Four headed southwest into the mountains and two north towards Wyoming. *'On which horse did John Tidwell ride?'* he wondered.

The Utes made no more attacks on The Dale, and it suddenly seemed deathly quiet. The men and women inside the big house waited for more than half an hour before they ventured outside. By then it was obvious there was no one left to shoot at them.

Now that it was all over, they found seven dead Utes around the house and an equal number of large blood spots on the ground where men with severe wounds had laid and probably died. The Utes had carried off all the dead they could get to, without exposing more to the likelihood of joining their ancestors. In fact, the last charge had been strictly to try and get to the bodies, but when two more of their braves fell to the hail of bullets that rained from the old ponderosa structure, they abandoned the idea and headed south into the mountains.

The survivors also found the bodies of eight white raiders, including one who had a scalp tied to his belt.

Just before sundown, Cliff rode back into Virginia Dale, finding a company of cavalry had arrived shortly before him.

These men had been en route to Fort Laramie, but while passing through Camp Collins, they were diverted by the news that had been received over the telegraph lines. When no southbound arrived in Denver, quondam Governor Evens had become worried about the gold shipment his stage line was responsible for. Also since the telegraph lines appeared to be down at Virginia Dale, he had used his influence to get the military authority in Denver to send a wire to the Colonel at Camp Collins for someone to investigate.

Luckily riding with the troopers was a camp surgeon, Doctor Smyth. He operated on Tom Smith and found the 36 caliber ball lodged in his right arm. His second wound was cleaned, and both his arms were placed in slings. The doctor also treated the now infected scalp wound of Spuds Lords, where the timber splinter had entered.

No other injuries had been received by the defenders of the old stage station.

Tom Smith was too weak to travel and had to remain there for several weeks. Porsche stayed with him. "He must have a nurse," she explained to Miss Lola in the note she sent with the other girls.

Cliff continued on to Cheyenne in his search for John Tidwell. It was there, a month later, he received the following wire:

REB BROWN DYERS HOTEL CHEYENNE WYOMING TERRITORY
STOP

THOMAS SMITH MARRIED TENNESSEE LOBELL YESTERDAY
STOP

COUPLE HEADED FOR TEXAS
END

He read the wire twice, then folded it and placed it in the pocket of his canvas vest. He smiled, remembering Tom once saying something about never marrying a whore.

Chapter Five
Wyoming Territory

Celeste Patay was born in the year 1839 along the banks of the Saint Maurice, near the ville' Trois Riveres, in southeastern Quebec, the result of a union between René Doiron and Marie Coltey. Doiron was a fisherman who provided food for the huge lumber industry along this tributary of The Saint Lawrence River.

In her eighteenth year Jacques Patay, who was ten years her senior, approached the beautiful blonde girl one afternoon and said, "Celeste, cheri de mon coeur." No one had ever said such charming words to her in all her life. Here, a man full grown, a proven hunter and trapper who had traveled to far away lands would say she was the darling of his heart, took her completely by surprise and swept her off her feet.

Patay would soon leave again for the vast wilderness of America, west of the territory claimed by those United States, into known Indian Territory, a place from which many never returned. However, he was spirited and had made friends with the Northern Cheyenne, a people whom he had traded with many years and whom he trusted. His only real danger was in passing through the lands of the Lakota.

He furthermore promised when he returned the next year, he would have sufficient gold to arrange their marriage and provide a home for them there. Not once during the long months of his absences did she doubt that he would do that very thing.

He kept his promise, to some degree. He did return with enough gold to arrange their marriage, but when it came to buying a home for them, he had a better plan for the money his furs had brought in Saint Louis. They would travel by river all the way to New Orleans. There he had friends who he could go into partnership with and in no time at all, they would be rich. He assured her that New Orleans was a city where she could feel at home, a large part of the population spoke French, at least a form of French, and she would not feel so much a stranger there.

Celeste simply did not understand why they could not stay there in Quebec. There were many jobs available to a man such as he, and she could be near her mother, to whom she was very close.

He would have nothing to do with any idea save their going to New Orleans and made it plain if she did not plan to obey his wishes as his wife, they should part now, and he would be on his way.

The very thought of being without him after waiting and dreaming of little else for so long was out of the question. They were married and departed before the sun set on the third day of his return.

Her mother had given Celeste a letter to take to her brother, who had gone to New Orleans many years before. At least she would have some family there.

The morning after their departure, a Constable arrived at the Doiron home with a warrant for the arrest of one Jacques Patay on the charge of grand larcyen. Marie Doiron assured him her daughter and her new son-in-law had traveled upriver to Quebec City.

The long journey south took many months and was a time for fun and passion for the new couple. Celeste suddenly realized that all those feelings she had, feelings that confused her and caused her so much pain, feelings she had been unable to understand for so many years, were the very ones, now that she was free to release them, gave her so much pleasure. Even though Jacques was the first man who had enjoyed her treasures, she realized she was not the first woman he had spent time with, but that made no difference to her. *'He is a man, men do such things before they marry, women do not,'* she reasoned.

They took the Saint Lawrence south to Lake Ontario. When they passed old Fort George, she remembered her grandfather telling about how his regiment had helped the Americans defeat the Red Coats there in 1813.

They traveled down the Niagara until the current became too strong, and there Jacques sold their boat and bought a small wagon that they used for the next several miles. Finally, south of the falls he was able to sell the wagon and buy another boat, a larger one.

She was concerned that he had eagerly taken so little for their original boat and paid more than twice as much for the newer one. Jacques did not bother to explain that the craft they had used so well for so many weeks was the reason the Constable was looking for him.

Soon they were once again in open water, staying just close enough to the north bank to see the shoreline, and after several days of sailing Lake Erie, they took the Detroit River into Lake St. Clair.

After stopping for two days at the Point Aux Basques lighthouse, where repairs had to be made to the boat, they were off again headed for Lake Heron.

Each day she placed several lines out and checked them hourly. Never had a day passed that her lines failed to provide them with the belly timber they needed and more. While in Potagamissag Bay, she had hooked a fish so large that it had broken the strong line. She never saw the fish, but she dreamed many times of how large it must have been.

Traveling through the Straights of Mackinac a canoe containing five Indians came close to them, and it frightened her considerably, but they never approached the Patays. Each had a good look at the other, each was satisfied, and eventually, she decided the redmen were as curious about her and Jacques as they were about them. Still the tales she had heard, for as long as she could remember, of the terrible things the redmen did to white women caused her for the first time to fear the strange people so many called savages.

That night she had a terrible nightmare; *'The five savages returned under the cloak of darkness, and began to repeatedly rape her. She cried out to her Jacques to help her but he did not come. After long hours of this humiliating and painful ordeal she was tied naked to a pony and led away with a coarse rope about her neck. After many hours of agony, she fell from the horse and the rope snapped her neck paralyzing her. She then saw the painted face of the savage who had held the other end of the rope ride up along side where she lay helpless on the desert floor, and look down upon her so unconcerned, as one might glance upon a frog they had unintentionally stepped upon, and then he pulled at the rawhide reins, turning his pony, moments before he heeled the beasts' ribs and trotted away after his friends, leaving her to the pack of wild dogs gathering about, snarling and snapping at her, and she screamed in terror, but there was no one to help, no one who cared.'* Celeste awoke screaming and in a cold sweat, but even her terrified cries had not disturbed her husband's sleep. From that night on she could not shake the fear she had of Indians.

The trip through Lake Michigan was rather unpleasant. Almost every day the winds were so strong that spray covered them and most of their provisions, thus the many days spent there were the worst of the trip in her mind.

When they reached the huge settlement called Chicago, they were able to restock with staple goods much of which had been so wet in the preceding days that they were useless.

After Lake Michigan, the journey down the Illinois River was a delight and she especially enjoyed the three days they stayed at Peoria, where they found some people who also were from Quebec, and she felt a touch of home.

Too soon for her, once more they were traveling south on the river, and on the third day out of Peoria, Jacques shot a deer that was swimming past, and they had roast venison and fried bread cakes, a nice change from the daily diet of fish.

It was the first day of June, 1859, when they almost overturned at the location where the waters of the Illinois River entered the mighty Mississippi. Celeste thought that surely she would drown on her birthday when she was swept overboard. Jacques had felled four strong and strait hickory trees that he formed into long wooden rods to use to pole should they become stuck on a sandbar; he quickly pushed one of them out to her, and she was able to grab hold. It easily kept her 110-pound frame from sinking until they reached calmer water where he was able to pull her back aboard.

That night she wanted him to hold her tenderly. After all, it was her special day of the year and a day in which she almost died, but he was distant and uncompassionate. This was the first night in their marriage he had acted this way, and it hurt her feelings deeply; she fell asleep with a tearful eye long after he had begun to make his nightly noises.

The next day he seemed to be totally unaware of her obvious hurt, going about business as usual. Now she was no longer feeling hurt, that had been replaced with rancor, and she did not bait her lines before she allowed them to trail behind the boat. Her trick had little effect on him; however, when the evening drew on and they should be locating a spot to camp for the night, Jacques continued south. As soon as full dark was upon them, they rounded a turn and she saw the glow of lights ahead of them on the river.

They had seen increasing numbers of watercraft in the last few days, some of which were as large as a city she thought, and now there seemed to be several of them ahead reaching from one side of the river to the other.

"We better go ashore," she called to him, but he paid her no mind, only lifting his arm and throwing it back down in what had become his gesture of disagreement with her.

On they floated, slowly getting closer and closer to the lights of the big boats that surely would swamp them, if not run them over entirely. Her anxiety increased with each passing minute, and every mile they closed on the huge craft. She simply could not understand Jacques' lack of concern. Finally, they moved around a big bend in the river, and suddenly she could see the lights were much farther away than she had thought. In fact, they now appeared to be stationary, no longer moving up river; they had all, save one or two, gathered to the right side of the wide muddy river. The more she strained, the more she was puzzled at what was happening until finally it came to her; these were not lights on a dozen riverboats but rather lights on shore, lights of a settlement, a huge settlement.

"Madame," Jacques suddenly said, "I give you Saint Louis."

Never in her life had she seen so many lights. Even Chicago had not appeared so large. She immediately became exceedingly excited, and she placed the top finger of her right hand between her teeth and bit down a little to keep from crying out with joy.

Their stay in Saint Louis was a joyful time to Celeste. Her husband was once again passionate, and they enjoyed several nights in each other's arms.

Jacques had friends there, people who he had done business with in the fur trade. Events that changed the course of history for the fur trade were spoken of, and she soon understood it was nothing in this day and time as it had been twenty years before. The beaver was mostly gone, and only the Reddies knew where the few remaining streams the busy creature inhabited were located and these were high in the mountains. Had Jacques not made lasting friends with some of these people, he would have been out of the fur trade altogether as so many others were.

An old French trapper she met explained to her, "Of course, beaver is not the only pelt there is a market for, there is the fox, the otter, the muskrat, and as everyone knows, the coat of the great bear is always in demand but nothing like the days of old,"

Celeste spoke almost no English, and her communication was only with those who spoke her native tongue, but there were enough of them among Jacques' friends that she was not left in the dark on all matters.

Jacques had promised to teach her to speak the language of the Americans as soon as he had time, but he was too busy these days for such things. "When we are en route to New Orleans, perhaps," he had said. This however was not to come about. Once they were again southbound, the traffic on the river increased rapidly, and he said he was too busy staying out of the way of the Paddle Wheelers and the ever-changing sandbars. She understood at first but soon realized it was only an excuse. He had plenty of time to give her lessons, had he so wanted to. She promised herself, '*I will find someone else to teach me and show him.*'

New Orleans was a place like no other she had ever seen. Excitement was found at every turn. The people spoke a language she could understand. Not the same French she knew in Quebec, but still French, and everyone seemed happy to have her around, everyone except Jacques that is. Once again he seemed distant, especially when bedtime drew close. Celeste began to wonder if she was doing something wrong with their lovemaking. He never seemed to desire her anymore. They only enjoyed each other once or twice a month and that was always at her initiation. Celeste greatly enjoyed their sexual activities and was never left unsatisfied. She was sure she could do it every day of her life and not get too much, everyday when 'Old Grandma' did not show her bloody face that is. Still many nights she was at a loss and deeply hurt inside by her husband's attitude toward her when the candles were blown out.

She found some people who had known her brother, but they gave her the sad news that he had left for the plains of Wyoming two years before she arrived.

It was during late November Jacques told her he was going to Texas. Explaining he had secured a position as a teamster on a freight wagon with a train that was carrying goods to the army post at Fort Worth. They would be returning with men and civilians who had been wounded fighting with the Comanche Indians there. She begged him not to go, but he was headstrong and never listened to the advice of someone ten years his junior, especially that of a woman.

Celeste had taken a job at *The Brown Pelican*, a fish house that served several of the finer restaurants in the French Quarter and would be safe and secure during the two months he would be away, but that was not the reason she so desperately did not want him to leave her alone. There was one Thierry Desmarest, a young man whose father owned *The Dixie Lady*, one of the most luxurious restaurants in the Quarter. Thierry was older than she but not near as old as her husband. He was also very handsome and very wealthy. The fact that she had caught his eye was not lost on several of the women who worked at *The Brown Pelican*. Celeste also was most aware of Thierry's attention and realized she, too, found herself attracted to him. However, she had been raised in the strictest of Catholic homes and knew it was a demon dwelling within her body that caused her to feel this attraction.

On each of the days she was required to deliver the fish to *The Dixie Lady* she prayed he would not be there, but she always felt a warmth rush through her loins when their eyes made contact. On nights after such experiences she would lie close to Jacques and hold him tight and long for him to take her body in the manner she knew Thierry desired to, but he seldom obliged her. Still, Jacques was her strength to fight off the demon, and she feared greatly when he told her he would be away for so long a time.

On this day, when she and Jacquelyn carried the fresh fish by cart to *The Dixie Lady*, they both saw him sitting on the front balcony reading a newspaper. Celeste quickly snapped the long thin leather on the mule's back and turned the beast towards the alley that led to the back of the restaurant.

Jacquelyn laughed at her before saying, "Celeste, you are a fool. This man could give you so much."

"I am a married woman. I need nothing from this man."

"You are a married woman, baugh. Your husband is a bum. He never works; he drinks all of your earnings. You should leave him."

"Never! Such talk is a sin."

Celeste entered the alley that ran behind the elegant restaurant and pulling hard on the mule's reins, stopped the single-axle cart. Their feet had no more than touched the cold damp bricks, when the smooth voice that so often tormented her dreams, filled her ears.

"Ah, two most beautiful ladies on such a beautiful afternoon."

Celeste immediately felt her loins tingle when she heard the voice, but she did not look his way.

"You are most kind Monsieur," Jacquelyn replied and smiled, looking first at Thierry and then at whom he was staring. She then giggled and took the basket of fish from Celeste's hands and rushed inside leaving the two of them alone.

Celeste looked at the paper he had folded under his arm and she asked, "What is the news, Monsieur?" hoping it would distract him from what she knew he wanted to talk about.

"News?" He looked at her and then at the folded paper and then opened it and read aloud the headlines, "Thomas Overton Moore defeats Thomas Jefferson Wells in the Governor's Race."

He once more looked at her face and smiled before asking, "Are you a scholar of politics?"

"Oh, Monsieur non. I can no read, but my husband he is going to teach me, when he has the time."

"Why not let me teach you? I have time right now."

"No Monsieur, it would not be proper."

Suddenly he dropped the paper, reached forth with both hands and pulled her to him. Her face was filled with fright as he easily lifted her feet off the ground and brought her lips up to his.

His kiss was gentle and warm and strange feelings rushed through her as she had never felt before. She wanted to scream out, to tell him to stop, to tell him to put her down, but she was afraid if he did, she would not have the strength to stand.

Finally, the sound of bare feet slapping the wooden floor behind them filled the air and he lowered her back as gently as he had lifted her and released her arms only moments before Jacquelyn appeared.

Celeste was so emotionally stirred she quickly looked away before rushing to their cart.

Jacquelyn stopped long enough to flirt with the wealthy young man before she too climbed into the cart. She barely had time to sit before Celeste dropped the reins on the mule's back and they were off around the building and out of sight.

Jacquelyn heard him laughing loudly but did not understand what he found so funny.

Celeste did not hear his laughter at all. She didn't know anything of the conscious world until they passed *The Bougainvillea* slave houses where their next delivery was to be.

"Hey stop, where is your head!" Jacquelyn yelled out and reached for the long leather leads to halt the mule.

The night before Jacques left for Texas, they enjoyed each other for the first time in two months.

A week later Thierry Desmarest knocked on her door just after dark. When she opened the heavy plank portal, he held out a newspaper, "It says here John Brown has been hanged in Virginia. You will allow me to begin your reading lessons tonight, non?"

Before the hard freeze came in middle January, Celeste realized she was with child. However, she didn't know who fathered it. Almost nightly this fear resulted in horrifying nightmares of the baby arriving and looking one hundred percent like Thierry Desmarest, and he grew to be a head taller than her husband, *'Then everyone will know the truth and Jacques will banish us and throw us both out.'*

One night she dreamt she had bore a son, but suddenly he was grown and somehow injured and hogs attacked and ate him; then the dream flashed to a time when she had just been awakened by his crying and saw he was no longer a tall handsome Cajun as in her earlier nightmare, only a hungry suckling once again. These dreams continued night after night until in late February when Jacques returned.

Her husband seemed genuinely pleased about her condition, provided it did not slow him down in his new idea.

With great enthusiasm, he explained to her of the news he received while in Texas. Moon Thresher, one of the men he met at Fort Worth, told him the sutler post at Fort Laramie could be bought. "I am sure it will be our gold mine, non. You know I have many friends, many among the Northern Cheyenne, and with this increasing talk about the secession here in this southland, it surely is the time for us to move west before the war, it breaks out, non?" Then with a twinkle in his eye he added, "Perhaps that is where your brother has gone, oui."

She ingested his news with mixed emotions. It would be good for them to leave New Orleans. She knew now she was unable to resist the advances of Thierry and sooner or later Jacques would find out and then there would be a killing. Either way, the outcome would spell disaster and disgrace for her. However, was she ready to leave the safety of Louisiana, a land she had learned to love? She thought she could talk him into moving to some other Parrish, but deep inside she did not believe it. Wyoming Territory would be their next home, and she knew it in her heart.

Spring once again found Celeste living on a flat-bottom boat. Moving only as fast as the men could pole them. This time however, she was heavy with child and could do very little other than fish and prepare the meals for several men.

Jacques had bought the boat from a man who had brought goods south all the way from the Ohio River. Her industrious husband then loaded it with bales of cotton and sugarcane and hired six men to help with the poling.

When they finally reached Saint Louis, it was early June, and after unloading the cotton they had contracted to deliver there, Jacques paid off the polers and still had a small profit. Almost immediately, he sold the boat for what he had paid for it in New Orleans. The money they made from the sale of the sugarcane was pure profit. She had to admire Jacques, 'He may not have the finesse of Thierry in the bedroom, but he is a businessman through and through.'

On his last return from the upper Missouri, he had deposited all his earnings from the sale of the furs in The Bank of Saint Louis on Cedar Street, save what he needed to go back to Quebec and retrieve Celeste. In only three days from the time they docked, he had withdrawn all his remaining funds and using some of it, bought a used army ambulance for their travel west.

The wagon, it seemed, had been abandoned on the prairie with a broken axle. A weary homesick traveler had made enough repairs to get it to a settlement where a new axle could be bought; from there he took it on east to the river city where it was sold for money to buy tickets on a paddle wheeler to Owensville.

Jacques and Moon walked into Blane's Livery just as the man from Kentucky was leaving, and the hostler made a quick profit.

Before they turned the little wagon westward on Rue de Rio she made Jacques take her to the Cathedral where she spent an hour on her knees praying to The Lady to forgive her of this great sin and not to hold it against her child. She also prayed for strength to fight the demon that lived within her loins.

Celeste made the best of the long trip across Missouri to Saint Jo. There they joined a train headed for California via the Oregon Trail through Nebraska.

The train with which they had contracted would start late, and everyone knew it would never make California before the winter snows came. However, the wagon master, Chance Wayne, a man of some foresight, had wisely suggested to the train leaders for them to pool together and buy two large freight wagons and fill them with necessary and prized goods. He explained they could sell and barter one wagonload in exchange for the right to winter at Fort Bridger.

It was a good plan and would result in them being the first train over the Sierra's the following year, when after the long winter months, their second wagonload of goods would bring premium prices at the settlements high in the California Mountains.

Jacques and Moon were hired to drive these freighters, as they both were experienced teamsters on freight wagons. Celeste would drive the small ambulance. The teamsters never gave Chance Wayne the slightest clue they had no intention of going beyond Fort Laramie.

Never in her life had she hated anything so much as she hated Nebraska. It was hot, dusty and barren. Nowhere, save along the banks of the Platte River, was there sign of anything that resembled a tree. She remembered the beautiful green forest of Quebec and longed for home. The larger her belly swelled the more she longed for her home and her mother.

Several times along the way, they had seen Indians on far off hills, sitting and watching the slow moving oxen pull the heavy-laden wagons westward, and a twinge of terror would suddenly sweep upon her, but never did they come close. Jacques said they were Sioux, but she wondered how he could tell from so great a distance.

She learned of the strange-shaped rock that was called The Chimney Rock and of the bluffs where the old trapper Scott, had wanted to be buried. The stories told around the campfires the night they camped nearby were of how up in Montana, he had been injured so badly that his friends could not move him, so he was left behind. Months later when these same friends arrived at the river below these very bluffs, they found his body there waiting for them. No one knew how it got there or how it could have stayed in an undecomposed condition. The story caused chills to run up her spine for she had no doubts sprits lived here, and perhaps they could see inside her and recognize the demon that lived within her. She did not sleep well that night and was up and had her team hitched before Jacques awoke.

The greatest difficulty she experienced while driving the team, was the crossings of the Platte River. It seemed almost daily the Oregon Trail would cross from the south to the north and then the next day back again to the south side. Some of these crossings consisted of steep banks and at others, the land was so flat it was hard to see where it ended and the river began, but these too could be treacherous. One wagon belonging to a Prussian family called Kurtz, strayed just a few feet from the tracks made by the forward vehicles and became bogged down in a large pool of quicksand; these pilgrims lost everything, save their animals and their own lives.

However, from Scottsbluff on to the Wyoming border, the trail stayed above the wide North Platte, and Rawhide Creek was the only gulch that still contained water from the spring runoffs. They were making an average of twelve miles a day and arrived at Fort Laramie on the eighteenth of August, 1860. Celeste was less than two weeks from giving birth to a male child.

Jacques made the excuse that Celeste's condition was too advanced to travel further as to why they could not continue the drive. Chance Wayne almost called him to fight over breaking the contract at such a location. Finally Herman Kurtz and his oldest son, who had helped Celeste with the driving after their loss, were hired to drive the big Murphy wagons on west. Both Jacques and Moon knew they would never make the grade, but said nothing to Wayne as a warning.

The Fort's surgeon, Archie Fauntleroy, was most helpful in the delivery of a boy child. Even though she lost a great deal of blood, she was strong and youthful and would recover soon. His words as he placed the beautiful flaxen-haired child in her arms were a little saddening though, "Raise him well; it is most likely you will bring no more children into this world."

Jacques was pleased beyond her wildest dreams when he saw the male child had the blonde hair of his mother and named the little boy Jacque Louis Laramie Patay, Jacque because it was his father's name, Louis because the child had been conceived in Louisiana and Laramie because the lad was born at Fort Laramie.

The transfer of ownership of the Post Store from Seth Ward to Jacques Patay went just as he had planned, and in no time they moved into the living quarters in the rear of the large structure. Three sections divided the store: the adobe section built in 1850, a stone connecting building added two years later, and a segment constructed in 1860 which housed the officer's club. Also, there was a small area in the open attic that served as a sleeping room for Moon when he was at the fort.

However, Moon left in the company of two other buffalo hunters in early May in search of fresh meat and never returned. The army sent out a detail to search for the missing men, but a sudden spring snowstorm forced them to return with no news.

There were mixed emotions among the Patays over his apparent loss. He had been a good friend to Jacques and a hard worker both on the trail as well as after they had purchased the store. Now with his disappearance, Jacques was the sole owner of a rather lucrative business, a point which he enjoyed greatly. Celeste too would not miss the partner.

He had many times made offensive gestures towards her when Jacques was not around, even once mentioning how quiet their bed was and suggested he could provide her with all her husband seemed unable or unwilling to give. She abhorred him for it, and although much of what he had said was true, she wanted nothing to do with the toothless, filthy man whose hair never felt the teeth of a comb.

The very night before he left, he ever-so-slightly let the name of Desmarest enter his conversation with Jacques, and when he did, he had a smirk on his face and glanced over at her and then at little Laramie. She knew how unscrupulous he was, and that if he knew what his expression indicated he knew, he would use the knowledge to blackmail her.

'I can not truly say I grieved Moon's disappearance, non,' she thought with a smirk of her own.

The Post Store at Fort Laramie

In the late spring of 1863, the personnel at the fort were relieved and sent back to the states. They were replaced by the Eleventh Ohio Volunteers. Commanding the Eleventh was Colonel William Collins[1] a steady and seasoned officer, who earned his cloverleaf chasing Bill Quantrill over much of western Missouri and more of Kansas than he liked to admit. Among the officers that arrived with the Colonel was one Lieutenant Casper Collins, the Commanding Officer's own son.

The young officer was dashing and educated. He spoke three languages well, and was learning to communicate in Sioux from one of the Crow braves that had agreed to be a scout for the army.

When he saw the light-haired beauty, who he learned was the wife of the post sutler, he was mesmerized. She too found his presence favorable, and the fact he could speak her native language set a bond between them. With permission from her husband, he began teaching her English and the letters that were the tools of reading.

Jacques paid little attention to the officer boy who was willing to spend of his private time on such a fool's errand. He had much more important things to do, making money being primary on the list.

A year earlier, he truly realized the value of having a well-stocked store. Just after receiving his stock of supplies from Saint Joe, a wagon train arrived and bought every single item he had unloaded only three days before. He then set into action a plan to become the best-stocked post on the plains.

One night while Celeste and Caspar were together, the young lieutenant interrupted her studies by asking, "Are you aware there is a ghost that haunts Fort Laramie?"

"Non!" she replied as she rapidly sent her hands up covering her face completely, save her eyes which were as big as large buttons, staring straight at his young face.

"It is true indeed," he assured her and began with his tale. "It all started some eight to ten years back when another sutler operated this very store. I don't recall his name, but soon after he arrived, his teen-age daughter also came here to live with him, as he was a widower." The young officer paused, making sure he had the lovely Celeste's total attention and only then did he continue. "Being a fine horsewoman, the young lady took a daily ride; first only here on the grounds or very near the post, but as boredom set in she be-

---

1 Colonel William Collins: Camp Collins, later Fort Collins in Colorado, was named in his honor.

came more adventurous and traveled out farther and farther with increasing distances, even as far as the iron bridge. In spite of her father's warnings, she rode alone when there were no officers free from duty at the moment she chose to ride. One such day, she departed the post on an unescorted ride and never returned.

Several search parties and patrols were sent out, but no trace of the girl or her mount, were ever found. Heartbroken, the sutler sold his store, took his few possessions and joined the next eastbound train[2]."

"Oh non!" Celeste exclaimed. "What happened to her?"

"Some thought the hostile Indians captured her or killed her and stole her horse."

"Non!" she again said with a quivering in her tone, "I am very frighten of the Indians. Savages they are, non? I have heard of horrible things they do to white women."

Casper reached over and drew her close and she hugged him tightly, and he could feel her trembling. He suddenly questioned his wickedness for telling her of the tale. Finally, he spoke softly in her ear as she clung to him, "Most thought her fate was such, but seven years to the day after the girl vanished, three troopers, just back from patrol, told a strange story in the enlisted man's bar here. It seems they each had pulled guard duty the night before, and each saw the same thing, although at slightly different locations. What they reported seeing was a young woman in a green riding habit quirting her already galloping bay as she raced close by the bivouacked patrol."

"Oh non!"

"Yes, t'is true, and thus was born the Fort Laramie Ghost, for the old salts all agreed that the troopers' descriptions could only fit the long-disappeared sutler's daughter. She obviously still had her hair and fine horse, and no Reddies would have left her those."

The ending of his story only left her holding him tighter and her body quivering more.

As soon as Jacques could manage it, he traveled to Kansas City where he purchased four new Murphy Wagons directly from the manufacturer and brought them back loaded and in a tandem train pulled by twenty mules.

---

2 Train: At this time and location, train would mean wagon train.

He soon would have two en route eastbound with loads of furs, as the other two were transporting his supplies west to the fort. This worked well during the months when the weather permitted travel on the Oregon Trail. The only real glitch in his plan was finding suitable teamsters to drive the huge vehicles, and often he himself would have to do so, leaving the store in the hands of his capable wife. May of 1864 found Jacques headed for Missouri and Celeste doing that very thing.

Murphy Freight Wagons

She now had learned enough English to converse with most of the men there. They tried hard to understand the pretty blonde woman and even though her words were swamped with a thick French accent, through repetition and a genuine desire to help the young mother, only a few could not carry on at least a small conversation with her.

She so brightened their lives at an otherwise barren and desolate spot in an endless sea of brown grass and boredom; it seemed without even trying, Madame Patay had become the shinning star of Fort Laramie.

By this time, she had enjoyed the pleasures of Caspar more than once, but it was in no way an every night affair. She still prayed daily to have the demon driven from her body, but at night, she longed for the strong young man who came to her when her husband was away. It was during one of his long trips east she realized that she had never loved Jacques. He had simply been her rescuer when she was so young, and Thierry had been only the flame that ignited the fires she had kept hidden deep inside her.

Ft Laramie Officers Club at the Post Store

Caspar, on the other hand, gave birth to a feeling deep within her heart, a feeling that grew stronger as each day passed. She loved his curly blonde hair, his dashing horsemanship and even his reckless-ness, some of which she believed he did to impress her. She did not mind his love of gambling, as he often won, and even though he had a taste for strong drink, which he introduced to her, she would smile when he would come to her late in the night staggering and snickering. She loved his every movement, and she knew she could never deny him.

The thought of Jacques returning would bring about a strong burning to her stomach, and the nights she slept beside him, even though he only pursued his husbandly rights three or four times a year now, were pure agony.

The personnel at the post generally knew of the relationship, but respect for both their Lieutenant and for the woman they all secretly loved, kept tight lips and stern faces when the subject was approached by strangers.

Jacques had just returned from a long trip in early July 1865, when Lt. Collins was commanded to escort a wagon supply train to the post at Platte Bridge Station, some one hundred miles up the North Platte. He never returned.

A couple years later, the post's name was changed to Fort Caspar, in honor of this young and brave officer who lost his life to a war club of a Cheyenne brave, while he was attempting to rescue a wounded trooper.

Forever after, when Celeste heard the words 'Fort Caspar', a lump would swell in her throat, and her eyes would become misty.

She went into a deep hole within the darkest part of her brain and only allowed herself to emerge when necessary for the store and in the raising of little Laramie.

This state lasted for almost a year, and then she began to drink. At first, only taking sips at night to help her get to sleep, but as the months slowly slipped by, her consumption increased until even Jacques began to complain about her making mistakes in dealing with the customers.

He had moved them from the back of the store to the room vacated by Moon in the attic and had turned their former quarters into a club for the enlisted men and non-coms to enjoy a game of cards and some relaxing beverage on their off- duty time. Soon most of the men at Fort Laramie owed Patay more on the tab than the paymaster provided, an arrangement Jacques found to his liking.

Of course, when it came to the immigrants who needed his provisions before they could continue their journey, he demanded cash. He even raised his prices when folding money was used by saying he gave a discount for gold.

Jacques Patay had few friends, but because of their devotion to his wife, most men tolerated him. He minded their attitudes little.

Celeste finally came out of her hole one day in the fall of 1868 and thereafter continued her life as the sutler's wife. She was known as a good woman who never short-changed you intentionally; though all should count their change on days when a body could smell the sent of whiskey on her breath. Also during such times, if her husband was away on one of his trips, there were a few men who knew other pleasures at times could be relished from the lady.

Jean Mouton had struck a trail west-by-northwest from The Dale, towards the Godfrey ranch, but seeing the buildings intact and activity apparently normal, he and his companion cut back east towards Cheyenne.

John was still using his French alias of Jean Mouton when they arrived two days later. Avoiding their earlier hangouts the two men took a room at *Dyers Hotel* and waited for the bank to open. The next day he attempted to have the remainder of Hickey's Denver holdings transferred to Cheyenne, but the bank in Denver would not send it without further proof of Mouton's identity. Rather than make a scene, and keeping in mind the conditions under which they had last left this town, he simply replied, "That is understandable. I will wire Mr. Hickey immediately and have that information forthcoming in a day or two." Then he bid them a polite adieu and left.

That afternoon after provisioning themselves, Jean Mouton paid in advance for the room covering a thirty-day period. He explained to the clerk he and his friend were going to Kearney, Nebraska, by rail, but wanted to leave their belongings in Cheyenne so they would not have to lug them around while traveling. The clerk understood; many wealthy men had done the same. Within the hour he returned to the bank, and from a window teller he withdrew half of his holdings from his account there, in folding money and left instructions he would send for the remainder when he established an account in Montana.

The two then rode north out of town without anyone noticing.

After following the old Indian trail northward for several hours, they stopped and rested the animals, as well as themselves, for two hours under the shade of a few cottonwoods along the banks of Horse Creek.

John wasn't sure how he would handle the next part of his journey. He was in flight, and he knew it, and he didn't like it.

Looking over to his left, he saw a man who had never seen the insides of a school and had probably never in his life enjoyed the pleasures of lounging in a porcelain washtub until the warm water became too cool to remain comfortable. A man who very likely never intentionally bathed in his life, his hair was long and full of tangles as was his beard.

John looked up at York's old kepi and seeing it was no longer blue but faded and dirty to the point it seemed to be more of a light tan, and were it not for the few places where the cloth had been mostly protected by the leather strap, one could have guessed it to be Confederate Butternut rather than Union Blue. '*A most disgusting man when one takes the time to look at him,*' he thought. Suddenly Mouton realized he had a growing distaste for the likes of York, and began to hate he was partnered up with the crude man. However, he also realized York knew much too much about several activities that he could in no wise allow to become known to others; so for the moment he was stuck with his partner. Still he had to admit to himself that in a fight, York was a good man to have around. '*Perhaps no match for that damn Reb Brown, but against Indians and other ruffians, he can be quite useful.*'

Jean Mouton's mind began to dwell on the man Reb Brown, and suddenly he felt a burning deep in his stomach. '*I should have killed him years ago. He is the main reason I'm not still in Georgia. Definitely the reason I had to kill Will Hickey and ruin the sweetest deal I have come across since China. He is the reason I have to move about looking over my shoulder; why is this bastard pursuing me so? Surely by now he realizes he can not be tried on the murder of Polk[3] without my testimony, and I will never return to Georgia. Could he be so afraid I might that he pursues me so?*'

He thought long and hard on Reb Brown before he agreed with himself, '*I must find some way to change my image, some new identity he will never connect. There is still hope of accruing more of the money Hickey placed in the banks for our land and cattle deal, and I must get on with that.*'

Near sundown, they came to Chugwater Creek within sight of a small adobe where a thin line of smoke rose from the chimney. Approaching the flat-roofed hut, York called out, "Halloo the house."

"Who you be?" came the reply.

"Just a couple a' riders headed to Fort Laramie. We would be obliged to stay the night."

"What business have you here on my land?"

---

3 Polk: For the shooting of Booker T. Polk see Gold in the Red Desert, Book one of The Owl Hoot Trail trilogy.

"Just passing through, didn't realize it was privately owned," John called back in perfect English, and then he added, "We would be happy to pay for a hot meal."

Shortly the door opened, and an old man stepped out holding a single barrel smoothbore. Behind him was a tall lanky boy of perhaps fifteen or so.

"Niles is the name," the man offered after looking the two over.

"Good evening, sir. My companion here is known simply as York, and I am," he hesitated a moment before adding, "John Brown recently of Georgia."

"We got a slab a' salt pork and some beans a b'iling."

"Sounds wonderful," John answered and then dismounted.

That night he learned Niles Hamm had homesteaded a section bordering the creek and then had his retarded nephew Jamie homestead another section touching his on the east. They ran a few head of beeves and were mostly interested in staying alive and being free of the townspeople who made fun of Jamie. Hamm was usually happy to see travelers and anxious for news of any kind. The number one question was always, "Heard a' any Indian trouble?"

The next morning after a restless night the two started out again, right after breakfast.

Later, just before the noon hour as the two men were moving across the vast sea of waving grass, suddenly John pulled up sharply and reached for his revolver; York followed suit.

The sound of hoof beats pounding hard and fast could be heard approaching. Their animals seemed not to be concerned, but they expected to see one or more Indians come charging over the little rise ahead at any moment. What they did see instead, was a green-clad woman, riding hard directly towards them. She passed without even giving a word of explanation or even a nod, only quirting her horse hard and steadily as she vanished from sight over the rise behind them. Not knowing what or who she was obviously fleeing, they stayed at ready for several minutes. Finally, when nothing appeared and no additional sounds of horses were heard, they moved on ahead. The next several miles were tense however, as they watched and strained their eyes in the bright noon sunlight, but they saw nothing more.

Near the two o'clock hour, they crossed the North Platte on the iron bridge, and within minutes, they could see the buildings of Fort Laramie.

Riding directly to the Post Store, they stopped and spoke to an old noncom who had just stepped from the door, "Say Corporal, did you realize there is a white woman out there riding alone?" York asked.

"White woman alone you say?"

"Oui," Mouton agreed.

"Dressed in green, I suppose."

"As a matter of fact, yes, and riding her horse as if she was hunting with the hounds of hell," York added.

"A tall bay, I suppose."

"Oui, it was a bay horse," Mouton agreed.

"Aye, we know of such a lass," Corporal Donahue replied and then turned and spit a long stream of brown juice from his mouth onto an anthill that was forming just a foot or so from the building.

The two riders were quite curious as to the unconcerned attitude of the non-com, but Mouton looked over at York and quickly gave his head two short shakes, directing him to say no more of the woman. He reasoned her rides were commonplace and wanted to attract no more attention to themselves than required.

The boy with very light hair who had come out with the soldier smiled up at the riders; reaching forth, he took the reins from their hands as they dismounted, then in a strong French accent asked, "May I ta' horse monsieur?"

Mouton replied, "Oui. Je future content de prep faire pron."

The boy's face lit up when he heard the man speak the language so well, and he replied, "You are French, non. Me-ma will be so pleased."

Not anymore pleased than Jean Mouton was when he laid his eyes upon the strikingly beautiful thirty-seven year old Mrs. Patay, who was folding dry goods behind a rough-split log table that served as a counter.

The sound of Jacques' French accent was undeniable as the sutler gave orders to two men who were carrying stacks of pelts from the store to the large wagons out back.

Jean scarcely gave the little man in the red tuque, a cap he remembered to be so common in Quebec, a second look. That he was French was obvious, that he was the lady's husband was likely, that he was not armed with a revolver was pleasant. No other areas of attention to him were needed at this moment.

"Oh, never have I seen such beauty in such a barren, unlikely location," he said as he approached her, and taking her hand, he placed a gentle kiss on her knuckles.

It had been a long time since she had heard her native tongue spoken so well and so correct to Quebec.

"Oh Monsieur, I too find this meeting exceedingly pleasant. You are from Quebec, non."

"Non, but let us say almost, oui. My mother was from Quebec, I, from New York," he answered by opening the palm of his hands expressing a gesture of sorrow, "but I long for the many childhood days I spent with my Grandfather in Quebec City."

Immediately she felt the warm stirrings flow through her loins, and she smiled at the handsome new stranger.

Cliff arrived in Cheyenne only two hours after his target had departed. Unfortunately, he had no way of knowing that and immediately began searching the saloons and hotels. By the two o'clock hour, he had made two discoveries. First, in *French's Saloon* on Eddy Street, he found the Adams brothers. Second, in the lobby of *Dyer's Hotel* he found where one Frenchman, registered as Jean Mouton, had prepaid for a room for a three-week period. The clerk remembered Mr. Mouton pretty well and described John Tidwell to a tee; he also provided Cliff with a good description of his companion York.

Cliff returned to *Ames Boarding House* with Ethan and Shep, where they had a room.

The two explained that they had heard that a new company was about to build a road into the Black Hills, and they were looking for work. Both had sent almost all the earnings Mr. Rumans had paid them, back to Paris to help out the folks there, and now were nearly broke again. The pair had decided to hire out and get some money before trying to make their way back to Texas.

Cliff also took a room there for the night before inviting the boys to a steak dinner.

He realized he was in somewhat of a predicament, *'If I pursue Tidwell to Kearney and find him, it will all end there, but if I am unable to find him and we pass on the trail I will have given him extra days to escape, for surely the bastard will find out I have been here askin' of him. On the other hand, if I wait here for him to return and the prepaying of the room was a clever rouse, then the murderer will have a long head start on me.'* Finally, he asked the boys, "Since you don't know when this Mr. Frank Yates will be here signing up his hands, I would like to employ you for a week or so."

They looked at each other and smiled, "Shor' Reb. What can we do fer you?"

Dyer's Hotel on Eddy Street

"I want us all to move over to *Dyer's Hotel* and get a couple of rooms there. One of you must keep your eye on room 17, day and night. Work it out; take shifts whatever you got 'a do but I want to know if anyone goes into that room. I'll pay each a' ya in Yankee greenbacks for it."

"You done decided to go on to Kearney," Ethan said.

"Yep," Cliff replied.

He was tired, and it showed. His forehead seemed much more wrinkled than when they first met him and that was only a short time back. He drew in a deep breath, slowly let it out and then pushed his old gray hat back where the hair showed before he continued. "It may be a wild goose chase, but I can't afford to let him get back into the northeast. That's his country and he could disappear in a place like New York City, where I would never find him. From Kearney he could just keep on going."

"What you want we should do if'n he do come back here and then high tail's it again?"

"Send a wire to me in Kearney, I'll check there as soon as I arrive, and I will send you one when I start back if he ain't there. If he shows back here, don't neither one a' you try to take him. You are two fine boys, but this man is cut from a different slab. He would kill you through trickery, never give ya' a fair chance."

Ethan started to object about him not being good enough to take on Reb's enemy, but Cliff read his thought and added, "Now I know Ethan can knock the left eye out a' a fly at three hundred yards with a good rifle, but I'm here to tell you he's a curly wolf; remember Tidwell's done already put a slug in me, back in Macon." This took a little out of Ethan for he surely never considered himself on par with Reb Brown.

Cliff pondered a few moments before he spoke. He knew there were times when two were better than one, but he also realized there were times when a partner would cause one or both to feel the need to display their courage, when it was better to stay out of a scarp and this led to his next statement, "Should he leave before I get back, one of you stay here and wait fer me, and the other trail him from afar, and I do mean afar."

He looked at each of them hard in the eyes before he added, "We understand one another?"

"Shor' Reb," they both assured him.

Before turning in that night, he went to the depot and confirmed there would not be an animal car on the eastbound in the morning and found it would be the following day before one would be available.

'Once again I must make a decision where the wrong choice could cost me. If I wait for the animal car and he leaves in the interim, I will once more be set behind. If I go on without Ola and then find Mouton has cut north or south, I would be without a trusted mount. I surely don't want to be that close to a killer like John, Jean Mouton, Tidwell, on a unfamiliar horse. No, I will wait.' So he booked passage for the Wednesday train.

From the beginning, even though he very much admired the gift Sam Brooks had brought him, he felt Ola was not the companion Big Red had been, at least that was his thinking for a long time. Now after being pals with the stout stud for a few years, unknowingly they had bonded, and he truly trusted Ola. Perhaps the Appaloosa would never replace the big sorrel in his heart, but he had learned to respect and depend on Ola, almost as much as he had Big Red.

Although the boys were twins, one would never know it. Ethan was a sinewy[4] Texican well over six-feet and had hair the color of Withlacoochee River water, whereas his brother was several inches shorter and more powerfully built. Shep had gotten his name because his blonde curly hair looked more like it belonged on a sheep rather than a man. A few hours after they watched Reb' s train pull out, Shep fell head over heels for a little red-haired saloon girl in French's place.

Cliff could see the faint flicker of lights on the prairie many miles before the train pulled into the depot at Kearney at precisely 9:00 PM.

After securing a stall for Ola at Tom Meade's stables, he checked in at *The Prairie Flower Hotel*. This was a two-story affair with ten rooms on each floor. The largest in town and most likely where John Tidwell would be found, if he was here at all.

Cliff made the rounds to all sixteen saloons before the three o'clock hour approached and barely was able to climb the stairs to his room due to fatigue and alcohol, when he finally called it a night. No where had he seen anyone who resembled his prey.

It was well past eight before he began to stir. The rising sun was shining through the thin material the hotel furnished as window curtains, and seemingly being directed straight onto his eyelids. Even when he squeezed them tightly closed, his eyes seemed to be staring at a strong red sun. It was no use, he might as well get up and about his business; the squeezing of his eyes was just giving his head something extra to complain about.

After dressing and having two cups of Arbuckles in the hotel café, he forced himself down to Meade's to pay for Ola's stall and feed, as well as to check out any good riding horses that might seem not to belong there.

'Horses are a funny breed of animal,' he thought as he walked the narrow boardwalk in front of the false fronts on many of the stores, 'when alone they crave company, even the company of a man, but they prefer the company of other horses. However, when they are in their home stalls or among their pals they shun the strange horse who they would

---

4 Sinewy: Lanky, lean, tough, and muscular.

love to be around were they otherwise alone.' He stopped long enough to look into the big window where a barber was plying his trade on a bearded gentleman. *'He's too heavy to be John Tidwell,'* Cliff soon concluded, *'however Tidwell will be keeping himself well trimmed when he can.'*

Arriving at Meade's he noticed the only horse the others seemed not to accept was Ola. The hostler was a lanky sort of fellow with a strange accent from some far northern country. His trousers were considerably large for his gaunt frame and stayed around him only due to the heavy leather straps he had fashioned into suspenders. He had no over-shirt, only the tops of his long johns to keep the suspenders from rubbing his shoulders raw, but he seemed not to notice them at all. He also wore a tall stovepipe hat like the one the Yankee President often had worn before he was sent to hell.

"Mighty fine fall day young man," he spoke as Cliff entered.

"Howdy," Cliff replied and walked towards the back where the white-spotted rump of his stocky horse could be seen. Ola was now raising his head so he, too, could see the approach of the man with the familiar voice.

"This Appie here is mine," Cliff said. "Got in late last night and took the liberty of stalling him here."

"Yep, I figured you to be the one when I seed you come in," he answered leaning on the wooden spiked pitchfork he had been throwing hay with. "Heard you come in last night. Could tell you were caring for your animal you'self, so I figured you would be in ta' morning and didn't bother with getting out of my warm bedding. A man what takes proper care a' his animals will be a man to trust," he stopped talking long enough to spit some tobacco juice from his mouth and then added, "these nights are getting a mite cool, wouldn't be surprised if the snows don't start presently."

Cliff stayed with him half an hour while he curried Ola and talked of one thing and then another, finally getting around to asking about any strangers arriving lately, perhaps with a French accent.

"Naw, none 'cept John Frenchy the scout for the army," he said.

The name John Frenchy alerted Cliff, and immediately he wanted to know more about the man but soon realized he was on the wrong trail.

"Yeah, ol' Frenchy is been in these parts a long spell. He happened as a mistake between a Frenchman, a trapper, and a Crow squaw, he don't cater to whites too much, but he hates the Lakota's more, so he makes a good scout, they says."

Disappointment swept over him as Cliff listened to the hostler. "No others then?"

"Nope none here," Meade assured him.

Walking back up the street he remembered, 'the clerk at The Union Pacific Hotel in Cheyenne said they were traveling by rail and very well might not have had horses at all, but Tidwell is crafty and I doubt he would get himself put afoot anywhere it was not planned to be to his benefit.'

Next, he went to the Town Marshal's office, a little two-room shadow of a building sharing the walls of Denny's Dry Goods Store on its north and The Prairie Fire newspaper office on its south.

"Joe Benifield is the name," the man behind the badge said as he shook Cliff's hand. "What can I do fer you?"

Cliff told him of his long hard run following hot and cold trails after the man who had murdered his wife back in Lowndes County, Georgia.

Benifield smiled when he heard the name. "Wouldn't have been in Troupville, would it?"

Cliff was taken back, this man who very definitely did not sport a southern drawl, speaking of so small a village in his home country. "Why no, south of Valdosta. You know of Lowndes County?"

"No, not really, my mother was a Folsom before she married Dad and moved to Illinois. She often spoke of Lowndes County; I don't think she ever accepted Decatur as her home. She was most upset when father joined up to fight against her home people and was so glad when his year enlistment was up and he had not gotten further south than Tennessee."

Cliff suddenly remembered the bloody fighting he had encountered with Illinois troops and their Henry repeaters. He almost asked what outfit the Marshal's father had been in but drew up short, thinking better of it.

"This man I'm after was one of the postwar appointees sent south to head up the Freedman's Bureau, what they termed The Civilian Branch."

"Yes, Ma's people sent us letters with many horror stories of these men who pretend to be the Negro's friend, only ending up stealing from both the conquered whites and the poor dumb Africans."

Cliff started to say something about the not-so-conquered whites but again thought better of it.

"Has such a man been in Kearney in the last month?"

"Naw, I don't think so. If he was he would have made an impression on someone here and I would have heard about it."

"Well, I thank you for your time and will do a little more investigating, but looks like I'm following a cold trail again," Cliff said sliding his hat back on his forehead.

"When you catch up to this gentleman, what are your plans?" the lawman asked knowing full well the answer but curious as to what kind of reply the Georgian would give.

"I plan to bring him to justice. Do you have a strong jail here?" Cliff added before he bade him good-bye accompanied by a knowing smile.

Reading well the answer and the expression, Marshal Benifield nodded his head. After Cliff had left his office, he eased over to the wood burner where he lifted the pot and poured himself a steaming cup of coffee; then looking out of the window he watched the man with the stalwart figure walk on down the boardwalk until he entered the tonsorial shop[5]. Then shaking his head slightly Benifield said quietly with no one to hear, "I shor' wouldn't want him on my trail, cold or not."

There Cliff got a shave and had his hair cut back. He listened keenly to the conversation taking place between the barber and the two other men who seemed to be there solely for the purpose of drinking free coffee and keeping the seats warm. It amused him to watch them, as they never seemed to return to the same seat from which they rose before heading to the pot that was boiling on the big potbelly.

Cliff realized he needed the cleaning up, but he was disappointed with what little information his stay there earned him. Next, he headed for the Union Pacific office where he got off a wire to the boys, letting them know he had arrived and wondering if they had found out anything there.

Walking back to the Prairie Flower, he passed a shop that had a long wooden shingle in the shape of a rifle, and it reminded him of Zimmermann's in Dodge City. Not really needing anything he should have passed on by, but being a man who appreciated fine weaponry, he didn't.

The shop was not well lit; still he enjoyed the works of a fine metal artist, as well as the smells of gun oils and powder.

---

5 Tonsorial: Barber.

The proprietor was a one-armed man who still wore his blue kepi, and Cliff immediately was on guard for any animosity born a decade past to spring forth. He was sure as soon as he opened his mouth, his homeland would be revealed, and he would have to deal with another bitter Yankee. He had seen more prejudices against southerners in Kansas than niggers ever received in Georgia, and he had little reason to believe Nebraska would be different.

With a friendly smile the gunsmith asked if he could help him.

"Naw, just admiring your stock," Cliff replied as he prepared himself for the onslaught.

"Sure," the short man said with no sign of hostilities, "let me know if I can help."

"I see you have several of the new Winchesters, have they chambered it fer Colonel Colt's 45 yet?"

"No, I'm afraid the rim on that round will never hold up to Winchester's extractors. I do hear rumors that Colt might be coming out with a version that takes the 44 Winchester, now that Remington has chambered their revolvers for it too."

"Oh, I didn't know that," Cliff replied.

He had seen the new guns offered by both Colt and Winchester and realized they were much stronger made than what he carried. Cliff was convinced the only way to go was to have ones long gun and short guns utilize the same cartridge, and that is why he stuck with the less powerful Henry round in his Open Tops and Yellowboy.

The man offered him a new nickel-plated pistol to hold. "I just got this one in and it is chambered for the 44 WCF which is our most popular rifle round these days."

Cliff could see the resemblance to the old Army Remingtons that the Union troops had so often carried, but this gun seemed to be better trimmed or something. The wide trigger felt good, and he believed it to be a great improvement. He had to admit the revolver had a good feel and balance.

It was tempting, he always was a sucker for a new gun, but to change would be more than just buying a new pistol and rifle. He had large stocks of Henry cartridges, and he had seen to it that both the Adams boys would be carrying Open Top Colts. "Naw, I reckon not at this time," he said and handed the silver pistol back to the man, who nodded his head.

Looking about again, Cliff noticed by far the majority of the store's stock consisted of former war guns, particularly a large number of Spencer carbines. It made sense and he started to leave when, almost as a joke, he asked, "You wouldn't have a Whitworth would you?"

"You know I do, with bullet mold and all. An ol' Johnny Reb came in here six maybe eight year ago, not long after I lost my appendage when a damn Sioux bastard buried his tomahawk in my arm; caused me to have to muster out," he said, and then turning, he added without looking back at Cliff, "now where is that ol' jewel?"

The man went into a backroom where he rummaged around for a couple minutes and then returned with the long rifle. "Here it is, I got 'a do some more looking fer the molds, that's one rifle what won't stabilize nothing but the right bullets, if you want to hit anything, that is," he added.

Cliff looked at the old piece. It had a long barrel, well over 30 inches. The lock was marked Whitworth in front of the hammer with sheaf and crown over a W at the rear of the lock. The barrel was marked "Whitworth Patent". It had '52 bore'[6]proof marks on the left rear of the barrel. The butt-plate was checkered, as was the trigger. The stock was also checkered at the wrist and forearm. He smiled when he saw the 'C.S.' stamped at the rear of the barrel and on the tang of the butt-plate. Of course, there were many dents in the wood, and there was some rust pitting on the top of the barrel near where the front sight should have been, evidence of blood, he suspected. There, on the left side was what he assumed was a mount for one of the telescopic sights, but it was gone; in fact there were no sights on the gun at all, but otherwise it was sound and tight.

Finally, the man came out of the backroom with sweat sprouting from his forehead. "I found them!" he exclaimed excitedly.

"Good," Cliff said.

"Have you checked the bore?"

"No," Cliff replied as if the man should have known he had no way to do so.

"Oh you'll love it, just as sharp and clean as the day it left England. That ol' Reb sure knew how to take care of a fine weapon."

"What happened to the sights?"

---

6 52 bore: The lands in a Whitworth were 0.52 inches and the grooves were 0.541.

"Oh, it had one of those new looking glass sights on it when he brought it in, but that thing was busted, and he didn't have the money to have it fixed. That's why I ended up with the gun. I traded him a new 50 Government trapdoor even and he let me have his ol' gurl here. I meant to fix her up and take some buffalo, but the truth is that damn Sioux finished my hunting days forever, so she just got pushed back in the corner yonder and was almost forgot about."

"How much?" Cliff asked.

"Oh, 'al you pay ten fer it, with the bullet molds? I had ten in the trapdoor."

"Sold," Cliff replied and reached into his vest pocket and took out one of the Yankee twenty-dollar greenbacks.

A Confederate Whitworth .451 Sharpshooter

"Don't see many civilians with payroll money," the old soldier said, folding and then pulling the bill out straight again.

"Yeah, I won it in a poker game from a Master Sergeant down in Wichita some time back, been saving it for just the right thing," Cliff lied.

"If you want to leave this here for a couple a' days I can get you some sights from Omaha and install them fer ya', iron sights that is, can't get them glass globe sights 'cept from England."

"No, actually it's a gift for a friend, and I will let him choose what sights he wants."

"Oh, I see, that's pretty nice of you, must be a good friend."

"Yes, he is," Cliff confirmed folding the two red backs he had received as change, and placed them into his pocket. Picking up the Whitworth, he started out, then stopped and looked back, "Been a pleasure a meeting ya mister," Cliff said and then went on out.

Heading straight back to his room to deposit the rifle, the clerk called out to him as he entered, "Sir, you have a telegram."

"Thank you," Cliff said and took the folded yellow paper and placed it in his pocket and headed on upstairs to his room.

Upon entering his room he laid the big gun on the bed. Cliff felt good about discovering the piece, he knew it would please Ethan immensely.

He then poured some water into the washbowl resting on the small table, and rinsed his face, hoping the cool water would ease his headache. Then after drying his hands, he reached into the right breast pocket of his vest and took out the telegram and unfolded it.

His emotions were mixed as he did so. Perhaps it would be good news, but a gnawing gall in his gut promised it would be otherwise. Still, he could not put it off so slowly he opened the wire and read:

> REB BROWN PRAIRIE FLOWER HOTEL KEARNEY NEBRASKA
> STOP
>
> SHEP DONE GOT THROWED IN JAIL OVER A WOMAN
> STOP
>
> NO SIGN OF MOUTON
> END
>
> SIGNED ETHAN ADAMS

Cliff took a deep breath and slowly let it out as he refolded the paper. *'I would have liked to stay longer and looked deeper, but the truth is, it appears either Tidwell did not get off the train here, and if that is so, it will be a long hard and cold trail to pick up; or he never got on the train to begin with.'* This was something he had been running around in his head ever since he began wondering why Tidwell would make a point of telling the clerk in Cheyenne of what his plans were to begin with. *'It is not like him to intentionally leave a trail, unless it is a wild goose trail,'* he thought.

"Cheyenne is where I will begin again," he said aloud.

The next day he was pleased to find the army had ordered an animal car, and there was room for Ola.

It began to snow before they left Kearney, and from the size of the flakes, he figured it to be a big storm.

James Donald Moore came to Cheyenne with the first herd Charles Goodnight brought this far north. He and his pal Clay Allison had been riding herd a few nights before trail's end and had quietly drifted off two hundred head into a box canyon just south of the Colorado border. The grass was plentiful there, and there was a small, fast moving creek flowing out of the mountains through the canyon. With little effort, they had the beeves settled down, and a make-shift rope gate to discourage their leaving and were back with the main herd before the other outriders missed them.

Carl Watson did ask Jimmy Don where he had been, as he had not seen him in his last pass, but Moore explained, "I got me a bout with the flux and have been off my horse in the bushes nigh on as much as I have been on it. Say Carl, you ain't got no Calomel with ya do ya?"

"Naw, but Cookey has some back at the wagon."

"Wal' I'll try and make out till I'm relieved, hate to wake 'im up, or I might not get no breakfast."

"Yah, he can be ornery at times," Watson agreed before he touched his heel to his cayuse's ribs and moved off into the night, softly uttering a drowsy hymn about riding an old paint and leading an old dun.

After being paid off in Cheyenne, the two rode back and checked on the little bunch and found them quite content with their new home.

Jimmy Don stayed on with the small herd while Clay hurried back to the city to sell them to cattle speculators.

While there, Clay found favors with a young lady. He was in her room at Frenchy's, when the noise coming from the room next to hers became so loud Clay, clad only in his new Boss of the Plains Stetson and tall boots, walked out onto the balcony in full view of everyone in the bar below, kicked open the door to the offending room, and started firing away with his 44 Colt. The gentleman in the room received a dangerous wound when he dove through the glass window and landed on his shoulder and back in the street below. Unfortunately, the lady, who had been so delightful in causing the noise, was hit by one of Allison's stray balls, and was found sitting in the bed with a hole in her naked chest.

Immediately, locals who frequented Frenchy's and knew the poor girl, started after the shooter. Allison, seeing he was out-numbered and holding an empty revolver, followed his earlier target and leaped from the window to the alley below, landing only yards from the previous jumper, who was being tended to for a broken collarbone by the local sawbones.

Ten minutes later, when the triumphant crowd had returned to the bar to rejoice their, running a Texican out a' town, Clay rode his pony through the front doors of the saloon. He was clad still only in his boots and hat, but now he was brandishing two of Colonel Colt's horse pistols, with which he shot the bar to pieces, scattering the crowd, before making good his escape.

Jimmy Don, of course knew nothing of his partner's escapade, and three days later, after becoming bored with his present company, also rode into Cheyenne. Finding others of the Goodnight outfit, he learned how Clay was last seen southbound, hooting and hollering and waving his new hat.

The young Texican considered the loss of Clay Allison as a partner a blessing. Jimmy Don waited three weeks, until all the men he had rode up from New Mexico with, were headed back south. Then he hired two vaqueros and brought his little herd north and west of Cheyenne. He had scouted around and had found a good spring that looked to always hold water, a tributary of South Crow Creek, some fifteen miles southeast of Laramie, and there he camped with his beeves.

Jimmy Don Moore was not yet twenty-two years old, but he had come from a family where money was precious; he knew how to skimp and save and not to waste it on foolishness like so many of his friends had done. His pay from Goodnight had been a sizeable amount, and from it, he retained one hundred dollars in folding money, printed by *The Bank of Denver*, as operating capital. The remainder he rolled tightly and placed in his slicker, which he folded as small as he could get it; he then tied this with a new rope and buried it next to a lonesome cottonwood that looked as if it only drank when snow was on the ground.

By the time *The Union Pacific* and *The Central Pacific* finally agreed upon a point of rendezvous, in May of 1869, Jimmy Don had filed on the land. Now, by trading steers for cows and accruing a few mavericks that seemed to stray from their owners, he had a small herd of some five hundred or more head hanging around his spring.

He only hired Mexican employees because they worked harder than coloreds, and the white cowboys required twice the pay as either of them.

He had a nice-sized one-room house that had first been built of sod, but he had rocked it in during his second summer; now only the grass growing on the roof gave away its interior structure.

The one thing Jimmy Don did miss was the company of a white woman, and his only vice was to ride into Cheyenne or Laramie a couple times a month to visit a house of pleasure.

One night, while in Laramie, he came upon a girl who had only started working there that week. Her hair was the color of corn silk during its early bloom, and her skin was as fair as he had ever seen. Before he left the next morning, he had convinced her he was an up and coming rancher and would be quite rich in a very few years. When he returned two days later she rode beside him in his buckboard to the *Circle Rocking AR Ranch*.

Jimmy Don had chosen to name his land and register his brand as such because he was originally from Amarillo, but he now lived in the Rockies. It also did not hurt that the Circle A was a large ranch along the Colorado line, near the old Willow Springs stage station and bordering Israel Godfrey's spread.

The Circle Rocking AR Brand

Elaine Dumas did see a future there when she emerged from the only door of her new home, however she had not been impressed with the accommodations offered at Jimmy Don's mansion.

None-the-less, Elaine obliged Jimmy Don in every aspect of a good and faithful wife, save one. They had never been married in the legal way. She was, of course, his common-law wife but not his married wife.

In return for her affection, he had built her a fine ranch home just a short hundred feet from the old rock one he had found plenty suitable as a single man. The new house was of clapboard with pane glass in the windows and a wooden floor. It was three steps from the ground and had a porch on both the front and the rear. There was a trap door that would allow one to either enter the root cellar he had dug under the house or serve as a means to drop down under the cover of the house to return fire in the event of hostile attacks. Elaine was well pleased with her new home. It was as good as, or better than, any other in south Wyoming, except of course for the very wealthy, which she did not socialize with anyway.

Their ramrod, Gilberto Rodriguez, now lived in the old house with his three sons and three nephews.

Fall roundup had located six hundred head wearing the Circle Rocking AR brand with several of the heifers expecting to drop calves come spring.

The first day of November found the ranch cold and still. The storm started the evening before but had laid for a few hours. Some time past the two o'clock hour it set in again, this time with steady large flakes of powder. By sunup, there was a white blanket covering the whole of Wyoming Territory. Before noon, the snow was nigh on three feet deep, and Jimmy Don and his Mexican cowboys were out trying to round up as many of their beeves as they could and herd them back to the ranch house area. In one draw, where the snow was accumulating rapidly, they found a hundred or more head bunched together for warmth, as well as the comfort of company. It took them the remainder of the day to get these back to safety.

The snow continued throughout the night and stopped only an hour after sunup on the second.

"It's so still; it's eerie," he said to her when they returned near the noon hour, "I never seen it so still out there."

"Wal', just wait an hour, and it will be blowing your shirt tail off. This here's Wyoming, you know," she replied, setting a heavy skillet of brown biscuits on the table. Reaching to the single kitchen shelf, she retrieved a can of molasses before placing it beside the skillet.

"How many did you find?"

"We did alright; got maybe three hundred around the ranch here and another couple hundred over next to the spring," he said, lifting his old blue cup high so as to down the last of his hot coffee before he reached for the bread. "I guess we're bound to have lost some, but it ain't too bad."

The next day, as sure as if she had brought a spell to the land with her remarks, a wind came rushing in from the southwest and blew ninety-percent of the snow to Nebraska and the Dakotas. Save for around the buildings and peeled fence posts of the corral, the ground was as clear of the powder as if it had never dropped the first flake.

It was then Gilberto Rodriguez came up on the front porch and spoke as he pointed, "Señor' Jimmy, there in the corral; you had better come see."

"What is it?" Elaine asked looking towards the barn and their old house where a large bunch of cattle was milling around.

Jimmy Don did not reply to either of them. Instead, he stepped from the porch and briskly walked where the vaquero was pointing.

When he returned, she could not tell if he was smiling or gritting his teeth.

"What's wrong?"

"That bunch we found huddled up in the draw."

"Yes."

"Wal', every head of them is Circle A stock. More than two hundred looks to be."

"What you gon'a do?"

"Don't ask stupid questions woman, just keep the coffee hot. We got some work cut out fer us today."

The remainder of the day was spent re-branding the rescued stock before setting them out to graze on their own.

That night she told him she was worried, "I just got this bad feeling. I don't know why or what brung it on, but for the first time since I come here, I'm scared."

"Scared a' what?"

"That's just it," she said as she lay beside him. "I don't know what it is; just scared." She reached over and placing her arms around him, drew herself up close to his back and held on tightly.

He could feel her quivering but was not sure if it was from fright or the cold, and he was too tuckered out to be doing any messing around if that was what she wanted.

After a while, she spoke, "Jimmy Don,"

"Huh?"

"I want to get married."

"What fer?" he asked annoyed.

"I want to have your name, that's why. If something wus to happen to you I would have nothing."

"Ain't nothing going to happen to me. Ol' Gil and his boys take better care of me than the army did General Lee."

"Still, I want to get married."

"We'll talk about it after we find all our stock and see how many we lost. We'll be a needing to go to town fer supplies by then anyway."

The same storm that fell on Moore's ranch almost kept Cliff from returning to Cheyenne. The build-up was so deep, that when the winds did come, they caused the tracks east of Cheyenne to be buried in a drift higher than the locomotive's smoke stack, and the engine almost was derailed before the engineer was able to stop her.

For several hours, the railroad workmen, and finally most every male passenger, were out in the ground blizzard, clearing the tracks with everything from huge shovels to their bare hands. Finally, just as the sun was rising on the third, Ol' # 17 pulled to a stop in front of the Cheyenne Depot and Hotel.

In town, there was twelve inches of snow still around any and everything that could cause a drift, some places more.

As soon as Cliff had Ola stabled, he walked back to *The Dyers House*.

Ethan was in his room looking pretty gloomy when Cliff walked in. He had a good sized shiner on his right eye and a cut that looked quite swollen on the left side of his lower lip. The tall lad was both glad and sorrowful to see his older friend.

"Alright," Cliff said as he removed his heavy coat, "tell me what happened."

"Wal', you know Shep. He's a sucker for a purty face an' he see'd this little red-haired gal working in Frenchy's. A new one, anyway, he just up and wanted to take her home with him."

"Seems like I've heard this before," Cliff replied.

"Wal', you know Shep."

"Yeah, I know Shep," he said nodding his head as he dropped his revolver belt[7] on the bed.

"Wal'," the boy twisted his head and nodded a little, "it do seem like she shines to him too, only Big Ed had invested in her trans

Ol' Number 17 stuck between Pine Bluffs and Cheyenne

---

7 Revolver belt: Until WW I the use of belts to hold up ones trousers was practically nonexistent. The only belt used by a man on the frontier was to secure his revolver holster to his body, sometimes simply called a gunbelt.

portation from Texas," he paused and again twisted his head some before admitting, "along with several other new girls. Seems he wants no new romances taking place until she has worked off his investment, and he says he wants $1000.00 before he will let her go," Ethan said and then asked, "That ain't legal; is it Reb?"

"It ain't legal in Dixie, but this here Territory is run mostly by Yankees. They seem to make their own laws."

"What can we do, Reb?"

"What kind a' charges they got on Shep?"

"Wal', he did cold-cock a deputy who tried to stop him from taking her out a' Frenchy's."

"Great," Cliff replied as he stood, and began rolling up his sleeves as he walked over to the table. There he poured water from a pitcher into the bowl provided for such. After washing his face he began to shave away the last several day's beard.

Wiping his face clean he looked at his reflection in the fading old mirror. *'Gaud, I sure look awful,'* he thought. *'This here man chasing will age a fellow before his time.'*

Finally, looking up, he espied the desperate expression on his young friend's face, so he tossed the towel hard on the table and said, "Tomorrow, I'll go to the Sheriff's Office and see what I can do." Taking a deep breath he turned and added, "Now, let's go to Frenchy's; I want to see the girl that caused all this trouble." Then looking at his young friend he added, "Oh, I near forgot; unroll my blanket yonder."

Doing as he was told, Ethan's expression suddenly changed completely. "Oh my Gawd, where ever did you find this?" he asked with tears building in his young eyes.

Ethan held the Whitworth in his hands, turned it over, and gazed at the old rifle as one would a long lost toy from their youth.

Feeling as though he needed to say something, Cliff spoke, "There in the little bag is the bullet mold; I understand it needs special bullets to shoot true."

"Yes, yes it does, they need the elongated hexagonal bullets because of the faster rate of twist," Ethan replied as if he was repeating the exact words an instructor said to him many years before.

"Sorry about the sights; it had one of them telescopic tubes, and it wus busted, but there are a few of them funny looking bullets in there too."

"No bother, I'll get some sights for a Sharps; should work just fine," Ethan said, and then looking at his old friend, he managed, "Thanks Reb, what do I owe you?"

"It's your birthday present."

"But it's not my birthday."

"Will be 'afore long," Cliff said, and then placing his hat on his head, he finished the conversation with, "Come on; let's go."

The walk to the saloon was short, and as soon they were inside, Ethan immediately walked to the long bar, but Cliff turned right and moved over to where several men were bucking the tiger[8] at of couple tables.

Cliff had given Ethan instructions that once inside, to act like they were strangers, yet somehow to point out the girl.

He walked slowly as he approached the men, his eyes scanning every inch of the saloon as he moved.

The room was perhaps thirty feet wide and fifty feet long. The bar was on the north side, with the tables along the opposite wall and a stairway leading to the second-floor rooms where the girls plied their most profitable trade.

Cliff could see three saloon girls moving around the room trying to get the men to buy them drinks, but all of them were dark-haired. Finally, one approached him and asked if he was new in town.

"Yes, as a matter of fact, I am, and I heard you got a red-haired lass working here."

"Oh, you mean Ethel, she's with a customer."

"I'll wait," he said moving over to the bar and stopping close to Ethan.

"Give me a rye," he said to the barkeep as the short man approached.

"And the lady?" the man suggested.

"Why not," he replied, "give her one too," Cliff agreed.

When the man returned, he set the two glasses down on the bar in front of them; then stepped over to where Ethan was standing.

"You again, didn't you learn enough already?"

"I ain't looking fer trouble. I just want a drink."

Cliff could see the glass the man sat in front of the whore was a much lighter shade than his, and while he was talking to Ethan, she

---

8 Bucking The Tiger: Playing Faro.

looked over at the boy with the beat up face. While her attention was on Ethan, he switched the glasses.

After looking back at Cliff, she said as she picked up her shot glass, "Why you want her? I can show you a lot better time than she can."

Cliff looked back at her and smiled, "I always wanted to see if them red- headed women were red on the bottom like they is on top."

"Wal', I can tell you that," she said giving him a smile.

Cliff raised his glass, "Here's to purty women," he said and downed the drink, immediately realizing there was very little whiskey in the water glass.

She did likewise, but when the strong drink rushed down her throat, she gasped and coughed. The moment she caught her breath, she shot a dirty look at the barkeep and tried to curse him, but the scalding of her throat only allowed a whisper to come from what would have otherwise been a scream, "Damn you, Charlie!"

She continued to cough for a few seconds as she tried to get her breath back. The bartender only returned a puzzled expression at her.

At that time, a door opened on the second floor, and a big man with a tall- crowned hat came out pulling a suspender over his shoulder; behind him followed a small girl with strawberry hair and freckles.

Ethan coughed himself, loudly, when he saw her.

"Sorry honey," Cliff said to the whore beside him. "I never mess with a woman who can't handle her liquor."

Moving away without giving her a chance to reply, he headed to the stairs.

When the little redhead reached the bottom step, he stepped close and said, "I'd like a few minutes of your time, Miss."

She sighed, and then in a soft voice replied, "Look mister, I just had a rough time with that big galoot, and I need some rest."

"You'll be pleased with me," he responded.

"Can't you go with one of the other gurls?"

At that moment, a big man stepped through a back door and immediately looked at her.

Cliff recognized a moment of fright sweep over her face, and he turned and looked at the man she was gazing at.

Big Ed was not more that five-foot-nine inches, but he had very wide shoulders and a huge belly that reflected his easy life. Still, when he moved towards them, he walked with a confidence that doesn't come from living a bluff. Cliff suspected he was not a man to get into a fist-a-cuff with.

Taking her by the elbow, and stepping on the stairs he whispered, "Come on; I ain't going to hurt you."

She knew she had to go with him, or she would be in serious trouble with Big Ed; from the beating he gave Shep and his brother, she did not want him hitting her.

As soon as they entered the room, she began to undress.

'*She is sure purty,*' Cliff thought and would have enjoyed having her continue, but he knew that Shep would not have wanted him to see the woman he thought he was in love with naked; so he reached over and touched her arm, stopping her.

"Look, I'm not here to enjoy your pleasures. I'm a friend of Shep Adams."

She looked up and then quickly at the door.

A moment later when she composed herself, she took a deep breath and asked, "What do you want?"

"I want to know about you. About what your intentions are with Shep," he replied softly.

She was frightened, but his voice was so soothing, somehow she suddenly felt safe being close to him.

Shaking her head, she said, "There ain't no Shep and me. Not a chance. Big Ed won't let me go."

"How much do you owe him, really?"

"I don't know, we all agreed to come here and work the winter. He said there was good pay in it."

"Did he pay your way?"

"Yes, I suppose so. Somebody did," she replied shaking her head slightly.

Suddenly, she realized she was standing there in a thin camisole and her bloomers and she felt indecent. She walked over to a hook on the wall near the window, removed a cotton robe, and covered herself.

"How long you been in the business?"

"This is the first job I ever had, where I had to do this."

"Why did you come here?" he asked now shaking his head.

"My sister lives here som'ers. She is married to a big rancher near here," she said looking through the window at the snow just beginning to fall again.

"You don't know who her husband is?"

"It's Don; she wrote saying she was marrying Jimmy Don, but I can't find no ranch around here owned by anybody named Don."

"How much do you make for bringing a body up here?"

"I charge three-dollars, Big Ed gets one for the room, one against my debt to him, and I get to keep one." She again let out a heavy sigh, "I reckon I'll be poking cowboys till I'm a old woman of thirty."

Cliff then stood, reached into his pocket, and gave her a twenty-dollar green back. Then said, "Go tell Big Ed I bought you for the remainder of the night. If he gives you a hard time, just scream out, and I'll come a runnin'."

She looked at him and seemed to have a huge load lifted from her. Smiling slightly she said, "Thank you," before she turned for the door.

"By the way," he said stopping her.

She turned back to look at him with an expression of question and a little fright.

"Thirty ain't old," he said, remembering he was now past thirty.

She smiled before saying, "I'm sorry. I'll be right back."

After they had talked over an hour, Cliff was convinced she was truly an unfortunate girl being forced into white slavery by either Big Ed or someone who Big Ed did business with. He was also convinced she did indeed have affection for Shep Adams.

"I'm going to try and slip out the back stairs, if I make it, I want you to go downstairs and buy a bottle from the bar, and pay for it with this," he gave her a silver dollar. "Then be sure the barkeep hears you say you have to go to the little house. That should let you out the back door, and if anyone starts looking for you, the barkeep may be able to delay them."

He looked at her, and she looked frightened again.

"Do you savvy?"

She nodded her head and looked up at him through big blue eyes.

When he reached for the doorknob, she asked, "What if they stop me?"

"Then just bring the bottle back up here and wait. If you don't show up in a while, I'll come back here."

She nodded her head in agreement, but he was not sure she had the courage to go through with it.

He had been standing in the dark behind the outhouse for almost fifteen minutes, and the falling snow and freezing cold were beginning to become almost unbearable.

Two people had come out to use the house, but neither were Ethel.

Just as he decided something had gone wrong, the door opened again, and dim light bathed a narrow strip across the alley with a yellow ribbon.

Once more, he moved back into the shadows.

This time there were two people, a large man and a small woman. When the two reached the little house, the man told her to go ahead; he would wait. She said no, she would wait. This went back and forth for several exchanges.

Cliff had long since recognized the voice of the woman to be Ethel, and he finally stepped out and dropped the man with a slap across the back of the drunk's neck with the barrel of his Colt.

"Come on," he said, and before the man was fully down, he had her by the wrist and was leading her away.

"Where are we going?"

"Just trust me and keep up," he replied as he made as much time as he could without running and attracting attention from anyone who might venture out of one of the other saloons that also backed up to this alley.

They went up the back stairs of *The Dyers House* and moved cautiously down the hall until they reached the room. He softly knocked twice on the door before a voice came from inside, "Who is it?"

"Reb."

The door opened immediately, and Ethan stepped out, "Man, am I glad ___," he stopped mid-sentence when he saw who was standing behind his friend. "How did you___?"

Cliff placed his hand on the young man's chest and shoved him back inside the room before he could say any more. Then he stepped aside and motioned her in also. Finally, after taking a quick look back down the hall, he too entered, closed and locked the door.

Lifting his finger to his lips, he motioned for them to be quiet. Then, softly, he spoke, "Ethel, do you have anyone that you can trust? A friend, anyone?"

She slowly shook her head, "There's a gurl, Jenny that works at Frenchy's, but she is afraid of Big Ed," she sighed. "Everyone is."

"Nobody else?"

"Only my sister, but I don't know where she is."

Cliff shook his head before he ran his fingers through his dark hair. Finally, after thinking for some time, he turned and looked her over really well for the first time. *'She's short and purty thin. Not much older than what a body would call a child, but she doesn't look frail, and I'm inclined to take a chance.'*

Turning to Ethan he spoke softly but with force, "Tomorrow, they will find her missing and start looking for me. It should not take Big Ed long to wonder if Shep had something to do with her disappearance, and then they will be looking for you too," he said nodding at him. "So Ethan, the first thing come morning, I want you to go to the depot and buy two tickets for Omaha."

Turning to her he said, "You stay here, and don't open that door for nobody; 'cept one of us." Then looking hard at her he added, "Do you savvy?"

She nodded her head before she softly replied, "Yes Sur."

"What are you going to be doing?" Ethan questioned.

"I'm going to jail," Cliff replied.

They both looked at him with astonished expressions.

That night, he and Ethan stayed in his room but he was up and dressed before first light. Awakening the boy, he said, "Get up and get dressed. I want you at the depot as soon as they open for the Six AM."

"Yes Sur," Ethan replied as he sleepily yawned.

"Should I wake her?"

"My guess is she didn't sleep."

Cliff left by the back stairs, and went straight to the livery where he saddled Ola along with the mounts he recognized belonged to the Adams brothers. Next, he awoke the hostler, paid their account, and rented a spirited little Pinto for two days.

Riding Ola and leading the other three, he headed into town.

First, he tied the Paint and Ethan's pony to the hitching post at the rear of *The Dyers House.* Then he led Shep's mount behind him, as he headed for the county jail.

There was no one in the front office when he went in. The room was still and cold so he placed a couple split cottonwood branches in the old flat stove and started a fire using some wanted posters as kindling. As soon as he was satisfied the fire would catch up, he placed the half-empty coffee pot on the stove with a loud bang and waited.

"What the hell?" came from one of the cells in the rear.

"Got your coffee going," he called back.

"Huh?"

"It's cold in here, thought I would start ya' fire and get ya' coffee going."

Soon a lanky man came out pulling his suspenders over his shoulders.

"Who the hell are you?"

"Name's Brown, I've come to bail out one of my boys."

"What you talking about?"

"You got one of my boys locked up in here, don't you?"

"I don't know what you are talking about," the jailer said.

"Shep Adams, you got him back there, don't you?"

"Yeah, but?"

"I told you; I'm Brown. I brung up four thousand head from Texas, and I'm supposed to deliver them to a Mr. Walcott here. He's expecting me," Cliff said, and then turning slowly and looking directly at the deputy, he continued, "And you got my Tally-man locked up. I can't deliver them unless I got my Tally-man to do the counting."

"I don't know, Big Ed said ___."

"I don't know, nor do I care about no Big Ed. I just know and care about them four thousand head out there in the snow with very little grass to be grazing on. Now Mr. Walcott done already agreed on a price fer the hold herd, and the longer they starve, the less they are going to weigh when he ships 'em, and the madder he is going to be at you."

Deputy Stillwell studied hard. *Walcott is the most powerful politician in the county, maybe the whole territory. It were him who put the Sheriff in office.*

"You need to get you another counter."

"Nope, he's the best. You don't want to cooperate I'll just go wake up Walcott."

"No, wait," he studied as he rubbed the whiskers on his chin. "You say you gon'a pay his bail?"

"Yes Sur," Cliff replied and then added, "And have him back for the trial 'cause I've done got witnesses what aim to testify that he was ram-rodded."

"His bail is a hundred dollars," Stillwell said back figuring the amount would settle his problems.

"Chicken feed, considering on the amount I could lose without him a' counting," Cliff replied as he reached into his vest pocket and retrieved a roll of greenbacks. Pealing off five, he stopped and looked at the Deputy and then laid one more down in front of the lawman. "Cause you are so understanding and need, I suspect, some entertainment yourself."

The deputy took the last bill and folding it, slipped it into a pocket in his pants. He then put the others in the drawer of the desk before reaching for a large ring of keys.

Shep was still asleep when they began unlocking his cell door. The noise awakened him and looking up he said, "Huh, oh howdy, Reb," with sleep still showing in his left eye. His right one was so swollen and blue, he couldn't get it open.

"What's this?" Cliff said harshly as he reached over and taking Shep's jaw in his strong hand, he turned it so the bruised eye was facing the deputy.

"He resisted," the lawman said back defensively.

"If this bad eye causes him not to make a good count, I'll be back, and there'll be hell to pay."

Shep looked at him questioningly, but Cliff hurried him along before he could say anything that would upset the applecart.

As they were passing the desk in the outer office, he paused and turning to Stillwell asked, in a most demanding voice, "Where's my revolver?"

The deputy stopped cold, then reluctantly turned and walked back to where he had been sleeping. There, hanging over a low bunk, was the cartridge belt, holster and Colt he had taken off Shep. It was obvious to all he had been planning to keep this prize for himself, but now caught in his own thievery, he retrieved it. Bringing it out, he shoved it at the young cowboy, "Here."

"Thank you, Deputy," Cliff said, and then taking Shep by the arm, he led the boy out the front door and around to where the horses were tied.

"Where we going?" Shep asked, surprised at the mounts waiting there for them.

"We're getting out of town before that lawman finds out I ain't got no four thousand head of beeves already sold to old man Walcott."

"I ain't going without, Ellie."

"Ethel is waiting with your brother, at the depot."

"What?"

"You can stand there looking like a blame idiot if you want, but the three of us are making tracks out of this here burg and pronto. Whether you are with us or not, is your business."

Ethan and the girl went to the depot as instructed and bought two tickets on the westbound. After making sure the telegrapher saw her board with him, they sat by the window waiting anxious minutes for the train to pull away.

Cliff and Shep headed south, leading the other two horses. As soon as they were beyond the view of anyone from town, they turned northwest and began the long uphill run to Sherman Station, where he knew the train had to stop after the climb.

Both men and animals were winded before they reached the 8000' elevation; however, they were only three miles from the little village when they saw the train slowly pass by.

While the locomotive was taking on water, Ethan and Ethel slipped off the north side of the car and hurried behind the small building, that served as depot and telegraph office. After the train pulled away, they waited there in the cold howling wind for almost twenty minutes, before spotting the riders approaching from the southeast.

Jimmy Don had indeed kept his promise. When they went to Laramie for supplies, he had made her his wife. As a wedding present, he employed Lawyer King to draw up and record a will showing she was a full partner in his ranch.

That night when they returned to the spread, Elaine made Jimmy Don realize just how much she appreciated him making her his wife.

The following morning, he and two of Rodriguez' sons were riding north, looking for a large bull Jimmy Don especially liked and had not seen since the big snow. An hour out, they spotted a couple of riders, laying low over their saddles, in a stand of trembling poplar[9] on the top of a small knoll.

---

9 Trembling Poplar: Local name for Aspen trees.

Jimmy immediately turned towards them, spurring his mount in their direction, "Come on; let's see who's on my land."

Just before the trio reached the trees, another dozen mounted men came into view.

"Holy Mother!" Carlos exclaimed when he saw the number, pulling up short.

Cliff's plans were to go on to Laramie and there wait until the weather broke, before heading on north in search of Tidwell.

As the four came over a hummock, they saw the lone horse standing with its head down. It was obvious it had been ridden there, as the saddle was still on, and tightly cinched.

Cliff dismounted and looked the old bay over. The Mexican saddle was not fancy and obviously belonged to a vaquero, rather than a caballero[10]. Walking around to the other side, his gloved hand touched the small trail of blood that had run down the left fender.

"The hombre this cayuse belongs to is hurt. We best spread out and have a look-see," he said rubbing his wet finger and thumb together.

Leading the bay, they began their search. In a few hundred yards, at the bottom of a small draw, they found Carlos. He had a rifle ball in his right thigh, and he had lost a lot of blood. Had it not been for the freezing temperatures, he would have been dead long before.

Cliff took a bottle of rye from his saddlebags and pressed it to the lad's lips. A small amount entered his quivering mouth, and he began to cough.

"Who shot you boy?"

"Help," he struggled out. "Señor Don, he needs help."

"Where do you live?" Cliff asked.

"Rock'n AR," he finally got out before returning his attention to what he considered his duty, "Señor Don, he need help."

"Where is this Rocking AR?"

"Southwest, three miles, me-bee, but Señor Don," he emphasized, pointing north with his last conscious movement.

Cliff lowered the boy back on the frozen prairie, then stood straight and shook his head. "Let's bandage up that wound and then we can tie him in his saddle. Then we'll go looking for Señor Don," he said.

---

10 Caballero: Wealthy rancher, a Cavalier, or gentleman.

They had difficulty following the tracks on the hard ground but finally cut a trail where several shod horses had come from the west, headed in the general direction of Cheyenne.

Cliff looked at the trail and knew it was not old. *'Is this the trail of Señor Don, or were these riders coming from the fight where the Mexican boy was shot?'* he wondered and looked to his left. *'The country here is rolling; and even though it appears rather flat, in reality, there are many depressions and hills that could hide a small army.'*

More on a hunch than solid evidence, he turned Ola west towards a knoll some mile and a half away, where a stand of timber could be seen.

They were a full hundred yards from the trees when Cliff suddenly pulled-up. In a motion as smooth and as quick as if it had been planned and practiced for hours, he pulled his carbine from its scabbard.

The others were surprised at his sudden move, and Shep said loudly, "What in tarnation?"

Pointing with his Winchester towards the aspen, Reb felt nothing needed to be said. Looking at his lead, they too soon spotted the pair of men swinging from the tree limbs, twisting slowing in the wind, and they all heard her gasp.

"Better stay back with your lady-friend, Shep," Cliff ordered before touching his heels to Ola's ribs. Immediately the stout stallion moved slowly forward, followed by Ethan's mount.

The dead men, another Mexican boy and a white man only a few years older, had been stiff a long time before Reb and Ethan lowered them to the ground. Pinned to the coat of the white man was a brown piece of paper on which was crudely written, with a charcoal stick, *Cattle Rustler*.

Cliff found in the man's vest pocket a receipt from a lawyer King in Laramie to Jimmy Don Moore, Circle Rocking AR Ranch, Albany County, Wyoming Territory.

"I think we have found Señor Don," he said, as he folded the paper and placed it in his own coat pocket.

"Look around, and see if you can find their horses," he added as he gazed out across the frozen desert.

Thirty minutes later, Ethan returned. "Looked good Reb, and they ain't no whar' close. No tracks neither; must a' been with that bunch what made that trail we cut back yonder," he said shaking his head, as he pointed to their back trail.

"Yeah, we'll put the boy there on the horse with the other Mex, and Ethel, you ride double with Shep. We'll have to put the bigger one on your little paint; can't expect that scrawny ol' bay to carry all three," Reb said, with a sigh.

It was no easy job getting the stiff bodies tied on the saddles, but after they all pitched in, it was finally accomplished.

"Where we taking them?" Ethel asked.

"The boy said the ranch was south west, and we are headed west anyhow," Cliff replied as he mounted the big Appaloosa. "Reckon we can look for it. If we don't find it, we'll take them on into Laramie."

The temperature dropped another twenty degrees as soon as the sun slipped behind the not-too-distant mountains, and Cliff started to worry about their own welfare. He had not figured on this diversion. They could have made Laramie City before dark, had they not run into the hurt boy. Now he had a shot up Mexican kid, two youngsters, and a half-grown girl out on the prairie. Also, the clouds that had held in some of the earth's warmth were slipping away to the east, leaving bright stars dancing in a clear sky.

'Back in Georgia, when the sun goes down the wind stops, but not out here,' he thought looking slowly around, as they continued riding facing the ever present zephyr.

Around six that evening, Ethan called out, "Look!"

Turning, Cliff saw him pointing off to the south at the dim glow of a man- made light. He studied it for a full minute before he spoke, "We'll ease on closer and have a look-see. Don't want to run into anymore vigilantes."

When they had stolen on a little farther, Cliff could make out the shape of two houses, a barn, and a corral. "Ethan and I will ride on down there and see what place it is. Shep, you stay here with your woman, just in case."

It was the first time either had thought of her as being his woman, but Reb's remark gave both of the young lovers a warm feeling.

Fifteen minutes later, Ethan and three more riders came towards them moving fast. The largest, a dark skinned man twice the age of the others, jumped from his horse and rushed to the old bay where the two bodies were tied. Touching them, he howled as loud as any wolf they had ever heard. This caused a cold chill to run up Ellie's back; it also startled their horses, which began to dance about.

Ethan reached over, took the bridle of her horse and calmed it before saying, "Reb said we should come on down. This here is the Rocking AR outfit."

Never had two people been more surprised than the two women who suddenly saw one another. Here in the middle of the frozen prairie, escorting the body of her dead groom, was Ellie, Elaine's little sister.

"What's with this Ethel?" her sister asked.

"I didn't want anyone to know my real name, didn't want to bring any shame."

Elaine Moore was in a state of total confusion with her emotions. Engulfed with delight about seeing her kid sister, and yet entrapped by a deep bitterness growing in her heart over the murder of her new husband.

That night, they laid the bodies in the barn. The men slept in the stone house with Rodriguez' remaining boys. The old man slept not a wink, rather tended to his wounded Carlos. The sisters stayed inside the house, alone with their joy and sorrow.

The next day, Cliff and the Adams brothers escorted Ellie and the relic[11] Moore to Laramie. Immediately upon exiting the pass, and dropping down to Laramie City, Ethan wrinkled his nose before snorting, "What's that awful odor?"

Elaine replied, "It's the new Union Pacific Rolling Mill. They re-roll old railroad rails and other metals. Some believe it will be the springboard for more industrial development here."

"What do you think?"

"I think he's right; it smells awful," she said and looked up at the Georgian who now side-rode her.

The first thing the group did was to contact Doctor Lathrop and ask him to go to the Circle Rocking AR to help Carlos.

The second on Cliff's agenda was to report the murders to the Sheriff. Cliff explained what they had found and handed him the sign that had been pinned to Moore's shirt.

They left his office with little hope anything would be done. The Sheriff had given Cliff the impression he would side with the big ranchers, should it come to that; so he figured the man had been elected by the influence of Cheyenne money.

---

11 Relic: A woman who's husband is dead when she dies, a widow.

While they were in Laramie; Ethan found a gunsmith and had sights installed on his rifle, while Cliff and Mrs. Moore sought out Lawyer King, who had an office on Second Street over Williston's store. After telling him about finding Jimmy Don Moore lynched, Cliff showed him the receipt he had found in the dead man's pocket.

Dennis King was a big man, a couple inches taller than Cliff and a full hundred pounds heavier. His voice was however, soft and almost soothing as he explained to them what Jimmy Don had done only a couple of days before. "I don't know if this will hold up," he said. "I explained to Jimmy Don about the law against women owning real property, but he was adamant about wanting it recorded. So I did just that, right after he left."

"What do you mean, I can't own property? The land was rightfully my husband's."

"Yes, that is true, but territorial laws are based on the Old English Law, and they forbade women from owning property. There is some talk that if we become a state, women will get more rights, but as of now, there is no precedent."

"Wal' by Gawd, we are aboot to make one," she said standing as she spoke.

Cliff could see she was a strong woman, but he also knew she was on the verge of bursting into tears at any moment. Thinking it best, he suggested they leave, before she said something to the lawyer that would anger him.

On the way back to the ranch, he thought hard on the situation he was in, '*My pursuit of John Tidwell, as well as the trouble I might be in for lying to the deputy to get Shep out of jail, both soundly point for me to move on as soon as possible.*' However, there in the back of his mind was this little voice that kept telling him it would be going against the grain to leave a widow in the mess Mrs. Moore was in. Finally he decided, '*I will stay around long enough for her to sell her place; looks like she's gon'a need someone for a few days. Then I'll head on after the bastard who murdered Nadine.*'

When they were three miles from the ranch, Ethan's sharp eyes caught the first signs of the smoke. Immediately, they whipped the horses into a fast gallop until they reached the rise, where they espied the new house fully aflame.

Several riders were circling the other buildings, and even though no sound could be heard, the small puffs of white smoke appearing here and there told the story a fight was still raging ahead of them.

The distance was too far for them to continue running the horses at the pace they had been. Still, he knew there were too many riders for the old vaquero and his boys to hold off much longer.

When they reached the last hummock above the ranch, Cliff called to Ethan to try his rifle. The boy jumped from his horse before the animal was fully stopped, and he almost lost his balance as he grabbed the Whitworth.

The shot was a long one, at least a thousand yards perhaps more, but a second after the gun roared, a horse fell, spilling its rider. *'Shor' glad that smithy let me sight her in before we left,'* Ethan thought.

Twenty seconds later, that man fell dead from Ethan's second shot.

P.C. Defray saw Billy Dees fall from his stricken horse and then from the bullet that snapped out his life. At first, he thought the animal had been hit by one of the men in the stone house, but when he saw the way Dees jerked as the hunk of lead struck, he realized the man had been hit in the back. *'That bullet could not have come from the house or the barn,'* he surmised.

Stopping his horse, he looked towards the west road just in time to see a puff of blue smoke appear amongst the ruddy rays of the sunset on the western hill. A second later, another of Defray's men fell as the heavy bullet tore through him.

P.C. also spotted the two riders coming hard at them from the same hill and decided they had done enough to satisfy the new boss. He then rode into the circle of moving horses and motioning for the others to follow, led them away to the northeast.

Old Rodriguez came out of the small house and took a shot at the trailing rider as the attackers sped away. His bullet struck the high cantel of the man's saddle and passing through the thick leather, entered his right cheek. The burning was terrific, but the man stayed on the horse and disappeared over the rise close behind his confederates.

Immediately, Rodriguez sent his boys into the barn to put out the small fire, which had just been started only a minute or two before help arrived.

There in the ranch yard, twisted and grotesque, lay the two dead men Ethan had dispatched. A third body was there also, the old man's youngest boy.

Rushing to his son, he saw the lad was bleeding where a revolver ball entered under the left collarbone. Gratefully, Gilberto realized he was still alive. With fatherly care, he scooped up Pedro and carried him inside the bunkhouse.

Cliff told Shep to stay with the women, and then he rode hard right past what was left of the ranch, following the outlaws' fresh trail. It was well after dark before he returned.

"Did you find them?" Elaine asked, as he entered the small one room house.

"I don't know for shor. They rode up to, or closely past, a big ranch some ten miles northeast of here," he replied. "I couldn't be sure if I was still following the same ones after sundown. There are a lot a' tracks around those hills. Tomorrow I'll go back and see if I can pick up where I last knew for sure I was on the right trail."

"That's the Wolf Crick spread," she said. "Jimmy Don told me they have been after him ever since he filed on this place, some four year ago."

"It's a big outfit. I could tell that," Cliff said, giving his head a quick nod.

"One of de' biggest," Rodriguez added. "De' dead men, who lay in the barn, 'da ees' hands of Wolf Crick."

"Yeah, owned by some English Lord or something," Elaine said. "He has never set foot this side of the ocean, just sends over some of his kin to sit around in Cheyenne and act almighty."

"It ees' true, Señor. No man has ever seen 'da owner. Only 'ees foreman and now 'da say he has brought a man, from 'ees country, to be 'da new foreman."

"That's what I need to do, import me a foreman that will fight this bunch," she said bitterly.

"No, what you need is to get the law on your side. I will go back to Laramie tomorrow and tell the Sheriff what has happened. This time we have evidence in the form of bodies. Now you women must stay here in this stone house," Cliff said, looking around at its construction. "It will not be so easy to burn down. Me and the boys will move into the barn."

There was silence in the small room for long seconds before she spoke, "Not tonight. Tonight, we will all sleep here where it is warm. That barn has too many holes in it. Tomorrow when you go, take the spring-wagon and bring back cut boards to make an area in the barn where you men can sleep. Buy another heating stove and chimney pipe as well."

After spending nearly an hour with the Sheriff, Cliff convinced him to come out and look over the dead men, as well as the remains of the ranch house in which the Moore's had spent their wedding night, less than a week before.

When Reb Brown dropped this load, Pike Pepper had been Sheriff for less than two years, having replaced Albany County's first Sheriff, Nat Boswell.

Boswell, while in office, was appointed Deputy United States Marshal for the area. This appointment dictated he also serve as the first warden of the Territorial Prison there in Laramie. Soon the workload became so demanding he resigned as sheriff, leaving the job open for Pepper to fill.

Pike had done a fair job in his position, considering this was his first experience as a lawman other than some duties in the army. He had not been elected by Cheyenne money as Cliff had thought. Still, there was no question Cheyenne politics did have an overwhelming hand in everything done in the Territory, and Pepper was well aware of that fact. He also was well aware that foreign money had a big influence on Cheyenne thinking. He knew anything he did for Mrs. Moore would have to be strictly within the responsibility of his position. He could not move on hunches or things that seem probable. He must have strong evidence, or he would be able to do nothing. It was with these thoughts he left *The Circle Rocking AR Ranch* and headed towards *The Wolf Creek Ranch*.

Riders were seen five miles before he got to the hill that overlooked the ranch plaza. Below, in the center of a cluster of several buildings, was the main house, a tall, out-of-place looking two-story affair. It was made of imported clapboards with a two-column supported roof over the front porch.

Off to the right, he spotted a couple of small corrals made of peeled lodgepole. However, it was at a much larger corral several cowboys were seen working green broncs.

Behind this stood the barn, which appeared more like a hotel, being even taller than the main house and painted a bright red.

Pepper asked for P. C. Defray. Instead, he was shown into a large study to wait for the new ranch superintendent, as the old colored man called his new boss.

When John Mouton left Fort Laramie with Celeste Patay, he knew he would not be welcome among any of the soldiers who had grown to know and feel favorably as her protectors. He too was sure Jacques Patay would be out to kill him. After initially going to Cheyenne, the two soon took the eastbound to Omaha.

He had promised to take her back to his home in New York, where she could see her mother from time to time. Truthfully, he had never had any intention of returning to an area where there could, and very likely would, be warrants of murder awaiting him.

Instead, he had planned to move north to Bismarck. There he was sure Will Hickey had set up an account for their joint venture in the cattle business. Of course, he was not sure it was still open, and if so, whether he could draw on it. There even was a good chance no one knew of it, as it had been set up while they were in Chicago together.

This was before he had the good fortune of meeting Allen Moreton, the nephew of Sir Frances Moreton. Sir Frances was the Master of *The Birmingham Social Society*, a position that gave him great influence on the investments of a fair size group of British Gentlemen of great wealth.

Young Allen had taken a holiday in America and was drawn westward after becoming addicted to the dime novels that were pouring off the eastern presses daily.

Allen had convinced his uncle that a fortune could be made by investing in the cattle business in Wyoming and Montana. There, land was free for the taking, provided the Sioux and Cheyenne didn't get in one's way. It was through him that *The Wolf Creek Ranch* had been purchased by *The Birmingham Social Society*, three years before.

During that time, over two hundred thousand English pounds had been poured into the ranch to purchase more cattle and land, as well as for the construction of the big ranch house. Only two weeks before, Allen Moreton was able to also purchase *The Circle A Ranch* taking their spread all the way to the Colorado line.

However, young Moreton had not found The Great American Desert to hold the glorious adventure he had imagined. Also, due to his having suffered rheumatic fever at the age of nine, the altitude of the high plains kept him indoors, more than out, as he had dreamed.

He was however, acutely aware of the predicament he had gotten himself into with his venture. Uncle Fran did, after all, hold the purse strings to the family fortune. One could easily end up disowned, so to speak, at the time Uncle Fran's Will was read, had he caused embarrassment to the good name of Moreton.

John Mouton was quick to pick up on the English accent and gentlemanly mannerism of this man and thus wasted no time moving to his side and buying him the next glass of brandy. On a whim and using his best British accent, he introduced himself as Major John Brown.

"I was with the 3rd Bengal Light Cavalry on that frightful Sunday back in 1856, when the blasted Sowars revolted. We escaped with our lives by the skin of our teeth. It was that bloody day, I received these two leg wounds that curse me with a slight limp, even now. Thankfully, in time we were able to overcome the rebels and put down the rebellion."

Immediately, he had young Allen's attention, and soon they were in deep conversation.

"Oh, Dear Lord! Thank God for British military power. Tell me, which regimental commander did you serve under?"

John thought carefully, not sure just how much Moreton knew of the Rebellion in India. The only commander's name he could remember was, Sir Hugh Gough, and it was this he said to Moreton.

"Oh yes, I've heard my uncle speak of him."

As the brandy flows freely, the tongue does likewise. In less than an hour, Mouton knew all he needed of this displaced Brit, and the enormous opportunity that had fallen into his lap.

He didn't have it all his way though. Try as he might, Moreton would have nothing to do with buying land in Montana until the Wolf Creek venture was a financial success.

Seeing he was getting nowhere, John offered to take over the Wyoming ranch for Moreton, on the condition the lad would agree, after seeing what a good foreman could do for a spread with sufficient money, to invest in land around Miles City.

That night, with a not so firm handclasp, a partnership was forged that would bring about rather profound events and would largely shape both of their futures.

Returning to his room, where Celeste was preparing herself for dinner, he explained that Jean Mouton would have to be a name of the past, at least for a short while. Also she must act as his wife and not let on to anyone she had ever been in Wyoming before.

He spent a full hour explaining her duties, when to speak and what to say. The most important point being, she was to act as though she understood almost no English, a part that she could play well, for she had never truly understood the language.

Her only protest was of them returning so close to where her husband and the men who had known her at the fort would be. He assured her that as his wife, and with him acting as an English gentleman, no one would recognize or suspect her.

"Besides, the kind of riffraff that patronized your husband's business will never be allowed in *The Inter Ocean Hotel*." The statement might have been true, of that she did not know, but the cut to her former life was insulting and hurt her deeply.

When her protesting became strong, he firmly stated he was returning to Wyoming. She could come with him, or make do for herself in Omaha, or wherever she could find someone to take her.

With no money and no one to turn to, she suddenly realized the predicament she had gotten herself into. She had to go with him; she had no other choice.

Two days later, while Moreton was en route to New York, they were disembarking from the westbound and were once again in Cheyenne.

Major John Brown, as promised, rented a room for Mrs. Brown and himself at *The Inter Ocean Hotel*, Cheyenne's finest. He also hired a messenger, sending him to *The Wolf Creek Ranch* with a letter of introduction from Sir Allen Moreton, explaining where he was, as well as instructions to have appropriate vehicles sent to transport him and his lady to the ranch.

The next day was spent buying proper dresses and other attire that any respectable English couple would be traveling with. Other purchases included the best in both silverware and fine china, all charged, of course, to *The Wolf Creek Ranch*.

P.C. Defray was none too pleased in receiving the note. However, he did recognize the signature and handwriting of Allen Moreton introducing Major Brown.

'I have not really minded being second in command to Sir Allen, after all he is but a boy, but this new dude could be more of a problem.'

A problem which would prove to be beyond his wildest foresight.

In less than a month from the time he arrived, Major Brown had employed twenty new men, all quite familiar with guns and had decided it was time to move on *The Circle Rocking AR Ranch*.

It was under his direct command and watchful eye that Jimmy Don and his young vaquero had been hung.

Although Defray was now just the Jigger[12], he immediately recognized the force and ruthlessness in his new boss. When ordered to burn out the Moore spread, he didn't hesitate one moment. P.C. had no doubt a refusal would not just earn him the loss of a job, but his dismissal could very well come from the muzzle of the Major's revolver.

Sheriff Pepper was ill prepared for the reception he received when he was introduced to Major Brown. He also soon realized even though he had the dead bodies of Wolf Creek hands, there was little he could do. The Major accounted for every man on his payroll. Defray agreed the accused men had been fired two weeks before, along with several others whom they had found drunk in a little line camp out on the south fork of Crow Creek.

Returning to *The Circle Rocking AR Ranch* was not going to be a pleasant task. The Lawman would be bringing news he knew would not set well with Mrs. Moore.

Cliff listened to Pepper silently, while the others moaned and groaned. All that is except Elaine, who screamed and shouted curses Cliff had not heard since his army days.

He had heard the tune all before, fifteen hundred miles away in South Georgia when the carpetbaggers ran the government and protected the criminal. Only this time, he really believed Pike Pepper was telling the truth and really did have his hands tied.

It was this conversation between the Sheriff and Mrs. Moore, which sealed his fate for some time to come.

Cliff understood if Elaine Moore was to survive, she had to have a strong foreman. He also recognized, were he to ride away leaving her in this spot; he would not be able to look at himself in the mirror.

That night after supper, he walked out to the corral and laid his elbows on the top rail. Taking a deep breath of the cold dry air, he spoke with nobody to hear, "John Tidwell, you will not escape me.

---

12 Jigger: Second in Command to the Foreman.

It might be some time before I catch you, but I have not forgotten my promise. I will find and kill you someday, or you me."

His thoughts were suddenly cut short when he saw the stream of light appear on the frozen ground and heard the door of the cabin open and close. Her footsteps were plain, with her leather soles crunching the tiny ice particles as she came towards him. He did not turn to look at her; he did not need to, he knew full well who was approaching.

"Mr. Brown, you shouldn't be out here. You'll ketch your death."

"Mrs. Moore, I could say the same thing to you," he replied.

She nodded her head in agreement, "Yes, I suppose you could at that, but I do wonder why you are out here in this weather."

"I was trying to figure out how to go about askin'," he paused and looked off into the night before he finished his statement, "if you would consider giving me the job as your foreman."

She looked up at the back of his head in amazement. "Why Mr. Brown, I came out to ask of you that very thing."

He took a deep breath, knowing well that he really wanted no part in the fight he was jumping into but also knowing he must do so. "Well then, I'll take the job on two conditions."

"Absolutely, you have the right to make reasonable requests. What are your conditions?" she asked.

"First, I will be the ramrod. We do it my way and not yours. If you do not agree with me, you and I talk it over in private, never in front of one of the men." He paused, then emphasized with a strong voice, "The men work for me, not for you. If you don't like my way, you can fire me, and I will fare forth as soon as I can get my possibles together, but if I'm the ramrod you can not give the orders. The men work for me."

"That is reasonable and your second condition?"

"You must stop calling me Mr. Brown. My friends call me Reb," he paused before adding, "and I do hope we will be friends when this is all over."

Elaine Moore realized she was hiring a man much stronger that she, a man just as she needed, but it did go against her grain to be stripped of her authority so soon after receiving it. "Yes, Mr. Brown, I too hope I will be calling you Reb by then." With that said, she turned and walked back to the stone house.

He still had his back to the structure, as he had throughout their conversation. The light from the open door momentarily flooded the small area before suddenly the land became dark once more, lit only by the stars and a sliver of a moon, and he knew she was back inside. Cliff then shook his head slightly, feeling the weight of the new yoke he had just agreed to bear. He stayed there another five minutes before he walked to the barn.

The next morning he had Shep and Ellie take the buckboard to Laramie with Carlos. The boy had not fared well during the night, and he was now fevered. *'Only a doctor can save him, and I'm not sure it wasn't too late for that.'*

He pondered his situation, *'I have two good men I know I can count on, when Shep is not moony-eyed over Ellie. The ol' Mexican seems to be sound and totally devoted to Mrs. Moore, as he must of been to her husband. The three boys he has left are untried. One is ol' Rodriguez' son and the other two the sons of his sister, Juanita Gaztambide, I think they called her,, who is still down in Chihuahua.'*

Cliff allowed his mind to rest a few moments before again he considered his predicament, *'Although both sisters are strong, considering their sex, they may or may not be counted on in an emergency. I need more men. Men who not only know cattle but also know their way around the smell of burning gun powder.'*

The next morning when Shep and Ellie took Carlos to the doctor, they also carried a written note to the telegraph office at the depot in Laramie.

A week later, when Rodriguez went to check on his son, Cliff rode with him. They both were pleased when they learned that Carlos would pull through, although it would be many weeks before the boy would be able to again carry out the duties of a vaquero, which was his greatest ambition in life.

After loading the supplies they had picked up at Grover's Store, Cliff said to Gilberto, "Go ahead; make Carlos as comfortable as possible in the buckboard, then pick me up at the railroad station. I'm going to check on a wire. Oh, here is some money for the Doc."

He was pleased to find that indeed there was a wire waiting there for him.

REB BROWN CIRCLE ROCKING AR RANCH LARAMIE WYOMING STOP

AS YOU REQUESTED FIVE TO ARRIVE CHEYENNE BEFORE CHRISTMAS END

SIGNED JOHN RUMANS

Ishté Shipite had been born in the Valley of the Greasy Grass in the summer of 1826, the fourth son of the proud Crow warrior, White Mountain. He had been raised in the traditions of his father and his father's father, for as far back as anyone knew of their people.

It was with a strong resentment that cultivated into a great hate the Sparrow Hawk people, as they called themselves, had given way to the invasion of the people from the rising sun, as well as from the face of the wind. People who began to arrive in great numbers before Ishté Shipite had been born. The Crow, being a much smaller nation had given in and retreated again and again.

Still, through it all, the Crow warriors had developed a great ability that was not matched among any other people on the Great Plains. The Crow was a master at stealing horses from these immigrants who called themselves Lakota and from their allies, the Cheyenne and Arapaho.

Ishté Shipite was no different, and as a young man, he had brought much pride to the tipi of his father, with the numerous horses he stole from these invaders.

Gradually, as the Lakota became more and more numerous, White Mountain hired himself out to the white soldiers as a scout to hunt his old enemies.

After the death of White Mountain at the hands of a Cheyenne war club on Powder River, Ishté Shipite likewise became a scout for the white soldiers. It was in this position he met and found a great fondness for the boy Laramie Patay, who lived at the white soldier's fort near the Frenchman's River[13].

Ishté Shipite had agreed to scout for the Sixth Ohio during the spring and summer of 1875, but when the cold winds of fall began and the soldier patrols became fewer and fewer, he was relieved of his duties and told to return in the spring for more work.

There was no more for an Indian to do during the winter months than that of an out-of-work white man. It was a time when food was scarce and the weather bitter.

When the boy came to him and asked for his assistance in finding his mother, the Crow agreed to help his young friend. It was this endeavor that brought the two to the banks of South Crow Creek, the second week of December, in The Year of Our Lord 1875. The

---

13 Frenchman's River: Laramie takes its name from Jacques LaRamie, a French-Canadian trapper who died in the nearby mountains.

little stream had long since frozen solid, and they had to use a hatchet to break the ice to let the horses drink.

Powder had fallen since just before the noon hour, and now a soft blanket covered the frozen clay. Had this not been the case, Ishté Shipite would never have been caught as he was.

Cliff had cut the trail of the two horses three miles from the creek. Finding it fishy that a shod horse and unshod pony seemed to be traveling together, he had led Ethan Adams and two of the Mexican boys in a slow but steady pursuit. It was, after all, possible that the white man was not traveling with the Indian, rather about to be his victim.

Seeing the trail lead over the bank and not come up the far side, gave him further concern. Dismounting, and leaving the boys to hold the horses, he and Ethan moved in on foot to investigate.

Ishté Shipite smelled them before he heard them. However, it was way too late to do anything about it by the time he whirled around to see, two men with rifles pointed at them from above.

Had he been alone, he would have tried to escape, but he knew the French boy had not been away from the security of the fort long enough to survive an attack from men with rifles. Instead, he spoke to the boy who was still on his knees drinking.

Standing and looking over his shoulder, Laramie's facial expression suddenly changed from questioning to fright when he saw the rifles pointed at them.

He quickly dropped his canteen and shot both hands high over his head while asking, "What do you want, Monsieur?"

Cliff, quick to pick up on the strong French accent replied, "You are on Circle AR Range. What are you doing here?"

"We are looking for my mother."

"Your mother?" Ethan replied questioningly.

"Oui," the boy said, nodding his head.

"Your mother is lost out here in this storm?" Ethan again questioned.

Cliff had now switched his attention to the Indian. The man had moved a little to his right where he had placed his foot over a well-rounded wooden stick, pushing it into the soft powder. *'Very likely the handle of a tomahawk,'* he thought. The red man made no other moves for the moment. Still Cliff was sure the Indian knew quite well the stick had been there and had intentionally tried to conceal it.

"Oui," the boy continued, "Me-maw left the fort in the company of a scoundrel who deceived her with his French charm."

Suddenly, Cliff was once more interested in the boy. "What is the name of this French scoundrel?" he asked.

"Jean Mouton," answered the boy.

Immediately Cliff lowered his carbine. "Where did you last see this Mouton?"

"Fort Laramie."

"How long ago?"

"Many months, he took my mother and disappeared. Ishté Shipite here is helping me find her."

"Why are you here? Do you think Mouton is here?" Cliff questioned, almost in a frightened voice, frightened he may not hear the answers he wanted.

"We crossed trails with a small band of Crow who were headed to the winter grounds. They told Ishté Shipite they had seen the fort woman in this area."

"This man she left with, Jean Mouton, is he still with her?"

"I think so, Oui," the boy answered.

"I am called Reb, Reb Brown. I work for the lady who owns this land. You are welcome to come and eat with us, and stay over in the shelter of our barn," Cliff told him.

The two looked at each other, then the Indian dropped his head.

"I think that would not be good," Laramie replied, "but I thank you. You are a kind man, oui."

"Look, it's going to get cold tonight. You are on Circle AR land now, but we are a small spread, if you make camp on another ranch's land they might not be so accommodating," Cliff pointed out.

The two again were talking between themselves when he added, "If you are worried about the Indian not being welcome, you are wrong. *The Circle Rocking AR Ranch* welcomes men from all over. Most of our wranglers are from Mexico."

Once more, they talked low between themselves, and finally the boy nodded his head. "Oui, we will accept your kind offer, for this night only."

"Good, come on then," Cliff replied and offered his hand to the lad. "What does this Ishto Shipmite mean?" he asked, and seeing the puzzled look on the lad's face he added, "I mean translate it into English."

"Oui, it means he has a black band around his eyes, it is his badge, uh, the way he paints his face for war."

Cliff nodded his head, and then looking at the Indian he said, "I will call him Black Band. I would never remember Ishto Shipmite."

"Ishté Shipite," Laramie corrected.

"See what I mean," Cliff said, and the boy smiled and then spoke to his companion, and the older man just nodded his head.

"He will answer to Black Band; he understands the ignorance of the whites."

Cliff wasn't sure he liked that explanation but said no more on the subject.

Returning to where the vaqueros held the horses, they mounted.

The Mexican boys both stayed a considerable distance from the Crow, who side-rode the young Frenchman.

"I have been hunting a man for a long time. I think he may be the same man you spoke of," Cliff said.

"Is he a Frenchman?"

"He is whatever he wants to be. He speaks many languages and often changes from one name to another. He does speak French as if it were his own language."

"What is this man called?"

"Sometimes he uses the name Jean Mouton, when he is pretending to be French."

"Oui, the man who left with my mother is called Jean Mouton."

"What does he look like?" Cliff questioned.

"Tall and dark, but quite old, even older than you," the boy replied. Then added, "His hair has streaks of gray in it. I don't understand what caused Me-maw to leave with him. He must have forced her to go."

"Even older than me, eh[14]?" Cliff said back with a slight smile but still not at all liking the fact that the boy thought of him as an old man. *'After all I'm only thirty-three.'*

Cliff moved forward in order to ride beside the boy so he could ask him questions about this Jean Mouton, and when he did, the Indian dropped back slightly. Some of the questions the boy could answer, some he could not.

They had ridden less than three miles when the Indian suddenly moved up fast beside them and pointed to the north, "Many riders come."

---

14 EH: Pronounced 'A' often used in the west especially in Western Canada.

Cliff looked in the direction he was pointing but saw nothing save the open ground for more than a mile as the lay of the land acclivitied[15] into a slight rise. Neither did he hear anything, save the wind. Nonetheless, he had learned to trust the Seminole and Choctaw, who had fought with the Confederacy, and he decided not to doubt this red man either.

Turning, he said sharply to Ethan, "Fall back to that buffalo wall'er we just passed, and lay low. If this proves to be trouble we might need your Whitworth."

Ethan only nodded his head as he spurred his horse and quickly galloped back in the direction they had come.

He had barely dismounted when Cliff spotted the first of the riders come over the rise. Glancing back quickly, he saw Ethan laying his horse down, as he had been taught to do during the war when they needed to remain out of the sight of passing Yankee Patrols.

Satisfied Ethan would not likely be spotted, he turned back to face the approaching riders. Cliff began to count under his breath as they approached, "Eight, nine, ten, eleven."

"Everyone get out your rifle if you have one. Don't point them at nobody but have them ready," he instructed just before the first horses arrived.

"You are on Circle Rocking AR land," he said sternly to the lead rider. "State your business, and be quick about it."

"Wal' now, ain't we got us a rooster here," the man said looking around, as a couple of the others moved up along side him. When he spoke, they laughed at his comment. Turning back to Cliff he said, "This here is Wolf Crick land. You is trespassing."

"We both know full well where we all are, so stop your foolishness and get on with explaining your presence here," Cliff replied. "Or else face the consequences."

Once more the Wolf Creek men laughed.

"I say you are the trespassers, and I got eleven to five that says I'm right."

"And just who might you be?" Cliff asked.

"I'm P.C. Defray, the foreman of The Wolf Crick outfit, just why do you want to know?"

"Foreman?" Cliff questioned and then paused, "That's fishy, word in Laramie is you got demoted, a new man done come and put you in your place," Cliff said back.

---

15 Acclivitied: Sloped.

Hearing this, a few of the men behind Defray snickered. He turned his head quickly to see who was laughing at him, but they straightened their expressions before he saw who the culprits were.

Facing Cliff once again, he replied as he narrowed his eyes, "Well, I'm the one in charge a' these men, and we aim to hang you fer trespassing."

Cliff rested his palm on the stock of his Colt, and remembering how well it had worked at Monia[16], he said without looking away from his adversary, "Boys, I want every one of you to put your guns on this here Jasper. Pay no mind to the others." He spoke slowly and surely, "If anyone shoots, every one a' you are to drill this big dumb one," he paused a moment and then asked, "You all understand?"

Defray suddenly realized the spot he was in, as every one of the Circle AR men suddenly had their rifles pointed directly at him.

"Si Señor Reb. We weel' all drop 'da bullet in 'da big dumb won'," Pedro replied.

"You ain't going to let them buffalo you, P.C., are you?" one of the riders behind Defray asked. He had been one of the ones who had snickered at him and had no love loss for his former foreman.

"Shet' up Slim," Defray replied harshly.

Cliff could see small spots of sweat suddenly burst upon the man's forehead and he knew Defray was scared almost to the point of panic. Realizing that could cause a reaction that would get a bunch of them killed quickly, he again said, "You are on Circle Rocking AR land, if you don't want to be buried here, best you turn those broncs around and head back to your own spread," he paused and then added, "and don't come back."

"Damn it, P.C., we got 'um out numbered more'n' two to one."

"Shet' up," Defray shouted. Then turning his horse's head sharply, he looked at Cliff and said, "You ain't seen the last a' me, Copperhead," as he spurred the buckskin and headed off up the slight hill with his men following.

When they had traveled some two hundred yards, the man who had been jabbing Defray the most stopped, then pulled a long-barreled Winchester from its scabbard and taking quick aim, let fly a round.

The ball passed through the very top of Cliff's Stetson, causing it to fly from his head.

---

16 Monia: See Gold In The Red Desert, Book One of the Owl Hoot Trail trilogy.

The other riders stopped and looked back at the sound of his shot, and then they turned their mounts around to make a charge on the men they had just left.

Suddenly the shooter flew from his saddle as if hit by a cannon ball.

Defray quickly spied the smoke of the Whitworth, and remembering how his men had been killed in the raid on the ranch, he immediately realized they were in grave danger. "Come on, they got them a sharpshooter down thar," he shouted as he whirled around, and riding low in his saddle, he led the others over the rise and out of sight.

Just before they reached the crest, Johnny Loomis shouted over at him, "You just gon'a leave Slim back thar?"

"He's dead," Defray shouted back.

"You don't know that."

"Wal' go back and save him if you are of a mind to. It'll serve the both a' you right for siding with that hombre back there," he shouted as he galloped on.

Cliff rode up to where the dead man had fallen and dismounted. "Better get him over his saddle 'afor he stiffens up." Then motioning with his hand to Pedro he added, "Go fetch his pony."

"Si', Señor," the young man answered.

By the time they had the body tied to the saddle, Ethan rode up. "I waited to make shor' they didn't come back," he offered.

"You did good. Probably saved a bunch a' lives," Cliff said back, without looking at him.

The young French boy then eased his pony next to Cliff's and said, "Black Band doesn't savvy why you take this bad man. He thinks you should leave him for others to see what will become of them if they attack you."

"I'd like that, but we need to be first in telling our side to the Sheriff. Bringing in the body will help with that," Cliff replied.

He didn't like having to explain himself, but he realized this boy was pretty young and had not had the experience of fighting in the war. *'I'll tolerate the boy's boldness some,'* he thought.

When they arrived on the hill overlooking the ranch, he sent the others on down but asked Laramie and the Indian to ride on with him into town with the body.

To say a Whiteman leading a horse carrying a body, being followed by a long-haired blond boy dressed in buckskins, who was being side-rode by an Indian, raised a few eyebrows, would be a short statement. That is, compared to the reality of the commotion they stirred up when they eased down C Street to the small office next to *The Laramie-Walden Stage Line* depot. It was there Philip Mandel, one of the first commissioners for Laramie County, had built an office for Sheriff Pepper.

"Brown," Pepper said, when he stepped out on the boardwalk, "why is it every time you come to town, you are bringing shot up men?"

"I reckon you have some undesirables living around these parts," Cliff replied.

"That's Slim Carver, one of Wolf Crick's hands. I reckon you better come on in and tell me what happened," Pepper said to him, and then turning to the thin man who was now standing just behind his right shoulder he said, "Take the body down to Jesse Owens' and have him lay 'im out fer a burial."

"What should I do with his horse?" the man asked as he walked past the Sheriff, brushing up against his arm as he went by.

"Take him to the livery," the Sheriff said, with a little sharpness in his voice.

"Oh, yeah," the man said nodding his head as he took the reins from Cliff's hand.

Cliff had just finished explaining to Pepper what had taken place, when Defray and several of his men rode in at a fast gallop, pulling up sharply in front of the same office.

Black Band had spotted them long before they arrived and motioned for Laramie to follow him across the street into an alley, where they could watch but not be noticed by the Wolf Creek riders.

Jumping from his saddle, Defray quickly pitched his reins to the man beside him and rushed inside.

Through Pepper's single front window Cliff spotted them riding in, and recognizing who they were, moved back to the left wall so when the man entered, the open door hid him from direct view.

"Pepper!" Defray shouted. "One a' my men was bushwhacked not a mile from Wolf's main ranch house," he said, stopping just short of the desk the Sheriff was sitting behind. "This time you ain't gon'a squirm out of it. I want a warrant fer that damn Copperhead on a murder charge."

"Who got drilled?"

"Slim, Slim Carver, one of my best men. Shot in the back by that damn new foreman a' the Circle AR's."

"You see him plug Slim?"

"Yeah, I seed him do it. Shot him right in the back. Several a' my men seed him do it too," Defray shouted. "Now you gon'a get me that warrant, or am I gon'a have to wire Cheyenne and have you removed?"

"Before you go to that much trouble, I want to ask you a couple questions," Pepper calmly replied.

"What questions?"

"Where is the body?"

"Huh?"

"I got to see a corpus delicti."

"What?"

"I got a see the body. Got a make shor, he's shor enough daid."

"He's dead alright. I'll testify to that."

"That won't do. I got a see it."

"Wal', we didn't have time to stay fer the burial 'cause we didn't want this here killer to get out of the country. The others back at the ranch is probably done got him laid to rest by now."

"Somehow, I doubt they done dug a grave in this frozen ground jus' yet," Pepper replied.

"Wal', maybe, maybe not. That ain't got nothing to do with what I come here fer anyway."

"You say he was shot in the back by the foreman of *The Circle Rocking AR Ranch*, less than a mile from your headquarters, and you and all your men let him ride away?"

"He had a good head start on us. He shot him with a government rifle from nearly half-a-mile away."

"Half-a-mile?"

"That's right, you deef? Now fill out that warrant so we can get after him."

"How you so dang sure it was this fellow, if'n he was half-a-mile away?"

"'Cause I was just talking to him, and when we rode off he started slingin' lead and plugged Slim in the back."

"You were talking to a man you despise, who was trespassing within a mile of you're boss' home, and you just rode off and left him there?"

"Wal', there's more to it than that. I aimed to cut him some slack until he murdered Slim."

"You sure Slim wus shot in the back?"

"Damn right I'm sure. I said, it didn't I?"

"Yeah, you did," Pepper agreed, as he looked up at the man who now had his palms lying on the Sheriff's desk leaning forward and placing his face only inches from the face of the lawman.

"Now do I get the warrant or not?"

"There's a problem P.C.," Pepper said, staring straight into the puncher's eyes.

"What kind of problem?" P.C. questioned rising up and turning his head slightly.

"One thing, it's a' gen' the law to make a trumped-up report to a lawman."

"What the hell are you talking about?"

"Wal', you see, first I done seen Slim's body, and he weren't shot in the back. He were shot square in the chest." Pepper paused and let this sink into Defray's mind before continuing, "And second, that fellow behind you thar, tells a different story."

Suddenly Defray whirled around and reached for the revolver he carried cross-draw in a belt holster.

Before he had the Remington fully out of its leather, he was looking down the barrel of Cliff's Colt. He immediately realized it was pointed straight at his middle.

"Easy now, Defray," Pepper said. "If he shoots you right now, I'll have to testify it were self defense, and he'll walk, while you'll be laid out beside Slim down to Owens', awaiting the spring thaw."

Defray was hot-headed and bold, and it was the second time in a few hours this Cracker had bested him, and it burned in his craw, but he was no fool. Releasing his grip on the big revolver, it fell quickly back to its resting place.

"You sidin' with him, Pepper?"

"I side with the law, and both of you roosters had better learn that," the Sheriff said back, just as stern as the question had been directed at him. "And this time, his story makes a lot more sense than your'n does." Pepper paused and let his words fall hard. "And I suspect it was you what was trespassing."

"Twern't neither, we were on Circle A land, and *The Birmingham Social Society* done up and bought that brand last month."

"Me'bee, that I'll check on, but right now get your men and ride on back out a' here before I throw you in a cell for making that trumped-up report. And tell that new boss a' yours, Pike Pepper ain't one to be fooled with."

"Tell Mr. Mouton, I'll be seeing him too," Cliff said.

Defray looked at him questioningly before replying, "Who?"

"Jean Mouton, your new boss," Cliff said again.

"Never heard of him," Defray said back in a sincere response. "The new boss of Wolf Crick is Major John Brown, a proper Englishman."

Cliff had been fishing, hoping he had stumbled onto Mouton, but he was convinced Defray didn't know the man.

After the Wolf Creek hands rode away, Pike asked about this Jean Mouton, and Cliff told him the whole story.

That night when they returned to *The Rocking Circle AR Ranch*, Elaine Moore asked Cliff to walk with her out to the corral. The temperature was hovering near ten degrees, but the wind had laid some. Nonetheless, he knew when she asked him to walk with her in such bitter cold, she an ax to grind about something.

"What is it, Mrs. Moore?" he asked resting one boot on the bottom rail of the larger corral.

"It's that 'Injun," she said hatefully. "I don't want no Reddies on my property. It was Injun's that killed my Ma, and I won't have none around me."

"Where did this happen?" he asked.

"Texas. On the Pease River of Texas," she said looking off into the darkness.

He could tell she was, for the moment, gone from him, drifting back to another time and another place, and now he would have felt the intruder, to disturb her thoughts.

When she began speaking her voice was soft, not harsh as it had been before, "Ellie and I had gone down to the crick, to fetch a bucket of good water from a spring there, when we heard the shooting.

Just after, I spied many Injuns cross the river south of us me'bee half-a-mile, and I led Ellie back towards the house as quickly as we could and still stay in the cover of the bushes along the river. Then we had to creep along in the tall grass as far as we could, but when we come to where Pa had cleared the land, there weren't no more cover." She paused and caught her breath before continuing, "We stopped thar because th' Injuns were already riding into th' yard.

Pa was out in the field plowing and when he began to run back to where Ma was, one of them filthy Reddies hit him in the back with a stone-club and knocked him down. He jus' lay thar, and I jus' knew he was daid." Again she stopped, this time more because she was attempting to hold back the crying that was seeking to overtake her emotions.

Cliff had to admire her strength as she fought back the tears and continued her story.

"Ma had been to the barn churning fer butter when they came, and seeing Pa fall, she screamed. It were that what caused them to see her." At this time Elaine Moore shook her head as if she was trying to stop her mother from making that scream.

"In no time, three or four of them were on her, and they stripped all her clothes off and began to violate 'er. I held my hand over Ellie's eyes so she wouldn't see it for a while, but they just kept it up one after the other. They just kept on doing 'er over and over.

Ma screamed for a while, then she sort a' sobbed and then she stopped making any sound at all. She just laid there while they took their pleasure with 'er. Finally, I guess each of them had spent their loins and they stopped, but Ma didn't move none. I could see a big red pool of blood on the ground under her, and I figured she too, was dead.

Aboot that time, one of the filthy Reddies laid down his hatchet and reached for his knife. He pulled her hair out straight and put the blade to her head, but she whirled around suddenly. I seed she had his hatchet in her hand, and she clobbered him with it in the side, under his left arm. It went in deep, and I seen the blood spew out even before I heard him scream.

With strength I don't know where he got, he cut her hair from her head and threw her back to the ground. Then he slowly stood and held a fist full a' her long yaller hair up. Ma was blond like me," she suddenly injected, "and yelped kind a' dog-like a few times, ya know how they do, and then he fell daid at her feet."

This time when Elaine paused there was no crying, he saw a change had taken place within her emotions and her voice. "Another one of them butchering Injuns rode up on his horse and shot a' arrow in her where she lay there on the red earth, and then they fired the buildings and rode away carrying that daid Injun, what Ma had killed, with them."

"How long ago was this?" Cliff asked hoping to bring her back from that awful day to the present.

"It were in '63. The Hill family, they lived down river a few miles, took us in. It were from their family, Hillsboro is named," she said in a little lighter tone.

Then she swung back and added bitterly, "They never caught 'em. Not the ones what done it. Most of the men were off fighting with the Yankees under General Hood som'ers, and what few Rangers there was left, weren't able to do much." She stopped and then turned to face him and said, "Pa recovered, but he never was the same. That lick he took from that stone-club did something to scramble up his mind, and he just sort a' existed mostly after that." Taking a deep breath she finished with, "Now do you see why I won't have no Injun on my property."

"Them were Comanche, Kickapoos, or Lipans, Texas Indians. Comanche, I'd 'spect. This here is a Crow, as different as French and American," he replied.

"I don't care. He's a' stinking Injun."

"Mrs. Moore, you're barking up the wrong tree," Cliff took a deep breath before speaking again. "I know you've been through the mill, both back then and here recently, but now you listen to my story. A man, a white man, is responsible for my father's, my two brothers', and my mother's deaths. He personally shot to death my wife, and I have been on his trail for nigh on four years. This here Crow Indian just might be able to lead me to him, and I ain't gon' a' let that chance slip away. If you won't have him here, then you won't have me, neither. I'll be packed come morning. I'll tell Ethan to stay with you. I know Shep ain't gon'a be leaving your kid sister. The two a' them should get you by," he said to her, knowing full well those he would be leaving behind would not be enough for her.

As much as he wanted to help this woman, he would not lose this opportunity to find John Tidwell.

Elaine Moore was a woman who had become accustomed to getting what she wanted. Her good looks and attractive figure, along with above average intelligence, had been the weapons necessary for her to survive and for the most part, live as she wished in a harsh land, during hard times.

She too, realized as good as the brothers were, they would not be able to stand up to Wolf Creek. *'I have to keep Reb here. Still, it is important to do so without it appearing I have given in to him.'*

Finally she asked tenderly, "Tell me aboot your wife."

"I wus raised in South Georgia," he began, and when he had finished he looked at her and then down to his boot and added, "That's twice I've told that story in only a few hours, and I don't intend to do it again soon."

Elaine suddenly reached around him and drew her body up close to his and began to cry. "I am sorry for askin' aboot it. I should have known better."

He too suddenly felt the load seem to slip away some as she held him close, and he was grateful for the feeling.

He placed his arms around her also and held her slim body tightly for many seconds before he released his grip.

She sensed his mood change, and she too pulled back. Then she said looking up at his face, "If the Crow will help you; he can stay." Thereafter, she immediately turned and walked back to the stone house.

Cliff was surprised when he moved; for it was then he realized the closeness of her body to his, had stirred his blood. A feeling he was not accustomed to much anymore, except when he first woke up of a morning, of course. He waited a minute or two for it to subside before he walked into the barn where the other men were sitting around a makeshift table, playing a game of cards.

Approaching Laramie and Black Band, who were off a ways from the others he asked, "You two not into poker?"

"Whiteman no like to lose to Indian," Black Band answered.

Cliff understood and nodded his head.

"Who the hell is this new foreman of the Rocking AR?" John demanded.

"Didn't catch his name," Defray answered. "But he is a damn Copperhead, I could tell from his drawl."

"My poor ignorant man, more than half of the men in the west have migrated from the south. They have nothing left of their high-faluting plantations, so they tucked their tails between their legs and ran west. That doesn't tell me anything."

"I'll find out," Defray said.

"Never mind. I don't care who he is. Just kill him, and get that woman off my land, I need that spring," he said before he lit his big cigar. "Now get out of here."

Defray didn't like being talked down to by this man or any other. He didn't like the man bringing his French wife with him either. *'She fired Peppi the first week she was here. Damn her!'*

P.C. and the housekeeper had a good relationship going for more than a year. Now he would have to go to Cheyenne or Laramie for his pleasure.

For over a month, Defray had the new men John Brown hired ride the line that separated the Wolf Creek brand from the Circle Rocking AR, in hopes of catching his target. Not once did anyone see him, or any AR men, except at a distance, then they seemed always to be as many as he had with him. He also had developed a great respect for the sharpshooter who rode with the AR outfit, and wanted no more crossing of trails with that marksman.

A week before Christmas, Pike Pepper rode up to the ranch. Looking down from his saddle, he reached inside his heavy coat, produced a folded yellow paper, and handed it to Cliff.

"What is it?" Ellie asked as she watched from the window.

"Looks like they finally got a warrant for Reb," Elaine replied. She jerked off her apron, grabbed her old bearskin coat, and started out the door ready to do battle with the Sheriff.

"I hope this don't mean what I think it do," she heard Pepper say.

"Just need some more hands, that's all," Cliff said, as he again folded the wire and placed it inside the pocket of his vest.

"Hands is one thing, but from where I stand, that looks sort a' like you done imported some gun hawks," he replied nodding his head at the telegram.

"These boys helped me drive a herd of Texas longhorns up to Kansas, nothing more. The same outfit where the Adams brothers came from."

"Yeah, and that Ethan Adams has done accounted fer more than his share of daid men here in Albany County."

"Sheriff Pepper, I will give you my word, we will do nothing unlawful here as long as I am foreman of *The Circle Rocking AR Ranch*."

Pepper looked over at Elaine Moore, who now stood beside Cliff, and saw in her face a different tune than that of her foreman.

"And what about you, Mrs. Moore, can I get the same promise from you?"

Elaine did not change her expression. She stared straight at the man who still had not dismounted and after a couple seconds of silence she said, "You heahed my foreman, what he says is law here. Now if we had law elsewhere in the county, someone would be out looking fer the men who hung my husband on his own land." She stopped and let her statement lay on everybody's mind a second or two and then she added, "Just you do your job and keep the Wolf Creek ootfit off my land. And when you ain't doing something for the good fathers of Albany County, you might take a few minutes of your time and find the men who murdered my husband."

Pepper knew she had no loyalties to the law whatsoever. However, for some reason he did not understand, he trusted the Georgian and believed the man would do as he promised.

"I'll do that, Mrs. Moore," he replied and touched the front brim of his hat as a salute to her. Then looking back at Cliff, he said, "I'll be taking you at your word, Brown."

Riding away, he thought of the irony in a Brown from Georgia and a Brown from England being such enemies. "Hell, they could be kin," he said to his horse, and then laughed.

"What was it that he brought?" Elaine asked.

Cliff glanced over at her and saw the same look Pepper had seen, and he didn't like it either. "It was a wire from Denver, the men I sent for are to arrive in Cheyenne on the four o'clock," he replied.

Then he walked over to the corral where he spoke to Ethan, "Get your long gun and tell Rodriguez I'll need one of his boys to ride with us."

"Where we going?"

"Cheyenne."

"Yee Haw!" was the only reply from the young man as he rushed off towards where his pony was tied.

The depot in Cheyenne was along the south side of the town. Most everything north of the tracks was respectable and of the "better" class of people. South of the tracks was where the Mexican, tame Indians, and poor whites hung out. It was much like the way Dodge City had been when he arrived there, and much like every other town he had seen in the west, a few with money separating themselves from those who were poor. "And they say we were the segregationists," he said just above a whisper.

"What?" Ethan asked.

"Oh, nothing," Cliff answered as he dismounted, before tying Ola to the hitching post on the south side of the depot.

Pedro parked the wagon just down the tracks, locked the brake and hunkered down as low as he could, keeping the cold wind to his back.

The engine of *The Denver Pacific Railway* was only 40 minutes late pulling into Cheyenne and stopped just south of the Union Pacific tracks and depot. It being no later than that was a surprise to everyone, especially the telegrapher. Immediately he set about his job of sending a wire back to Denver, notifying them of its arrival.

Several passengers offloaded before Cliff recognized little J. J. Carlson jump to the frozen ground.

"Damn, it's a mite cold up here," he said to someone behind him. Next to hit the ground was Billy Ellis, and he agreed with the little man's statement.

Cliff walked up to them and stretched forth his left hand, extending his welcome. "I hope it ain't just you two loafers."

"Come on now Boss, you know we's top hands," the short man replied smiling widely.

"Naw," Billy answered. "Tommy, Nathan, and Tyrell, rode back in the animal car. They said it was to keep an eye on the stock, but I bet it was a mite warmer back there."

"Yeah, I bet ol' Tyrell burrowed into a pile a' hay and slept the whole way," J.J. said, at the same time he was slapping Ethan on the arm.

"Do you all have mounts?" Cliff queried.

"What do you think we be, a bunch a Kansas Jayhawkers?" Billy asked. "Shor' we all got mounts. We's from Texas, Boss."

"That's good," Cliff said, then added, "I brung a wagon just in case. Come on, I got us a room at *The Ames Boarding House*. Ain't much, but it's a bit warmer than that thar train."

"Hey Ethan, they got any purty whores in Cheyenne?" J.J. asked.

"Hell, Shep done snatched the purtiest one of all and lit out with her."

"Naw, not Shep."

"Shor' did."

"Reb, he telling it straight?"

"I'm not so sure I'd be calling her a whore around Shep, if'n I was you or her sister neither," he replied.

"Wal', I want the purtiest whore in Cheyenne, if ol' Shep done stole the purtiest of the wimmen."

"Stole is damn near what he did too," Ethan said.

"What?"

"Tell you about it another time," Cliff offered as the horses began to come down the off loading ramp along with the remainder of his men.

When everyone had saddled up and were about to mount, Nathan looked back and elbowed Ethan, "That Meskin boy yonder, he looks like he's following us."

"That's Pedro; he's the foreman."

"Huh?"

During the short ride from the depot to Ames Hotel, Billy Ellis eased up beside Cliff and asked, "Hey Reb, what we up here fer?"

"Didn't Rumans tell you?"

"He just said you were in a little trouble and needed some help. We all up and volunteered."

"I'll tell you more about it tomorrow. This here town is full a' trouble, and the quicker we get away, the better I'll like it."

When they arrived at the boarding house, Pedro tied each of the horses to the wagon and started on to the livery, a block up the street.

"As soon as you get them taken care of, hotfoot it back here," Cliff said to him.

"Oh, no Señor. I'll stay with the animals."

"Not a chance. Too damn cold in that barn. You do as I tell ya now, and on your way back stop by that Cantina and pick us up some of them skinny little slices of cornbread, and get some meat and beans and stuff in them. And Pedro, bring some fer yourself too. Here's a dollar, shouldn't be mor'n that."

"Si Señor," the boy replied, but Cliff could tell he was uneasy about staying in a white man's house.

Cliff had rented two adjoining rooms on the second floor. As soon as everyone got their gear stowed, he called them into his room and began to tell them the rules of the evening. "I know J.J. there aims to wet his pecker, and I 'spect the rest a' you do too, but I got 'a tell ya something first."

Cliff stopped, and looking as serious as he could, hoping they might heed a little of what he was going to share, he began, "The last time we wus here, I had to stretch a tale a mite, to get Shep out of jail. I wouldn't be surprised if'n there ain't some law still a little huffed over finding out I tricked him.

Go ahead and have some fun but don't get into no trouble. You ain't no good to me beat up, shot, or in jail. I doubt if'n I can get another one out a' that **hoosegow**."

He looked around at their faces, all of which were showing signs of strained anxiousness. "We leave at first light. Anyone too under the weather to ride, can catch the next southbound back to Texas, when you feel up to it."

"Damn Reb, you are a hard one tonight."

"We are up against a hard fight boys," he said, and reached into his vest pocket for his makin's[17] but also brought out a twenty-dollar gold-piece and added, "I'll expect some change from this Double Eagle," before he flipped it to them. "And stay out of Frenchy's."

The men had not been gone more than ten minutes, when a soft knock was heard at the door.

Cliff reached for his Colt hanging by the bed before he rolled off onto the cold hard floor in his stocking feet.

He was about to jerk the door open when a voice whispered, "Señor Reb, it 'ees me, Pe'dro."

Cliff opened the door and lowered the hammer on the big revolver. "Come in Pedro," he said. He then carefully looked out in the hall, checking both ways until he was satisfied the boy had not been followed.

Then he stepped back in, closed and locked the door, before asking, "Everything go alright?"

"Si' Señor. De man at the livery, he sa'de he knew you, and would feed all the caballos, pronto."

"You did good Pedro. Now let's dig into that chuck, then you can find you a warm spot so we can get some sleep."

"Señor Reb, I should not be here, I t'ink. I should stay wi've the caballos."

Cliff knew the boy was afraid the white men would object to his being in the same room with them, and he appreciated his loyalty in not wanting to be the cause of trouble among the Texicans. However, he had always treated his good men the same, weather they

---

17 Makin's: Paper, and tobacco bag to roll a cigarette.

be white, black, red, or brown. He had no intention of changing now, so he said, "If I needed you to stay with the hawses, that's what I would have told you to do. I need you here with me. I want to get some sleep, and I need you to be here in case there's trouble, so you can wake me."

"Ah, Si. I weel' wake you," Pedro said, smiling broadly at the great responsibility that had just been given to him.

Cliff lowered the fire in the lamp until just a dull glow caressed the room, and then he stretched out on the only bed. For a long time, he laid there looking at the ceiling thinking first of Nadine, then of John Tidwell. When his thoughts came to this subject, his stomach began to burn. Sometime later, he felt Pedro touch his arm. "What is it?"

"Someone 'ees outside, I t'ink."

Cliff listened and recognized the voices of Ethan and Billy Ellis. "It's just a couple of the boys," he said.

"Si, Señor," the boy replied and then moved back to the corner of the room.

The two cowboys were less than quiet, although it was obvious they were trying to be, but the alcohol they had consumed made quietness impossible.

Cliff could hear them in the other room telling each other about the whores they had enjoyed, and the thought suddenly crossed his mind, *'Perhaps I should have gone with them. It certainly has been a long time since I tasted the pleasure of a woman.'* As these thoughts wove their way through his mind he suddenly realized he was thinking of Elaine Moore and the feeling he had experienced the night before when she had hugged him tightly.

'She is a looker,' he admitted to himself but then tried to dismiss the idea by saying under his breath, "Hell, her husband ain't hardly cold yet and you thinking such. You should be ashamed a' yourself, Reb Brown."

"You call me, Señor?"

"No Pedro, I was just figuring on what supplies we should get before we leave," he lied, knowing full well he had already decided against waiting for the store to open before departing this burg.

Late in the night, he heard a window being opened and someone in the other room throwing up, then the window being closed again. *'I reckon it was best I didn't go with the boys after all.'*

They slipped out of town just as the city man was putting out the new gas streetlamps. He gave the six riders and the following buckboard a curious look as they moved into the fog that was forming along Crow Creek.

They stopped ten miles west of town and built a small fire under the limbs of a big cottonwood, and Pedro soon had a pot of Arbuckles next to the fire and bacon sizzling in the pan.

The boiling coffee was a pleasant aroma to J.J., but when the smell of the bacon reached the wagon, he rose up and began heaving over the side of the Studebaker.

He had been too sick to sit a saddle, so Cliff had him laid in the back of the wagon thus far, but when they moved out from this short stop, his horse was no longer tied to the tailgate.

The next ten miles were some of the worst the lad had ever remembered in his life. Had it not been for Tommy Walker helping him from time to time, he would not have been able to stay aboard that bronc.

By the time they reached the ranch, J.J. was sitting pretty much straight, even though not always totally upright.

Cliff rode up beside him just before he dismounted and asked, "Was it worth it?"

"That's just it, Reb, I can't remember what she looked like. I remember going up to her room alright, but that is about all, and that's kind a' a blur."

Cliff couldn't help but laugh inwardly. He had been in the same condition more than once in the early days of the war, but he didn't dare let the boy know that.

Nodding his head, he said to J.J., "Let this be a lesson to you. I almost left you back there in Cheyenne."

Then turning to the other men he said, "Get yourselves cleaned up and presentable. I'll bring the real boss down to meet you after chuck, and I want you to show proper respect." He then handed his reins to Pedro and headed towards the stone house.

Elaine Moore was watching from the window as the tall, lean man started her way. She had to admire his appearance. His slow deliberate stride, the way his fringed chaps were slapping against his legs as he walked, the straightness of his back, the square, wide shoulders and the dark hair, now a little too long and bushy, showing from under his Stetson.

Suddenly she felt a dampness in her loins, and she thought of the night before when she had laid awake, remembering the hardening of his manhood pressing against her leg, as he had held her close.

'Damn, why didn't I meet him before I did Jimmy Don,' she thought, and then suddenly she realized what she had been doing, and she shook herself back to reality.

"I see you made it," she said sharply as he entered the small building. "Any trouble?"

"No, one of the boys got a little drunk but no trouble," he said removing his hat.

"I would have thought you could have prevented that sort of thing," she spat back sharply.

"You got a burr under your saddle or something?" he replied suddenly.

She was taken back at his roughness, realizing he was not one to be scolded. However, as much as she tried not to do so, she still retorted, "I just think a foreman should be able to control his men, that's all."

"Anytime you want a different foreman, just let me know," he slung at her as strongly as she had to him.

Returning his hat to his head, he started for the door. Upon opening it to the cold wind, he stopped and spoke without looking at her, "I told the men you would be out to meet them after supper." Then, just before he stepped outside, he added, "If you are of a mind to."

Suddenly the wind stopped whirling around in the room as the door closed, and he was gone.

She didn't look at him as he walked back to the barn, and she had to bite her lower lip when Ellie spoke, "Gee Sis, you were shor' a bitch to him. What's the matter with you? The man is doing his level best to keep this ranch fer you and you go and bite his head near off."

"Wal' ain't you the one to be complaining. All you do these days is lay around with that no good saddle tramp. You'll be turned up pregnant here a'for long, and he'll be high-tailed it out of the Territory," she snapped. Then removing her apron, she threw it across the room before grabbing her coat and charging through the door, towards the outhouse.

Elaine felt the tears building long before she reached the little one-holer, but she couldn't help it. As soon as she was inside with the door closed, she let her emotions go and began to bawl openly.

She had been sharp to him because of her own thoughts, not because of anything he had done, and she realized it. She also realized she had said some awful things to her little sister, and she was equally sorry about that as well.

"Whatever am I going to do?" she asked with no one to hear.

Two hours later, she and Ellie, now changed into new prairie dresses, were as pleasant as two young girls could be as they walked into the barn.

They both moved around speaking to the new men, as well as their loyal hands.

Finally, Elaine called out asking for their attention, "I want you all to know, that I fully realize the sacrifices you are making coming here to help me. I also know, were it not for my loyal friend Rodriguez and his sons and nephews, as well as the best damn foreman on the Snowy Range, I would have lost everything several months ago."

She stopped, looking first down at her feet, and then directly at Cliff. "I fear, perhaps I might have been swinging from a limb like my husband did, were it not for you Reb Brown, and I deeply appreciate it.

I also want to say that in all my born days I never knew a 'kaboy from the Lone Star State who weren't too loud, or too drunk to be pleasant, but if you boys are half the men that these Adams brothers are, I will forever change my mind on the subject."

"Hey, hey," Tommy Walker yelled.

"Ma'am," Billy Ellis began as he removed his big hat, "I, err, we, that is err, well we ain't never worked fer no wimmen' 'afore, and I reckon it's fair to say were it not fer Reb askin' fer us, we never would have come here in the first place but___,"

"Hell Billy, stop stammering around and say what's on your mind," Shep said to his friend.

"Wal', I just wanted to say ___, well; you shor' are the purtiest boss I ever had."

"Thank you for the compliment, but I'm not your boss. Your boss is standing right over there," she replied nodding her head at Reb.

That night when Cliff pulled his blanket over him, he shook his head and whispered to himself, "I'll never understand women."

"What did you say boss?" one of the boys asked.
"Nothing."

Celeste Patay had been exceedingly pleased when Jean had taken her away from the fort. It was an adventure even greater than when her husband had brought her, by boat, from Quebec.

The first few weeks, she had enjoyed her life as she had not done in many years. Her new man was truly a great lover. He never pleased himself until after she was satisfied, which was something her husband had never even considered. However, recently she began to notice that Jean was becoming more and more moody as the winter months approached, and he seemed to worry a great deal about something concerning his operation of the ranch.

Her poor understanding of the English language often left her confused, especially when she heard the talking of the men who worked for Jean. However, she had heard and fully understood what the man called PC meant by saying something to one of the hands about, "His French Whore."

She had been in the kitchen overseeing the Mexican cook prepare the evening meal, when the man opened the rear door as she was going to the root cellar to retrieve eggs for the desert. At that very moment, the two wranglers were passing, obviously discussing Jean Mouton.

It was the first time she realized the men thought of her as a whore. She did not think of herself as such. Jean had told her she should respond to the name Mrs. Brown if so approached. She had no idea any of them knew she was not Mrs. Brown. That night she wept after he was asleep.

The tension Celeste had detected in him was indeed working on his mind. He had not planned on this Moore woman being so stubborn. The failure of obtaining the water rights to that spring and along the creek, would not go well were his bosses to find out the significance of these losses.

John had received a wire from Allen Moreton informing him he would be arriving in Cheyenne with news from home, and needed to talk to him. Mouton did not like this at all. *'Why can't the young bastard stay back east where he belongs, and let me make him and his family rich?'* he questioned in his mind.

Nonetheless, it was times like this that made him realize he, too, was little more than hired help and could be replaced with the snapping of an English finger. Immediately, he felt a burning deep in his gut, and cursed under his breath.

'What am I to do with Celeste while meeting with Moreton? I could leave her here at the ranch. Perhaps it would be better to take her with me. Should I leave her, the men might try to question her about our relationship. Of course, if I take her and any of the soldiers from Fort Laramie were to see her, she will most surely be recognized, and that would be unacceptable. No, I must leave her here, and she will not like that.'

Rodriguez approached Elaine, looking carefully around making sure no one else saw him talking to her. "Señora, I was with Juan two days ago, and we came upon the ol' cabin at Sandy Hill. It is in mucho, how do you say, bad building."

"Poor condition?" she suggested.

"Si poour condis'eon," he agreed. "But no one goes there. It would be a good place for you and the little one to hide if the hombres from Wolf Creek come again, I t'ink."

She thought a few moments, *'I can't recall Jimmy Don ever talking about such a cabin, or Sandy Hill.'*

"I don't know of this cabin, Gilberto. Where is it?"

"It 'ees the first place Señor Jimmy Don and me stay, when we come to dis place, but it was not near the rio, only a leetle' arroyo, not grande, thet 'ees why he moved here and build the stone house, to be close to the rio."

"Where is this place?" she asked, still not sure of what or where he was talking.

"There, cinco miles, me'bee more," he said, holding up an open hand with all fingers extended, before pointing to the north.

"Tomorrow, you will show me this place," she said. Then added, "Tomorrow, after the others are gone."

He nodded and returned the large sugarloaf[18] to his head. He then headed back to the corral, where the other men were working on a wild mustang one of his nephews had caught.

The weather on the high plains in the fall and winter is usually a perfect circle. Today it snows, tomorrow it will be calm, the following day the wind will come up with such a force, it often seems a slight man could be blown from his saddle, and sweeps most of the

---

18 Sugarloaf: Large brimmed sombrero with a peaked top.

powder to some unknown place in the east. Then on the next day, the circle begins all over again with a strong snow storm.

The next morning was quite different from the norm. For some reason no one could explain, the morning broke with heavy clouds moving low and fast toward Dakota Territory. Elaine thought snow would surely begin falling at any minute, destroying any hope of Gilberto Rodriguez showing her this mysterious cabin, but it was not to be. By the ten o'clock hour, the sky was clear and deeply blue, as only a high country sky can be. The wind, though still blowing with its usual gusto, was unusually warm. She and the older man were almost out of sight when her sister missed her.

The country there is rolling, with small hills and shallow depressions where scattered trees grew.

Their pace had been swift at first, but gradually the track he was taking began to ascend, and before long the acclivity was working on the horses. Eventually they were moving at little more than a slow walk.

The Cliffs Elaine saw off in the distance

At the very northwestern edge of her property, they came to a hummock that shot up quite suddenly from the norm of the land. Again, scattered pinions grew here and there, but it was too high for sage. Mostly it was rock, with several areas of short crags where the melting snows of summer had let erosion work its course. Off in the distance, she could see very large rocks where at and near the top, were huge boulders and steep cliffs. It was towards these he led her until they came upon a ravine in the desert, unseen to the traveler, until a few feet prior to arriving at its steep bank.

Rodriguez carefully guided his horse down the thirty feet to its snow-covered bottom, and she followed.

After easing off the bank into the ravine, she immediately realized the force of the wind was no longer felt. The snow was almost up to the horses' bellies here, where it had been protected from the gales.

He moved on northward in the gully for what seemed to her like another mile, and she had to admit she didn't like it down there. Finally she spoke, asking, "Are we still on my land?"

He looked back at her and slowly shook his head, "No. Open range here." At this time, he stopped his mare for a breather, and then once again looking at her he completed his answer, "No man owns des' land."

"I see," she replied.

Although there was no wind, the temperature was considerably colder in the gulch than on the level ground where the warm wind was blowing. She shivered and reached for the bearskin coat tied on the rear of her saddle.

She was riding a standard saddle, rather than the sidesaddle she normally used when side-riding a man. She had considered one, but after debating on it with herself, changed her mind and told him to use one of the men's saddles from the barn. Elaine was satisfied Rodriguez was too old to be inspired by her boldness, and she realized this would not necessarily be a pleasure ride, considering the area to which they were going.

She had been wrong about Rodriguez' attention to her forking a man's saddle, but he was much too respectful to allow her to see his interest.

When they had stolen on some two miles up the arroyo, they came to a small rift in the rock wall, to their left, scarcely four feet wide. Its mouth was surrounded with stunted shrubs and overhanging vines to the extent if one had not known of its existence, or were not following a trail left by another, it would have easily been passed by.

Rodriguez pushed his cayuse into this cut, some one hundred feet of curvy trail-bed, which turned first to the right, and in no more than the length of a horse's body, back to the left. Finally it opened into a canyon that was bounded by high ridges on all sides, rising perhaps 300 feet or more at their highest.

She had seen these steep rough masses of rock, which formed the cliff walls, before they had come upon the ravine. However, now realizing when viewed from afar she had not appreciated they held such magnitude.

The canyon, a true amphitheater, was bedded with shin high grass and shaded by scattered piñon pines and cottonwoods, proving either a creek was near, or slow melting snows kept the secret place well-moist during the dry months.

Gilberto moved into the small flat valley, to the little stand of trees, and there he dismounted and reached for her, helping her to do likewise.

"Is the cabin near?" she asked, looking around.

"Si, there," he replied pointing ahead.

She followed the line of his hand with her eyes but saw nothing. Nonetheless, when he began to walk, she followed.

The snow here was halfway up her calves, and she feared her boots would fill, causing her feet to become frost-bitten, but Rodriguez made sure when he walked, his steps were short and wide, thereby cutting a trail for her to follow.

In less than two hundred feet, he broke a limb from a felled tree and began probing the snow.

She watched until finally his hand went deep into the white powder. Turning to her, he said, "Crick here," before he jumped.

He landed only a yard ahead and almost lost his footing but was able to keep his balance. Then he turned, and he held out his hand for her to follow.

"Ees' leetle ice in the crick, me'bee."

She too jumped after him, and he caught her outstretched limb, pulling her forward and clear of the creek.

She took a deep breath and then blew most of it out. "Glad you knew aboot thet," she said.

He then pointed, and there through the trees, she saw it ahead. She would have never recognized it as a cabin had he not shown her.

The small one room structure had a low roof that was completely covered with snow and the sides had rocks and dirt piled up to the wooden poles of the roof. There were no windows save a small cut in the only door. Looking at the cabin as a whole, she was amazed at it even being man made.

Rodriguez experienced great difficulty getting the door to swing out so they could enter. Once inside she stood in almost total darkness, save the light spilling past the entrance.

Moving to one wall, he began feeling around until he came upon a lantern, which he soon had lit. The dull yellow glow, given off by the dusty globe opened a whole new world within the small retreat. At least it appeared small from the front, not necessarily so from the inside. There was no apparent rear wall. Instead, she realized a cave was there, opening into the side of the cliff.

Just beyond, she espied a few small pieces of partially burned limbs and a circle of charcoal, giving evidence of a long past fire.

"I don't savvy Jimmy Don building this place, if there is no water," she said looking around.

"Oh Señora 'dare 'ees water but no more," he said shaking his head. "Da water come from 'dare in 'da cave. 'Dare 'ees water in the summertime wheen' the snow is no more. Not so in 'da winter."

"I see," she replied nodding her head. *'So it takes the thawing of the snow before there is water here. Most likely in late winter, when it had been many months since the thaw, Jimmy ran out of water, and he decided to make the move,'* she thought.

Looking at Rodriguez she asked, "Is there water here now?"

"Si, me'bee. We can go and look," he said, looking into the dark cave.

"Let's do," she agreed.

Taking the lantern, he led the way. The cave was large, almost tall enough for him to stand straight, and the further they walked, the warmer it became. When they had gone perhaps fifty yards, he stopped and pointed to a crack in the stone wall. There, she spotted a steady drip of clear water falling onto the sandy floor or before soon disappearing into another crack along the same wall, she was not sure which.

"In the June time dare ees mucho water here, and the crick it 'ees full."

"Who all knows aboot this place?"

"I do not know, no one, Indians, me'bee'?" he said, raising his shoulders and palms.

"I think Reb needs to know of it, just in case we need it sometime," she said and turned back towards where they had come.

"De' Señora knows as bes' too, I t'ink."

After she did some dusting and straightening of what little furniture there was, a table and two chairs, they returned to the light of the day.

Rodriguez made sure the cabin entrance was well secured and reasonably hid before they walked back to where the horses had been left. "I t'ink the door, we should me'bee fix, no? An' some of the front, no?"

"Yes, but only from the inside. I do not want it to look new outside, be too easy for others to spot," she said, as she looked back at the cabin.

The older Mexican just nodded his head in reply and moved on ahead, making sure he was breaking a wide trail for her through the powder.

Snow had begun to fall, and she was glad to see it soon covered their tracks.

Their ride towards the ranch was uncomfortable. The wind was almost squarely in their faces, and the snow was beginning to bite, even though the temperature had not fallen much as the storm approached.

They had traveled less than two miles when she saw Rodriguez rise suddenly in his saddle, before falling forward and off his horse onto the frozen ground.

She looked at him as he just lay there not moving, and she was mesmerized by what had just happened before her eyes. It was the wind-muffled sound of the second shot that brought her back to reality.

Suddenly, she spotted three horses off to her left. On two were the shapes of riders, but the third had an empty saddle. It wasn't until she recognized the contrast the gun smoke made to the color of the falling snow did she realize the third man was down on one knee taking careful aim with his rifle.

The sound of the heavy slug slicing the air only inches from her head caused her to turn her mount back towards the cut and whip him hard with the quirt she carried.

She knew the chase was on although she did not look back. On she dashed, hoping she could reach the arroyo, hoping more she would be able to recognize it in time so as not to plunge head first into it.

The fast moving storm only lasted another hour, and then a strong wind came up and began blowing the fresh powder towards Nebraska.

It was just after the noon hour when Gilberto Rodriguez' horse came trotting into the ranch yard, and stopped in front of the barn and lowered its head.

It was Juan who saw him standing there. Digesting the strange sight, he walked to her slowly.

Juan patted the animal and eased around from one side to the other trying to figure out why Gilberto had chosen this place to leave his favorite horse. When his gloved hand touched the horn, he felt the slipperiness of it, and removing his hand, he rubbed his thumb and forefinger together trying to discover what it was.

Finally he realized it was frozen blood he had touched, suddenly his eyes opened wide, and he began to yell.

Shep was working in the barn and heard him. However, it was Ellie who reached the boy first.

As soon as they realized the significance of what Juan had discovered, Ellie screamed, "My sister left with him! Right after breakfast!"

Shep immediately saddled his horse and headed out for the river where Reb and several of the other men were working strays out of the cuts along its banks.

One hour after Rodriguez' horse had arrived at the ranch, Cliff and Black Band were ready to move out.

Several of the men wanted to go with them, but he thought it might be a trick to get most of them away from the plaza so it could be overrun. Reb thought strongly on their wants but decided to insist everyone else stay there.

"Shep, if we are not back by dark head into town and fetch Pike Pepper," he said, then spurred Ola and they were off.

The wind clearing away the snow was of some help, but they would have been at a total loss as to which direction to take at all, had it not been for Tommy Walker having seen the two leave. He assured Reb they headed out to the northwest.

Cliff considered himself a fair tracker. He realized he was not what would be classified as having a hound scent. Nonetheless, he had made a good effort at staying alive through several years of hard fighting and many more since the sabers had been turned in, simply by being able, often times, to watch and read sign. Still, he was always amazed when he could watch an Indian track.

The Crow walked his horse slowly in a large semi-circle, first to the right and then crossing over the aim of their trail, an equal distance to the left. He did this for perhaps two miles before he suddenly stopped and quickly dismounted, stooping to the ground. In a short time, he stood and waved to Cliff.

"There, two riders come this way," he said, when Cliff reached his position.

"You think it's them?"

"One rider heavy, one not heavy. One horse make same track as Señor Rodriguez' horse."

"Let's go," was all Cliff said, as he touched his heel to Ola's side.

Two hours later, they found the body of the old Mexican. The bullet had struck him just aft of his left elbow and passed through, exiting his right chest, tearing his tobacco pouch to pieces in his vest pocket.

Cliff could see small specks of blood, but no pool as one would have thought with such a large wound. It was obvious to them both; the man was dead when he hit the ground.

"Look around for Miss Elaine," he ordered.

The Indian once again placed his attention to the surrounding ground, often using his hands to brush away the fallen snow.

Soon Black Band stood straight and pointed to the frozen clay he had uncovered. "Many horses," he said.

"Can you follow them?"

The Crow lifted his shoulders as if to say maybe, maybe not, but he immediately returned his attention to the earth. His circles widened as on he looked.

Cliff was becoming both nervous and aggravated the longer the Indian took. He could not understand why he was doing his circles rather than just following the trail he had found. Also, the thought of Elaine being taken by the riders of those horses was building heavily in his mind, causing heartburn, and bringing pain to his chest to the point he belched loudly. "Damn sorry Government

Java," he said just above a whisper, knowing full well the coffee had nothing to do with his indigestion.

Several minutes passed, and the Indian continued in his circles. Finally, Cliff called out to him over the wind that was beginning to build, "Those hawses, are they shod?"

"Whiteman," was all Black Band said in reply.

Cliff nodded a reply, even though his companion was not looking in his direction. He had suspected they were Wolf Creek horses all along. Rodriguez had been shot and left to lie where he fell. Had Indians done the deed, most likely he would no longer have his hair.

Finally, Black Band stood straight again and after mounting his horse, waved Cliff over.

He wasted no time heeling Ola over to where the other rider was waiting.

"Woman rides this way," Black Band said, pointing towards the distant mountains.

"Let's go," Cliff ordered.

Black Band did not head out as quickly as the command suggested; rather he straightened his back and looked deeply at Cliff, "Four cayuse follow her. All run fast," he said, moving his open, down-turned palm across the ground before him.

Cliff nodded his head and again touched Ola with the heel of his boots.

Their progress was slow, but the snow had stopped, and the wind was increasing. Within half an hour these high plains were more tan than white, except for the places where pine or larger than normal sagebrush stood, allowing the powder to drift around and behind it.

Finally, the Indian pulled up and held out his hand to stop Cliff; then he slowly moved forward. Cliff followed and soon saw the dark depression of the cut. Stopping at the rim, there below, they saw a dead horse. The brand on his left hip was a Circle WC.

Carefully, Black Band moved down the frozen bank until his pony was belly deep in the snow. Stopping beside the dead animal, he dismounted to inspect it. When satisfied, he looked up at Cliff, who was still on the level of the plains and spoke, "Horse fall, break neck. Man dead."

"Man dead?" Cliff questioned. "Is there a man down there too?"

"Riders carry him off."

The Circle Wolf Creek Brand

Cliff was amazed the redman could determine such in this cut three feet deep in snow.

"What happened to Mrs. Moore?"

Again Black Band pointed up the arroyo, "Woman go that way."

"They didn't follow her?"

"One follows."

"Let's go," Cliff replied, as he heeled his mount once more.

Ola was not at all pleased with what he was being asked to do. He fully recognized the danger in descending the slippery bank and also was quite aware one of his kind was lying below dead. Nonetheless, he moved forward and as cautiously as he could, eased down the steep bank.

They continued on much more slowly now because of the deep snow, but the need to locate a trail was no longer necessary. Should either of the people they were after leave the cut, their tracks would be clear where they ascended the bank.

After another mile, they came upon the cut in the steep stone wall, and Black Band pointed to the narrow opening. Cliff nodded his head, and soon they were moving towards the canyon that contained the old fronted cave.

After traveling not more than a hundred yards, the faint sound of a gunshot was heard ahead. It was soon followed by a sharp crack, easily recognized as that of a rifle report.

Cliff suddenly had a warm feeling sweep over him. '*She must be alive and fighting back,*' he thought.

"Come on!" he said reaching for his carbine and urging Ola ahead.

They heard no more shots as they entered the wide meadow but did see the tall bay horse standing under a cottonwood, pulling bark from the trunk with its strong teeth. The Circle WC brand was clearly seen on his left hip.

Dismounting, they moved ahead, drop reining their mounts where they abandoned them.

Cliff swiftly loosened the saddle cinch on the bay only enough to present a problem if a rider tried to mount him without first re-tightening it.

The snow here was waist-deep again, but the trail cut by her horse was clear and easy to follow. Also, boot tracks could be seen in the white powder.

When they came to the small stream, it was obvious she had been pushing her horse hard, and it had lost its footing here and fallen. Ahead was a trail left by the horse as it cut through the snow and that of two humans afoot.

Her tracks clearly indicated she had been running. Cliff spotted where more than once she had fallen only to get up and hurry off again. Her pursuer was more deliberate. He had not rushed after her, obviously thinking he had her trapped, and was moving in for the kill.

Presently, they came to a place in the patch of trees where more clearing could be seen ahead. There they stopped, watched and listened.

There was no sound of any kind. The ever-present wind of the open plains had not found its way into this hidden valley. Total silence was observed until they again moved slowly forward, and then only the soft sound of his boots crushing the powder was heard.

Cliff felt a moment of pride sweep over him as he spotted the movement through the trees a moment before Black Band. They both suddenly crouched lower, as if to hide from what ever was moving ahead.

Keeping a keen eye on the dark figure off to their right, they eased on until they reached the edge of the trees. From there, they quickly realized it was a man slipping along the rock wall towards the partially exposed wooden front of Jimmy Don's old cabin.

Cliff strained hard to recognize him, but he had the collar of his plaid coat turn upwards, trying to get added protection from the cold. From this distance, it was difficult to distinguish where the frozen collar ended and the frozen beard began.

Finally, Cliff took a fine bead on the man and called out, "Drop your rifle and identify yourself."

The startled man quickly turned and fired wildly at the sight of the two men below him.

Cliff squeezed the trigger, and the little carbine reported immediately, sending a Henry conical onward rapidly, striking the man in his right shoulder. He had been trying to reload the Number 1 Remington as fast as he could, but the blow of the heavy lead slug caused him to immediately drop the rolling-block rifle, before he too fell backward and then slid down the bank into the deep snow below him.

Elaine Moore had heard the sound of first Cliff's call to her attacker, followed by the gunshots, and lastly the scream the stalker had made when his shoulder had been smashed by the 44 caliber bullet. She had been unable to make out who had called before the shot. However, there was no question that the cry immediately after the second shot was from someone very close who had been hit. Still, she wisely did not remove the heavy timber securing the door.

The next minute seemed at least an hour long, as she strained to see anything out of the small gun port cut in the heavy timber of the door.

Finally, she spotted two men pass in front of the cabin, and even though they were still almost seventy-five yards away, she did not fail to recognize the deliberate swagger of her foreman.

A rush of relief swept over her, and she suddenly felt weak and queasy in her stomach. Almost immediately, she began to weep uncontrollably and slumped into the chair behind her. Elaine was still sitting there when they reached the cabin front, and Cliff called out to her.

Suddenly, she realized she did not want him to see her so weak and afraid. *'I remained calm most of the time, even after my horse fell into the creek down in the trees.'* She had been mad as a wet hen at herself for not remembering it being there. She now knew it was that anger which overrode the emotion of fear. '*Now I must clear my head of this nonsense and open the door for them.*'

Standing, she laid her revolver on the table and using the backs of her gloved hands, wiped the tears from her eyes and cheeks. When satisfied with her appearance, she removed the thick board that secured the door and pushed it open.

The moment she saw him appear in the doorway, she again lost all control of her emotions. Rushing to him, she burst out in uncontrollable sobbing as she held tightly to his body. Over and over again, she pulled him closer to her, hugging this man with all her might as she bawled openly.

Cliff still held the Winchester in his right hand, but he placed his other arm around her and carefully patted her back, trying to assure her everything was all right now. However, when she did not release him, he became embarrassed knowing Black Band was seeing her hold onto him as she did.

Only the sound of Ola's whinnying stopped her clinging. Cliff pointed for Black Band to see what was causing his horse to call out so.

Soon the Indian returned and explained that the man Cliff had shot was not dead and had tried to lead off their horses. However, Ola had revolted and caused both to bolt. He had got there, just in time to see the man entering the cut riding bareback.

"Can you catch him?" Cliff asked.

"I catch my horse, first," Black Band said, and then hurried off.

"Come on," Reb said to her. "Let's see if we can catch your horse."

"I twisted my ankle when I fell," she said. "Could I just wait here for you?"

"Sure."

When he did find her horse, he realized it sported a bad limp and assumed it too had sprained something in the fall, so he left the gelding there.

Black Band had just caught his pony when Cliff started back, and he called out to him, "After you finish with the bushwhacker, go to the ranch and bring back the buckboard. Miss Elaine has a bad leg."

The Crow nodded his head before pulling on the right rein and turning his pony towards the mouth of the canyon.

"Bring some of the boys too," Cliff called out to him as he rode away following the path cut in the deep snow.

Cliff thought about shooting her horse but decided against it. *'Here in this meadow there is a good chance nothing will bother him until he can make it on his own,'* he reasoned, then as an afterthought, *'less there is a bear or painter hereabouts.'*

Black Band found the trail of his prey with ease but did not seem to gain on him much after they each had returned to the high plains. The white man's horse was larger and stronger than his pony and began to out-distance him. Only once did he see the rider, some two miles ahead. Unfortunately, shortly after, the snow began again. This time large flakes fell, slowly at first, but within a mile or two the snow was falling at such a rate he lost the trail.

Three hours later when he topped a hummock, he spied several riders huddled together. Two were assisting another off his mount and laying him on the ground.

He was not sure just who they were, but he had learned long before it was not healthy for a single and especially a strange Indian to ride up on a bunch of white men. Thus, he wisely turned south and headed for *The Circle Rocking AR Ranch* before they saw him.

Long before he reached the ranch plaza, the storm had intensified to the point he could no longer see ahead, and he simply loosely tied the reins together and let his pony find his own way back to the warmth of the barn.

Ethan was the first to see the lone rider coming in, and he quickly summoned his brother and Ella.

When the Crow had told his story, a cloud of relief seemed to hover over the whites there. "At least they are safe," Ethan pointed out.

Not so among the Mexican hands. The murder of their father, or uncle, as the case may be, stirred much heartache and gloom, which soon turned to anger and then rage. Only the cool head of Ethan kept them from heading over to the Wolf Creek spread right then for revenge.

"No. You will be playing right into their hands," Ethan told them. "Wait, presently Reb will git back. He is our leader, and it is him we will follow."

This only caused much grumbling in a language he only knew slightly, but finally Ella spoke, "If you have no more care for my sister than thet, go ahead and get yourselves killed to prove a point, but if you will remember it is Miss Elaine who was the friend of your father, your uncle. He would be most ashamed of you all if you let her down and fail to help her when she needs you most. You all know Gilberto Rodriguez would not have let her down."

The storm lasted all the night and on into the next day. Just before the four o'clock hour, it suddenly stopped, but the snow was too deep, and it was too near darkness for them to start out.

The bullet had struck P.C. in the upper right shoulder, cutting his collarbone in two before passing on straight through, to spend most of its energy against the rock of the canyon wall.

The shock and pain was so intense at first, he lost consciousness, but his falling back into the snow bank had been a blessing. The cold powder soon caused the bleeding to stop and also awakened him in a matter of minutes.

His intention had been to take their mounts, thereby trapping the trio, until he could send other Wolf Creek hands to finish them off.

He had been able to catch the pony easily enough, but when he took hold of the reins of the Appaloosa, the big animal reared and kicked at him with its front feet. This caused him to drop the lead on the Indian pony, as he scrambled to get to his own mount. His anger was great, and he intended to still lead them from this canyon, but as he tried to mount his horse, the saddle slipped and spilled him. Then once more, that crazy stud charged, and he had to leap aboard his mount before he was stomped to death in the snow. Reaching down, he pulled the cinch completely loose, and the saddle and blanket dropped. Cursing, he rode away for help.

P.C. never knew he was being pursued but was plenty grateful when he cut paths with several of his men.

That night, John Brown openly displayed his displeasure with the wounded man in front of the others in the bunkhouse before he stomped away.

"You leave a dead body out there for them to use as evidence, let the girl get away, get one man killed and yourself shot up. Some leader I have inherited," he shouted. John slapped his gloves in the palm of his other hand and added, "Come first light, I want ten of you to get out there and get them if they are still at this hidden cabin. Find that body and bring it back here so we can dispose of it." Then in a somewhat calmer voice he asked, "Who shot you?"

"I don't know for sure," Defray replied. "I'm hit in the back, you know." He paused a moment thinking back and then added, "I spotted that big Appaloosa the Copperhead rides there," he paused again, "and there was a' Injun with him."

"Too bad they didn't scalp you."

"Bastard!" was all P.C. said and that just above a whisper as his boss slammed the door upon his exit.

They tried the next day, but the storm was too intense, and they had to return to the shelter of Wolf Creek's bunkhouse.

Omaha, who was leading them, did not take the chewing out as P.C. had done the night before. When John Brown began cursing him, he took a swing at the older man. To everyone's surprise, the slim graying man sidestepped the blow and came up with a small Arkansas Toothpick, sliding the thin blade neatly between the cowboy's ribs.

There was a strange expression on Omaha's face when he turned back and faced his fellow workers. He then grabbed his side and began walking, almost staggering, towards the bunkhouse. He fell about half way there, and before his friends could get to him, his dark blood had stained a large circle in the fresh snow. Later that night his soul departed, as did three of Wolf Creek's old wranglers.

Cliff realized the snow was beginning to settle deep in their little hidden meadow, so he decided to bring both Ola and Elaine's chestnut, into the cave with them.

Gilberto had lain in enough wood for future fuel before leaving the cabin earlier that day. Now as a result, they were really not uncomfortable at all. Both had some provisions in their saddlebags, and the steady dripping of fresh water kept his canteen full.

Cliff moved back deeper into the cave, exploring for an escape route should the need arise. Finally, he decided not to venture farther for fear of not finding his way back to her.

That night they slept next to one another for warmth, but nothing more was ventured.

The next morning, when he tried to open the door of the cabin, it did not budge. After he struggled with it for a couple of minutes, she opened the rifle port only to see packed snow completely covering the hole.

The feeling of being trapped swept over her, and Elaine almost screamed. However, with determination and gritted teeth, she was able to control herself. *'I did display my weakness yesterday, but I do not intend it to happen again.'*

Cliff, realizing Black Band may not have survived himself, also knew their danger just might be quite grave. *'It could be next June before the snow in here melts enough for that door to be opened from the inside,'* he thought. *'I must find another way. At the very least, for her benefit, I must look like I am finding another way.'*

He ventured once more into the cave but again had to return. "There are so many cutoffs in there, it is next to impossible to know which is the main route," he told her.

Looking around, he discovered a decaying leather bag next to the stone wall, and in it he found a hammer. *'Surely this is the hammer her husband used to construct the cabin front.'*

Soon they both were working at the hinges on the door, and within an hour, the door was off and out of its frame. It sickened her to see a solid wall of snow, packed tight by its own weight.

Another hour passed before he had tunneled out and stuck his head into the cold, clear air.

"What do you see?" she called to him.

"It's still snowing," he called back, "but we can get out if we need to."

He knew the snow was at least eight feet deep there in the canyon and was not at all sure they could get out. Nonetheless, he didn't want to alarm her and decided to wait the storm out before trying.

"We are better off waiting here until the men arrive with the buckboard."

"Do you think they will find us?"

"There is one thing I am sure of, Black Band can find anything." Even though the words were true, his thoughts were, *'If he is still alive.'*

That night they ate the last of the food, and he knew their fuel was running low. Cliff decided to let the fire go down, saving a few pieces of wood in the event help did not arrive the next day.

Not long after the fire went to embers, she began a steady cough. Remembering a pint size fruit jar of whiskey he kept in his saddlebags, Cliff retrieved it and handed it to her.

She gave him a grateful smile just before she took a long draw. It had been some time since she had allowed strong spirits to burn her mouth, and the whiskey took her breath at first, but she did not let him know it.

Jimmy Don and she had enjoyed many a night of play after they had consumed too much alcohol, but since his death, she had not touched any.

Tonight the whiskey seemed to be just the right remedy for several things that were troubling her mind.

He had placed his saddle against the rock wall and was now leaning against it. She moved over and leaned her back up against his chest and then said, "Will you warm me a spell?" knowing full well he would.

Within less than an hour, the pint jar lay empty on the earth beside them, and she was busy tugging at the buttons of his fly.

Her clothes were already gone, and she stopped kissing him only long enough to struggle with his top button.

Soon they were wrapped in an embrace, with her legs and arms tightly wound around his hard, lean body.

He had not enjoyed a woman since he left Cheyenne several months before. Even though he had made a sure deal with himself that, save an occasional whore, he would not get involved with any woman again until he finished his promise. Yet this night, it all seemed right.

They enjoyed each other twice more before finally falling asleep.

Several hours later, he was awakened by Ola nudging him with his nose. Cliff arose and eased away leaving her to sleep.

The embers were almost a thing of the past, but he blew on the ashes several times and finally saw a bright yellow flame jump from their midst. Dropping a few splinters on the small blaze, he soon had a fire going. Beside that he set the coffee pot, then dressed and went to see what Ola was concerned about.

The big horse was staring deep into the darkness of the cave. Cliff tried as hard as he could but saw nothing, save the blackness of the cold hole. Then suddenly, Elaine's gelding whinnied and began to prance about.

Cliff reached for his Colt before placing his arm under the horse's neck, and opening his palm, he covered the gelding's nose gently in an effort to calm the animal.

Elaine stirred but did not awake; she had consumed much of the alcohol, and he knew she would not be feeling too swift when she did.

The horse calmed down a great deal with Cliff holding him so closely but never took his gaze from the darkness of the cave.

He was just about to let go of the chestnut when Ola sounded off loudly. With that, her horse lost all confidence and reared up breaking Cliff's hold.

Elaine sat up and looked around. Her breasts were cast as golden pears by the small flames, and Cliff immediately felt a stirring of his own, but he knew well enough this was not the time for such thoughts.

"What is it?" she asked, obviously concerned.

He moved his open palm up and down several quick strokes as he spoke, "Doe-no."

Then he stepped sideways, away from the fire, against the far wall. The short flames were giving life to strange dancing shadows about the interior of the rock walls, and when she looked back at Cliff, she saw nothing at first.

The protective coating applied by the folks at Hartford, some fifteen years before, had now almost entirely faded or worn away from his revolver, and only the dull gray of the metal itself was left for one to appreciate. It was this finish reflecting the light of the fire occasionally, which allowed her to realize where he was standing.

For a long minute, all was quiet. Then suddenly, both horses began to dance about.

She was not sure if she really saw them, or it was her fright that caused her to imagine them, but she thought she saw two eyes suddenly shine brightly from the blackness. All this happened only a split-second before the deafening roar of his Colt, discharging inside their close quarters, almost caused her to lose her bladder.

She screamed loudly, and then taking a deep breath she asked, "What is it you are shooting at?"

"A painter," he replied.

"A what?"

"A big painter," again he said.

Now she was totally at a loss as to what was happening. His explanation was more confusing than had he not replied to her question.

"A painter?" she screamed back.

"Yeah," he said, as he stepped from the shadows. "A painter, you know a big cat."

"You mean a panther?"

"Yeah, I heard some folks call one that a few years back. I think they wus from Pennsylvania or Ohio or sum-ers up there. Panther, that must be a Yankee word. Anyways they's painters in Okefenok' Country."

Taking a small splinter, he held it in the flames and then took it over and lit the oil lantern. "I think you call them lions out here."

Slowly he brought the wick up until it gave a good glow ahead, then he moved forward into the cave.

"Mountain Lions, yes, yes we do." She suddenly was not the least bit cold, and she jumped from the bedding he had made from their saddle blankets. Grabbing her 32 revolver, she pointed it into the cave also. *'I must be careful not to shoot Reb,'* she subconsciously cautioned herself as she stood there buck-naked, with both hands out-stretched and gripping the small revolver tightly.

After what seemed like half an hour, he suddenly appeared from the darkness.

"What happened to the lantern? I was expecting to see the lantern."

"I turned it out when I didn't need it no more," he replied looking at her standing there behind the fire.

"Damn, you are a fine-looking woman," he said.

Suddenly, she realized she was naked, and for the first time in years, this embarrassed her. "Wal, I didn't have the time you apparently had," she shot back reaching for her coat.

"Wait."

She stopped and looked back at him.

The sight of him moving from the dark cave towards her was extremely arousing, and she suddenly dropped the coat. "What aboot the mountain lion?"

"He won't peek."

This time their sex was furious at first. Then he slowed, and finally laying down himself, she mounted his body. Slowly and deliberately, she rode him as the lust built deep inside her, until an explosion caused her to pass out.

Later, when she awoke, she was again covered by the blankets and he was dressed and pouring hot water down the barrel of his revolver.

She had not enjoyed a sexual experience like the ones of the night before in a long time. In her youth, sex had been pretty gratifying, but after she began whoring, its pleasure simply was no longer there. Even though she did have a great deal of fun with her husband, she never really expected to experience true sexual satisfaction again after selling her body to so many men. This morning she knew those feeling were not dead in her after all, and she was incredibly grateful for the knowledge.

Her head ached a little, but her stomach only felt the need for food, which she thought strange.

"Did you kill him?"

"Yep."

"Where is he?"

"Back a ways," he said nodding toward the cave.

"I want to see him."

"Go ahead," he teased.

"No!" she shot back sharply. "You show me."

He reassembled and loaded his revolver and then let it drop gently into its leather home before he stood.

Picking up the lantern he said, "Get dressed first. You cause me to lose my train of thought walking around naked."

"I like thet," she said. However, only after standing and giving him another view of her body did she slip on her heavy coat and then her boots. With both her hands around his upper arm she walked at his side, if not slightly behind, into the cave.

The big cat was lying on its side in a pool of blood some eighty feet from where he had been hit. The bullet entered just below his jaw and passed on deep into his body, destroying his heart as it did so. Only the instinct to flee from great pain had driven him this far, for surely he was dead before the lead lodged itself in his left rear hip.

"My, he is big!" she exclaimed, when Reb held the lantern over the carcass for her to see.

"Yep, he's as big as I ever saw alright," he agreed.

"What did you call him, a painter?"

"Yeah, a painter."

"Why did you call him thet?"

"Cause that's what we call them in South Georgia."

"Never heahed thet before," she admitted.

"That's because you ain't never been to South Georgia," he teased back.

"You gon'a take me?"

"Nope."

She slapped his arm, "Wal', a gurl gives herself to a man, and then he just plans to up and leave her. I reckon thet's the way things work out for us wimmen folk."

"That ain't it at all."

"Wal' then, why not?"

"I took my wife back to Georgia and got her killed," he said and then stopped and looked off into another time where she dared not enter. After several moments, he finished, "I don't plan on going back there myself."

Then he looked down at the big puma, "Come on let's cut him up. I'm hungry."

"I ain't going to eat no cat!" she exclaimed shaking her head.

"Oh yes you will, when you get hungry enough you will fight me for a chunk of this ol' cat."

"Reb," suddenly her voice became very serious. "Are we going to be able to get out of here? I mean I know the meadow is pretty deep, and since the wind doesn't blow in here it might be so deep we can't get out."

"Not to worry. We will be out of here tomorrow, if not before."

"No, I mean it. The boys might not be able to find the gulch and miss us altogether."

"I looked closely at the tracks back there where I shot this painter, and he didn't come in from the cabin side. His tracks lead in from the cave. All we have to do is follow his tracks back and find his entrance. I bet it will be up on the ridge someplace, where the wind does blow."

"You think?" her voice was now spirited again.

"I think," he said back nodding his head. "Now help me."

"No."

An hour later, she was sitting beside him fully dressed and using a small splinter to pick a tiny piece of meat from between two molars. "You know Reb, them mountain lions," she started and nodded her head agreeing with her thought, as well as him, "is good eating."

"Glad you told me," he replied smiling.

"Reb?"

"Yeah?"

"What are we going to do?"

"I told you not to worry, we will get out alright."

"No, I mean, are we going to tell the others?"

"I reckon they will know soon enough," he replied as he cut away a large piece of cooked meat and stuffed it in one of his saddlebags.

"You suppose so?"

"Yep."

"I guess you are right," she concluded, and then smiled as a warm rush swept through her. "You'll just have to move into the house with me."

"Nope."

"Why not?"

"My place is with the men. We will find time for ourselves when the time is right."

"I don't like it," she said back.

"That's the way it has to be though. Mee'be when this is all over, we can do more as a team."

That warmed her again, as she took his statement as a proposal.

The morning broke to a clear sky of brilliant blue that only areas of extremely low humidity can reveal. The ever-present wind was hiding somewhere far off, and the temperature hovered near ten below. The snow in the hill country was some three feet deep, as a rule and much worse where it had drifted.

Ethan suddenly was in charge, not by appointment or agreement, simply because someone had to be, and his natural leadership sprang forth.

"Shep, you keep Ron and Howard here with three of the Meskin boys, just in case they try to burn us out again. I'll take the others and go get Reb and Miss Elaine."

There was some commotion among the Mexican vaqueros, as to who would go and who would stay, as all wanted to be there in case a settlement with the Wolf Creek bunch arose.

Ethan settled it with one strong statement, "We're riding out; when I look back if half of you are not here with my brother, I'll not stand for any of you to come with us." With that he mounted, and turning, he told his men to break trail ahead of the buckboard. Half a mile up the hill, he turned back and saw six of the vaqueros following close behind, and a slight smile came to his face as the feeling of satisfaction filled him. Until they found Reb, he was in charge, and the weight of that responsibility lay heavily but proudly, on his strong young shoulders.

The going was slow, but with proper resting and rotation of the lead animals, they continued at a steady pace.

Six miles to the northeast, another group of riders were also busting a path through the deep snow. They lacked the leadership of the Rocking AR bunch, as well as a guide, and their progress was slower. However, with fewer miles to go they were slightly ahead on the collision course that would intersect at a point near the big rocks ahead.

Before he returned to the warmth of the bed shared by Celeste Patay, John Brown had appointed Gab Easterman to lead the ten men he sent out that morning.

For some strange reason, the killing of a man up-close like he had done to Omaha had always aroused him, and when he learned his victim had surely succumbed to the knife wound, he felt the need of a woman.

The first time he had experienced this was long before, when he killed Frank Coleman[19] with the fire poker, unfortunately when he had turned for the lovely Diane to relieve his new found passion, he realized she too was dead.

Celeste was surprised when she felt his naked body suddenly reappear next to her under the heavy comforters. He had not shown much interest in her for several days, and she had begun to worry he was tiring of her; the attention this morning was more than welcome.

After building up the fire and carefully packing the things he thought they would need in their saddlebags, Cliff told Elaine to stay put while he tried to find the entrance the cat had used. She protested, but he was firm and she finally agreed.

Taking the lantern, he moved back into the cave, and soon the faint glow of his light was lost to her in the blackness.

She knew he had only turned into one of the many cutoffs, still when she could no longer see the light, she suddenly felt very alone, and she feared for his safety.

An hour passed, and when he had not returned, her concerns began to grow. Recognizing the signs of panic were beginning to overtake her, she boldly fought them off. "Reb told me to stay here, and I will do as he said," she spoke loudly.

Ola turned and looked at her when she did, and suddenly she felt embarrassed, as if the horse knew her fright and was looking on

---

19 Coleman: For more on the deaths of Frank and Diane Coleman see The Withlacoochee Renegades Chapter Fourteen.

her as a weakling. This seemed to give her strength, and she then stood erect and looked him back straight in the eye. "Don't look down on me," she snapped at the stout horse.

He shook his head and then nuzzled the neck of her smaller horse, which stood close by.

Shortly after this encounter with Ola, the faint glow of the lantern appeared, and she again felt weak with relief.

"Did you find anything?"

"I think so," he answered as he blew out the light.

"You think so, don't you know?"

"I found a place high on the rock wall that is caked with snow. It was too high for me to get to, but I think I can reach the ledge below it if I stand on Ola's back."

"Are you going back?"

"Yeah, after I eat something."

"This time take me with you," she said, more as a statement than a request.

He started to say no, but the look on her face showed the signs of the strain she had endured, and he smiled instead. "Missed me, did you?"

"Don't get too puffed up. You ain't the only cowboy thet shared these blankets," she snapped back quickly, then immediately regretted her statement.

At first, he considered the statement as an affront but quickly saw it as her defense to his being in command over her. Instead of popping back at her, he smiled again and added, "But never so good a one, eh?"

This time she slapped his arm and smiled back, "You are purty good, cowboy."

The struggle he experienced moving from Ola's saddle up to the narrow ledge had bruised his right hand, and it worried him some, but it did not stop him. After several minutes of careful climbing up the steep ledge, he reached the snow-caked opening.

From there, he dropped the rope he had slung over his shoulder and lowered the lantern back to her. "Tie off the hammer so I can use it to break up this packed snow."

Cliff looked back and saw Elaine trying also to attach the lantern to her end of the rope. "You keep the lantern. I can see well enough without it here," he called down to her.

This was welcome news to her ears, as she had again felt the knife-like pain of panic trying to grab her while she had been standing there in the darkness.

Within a couple of minutes after he pulled up the hammer, she saw the sudden appearance of light bathe the top of the cave.

"I'm through," he called to her.

She now almost burst out crying but fought it back. "What can you see?"

"Blue sky, but the wind cuts with the keenness of a knife up here," he shouted back.

Feeling enraptured, "Wonderful!" was the first of many words that seemed to spring from her lips, and finally he had to shout at her to be quiet.

"Why?"

"Just be silent for a minute."

After what seemed like a long time he finally spoke, "Gunfire," was all he said before she saw him frantically digging away at the opening.

The two outfits had arrived at the point of their collision course at the same time, and immediately a firefight broke out. Two of the vaqueros charged the Wolf Creek gang and were cut down before they had gotten within fifty yards of their intended prey.

One of the fifty caliber slugs from a trap-door Springfield crashed through the head of the near mule, and he jumped high on his hind legs before crashing into the snow. This caused his teammate to panic, and Laramie Patay had a terrible time keeping this animal from overturning the wagon.

In the next minute, two dozen shots were exchanged between the opposing sides before each settled down to finding cover and began serious shooting.

Ethan eased over behind the wagon-bed and began taking careful aim with his Whitworth. One by one, the Wolf Creek men began to fall to his shots.

Finally, Gab realized they were out-gunned and told his six uninjured men to hightail it out of there.

When Ethan saw they were leaving he had just put a fresh load in his rifle; he waited until the riders were topping the rise, some three hundred yards off, and he dropped the last wrangler. The others did not look back to see if their friend had survived or not.

It wasn't until they stopped a mile away, did the rider-less horse catch up to them.

"Damn," was all Easterman said, knowing full well he was in for a double-barrel ass chewing when he got back.

Cliff fired off a couple of rounds from his Colt when he was sure the fight was over below. From where he was he had not been able to see the encounter, but he did see the men hightailing it over the rise and witnessed the last in line fly from his mount.

'Only a Whitworth bullet hits a man like that,' he thought as he smiled. Then almost as in an apology to Christian[20] he added, *'Or mee'be a Sharps.'*

It was the keen ears of the Crow that heard the faint report of the pistol, and he pointed towards the ridge to their north.

Half an hour later, Cliff was yelling to Ethan, "Nice shot there, boy."

"Boy?" his young friend shouted back.

Cliff dropped the rope back to Elaine and pulled her up to where she could slip through the opening he had made in the hard-packed snow. With much effort, two of the Vaqueros began the climb up the face of the steep rocks.

When he finally arrived where they waited, Pedro removed his big sombrero before saying, "Señora, Señor Reb, Pedro 'ees most happy to see you both well."

"We're rather glad to see you too," she replied and gave him a hug.

With the rope tied under her arms, the three men lowered her down to a ledge from which she could make her way to the prairie floor.

Cliff scribbled out a note on the back of the white bag he had brought his makin's in and told the Mexican boys to give it to Ethan. Then he sent them back as they had come.

When the boy handed the note to Ethan, he read it and then shook his head.

Elaine seeing this, demanded to see the note. "I am still the owner of this ranch and you do work for me. Now give me thet bag."

Looking at the faint writing, she too shook her head at what he had written:

"Ethan, get Miss Elaine back to the ranch as soon as you can. Send for Sheriff Pepper and let him know about the

---

20 Christian: Christian Sharps was the inventor of the famous buffalo gun.

murder of Rodríguez and the attack on Miss Elaine. And have Black Band and two of the men work around into the meadow where I will meet them."

When she finished reading it a second time, she looked up to protest, but Reb had slipped back into the small opening in the cliff and was gone.

"Has he gone mad? He must come down this way!" she exclaimed.

"Now Miss Elaine, you don't really expect him to leave his hoss there to starve, do you?" Ethan said to her.

She thought a minute and realized of course, the boy was right. Reb Brown would die himself before he allowed that Appaloosa to starve to death. "Damn him," she said. "Damn thet horse!"

"Yas, Ma'am."

"Ethan, I want all of us to go around and help him get out. The snow is perhaps fifteen feet deep in thet meadow."

"Ma'am please don't give me no hard time. Reb done told me to take you back to the ranch as fast as I could, and thet is just what I aim to do."

"I still run my own ranch," she said sternly.

"Yas Ma'am, and it would shor' grieve me to have to tie you up to get you to go, but I work fer Reb, not you, not your ranch, and he done told me," he said removing his hat.

She could see he was determined and just might make good on his threat, so she decided on a compromise. "Alright, I'll go with you but just me and you. The remainder can stay and help get him out."

"Miss Elaine___," he began, but she cut him short.

"I know Reb done told you, and I'll go with you but you alone. The Wolf Creek outfit won't give us anymore trouble today. They are limping home licking their wounds; we will be alright, and Reb will need everyone he can get, if he is to get out of thet meadow alive. I know; I've seen it, and you ain't."

"Ma'am."

"Now, Ethan I have set my mind to this, and I won't have it no other way."

He could see he was up against a mighty strong woman, and that was one thing he had very little knowledge of how to handle. So, somewhat embarrassed, he agreed and told the others what was happening.

It was late that afternoon when they made it to the meadow. Cliff had beaten his way through only half an hour before. He was resting from his laborious ordeal when he heard the sound of trotting horses emerging from the rock rift where the storm had not deposited too much snow.

He was very grateful Ethan had the foresight to bring extra grain for the animals, as was Ola and the chestnut she'd left behind.

That night they all stayed in Jimmy Don's retreat. It was an hour before the broad light of day when the outfit moved out together.

The wind was up again, and upon reaching the open prairie, they saw most of the powder from the heavy snowfall had been blown to Nebraska or the Black Hills. The travel back to the ranch was painful, as a twenty-five mile an hour gale cut into their faces, but with little snow on the frozen ground, their progress was swift.

When they arrived back at the ranch, everyone was surprised, for none had expected to see Miss Elaine run from the stone cabin, throw her arms around her foreman and begin kissing him long and hard, right there in front of them all.

'Well, I reckon there won't be no doubt now,' Cliff thought as he cut his eyes around at the others, who stood there with astonished expressions on their faces.

There was a lot of local gossip around the Rocking AR for the next several weeks. Even a pool was taken as to whether or not Miss Elaine and Reb would be married before Christmas, but the New Year came and passed, and the couple announced no date.

Neither was there any more trouble from the Wolf Creek outfit.

Pike Pepper had full intention of arresting P.C. Defray, but when he arrived at *The Wolf Creek Ranch*, the foreman was no longer there.

Major Brown assured him that he had fired Defray a week before Rodriguez had been killed. Pepper knew full well he was dealing with the alpha wolf, but the only man Elaine Moore had identified was Defray, so all he could do was read them the riot act, and that he did before leaving.

Jean Mouton was no fool, and he knew Pepper would now be watching them closely. Unfortunately Allen Moreton had wired they were no longer to harass the neighbors. Nonetheless, Jean's instructed his men, should they find Elaine Moore or her Foreman away from the others, they were to bring them back to him at all cost.

This gave the Rocking AR time to gather and rebuild. Even though the winter was typical for this high country, they reconstructed her house and cared for her stock. When spring began to break in April, many a new maverick was found tagging along behind its mother.

The sons of Rodriguez took their father's body back to Guadalupe to be buried along side their mother. Cliff had paid for the train tickets for as far south as they could ride the rails, thereafter their travels would be by horse and a single buckboard.

The other vaqueros stayed the winter out, glad for a job with such good pay. An American dollar for each day worked was riches unheard of in Mexico or even elsewhere north of the border, for Wetbacks.

Elaine was not so happy about the calm that swept over the valley. Sure, she was glad to have her home again. Now she let Shep and Ella use the stone house. Her herd was increasing, and she and Reb found time often to enjoy each other's company, as well as her new bed. Nevertheless, her plans of getting the men responsible for her husband's lynching were not being pursued, and that was, after all, her real goal.

It seemed, out of nowhere, a hot wind suddenly appeared the last week in May, and the deep snow in the mountains began to melt early. This caused the streams to suddenly rise, sometimes without warning. One such occurrence happened while Laramie and Black Band were moving a few dozen horses across Little Crow Creek, and they just barely were able to get themselves and most of the animals to safety.

Elaine overheard them telling Reb about it, and immediately a plan began to cultivate in her mind.

A week later the Rodriguez boys returned, bringing with them Absalom Gaztambide, the son of their mother's sister.

Absalom was quite tall for a Mexican. His face showed a faint, but long, scar of a ghastly wound from many years past, and he seemed to have a much harder outlook on life than his cousins.

Reb didn't like him right off, but Elaine asked him to give the boy a chance for Gilberto's sake. "After all, he is their family, and I'm shor' they all need as much help as they can get." Cliff nodded his head to her but was still uneasy with having the lad around. He also noticed, come payday, Absalom did not send any money home like his cousins did. This too did not set well with him.

Reb had not been in the Rockies more than a week when he had heard the saying about the region, "If you don't like the weather, hang around a couple of days, and it will reverse itself." The first day of June proved this to be so true. The warm weather that had slipped in during May was suddenly replaced by a heavy, wet snow that blanketed the sage-covered range with six-inches of the sticky stuff. The mountains off in the distant west showed the presence of new and thick white tops.

Snow that comes in the spring and early summer is not at all like the powder that floats down in the fall and winter. Spring snow is heavy and wet and pretty difficult to move through. It's also quite dangerous to man and stock alike. Although the temperatures rarely drop below the teens, the stuff soon becomes a sheet of ice, that when broken through, can cut to the bone, leaving animals bleeding and easy prey for wolves and bear.

Reb had most of the men out trying to locate any injured beeves when the rain began. It was not at all the usual rain of the high country, rather a heavy drizzle, drenching everything in its path. When Elaine first felt it, she had just emerged from the barn where Carlos and Absalom were attending to a couple of mavericks the Adams brothers had brought in from the prairie.

The warm shower had wet her to the skin, before she could get in the wash her sister had hung out only an hour before.

After placing the clothesbasket on the back porch of the stone house, she immediately returned to the barn. She looked closely and when satisfied no one was there other than the two boys, she motioned for Absalom to come to the stall, where she stood slightly concealed from Carlos.

The tall boy approached her with a slight grin. He knew she was calling him for something she did not want others to know about. He hoped it was for favors she was not getting from the Señor Reb, although he wasn't certain how they would manage it without Carlos finding out.

She told him what she wanted him to do. She also added, "I will make it worth your while, if you can pull it off with no one else finding out about it."

This was all he wanted to hear, and with a large grin on his face, he pulled the big sombrero from where it hung down his back and placed it firmly on his head. "Si', Señora, for you I will do dis."

Elaine did not like the expression on his face but nonetheless replied, "Good, but remember, no one must know it was you."

He nodded his head and repeated his last statement.

Returning to her house to change from the wet outfit she had on, to a bright yellow prairie dress, she thought about the lad in the barn, *'I must agree with Reb, this boy is not at all like Gilberto Rodriguez, or his sons.'* After digesting her thought, she realized she also hated to admit it.

The rain lasted all night and was still falling when dawn broke. By this time, all the rivers and dry creeks in the area were filled to the brim. Many were overflowing their banks, with the muddy water being pushed by very swift currents.

Late that afternoon, Absalom rode into the ranch yard and fired his percussion revolver in the air once to attract attention.

Reb came from the barn at a run, followed by half a dozen other men. Looking around and seeing no one other than the lone rider, he returned his own Colt to its leather home and looked with narrowed eyes at the young Mexican. "What the hell are you doing?"

"Many riders come from da north. Da shoot and yell and drive off the bovines," Absalom said back then added, "Da go towards the rio. Carlos, he 'ees shot, dead I t'ink."

"What is it?" Elaine asked, as she came rushing from the house.

Cliff was loading his Winchester when she called out, he finished and shoved it hard into his scabbard before answering, "Sounds like Wolf Creek is up to no good again," he replied without really looking at her.

"Ethan, get your Whitworth."

"Yas Sur."

The afternoon sky had darkened with the coming of a new storm, and the men, now mounted and gathered in posse strength, looked to their leader for the word to head out.

Cliff glanced about him, and then at Shep, who was standing with the women. "Keep close boy, this may be a diversion."

"I will Reb," the blond youth replied, as he placed his arm around the young woman he planned to soon marry.

Cliff then added, "And send the Indian on, when he gets back." Then looking at Elaine, he pulled slightly at the front of the brim of his hat before he heeled Ola, and they began moving out at a fast pace.

Absalom was the last to leave. As a bolt of lightning lit the plaza, Elaine saw the fiendish grin on his scarred face, and the sight sent a cold chill up her spine, for she knew well its meaning.

Laramie and Black Band had been rounding up some strays they found bunched in a little draw, some five miles north when the storm hit, thus did not arrive back until well after dark.

Shep told them what had happened, and the Crow turned without reply and moved his saddle from his tuckered out mount to a fresh one he selected from the corral.

Laramie began to catch himself one, but the older man stopped him, and after some conversation Shep could not hear, the boy threw his saddle over his shoulder and headed for the barn.

Black Band did not stop by the house; neither did he look at Shep as he rode past.

The fast moving thunderstorm raced over and ahead of the seven riders and on into the darkness of the early night. They were glad to see it pass. The lightning was sharp and often, and even though it seemed not to be hitting the ground, it caused the horses to be difficult.

On they rode into the darkness without speaking to one another. Only the distant rumble of the thunder ahead interrupted the sound of many hooves splashing in the newly formed mud.

Each man knew if they over took the Wolf Creek gang there would be a gun battle like they had not seen since the war. Each was alone with his own fears, his own determination and his own loyalties. Only one wanted to be somewhere else.

Six miles from the ranch, they came upon the body of Carlos lying in the mud. Cliff dismounted and rolled the boy over. His young face was covered with yellow earth, mixed with the rain and blood, which had gushed from his head where the ball struck him a little above and a little behind his right ear. Cliff could feel the softness of his crushed skull with his thumb as he cradled the boy in his hands.

"Why he is not dead, I will never know," Cliff said just above a whisper.

Then turning to Tommy Walker, he spoke, "You and Billy make up a travois and get this boy into Laramie, to the sawbones as soon as you can." Then looking at the other men who still sat their saddles, he added, "Take his brother with you."

"I will go," Absalom suggested.

Cliff looked over at the tall boy and said sharply, "No." Then turning away from him, he added simply, "Tommy."

"Yas Sur," came the reply. No more was necessary for them.

"And boys, tell Sheriff Pepper what has happened."

"Yas Sur," Tommy replied again, nodding his head.

Cliff didn't wait to see that his men did as he had instructed, he knew his word would be followed to the tee. Without looking back, he mounted and moved beside Absalom, "Lead us out to where you last saw our beeves."

The Mexican boy looked at the men who were now tending to his wounded cousin, and then turning back without reply, started off into the rainy night.

Less than an hour later, they came to the river. It was nearly out of its banks and moving with such force a Mississippi Sternwheeler could not have crossed it.

The muddy ground was torn right up to the riverbank. Even in this rain, the scars left by so many hooves had not been washed out. It was plain for anyone to see, the herd had been driven at full gallop into the raging waters.

Cliff took a deep breath before turning to face his men who were awaiting his orders. He realized the night was black, and they had no means to make torches. Following the trail of a herd of over a hundred head of cattle had been one thing; to track a few men on horseback was something else. Once more, looking up at the dark sky, he shook his head before speaking, "No way to stay with them tonight boys, let's hold up till first light and try and pick up their trail."

Ethan dismounted, but instead of loosening his cinch, as were the others, he approached Cliff. "We know where they are headed. Why don't we just cut across country and be at the Wolf Creek when they get there?"

Cliff took a deep breath and slowly let it out before he answered, "No, not in this weather. I ain't about to lose another man tonight, and that is just about what would happen in this blackness. We could ride right off into a gulch and not know it till the bottom hit us in the face. Besides, they probably are already sleeping in their dry bunks by now."

"Alright, Reb, you know best," the boy said and turned away but stopped and added, "It's just I can't stand to think they's gon'a get away with shooting little Carlos in the back like thet."

"They won't get away with it," Cliff replied. "Now get some rest."

He instructed everyone to hobble their mounts before bedding down, then he laid out his soogan[21] on the muddy bank and placed his saddle on top of it. After wrapping his slicker around him, he slipped down on the cold wet ground, pulled his Stetson over his face and closed his eyes. However, sleep did not come easy. There was something that didn't set right about all this, only he couldn't lay his finger on it. Sometime later, he drifted off.

The sound of his horse awoke him and looking where Ola was staring he saw the lone rider on the hill in the purple light of dawn. At first, he was not sure of it's meaning, but quickly he realized it was the Indian.

He too, was not sure of who he was watching until he saw his boss stand and shake out his wet blanket. There was something about the stature of Clifford Brown that left an impression on any man who had ever met him. An impression, they would never forget. To the keenly honed eye of a plainsman who was native to the land, it was no contest at all.

The rain had stopped hours before, and now a cold wind was blowing from the southwest.

They made a small fire and boiled a pot of Java while the Crow made a wide circle looking for tracks.

After nearly half an hour, he returned and spoke, "No tracks," he said, pointing towards the northwest where they all knew the Wolf Creek Outfit's land was.

"You didn't find anything?" Cliff questioned.

"No tracks," the Indian repeated.

"Damn. I thought we would find something."

"Wal', thet don't make no difference, we all know who done it. I say we go on and cut them to pieces while they sleep," Tyrell ejaculated.

There was a considerable agreement among the other men on his suggestion, but Cliff put a stop to it. "No. We'll let Pepper take care of it. Let's go see what Tommy has to say on that."

The men didn't like it, but they knew he would not be swayed and also knew he was right.

When they returned and no Wolf Creek men had been killed, Elaine didn't like it either.

---

21 Soogan: Quilt or covering in a cowboy's bedroll.

For the second time in a few days, Pike Pepper was approaching *The Wolf Creek Ranch*. He was all too aware of the danger he was riding into, but he too knew he was riding under the protection of his badge, a small seven-point star that had been cut from an old Mexican peso many years before. Not a shield in itself, and something that would be a subject of laughter in so many locations in this wild country. Pepper however believed this would not be the case on the Wolf Creek spread. Here, despite what the Wyoming cowboys and their foreman may think of him and his authority, the ranch was under the umbrella of Sir Frances Moreton and *The Birmingham Social Society*.

He knew well, should the news to get back to England, that the local 'Reef of the Shire'[22], had been killed by employees of a gentleman of this society, the resulting wrath would be more than Major John Brown would be able to overcome. Pepper knew Brown too was fully aware of this.

Another ace Pike Pepper held, that he didn't even know he had, was that at the very same time he was leaving Laramie, Allen Moreton was arriving at Wolf Creek.

The Englishman's agenda was one of assignment as well as pleasure. He had never gotten over the lure of the Wild West and the roughness that seemed to ooze from the men who worked at the ranch. Although he had to admit, they were not the spitting image of what he had dreamed of while studying so deeply the dime novels. Still, he had been directed by his uncle to place certain restrictions on Major Brown.

Word had been received that there was unnecessary violence in the area, and some of it may have been caused by men who were employed by Wolf Creek. This was something that their Society simply would not allow to taint its image. Thus, Allen had been instructed, in rather strong words, to deliver with full British sternness their feelings on the subject to their head caretaker, a task Allen Moreton did not relish.

Although he considered John Brown to be his friend, he had experienced an uncertain fright, deep within him. Once in the past he had challenged his employee's authority over the operations of their investment in this savage land, and the results chilled him.

He knew Major Brown was a most pleasant and well-educated man from a prominent family, as well as a trained military officer

22 Reef of the Shire: Origin of the word Sheriff.

of the British Army. However, this man also oozed his own kind of roughness, a roughness far greater than what the lesser employees seemed to display.

Allen experienced a feeling he was in the presence of an evil spirit, when he had on a couple of occasions, glimpsed the anger of the man, and he could not escape from it.

Delivering this order to Major Brown was setting very uneasy on his mind. This surely was a task he would have paid dearly to have pass from him.

They had just settled into afternoon tea being served by the very pleasant Mrs. Brown, when one of the cowboys came in and approached John.

Immediately a change swept over the man, and Allen recognized the spirit he so feared had been awakened in his friend. *'Whatever the news delivered by the peasant, it is not good news. Of that I am positive.'*

John stood, threw his cloth napkin hard at the table before turning and walking from the room, without giving either of them the slightest explanation.

Celeste's face showed her worry; seldom had she seen him act in such a manner, especially in the presence of so important a person as Mr. Allen Moreton. *'What could be the matter?'* she wondered.

"What is it?" Allen asked Bunyan White.

The lean cowpoke looked at Moreton, giving him the usual expression a man of the west feels for an eastern dude and left without an answer.

Celeste, realizing the implications, called out, "Bun, do tell us what it is."

White took another step after his boss and then thought better of ignoring the lady of the ranch, "The Sheriff Ma'am. Sheriff Pepper is here."

"Whatever could he want?" she replied.

Both she and their guest moved near the large door that opened to the front veranda.

The voice of John Brown was loud and clear as he spoke, "I do not know anything about any killing or any stampede."

"One of Rocking AR men swears it was you leading your men. He says he saw you and can identify you," the Sheriff replied.

"I don't care what this so called witness says. I have not left this house in the last three days, and I have two dozen witnesses to verify that."

"That may well be Major Brown, and you will have every right to have each and every one of them testify for you in court, but I have a warrant for your arrest, and I am going to serve it."

"Non' you are not. No one is putting me in jail."

At this moment Allen Moreton stepped onto the porch and spoke to his Overseer, "John, go with him. I will have you out on bail within a few hours."

"That won't work here. There is no bail for murder; is there Pepper?"

"Thet's right," the Sheriff confirmed. "Now let's get on with it."

The moment Pike's boot sole touched the first of the ten steps that separated the two adversaries, Major John Brown ceased to exist, and Jean Mouton emerged from within him.

In a flash so quick no one saw him move, suddenly the shiny Colt Navy, that had served him so well on so many occasions, appeared in his hand and was being cocked.

Not believing what he was seeing, Allen Moreton stepped forward and yelled at his friend, "No, John. Go with him."

Mouton turned only slightly before he fired. The 36 caliber ball struck the Englishman full in his right breast, snapping a rib and severing the artery behind it.

Celeste Patay screamed.

Pike Pepper's hand shot forward for his own revolver, hidden in the holster that swung from his right shoulder, behind the unbuttoned vest, but he was not fast enough. Bunyan White poked the barrel of his own revolver into the side of the Sheriff and pressed it hard towards the kidney. "Don't even think about it star packer."

Pepper stopped his draw, and the man on his other side took the pistol from his hand.

"Oh Jean, what have you done?" cried his lady.

"Stupid bitch!" was the only reply she received.

Pepper watched the left leg of the nobleman jerk three or four times before the body lay still. Looking up higher, he saw the terror in Celeste's face before she hurried into the house after her lover, screaming, "Jean, Jean Mouton, don't leave me."

It was early the next morning when Ethan came upon the bodies. He and Arturo Mendoza were looking for any beeves that might have strayed from the herd before the stampede.

Both men had been shot at close range, that was apparent. One lay in a pool of frozen blood and the other showing no signs of bleeding at all, except on his fancy white shirt.

Anyone who saw the scene would have easily understood there had been a shoot out between the Sheriff and the Englishman. Each man held a revolver in his right hand, and each pistol had been fired. The case would have been closed as soon as the evidence was presented to any coroner's jury; had it not been for Ethan's sharp eye catching the slight twitch of the little finger on Pepper's left hand.

Remembering how the surgeons had used the snow to stop bleeding during the war, he instantly packed the Sheriff's wound with the white stuff and sent the lad to the ranch for a buckboard.

When Cliff arrived ahead of the wagon, he immediately saw something was amiss. During the war, he had observed many a man die and equally as many who had died a day and some two days before. Almost always they came to their final rest in some twisted and grotesque position. Arms out or under them, often legs twisted and on occasion completely turned from the norm. It was common to see their mouth's open and totally round, as if their final breath had exited the body with such force it blew a round hole there. This was not what he viewed here.

The man who apparently had shot Sheriff Pepper was lying on his back, both legs straight and close together. His arms along side his body as if he had laid down to go to sleep. In his right hand was a revolver, but otherwise one would surmise he was simply resting. The Sheriff likewise was lying on his back; of course Ethan might have moved him thus, to ease any pain, but he would not have done so to his dead assailant. Also the Remington held by Pike was in his right hand. Cliff had made a mental note the first time he saw him, '*Sheriff Pepper is left-handed.*'

Lifting the vest confirmed his memory. The holster was strapped from the Sheriff's right shoulder, not his left.

In addition, he recognized the wound of the other man as a bleeder, and there was no blood under the body. '*These men have been shot elsewhere and then brung here,*' he thought. '*Why?*'

Cliff lifted the short barrel New Model Police Revolver from Moreton's hand and looked admiringly at the highly engraved nickel-plated piece. *'It truly is a work of art,'* he thought running his thumb over the etching a very talented artist had performed on the gun.

He also took note the dead man wore no leather at all, save his pricey suspenders and boots. He had no identification his person except the obvious expense of his attire. *'This is no run of the mill Dude,'* Cliff concluded. *'Somebody will be missing him sooner or later.'*

On the way back to the ranch with the wounded man, Arturo said softly, "I should 'ave told you."

"What?" Cliff asked.

"No, no-thing," the boy replied not looking at his boss.

A few seconds later Absalom Gaztambide moved his mount close beside the wagon and gave Arturo a sharp look. At the same time, his left hand rubbed the old broken handle of the big knife he carried stuffed behind his holster belt.

An immediate dryness enveloped the smaller boy's throat, and fear swept his face. The sudden expression change did not escape Cliff. He decided to question the boy about what Absalom held over him, as soon as he had the two separated. Right then he had a dying Sheriff on his hands, and that was the most important thing he had to consider.

When they arrived at the ranch, they carried Pepper inside the stone house and sent for a doctor. Cliff just didn't think the man would survive the trip into Laramie bouncing around in that wagon. He was surprised he had survived this far.

When Doc Lathrop arrived, he immediately went to work. After three hours, he emerged from the room where his patient lay so near death.

"Snow," he said and then paused. "It was the cold that has kept him alive. Whoever thought to pack the wound with snow saved his life."

"I'll see Ethan knows you said that," Cliff replied to the tired-looking man.

"Would you like a cup?" Ellie asked holding the big pot she had just removed from the fireplace iron. "We have Arbuckles."

"I would love some of your Ariosa," the tall man replied, as a smile slipped over his face, erasing the previous frown.

The doctor eased his body into the straight-backed chair and slowly shook his head, as if he was debating with himself.

"Will he live?" she asked, pouring the dark liquid in the blue-speckled cup setting before him.

"I don't know. He is very pale, lost so much blood. He is very weak," the doctor replied, as he reached for the coffee. "Maybe, if infection doesn't set in. He was shot at point-blank range. The ball took much of the burning fabric from his vest in with it. I had a lot of difficulty removing it." Lathrop stopped and took a slip of the hot liquid. "I don't know if I found it all."

"Just how close was the shot?" Cliff asked as his curiosity caused his eyes to squint.

"Very. Much of the powder was burned inside his body. Maybe the barrel was against his chest when it was fired," he again shook his head. "Someone wanted him dead very badly."

Cliff lifted his eyes toward the opening door.

Immediately upon seeing the pretty woman enter, Doc Lathrop rose from his chair.

"Please stay seated, Doctor," she said. "How is he?"

"Alive."

"The Doc said he might make it," her sister added.

Elaine looked at her man and then back at the Doctor. "Has he told anybody who shot 'im?"

"No, he has never regained consciousness," Lathrop replied shaking his head again.

"Does Pepper have a sworn Deputy?" Cliff asked.

"No, I don't think so," the Doctor replied. "He has a helper that tends to the jail."

"We all know who did this. The same people who stampeded my beeves into Crow Creek, the same people who murdered Gilberto, the same people who hung my husband."

"Yes, we know, but we still need the law before we go after them," Cliff said.

"Oh!" she said in disgust as she shot a hateful look at him, before stomping out.

"I think she is right Reb," Ellie added, looking also at Cliff, only with a much more pleasant expression.

Shep placed his hands over her shoulders in a caring gesture, letting her know she should not give her option at this time.

The next day, Cliff and two of his Texicans in a buckboard, followed behind the Doctor's buggy as he returned to Laramie City.

While there, Cliff planned to get a month's supply of necessities, but his main purpose of the trip was to let the Powers That Be know about the shootings and what evidence he and the Doctor had discovered.

However, the news was already out about the gunfight between Sheriff Pepper and some Dude he found butchering a stolen calf on Wolf Creek range.

The town was in an uproar over their only Lawman being killed, and was demanding the county officials appoint an interim officer until a new election could be arranged. Cliff and Doctor Lathrop arrived just in time to stop such happenings.

The news Sheriff Pepper was not dead, was a shock to most of the townspeople, especially those in *The Bucket of Blood*, a saloon formerly owned by Big Steve Long, before the Vigilance Committee lynched him and his two brothers. It was now operated by a less threatening manager and was also often the hangout of Wolf Creek hands, when they were in town. This afternoon several were gathered there encouraging the crowd to demand Bunyan White be appointed the new county officer.

Doctor Lathrop's news of the Sheriff being alive put a stop to any immediate appointment, and Bun White quite suddenly disappeared from the scene.

When no longer anyone suggested a new appointment be hastily made, the Circle Rocking AR bunch headed home early that evening.

That night Reb and Elaine had a big argument in the new house, and both the men in the barn and the couple in the stone house heard the yelling, although exactly what was being said was not clear to the listeners.

Later, after their emotions had cooled, Elaine enjoyed the most satisfying sexual encounter she had ever had in her life.

The next morning, two hours before sunup, Reb was in the barn awakening his men.

Elaine watched from the glass window as the dark figures of men and horses moved, first out of the barn and then out of the yard. A feeling of triumph filled her. It was the first time since she had met this man that she felt she had control of him. *'Our fight sure was fierce, but before he fell asleep, I conquered this mighty man. Now he is heading out to destroy the men who murdered Jimmy Don fer me. When he returns I will make him my husband, and there will be no one who would dare to take my spread, and the threat of the law forbidding a woman to own real land, will be null and void.'*

Cliff thought about the campaign he was undertaking. *'We will be out-numbered, so the element of surprise is essential. We have the advantage though as their ranch yard is in that little valley, much as Elaine's ranch is, only the creek runs right near the plaza. That will be of help.'*

The surrounding hills blocked a lot of the wind in these slightly low areas, and this could be of great value on the worst days when the weather was treacherous. This in turn was an equal deficit as a point from which to do battle.

Cliff's sharpshooter with his Whitworth, could keep many a man entrapped within the safety of the walls of the buildings, while his mounted men moved in to carbine range and surround the ranch yard.

The only thing was, Ethan had not been at The Circle Rocking AR when they returned from Laramie, and no one seemed to know where he was. This caused Cliff much worry, he really liked that boy, and he prayed harm had not come his way.

Instead of Ethan, Cliff would rely on his brother Shep who carried his Sharps. Cliff knew Shep was also a wonderful long-range shooter, and the Sharps was almost as good a weapon as the Whitworth. Shep was also almost as good a marksman as Ethan, still Cliff felt he was short-handed.

He also knew Elaine expected him to kill all or most of the Wolf Creek men, but he had no intention of killing anyone, if it could be avoided.

He planned to leave Shep high, well out of range of any rifles the Wolf Creek men might have. Should the need be, the boy could keep them in check, while he and the others slipped into the positions they needed along the bank of the creek, where they could cover the buildings with their Winchesters.

Another ace Cliff held was Arturo Mendoza following in the wagon. He brought enough supplies for them to blockade the Wolf Creek outfit for several days, should that become necessary. It was a good plan and would work, of that he was certain. He also was certain it depended on them arriving with the element of surprise.

When they were close, some half-hour before sunup, the distinct report of gunfire could be heard. Immediately, Cliff felt a rush of acid in his stomach. Something was wrong, and likely this meant his plan was in shambles.

Dismounting, and Cliff and Shep slipped over the rise on their bellies to survey the source of the gunfire. They had barely reached the crest of the hill when the report of a rifle was heard close by. Cliff again felt the acid in his stomach because there was no question in his mind that that rifle was anything but a Whitworth.

When they located the rifleman some fifty yards below the hill's crest, they saw he was pounding the ramrod deep in the muzzle of the big gun as he hurriedly reloaded.

Before Cliff could call to his friend, the flash of another gun was seen some forty yards to his left, a split second before the sound reached them. He witnessed the boy throw his arms high before dropping the long-gun.

Cliff swung his Yellowboy at the muzzle flash and fired four rounds as fast as he could work the lever.

A scream was heard, and then all was silent. Cliff moved toward the man he had just shot, while Shep headed for his brother.

Satisfied Bullbat Drew was dead, he turned his attention first toward the large rock where the two boys were and then at the ranch plaza.

The sun was high enough now to shed a faint light on the scene below, and he saw several men dashing about here and there between the buildings. A couple of shots were sent up at the rock, but it was just too far for their slugs to reach.

At that moment, the thunder of Shep's Sharps reported, and a second later one of the figures below flew backwards.

"Hold up," Cliff shouted at the young man.

Shep stopped his reloading and looked toward his Boss, who was now almost to his side.

"They done shot Ethan!" he screamed.

"I know, still hold up, and let's get a fix on what is going on here."

The boy's face was covered with beads of water, and Cliff recognized he was at the point of panic.

"Easy, Shep. We'll take care of Ethan first."

Shep looked wildly at him for a couple of seconds and then seemed to return to his senses.

Satisfied, Cliff said, "Watch they don't try and rush us while I look after Ethan."

Shep nodded his head without speaking, and then he turned and looked back at the ranch yard some four hundred yards below.

Cliff checked Ethan's side where the rifle bullet had entered. The wound was bad, but the boy was alive and seemed to be in a state of shock. He looked at Cliff and smiled, "Hi Reb. Thought you would never get here."

"What are you doing here?" Cliff replied, as he stuffed his neckerchief in the big hole in the boy's side.

"Doing what you said. And doing it right well until just now," the boy replied.

"What 'a you mean, doing what I said?"

"What you said fer me to do. Kill every one of them bastards."

"I never___," Cliff stopped and narrowed his left eye into a squint, "Who told you to kill them?"

"Absalom, he gave me the note you writ'. Said I wus to come here and keep them holed up until you arrived, been here since yesterday afternoon. Near out of lead too. I thought you would a' been here hours ago."

"Absalom? You still have the note?"

"Yeah, I think so. In my vest pocket," he said, then coughing he grinned and added, "I can't seem to move my arm."

"You just rest," Cliff told him before he removed the yellow paper.

Unfolding it, he struck a Lucifer, and holding it close to the paper he read the neatly written words:

> Ethan,
> Go to the Wolf Creek spread and kill as many
> of them as you can. Keep them holed up until I
> get there with the rest of the men.
> Reb

There was no question about the note. He immediately recognized Elaine's handwriting. What he was unsure of was her connection to Absalom.

"When did Absalom give you this?"

Ethan coughed again, this time blood shot from his mouth in tiny droplets as he did. Finally, he answered, "Yesterday aboot an hour after you headed into town."

"Alright, just you rest easy," he replied and then took a deep breath.

He thought a few moments, and then he tapped Shep on the shoulder and spoke, "Don't kill anymore unless they try and rush us."

Shep nodded his head.

Cliff then slipped over the hill to where the other men waited.

"Move out and around the ranch in a big circle," Cliff said motioning with his arms what he wanted them to do. "Don't shoot anybody unless you have to. I will try and talk to them as soon as there's light enough for them to see a white flag."

The men looked questioningly at him, but none of them spoke.

He removed his heavy coat and suede shirt, and then with his knife, he cut his long johns just above the belly, removing a large portion of the white garment to use as a flag of truce. Replacing his shirt and coat, he moved back to his saddlebags, took out a spare pair of johns and carried them back to make bandages for his friend.

When full light finally arrived in the valley where the Wolf Creek spread lay, Cliff counted seven bodies laying about in the ranch yard. He shook his head just a little at the sight and thought, *'Ethan has been busy.'*

Then he stood, and with his truce flag tied to the muzzle of his carbine, he started down the long hill.

'This could be the longest walk of my life,' he thought and then realized, *'or the shortest.'*

At a distance of two hundred yards from the bunkhouse, he stopped and called out, "Who is in charge here?"

"Who wants to know?" was the reply.

"I'm Clifford Brown. I want to talk to whoever is in charge."

"The man in charge is lying out there in front a' the steps a' the boss' house."

Cliff did not like the way this was going. A good shooter could drop him from this distance, and there was little or no cover for him to seek should this go bad. Finally, he called out again, "He was in charge. Who is in charge now?"

No one answered for several seconds, and then someone called out from the main house, "What do you want?"

"I want to stop the killing."

"You the law?"

Cliff suddenly realized they thought it was a posse who were there with him. "Yeah, I'm the law, and I only want the man who shot Sheriff Pepper."

Again there was a pause before the voice in the big house replied, "He ain't here. He lit out a' here just after they wus shot."

Cliff now was sure the Dude had been shot here and carried off to where he was found.

"Alright, then we have no more arguments," he said back. "Come on out, and let's all lay down our guns."

No answer came for almost a minute. Then, very cautiously, with his eyes continually jumping between Cliff and the big rock behind him, a man in an old buffalo coat emerged out on the big porch, standing where Major John Brown had stood only a few days before.

Cliff now looked around and saw his men were standing along the rim of the surrounding hills. It was an impressive sight, and he felt that it may have been the straw that broke the back of their resistance. Slowly, two more men followed the first man out onto the porch, and then others came from the barn and the bunkhouse.

"Lay your rifles down, and no one will hurt you. I want to know what happened here, then you will be free to go."

Seemingly, as if being mechanically controlled, they laid down their guns and stood back up straight.

"What happened to Drew?" the man in the buffalo coat asked.

"Don't know him," Cliff replied as he moved in closer.

"He went out two hours ago trying to get thet damn Sharpshooter."

"He's up there with my men," Cliff replied.

"He alright?"

"He ain't hurting none. My man Shep is with him," Cliff assured them then added, "Now all a' you move over here away from them rifles and shuck your side-arms too."

"You talk mighty big down here all by yourself."

Cliff recognized the voice as the same who had questioned him from the bunkhouse. "Listen, big shot. All I have to do is drop this flag and that sharpshooter will drop one of you before it hits the ground."

"Shet' up, Russo," the first man to come out commanded.

"When did you get to be in charge?"

Cliff slowly pointed his carbine at the man who was causing the trouble, and immediately the men who stood near him began to move away.

"You don't scare me. You can't hit me from there with that short barrel thing."

"I don't plan to hit. I only pointed you out as the next man for Shep to kill with the Whitworth."

The man quickly cut his eyes toward the big rock high on the hill.

At that moment someone with a strong, sharp accent gulped, "No wonder he never missed. I seen them Rebs with their Whitworths in the war. It are the straightest shooting gun ever made."

The troublemaker dropped his pistol in the dirt at his feet and walked away from it.

An hour later, Cliff was looking at the large dark stain on the front porch, realizing most likely it had been the blood of the dude they had found with Pepper.

"Who shot the Dude here?" he asked.

Snake Canyon shifted his narrow shoulders within the big buffalo coat before he replied, "Major Brown shot him."

"Major Brown, the foreman here?"

"Yep."

"Where is he now?" Cliff asked, hoping his source of information would not dry up.

"Took off, right after he killed Moreton."

"Moreton?"

"The Englishman who owned this place," Snake added.

"Who shot Pepper?"

The skinny lad spoke again, "Bun White."

"Which one is he?" Cliff asked looking at the men who now stood bunched over near the corral.

"That's him thar'," Snake replied nodding to the body at the bottom of the steps. "He were one of the first to get hit yesterdee."

"Thought you said he lit out a' here."

"Well, he did when that Whitworth hit him. You Pepper's deputy?" he asked Cliff.

"No, I'm a State Man," he answered, hoping it didn't dawn on any of them that Wyoming was still a Territory, not a State.

Finally satisfied he had done all he could here, Cliff told Snake he was to come with him to explain the shooting of Sheriff Pepper to the authorities in Laramie, and then he told his men to pick up the firearms laying about.

"We need our guns. What if Injuns come?"

"We will leave them over the hill yonder," Cliff replied. "Don't want nobody taking a bead on my back while I'm climbing up that hill."

The statement made sense to them. They would not have wanted to walk up that hill with guns behind them either, so no more was said.

When Cliff reached the big rock, he found Shep weeping over the body of his brother.

Seeing the supply wagon had arrived, he yelled out, "Where is Arturo?"

The small Mexican boy sheepishly came from behind the vehicle. "Si Señor Reb, here I 'ees."

"Arturo," Cliff's voice rang strong and forceful, and everybody there realized he meant business. "You see Absalom here?"

"No Señor."

"You think he can hurt you now?"

The boy looked around him and then at the ground in front of his feet without replying.

"I asked you a question!" Cliff shouted.

The boy jumped, and everyone saw a dark stain begin to run down his dirty white pant leg as his bladder failed him.

"No Señor," he whimpered. "He ees not here."

"What is it you know, that Absalom doesn't want you to tell me?"

There was another long pause, and Cliff shouted in the boy's face, "Tell me!"

"Oh Chihuahua, he, he ees da one what shoot Carlos. He shoot him in the back of the head. Carlos would not help him stampede the beeves."

"Absalom stampeded the herd?"

"Si, the Lady," he suddenly stopped.

Cliff squinted his eyes tightly before grabbing the boy's shirt and twisting the collar tightly in his left fist, "The Lady what?"

"She told us we should do it. She say it will get you to go after the men who killed Gilberto."

Cliff felt a blow strike him from inside. The words were as hurtful as a hot pistol ball would have been. "All of this, all these men dead because she wanted me to get after them?"

"Si Señor."

He released the boy's shirt, and then took a deep breath. Turning, he looked at the men, and slowly he took a step, almost losing his balance.

It was late in the day when they arrived back at the ranch. Everyone waited anxiously, they all knew Reb and Mrs. Moore were about to clash, and no one wanted to miss it.

She was the first to see them returning, and she called out to Ellie.

The two women and the three hands that Cliff had left to protect them stood watching as the column of riders entered the ranch yard.

As soon as Cliff dismounted, he walked up to Absalom and struck him a swinging blow in the jaw with the butt of his carbine. The tall boy dropped instantly to the ground.

"What the___?" Elaine questioned loudly.

Cliff reached down and removed the rifle, pistol, and old knife from the semi-conscious lad, and tossed them to Billy Ellis.

"What's got into you!" she screamed at Cliff.

He completely ignored her, walking back towards Ola. Cliff felt tuckered out, the most he had felt since the war, and his walk showed his fatigue when he moved towards his horse. Ramming the carbine in its scabbard, he then released his belt buckle and swung the heavy revolver over the horn. At the moment, he suddenly wanted nothing to do with guns.

That feeling lasted only as long as it took him to make that walk and then go to the water trough to wash his head.

It was Tommy Walker who screamed, "Reb, look out!"

Instinctively, he whirled to face the obvious danger, his hand shooting to his side where the Colt rode, but it was not there.

There in front of him, only yards away, was Absalom with the heavy new Winchester they had recovered from the body of the man who had shot Ethan.Someone had decided it was too much a gun to leave for the Wolf Creek men and had laid it in the bed of the wagon, where Absalom found it.

The tall Mexican pulled back the hammer and aimed the long barrel at Cliff. "Now you weel die," he said hatefully, as he began squeezing the trigger.

"No!" Elaine screamed.

The boy Laramie shouted at that moment, "Reb," as he tossed his seedsower to his boss.

The act would have been a brave but a useless gesture had not the firing pin of the Centennial Winchester struck hard on a spent primer.

The tall boy looked surprised when instead of the loud report he expected, he heard a loud click. Cliff then realized no one had ejected the shell that had killed Ethan.

With a fury Absalom worked the lever, but he had not gotten it closed fully when the buckshot of the old single barrel shotgun hit him full in the face. The force of the blast knocked him backward, and he threw the Winchester high in the air before his lifeless body slammed on the hard ground, behind where he had stood.

"Why did you hit him?" she again shouted at Cliff.

"Why did you have him stampede your own beeves?" Cliff replied, without looking at her.

The words hit her equally as hard as the news had hit him a few hours before. She suddenly felt totally defeated. *'How could this happen?'* she questioned herself. *'I had him, just this morning I had him.'*

Ellie had seen the pain on Shep's face when he arrived and rushed to his side; he took her arm and walked her over to the wagon, there removing the horse blanket that covered his brother's face.

"Oh, no!" she uttered, and her sister heard her pain and turned and looked at the body.

"Oh my Gawd," she said softly.

That night, he after he had regained consciousness, Cliff spoke to Sheriff Pepper and explained all that had happened.

Pepper confirmed Snake's description of the killing of Allen Moreton, as well as the account of his shooting, being pretty much on target.

"Did you get the man who shot Moreton?" he asked Cliff.

"Naw, they said he fled shortly after they took you off."

"Yeah, that makes sense," the Sheriff weakly nodded his head, affirming the idea. "I remember her calling out to him when he went back into the house, something about not leaving her."

Cliff took a deep breath and then sighed heavily.

"You know, that was the first time I ever heard her speak American. I didn't even know she could talk the language."

"What?" Cliff questioned. He had been thinking of Ethan lying out there in the barn and had barely heard the Sheriff.

"I said I didn't even know she could speak American, until she called him Jean Mouton, in pretty fair English too."

Cliff heard this very well. "She called him John Mouton?"

"Yeah, you know the French can't really pronounce John, but that was what she was trying to say."

Suddenly his tiredness was gone. He no longer felt weary, instead realized he had been on a tangent. Now it was necessary to get back to his real goal in life, to find and kill the man who had murdered his wife.

That night he slept in the barn with the other men, and the next day, as soon as they had laid Ethan to rest beside Jimmy Don, he turned and walked heavily towards his big Appaloosa.

"Reb. Reb please wait," she pleaded as she tried to keep pace with his long strides.

"I'm sorry. I was wrong. All along, you were right. I admit that, but now don't you see? Now we can be married, and this place will be yours, yours and mine, with no more troubles."

"No."

"But Reb, I need you. I love you. You can't leave me. Not now," she pleaded.

"Shep will take care of you until you find another man," he replied as he shored up his cinch, "and that shouldn't take you too long. I'll leave the men with you," he paused shortly before adding, "for now," he nodded his head approving his last injection. "I done told them to stay with you as long as you need 'em."

"But I want you. I want to have you forever."

"You don't have me Elaine. You never did," he said back, and for the first time since he returned to *The Circle Rocking AR Ranch*, he looked at her.

Seeing the expression on his face, she knew he spoke straight from the horse's mouth, and she realized there was nothing she could do to change his mind; suddenly she felt totally defeated.

They all watched as he rode away, save Black Band and Laramie who followed him from a short distance. The boy was determined to find his mother, and now he knew Reb Brown was on the trail of the man she was with.

Chapter Six
Big Sky Country

The moment he returned to his senses and saw Allen Moreton dying there in front of Sheriff Pepper, Jean Mouton realized his future at Wolf Creek was to be very short. Immediately, he motioned to Bun White, and they went into the house for a few moments.

When White emerged, he and a couple of hands took Pepper off. While this deed was being completed, Jean opened the big safe located in the study and removed all the money. Next, he went to Allen Moreton's room and found his dead boss' large wallet containing over one thousand pound notes. In addition, among Allen's personal effects he kept in a soft leather traveling bag, he discovered a bankbook on *The First Union Bank of Omaha*, which contained figures of some twenty thousand pounds in *The Wolf Creek Ranch* account.

Inside the bankbook was also a key. He recognized it as the type pertaining to a safety deposit box so many of the larger banks were now installing.

'Perhaps this is my biggest prize yet,' he thought as he squeezed the key tightly and affectionately in his palm. From behind him, her voice interrupted his planning, "You are leaving me, non?"

At first he thought, *'Leaving you, oui.'* However, his eyes narrowed as he considered the ramifications of leaving her here. *'Here she might give evidence to my true identity. She can be left anywhere.'*

Satisfied with his last thought he turned and smiled at her, "Get your things if you want to go with me," he said, turning his face from her.

Only the cook saw the two leave, and before the sun set in the western sky, they were approaching the outskirts of Cheyenne.

Sunday morning, the 25th day of the month near the ten o'clock hour, he watched the passengers board *The Cheyenne and Black Hills Stage* in front of *The Inter-Ocean Hotel*, and he gave the first sigh of relief in several days. He was, at last, once again headed towards Montana, even if his route would be through Dakota Territory.

The Union Pacific Hotel and Train Station at Cheyenne

'The stage is the best means to get there, no question,' he thought as the new Concord rolled away. 'Should anyone follow, they will assume we took the train east. No one will suspect we went by stage, especially if we do not board with the passengers.'

The night before he had bought Celeste a bright red dress, and then the two of them strolled boldly down to the depot where he purchased two tickets for the sunrise train to Omaha. At the time there were several men in the large depot office, and not one could resist being heedful of the lovely lady in red.

Later that night while she slept, he slipped his thin stiletto under the fifth rib of a drunken man, who had mistakenly stopped in Cheyenne before heading on to the Black Hills gold fields. This poor little devil had the unfortunate experience because his size so closely matched that of Jean Mouton's traveling companion.

When she awoke the next morning, she was told to dress in the man's clothing. Then without breakfast, they slipped out the back of the hotel to the livery where their horses were boarded.

Overtaking the six-up[1] was not too difficult, and they watched from afar the changing of horses and the relief taken, one by one, of the passengers in the small house behind the main building. When the coach pulled out behind a fresh team, Jean and Celeste skirted *The Horse Creek Stage Stop* and followed just far enough behind not to be seen.

Metal Bridge to Fort Laramie

Bear Creek, Chugwater, Chug Springs, and Eagle's Nest too were avoided. When the rocking coach pulled to a stop across the military bridge on the Fort Laramie side of the river, the mounted couple gave the Post a wide birth. Instead, that night they camped up river some two miles in a small grove of cottonwoods.

For them to be seen at Ft Laramie would have been a sure disaster. Neither knew of her husband's death, nor of the pursuit being made by her son. However, both knew full well, half of the men stationed at the fort would recognize her, and their carefully planned escape would come to an abrupt end.

1 Six-up: A stage coach pulled by six horses or mules.

Jean realized he had become tired of her and needed a new relationship. He considered leaving her there and pressing on alone, but thinking more on it, he remembered just why he had not left her back at Wolf Creek. *'She simply possesses too much knowledge of my plans to be found abandoned and perhaps, with her back up.'* He also realized many people had seen them in the U. P. Depot, and for her to turn up abandoned or even as a body so soon afterward, would likely be disastrous for him. *'No, she must be taken along.'*

He was not alone in these same ideas. She also thought of slipping off to the Fort while he slept, but she was ashamed of her abandonment of her husband and child. She also suspected her reputation would be that of a whore, were she to return to her former home.

Besides, when this man did take her body, he lit a fire in her as no man had ever before, and she would sometimes become sick to her stomach at the thought of never having him sharing her bed again.

Although, she had to admit, his interest in her treasures were not as keen as they had once been. *'It is the difficulty we are experiencing these last few days,'* she thought. *'When we reach Montana Territory, he will be his ol' self, and I will be able to attract his blood as before, and he will give me all I need once again.'* It was with these thoughts she drifted off to sleep under the stars of the cooling June night.

The white man has come to remember it as something totally different from that of the Indian. Ask anyone of European descent, and they will either tell you about *The Battle of the Little Big Horn* or perhaps say, "You mean, *Custer's Last Stand.*"

Not so, among those whose fathers roamed these lands many years before the first United States citizens, Lewis and Clark, set foot on what was to become Montana Territory. To these native people, the rolling hills that fall to the shallow stream below are known as *The Valley of the Greasy Grass,* a special place where food and water could always be found and grazing was bountiful, a haven in this rolling desert for their herds and their families.

When Yellow Hair and his long knives attacked the villages that hot June morning, most were completely caught by surprise. Of course, they knew the pony soldiers were east of the Elk Mountains. They had watched when the two great columns separated and rode off in what appeared to be different directions, each of which would pass well away from the village hidden among the thick cottonwoods along the banks of the little stream.

All they had to do was wait until the pony-soldiers passed and then slip off towards the White Rain Mountains.

Gall, War Chief of the Hunkpapa Lakota, had been confident all would be well if they waited. He had sent his two wives and three children to the southernmost part of the village, where there was a little grove of timber near the river. There his children could play in the water while the women did their wash. After seeing to their safety, he mounted his pony and rode back to speak with several Cheyenne, who were watching the vast pony herd that was grazing over the hills, west of the village.

He had only just arrived among the Cheyenne, when the sound of gunfire was heard. Immediately he rushed back to where he had left his family. By the time he arrived, much fighting had taken place. The air smelled of sulfur, and the sing of bullets seemed to be everywhere.

It did not take him long to find his family, all had been shot by the advancing soldiers. He picked up his three-year-old daughter and holding her to him, wept. Oh, how he loved this girl child.

Gall was still holding her limp and bloody body close to his heart when a heavy slug struck her again, penetrating her small lifeless form and burning against his chest. The impact of the fast moving lead resulted in her being knocked from his arms, and he looked first at her lying there in the shallow water and then at the spent lead that was stuck to his skin. Reaching down, he pulled the revolver ball from his chest.

The huge man then raised his gaze to the young soldier who was standing, perhaps fifteen paces away, on the opposite bank. The man was desperately trying to reload his pistol, and Gall could see there was a dark stain in the front of his blue pants, where fear had overtaken his ability to control his bladder.

The big Indian had laid his short rifle beside his youngest wife when he had found her dead and now had only his tomahawk for a weapon. He knew it would be a long, almost impossible throw, but he also knew his aim would be true. This man, who suddenly represented all those who had killed his family, needed to die, and he needed to be the one who killed him. With a mighty swing of his powerful arm, he released his grip on the old wooden handle, and the hand axe was on its way, tumbling over and over until it buried itself deeply into the upper chest of the tunic-less soldier.

Gall watched the man drop his little gun and grasp at the hatchet, but he had not the strength to remove it. He stood there for only two or three seconds, but to them both, it seemed like a lifetime. Slowly, his knees buckled. However, as if in a last act of defiance, the young man released his grip on the battle-axe and slowly brushed his blonde bangs from his forehead. Seconds later, his body fell forward as his soul raced away to meet Lucifer.

The Great War Chief walked over to the body and removed his hatchet. He looked at the new Colt pistol that lay beside the dead soldier, but his heart was heavy with sorrow from the loss of his wives and children. Dismissing the small gun, he moved at a trot towards the sound of other women screaming with his battle-axe in hand.

Passing close by as he hurried towards the sounds of gunshots, he saw the son of Jumping Bull[2] race towards his tepee and close the flap, as if it would deflect the bullets that still filled the air. Gall, having never carried a huge respect for the holy man, mumbled these words barely above a whisper, "Squatting Cow now makes medicine." He rushed past the tall tent on towards the sounds of heavy fighting. Before that day was over, he had used the hatchet to send many pony-soldiers to their reward in the hereafter.

Word of the destruction left by the hostiles in southern Montana had not reached Fort Laramie by the time the stage pulled out the next day.

Jean Mouton and Celeste Patay had already broken camp and would be waiting for the coach to arrive at *The Rawhide Buttes Station*. No one would ever again see her dressed in a man's outfit. When the six-up pulled into the dusty stop, both were dressed to the tee in their Sunday best. Looking for all the world like the easterners they really were.

The Rawhide Ranch was owned by an old devil of a man, who had a bit of wit cut deep into his otherwise crusty nature. That is not to say Russell Thorp was an unfriendly cuss, on the contrary, he was a sporting man, especially when it came to the ladies. He was not an unknown caller at *The Ecoffey Hog Ranch*[3], west of Fort Laramie. Of course, he often said, "I only go there to carry the gospel to the poor unfortunate creatures who struggle to make a living in these

---

2 Son of Jumping Bull: Sitting Bull, Medicine Man of the Hunkpapa Lakota.

3 Hog Ranch: A whore house on the prairie, equal or at least no higher than a crib in the towns.

desolate and barren plains of eastern Wyoming." All of the hands who worked the R bar T brand, knew that to be the holy truth.

The Rawhide Ranch itself was considerable in size. However, it was the plaza of buildings clustered in a little valley along the creek that most called the ranch. Several buildings had been hewn from the nearby timber, including a rather well-constructed ranch house. This main house served also as an overnight stop for *The F. D. Yates & Co. Stage Line*. It was listed as *The Rawhide Buttes Home Station* on their schedule of stops advertisement hanging on the wall in *The Inter-Ocean Hotel* in Cheyenne.

It was here under the shade of the front porch roof, Russ Thorp was standing as he watched the two riders approach from the south. He had realized from a distance the smaller rider was not a man and that surely the other was not a western man. Neither sat a saddle in a manner common to those who made their living from it. Russ had little, perhaps no, interest in the tall, lean man who reined up in front of the hitching post. His eyes were glued to the lady. He was sure he had seen her before but just couldn't put a time or place on when or where.

"Monsieur, we understand my wife and I may obtain traveling arrangements on the northbound coach here, non," Jean said, once more using a strong French accent.

"Yep. That you can," the man replied. Then added, "Your wife, eh'?"

"Oui, my wife and I."

"Tomorrow, you can," Russell replied nodding his head, yet not looking once at Mouton.

When he did take his eyes from her, he turned only his head and spoke to one of the hands, who also was staring at the lady still sitting astride the big black mare. "Stoner, take the lady's baggage in the house."

"Yas, Sur," Jake replied and moved towards the pack mule Jean had rented from the livery in Cheyenne.

Russell Thorp moved off the porch and walked between the two horses. He pushed her mount hard, insuring enough room for her to dismount. "May I help you down, Ma'am?"

Jean felt a sudden moment of anger at the obvious dismissal he was receiving but quickly decided that this might work well for him after all. Releasing his clasp on the small ivory grip of the Colt he carried under his jacket, he dismounted himself. Then he walked around and tied the two horses to the twisted old hitching-rail.

"I, sir, am Louis de la Motte, and may I present Lady Marie."

She turned and looked strongly at him when he spoke but did not otherwise expose his new lie.

Jake Stoner placed their luggage in the only room that was not occupied by Mr. Thorp's people. It was a small room with a loosely fitting slab door and one window. This gave view of a large corral at the backside of a two-story barn, where several strong horses were milling around.

Jean first checked for the non-existing lock on the door and then moved over to the open window. There was no glass, only an opening cut in the logs, with a wooden door to keep out some of the cold in the winter months. Through it he espied half a dozen wranglers working around the corral and two other men pitching freshly cut hay from a wagon to the upper door of the barn.

"You make up such names, why? I will never remember them, you know. You get this de la Motte from where?" she spoke in a steady flow, not stopping between sentences, as she opened one of the leather bags. Had he not been accustomed to her form of French, he would have not been able to distinguish her meanings.

"Ah Marie, you are so beautiful when you are angry."

"Ah Marie, who is this Marie?"

"Why Mademoiselle, it is you of course," he said, as he placed his hands on her shoulders.

"Huh!" was all she said in reply.

"If you must know, Louis de la Motte is a hero of mine. It was he who seduced the Queen Marie Antoinette, before her unfortunate beheading."

"Ah, a pleasant thought," she said, tossing the new red dress over the bedpost before digging deeper into her bag.

"It does seem our host has taken a fancy to you, my Dear. I do think that might work to our benefit."

"He is a rough, smelly man," she said back still digging for something in her bag.

"Oui, that he is, but you shall be nice to him."

"I will not."

"Oui, you shall," he said, pausing before he finished, "or I will leave you here." Then he walked out of the door, and left her to dwell on his statement.

That night Jean made it a point to go to bed before the dinner meal, stating he had severe pains in his stomach. She cut a sharp eye at him as he spoke, knowing full well he was leaving her to face the wolves alone.

The northbound stage arrived an hour after the sun had dropped behind the low hills to the west. The driver and messenger both immediately headed to the big wooden water barrel, which always contained a jug of new whiskey for their pleasure.

R bar T hands were at the front of the coach before the driver's feet hit the ground, guiding the vehicle over where the horses could be removed and fresh grease applied to the squeaky wheel, which all heard as the stage approached.

The six passengers, who struggled through the small coach door, were all obviously headed to the gold fields, to make their fortune as soon as possible. Four seemed so out of place that no one even gave them a second look. Of the other two, one appeared to have been making his living as a buffalo hunter or wolfer and from his smell they suspected it to be the latter, the other appeared to be a gambler.

'I do suspect he will find his gold on the tables of a saloon in the Deadwood camp,' the ranch owner thought.

Russ had sent two of his men out to kill a few prairie chickens for the meal, a most unusual move on his part, which raised the eyebrows of more than one of the punchers[4] who worked there.

All the passengers and the two stage employees, along with the regular hands, were served a good meal of antelope stew in the bunkhouse, where they also were shown their bunks.

The grouse, prepared by a Chinese woman Thorp had hired to cook, was served only in the house and only for the special guest.

Later Jean could hear the sounds of passionate play in another room, but he did not venture out to see who was enjoying Celeste's treasures. He was surprised that the sounds gave him a powerfully hard erection, something he had not found so frequent during the last year.

An hour before dawn, she entered the room and slipped into the bed beside him. Her movement in the squeaky bed awakened him, and he realized the thought of her being so recently used by another man still aroused him. Quickly he moved close to her, but

---

4 Puncher: Cowboy who punched cattle with a probing stick into loading pens.

she turned away, a gesture that he did not appreciate at all. He immediately jerked her back and mounted her, relieving his passion.

After having a quick breakfast of salt pork and coffee, Russ Thorp paid $20 apiece for their horses and another $30 for the pack mule. Louie de le Motte presented him with a bill of sale, then assisted his lady into the stage

As the coach moved out onto the dusty road Jake offered, "That Mrs. De la Motte was sure a fine looker fer a' older woman, huh boss?"

"Marie de la Motte my ass. That thar is the trader Patay's wife, from down to Ft Laramie, I seen her several times, a year or two back. She must be a California Widow[5] these days."

"You shor'?"

"Yep, I'm shor'."

"Well, I'll be damned!"

Bill Mansfield checked the new Smith seedsower[6], which had been given to him for this trip before they left Cheyenne. Satisfied it was loaded, he closed the action. Jack Gilmore smiled a little behind his thick mustache, before he spoke. "Them is the same two shells that were in 'er half a' hour ago, when you checked 'er for the fifth time."

"I'm a mite nervous, I reckon. There is so much talk about Injuns being all riled up cause of this Black Hills invasion," he paused before he added, "of nigh on every easterner west of the big muddy."

"Injuns always git a mite riled up when the Whiteman breaks his word, and he done up and broke it again, this time a plenty," Jack replied, just before he spit off the right side of his seat.

The tobacco juice was caught in the turbulence and dust caused by the front wheel and carried back into the rear window, some striking Emmett Parkhurst in the face and some also landing on Dale Yukon's sleeve. The wolfer never gave the stain more than a glance. On the other hand, Parkhurst felt his anger shoot straight up long before he removed a white linen kerchief from his inner coat pocket to wipe his face clean. The urge to send a couple of balls through the thin wood that separated the interior of the coach from the driver's seat above rushed through his mind, but he resisted it.

---

5 California Widow: A woman separated from her husband, but not divorced. Derived from when forty-niners went to seek gold, leaving their wives to follow later.

6 Seedsower: Short double barrel shotgun.

Jean Mouton saw the expression on the gambler's face and knew full well his feelings. He also appreciated a smirk of humor in the whole incident. He had learned many years before, to avoid much of the dust and other such displeasures as the gambler had just experienced, one should always ride these disgusting vehicles with one's back to the front bulkhead.

The horses were changed every 15 to 20 miles, and that evening when the stage pulled into *May's Ranch Station*, everyone aboard felt the dire need for a night's rest.

The accommodations were not as good as the night before for Jean Mouton, but his traveling companion did not dread the night as she had at *The Rawhide Ranch*.

Not once did Celeste mention anything to him about what had happened the night before. In fact, she had avoided speaking to him as much as she could. Once, she started to tell him about Russell Thorp passing out, but she thought it better to let him think it was she who had secured their escape. Thus, he would be in her debt. Only she and that nasty smelling saddle tramp would ever know the truth. Celeste also fully realized he had sent her out as his whore, and she did not appreciate that one bit.

The entire conversation at the supper table was of the Indian trouble that seemed to be brewing over the discovery of gold in The Black Hills, and it frightened her, as did any talk of the savages.

Jean Mouton didn't seem to let it concern him in the least. His mind was on the bank key he kept in his vest pocket, close to his heart.

His lack of concern also frightened her. *'Has his determination to reach Montana Territory blocked all his sense,'* she wondered.

The next morning, just before they were to board, one of the stage employees came in to report he had seen riders on a distant hill in the early morning light.

"Wus them Injuns or Whites?" Gilmore asked him.

"Doe' no. It were not light enough to see more than men on horseback. There yonder," he added, pointing towards the small hills, a mile east of the station.

"You sure boy?" asked Mansfield.

"Yep, I'm sure. Sure," he replied nodding his head.

"I don't like it," Mansfield said.

"Could a' been anybody," Yukon contributed. "Maybe just drovers moving cattle by."

"What about it boy? Were it drovers?"

"Doe' no, mee'be. I just seen riders, three, mee'be four."

"Well, I ain't taking no chances," one of the top riding easterners said. "I'll wait right here until we find out."

"That'a cost you a dollar a day fer bed and grub."

"I'll pay, and you others should do the same. There'll be another stage along in a day or two; things may have quieted down some by then."

"In a day or two, them diggers may have all the gold done dug up and in that Deadwood bank," another added.

"Is there a bank in the Deadwood Camp?" Parkhurst inquired.

No one answered.

"Yeah, staying here is pure stupidity," Yukon said. "Hell, if'n it are Injuns, they might just come right down here and massacre every living soul still around and burn this place to the ground."

"Make up your minds; this here stage is pulling out in five minutes," Gilmore said, as he double-checked the tie-down ropes and leads.

When they did pull out, there were two would-be miners on top, Ben Maynard[7] and Stony Silverton, each with a shotgun they had purchased from the station manager. Yukon and Parkhurst were the only two inside with the French couple.

No one really made any mention, or other acknowledgement, when the team pulled the coach through the knee-deep water of the Cheyenne River. However, it was only a few miles after the crossing a round ball hit the easterner who wore the yellow jacket, square in the back.

Jack Gilmore had seen the flash off to his left and heard the hot lead as it passed inches from his ear. He also heard the dull thud when it struck T. S. Silverton's beefy back, but he did not hear Silverton's body hit the ground only a second after. In fact, he heard

nothing else for a time because of the blast of the messenger's shotgun so close to his head. Bill had cut loose with both barrels and the explosion was deafening.

The Arapaho who had killed the miner felt the stinging bite of the buckshot, but he was too far away for it to penetrate his skin. His pony was less accommodating of the hot lead balls and began

---

7 Ben Maynard: Nadine's brother, who would later be playing poker in The Number 10 Saloon just moments before Bill Hickok met his maker.

to buck wildly. The last Gilmore or Mansfield saw of the attacker was when he was flying backwards from the jumping horse.

"I got 'em," Bill shouted.

"You got his horse," the Jehu yelled back and then added, "You better get reloaded 'cause he's bound to have friends."

Bill looked first at his companion and then back to the left side of the road where six more mounted warriors were seen. "Holy shit!" was all he said as he opened the shotgun.

Celeste had seen the man in the yellow coat fall from the coach and was about to yell to the others, thinking his fall had been an accident, until she heard the sound of the gunfire. Then she suddenly could not utter a sound. From the time the savages passed so close to their canoe in Lake Michigan, she had an inner terror of the red race and her nightmare so long ago only added fuel to this fear. Over the years, while working at Ft. Laramie, she had seen many and knew most to be beggars. However, occasionally some would come by, and the hatred in their eyes caused her to cringe with fear. It was just such a fright she now experienced.

Several arrows were sent at the fast moving coach as it passed the Indians, but none found flesh.

The ambushers were not worried about the misses; they knew the stage would not go far.

The attack had occurred as the road curved down a small hill, and Jack had given his six-up a full snap of the long fly killer on each of their rumps, to alert them to the seriousness of the situation.

The horses were pulling with all their might up the next little rise, when he saw the Indians pass them out of the corner of his eye. They were fully a hundred yards away and riding hard and fast to get ahead of the fleeing coach. *'I'll, by Gawd, give them a taste of good draught animals,'* Gilmore thought, lashing out with his long whip and snapping it only inches above the animals' heads. Unfortunately, topping the rise he saw the uselessness of his attempt and had to pull hard on the long reins as he stomped the brake with his right boot.

Bill Mansfield almost tumbled forward and out of the boot as the vehicle suddenly lost much of its forward thrust.

The horses, too, had spotted the danger ahead and were now trying hard to stop without being overhauled by the coach behind them.

"Holy Shit!" Bill again exclaimed when he saw the stack of dead wood across the trail at a point where two larger-than-average rocks rested, one on either side of the narrow road.

The men inside were firing, along with the others on top, at the passing raiders. Someone suddenly, from inside or on top, connected, resulting in a young warrior throwing both his arms high into the air and releasing his weapon before falling off the left side of his mustang. This only caused the others to bring their wild yelps to a louder volume.

Jack, or the team, he was not sure which, stopped the stage some five feet before the horses would have plowed into the tall stack of timber.

Immediately, the driver jumped down and tended to the lead animals, knowing he had to calm them before they panicked and turned the coach over.

All the men were now firing steadily at their attackers, but few hits, if any, were seen.

The Sun People[8] had picked their spot well. To the west of the road at this very spot were several rocks and a shallow washout that gave the attackers good cover. To the east, the hill rose another thirty feet in a steep bank.

The siege lasted for the remainder of the day, however when darkness came upon them, Jean decided it was time to depart company with the others.

That night a partial moon lit the area just enough for a man to see but not be seen if he was careful; it was enough for Mouton. Just after midnight, he slipped away, disappearing within a few steps.

He moved southwestward towards where they had last seen the hostiles. His thinking was, the savages would surely be closely watching the other directions for an escape but would never think a Whiteman would dare approach them.

It had taken him almost an hour to cover the two hundred yards when he saw something move ahead, and he froze in his tracks. After over a minute, he again saw the movement off some distance and realized it had to be the animals of the savages.

Just as he was about to inch forward, the sound of something rubbing against a greasewood bush behind him sent a cold chill up his spine. Immediately he froze and listened intensely. *'Yes, there is no doubt. Someone is coming up on me from the east,'* he agreed with

---

8 Sun People: The name the Arapaho call themselves.

himself. Lifting his Colt from its holster, he slowly eased down into a crouching position, from there he waited.

After several seconds, he realized the folly of firing a shot so near their camp, and he slipped his hand forward on the revolver until he was holding the barrel with the stock up. *'It will make a fine club for this savage,'* he thought.

Jean Mouton waited patiently, an emotion he had learned as a young man. *'To wait on the savage is easy, far easier than taking an arrow, or war club to the head.'*

He peered keenly into the semi-darkness, determined to be the first to see the other. Unfortunately, a small cloud passed between the moon and that tiny portion of the Great Plains, and suddenly it was quite dark.

A few seconds later, he realized something or someone was behind him and slightly to his left. He wasn't sure how he knew it, but he was certain of it.

Suddenly, being patient was not so easy. At any moment, the cutting blade of a tomahawk could come crashing down, splitting his skull in less than a second. He wanted to jump up and give the invader a fight of it. This would be almost certain death, but at least he might be able to take his foe with him. Jean slowly and very carefully, moved the Colt around in his hand to where once again he had the grip tightly in his palm, but it was not cocked. The sound of cocking it would be a sure exposure of his location, should the savage not be able to see him in this unexpected darkness.

His years as a warrior and self-discipline began to slowly root out the urge to panic. Now, he was determined to remain perfectly still, until he knew for certain he had been seen.

Seconds crept like hours.

There was slight movement to his left, and there, out of the corner of his eye, he could make out the figure of a man's leg, a powerful leg, standing almost next to him. Only the leg was not turned towards him, rather it was beside him. *'He is looking for the source of the same noise I heard only a minute ago.'* Jean was now certain he had not been seen.

The cloud gradually moved away, and the silver light, so very dim, was again capturing the prairie in front of them.

Mouton's eyes moved first to his left and then ahead to the east. *'Either place very likely contains a deadly enemy, but which will see me first, if either?'*

The light swept past his hiding place, and he was relieved to again see he was concealed behind a six-foot tall greasewood bush.

There, less than two yards away, stood a tall, strongly built man, dressed only in a loincloth. In his hand was a small stone club with several feathers hanging from the hide that had been wrapped tightly around its wooden handle.

Jean saw no other weapon.

The savage was semi-crouched, not as low as he, but neither was he standing fully, waiting to pounce upon whoever was approaching if need be.

Jean looked back just as the light of the moon swept the trail he had left in his escape from the stage. There, standing and gazing into the darkness, was Celeste.

The man moved like a cat. Not stealthily, but rather with a lunge, as would a cougar. One second she was standing there and the next he was upon her. His left hand moved with such force, he never needed the war club.

Jean could hear the wind rush from her lungs as the man's palm crashed into her solar plexus, and she went limp in his arms, gasping for air.

The Arapaho lifted her over his shoulder, as one would carry a sack of grain, then he turned, walking back past Mouton and on down a dim animal trail.

Jean could have killed him with ease. He could have stopped him with a swift blow of his revolver to the head. He could have reached out and touched his arm as he passed, he was that close, but he did none of these. What he did was to wait and watch.

When they had been gone some five minutes, he followed cautiously. Soon after, he heard her scream. There was no doubt the others back at the stage, heard her scream also. Her cry was like a knife cutting the silence of the deathly quiet night.

Once, maybe twice, he heard her cry out his name and slowly he inched his way toward the sounds.

Some of her emissions equaled her first scream but most now were more like sobs. There were very few seconds when some painful sound was not coming from her location, as well as grunts and laughter.

Finally, he slipped into a ditch like depression, where the spring rains had cut a shallow washout into the prairie floor. From there, he could move forward and to his left, moving ever more closely to the sounds she was making until at last he could see them.

There were three men standing in a semi-circle, intensely watching the fourth who was on her. He was using her as rapidly as his back and legs would allow. One of the others stood close by naked of his loincloth, with a full erection waiting his turn. Another who was standing above her head, also no longer wore his loincloth, but he was only laughing at what was taking place.

Jean recognized him as the one who had carried her off, and surmised he had been the first to use her.

Soon another came out of the darkness and began talking. An argument ensued between him and the savage who had captured her, finally the new arrival won out, and the captor moved away in the direction the new arrival had come.

Celeste looked up at the many savages surrounding her and screamed again, as if she had been through this ordeal before, and knew of its conclusion.

Jean took one last glance at the scene before him just in time to see an exchange of males take place on the woman he had kept for so many months. He then eased off, following the savage into the darkness.

When Jack Gilmore heard her first scream, he was totally surprised. Suddenly he turned and looked for the lady passenger. She was not there.

"Bill, whar is that woman?"

"I doe' no," replied his partner.

"Her husband, whar is he?"

"Doe' no that neither."

"You, did you see where they went?" he asked Yukon.

"Naw, I've been too busy looking fer Injuns."

"Anybody see the two Frenchys?" Jack whispered out to the others. Each looked around, then at each other and raised their shoulders or shook their heads.

"Damn!" the driver exclaimed from behind clinched teeth. "Damn fools."

It was at that time they heard the sounds of a revolver discharge, followed immediately by several horses charging away into the night. Soon the sounds of excited talk was recognized off in the darkness, and then all was quiet.

The next morning, Bill Mansfield and Emmett Parkhurst slipped out to scout the area where the screams had come from the night before. They soon found where the Indians had made a small camp, and there was much sign of moccasin prints in the sand. They even found the undergarments and blue dress Mrs. De la Motte had been wearing. There was some blood on the white linen things but not a large amount.

When they returned to the stage, they reported that all the Indians were gone. "They must a' killed Mr. De la Motte as he tried to steal some of their horses, then captured his wife and took her away with them."

"What makes you think that?" Jack asked.

"There was a large red stain out where the horses had been, and we found these," he said holding up her dress and bloomers.

"A Gawd, they stripped her?" one of the miners asked.

"Sure do look that away."

"No bodies?" asked Yukon.

"Nary a sign," Mansfield replied.

"Damn fools, should never have tried to slip off like that," Jack said. Then he added, "Come on let's get this road cleared afore 'em butcherin' Redskins comeback fer us."

It did not take Cliff long to locate a hotel clerk who remembered the tall man with a French woman. "Yes, I do remember an odd stick with a French accent, a handsome woman with him, Frenchy also."

Cliff dropped a gold eagle on the desk. In a smooth motion, almost too quick for the eye to detect, the coin disappeared.

Aucilla Plymale began working at the hotel some six months before; it gave him a grand opportunity to observe the guests as they checked in.

He had been quite a rancher in Arkansas some time back. Unfortunately, his passion for poker had stripped him of his land and riches one night in Fort Smith. He played too long after drinking too much and slowly watched his riches and property peter out. Thereafter he drifted west, hitting one boomtown and then another, making a living by his incredible ability to remember exactly what he had recently seen, an attribute that was without price in a card game. He also made it a point never to play while roostered[9] again.

---

9 Roostered: Drunk.

It was this ability that Cliff Brown was most interested in, not for a card game, rather in his description of the man and woman.

Aucilla had taken the job as day clerk at *The Leighton House,* after drifting into Cheyenne just before Christmas of seventy-five. It would have not been his choice of day jobs; in fact, at 68 years old he no longer really wanted a day job. However, he found the meager pay and benefit of a room in such a fine hotel worth the time spent at the front desk.

The position also gave him an unlimited opportunity to distinguish between the men with means and those who would only try to obtain their means at the tables. He really had no time for the latter. It would be the men with money he would be seeking for a good game of poker in the wee hours of the morning.

"He were a flannel mouth Dude if 'eir I see'd one," the clerk said. "I wus trying to make out if he were a big bug, flush and all, but I didn't go through the mill fer nothing. I see'd right off he couldn't hold a candle to a real thoroughbred."

The best information Aucilla gave Cliff was a small comment he had overheard the Frenchman ask of one of the Chinese workers. "It was not so much the question itself that was impressive, for surely a heap a' men have expressed the same desire, but it was the manner in which this man seemed to want everyone else to know of his askin' the question," Aucilla stressed.

"Well, what did he ask?"

"He done asked me directions to the depot. I mean every man in Cheyenne knows which direction that ungodly sound comes from," Aucilla replied. "Obviously he wanted me to think he had business at the depot."

"What wus it he asked the waiter?"

"Where he could rent a pack animal," Aucilla answered.

"Do you know which livery?"

"I do."

"Are you gon'a tell me?"

"It is quite obvious from your speech you were not raised in this awful place; may I ask of your up-bringing?"

"Georgia. South Georgia," Cliff replied almost in an aggravated voice.

"And your ootfit?"

"I served General Forrest, proudly," Cliff shot back.

"Ah, The Army of The Tennessee."

"Yep," Cliff said, this time narrowing his eyes.

"I served General Shelby," the older man replied and then added, "Proudly as well."

Cliff was not sure where this was leading, but he had now decided to give the clerk his head with their conversation.

"This Frenchman you seek, he be a friend of yourn' or no?"

"He's the dirty carpetbagger what murdered my wife," Cliff replied with a voice strong and stern, and the man instantly knew he was telling the truth.

"I do believe you will find the information you need from Patrick Pence. His place is on 17th Street behind *Mearea's Saddle Shop*. Look for the shingle, *Six Pence Livery* and go down the alley."

Cliff looked at the clerk deeply, and his expression changed. He now was positive the man had only been waiting to make certain his need for this information was legitimate.

"Obliged," was his only reply to the clerk, but the seriousness in his eyes was now gone, and a grateful expression could be read on Cliff's face.

As Cliff turned, he heard Plymale add, "My guess is they skedaddled out a' hyar on hawses. You be powerful careful, I 'spect him to be a curly wolf in dude clothing."

Cliff raised his right arm as a gesture of reply, without further conversation.

An hour later, he was in his room packing when Laramie came in. "Reb, I found them. They took the train to Omaha. Several men down at the depot remembers Me-Ma. She wus wearing a bright red dress."

"Find Black Band, we'll be lighting a shuck north directly," Cliff replied without looking up from his rolling of the bedroll.

"North, but they qui a voyagé, ah, how do you say, ah, took the train to the east?"

"Go east if you are of a mind to; I'm riding north."

The boy was confused. He had been so certain this man would lead him to his mother, suddenly he was no longer so sure.

Half an hour later, Laramie was telling Black Band what had happened and in doing so, explaining that the train people might not let him have a ticket, just as those of the hotel had not let him stay in a room.

The Crow listened and then said, "We go north."

"Non, do not you understand, Me-Ma bought a ticket to Omaha. The man there described her perfectly."

"She buy ticket. She no ride train. We go north with Reb Brown."

Laramie suddenly thought hard on what he had just heard. It made sense.

That night they stopped at *Horse Creek Ranch* and the next at *Fort Laramie*. Everyone at the Fort was proud to see the boy. He too seemed happy. So many of the men that had watched him grow up were still there, and it seemed they all wanted to do something to befriend him. Unfortunately, no one had news of his mother. No one had seen her, and she definitely had not been on the stage when it passed through a few days before. He was also informed of the death of his father and that he now owned the Post Store, but his drive to find and rescue his mother was much too great to stay there. So he asked Corporal Donahue to see to the sale of his business and keep the money for him. "I will leave you know where to send it, when I know myself."

Some two hours after dark, the stage came rumbling in, and everyone who was still awake rushed out to investigate.

"What is all the ruckus about?" Charlie Russo asked, looking up from a full house of threes and sevens.

"Stage coming in," Sam Horton said. Then added, "Three days early."

The tale of their attack was not totally a surprise to anyone, save perhaps those who had thought of deserting and heading for the gold fields. There had been sightings of marauding Indians ever since Custer led his expedition into the Black Hills the year before. It did seem these were becoming more and more frequent all the time.

Ol' Iron Nut was quick to point out, "Why just last week Leo Roberts was chased by several savages near Hat Creek but was able to avoid going under by sending a Sharps 50 slug into the lead pony's head. Then the others decided his hair wasn't worth their effort after all." The name Ol' Iron Nut amused most of them stationed there, after the First Sergeant had given it to the company's blacksmith.

The telling of the fight with the Arapaho was of great interest to all, but giving the details concerning the loss of the three passengers seem to set an atmosphere of despair.

"Them no good Injuns killing a white woman like that, it just ain't human," Terry Gittemeier said.

"You are right as a trivet thar, my friend."

"Weren't thar nothing you could do fer her?" the kid asked.

"Hell boy, thar were nigh on thirty of 'em varmints. Well heeled and popping lead and arrows at us all the time," Bill Mansfield lied.

"Yeah, we had to listen to her screams, but twern't nothing we could do," Maynard added.

"I don't think there's enough gold in all a' Dakota Territory to make me head north again," Parkhurst said, shaking his head and looking down at the ground.

"Not me. I'm headed north as soon as I can," Maynard offered soundly.

Ignoring this last statement Laramie asked, "This woman, could she be Me-Ma?"

"Now, I never see'd your Ma, cause 'afore me getting this here job a' reinsman I 'haint been here to the fort in many a year. She wus done gone when I started driving through here, but I don't see how she could a' been," Jack answered the boy. "Asides, been your Ma, she would a' boarded here, not up to Rawhide."

"Oui, I guess so," he agreed lowering his head.

"You say they boarded at Rawhide?" Cliff questioned.

"Yep, they wus there 'afore we got there. Her and the Dude," he said back to Cliff and then turned to Laramie and added, "As I said, I never seen your Ma, Kid, but I can tell ya' these two were easterners, that's fer sure. Real dudes they were."

"You sure they are dead?" Cliff queried.

"Yeah, we heahed them screaming, then a shot rang out in the cool night air and then right smartly after, them Injuns all rode off together." Bill Mansfield paused then finished with, "They is all done in, fer sure."

"You find their bodies?"

"No, but that don't mean nothing. We never looked. As soon as we saw clear, we hightailed it out of there," Jack replied a little irritated at the stranger questioning their mighty good tale. "Come on I need a drink."

"I'll buy that drink," Dick Davis said, slapping the teamster on the back.

Laramie was awakened early the next morning by the sounds of Reb Brown packing.

"Where you off to now?"

"North."

"Ain't no need, you heard the stage driver say it couldn't been my Me-Ma and the Frenchman."

"It was them," Cliff said as he placed the box of 44 Henrys, he had purchased from the Post Store, in his saddlebags.

"What makes you so sure?" the boy questioned. "Like he said, she would have boarded here where so many of her friends are."

"That's exactly why they boarded north a' here, too many people to recognize her here. Besides, how could she have known your father wus dead?"

Cliff belted on his revolver and opened the door, then looking at the confused youngster, he asked, "You coming with me, you better pony up; or are you still headed fer Omaha?"

The kid shook his head, then jumped up and started pulling on his boots.

In another thirty minutes, three men were crossing the iron bridge headed north. They had just topped the hill when the sound of reveille began to awaken the sleepy fort.

It was near the noon hour when they gazed down on the collection of buildings that comprised the headquarters of the "Damfino" a nickname the boys who worked the R bar T brand affectionately and sometimes not so affectionately, called *The Rawhide Ranch*.

The new intruders had seen a few wranglers moving some horses out of a draw an hour before but stayed clear and moved on to the ranch plaza. "No need to have to identify ourselves twice," Cliff had said, and the others did not disagree.

"Who do you make it to be?" Jake Stoner asked as he and his boss studied the three riders easing down the distant hill.

"Doe' no, but that second one is Injun."

"How can you tell?" Stoner asked as he narrowed his eyes, trying to see what his boss had seen, that he missed.

"Well, Stoner, when you been here as long as I have, you will know them things too," the older man replied. He then spit a long stream of tobacco juice to the ground under the hitching post before he wiped his mustache clean with the thumb and forefinger of his right hand. "You'll surely know."

"Better get you a rifle and wait in the barn yonder, just in case."

"Yes, sir," the hand replied.

Russ never could figure out why he let Jake Stoner hang around the ranch house. *'He 'taint a better hand than half a dozen of the other boys, and he sure 'taint no friend, but for some reason when the work assignments get handed out I always seem to give Stoner chores here, rather than out on the range,'* he thought as he watched the lanky Ohio boy slip over to the barn with his new Kennedy rifle. Russ shook his head in wonder on the subject.

Cliff stopped some twenty yards from the porch where the man stood.

"Like to ride in, if'n you have no objections."

"Why ask now? You been trespassing for five miles."

Cliff touched Ola's rib with the heel of his old brown boot, and the big horse moved slowly forward. The kid rode up beside him, but Black Band stayed a few feet behind the others.

"Hard to get here without trespassing," Cliff replied when he was near enough to talk without raising his voice.

The Rawhide Buttes Station

"Yeah, I reckon it is at that," Thorp agreed. "Why are you here?"

"We were at Fort Laramie when the stage came in last night," Cliff replied, shifting his weight in the saddle.

Russ Thorp noticed there was little squeak to the leather, as he sized up the tall man with the drawl.

"Looking for a man and woman that might a' been on the stage when it left here, northbound."

"What fer?"

"The woman, she might be my Me-Ma," Laramie said boldly.

Thorp looked keenly at the kid, and then he recognized him. It had been a couple of years, and the lad had grown quite a bit, but he knew it was the Patay boy all right, that blonde hair was a dead giveaway. He was not sure if he should tell him the truth or not. Gilmore had said she and her dude had been killed. He thought long, and then decided the boy would find out sooner or later, so he replied, "It were."

The news was both good and bad to the youth's ears. A moment of excitement shot through him for being so close to finding her, but then a dreary cloud eased over when he thought of her being dead, perhaps scalped by some hostile Indian.

"The man she was traveling with?" Cliff asked.

"Some dude from the east. A sissy fellow I would say. Called himself De la Motte I think," Thorp replied showing his disapproval of anyone from the east.

"He murdered my wife," Cliff said back and then added, "Easterner he may be, but he is no sissy. I've been on his trail nigh on three years, and the dead bodies I can account to him could stretch hence to The Jenny Stockade[10]."

Thorp just nodded his head as if he believed him.

Cliff, satisfied with what he had learned, was ready to move on. "Well, if we might water our horses, we will be on our way."

"No need, get down and stay a spell, I'll have the Chinnie gurl rustle up a little chuck, getting a mite hungry ma'self."

Cliff looked at the man and then at his companions, both of them seemed keen on the idea of food but neither said anything.

"We all invited?"

Russ looked hard at him and then at the Indian. "Crow, ain't he?"

"He's Crow. Black Band, a good tracker and a good man to cover your back."

"Really?"

"Yep, had I given him the nod, your man there in the barn would be eating that carbine by now," Cliff said back, without even looking in the direction of the tall structure where Stoner was hiding.

10 The Jenny Stockade: The first Whiteman killed in the Black Hills gold rush was at this location.

Thorp thought a moment and then said, "If I can eat what a Chinnie woman cooks, I reckon I can eat it with a Injun."

Cliff recognized the concession this man was making to be hospitable, and even though he had rather be on the trail, he nodded his head before touching the front brim of his hat. "You are an understanding man, Sur."

The meal was not well-prepared grouse, as had been served a few nights before, rather antelope. However, it did share the stew pot with a little beef and some vegetables. To these had been added spices and other seasonings Cliff had never tasted before. There were also little logs of wrapped bread with some other meat and cabbage in them, which likewise he did not recognize.

"This here is a tasty meal," he said to his host. "I'm obliged."

"It's good to have another man around," he said, emphasizing the word man.

Cliff looked over at Jake Stoner, who was bringing in a few split logs for the cook stove. Stoner had not been invited to the table, and everyone could tell he was insulted by being left out.

"Employees are not really considered men. They are my hands. Of course I have them around, but I like the company of a real man on occasion, and you Mr. Brown, seem to fill that position powerful well."

"The compliment is appreciated Sur, but I'm not sure I deserve it."

Offering Cliff a cigar from his coat pocket he added, "Any man who would pursue a murderer from Georgia all the way here, is a man of my liking, and I do believe you deserve the description."

Cliff raised his hand at the cigar before he said, "I have my makins, I'll quirley[11] my own, however my friend here enjoys the richness of a ci-gar." With that, he took the twist and handed it to Black Band.

Thorp did seem somewhat offended that his guest declined his offer of the fine tobacco, as much so as what he had done with it, but he said nothing to that effect. He did raise his eyebrows when the Indian began biting off plugs of the cigar and chewing them.

They continued the conversation for another twenty minutes and the man could see Cliff was becoming restless, so he broke up the noon gathering by turning to Laramie and saying, "I do hope you find your Ma in good health and soon, boy."

"Oui, Monsieur," Laramie replied, "I also want that."

---

11 Quirley: Roll your own cigarette.

Black Band easily found the place where the stage had been ambushed and the shallow grave where they had hastily buried Silverton before making a rapid retreat back towards Cheyenne. Wolves had dug it out and were scattering his remains across the prairie as they arrived on the scene. His bright plaid coat had been shredded by their sharp teeth and long claws. Small pieces of yellow were seen laying here and there, some caught on sagebrush where the wind had carried it.

The sight and thought of his mother being so desecrated turned Laramie's stomach, but he hid his sickness from the others. However, the look on the lad's face did not go unnoticed by Cliff, and he sent Black Band to see what he could find.

Half an hour later, the Indian returned.

"Six Arapaho. One dead. Much blood. Whiteman leave on pony, white woman leave with Arapaho."

"Are you sure the blood was not Me-Ma's?"

"Blood Arapaho. Six come here, five walk away. White woman walk with them."

"He got away then?"

Black Band nodded his head, "Man in white man's moccasins catch ponies. Five Indians walk away."

He handed Cliff the Colt and explained he had found it laying where the ponies had been grazing. Immediately the Georgian recognized the weapon. It was Tidwell's all right. *'This man Jean Mouton, without question is John Tidwell.'* He now was certain beyond any doubt.

"She is alive then," Laramie said joyfully. "She is alive."

'I bet right about now, she wishes she weren't,' Cliff thought looking at the revolver, but instead he said, "Let's get going." Then, turning, he spit before adding, "Kid go back and get our horses."

When the lad was out of hearing range he said, "Black Band, you ride in front."

"We follow him trail?"

"Is she still alive?"

The redman looked hard at him and then slowly shook his head, "No, too long."

"Follow the man," Cliff nodded. "Don't tell the boy."

The Indian said nothing in reply.

Jean Mouton had followed her captor as the well-built man moved off into the darkness about a hundred yards. There he came upon a small area that had an unusually good stand of grass, and he saw their ponies were cropping on the rich buffalo feed. It was there the Indian squatted and waited as the night stillness was interrupted by Celeste's screams.

Jean inched up behind the stout man, having every intention of slipping his Arkansas Toothpick where it would kill rapidly, but the keen ears of the plains warrior heard his approach, and the big man whirled suddenly.

Mouton had no choice but to put a bullet into his forehead. This sudden blast in the night startled the ponies, and they began to run. He was just able to grab the mane of the last one and swing onto her back. In doing so, he dropped his Colt.

It was not easy hanging on to the pony as she ran across the uneven ground. It had been some time since he last had ridden bareback and twice he almost fell, but he did manage to hold on. After two or three miles, the horses ahead began to lose interest in this and slowed, his mount did the likewise. It was then he found the rawhide reins that hung from her mouth and he turned her north-by-northwest, and slowly the two moved away from eastern Wyoming, towards Montana.

The next morning, as he rode across the vastness of the Great Plains, he saw several buzzards circling off in the distance. At first, he thought it would be best to take a wide circle around them, but then curiosity overtook him.

'It could be a freshly killed Buffalo or deer,' he reasoned as the hunger in his stomach growled angrily at his mind.

Finally, he saw one of the large birds dip and disappear into a ravine ahead. Immediately thereafter, several magpies screeched and scattered from the cut in the prairie.

When he arrived, he saw a body. It was that of a white man, killed not more than a day before. He lay flat of his back with his arms out to his sides and his feet slightly apart. Had one not seen the blackened area, where the dried blood covered his head, or the sockets where the scavenging birds had picked his eyes away, one might think he was just resting peacefully. But he was dead, of that Jean had no doubt. He had been scalped, and there were at least four bloody holes in his checkered shirt where arrows had penetrated his upper body. The arrows had been retrieved, and now only the torn and bloody holes told the story.

Jean knew this had been done by a small band, a war party moving swiftly. Had there been women and children with them, this poor devil would have been stripped, and his high brogans would have been salvaged for their leather by the squaws.

Mouton turned him over, and there in a pocket he found a leather billfold containing a $20.00 note on *The Bank of Denver*. Also in a coat pocket, he found a small Marlin revolver. It was fully loaded, but he could find no additional cartridges.

'Five small rounds,' he thought shaking his head, and then he concluded, *'An hour ago I did not have these.'*

The man was a miner, of that he was sure. Not far from the body lay a shovel and pick. They had not been used but apparently had fallen from a pack animal.

Mouton then mounted and followed the gulch. About a mile on, he came upon a mule standing alone in a small pool of water. There was an arrow buried deeply just behind his ribs. The animal was slowly dying and had lost all will to flee.

Mouton led him from the water and then, placing the barrel of the Marlin behind the mule's right ear, he pulled the trigger. The little 30 caliber slug did not go very deep, but it did reach the animal's brain and he fell, kicked several times and then giving a long and loud call, died.

Mouton butchered the mule there in the cut and ate heartily. He was surprised how sweet mule tasted. He had eaten it before, but he did not remember it to be this good.

Returning to the camp of the dead miner, he rummaged around until he found a bag of salt and an old canteen marked with faded letters 1st M. HA.

Taking these, he returned to the mule, salted some of the meat and filled the canteen before once again taking a heading of north-by-northwest.

Jean Mouton was not what a westerner would call a savvy man. However, he had not lived this long, being involved in many deadly fights, wars, and world travels, to be without the knowledge of basic survival.

Two days later, he cut Powder River and camped in a stand of cottonwoods. Soon after dark, he moved a short distance from where he left the pony hobbled and went to sleep. A short hour had barely passed when he was awakened by the sounds of approaching hoof beats.

Digging out the little Marlin, he eased the hammer back and stared out into the black air at the sounds, it being too early for the moon to have risen.

He was sure there were three, perhaps more. Their voices were higher pitched than most, and the tongue they spoke was strange to him, although from this distance, he was not sure he could have understood what they were saying had they been speaking a language he was familiar with.

He waited and breathed cautiously in the warm night air. After some long minutes, a time that seemed like two hours to him but in reality was quite possibly less than ten minutes, he heard them gathering dry wood. Shortly thereafter, he could see the flicker of a small fire.

An hour passed before he moved again, slowly easing toward the light of the fire. The moon was rising now and a pale glow of silver cast itself across the sage-covered prairie. He could see his mount off some fifty yards from where he had been sleeping and was thankful the Indians had turned in before the moon had risen.

His pony saw him moving and made a snort. This aroused the attention of the other ponies nearby, and they began moving closer to investigate the intruder.

Jean Mouton lay frozen behind the exposed roots of a huge cottonwood and waited to see if this new action would awaken his adversaries.

Finally, after several minutes passed, he moved towards the ponies, which now had surrounded his own. The animals seemed to be greeting one another in some strange mannerism as members of the horse family often do, and they paid little attention to his approaching.

He decided his best avenue of escape would be to run off their mounts and beat it with them, but as soon as he removed the rope that hobbled his paint, he caught a movement in the corner of his eye, and slowly he lowered himself behind the short animal.

With only the top of his head above the horse's back he watched anxiously. The squatty man was speaking softly to the animals as he approached, and they began to mill about.

Jean held the rawhide reins tightly so his pony would not move away and reveal him to the stout savage, who was now a distance of less than forty feet.

The Lakota moved slowly forward, continuously speaking softly to the ponies ahead of him. When he finally reached the nearest, he stretched forth his hand and touched the nose of the little filly. A moment later, his eyes focused on the image of the man behind the other horse. It was the last sight he saw in this life.

The sound of the little 30 caliber revolver thundered through the night air, awakening the dead man's companions.

Long before they realized the source of the thunder, Jean had grabbed the Springfield carbine from the Indian's back, along with the cartridge belt he wore as a bandolier and had mounted his own pony. Discharging his last three revolver rounds, he stampeded the other horses as he followed them in their dash across the dimly lit prairie.

Near the noon hour on the first of July, he saw the dust of another horseman moving fast in a little valley some two miles away. Jean studied him until he was out of sight.

'He is heading in the direction I am,' he thought, *'and he appears to be in a tremendous hurry.'* Mouton rubbed his chin with the palm of his hand, taking notice of the unshaven condition he was in. *'I wish I knew if he is white or red.'*

With extreme caution, he moved slowly towards the fresh trail left by the anxious rider. The man had crossed a small damp spot in the otherwise dry valley, and there left the clear print of a new shoe. *'He is no Indian,'* Jean told himself and then followed the trail.

It was just dark when he saw the dim light on the prairie a few miles ahead. It was in direct line from where the trail had led thus far, and he felt sure it would be the mysterious horseman. Still, he approached cautiously.

Finally, when within a couple hundred yards of the light source, he slowly began to see an object ahead near the light. Stopping, he studied it for a long time until something moved between the light and him. He caught his breath at the sight, and then cursed himself for the fright when he realized the object that had so mystifying was a cabin. Then he moved forward without so much concern.

The months of June and July in the northern plains are a mystery when one thinks of weather. Much of the time the days are hot and dry, but at times, when one least expects it, a storm can sweep in and lay a blanket of wet snow over the region. This year there had been no snow in late June; in fact, it had been unusually hot and, as usual, very dry. These conditions increased his need for water, to say nothing of his need for food, which was almost overpowering. Now suddenly both appeared to be only a few yards away.

The inhabitants were quite cautious at the sound of a horse approaching, at a good pace, on a dark night, and he was met with the muzzle of three rifles protruding from the gun ports in the cabin windows.

"Hold everything," he shouted. "I am white." He wisely spoke pure and plain English, not wanting anyone to link him with the Frenchman who had been with Celeste Patay on the Deadwood Stage.

Once inside, he explained he had been jumped by a small band of Indians who had killed his horse, and he had only escaped by killing one of the hostiles and riding away on his pony.

They looked at him in astonishment. Finally, James McAndow, his host, asked, "When did this happen?"

"Two days back."

"What are you doing oot here?" another asked.

"I'll tell you all you want to know, but please, after I have enjoyed some of whatever is boiling in that kettle."

McAndow looked over at the black pot hanging a couple of feet above the fire. "A' Gawd, what are we thinking, this man must be half-starved," and immediately he went to the stone fireplace and filled a wooden bowl with the stew, made of antelope and several mussels they had gathered from the Yellowstone River the day before.

He returned to the pot, dipped a second bowl and set it before the man in buckskin. "Here Muggins, I should a' fed you 'afor now."

The other man asked, "You only see them little bunch a' Injuns?"

"Ahuh, only the one small bunch, three or four."

"That there be a Sioux pony you got," Mr. Kelly said.

"Yes, I suppose it is," John replied.

"What be your name, if'n I ain't being too nosey?" James asked.

He had just taken a mouthful of chewy antelope, and he nodded to the man's question, being thankful for the opportunity to think while chewing before he answered.

"John, John Ferris Pell[12]," he finally replied, "and you?"

---

12 Ferris Pell: For more on William Ferris Pell see Book Two, The Withlacoochee

"I'm James McAndow, and this be Luther Kelly[13]," he answered and then nodding to the other man added, "And that rung 'oot piece a leather thar' is Muggins Taylor. He is riding dispatch fer General Terry. And a sad dispatch he be a carrying too."

"Is that so?" John Pell replied, not really interested in the gossip.

"Yeah," James said, not giving anyone else an opportunity to enter his tale. "His sealed report yonder is the news of General Custer's murder by ten thousand hostiles."

"Custer's dead?" This was news, news that even John Pell was interested in.

"Yep, he and all of the Seventh," Kelly added.

"Well, not all of the Seventh," Taylor corrected.

"Well, most a' them," the skinny man added, showing his dislike for being contradicted.

John had detected the New York accent on Kelly, and hoped he had not given himself away, before he realized who all was in his company.

"I'm just at sea and purely balled up how a man alone could a' got through all those stinking Redskins without being beefed," the blowhard questioned.

"Now Kelly, Muggins got through," McAndow pointed out.

"Yeah, he did," the man agreed as he walked away, towards the stone jug, setting on a nearby table.

"Where am I?" finally John asked, after emptying his bowl of soup.

"You sir, are at the table of the honorable James McAndow, Esquire, owner of the only stage stop the Bismarck to Bozeman Route has in these parts," Kelly answered peevishly.

"A stage will stop here?"

"It will. Day after tomorrow, if it gets through," his host answered.

"No stage is gon'a make it now. With Custer gone up the flume, the air betokens a true storm, like no other these sage-covered hills have known."

"Come on Kelly, don't be such an old croaker," James said. "They might just make it this far, most a' them Injuns aire east a' here."

"Maybe."

"I'm powerful dragged out myself, and I got me a long ride come morning," Taylor then offered. "I reckon I'll be hitting the hay."

Renegades, Chapter Fourteen.

13 Luther Kelly: Ex-Union Soldier turned scout, turned trapper. Often called Yellowstone Kelly, also known as, The Biggest Liar On The Plains.

"Can't blame you Muggins, take my bunk yonder," McAndow said, pointing to the bedroll that was ruffled near the back wall.

When the eastern sky was turning a light purple, Muggins Taylor headed out for Fort Ellis[14] on the stage road.

"I be surprised you ain't a riding with him Kelly," McAndow said to the scout.

"I'm a thinking I'll light a shuck east and try and overtake The Far West[15]. Muggins said she were in need of taking on wood before steaming on, and I reckon that I can catch up.

What about the dude?"

James looked back at the cabin, "Still asleep, but he said he would wait on the stage, and I reckon that's what he'll be a doing."

"I'll just take along that Sioux pony with me. If'n he's gon'a ride the stage, he won't be needing him, and I might, should I get some Injuns after me."

"Horse stealing is horse stealing."

"Hell, he stole it from the Sioux, all's fair," Kelly replied as he cinched up the saddle on his big gelding.

Black Band had no trouble following the trail left by their quarry.

The next morning they came across the butchered mule and the scalped miner. Black Band pointed out the same hoof print they had been following and the direction it had left in.

After filling their canteens, they too headed on, following the trail of the man Cliff was determined to kill.

They might have overtaken him had it not been for the many dust clouds they saw moving from the northeast towards the Big Horn Mountains.

Once, after waiting on a high knoll for almost an hour while they watched the passing of a large number, Black Band led them down to investigate.

Dismounting, he examined the torn up ground and then picked up a small doll a child had dropped. He handed the toy to Cliff before saying, "Sioux, many Sioux. Big village."

In another trail, they found the remains of a leather stovepipe that had been cut from a boot. There was a dark stain on the underside. Cliff looked at it and flicked some of the dried blood with

---

14 Fort Ellis: US Military Post near Bozeman, Montana.

15 The Far West: The steamer that carried the wounded from Reno's command back to Fort Abraham Lincoln.

his thumbnail from the black leather. "Yankee Cavalry," he said, before discarding it back to the prairie.

On they moved but more cautiously than before. It was obvious to each there were more hostiles in these parts than any of them had ever seen before.

When they passed a few miles west of the Crow reservation, Cliff could see the longing Black Band had to go to his people, but he did not abandon them. Cliff surmised his loyalty to the boy was as great as to his people.

They heard the sound of gunfire before they came in sight of McAdnow's cabin. Approaching cautiously on foot, they eased to the top of a small knoll and looked at the scene ahead. Immediately they spotted white puffs of gunsmoke coming from the cabin, and a dead horse lay some ten yards from the front door. They couldn't tell from this distance if it was an Indian pony or not. Also, smoke puffs could be seen from two locations nearly a hundred yards in front of the log structure.

Cliff motioned for them to follow him, but Black Band stretched forth his hand catching Cliff's arm.

Cliff looked where the Indian pointed and at first saw nothing. Then he spotted two more men easing up from a cut, towards the cabin's rear wall. It was obvious there was a single man shooting at the attackers, so there would be no one available to cover the back of the little refuge.

Black Band motioned for Cliff to take on the two in the front, while he and Laramie would skirt around and come up on those in the rear.

Cliff waited until he heard the two horses move out before he began to inch his way forward. He wanted to kill both of these, before his friends arrived at a location where they could be spotted. From these hostiles' point of view, they would easily see the stalk of his friends when Black Band and Laramie closed in on their companions, who most surely intended to fire the cabin. Cliff didn't want to take any chance on these two warning the others.

It took him a quarter of an hour to get in the position he wanted. He had determined from the time between shots, the man in the cabin was using a single shot and from the reports, it was a heavy one.

Both Indians ahead of him were also firing single shots, but the reports from their rifles, although loud, were not as strong as that from the cabin.

The smoke had just begun on the sod roof when Cliff fired at his nearest foe. He had waited until one of the Indians had shot, and then he took a bead on the other one and squeezed off a round. Immediately his friend turned, looking for the sound of the rifle behind them, as he desperately tried to work the trapdoor of his rifle. In doing so, he exposed himself and screamed loudly as his body shot forward a half a second before the report was heard coming from the cabin. Almost immediately thereafter, more shots were heard, but quite a bit fainter, and then Cliff saw a man on the roof stomping out the burning sod.

He turned to go back when a heavy slug struck the ground a little ahead and off to his right, less that a foot away. Soon thereafter, he once again heard the report of the big gun at the cabin.

"Som-bitch, that bastard is shooting at me." Immediately, he fell flat on his stomach. After laying there a couple of minutes he ventured a look back at the cabin and saw three men standing in front. Getting up then, he waved and watched for the return gesture, before dusting off his buckskin shirt and heading back over the rise to Ola.

That night was a solemn one at McAndow's Stage Stop.

They learned of the loss of Custer and the Seventh, a loss that did not sorrow Cliff Brown all that much. He had fought Custer during the war and had found him to be a ruthless man, who would kill any armed, unarmed, white or black, male, female or child, who stood in his way to glory.

However, there was little doubt but that the man they had followed was John Tidwell, now calling himself John Pell. Laramie also realized his mother was not with him. This could only mean she was a captive or dead.

Cliff watched the lad as he sat quietly staring off into a distance that didn't exist. Finally, Cliff turned to his host and asked, "What are you shooting in that stove pipe anyway? It sounded like a Parrott Gun from where I was."

James reached down, took a round from his vest pocket and pitched it to Cliff. "50 Sharps," he replied. "Throws a 475 grain hunk a' lead a fer piece."

"How much powder do this thing use?" Cliff asked, pitching the paper cartridge to his young friend.

"Oh, 'bout half a keg," James said smiling and reaching for the jug, he swung it on his upper arm and took a long pull.

"Sure glad you children showed up when you did. I wus a thinking I wus about to go under." He took another pull, and after a short gasp he continued his story, "Afore you come, it were getting as hot around here as a whorehouse on nickel night."

"Hell, a' we knowed you had this jug a' shine, we'd been here last week," Cliff replied and accepted the offer of the strong drink from their new friend, before passing it on to Laramie.

Black Band knew better.

Later that night, Cliff and the boy had a long talk before turning in.

"I know she is likely dead or worse," Laramie said shaking his head and fighting back the tears, "but I got a' keep looking, I just got a'."

"The thing I aim to set straight in your mind is, the same man what murdered my wife, got your Ma killed. We both got a' stay on his trail till he is dead. Sompin' happens to one, the other keeps on a' going. Nothing must stop us, till he's Lucifer's guest."

Laramie nodded his head and turned away so his mentor would not see the tears. "You can count on me, Reb. I'll never stop until I know fer sure," he finally choked out.

The next morning, after a breakfast of slapjacks made from Indian meal and haslet[16], fried in buffalo grease, they found themselves westbound towards Bozeman.

The eastbound stage had indeed arrived at McAndow's stop but upon hearing of the massacre, had turned back until an army escort could be arranged.

John Pell was aboard when it departed to the west once more. However, accompanying him was a most hysterical woman, who he judged to weigh half as much as one of the wheeler horses. She whined continually and screamed at the top of her lungs every time a tire struck a stone, which was several times each mile. When they pulled into *The Stillwater Station*, he was certain he and that woman would not share another mile together.

---

16 Haslet: Liver or other organs.

A good turn of events did occur for him as a result of this abominable creature though, and that was the fact he and Horace Countryman became instant friends.

Horace introduced him to Frank Quinn, the owner of the largest ranch in the area, and John saw it as an opportunity to perhaps repeat the business venture he had with Hickey.

In the course of conversation with Countryman, he mentioned a murderer had been reported following him. "You see I overheard this man talking with some of his other confederates, and it was obvious they were planning to rob an army paymaster. I, of course, told the authorities about his plan, but the incompetence of the local law allowed this murderer to escape. Now he has vowed to hunt me down and kill me also."

"Oh, you poor, dear man," said Mrs. Countryman.

John Pell did not fail to look hungrily at the handsome bride but seeing her devotion to her new husband and his need for a safe refuge in this storm, he restrained himself and smiled a thankful reply.

The following day, when the trio of men reached *The Stillwater Station* and inquired of him, Horace Countryman confirmed a man meeting the description of their quarry had indeed been on the westbound. "If'n you hurry you might just catch up to him."

Cliff thanked the station owner, and after resting their horses and taking on some food for themselves, they were once again headed towards Bozeman.

Jim Fesslor, known to his friends as Bearpaw, had been a teamster since his enlistment in the Kentucky Volunteers back in '62. He drove an army ambulance throughout the war and continued with the trade after the surrender. First, he had driven freight wagons from St Louis to Kansas City and later Murphy Wagons on the Santa Fe Trail. In '69, he hired on with *The Overland Stage Line* and drove from St Jo to Lincoln. Then when *Wells & Fargo Company* bought out Ben Holliday, he drove for them from Denver to Cheyenne. Two years later he got the gold fever and cut a shuck for Montana, only to arrive after most of the color had been picked up, so he hired on driving from Bozeman to Miles City.

Bearpaw liked being a reinsman, he liked horses, and he liked the way they seemed to appreciate his handling of the ribbons. He liked the people he met along the way, and he liked having a wife in Bozeman and another in Miles City.

Jim Fesslor would turn 36 years old the night he was to hit Miles Town[17], and he knew Jessie had a hog-killing time planned for him. In his mind, she cut a swell as a woman. He liked the fact she was tall with hair as red as a prairie fire and freckles to boot, and he dearly loved to bury his face between her mounds. However, because of this new Indian trouble, he would be staying with Rosie instead. Not that he didn't love Rosie, for he surely did, but Rosie had gotten herself with child, and these days she was not the fun gal she normally was. He just prayed it was one of his and not belonging to a passing deadbeat she had met at the saloon, where she worked when he was away.

Bearpaw tried to explain to Yukon King before he pulled out, "You know, I got a bad feeling cloudin' over me from the beginning of this trip. Dutch Roberts, who was to ride shotgun, got himself all roostered up and scooped into a card game with a chiseler. The bastard bilked him until his plunder was all played out and then shined away with Dutch's dineros." Bearclaw stopped and looked out the window of the old log building and wiped his mouth with a stained gloved hand before he continued, "Finally, Dutch caught up with the four-flusher, and they kicked up a row like kilkenny cats until Dutch had cleaned his plow and took back his money. Unfortunately, the dude had friends in high places, and Dutch ended up in the hoosegow."

Yukon listened to his tale but offered no escape for Bearpaw from his duty. There simply wasn't time to find another shotgun, so the teamster pulled out sitting alone atop the Concord.

Bearpaw could tell the horses were tired as he approached *Walker's Station*. The last fifteen miles was mostly upgrade, and they were nearly played out when he topped the rise for his fifth change since he had turned back that day. He stopped at the top of the hill, blew his horn and waited.

The reply did not come. *'Something is amiss, and here I am with a hysterical woman the size of a full grown hog, no messenger[18], and played out horses.'* "Well shit!" was his only comment.

---

17 Miles Town: Original name for Miles City, Montana, however even after the change many an old timer continued calling it Miles Town.

18 Messenger: Armed guard on a stage often called a shotgun because this was the weapon of choice by them.

He dismounted and walked around to the rear boot, where he had packed his own belongings and retrieved his new 44 Winchester, a gift Rosie had just given him before he left.

"What is wrong? Why are we stopping?"

"Just hobble your lip, lady. I'm giving the animals a breather."

"Well, I never___."

"Yas Ma'am, I 'spect you never did," he replied and then climbed back to the whip's seat. Bearpaw was sure Indians were about. The thought of mudsill bandits, never entered his mind.

Black Band raised his arm stopping them when they came in sight of the log buildings ahead.

"What do you see?" Cliff asked.

"No smoke," the Crow replied pointing toward the distant chimney. Cliff nodded his head.

"So, it's not cold," Laramie added.

"No, but it is time for chuck," Cliff reminded him.

"Yeah," the boy agreed, thinking of a bowl of stew these stage stops were known to provide.

Moving in a little closer, they found a coulee that led north passing less than a hundred yards of the barn. Dismounting, they slipped down into this deep ravine and eased forward in tandem, with the Indian in the lead.

When they reached the closest point to the buildings, each exercising great caution, they climbed the bank for a quick look over the top.

Everything was quiet, save the team that was still hitched to the stage in front of the smaller log building. *'Too still,'* Cliff thought.

The horses were restless; it was obvious they had been there for some time and didn't understand the reason. The lead pair twitched their ears at every sound, and once the big white kicked at his trailing companion.

"Bad," was all Black Band said.

Cliff knew he was right.

"What do you think?" Laramie asked.

Cliff then pointed toward the arrow that was just visible protruding from the coach door.

Ever so slowly, each moved over the top and inched forward, working from one bunch of sage to another, until finally they made a dash for the rear of the barn.

Inside were several draft animals and one saddle horse.

From the front of the barn, they had a good view of the main building, some forty yards away. All was quiet.

After waiting a full ten minutes, with nothing moving except those six hitched horses, Cliff decided they needed to do something before the team made a bolt and spilled its load.

He spoke to the other two, "Laramie, I want you to run to the back of the building and wait until you hear me yell. Black Band, you stay here and cover us. I don't want anyone inside to mistake you for a hostile. I'll go to the front."

His companions both nodded without other replies.

Cliff dashed for the lead horses and held tightly to the harness on the big white. The horse seemed glad to see the man and immediately calmed down.

Satisfied with the reception the animals were giving him, he eased on until he was at the coach door. After slowly opening it, he looked quickly inside but saw nothing. His attention was drawn to the arrow that had penetrated it. It had a metal tip that looked as if it had been made from a discarded blue hen[19].

'*Strange,*' he thought.

Closing the door, he moved to the rear of the stage and again took his time observing everything he could from his new position. Finally, he leaned his Winchester against the side of the boot and pulled the long barrel Colt from his gunbelt. Then, just after taking a deep breath, he dashed for the front of the building.

Flattening his back against the rounded logs, he waited and listened. Hearing nothing, save the sound of the once more irritated team, again he took a deep breath and lifting the latch, pushed open the front door.

He rapidly shot his head forward and then back to the sanctuary of the thick poplar logs. He had seen nothing out of the ordinary, unless one would call an empty stage station out of the ordinary. A few seconds later, he did this again, and when satisfied no one was inside, he entered and called out, "Anyone to home?"

There was no answer or any other sound.

Now Cliff entered the front just as he saw the boy come in from the rear door. Both looked at one another, and Laramie lifted his shoulders and turned up his palms. Cliff didn't fail to see the barrel of the boy's revolver pointing dangerously close when he did. To

---

19 Blue Hen: The can tomatoes were sealed in.

this, he just shook his head slightly and thought, *'I must take the time to teach the boy better.'*

Cliff moved around looking any place one could hide but found nothing before returning to the front door where he motioned for Black Band to come.

"Kid, check that back room," he instructed without looking his way.

Laramie nodded and moved forward. A couple of moments later he suddenly gasped, "Augh!" Followed by, "Reb!"

Cliff swung his Colt towards the sound.

The lad was standing at the entrance to the back room; the old brown army blanket that was used as a privacy shield was drawn back, and all the color had drained from the boy's face.

Cliff moved swiftly to his side and looked in. There he saw the bloody nude body of Jenny Mauser, all 450 pounds of her. Her throat had been slashed from ear to ear; a small patch of her scalp was bare as well, where a portion of her salt & pepper hair had been removed. Cliff noticed her privates had oozed blood before she had given up the ghost. Her expression was a combination of terror and peace at the same time.

Black Band was heard entering the cabin, and Cliff was glad, as this gave him an excuse to turn away from the ghastly scene.

"Take care of the team," Cliff said to the boy.

"Oui," Laramie answered holding back his tears.

"What do you think?" Cliff asked.

The Crow looked about for something short of a minute before returning to Cliff and saying, "Whiteman do this."

Laramie was just about to exit the front door when the Indian spoke. "Non. No way, just take a look at that scalped woman back there, and then say it were white men."

Cliff pulled back the blanket for Black Band to enter the back room. He was in there for a full two minutes before he came back.

"Whiteman," he said and then walked over to the stew pot that still hung over the cold, half-burned split wood. There he began to relight the fire.

"I don't believe it," Laramie said.

"Go take care of the team," Cliff said; this time it was a command, and the boy understood it as such. He turned and walked on to the stagecoach fighting back his sickness.

"You sure about the whitemen?" he asked his companion, as he picked up a nearly empty jug and smelled it. *'Bad whiskey,'* was his only thought before he sat it down on the table.

"Whiteman," was the only reply he got. It was enough. He had been suspicious when he first came into the barn about why the horses had been left, as well as to why Indians would leave a perfectly good metal point arrow in the side of the stage but had not drawn an absolute conclusion until Black Band had confirmed his thoughts.

Before leaving, they searched widely for other bodies but found none.

"I suppose the bastard we are after, lit a shuck out a' here before they came," Laramie said to him.

"Mee'be," Cliff answered.

"He and the teamster," the boy added.

"Mee'be," Cliff answered again, but he was not satisfied with the answer.

'No. John Tidwell was never on that coach.'

When they got back to Stillwater, they explained what they had found to the other members of the stage line.

"There weren't no sign 'er ol' Sage Walker or Dusty?"

"No one but the woman," Cliff replied.

"Not even Bearpaw?"

Cliff shook his head.

"Som'-Bitch!" Emmett Rider said, before spitting, then adding, "Rosie's sure gon'a take this hard, her being with child and all."

"Ol' Sage run a good station. He did," Red Mesa said, just before he too, spit.

That night they ate with the folks at Stillwater, and the discussion about the incident at *Walker's Station* dominated the conversation. The later the hour grew, the more the whiskey flowed, and the looser the talk became.

Some just didn't want to believe that bandits had been to blame. "Nobody knew Bearpaw was a returning. Why would white men be waiting fer him?"

"Yeah, just don't make no sense, the boy yonder said she were scalped."

"Indians wouldn't never left 'em horses," Horace Countryman reminded them. "It was bandits alright." Then he stood and headed for the next room, just before he started up the stairs, he called back, "Don't you boys spend all your money on that Who Hit John. I'll be a needing ya come sunup."

Countryman had tolerated the presence of the trio because they had brought convincing news about the stage and *Walker's Station*, but he had been pretty leery of them. He liked the man John Pell, and was convinced these three were the men who were out to kill him; still in these troubled times, no Christian Man could refuse sanctuary to another white.

Sergeant Skinner rented two of the downstairs rooms of *The Stillwater Stage Station* where he ran the little store out front, and in the back room, a bar, and he resented the advice of his landlord. *'It ain't often when the men of Stillwater gather around and run up a whiskey bill, save on Saturday nights. God forgive, I am thankful for the news of the slaughter at Walker's station,'* he thought. "Not the slaughter, mind you, but the news," he said just above a whisper, easing his conscience.

Red Mesa was a Relief Charlie[20] as well as a station hand, and the more he drank, the more he took on the mood of gloom. *'It could a' been me 'stead a' Bearpaw,'* he thought.

An hour after Countryman left, Cliff saw Red Mesa was near passing out. He moved over to the table and asked, "Mind if I sit with ya?"

The part-time whip raised his palms and shook his head.

"Can I buy you a drink?" Cliff asked, sitting across from him.

"I reckon."

"You know, I wonder what happened to the driver," Cliff said.

"Me too," Mesa replied, and then looking up from his glass he implored, almost pleaded, "You ain't seen nothing of him?"

Cliff shook his head.

"I just don't see Bearpaw riding shanks mare[21] when there were good horses about," he said looking back into the clear liquid in his glass. "Like he just up and flew away."

"Same thing happened to the Frenchman," Cliff added.

"What? Who?"

"You know, the dude who was also riding the stage."

"Augh, he weren't there," the sandy haired man replied.

"No?" Cliff queried. "I thought he was on that stage."

---

20 Relief Charlie: Slang for Stage Driver along with Whip, Reinsman, Jehu, and other nicknames.

21 Riding shanks mare: Walking.

"Naw, he went up to the Quinn Ranch after the stage pulled out a' here. I seed him leaving with ol' Frank he-self, but he weren't no Frenchman."

Cliff ingested this information and then handed him the bottle he had bought earlier, "Here, keep this. I won't be a needing it no more."

"Obliged," the hand slurred, as he reached for the two-thirds full bottle.

John Pell enjoyed the hospitality of his new friends. *The Quinn Ranch* was the largest he had seen in Indian Territory. Most of the spread had been Blackfoot land in years past, but with the Army's generosity at the *Fort Benton Trading Post* in giving blankets which were infested with small pox virus to this mighty nation, their numbers had diminished to only a few hundred. A few hundred who truly hated every white they saw but who were too small in numbers and many too sick or weak to fight effectively anymore.

In December of '69, Captain Baker and the Second Cavalry attacked a pox-riddled village of Blackfoot Piegans and killed nearly 200 men, women, and children, all sick with the pox. After that, the Blackfoot moved farther north and west avoiding contact with the massacring white soldiers.

The Crow then took possession of this land the Blackfoot had abandoned, but it never was totally a safe area for the invaders. The Sioux hated the Crow almost as much as they did the Whiteman, and never allowed the Crow to be at peace on it. The treaty of 1866 reduced the Crow Reservation to south of the Yellowstone River. This rendered everything north of the river, open range, belonging to the United States Government. Frank Quinn realized the opportunity and successfully moved longhorns on it.

This all was the proof in reality, of John's vision. The very idea he had struggled so long trying to convince Will Hickey of, the real fortune was in the ownership of the land. Free land at this time, land that one day a well-established man could get title to. All one had to do is claim it, improve it and be strong enough to hold it until Montana Territory became a state. John was convinced he was such a man, only this uprising with the Sioux could be a real problem if the army didn't act quickly and annihilate them all.

That night over cigars and brandy, Frank told him of thousands of acres north of his spread, which was prime country for grazing beeves.

"Up near the copper mines on the Carroll Trail," he said. "There is a stage line that runs through the area, when the Indians let it and some settlements already, mostly miners. The stage station at Copperopolis is in the heart of where I would go were I venturing out again."

'Copperopolis,' John thought on the name for some time.

The sky towards the old states[22] was just beginning to show a trace of light when the trio moved through Countryman's gate onto the Bozeman Trail. Cliff looked at the near black sky and took in a deep breath of the cold desert air and thought, 'South Georgia never had air as pure as this.' He shook his head remembering the humidity of the summer nights in the Deep South.

Then for just a moment his thoughts seemed to shoot straight to a night he had enjoyed with Nadine. They had taken a dip in the Little Withlacoochee River and then lay on a blanket on the little sandy beach that was at the north end of their property. Her white skin was like a silver statue bathed in the moonlight, and his lust was stronger than his good sense. Soon they were passionately enjoying each other's body, and neither saw the approach of the big gator until he made a large splash among the cypress knees near the shore. It was then, hell bent for leather, as they grabbed their clothes and climbed the steep bank escaping harm's way as quickly as possible.

At first, the remembrance brought pleasure to him but quickly the joy vanished and the bitterness for the man he pursued blanketed him and his determination became all the stronger to finish his self-imposed assignment. "I will find and kill you, John Tidwell," he said softly to himself with the utmost confidence.

John Pell had departed *The Quinn Ranch* the same morning his pursuers had began their ride to it, however, he only rode towards Copperopolis for a few miles when an idea struck him, and he turned southwest.

Late in the day, Reb Brown and his foe passed one another with only a hill and less than a mile separating them.

---

22 The Old States: A western term meaning East or the actual United States.

John entered the stage road and turned his horse westward. He rode now with a determination and a definite plan. Upon reaching Bozeman, he sold the horse Frank Quinn had loaned him and bought a stage ticket to Helena. There he identified himself as the Frenchman Jean Mouton and sent a telegraph to *The Bank of Bismarck* requesting funds be sent from his account in the name of Hickey and Mouton. To his surprise, two days later, an answer came back requesting certain identifying information, of which he had sufficient knowledge to satisfy the agent at *The Capital Bank of Helena*. His request for $1000.00 was approved.

The last time he had made such a request, it had been denied. Whether it was someone new working in Bismarck or some legal action that had occurred without his knowledge, he did not know or care; only once again, he had access to Hickey's money.

In reality, his success had not been a mistake at all, rather a clever plan by Augustus Spade to locate the elusive Frenchman. Spade, known as Ace by his fellow workers at *The St. Louis Detective Agency*, had been assigned the case after Leslie Hickey employed them to find and jail Mouton.

Ace had quickly located the account in Bismarck. At first, he had Mrs. Hickey put a stop order on all transfer or withdrawal of funds. Later as he began to learn more and more about Mouton, he decided there was a good chance his man would try again to withdraw money from the account.

He suspected since the account contained such a large amount, Mouton would go directly to Bismarck in an attempt to withdraw the funds, and he had traveled there, so when this happened he could make the arrest himself. A feather he would proudly wear in his cap and a stone he was sure would lead to a promotion within the agency. However, after his first attempt failed, Mouton had not again attempted to contact the bank. Finally, after months of waiting and nothing coming in, Ace was assigned a new task. Nonetheless, before leaving he had slipped $50 to one Beatrice Desmond, a bank clerk there, to notify him of any activity on the account.

He was finishing an assignment in Omaha when a wire came to him from North Dakota:

MOUTON HAS TRANSFERRED FUNDS TO THE CAPITAL BANK IN HELENA MONTANA END

SIGNED BEA DESMOND

Immediately he sent messages to the home office, as well to Pine Bluff.

His office advised him not to pursue it at this time, as they had another more pressing assignment for him in Missouri, but just before he boarded the train for St Louis, a new wire was delivered to him:

PROCEED AS RAPIDLY AS POSSIBLE TO HELENA MONTANA STOP

GATHER ALL INFORMATION POSSIBLE ON JEAN MOUTON STOP

REPORT ALL FINDINGS HERE END

SIGNED CAPTAIN JACK FARR

He was sure Mrs. Hickey had laid down the law to his boss, and now he was again on his way to end the case that would advance his career.

On the train west he read the yellow paper once more and smiled, even chuckled a little before he said aloud, "Sure," with no one to hear but himself. However, there was one thing Ace Spade had not counted on and that was the intelligence and shrewdness of his quarry.

Jean Mouton had immediately upon receiving his transfer, opened an account there in his name. The next day he withdrew half of it in gold dust and proceeded south by stage to Jefferson City, where he opened an account in *The Great Divide Bank* in the name of John Pell.

Slowly, over the next month he moved thirty-thousand dollars from Bismarck, leaving almost no trace of his transfers into the new account. Never once did he make direct transfers from Helena to Jefferson City. Only cash and gold were ever withdrawn, with dust being far more often the currency preferred to that of folding money.

He knew placer mines around Jefferson City were bringing in both dust and nuggets at a steady rate, and no one in Jefferson City gave him any notice other than being a wealthy businessman. He had explained to the bank officials he had investments in several claims in the gold fields, both here as well as down in Alders Gulch. It all seemed legitimate to them.

By the time Spade arrived in the new capital city, John Pell was well on his way back to the land of his dreams.

His first stop was to establish an account at *The Bank of The Yellowstone* in Bozeman and then another smaller account in the not so secure *Bank of White Sulphur Springs*, located a short half a day's ride west of Copperopolis, which had no bank.

The winter of 1876 passed with no advancement for the hunters but with much for the quarry. John Pell had hitched himself to a train of soldiers from Fort Ellis. They received orders to move goods and supplies eastward from the post at Fort Parker to an advance scouting party of *Northern Pacific Railroad* engineers.

The railroad men had been retracing the survey route of the 1871 party, when they encountered heavy resistance from a large band, said to be lead by Crazy Horse. A fight ensued but the party, some fifty strong, had been attacked near the banks of the Yellowstone where the river made a horseshoe bend providing a peninsula, a place where cottonwoods and pines grew thickly. The men of the party were able to make their stand initially by hiding behind the trees, but by nightfall, they felled trees and built breastworks, and that, along with their Spencer repeaters, was sufficient to stand off most attackers. They also sent two volunteers for help.

Nevada Dewitt headed west towards Fort Parker and Tony Sheffield east in the direction the engineers had come.

Nevada got less than a mile before being overrun and the party had to listen to his screams for most of the night, as the Lakotas skinned him, one piece at a time.

Sheffield however, made good his escape and eventually reached the new fort under construction across the river from Miles Town.

There were not sufficient troops at Miles Town to engage in such a rescue attempt, but the telegraph was still operating, and soon the call for help reached Fort Ellis.

Captain Baker left Ellis with a company of infantry now in command of the relief column, which included the troops Pell was with. Within four days, the rescue had been accomplished. The Northern Pacific survivors were escorted to a location where they encountered a steamer, and soon John Pell was also among them moving east on The Far West[23], headed down the Yellowstone for Coulson.

---

23 The Far West: For more on this steamer see T.H.Bear's The Withlacoochee Renegades Chapter One.

Beatrice Desmond was what westerns called a Grass Widow; her husband had left her a dozen years before, after he had learned of her social activities in the company of a young Lieutenant who had come home from the war as an amputee. It seemed the Officer had lost an arm but not the limb a young man holds most important.

Corporal Desmond, upon mustering out, found the knowledge of his cuckolding by the lover of his unfaithful wife, to be an embarrassment he had to suffer at the local pubs every time he entered one. Only months after returning, he again departed, this time for the west. She never saw or heard from him after that except when served with the divorce papers. Her one-armed Lieutenant was quickly transferred to another post, and she was without a means to support herself.

Bea was a tall, big-boned woman; her figure was large, though not out of proportion. Some might even call her plump, though no one would say she was fat. Her face seemed to always carry a stern expression, and she found office work easily, especially in the banking field where her honesty seemed impeccable.

She had worked with *The Bank of The Mississippi* in Saint Paul, for three years before Vice President Horace Kirkland began to give her special assignments. These soon materialized into special hours, hours that paired the two of them alone together, working late at the bank.

Bea did not really like Mr. Kirkland all that much, but it had been he who had given her the job and the opportunity to move from Northfield, leaving her past and reputation behind her. Of course, Kirkland knew of her divorce and the reason for it but not once had he mentioned it, or let on he possessed such knowledge.

She also was well aware he was married with a son and daughter and a Deacon in the Seventh Street Methodist Church. Other than lustful glances and an occasional brushing by a limb, he had never been anything short of a gentleman; that all came to an end the last Saturday of August, 1870. On that night, they had worked quite hard, both on the books and on moving several files from the front to the back storeroom. Shortly after eight, they finished, and both simply sank onto chairs, exhausted.

Beatrice had dropped a box of heavy books on her foot and had been limping since seven-ten. By eight, it had begun to swell, and her tight-laced boot was causing her pain more and more as each minute passed. She was just about to suggest she leave, while she could still walk the three blocks to her apartment, when a bright bolt of lightning lit the upper windows, followed almost immediately by an alarming clash of thunder. In a matter of less than a minute, a forceful storm was upon them. Lightning and thunder played a steady tune while a fierce wind drove cold rain hard against the windowpanes. They were temporarily trapped and each knew it.

After a few minutes, she asked if he would mind if she removed the offensive shoe. Of course, he did not mind, in fact he immediately dropped to her aid and assisted her in removing it. While doing so, he placed his hand on her calf. Even with the thickness of her heavy skirt, he could feel the well-shaped leg, and his forty-five year old blood rushed to his manhood almost as fast as the lightning bolts were appearing overhead, and he feared standing, lest she see his problem.

Finally, Horace remembered the decanter of peach brandy he had received as a gift from a salesman two Christmas' past. In his younger days, he had found a weakness for strong drink, but after meeting and marrying Charlene, he had abstained. This night he would return to his old ways.

"Here try a sip of this," he suggested, passing a half-filled glass to her. "It will relieve your pain some."

Unlike Horace, Bea had not given up her use of the pain reliever. Her friend, Lieutenant Farnsworth, had introduced her to the pleasures of a strong buzz. When she had been so humiliated by the revelation of their affair followed shortly by her husband divorcing her publicly, she often sought its comfort. She still did, every night after work.

Long before the storm subsided, they were deep in passion on the hardwood floor of Horace's office, starting a weekly event that occurred each Wednesday night after closing.

A year later, when he was offered the Presidency of the new bank in Dakota Territory, he took her with him, an arrangement that worked out fine for them both these several years, however shortly after he turned fifty, he began to have problems, and his weekly visits became less and less until she knew their affair was over. She did not let this concern her too much. They both knew well she had much too much on him for anything to happen to her position with the bank, but she had to admit she did miss the feel and attention of a man on occasion.

It had been in the spring of 1874, while she was on a trip to St Louis, she met Jean Mouton. They hit if off quickly and spent a joyful night together before he had to leave on business. When the inquiry came through on the Hickey account, she immediately recognized the name and made sure there was no delay in his request for the transfers. What she did not know was Horace Kirkland had been contacted by Ace Spade concerning the account.

As he watched the manner in which she took such a personal interest in the account, he began to suspect she had some connection with this Mouton, the Detective Agency was interested in. *'Perhaps here is a solution to my problem,'* he thought.

Little Spotted Calf, a Piegan[24] Blackfoot maiden of fourteen years, had gone south with her father, Black Eagle, to trade at the great Rendezvous, a place, each summer where the red man and the white man pointed not their weapons of war at one another, rather made peaceful trade with otherwise enemies. In the early summer of 1837, it was held at the junction of the two rivers[25] in Shoshone land.

Black Eagle appreciated it would be a long trip for a girl of her age, but she had learned much of the white man's language from the soldiers at Fort Benton, and her father realized the value she would be in making trades with the white trappers.

She was a beautiful little girl who had caught the eye of a Siksika brave, and an arrangement had been made where she would become the second wife of Red Wolf, upon their return. She liked Red Wolf, he was a strong brave and possessed many ponies. His wife was much older than she, and wanted someone to help with the work. Their lodge was never without food, and it gave her much pleasure to think such a mighty warrior looked in such a way upon her.

The trip south to the Wind River Rendezvous was a pleasant time for Little Spotted Calf. Although it took eleven sleeps, it was during the warm days of late spring when the great herds of buffalo were migrating north, thus food was plentiful. Her father, who loved his last-born child very much, always made their days together filled with games and adventure. She was the only young one of the sixteen Blackfoot making the journey and always seemed to have a

---

24 Piegan: One of the three divisions that comprised the Blackfoot Nation.

25 Junction of the two rivers: Where the Wind River and the Little Wind River intersect. Near present day Riverton, Wyoming.

special place among the other women. Her joy, however, would be short lived.

During the second night they had been at the Rendezvous, several of the white men had gotten drunk on whiskey, and one of them chased her across the high grass. When he caught her, he tore her new buckskin dress away and beat her about the face. Her father, hearing her screams, came running to her assistance. Unfortunately, her attacker's partner, using a Hawkins rifle, shot him in the upper leg, and he fell short of her.

After they saw her father was no longer a danger, her attacker and the man who had shot her father, each took her.

One of these men had very dark skin and spoke a language she had never heard before. She did remember hearing the other man say to him in the Whiteman's language, "Cisco get off, it's my turn." She could not understand what this man said in reply.

Black Eagle was not in condition to travel when the Rendezvous broke, and he and his daughter were left behind as the other Blackfoot departed for the north. The return journey was anything but a pleasant time for Little Spotted Calf. Both their horses had been stolen by the white men, as were most of their possessions. She was emotionally distressed by what had happened to her, and Black Eagle could not travel more than the distance of one half hour before he had to rest. They made sixty sleeps before their return to the Milk River camp was completed.

The news of their injuries had reached the village long before their return. Red Wolf, believing she would never come back, had taken another for his second wife.

Little Spotted Calf was pregnant with Cisco's child eight months, when the pox hit her. On the day her son was born, she gave up the ghost. Black Eagle, who had been lame from the time he was shot, also had the Whiteman's spotted fever. He realized the only chance the boy-child had to survive was to be with a strong family. The day after her death, he gave Little Spotted Calf's son to Red Wolf and asked him to raise the child. A week later Black Eagle also died.

Two Bucks, as he was called by Red Wolf, grew to a lad feeling dejected and unwanted. Travois Woman, Red Wolf's first wife, resented having him around, and she beat him for the slightest imperfection.

Pretty Moccasins, his second wife, was more compassionate towards Two Bucks, but she was subservient to Travois Woman and could not stop the beatings.

Pretty Moccasins had been heavy with her own first child when Two Bucks came to the lodge of Red Wolf. It was her milk that had nursed him after his mother's spirit had departed. She had love for the boy, but her own son was first in her heart, and Two Bucks felt this all of his young days.

Late in the summer of 1848, he was captured by a band of marauding Shoshone and taken south. Not one of the Blackfoot, from his village, attempted to rescue him.

Life with the Shoshone was worse that with his native Siksika[26].

Five years later he escaped from the Shoshone but ran south rather than north towards his people as they expected, thus avoiding recapture.

In 1858, as a twenty-year-old man, Two Bucks had lived and raided with the Comanche, the Comancheros, and a band of deserters from the Mexican army. He spoke the language of five nations, as well as Mexican, and the tongue of the white Americans. His fear was so deeply covered by the years of abuse; neither he nor anyone who rode with him realized it even existed.

Two Bucks stood less than any member of the band he rode with, but all understood his shortness in height in no way impeached his courage and ruthlessness.

Once some years later, one of the men had said after returning from a two- week raiding party in Texas, "The short one hates every man equally."

The reason for this statement was once again confirmed a few days before, while they were raiding along the river west of Benficklin. The little band led by Two Bucks had come upon a ranch hacked out in the dry soil, containing only a few head and a small area where they had cleared away the Yucca, Creosote, and Mesquite to plant a garden near the river.

The farmer never once looked up at the group of riders who sat atop a low sandy rise viewing the scene below. This man was working behind a mule, some one hundred yards from the mud hut he and his wife had built to satisfy the Homestead Act.

The man meant nothing to them; it was what they saw at the cabin that had their interest, for it was there the woman stood in front of the hut, under a canvas awning that had once covered their wagon, a vehicle that now sat nearly useless behind their home.

---

26 Siksika: Another of the Divisions of The Blackfoot Nation.

John Regis Edwards had placed the canvas there for his wife a year before, when she was with-child. Under it, she could do her chores in the shade and out of the stifling heat that consumed the hut during the summer days of bright sunlight.

She too did not look up from her work, as the riders began to descend towards the little farm. In fact, no one paid any attention to anything other than the daily chores, which had become such a routine to them, as to be almost mechanical. Not even the old black and tan hound who shared the shade with his Misses awoke, until one of the horses blew after stopping only twenty feet from him.

Slowly he lifted his head and gave them a queer look before rising on his front legs, and baying loud and long, before he stood completely.

It was only then Becky Edwards looked up and saw them. She immediately screamed from the start of so many unexpected men in such filthy attire.

Regis had heard Rocky howl and wondered the why of it in the heat of the day, but he was just near enough the river not to be able to see the front of the hut. He decided to continue with the row he was almost to the end of, before going to see what had brought his old hound out of his daily siesta.

In his younger days, back in west Tennessee, a rabbit or a coon would be in danger anytime Rocky was not on a leash, but that was then and this is now, and his days were numbered; Regis knew too well.

However, when he heard his wife scream, he threw the leads from his shoulders and abandoned Henry, still attached to the plow. Running to the top of the bank, he suddenly froze at the sight of seven riders, still mounted, in a semi-circle around the front of their home.

Regis was unarmed, save the small 1849 Model Colt revolver he kept in the pocket of his overalls. It was really too small for the taking of game, but it did serve well dispatching the all too prevalent rattlers, which seemed to appear from nowhere in the summer. Suddenly he realized the peril he and his family were in, having nothing larger for defense. Surely the light 31 caliber ball of his revolver could kill at a short distance, but from where he was, even if he were lucky enough to hit one of them, it surely would not stop him from whatever he intended to do. *'No, I must get closer if I'm to help Becky and little Phoebe.'* With all the courage he could muster, he walked towards his wife and her unwanted guests.

Hilario had just started to dismount when Regis called out, "Helloo, can we help you?"

They all turned his way, and immediately Rocky's tail slapped the side of the hut a couple of times before it stopped. Wagging one's tail in this heat is most tiring.

"Ah, the man of the house," Lobo said, looking at the thin shirtless Whiteman in bib overalls approaching slowly.

"We need food," Two Bears said.

"We can't spare any," Becky quickly replied, not wanting to give them any reason to linger. "There is water down by the river," she offered and then added, "fer your horses."

"Now Becky, I think we can spare some sowbelly."

She looked at her husband questioningly as he walked the last few feet to get between his family and the strangers. "Alright Regis, if you say so."

"It's best. We can manage without it, and these men probably need the nourishment."

She turned and started for the open door when Two Bucks spoke, "Wait, Uvaldo will go with her, just in case she finds a scattergun instead of sowbelly."

She turned and gave her husband a exceedingly frightened look, beckoning him to do something to protect her and her child, only she had no idea what he could do.

"There is a gun in the house, but it isn't loaded," Regis said. "She will do only as I tell her."

"You are wrong, Señor Texican. She will do only as I tell her," Two Bucks said back. Then with his head, he motioned to the gaunt Mexican who rode beside him to do as he commanded.

The man pushed his big hat back until it fell off his shoulder, hampered only by the rawhide string that hung around his neck, "Si," he said, as a big grin crossed his face revealing he had lost several front teeth at one time in the past.

"Wait," Regis said. He did not know what to say next. They were in trouble as they had never been before, and he fully realized it.

Two Bucks motioned with his head to the tall man, only this time the gesture was quicker and more forceful, "Uvaldo, do as I say."

The man dismounted and headed the few steps toward the woman. Grasping her elbow, he pushed her forward towards the dark interior of the hut.

Regis knew he had to do something now. Reaching in his pocket, he cocked the revolver as he pulled it from his overalls. The small ball struck the right shoulder of the Mexican and burned a shallow trench across his back as it passed under his gingham shirt, exiting on the far side and spending itself on a rock some fifty yards away.

The man released his grip on Becky and yelled loudly, but his complaint was unheard due to the loud report from the Dragoon, discharging in Lobo's hand.

Betsy saw the mixture of flesh and blood fly from Regis' back as the big ball exited, knocking her husband backwards a couple of steps and dropping him to his knees. He lost his grip on the pocket pistol, and it fell onto the sandy soil near where he had been standing when he fired.

Regis felt no pain, not of the physical kind, rather he now was enduring the greatest pain a loving husband could.

"Pretty good Lobo, you shot fast and straight. For this you will have the woman first," the short leader said, and again he motioned his command with a nod of his banded head.

The smile now belonged to Lobo, and he wasted no time dismounting the gray mare he had stolen two nights before from a Mormon drover, whose throat he had slit.

Uvaldo looked with resentment as the half-breed approached him, but he pushed her forward and placed the hand he had held her with, to his wounded shoulder.

Lobo began pushing the flaxen-haired woman towards the door, but Two Bucks stopped him.

"No. We take her out here. Her protector must watch."

The baby who had been asleep in the wooden cradle had been awakened by the explosion of the revolver fire and was now crying loudly.

"Shet' that thing up," Two Bucks shouted, not particularly at anyone.

Uvaldo, who had his anger up for losing the choice turn at the woman and being grazed at the same time, took the baby by its ankles and bashed it twice into the hard mud wall. With the first blow, the child went silent, upon receiving the second, its head cracked open and blood covered brains spilled out.

Betsy fainted and Regis began to lose what was left of his breakfast.

Lobo reached for the long thin knife he had killed the drover with, and cut the work dress from the woman. She lay there on the pale yellow soil shining white as snow, save for her lower arms, neck, and face, which all had burned dark by the wind and unforgiving sun.

Regis was on his knees and tried to reach for his fallen gun, but his gun arm was useless. The 44 ball had entered his right chest just below the collarbone striking the top rib before ricocheting up and out his back, shattering the shoulder joint as it passed.

Two Bucks saw his attempt and smiled, "Hilario, get the Señor Texican's peashooter before he wings another one of you, and we have to keel him. It is not nice to keel a man when his wife needs him so."

Regis looked at his wife's white skin as it contrasted so greatly with that of the dark Mexican who was now violating her, and he just shook his head helplessly.

One by one, they took Betsy. She had been awake when the first man entered her, but she pretended unconsciousness. Instead of thinking of what was happening to her, she let her thoughts return to her home in middle Tennessee, where this time of the year everything was green and beautiful. She remembered sitting beside her older sister along the banks of Otter Creek and letting the cool water wash the mud from between her toes.

She had enjoyed a happy early childhood and had never thought of traveling more than the twenty miles to Nashville each Christmas to see her Grammie. However, that was before the war and before the men with the strange accents came and told her mother they would have to move from their farm, because they had not paid their war taxes.

Her father had gone away when she was fifteen to fight the Yankees and never returned. She learned her grandmother had also died in the winter of '62. A month later, word was received of her father's death in a prison in New York. It was then her mother had taken her to live with Uncle Bill in Arkansas. The small note that came had simply said her father had drowned. She never understood how a man could drown while a prisoner in a camp[27].

Becky had married Regis when she was seventeen and bore him a son the following year. Unfortunately, it had succumbed to chol-

---

27 Drowned Prisoners:When the Elmira River flooded, many southern prisoners who were too sick to get out of their bunks drowned as the towns people watched and often laughed.

era, and was buried along the Santa Fe Trail in west Kansas. This day, she did not think of those bad times, she only thought of the good times. The times she had spent in Tennessee as a child and the first year of her marriage. These very happy times were the thoughts that kept Becky from losing her mind as the seven men raped her repeatedly.

Finally, the short one drenched her with a bucket of water to make sure she was awake. Two others then held her up, so she had to watch, as the leader cut the shoulder straps of her husband's overalls and then pulled them down and off his legs.

No matter how hard the wounded Regis tried to stop him, the half-breed stripped him naked with ease. Then, while she was forced to watch, he grabbed the helpless man and used him like a woman. When finished with his humiliating deed, he walked around in front of the man, and laughed loudly at his victim. Two Bucks then turned to make sure she was watching, and slowly removed a rusty jack knife from his pocket, and in a motion so quick she hardly believed she saw it, he cut her husband's privates off and threw them into the hog pen. She was on her knees as she watched, helplessly, as the blood spilled from his body, and she sobbed.

At the time of his death, Regis Edwards was 31 years old. He owned one hundred and sixty acres of burned-over sand, along the Middle Concho River near the eastern most point of The Chihuahuan Desert. His riches included his mule, Henry; twenty two head of wild longhorns he had managed to catch and place his brand upon; a Jersey cow, which had followed along tied behind their wagon all the way from Conway, Arkansas; one boar, and two sows, one with seven piglets; a single red rooster; and eleven laying-hens; and of course, his faithful old Rocky.

That night, the raiders stayed at the Edwards homestead and ransacked the hut taking everything of value, which wasn't much. They ate heartily on freshly roasted pig and drank the last of the homebrew Regis had brought all the way from Tennessee in a stone jug.

The next morning as the sky began to turn purple in the east, Becky Edwards was riding Henry bareback, with her hands were tied in front of her. A long coarse rope was looped around her neck with the other end tied to the horn of Uvaldo's saddle. She was wearing the only other dress she owned, the blue one she had married in. Before heading towards Mexico, they shot the remaining stock. The animals, which only one morning previously had been the future of Regis and Becky Edwards, lay dead or bleeding to death from Comanche arrows the party had shot into them.

A month later, when they sold their six women prisoners to the slave traders along the Mexican coast, had it not been for the scar the rope had caused, the woman with the flaxen hair would have brought considerably more dinero.

When word of the gold strikes in Montana Territory filtered its way to the band of Comancheros Two Bucks was riding with, he decided it was time he returned to the land of his birth. Less than a week after he made the decision, he took two loyal companions, Lobo and Lefty, and headed north.

For ten years, they had raided throughout the territories, every time leaving just enough evidence to make the investigators believe it had been Indians who had committed the crimes. Always riding unshod ponies, stealing, killing and raping, Indian fashion; no one ever questioned a band of renegades were responsible.

Two days before the raid on *Walker's Stage Station* and some twenty miles to the north, Two Bucks and Lobo watched, crouched behind a large rock, as three Lakota braves approached from the sage-covered prairie. As they rode closely by, the ambushers let them pass and then opened fire with their Winchesters. The Indians never knew they were in trouble until it was too late.

Two Bucks walked up to the bloody body of the leading Sioux and removed the bow and quiver of arrows from his back.

Lobo started to take their scalps, but Two Bucks stopped him, "No, let his people think Whiteman do this."

Lobo nodded his head and laughed, then began removing the other weapons from the three bodies.

It had been one of the arrows from this quiver they had sent into the stage door an hour after they had repeatedly raped, before killing, the fat woman at Walker's Station.

Two Bucks knew Indians of all tribes raped their women captives. It was part of their culture, part of their trophy in the victory. This was true, no matter whom the victims were, but there had always been a special esteem in the raping of white women. The whites left the impression on all redmen, they thought themselves above other races. All the nations received great pleasure from depriving white women of the pedestal they aired to be sitting upon. It made no difference if she was young, old, pretty, or totally undesirable, she would be raped. It was an act of humiliation, of revenge, more so than that of sexual pleasure, almost a duty. The pleasure came in the satisfaction of the degradation, rather than the act of sex.

To have killed a white woman without first degrading her, would have immediately brought suspicion that the crime had been committed by someone other than an Indian, something Two Bucks never intended to allow to happen.

Many a man had found himself on the Owl Hoot Trail, and most regretted the actions and decisions that had led them to follow it. The lack of sufficient provisions, the biting cold of winter, the misery of a smoldering summer sun, the lack of proper food, and always, at least mostly always, the lack of proper drinking water, made life miserable, to say nothing of the loneliness for the want of a good woman. Very few who had experienced it would not go back and correct the mistakes that brought them to it, if they had the chance to do so.

This was not the case with Two Bucks. He had never known a better life than what the trail gave him. From his earliest remembrance, life had been miserable. First in the lodge of Travois Woman, then with his Shoshone captors, and later with the Comanche, life had always been miserable.

Since he broke away and began his own band of renegades, he could do as he pleased and be beholding to no one. For the first time, life was not so miserable to him.

On the day Lobo led the raid on Walker's Station, Two Bucks had ridden into the Little Belt Mountains. He was scouting for a place to make a winter camp which was near the *Carroll Stage Route*, as well as near good water. Equally important was to find a location with shelter from the bitter cold he knew, more than the others who rode with him, was coming.

Later when he found out Lobo had made the raid and not taken the horses, he was furious. Lobo tried to explain it had been their intention to do so but after Ben Curry found a large jug of whiskey in the station, their reasoning was lost as they drank until they passed out.

However, had it not been for Ben, they could all have been caught passed out, with their hands in the cookie jar. It was while Curry was relieving himself; he spotted the approaching riders and alerted the others. With great haste and splitting heads, the four bandits retreated to a distant hill. From there, they watched Reb Brown and his companions slip up on the death scene.

Lobo's excuse made sense, but it in no way relieved him from Two Bucks' anger. "Mistakes like that can ruin my whole plan in these parts. Someone is bound to suspect the raid was not made by Lakotas!" he screamed at the much larger man.

"But we did as you told us; we shoot the Lakota arrow into the coach."

"Stupid, pure stupid. I guess if anything is to be done right, I must do it myself," he shouted, before stomping off, leaving Lobo embarrassed at getting both barrels of Two Bucks' anger blasted at him in front of the others.

The very day John Pell left Helena, Mr. Kirkland called Bea Desmond into his office. There she was introduced to Augustus Spade. It took the Detective less than half an hour to get her to admit having met Mouton when she was in Bismarck. She strongly denied knowing of any of his wrong-doings. Cleverly, she made no mention of their earlier chance rendezvous in Saint Louis.

"He had the proper credentials, and he was on the account with Mr. Hickey," she protested.

Ace knew she was correct, but he doubted she was as innocent as she pretended, and he made his thoughts open in the form of a threat.

Her expression suddenly changed when he explained to get to the bottom of it, he would bring the incident before the Territorial Court and have them make the determination of her guilt or innocence.

Having immediately spotted her expression change, he was confident he had her. "I will give you an opportunity to prove your loyalty. You will work as an undercover agent for the bank. If you are successful in bringing this thief to justice, you will avoid any possibility of having a court decide further. Of course, you will report directly to me, especially any and all information you uncover."

The unrealized problem was in truth, she knew, or thought she knew, Mouton was a resident of Helena, Montana, which of course he was not, a problem that would plague her for the next several months.

April Fools Day, 1877 found John Pell the new owner of *The Little Judith Ranch,* carrying the Lazy R bar J brand. The actual deed was for a mere 640 acres, but it was surrounded by open range, which only two years previous had been the undisputed land of the Teton Lakota.

When Two Bucks was born, this land belonged to the Blackfoot, and no one else dared to transgress it. Now John Pell owned it and laid claim to the surrounding one hundred thousand acres, some of which was on both sides of The Musselshell River.

Pell, of course, knew to claim such a vast land was as simple as the Spaniards sticking a staff in the sandy soil of Florida with a flag attached to it. He also knew the Spaniards no longer could claim Florida; they had lost it by being weak. It took force to hold land, and force meant numbers and money. He now had the money, Hickey's money; he needed only the manpower to make this dream come true.

'Where will I get the manpower?' he pondered. *'There is the army. Men whose enlistment is coming to an end and men who left before their enlistment came to an end.'* He liked the thought of men used to taking orders.

'Also there will be the men who come north driving my herds. Perhaps some of them will want to stay for good pay. I will need men with the knowledge of handling wild cattle.

There also are men who travel the Owl Hoot Trail. Men who would be good with their firearms and perhaps in need of a safe haven from the law,' John nodded his head approving his thoughts. *'Yes, there are men to have.'*

The winter and spring of 1877 found Reb Brown and his companions following one lead after another, up one blind trail and then back again. Nonetheless, Black Band was a tracker, and Cliff had learned a great deal of the art from the many months they rode together. The one thing he learned the best was, if a trail plays out, you simply return to the last known location of your quarry and begin again only with more diligence this time.

They found a man who remembered overhearing just such a jasper as they described speaking French to a French whore at *The Red Light Saloon* on Wood Street in Helena. He also remembered this man had mentioned something about his holdings in the Alder Gulch area.

They arrived in Virginia City on the first of August, to scattered thunderstorms with the high near the mid-eighties and a damp ten mile an hour wind coming from the west-southwest, keeping everyone on edge.

Virginia City was one of the first strikes of color in the then Idaho Territory. She, along with her sister Nevada City, shared many of the same rewards and fates. Both gained their resources from near-by Alder Gulch.

Only a few miles from the town limits of Virginia City, stood the stone home of Virginia and Jack Slade. Virginia City was not named for Virginia Slade, rather in honor of President Jefferson Davis' wife Varina. Virginia Slade did have a place in history named after her. Jack and Virginia Slade were the same couple who also had built *Virginia Dale Stage Station*, where Cliff had had the fight a couple of years before with the Utes at Spuds Lords' home.

Most agree, the hanging of Jack Slade was because he had caused a disturbance in a saloon. However, the straight of it is, Jack Slade was from the south and thus labeled a Democrat. By 1864, in the new Montana Territory, being a Democrat was an unwritten crime.

Politically, Montana belonged to Sidney Edgerton. Edgerton, appointed Montana's first Governor by his personal friend, Abraham Lincoln, had made it well known his beliefs to be all Democrats are guilty of treason. This of course, would never fly openly; as at the time, Montana was highly populated by Southerners.

Edgerton being aware he was out-numbered vote wise, shrewdly organized and led *The Vigilantes of Montana* to rid the Territory of Democrats under the ruse they were bandits. In fact, all the men and women who were hung by these vigilantes were Democrats, both southern Democrats and northern Democrats.

Neither Clifford Brown nor his two companions had interest in any of the area's history, although had they known, Cliff would have felt a kinship to those who had been hung. They only wanted to find the murderer they pursued. However, the fact Cliff still sported a strong southern accent, and one of his men was an Indian, did little to encourage their welcome by the authorities in Madison County.

When John Pell arrived as the new owner of the Lazy R bar J, Copperopolis was a growing community, with Noel Coker's newly built General Store and *Bragg Crouch's Blacksmith Shop*, which was next to Fannie Sharpshire's. Fannie had attached a fair size room on the side of her two-story boarding house, which was to become the town's first restaurant.

Across the street was a long log building called *The Bunkhouse*, owned by Rufus Orr and his wife. It was one of the most profitable businesses in Copperopolis; offering shelter from the cold winds, at a price the off-duty miners could afford.

Rufus' wife had come west from Indiana with her brother, Gentry Beck, to the Cherry Creek gold rush in Colorado back in the 60's. It was there Sophie had met Rufus and fell hopelessly in love with the big drover from Texas.

There was more than a little friction at first in the new Orr family, with he being fresh from Camp Douglas[28] prison in Chicago and her brother being freshly mustered out of the 104th Indiana Infantry. However, Sophie being her charming self with fiery red hair to stir the blood of her new husband and big blue eyes to warm the heart of her younger brother, finally succeeded in the hatchet being buried between the blue and gray in her world.

When they moved north to begin a new life, she convinced Rufus to invite Gentry to come and start a livery next door to their Bunkhouse, even though all knew the hatchet was not buried too deeply between the brother's-in-law.

To John Pell, what seemed to be the most important sign that this little community was here to stay was the opening of the *Big Sky Bank,* at the corner of North Street and the Martinsdale Road, the very day he stepped off the stage.

The only business he saw missing in this new community was that of a decent saloon and gambling house, a matter he planned to resolve as soon as he could muster his crew at the ranch.

Within an hour after stepping on North Street in Copperopolis, he had arranged a room at the Widow Sharpshire's and was having lunch with Ephraim Glaze.

Mr. Glaze was most impressed with the new owner of the Lazy R bar J. He could see John Pell was just the man to give his new bank the start in cash deposits it needed to get off the ground, thus a business friendship was created then and there.

Glaze also suited John Pell well. The short, over-weight quondam mayor of Sherman, New York, was ambitious and hungry

---

28 Camp Douglas: A POW camp some believe to have been the most horrible of all during the war, in that the commandants deliberately withheld proper food, medical supplies, and clothing from the confined Confederates.

for just what John Pell had, a seemingly unending supply of cash. John Pell also needed just such a place as Glaze's bank to hide Hickey's money.

They both agreed the best way to reap gold in copper country was in the ownership of a saloon. They also agreed, as soon as one would become successful in such an enterprise, someone else would realize their gold mine, and build a second such establishment, a competition they did not need. The town was growing, but it would be some time before it could support more than two saloons, so a secret partnership was formed.

John did not need Glaze's money to build the two saloons. However, he did need a bank and having a silent partner who also was owner and president of *The Big Sky Bank*, Copperopolis' only such establishment was a tremendous benefit.

Before *The Musselshell Saloon* was completed, *The White Castle Mountain* began to rise. It was located next to *The Carroll Line Stage Company*'s depot on the Martinsdale Road, only a short distance from the bank.

John knew his first love for this country was the success of his ranch and for that he needed a foreman he could trust and enough wranglers and punchers who were good with their guns, to make both the Sioux and the squatters stay clear. For the job of foreman he wired York, who was still in Cheyenne.

To run *The Musselshell Saloon*, he sent for Sally Mustang. For *The White Castle Mountain*, he hoped to get Bea Desmond. Unfortunately, when he wired her in Bismarck, his wire was returned, an inconvenience he did not like, but he knew for the time being, he would have to deal with.

Brigitte had been born in the bayou country near New Iberia, west of New Orleans, in the summer of '49. Her mother was a yellow nigress named May Day Le Petit. Her father, Beau Daiquiris, had a good position with Mr. Weeks at *The Blue Bonnet Plantation* where Brigitte was born and spent her early life.

When Sergeant Daiquiris failed to return from General Sibley's invasion of New Mexico, Brigitte's mother was forced to move into town. There she took in wash and did other odd jobs to put food in their mouths. Eventually however, with the occupation of New Iberia in the spring of '63 by the 114th NY, she became the mistress of a Major Hudson. He provided her and her four children with enough of the new Yankee greenbacks to keep them well-fed and in warm clothes during the cold months. He also saw to it they had a decent shack in the working quarters on the Bayou Teche.

On Brigitte's 14th birthday, her mother had left to fetch a basket of peaches she had arranged to get as a special present for Brigitte's special day. It was during her mother's absence, Major Hudson arrived half drunk and looking for the loving he was paying for.

Brigitte, being an early bloomer, had already found the pleasures her fingers could bring while she watched, through the cracks in the backdoor, her mother paying the rent once each week.

This day she purposely leaned over a little extra when she poured the wine for the Major, allowing her ample breasts to be exposed from the top of her loose- fitting cotton dress, a dress that once had held a hundred pounds of Amish flour.

It pleased her to see the eyes of this man swell as he gazed at her melons. She also knew her dress was so worn, that it was almost transparent, especially when the light was behind her, and she soon walked towards the window where the only other chair they had was located.

Before sitting in the rough-cut pine chair she slowly stretched, then looked down the road her mother would be approaching on.

The Major had just taken a large swallow of the hawberry wine when she stretched, and the view of her almost naked young body silhouetted through the thin material by the light coming through the door, caused him to allow the deep red drink to go down the wrong pipe; immediately he was bent over coughing and the incident caused Brigitte to snicker.

As soon as he could speak, he yelled at her, "You little wench, I'll show you to laugh at me," at which time he jumped up and rushed over to her. She screamed playfully when she saw him coming and again when he began tickling her.

Brigitte was not really all that ticklish, but she loved the attention she was commanding from her mother's lover, and she played it up as much as she could.

In less than a minute, the motion of his large hands on her sides had pushed the hemless dress up, exposing the dark patch of curly hair covering her privates. Upon seeing this, he stopped his tickling and moved his hand to her triangle.

They both were still naked in her mother's bed when May Day walked in with the basket of peaches.

When the 114th New York moved into New Orleans the next winter, it was Brigitte who went with Major Hudson and not her mother.

In the fall of 1876, Brigitte Daiquiris was working in Squirrel Tooth Alice's *Red Light Saloon* in Helena, Montana. Now she was known as Sally Mustang. It was there she met the rich Mr. Pell and enjoyed being able to converse in French with this handsome older man, who tipped so well.

John Pell, for the first time since he left New York, had found a woman who he genuinely enjoyed being with. Of course, he had always loved the pleasures a woman brought to a man, but so many of them had been little or nothing more than a necessity his body required. Brigitte was more than that to him. He realized he was older than her father, but she made him feel good, made him feel young again, not since Diana Roland had he felt this way about a woman.

Bea, on the other hand was just another port in the storm. She was attractive and certainly fun in bed, but she was not keeping material. What attracted him most to Bea was her knowledge of the banking business. She was a pretty, practical woman. She had a good head for numbers, and she knew when and what numbers were most important. He really was disappointed when he found she was no longer at *The Bank of Bismarck*, and he wasn't sure who he would get to replace her. In the meantime, he would let Sally Mustang head up *The Musselshell Saloon*, at least until construction of *The White Castle Mountain* was completed.

He always referred to the dark-haired she-devil as Sally Mustang when in conversation with anyone, including her, except on occasion when they were alone and he was feeling close to her. During those times, she was Brigitte, his special Brigitte.

The Musselshell was a one-story, three-room tiger[29]. The front had space for three gambling tables and a long bar. In the rear there was a storage room and off to the west side of this, he created Sally's living quarters.

His other saloon was to be a two-story affair with space for ten tables and rooms on the second floor for the girls to rent, where they could ply their trade. There was also a room in the rear that traversed the entire width of the building. This would serve as an office and still have plenty of space for nice living quarters, his living quarters when he was in town.

---

29 Tiger: Name often given to small dive bars during the nineteenth century.

The White Castle Mountain would be the finest saloon in middle Montana, and he knew it was just such a place to relieve the miners of their money. Once when talking to Ephraim Glaze, he referred to it as, A True Gold Mine in Copper Mine Country. Later when he reflected on it, he greatly admired his description.

The one thing John Pell had not counted on was a lawman. This came in the form of one Elon Traven; a Marshal hired by the townspeople after several miners had gotten into a drunken brawl, busted up Orr's Bunkhouse and offended his wife.

After reflection this town marshal did not worry Pell all that much, Traven's salary would be from the town's funds and Glaze controlled that for the most part.

John spent a long absence from Copperopolis in October of 1877. York had arrived with ten hands from Colorado and Wyoming. A few even from the Wolf Creek spread, and there was much to be done getting the ranch on track. However, immediately after he was satisfied with the progress he saw there, he took the stage west to Helena to arrange for more of Hickey's Bismarck funds to be transferred to Montana.

It was there, as he was leaving the bank, Bea saw him. She reached for the arm of Ace Spade to get his attention, but he had just turned and begun talking with the bank president. She stopped a moment and thought, *'Why would Jean Mouton be so bold as to come here when he was so elusive everywhere else?'*

"I'll wait outside for you, Mr. Spade."

She heard his reply, but paid little attention to him as he obviously was in deep conversation on his own agenda. Just as she reached the door, she saw her quarry entering a buggy and pulling away.

The night before, a wind had swept in from the northeast bringing a drastic drop in the temperature, and this morning low and dark clouds hid the mountaintops as well as the sun. A light powder was beginning to fall on the frozen street, and she watched as the horses' hooves broke through the thin layer and kicked up small clods of mud and ice behind them.

'He is getting away. What should I do?' she thought as she watched the black-topped buggy grow smaller. She knew she could not keep up with him on the icy street, and when he turned the corner, she lost hope of reaching him.

Of course, she knew she was being a fool for not telling Spade, but she did have a tingle deep inside her that this Frenchman awoke, and she could not deny it.

"What are you doing out here in this weather?" Spade asked breaking her deep thoughts.

"Oh, I was just about to come back inside."

"Why would you stay out here in the first place?"

"The cigar smoke upsets my stomach. I need fresh air often when around you."

"I'll never savvy a woman."

"I don't doubt that one minute," she replied with a hint of sarcasm, which he immediately detected; so as a thrust in their fencing match he added, "And neither do I believe for one minute, you are nearly as honest as you would like us to think. I will prove that very thing one day."

That night she thought long on his statement. It was true her honesty was less than perfect but for the great Ace Spade to prove it, was something else. She had almost decided to tell Spade about seeing Mouton when he made that threat. It was now somewhat of a challenge, and she felt she had the better brain in this match.

It took her some time to learn enough to suspect the Jean Mouton she had met in Saint Louis was the same John Pell, who she had seen that snowy day in Helena. Once she had put it all together, she realized with this knowledge she only had to work out some way to be rid of Spade and fortunes might be made.

She could tell John about Spade as soon as she found him. However, should he choose to kill Spade, the detective agency would only send another agent. *'No, I must come up with something else, some way to discredit Spade.'*

One morning she awoke with a terrible sore throat. It just so happened that this very morning Ace had uncovered a man meeting Jean Mouton's description had been seen headed for Alder's Gulch, and he wanted the two of them to go immediately. She explained she was too under the weather and begged him to send for a doctor.

Spade did not take this news well. He wanted to pursue his new lead, but he did not feel at all good about leaving her. He had never trusted her, and this was grinding on his gut.

Doctor Stick confirmed she had a bad case of strep, and after leaving her with a three days supply of ginger root, he warned Spade it could be scarlet fever.

"Damn!" the young detective said angrily. "When can she travel?"

"I don't know; my guess is she will be in that bed for several weeks, maybe until spring."

"Damn, damn, damn," Spade repeated slapping his fist in his other palm. "I'll just have to go without her," he added under his breath.

"Is she your woman?" the doctor asked as he reached for his weathered beaver bowler.

"No. She is a business acquaintance only; we are working together, nothing more."

"I see. I will have someone look in on her then."

"Yes, please do that."

Beatrice Desmond knew a little about herself, which neither of these professional men did. That very day, as soon as she was certain Spade had departed on the noon stage, she sent for a bottle of rye.

The next morning when Marion Mix reported to Doctor Stick, she told him "The only thing I found in Mrs. Desmond's room was an empty bottle."

The Doctor looked at her in surprise. "I told her companion not to move her," he said disgustedly, shaking his head. "And I was convinced she was only his business acquaintance. What men will do sometimes for a woman," he said shaking his head again.

"Yes," Miss Mix agreed, smiling secretly.

John was stepping out on the snow-covered boardwalk from the stage station where upon he spotted her coming down the opposite side of the street, in front of one of Louis Reeder's stone cabins. He could hardly believe his luck, and he wasted no time in attracting her attention.

That evening they stayed together in *The Rocky Mountain*, Helena's best hotel wrapped in each other's arms. The next day they were eastbound on *The Salisbury Stage*.

Two of the other passengers left the Concord at East Helena, and another got aboard there. That afternoon, they lost him as well at *Nine Mile Station*, and for the next fifteen miles, they were alone in the coach. It was during this time John told her about his new ranch and the two saloons he was building in Copperopolis. He also detailed the plans he had for her.

When asked what she was doing in Helena she replied, "I'm still working for the bank. Mr. Kirkland sent me west to look over the established banks in Helena." Which was not the whole truth but not totally untrue either. She decided to hold back anything about Ace Spade for the time being. She didn't want to put a fright in John. She wasn't sure he would not vanish again if she spilled too much, after all, she was not totally sure which side of this line she would come out best with, at least not yet.

"Tell me Jean, why have you changed your name to John Pell?"

He took a deep breath and looked out of the window. The landscape was a flatter terrain than they had been seeing, and he knew The Divide was slipping ever so slowly behind them. "You know I have a partner, William Hickey."

"Yes."

"Well, what you didn't know is that Hickey is dead. His adulteress wife and her lover killed him. She now is trying to keep me from getting the money I loaned her husband to start this business.

You see, Will was a rather wealthy man in Missouri, but he had made some bad investments, the largest of which was the purchasing of a stern-wheeler that ran aground on a sandbar and broke up. Several people drowned, and he had not secured sufficient insurance. He was on the very verge of bankruptcy.

Being his long-time friend, I loaned him a large sum of money to get him back on his feet, and we entered in this partnership to establish a ranch on the new free land in Montana.

My part was to come west and locate the land, and he was to stay back east and make the arrangements to ship our cattle up the Ohio to eastern distributors.

Sometime after I left Kent, his wife's lover shot poor Will, and she covered up for him by blaming it on me. I would return and clear it all up, but to do so right now, would cost just too much. With these new enterprises just getting off the ground, I must stay here until I get the ranch and the saloons well established. As soon as I do that, you can bet I will be headed back to Poplar Bluff, Missouri."

'Most of what he said makes sense,' she thought. *'From what I have heard it was Mrs. Hickey who had hired the Detective Agency to locate him, and it was on her orders that the bank accounts had been frozen for a time.'*

She swallowed, and the rawness in her throat caused her to cough.

"That sounds bad."

"I will be fine as soon as we can get inside a decent structure."

That night they stayed at *Toston Station*, a low-roofed log house that had a large fireplace and a long table, which could easily seat ten hungry mouths if they only had more than the four home-made chairs.

Mic Markarian, who ran the station with the Hatch boy, had made an edible stew from a combination of a leftover elk's ribcage and a few other lesser critters that had been trapped before the last storm. Mic had learned from his days in the navy that nothing will flavor a stew like the grindings of the Asian spice peppercorn, and he always gave his a generous amount.

The logs were well-packed and the roof being so low allowed the fire to warm the small building quite well, much to Bea's pleasure.

Later, after she and John had enjoyed each other in the single room off the back, she could hear the men on the other side of the old army blanket, which served as a door to their room, breaking out a jug and playing a game of cards.

"Jean, or should I just call you John?"

"I think John will do nicely."

"Alright then, John?"

"Yes?"

"Do you think a swallow or two of that beverage would help my sore throat?"

"It just might, Bea," he replied, knowing full well her needs.

John Pell did not bother with pulling on his high-topped boots. Slipping on his trousers and pulling the suspenders over his red cotton johns would be sufficient for his venture into the outer room, and so he moved out of her sight.

That night she slumbered deeply holding tight to her old lover.

The next day, as they talked of his plans concerning her management of his saloon, he said, "I not only want you to manage *The White Castle Mountain*, I want you to handle my money; take care of my banking when I am away; look after all the financial business from both saloons, as well as my ranch.

Only no one must know Ephraim Glaze and I are the true owners of *The White Castle Mountain*. You will represent yourself as the investor and manager of the saloon and move the profits to separate accounts in the *Big Sky Bank*."

It all seemed like a working situation to her, and she was more than glad to rid herself of Ace Spade, only she wondered ___.

"John, I think it would be better, if I too change my name. Were someone to recognize my name on some banking accounts, they might connect me to you."

"I can't see that happening, but if you wish." He paused, "What would you like to be called?"

She thought a moment and then said, "You pick it. I trust your judgment."

"Let's see, what do you think of Judith Willow?"

"Judith?" she turned up her nose in opposition.

"Yes, it is for the Judith Mountains a few miles north."

"I don't like it," she replied.

"Alright, what is your idea?"

"What do you think of Windy Willow?"

"Windy Willows, would sound better," he offered.

"Yes, I like that," she agreed. "From now on I will be known as Windy Willows, unless you want me to be known as Windy Pell."

"Listen Bea, nothing would make me happier," he lied, "but until I can clear up the trouble that damn Hickey woman has stirred up, it would be better if the folks in Copperopolis think we met on the ride here. Of course Ephraim Glaze must know, but I can keep him under control."

"Does this mean we will not be seeing one another, John?"

"Not at all, but it will have to appear only as new friends in public. In private I will need what you do so well, and often."

She smiled and pulled his arm close. "I think that is what has made my sore throat feel so much better."

"Perhaps," he agreed. "Perchance we should make sure you don't get a relapse."

"I'm with you, Honey," she said and squeezed his arm again.

When the stage pulled into White Sulphur Springs, he got off and sent her on alone.

Arriving in Copperopolis just before the sun hid behind the western mountains, Windy Willows checked into Fannie Sharpshire's boarding house and enjoyed a nice beefsteak along with lots of hot Arbuckles, heavy with fresh cream.

Fanny had baked three peach pies that day for her guests, and this touched off a near perfect meal, after the long 90-mile trip from Helena. Her only regret was she did not have an opportunity to enjoy a stiff rye with her meal. A problem she planned to soon remedy.

The next morning, after a light breakfast at Fannie's table, she headed to the *Big Sky Bank*.

Tuff Kohrs was the banks only clerk. He was a small wimpy sort of fellow that everyone laughed at behind his back, and a few to his face, about being named Tuff. His last name was also a point of debate. Conrad Kohrs was considered by many to be Cattle King in Montana and Tuff claimed to be related, but many doubted this.

When this big-boned lady, who stood some two inches taller than Tuff, asked to see Mr. Glaze, Tuff bit hard on the wooden pencil he had placed in his mouth only moments before she walked in as he was pondering the figures on the yellow tablet before him.

"Mr. Glaze?" he replied looking up at her.

Bea had chosen a bright yellow plaid dress to wear that morning, which sported one of the new bustles that were becoming so popular back east. She had only worn it once before and that was when she bought it on her trip to Saint Louis; the day she met Jean. Today, she would make her first impression on the town of Copperopolis and its business people, and this dress would give them just the impression she wanted.

"Yes, Mr. Glaze," she replied to Tuff before handing him a small envelope. "For Mr. Glaze; and him alone," she added sternly.

"Yes, yes ___, yes Ma'am," he said turning quickly and knocking on the door to the back office.

"What is it Kohrs?"

"A lady sir. A lady to see you."

"A lady?" the gruff voice called back through the closed door. "Which lady, Kohrs?"

"I don't know Mr. Glaze, but she has a letter fer you."

Bea could hear a chair being pushed across the wooden floor and a man clearing his throat.

The door opened partly and a hand extended, but Tuff did not see it. He had turned so he could again look at the tall woman standing at the counter. When nothing was placed in his hand, Glaze said roughly, "The letter Kohrs."

"Oh, yes sir, the letter," the small man said, as he hurriedly handed the paper to his boss.

Bea had waited long enough. She reached over and raised the hinged counter, walking into the clerk's cage, bumping him with her strong hip as she passed by, just before she pushed the door open.

"Mr. Glaze, I'm here to talk business, not to stand out there listening to the yackin' of that square-head[30], you have obviously employed in error."

Ephraim Glaze was himself not a tall man, although he did not have to look up to the stout woman standing before him. He had served under General Dashwell Bayard in the war but only for the first year and that was spent in New Jersey. He had come down with pneumonia that winter and was in the hospital when the regiment moved south. By the time he was healthy enough to be released, his enlistment was up. He chose not to rejoin his company, which by then was in Maryland.

Figures had always come easy to him. Soon he was employed steadily at home, keeping books for several of the more wealthy families, whose men were off to fight in the rebellion. Banking came naturally as well, and by 1864, he was working in the largest bank in Jersey City.

Six years later he was with *The Bank of New York,* and when they branched west he was glad to get the opportunity, first in Chicago and then Saint Paul.

It was in Saint Paul where he heard about the copper strike in the Belt Mountains. Soon he gathered all his assets and left for the newly opened Montana Territory.

Most of the capital in *Big Sky Bank* was his until the arrival of John Pell. He had had many a sleepless night wondering if he had made the right move leaving the security of *The Bank of New York* for his own business, but he held on and prayed. John Pell, he was sure, was God's answer to his prayers.

Ephraim,

The young lady presenting this note to you is a dear friend of mine.

Miss Windy Willows is the one I have been telling you about, who has much experience in the field we both love, money management.

Please introduce her around as the owner and manager of The White Castle Mountain, and establish the three accounts as we discussed before

---

30 Square-head: A late 19th century ethnic slur directed at German and Scandinavian immigrants.

I left.

I think it would be best for our venture if no one else knew she and I were old friends.

Will see you soon, John Pell

Glaze read the letter twice before he spoke, "Miss Willows, please sit down."

She immediately noticed the gruff voice he had used with his employee was nowhere to be found when he spoke to her.

Half an hour later as she left the bank quite satisfied, she walked immediately to the construction site of her saloon. Finding the workers taking a break behind a canvas tarp where they could escape the wind, she walked right up to the circle.

"Shu-Be-Do," Ed Meeks said, when he looked up at the woman who had just invaded their little pow-wow.

"Who's the ramrod of this bunch of goldbricks?" she inquired looking him straight in the eye.

"I reckon I am," a slim, dark-haired man in ragamuffin overalls shot back.

"Then you work for me. And I don't pay good wages to a foreman who hides behind a blanket when there's work to be done."

"Work fer you? Haw!" he said, with a big grin on his face. "I don't work fer no squawking woman."

"You are right. You don't work for me," she said and then paused looking around at the others. "You," she said nodding at Ed. "You are the new boss of this bunch; he just got himself fired."

A strange expression crossed all of their faces. They just couldn't tell if she was for real or not.

"Now, just wait here a minute, these here men are mine. Nobody tells them nothing but me. 'Asides Mr. Glaze hired me, and only he can fire me."

"You need to take that up with Mr. Glaze and do it now; I don't want you around here slowing down my good workers. I have a saloon to run, and I don't want to wait until next spring to start making money in it," she replied with strong conviction.

"Now, what's your name?" she asked the slim man she had just promoted.

"Ed, Ed Meeks."

"Alright, Ed Meeks, get your crew back on those scaffolds, and let's get a roof on this thing."

"Yes, Ma'am," the dark-complexioned man replied.

Gary Boyd stomped off in the direction of *Big Sky Bank* as the others climbed back up to the rafters.

By the time the bull-train pulled into Copperopolis three weeks later, *The White Castle Mountain* was ready to accept her furniture.

Among the freight wagons in that train were two Conestogas, carrying the James family and the newly wed couple of Hank and Marsha Groll.

Otis James, known to all his friends as Blackcat, was from the mountains of North Carolina, and had served in the Army of Northern Virginia, from First Manassas to the end of the conflict in the Old Dominion State.

He was the Sergeant who carried the last Battle Flag of the Old South ten paces behind The General, as his hero rode up to Appomattox Court House. That day he had fought valiantly but unsuccessfully, to ward off the tears. To this day, he had never cried again, even at the burying of his first child back along the trail between the ruins of old Fort Kearney and where Fetterman had been massacred. His wife Ginny had not suffered the same curse.

Marsha Groll's father had moved from South Carolina to the wilds of Alachua County, Florida, just after the third Seminole Indian War had come to a successful end. At first, he settled in Alligator's Town[31] where Marsha was born, but a year later he built a small cypress log home along the banks of the Alapaha[32] River near what was to become Jennings. It was there Marsha grew up, and it was there she first saw the young man from Connecticut, Hank Groll. Although she was only eight years old at the time, she was instantly infatuated with the tall, strange-talking man.

She did not see him again after that summer. Although, when the war broke out, she feared for him above all others, and she often had the same nightmare:

Her brothers, being loyal to their state, had ambushed a column of blue-clad horsemen being led by Captain Henry Groll, and there she saw, time and time again, night after night, the life blood flow from his wounds onto the red clay of North Georgia.

---

31 Alligator's Town: Once the home of the Seminole War Chief Alligator, now Lake City, Florida.

32 Alapaha: Pronounced A-lap-a-haw.

What Marsha did not know and did not find out until ten years after the fighting was over, was that the tall, young man from Connecticut had not been loyal to his state. He was one of the many who did not believe in Mr. Lincoln's war and had enlisted in the Confederate Navy. He was aboard the CSS Alabama when she was sunk off the coast of France in 1864. Ship's Officer Groll, being one of the few who were rescued by the English yacht Deerhound, spent the next ten years in and around the Old Roman City[33].

However, he too had not forgotten the little barefoot girl who had smiled so prettily at him while the older boys and girls swam in the black waters just north of where the Alapaha disappeared into the ground.

She had been standing under the low branches of a big magnolia, and the sweet smell of its blossoms had forever haunted him with her image. She was just too cute to forget. Returning to Florida, he

Hank and Marsha Groll's Wedding Picture

---

33 The Old Roman City: London.

found she had grown into a most beautiful young woman, and in less than a month, they were joined in Holy Matrimony.

Now these two families, the Groll's and the James', were both uprooted from their homes by the tyrannical rule of The Reconstruction Government. They each sought a better future in the promises of the west, and their trails had come together in the river town of Coulson, Montana. The James' via a wagon they had bought in Saint Louis and the Groll's who stepped off *The Sacajawea* on to the dock, on the deep side of the Yellowstone, the same day.

Ginny and her two children, Otie and Ginger, were in *Bettie's Store* in Coulson, when Hank and Marsha came in to get some supplies. Ginny and Marsha became instant friends, and it was this bond that convinced Hank to go on farther north to the new towns along the Musselshell River.

Ginny pointed out to her and she to her husband, "After all, Coulson already has a paper."

Hank was much too much in love with his bride to deny her anything that might work, so with a huge smile, he said, "If that's what you wish, Sweetheart."

It might have been Samuel Coulson's riverboat that had brought the Groll's to this part of Montana, but it was with *The Benton Transportation Company's* wagon train, they would travel north to set up a newspaper office in central Montana. Traveling in tandem, one wagon behind Henry and Marsha were the James'. Their hearts set on trying their hand at ranching on this free land so recently stolen from the Lakota.

Renting a small room in the back of *Coker's Store,* Hank had his printing press set up within a week of their arrival.

He had learned the printing business while living in East Sussex, after the sinking of The Alabama. Hank had studied directly under Thornton Leigh Hunt, the first editor of the British paper, The Daily Telegraph, the only real competition to *The London Times.* When Hunt died in June of 1873 the young newspaperman was devastated over the loss of his mentor.

Hank had saved a small, but strong bank account of English pounds and feeling a twinge of homesickness, booked passage for Charleston and headed back to the States.

Although the journey from Florida to Montana had not been an inexpensive endeavor, it was buying his press and typesettings that had eaten into his stake the greatest. Nonetheless, he knew his first paper would have to be complimentary.

He did have a small ace in the hole. George Saddler, better known as Whisky George, one of the bullwhackers on the Benton train, had

Creek Dividing the James Homestead

taken a fancy to him and Marsha. Thus George had agreed to bring them any papers, or other news, every time he made the trip north.

It was with this plagiarized information Hank reserved a quarter page in every publication of his thereafter. Hank entitled this column: **News From The United States**. This became a big hit with the people of Copperopolis and the surrounding mines.

Blackcat and Ginny located a small creek running through some of the best grazing grassland in the west. It cut off from the Musselshell River and promised to be wet year round.

Blackcat filed on the south side of what they were told was called Yadkin Creek, and his son Otie, filed on the north side across from his father. Both of these homesteads had been recorded before the foreman at *The Little Judith Ranch* knew anything about it.

Upon returning from his trip and learning of this, John Pell screamed in a loud and stern voice, "What!"

"Yes sir, they is there. Done built a soddy and sank a well. They got fences up fer a small plowed area that looks to be a vegetable garden," York replied.

"You let squatters on my range?" John screamed again.

"Well now Jean I didn't let them, they done filed with the land office over to White Sulphur Springs. What could I do?"

"You can get them off. That's what you can do."

"You know they got the law on their side."

"Here, I am the law, and if you ever call me Jean again I will cut your stupid liver out and feed it to that stupid dog of yours."

"Sorry, John."

"Get out of here, and get it done."

York had not seen him so angry since they were in Colorado, and he wanted to be well away until John calmed down.

York immediately headed to the Foreman's Room, a partitioned off section at the end of the bunkhouse, to get his gear. As he passed the corral, he shouted towards the group of men there watching a cowboy bucking out a bronc, "Loco."

The short, dark-skinned man under the Mexican sombrero looked up. When he saw York wave his big arm beckoning him, he spit and said, "Crap!"

Walking into his boss' room, he pushed his big hat back on his head where his wrinkled forehead was fully exposed. "You need me, Señor Boss?"

"Yeah, get five or six of the boys and get saddled up," York said, as he reached for his new 45-75 Winchester. "And Loco, choose the boys we brought up, not the new ones."

"Si Boss," the short man said.

Just as he was walking out the door, he heard York add, "And tell them to bring their rifles."

"Si Señor Boss," again he replied and waved a quick salute at the foreman, knowing York would not see his gesture.

Two Bucks had watched with interest, the building of the ranch that used the Lazy R-J brand and pondered what he would do with it. Lobo wanted to raid it right off, but he had stopped him. *'A ranch this size will bring many beeves, and beeves are just dinero on the hoof.'*

They stole a few head for food, and a few more they drove north and sold to a comrade who worked the Fort Benton area. On their return from Benton, they swung wide and came upon, quite by accident, the new family building on the river.

The old bandit suddenly realized what Tidwell had; it was only the beginning. *'Now, I am not so sure I had been right in stopping Lobo,'* he thought.

The following morning, Two Bucks and four of his men were watching from a distant hill, as York and his bunch headed west from the cluster of buildings that made up the plaza of *The Little Judith Ranch.*

The breed studied them for several minutes as the small group moved closer to where they waited, and finally he decided what he would do. When the Lazy R-J bunch neared the hill he and his observers were hidden behind, the raiding party turned straight west, moving down the old Indian trail which led to the Musselshell River.

The tip that led the trio to Virginia City had played out, and Reb Brown decided to go back to *The Stillwater Station.* It was there the last real piece of good evidence had ended.

'Perhaps there we can pick up the cold trail John Tidwell left,' then he added to his thought, *'or Jean Mouton, or J.D. Mather, or John Brown, or whatever the bastard is calling himself these days.'*

Black Band had cut the trail of unshod ponies earlier that day and pointed them out to Cliff. He held up his hand extending all of his fingers as he spoke, "They follow many whiteman."

"A war party?"

Black Band nodded his head at the same time he raised his shoulders indicating a maybe answer.

Cliff thought about it a while. *'One of Horace Countryman's hands mentioned he had seen a man meeting Tidwell's description at Stillwell last year and remembered he had spoken a little French to one of the Canadian wranglers who had been working there at the time. Also that part-time teamster, Red something, he said a fellow that was suppose to be on the stage with the butchered fat woman went to the Quinn Ranch, wherever that is. Only he was sure he wasn't a Frenchman. I wonder.'*

Neither was much of a lead, but Cliff Brown had long past learned it was often the small tidbits that would make a determined tracker successful, and he was short on big leads at the moment. Now, he had to make a decision: Continue on to White Sulphur Springs after Tidwell or follow this war party and make sure they were not up to another atrocity like he had found at *Walker's Stage Station* last year.

At that moment Black Band added, "Bandits, maybe."

That was enough to make the decision for him. *'Tidwell's trail will not be any colder tomorrow than it is today, and just maybe we can stop another massacre.'*

That night while the Lazy R-J men camped along the bank of the Musselshell, Two Bucks and his bunch watched from a cold camp a mile away.

"We can take 'em while they catch a leetle siesta," Lobo said as he waited for Two Bucks to give the order. "It will be simple. The stupid gringos are all bedded down around their fire, so cozy."

Two Bucks was not so sure. There was a bug buzzing around in his head. He wondered where the white cowboys were going, *'Me'bee they would cut south the next day and head into the town. Me'bee they would be a better prize on the way back to their ranch than on the trail away from the ranch.'* He thought long on this, much to Lobo's aggravation and finally he spoke, "No, not tonight."

Lobo lifted his arms in the air and turned his head looking up at the bright stars above. *'I will never savvy Two Bucks, of this I am sure.'*

Black Band returned to where Reb and Laramie were waiting in their own cold camp.

"The men we follow are bandits. They speak the tongue of the Mexicans. They wait. I think they attack at dawn. They will come from the hill from where the sun comes. It will make them invisible to the ones who sleep at the fire."

"Who is it they plan to attack?"

"Whiteman. Many riders make camp there, three miles."

"Cowboys?"

The Indian only nodded his head in reply.

Cliff thought long on this and then asked, "Can we be in a position to cut into them when they attack the cowboys?"

The old Crow nodded his head, and then made sign showing it will be a long distance away, before he spoke, "It can be done."

"Let's move there now and be ready, just in case they make their move before sunup."

The Indian nodded his head and then reached for a piece of salted pork belly that they had smoked two days before.

The next morning they observed as Two Bucks and his four slipped up to the hill and watched the Lazy R-J crew break camp.

Cliff was reluctant to use his field glasses for fear of the rising sun reflecting off the lens, but he did want to get a better look at both parties. Finally, using his big hat as a shield to shade the glasses, he focused on the bunch nearest him.

'No question, they are not Indians, at least not pure Indians,' he was convinced. He also was pretty sure the small one wearing a sombrero and a silver-studded gunbelt was the leader. 'At least he seems to be giving the orders.'

Then he turned the glasses to the cowboys, and he noticed each loading their rifles and checking their revolvers before they mounted. Cliff narrowed his eyes as he observed this. Turning his head to his companions, he said just above a whisper, not really speaking to his friends as much as to himself, "They are getting ready to hit someone themselves."

"Maybe they seen the others," Laramie offered.

"No. I don't think so. They seem to be powerful keen in something ahead."

"What are we going to do?" the kid asked.

"Wait," was Cliff's only answer.

The night before, Ginny had mentioned they were low on meat and needed to go into town, but Blackcat said they just couldn't go right now. "The corral is almost finished, and I need to have it ready before we go. I want to buy a few riding horses from which to work the steers."

Otie James had left before sunup to try and find some game for his mother. He took the Government Issue Springfield carbine that his dad had traded a drunken soldier out of, back at Hays, Kansas, on their way west.

Otis had long before bought a Henry repeater to protect his family, but the Henry round was too under-powered for game of any size, and the big 45 Government was just the ticket for that chore. He wisely reasoned he would need it far more than the jug a' shine he traded for it. This day would prove he made a good trade.

The old dry doe was walking slowly off the rim of the ridge, headed for the creek below, where Otie waited. She was reducing the distance between them, and that meant she was reducing the distance he would have to haul her. Ever so slowly, she moved closer to the water she needed; still she had not lived this many years being reckless.

Otie cocked the big hammer on the rifle and brought it up to his shoulder. Taking a fine bead on her neck, he slowly began to squeeze the trigger. He thought about his father teaching him how to squeeze a trigger rather than jerk it. He knew he was a good hunter and knew he owed it all to his father. In fact, he knew he owed just about everything he had, or was, to his father, and for just a moment he felt small.

Suddenly his thoughts were interrupted when the doe jerked up her head and looked back towards his house. He started to shoot, but he waited, wondering what she had heard.

Then he heard it too, or at least he thought he had heard something. Veering his head slightly, he glanced eastward.

A soft thud came from off in the distance. "What was that?" he asked himself as he frowned and turned his head and looked fully in the direction the muley was gazing. This movement did not go unnoticed by the deer, who immediately bolted off. The young man in blue coveralls over red johns didn't even see her go, his attention was instead on the strange popping sounds over the hill.

It suddenly hit him like a bolt of lighting. "Them is gunshots!" he said aloud. Immediately he began running back in the direction he had come.

Cliff watched the bandits, who were watching the cowboys shoot at the small soddy, some one hundred yards from their cover.

Most of the reports were light, and Cliff could distinguish between the different rifles. He was sure the man in the house was shooting a Henry or a Yellowboy. He had heard the sound of that little round too many times from both ends of a rifle. He also knew one of the cowboys was using a much larger gun, and from the speed between the shots, he was sure it was a repeater.

The little firefight had been raging for five minutes or more when he saw two of the men move from their cover and run across the creek in a maneuver to flank the house.

Cliff guessed there was no back door and possibly no windows on the south side of the house. It would be a simple matter for these two to reach it from where they were headed, and from there he expected them to fire the house.

'That just don't seem fair,' he thought, and he started to slowly rise, then suddenly he dropped back to the ground. One of the flankers had suddenly thrown both his hands up, and his rifle flew high in the air before he fell backwards. His buddy stopped and took a moment to look at his dead pard before he raised his rifle and fired at the gunsmoke ahead, but he had waited too long.

'*Whoever is in front of these cowboys is firing a heavy rifle of his own.*'

Otie had lost sight of his target for a second while reloading the trap-door carbine, but when the cowboy fired his carbine, the blue smoke gave away his position, and the boy sent a 405 grain hunk of lead true on its course.

Had they been closer, he might never have gotten off his second shot. The cowboy had a good bead on the shooter, but his Winchester just didn't have the power to cover the three hundred yards to where the boy stood clearly visible, out in the open.

Two Bucks did not fail to see the new shooter either, and decided it was not a good fight to become involved in. He motioned for Lobo and the others to move back, and Cliff watched them mount and head north.

Otie ran forward, right past the two dead men, towards his home and family.

'*He should 'a stayed where he was,*' Cliff thought as he watched the man run around to the back of the house, where he disappeared.

Cliff realized the man suddenly was no longer there and he concluded, '*There must be a backdoor after all or mee'be a root cellar.*'

"Come on let's move in closer," he said to his two companions. "That fellow just tossed in the best card those folks had."

Black Band nodded his head. He knew from the start this man Reb Brown, who he had followed for so long, would not stay out of a fight where bad men were hurting small people. It was not his way. '*A good way to be,*' the old warrior thought.

They watched as the cowboys moved forward. Slowly at first, and then when there was suddenly no more return fire from the soddy, they rapidly advanced to the creek where several large cottonwoods were standing among other smaller growth. Young willow trees and other brush that clung to life along the bank where moisture was most prevalent, offered little protection from a 44 slug. However, they did hide a man safely enough for him to fire a shot, before returning in a quick roll to hide behind the thick trunk of a cottonwood.

Ginny was overjoyed at the sight of her son's head appearing from the trapdoor at the rear of their cabin. It was the only wooden part of this otherwise dirt floor. Blackcat had seen to it they would have a means of escape should they ever need it.

He had just fired his last round at a man on the ridge across the creek. He knew it would be a lucky shot to hit anyone at that distance, but he figured he perhaps could keep them as far away as possible, even if he didn't hit anyone. He was reloading the tube of his rifle when his son appeared.

"Where you been, boy?"

"I went out 'fore sunup to try and get Ma some meat."

His father looked away and nodded his head, remembering their conversation from the night before.

"I was about to take me a big doe when the shooting started. I was well hidden and just squeezing the trigger on 'er when I heard it."

"Glad to see you boy, but you should have stayed hidden," he said giving his head one quick nod.

"I had to come and help, Pa."

Otis understood the boy's feelings and was sure had he been in the same place he too would have come back. "Well, come on over here and give them a round of that 45 Government. That ought to dampen the spirits a' 'em red devils."

Just as Otie moved forward towards the front of the little room, his sister Ginger jumped up and ran towards her mother. It was at that moment, a 44 Winchester bullet managed to find the small slit Otis had been firing through, and entered the interior of the cabin to strike her in the left rib cage. She simply let out a small cry, fell to the dirt floor and moved no more. Ginny screamed at the sight of her daughter falling, and Otis and his son turned and looked in horror.

During this lull in firing, Cliff sent Black Band around the hill to where he could cut off any more cowboys who might try to fire the soddy from the rear. At the same time, he and Laramie moved forward to where the attackers had been only a short time before. It was there they came upon Mesquite holding the horses.

A quick shot from his Yellowboy and Cliff was satisfied this one would be of no further distraction. He was just about to tell the kid to scatter the horses when he heard the muffled, but unmistakable, sound of a woman's scream. He stopped a moment and listened but heard nothing more. He then motioned Laramie to follow him to the top of the ridge, where they could see what was happening ahead.

York didn't understand why Curley Joe and Prescott had not gotten the fire going. "What the hell are they doing?" he cussed just above a whisper.

"Me'bee 'dey go to town," Loco suggested and then laughed at the frustration showing on his foreman's face.

"My ass," York responded, as he removed his hat to wipe the sweat from his forehead.

"Me'bee they are daid," Loco then said.

"They had better be," York shot back. Then he wondered, *'Dead, what would have killed them? That nester doesn't have any horses, and both of his mules are in the rope corral there. Everybody's in that make-shift house.'*

"No more shots come," Loco pointed out and nodded his head towards the soddy before he added, "from inside."

"Come on, let's pour it to them and rush the place. He's either shot or empty a' shells."

York and his five remaining men suddenly began firing with a vengeance. He told them to concentrate on the two small openings in the otherwise solid wall of grass and mud, which composed the front of the soddy. Then he stood and beckoned the others forward, as he rushed towards the house.

It was at that moment Cliff and Laramie opened up. Although they were experiencing the same distance disadvantage York and his bunch had had a short time before, one of his first rounds did strike Hatchet Jac in the back of his thigh. Immediately he went down, yelling in pain. Surprised, they all stopped and looked around.

The tell-tale smoke of gunfire was on the hill behind them, and lead was hitting the hard sandy soil all around them. Before York could think clearly about his situation, he saw Billy Scarborough fly backwards, as if he had been hit by a steam engine. A red mist of blood and lung tissue showered over Gila's face, who had been behind him. A split second later, the roar of Otie's military carbine burst into the affray, sending a sickening signal to the cowboy boss.

"She'et," the half-breed Mexican screamed, and before York could say anything, his men were headed for cover. A second later, one of Cliff's 44 Henry rounds took York's new Stetson off his head. That was all he needed, and he too, followed his fleeing men to the cover of the creek bank. From there they ran, crouched over, away from the soddy until they could no longer keep up the pace.

York breathed heavily as his lungs cried for more oxygen; he fell back against the yellow bank and considered the situation. *'I have a man with a bad wound in his leg. Billy is dead fer sure and no telling what happened to Curley Joe and Prescott. Our boots is soaked mostly through, and we are low on ammunition.'*

Loco broke his line of thought once again when he said, "Dem bad fightin' Som'Bitches, Boss."

"Must ta' been ten or more behind us," York said shaking his head.

Catching their breath, the men continued for several hundred yards before stopping again.

"Why didn't Mesquite warn us?" he finally said, after looking quickly in the direction of where they left their horses.

"I t'ink' he's daid," Loco suggested, then nodding his head he added, "Me'bee."

"Well, we need them horses," York yelled. Then pointing with his rifle he added, "Let's go see. And then get out of here." Pausing and taking a deep breath before he added, just as he again began to trot up the grade, "And I got 'a tell Jean about this."

Loco squinted his eyes and half-cocked his head as he repeated quietly, "Jean?"

By the time the Lazy R-J bunch reached their horses and got the wounded Hatchet Jac mounted, Black Band was bringing their own horses to the cabin.

York eased over to the ridge and took one last look before he returned and rode away with the others. *'There is only a handful down there. Shit, I can't let Pell find that out.'*

"We sure are mighty obliged to you fellows," the rancher said stretching forth his hand to Cliff. "I'm called Blackcat James, and this here is my son Otie."

"I'm called Reb Brown, the kid here goes by Laramie, and my friend here is Black Band."

Blackcat looked hard at the Indian before he offered his hand also to the redman.

"Obliged," he said.

"Are ya'll alright?" Cliff asked looking at the cabin door.

"No. No we aren't. They shot my daughter."

"How bad is she?" Cliff asked looking into the darkness of the soddy's interior.

"I don't know. We wus so busy there at the last but bad I think," her father answered as he started for the cabin.

Two hours later, they had buried the teenage girl on the small hill behind the cabin.

"Dust to dust. Ashes to ashes. The Lord giveth, and the Lord taketh away. Blessed be the name of the Lord," Otis James said, enduring his grief.

The small group stood there for long minutes with no one speaking. Finally Otie broke the silence, "Pa, I killed two a' them up yonder, reckon we should bury them too?"

"No. Not here, not with my baby," Ginny said strongly.

"We'll take care of them," Cliff said, returning his hat to his head.

An hour later, he and Laramie returned, carrying the gun belts and rifles of the dead men. "Here boy," he said to Otie. "I learned a long time ago never leave a dead man's valuables to the elements. You killed 'em, you earned these."

The young James looked at the plunder, and at first, his stomach began to squirm, but then he turned to his Pa, and seeing him nod his head, Otie reached for one of the rifles they had brought down from the hill.

"Who were they?" Blackcat asked, not really directing his question to anyone in particular.

"Doe no," Cliff replied. "Nothing on them two, to tell much," he replied digging his boot toe into the pale yellow soil. "Cowboys fer sure. I noticed a Bar brand when we took their horse wrangler, but things were happening so fast then, I really didn't get a good look see." Pointing to the steep ridge across the creek he added, "Black Band is up there now looking to see if they left any of their mounts when they ski-daddled out a' here."

Cliff walked back to the front of the soddy, where York's new Boss of The Plains still lay. Picking it up, he looked inside and then twisted it around until he came to the hole in the brim where his bullet had passed through, and there he stuck his finger. "Mighty lucky fellow," he said and then tossed the hat to Laramie. The kid tried on the beaver, but it was too big for him, and he just laughed when it fell over his ears.

When the Indian returned, he told Cliff, partly in speech and partly by sign, what he had found.

"Does he know who they were?" Blackcat asked.

"No. The one I shot yonder who was with the horses," Cliff said pointing in the direction of the far hill, "must have not been dead, least ways they took him with them."

Cliff then looked at the spent brass shell the redman handed him. "45-75. Someone's got a Centennial Winchester. This may be a lead."

"But why did they attack us?" Otie asked, almost as a plea, searching for an answer.

"My guess is, somebody don't want the competition," Cliff replied.

"We ain't gon'a hurt nobody, we just got 320 acres," the boy said fighting back tears.

"I'd bet there is some big outfit that sees you as a seed. If he lets you grow here, others will come too."

"But this is our land. We filed on it, paid our filing fees, legal. It belongs to us," Blackcat protested.

"That ain't the point, Mr. James," Cliff said back, as he looked out over the vast rolling plains before him.

"Well, just what is the point then?"

"Greed, Mr. James," he replied, just before he spit on the earth. "Greed, pure and simple."

"Tomorrow we must go into Copperopolis and see Marshal Traven," Blackcat said as he shook his head, still disbelieving what had befallen his family that day.

"You let a dirt farmer kill three of my men and shoot up two more!" the man slapped his beaded gauntlets across the back of a wooden chair. "A damn squatter run off my men," John Pell screamed, loud enough the hands outside of the newly built house heard him.

York tried to inject a reason for his failure, "Listen John, it weren't no dirt farmer that done this, it wus ten or more well-armed men."

"Ten armed men. Where the hell would a dirt farmer get ten well-armed men?"

John Pell moved over behind his desk and picked up a small, dark, tightly-wrapped tobacco stick and placed it unlit between his teeth. "It's beginning to look like I have sent for the wrong man to do my work."

"There's one more thing you need to know," York said, hoping this would relieve some of the attention from him.

"And what now?"

"I went back and watched them a spell before we pulled out. One a' them was riding a big Appaloosa, looked mighty like the one that fellow back in Colorado rode."

"Reb Brown here? Get out of my sight York, before I lose my temper."

When his man had left the room, John dropped his unlit cheroot into the horned ashtray and rubbed his chin with his right hand. *'No way, he could not have found me here. No way. I covered my tracks too well.'* Shaking his head he yelled, "Sing Lee!" Then turning towards the kitchen, he yelled again, "Sing Lee, where the hell are you?"

Throughout the remainder of the day York's statement lingered in his mind, sometimes quite consciously and sometimes just on the fringe, where it created trouble in everything he did. That night he slept restlessly, tossing and turning, and twice during the night, he rose to take a cup of brandy.

When the morning broke, he was up before Sing Lee and therefore before coffee, which again set off his day in a bad direction. Sometime near the nine o'clock hour, he decided to go to Copperopolis.

John walked out on the front porch and yelled, "York. York, get up here."

"Shit, he's still in a hissy," the foreman said, as he started across the fifty yards of well-trodden ground between the bunkhouse and the main ranch house.

"York, take all the Wolf Creek men," he paused and added with a sneer in his voice, "that are able to move and Bitterroot." Again, he paused, as if to take time to think clearly before he continued, "Take The Deacon too, and burn out that damn squatter. And York, if you fail this time, don't come back," he said, then turned and walked back inside without waiting for a reply.

"Yes sir," his foreman replied to John Pell's disappearing back, before slapping a new hat against his chaps. The hat was new to his head but not really new; it had been Mesquite's party hat, but he no longer needed it and York did.

Walking back to the bunkhouse he yelled, "Loco, get the men out here I need to talk to them."

When the raiding party arrived at the squatter's ranch, they met with no opposition this day. The James family was in Copperopolis searching out Marshal Traven.

Elon Traven was a tall lean man who had come to Montana five years before, as a scout for the army. He liked the big open country, and when his hitch was up, he stayed. Drifting to the gold fields first, where he became a deputy to Sheriff Ben Hill, but Traven was long on law and short on politics. Before too much time had passed, he and the sheriff realized they would both be better off if Traven moved on. After that, he rode shotgun on the Helena to Fort Ellis Stage, until he heard Copperopolis was in need of a Town Marshal. That would be more to his liking, and he decided to give it a try.

The town fathers had paid $200 for a Marshal's Office to be erected in what had been the alley between *Coker's General Store* and Jack McGinnis' new drug store.

At the same moment in time, as Blackcat James and Reb Brown were telling their story of murder and siege in this office, John Pell was stopping his buggy in front of *Big Sky Bank,* just down the street.

The conversation between Ephraim Glaze and John Pell was less than friendly. Pell demanding Glaze put a stop to the squatters moving into the area, and Glaze replying with equal fierceness he had no power to interfere with the Federal Homestead Act. Neither man giving an inch on their position. Finally, Glaze agreed he would place in effect a policy that the bank would not loan money to anyone who owned less than a thousand acres. Pell was not satisfied but realized Glaze was doing all he could without bringing down Federal Officials on them. Glaze was just glad to get John Pell out of his office.

The conversation taking place in the Marshal's Office was not going much better. James had come to town seeking help from the law, and the only lawman anywhere around was saying this all happened outside his jurisdiction.

Both parties stepped out of the buildings they had spent the last half hour in, spilling their frustration at the same time. John Pell stomped down the steps of the bank and into his buggy; Blackcat James and Reb Brown stepped from the Marshal's Office and onto the boardwalk.

Brown and James turned and walked into Coker's Store just as the black buggy of John Pell passed enroute to Sally Mustang's saloon.

Noel Coker was one of the early proprietors of the town, and business had been so good, he had already enlarged his building. He carried most everything a miner would want and was expanding his inventory of goods for the cowboys that seemed to be ever increasing in the area. Noel had even started a line of dry goods for the few women who lived in Copperopolis.

That very morning when the bull train arrived from Coulson, the Ezzard family was among the wagons. Micajah Ezzard was a tinsmith and a good one. He had worked in Denver, back when the Cherry Creek mines were in their glory and had built quite a reputation for himself.

A couple of months before, the 24 permanent residents of Copperopolis decided it was time to hire a town marshal. They realized only a town council could do that, thus one was formed. Ephraim Glaze as mayor, and as the town councilmen they selected Rufus Orr, his brother-in-law Gentry Beck, the newly arrived newspaperman Hank Groll, and Noel Coker. It was Noel who pointed the town's need for a good tinsmith and suggested they send for Ezzard.

Blackcat and Reb walked in just as Micajah Ezzard was introducing his family to Coker. "This is my son Kyle, and my daughters Alida and Alvah," he said, tapping his hands on the heads of the twin, blonde, ten-year-old girls. He then turned to a woman, who was admiring a roll of new cotton material that had only arrived the week before and was already a third gone, "and my wife, Jewell."

Cliff noticed standing behind the others was a woman in her late twenties, perhaps early thirties. She was shorter than the other woman, but her corn-silk hair convinced him she was related to the twins.

"Micajah," Mrs. Ezzard interrupted her husband, "don't forget our oldest."

The thin man turned seeing the girl behind him, he smiled. Then placing his arm around her, he shook his head, "I will never forget my Darlin'." Turning back to the storekeeper, he added, "And this is my beautiful daughter, Cimarron."

"Purdy gurl," Cliff said, just above a whisper to Blackcat.

"Ooh yes," was his friend's reply.

Cimarron was wearing a gingham shirt tucked into a pair of men's pants. Her well-shaped hips were obvious under the denim trousers.

"She don't look bad from the back either," Blackcat added.

Cliff cleared his throat and said, "I hadn't noticed."

Blackcat just rolled his eyes at that statement.

"Well now, Miss Ezzard, it is a real pleasure to welcome such a lovely lady to our little outpost of a town," Noel said to the young lady.

"Thank you sir, but I am not Miss Ezzard."

Her mother stepped forward quickly and offered, "Our dear Cimarron's husband is a miner, who went to the gold fields near the Deadwood camp several months back, and we fear he has come to some unfortunate fate."

"Oh, I'm sorry to hear such news," Coker said, looking back at the blonde girl.

She didn't reply, rather turning and looking off, as if she was trying to remove herself from the conversation.

Small talk continued between the store-keep and Mr. and Mrs. Ezzard for a couple more minutes until finally Blackcat walked up to the counter and said, "Don't mean to interrupt, but could I get some cartridges?"

"Oh, course," Coker replied, and then turning back to his new friends he said, "Please excuse me. You know business is business."

"Oh sure, you go right ahead, we'll just be looking around," Jewel Ezzard replied before directing her son away from the large jars of striped candy.

Walking over to where the two men were now standing, he asked, "Now___. Oh Mr. James, it's you. I didn't recognize you. What can I get for you?"

"A couple a' boxes of Henry's," Blackcat replied.

"44 Henry's. Yes, here we are," the skinny man said, as he reached for the beige cardboard boxes. "Getting low on these," he added, seeing there was only one box left.

"Better get some more. I think you will be having a call for them soon," Blackcat said and then added, "Hell, give me that last one too."

"Sure thing," the man behind the new wooden counter said, as he reached back and retrieved the last box.

Cliff laid the spent shell on the counter and asked, "You got any of these?"

Coker picked up the shell and looked at the rim. "45-75 Winchester. Yes, I do," he replied, and turning back he picked up a box of UMC[34] cartridges marked Centennial Winchester, across the front. "Mr. York always wants us to keep them in stock."

---

34 UMC: On August 9, 1867, the Union Metallic Cartridge Company was incorporated.

"York?" Cliff replied in a questioning expression.

"Yes, Mr. York. The foreman of *The Little Judith Ranch*."

"I'm new in these parts," Cliff said back. "You don't reckon they'd be hiring?"

"Now, I wouldn't know that," Coker said waiting for the tall man to pay for the 45-75's.

"No. I reckon that wouldn't be in your line, but if you would help me."

"What can I do?"

"Where is this outfit anyway?" Cliff asked.

"Why, it's the biggest cattle enterprise this side of the Rockies," Coker said back giving a little chuckle at the man's question.

"I still don't know where it is."

"It's to the northeast. Up on the Musselshell."

"And you say this York, he has a 45-75?"

"Yes, he's the only one I know of that does, except now, you."

"How much we owe?" Cliff's partner asked.

"That'll be, let's see, three boxes of 44 Henrys, and a box a' Winchester's al' come to ____, three times a dollar forty-five, and another dollar twenty ____, is five dollars and ten cents, and a nickel tax comes to five-fifteen."

"A nickel tax?" Blackcat questioned.

"Yes sir, a penny on the dollar for the town treasurer."

"Well in that case," Cliff said, "just forget the 45-75's, I ain't paying no town tax on cartridges."

"Oh," the man looked at his customer, being both surprised and disappointed. "Well, you know we have to pay Marshal Traven's salary with something."

"Traven, you mean the man who can't walk out of town?"

"Yes sir. He is the town's marshal after all."

"Here is the money for the Henry's and four pennies for the town," Blackcat said laying the coins on the counter.

When the two turned and started for the door, Coker called out to them,

"You sure you don't want these Winchester shells?"

Cliff twisted his head and shoulders back so he could look at the beige colored box in the man's hand, shook his head a couple of short strokes and then said, "I'll get some from York." Then as he veered away, his eyes locked with those of the pretty blonde woman, and he touched the brim of his hat before finally turning again towards his new friend. He glanced over at James and then walked out of the store with the shorter man at his side.

"Strange," was the only comment Coker offered as he placed the box of rifle cartridges back on the rough-cut wooden plank, which served as a shelf. "Now Mrs. Ezzard, where were we?"

When John walked through the swinging doors of *The Musselshell Saloon* his eyes took a second or two to adjust to the darker environment of the log structure.

It had only been during the last year he had become aware his eyes were not as sharp as they had once been. Of course, when he thought about it, he realized he was no longer a young man, no longer a middle-aged man for that matter, but he still did not feel old.

It seemed impossible so many years had passed since he had fled New York, ahead of a hangman's noose, so many years, so many miles, so many places, so many women. It was these thoughts that ran at high speed through his mind as he stood there waiting for his pupils to adjust to the semi-darkness.

'Yes, so many women, and yet only two had ever meant anything to me, really.' One who had died in his youth, and this one now who was gradually appearing ahead of him behind the rough bar.

Brigitte was not a tall woman, perhaps a half a foot shorter than him, perhaps more. Her hair was black as a crow's wing and when the sun shown on it, it would shine with a silvery glitter. Her quadroon[35] skin tanned well in the hot Montana sun, almost to the color of the redman, who all too often made his presence known to the new invaders of his land. Her figure was almost perfect, and he never failed to feel a stirring in his loins when he saw her.

Her face however, was what he lusted after most. "A face an angel could envy," he had said once to himself. Now as she slowly came into focus he was convinced he had been right in his statement.

There were three other men in the room, two leaning on the bar trying to carry on a conversation with the woman and an aged Mexican, who she had hired to strum slow tunes on an old, well-worn guitar.

He motioned with his head for her to come over to the table where he was headed. When she reached below the bar and retrieved a bottle of the bourbon he had imported from the states

---

35 Quadroon: A person who is one quarter Negro.

for them to relish when he was in town, one of the miners spoke up, "Hey Sally, how come you don't reach down there and get us some good whiskey from time to time? Hell, ain't our money good enough to get the stuff you hide down there?"

"She done snatched that bottle from her snatch, Frog. She didn't have it hid behind the bar."

"You think so, Shotgun?" his friend replied and snickered as the two turned and watched her move toward the table.

"If it did come from that snatch, I bet it shore smells good."

John started to rise from the chair he had just sat in. In doing so, his right hand moved quickly and smoothly to the five-inch Arkansas Toothpick he sometimes carried in his right boot, a movement that she did not fail to see.

"No Jean," she said, placing her hand on his forearm. "They don't mean nothing. Just whiskey-talk."

"I don't like it," he shot back, but he knew she was right, and he was a little irritated at himself for letting such a small thing get to him.

"I know, but its part of the business."

He just nodded his head and lowered himself back into the chair.

"You look troubled my Jean. Is there something wrong?" she asked as she slowly rubbed the back of his head with her open palm.

"Oh, just nesters trying to move in on my land, and the damn government is helping them."

"Hey Shotgun, will you look at that? Sally done up and left our company and is now rubbing that old man, like he was some fine thoroughbred or som'ping."

"Yeah. Hey Sally, you need me to fetch a curry comb fer you to use on him?"

"Get out a' here, you two. You drunk," she spat at them.

"Come on Sally, get me another drink," John Fleetwood, known to his buddies as Dancing Frog, said as he beckoned her with a wide swing of his arm.

"No. You leave now," she said and spat in their direction.

"Ah come on, Frog. This is a low-down place anyway," the thin man said.

"Yeah, but Shotgun, it's the only saloon in this here burg."

"Fer now, just fer now Frog. There's another one in the making just down the street and then see where we'll spend our dineros, Sally."

"Let's go in the back," Jean said to her.

She didn't like closing in the daytime, but he looked like he needed her right then, and after all, the Musselshell was his saloon.

She got up and following the miners, closed and bolted the door behind them. She then took a deep breath before she turned, "Now what is on my man's mind? A little pussy from Brigitte Non? Oui?"

When she was working in Helena, one of the men who preferred her to the other girls at *Alice's Redlight Saloon* had sent east for a beautiful French gown. It was made of a thin and transparent silk like material with lace about the shoulders. The fabric was just thin enough to reveal the shape and beauty of the body under it. Brigitte knew Jean loved her to wear it, and she now never wore it except when he came to her. It was this she was had on, when she stepped from behind the dressing curtains.

He watched her as she approached. Her beauty caused him to catch his breath, and he felt both strong and weak when he gazed at her slowly walking towards him.

Brigitte's body was as near perfection as he had ever seen. She was not tall, yet taller than many women he had enjoyed. Her skin was tanned to a stunning copper color but not dark or having the slight yellow tint so many of mixed races displayed. Her breasts were not huge, but ample; not melons, nor pears, but a happy medium between the two; much like Dianne Roland's had been, save for the dark areola. In fact, the only portion of her body that revealed her grandmother's blood was this very dark areola that surrounded her erect nipples.

Her waist was small, sporting a flat stomach which gave way to round hips that stirred his blood as it had not been stirred in years. The smell of her womanhood stole his strength. When he was in her room, he was almost helpless to resist her requests.

"What troubles my man?" she asked as he buried his face between her breasts.

"Just nesters, just nesters. Oh how I hate the thought of such undesirable weeds moving into this prime land. My land. They are the sandspurs of the human race. Let them start, and they are notoriously hard to get rid of. They can withstand drought, cutting, and most standard methods of control; however, that doesn't mean you can't get rid of them at all. They are very susceptible to lead poisoning and fire," he said back with bitterness in his voice.

"Man, did you see that blonde?"

"I saw you tipping your hat at her," Blackcat replied.

"I thought she was a boy, with them britches on and all, but when she turned, I seen that boy had the cutest face I've gazed upon in awhile."

"Yeah, she is a looker alright, but it is hard for me to think on such when my little girl has just been murdered."

"Yeah," was all Cliff could think of as a reply. Finally, he said, "Come on. I'll buy you a drink."

"Sure," Blackcat said back. "I could use one right about now."

However, when they reached the Musselshell, they found the door locked.

"Now don't that beat all," Blackcat said. "Closing a saloon in the middle of the afternoon."

Cliff could see movement through the slight cracks in the big door, and he started to beat on it but decided against it. "I reckon a body has the right to close whenever they want," he said.

"Still, just don't seem right," Blackcat offered as they turned away.

When the Lazy R-J outfit arrived on the low ridge which overlooked the James' spread, from the east, no life could be seen. They moved slowly and cautiously down the slope and into the creek bed towards the soddy, stopping near the same place they had during the last raid. After several minutes of watching and listening, York decided it was obvious the place was deserted.

"Come on, let's git on with it," he said to the others.

They ransacked the small house bringing everything of value outside where it was set afire. Then with the five gallons of coal oil they had brought with them, they set the interior of the soddy ablaze. Black smoke caused by the oil fire was soon billowing high and wide in the big, blue Montana sky.

York, satisfied with their labor, motioned the others to mount up. Then as a final gesture against his boss' enemies, he threw a loop over the corral fencepost and tying the lariat around his saddle horn, heeled his mount. The rope tightened and the horse pulled but defiantly the post held. It wasn't until Bitterroot also threw his lariat over the stubborn old cottonwood did the gate post bend and give up its earthly home. Then following the horses, it bounced across the dusty yard.

When The Deacon gave out a cheer, almost all the others followed suit with their yells and ropes, taking down the other posts of the corral. As a final act of destruction, York deliberately led his men through the small vegetable garden Ginny had begun.

The next day when the James family arrived at the burned-out scene that had been their home, Ginny screamed, "Oh God! What will we do now?"before bursting out in sobs.

Blackcat sat silently and gazed at the destruction, but Otie had a totally different reaction. His anger was great, and he could not control it. Jumping from the bed of the topless wagon, he grabbed a fence rail that had been broken to a little over four feet in length, and he began to beat it over and over on the ground.

That night they slept under the wagon and asked The Lord for guidance.

The weakness Jean Mouton displayed the day before, in the arms of Brigitte Daiquiris, was nowhere in sight when John Pell questioned his foreman about the nesters.

"They's done for. They done cleared out a'for we got there, and we burned the soddy and tore down everything else. They is history, Boss."

"You had better hope they are," Pell said, as he looked through the window of his den onto the yard. It pleased him to see several men were finishing the roof on the three-story hayloft there between the house and the bunkhouse.

"Now get that barn finished and a good size corral built. I expect another herd of beeves to arrive in a few days, and we will need a place to bust some mustangs for a decent remuda."

"Sure Boss," York said, backing out of the room, which had been turned into an office and den.

After making sure his foreman was no longer in the house he called out loudly, "Sing Lee."

When the small Chinaman arrived, he stopped just inside the door and lowered his head without saying a word.

"I will be having guests on Saturday. Prepare a table for at least twenty," John said without looking at his servant.

The Chinaman nodded his head and likewise did not look at the other man.

"It's not enough they attack his family and murder his daughter. When he is gone, they come and burn out his home," Cliff said, with obvious displeasure, to the man who was sitting behind his desk.

"I told you before; I'm a Town Marshal, not a Sheriff. It's outside of my jurisdiction. Besides, I have my own problems. Somebody slit two miners' throats a couple nights ago," Traven replied and then raised his eyebrows accenting his next statement, "in the alley right behind this very office."

"Well, I'm glad you have something to do instead of sitting behind that desk all the time," Cliff yelled back at Traven.

"Look, I know you are frustrated, but I can't help you. You need to send to Coulson. There is a U.S. Marshal there; he's the only one that can help until this county elects a Sheriff, and that ain't likely to be soon. Hell, Diamond City was the county seat 'till the gold run dry and now there ain't 60 souls left in the whole of Confederate Gulch. Word is, White Sulphur Springs will get the honor of being county seat permanently, though I think we are the better choice right here."

"Mee'be, Mee'be not, the copper might run out here just like the gold did over there," Cliff offered.

"Never happen," the Marshal replied. "We got 21 mines bored into the southern slop of them Castle Mountains. Copperopolis is here to stay, of that I'm sure."

"Nice to be sure," Cliff said back.

Traven removed his hat revealing an early baldness approaching his young head. "Look Mr. Brown, I wish I could help you," he paused, "and James, but my hands are tied."

"Well, mee'be you are right. I'll see about that U. S. Marshal you mentioned," the tall man said, slapping his hat against his leg before he turned and reached for the door. However, just as he opened it, Cliff looked back and added, "Thanks." Then he disappeared from Traven's sight.

"Shit!" was all Elon found to say when he looked back at the rough-cut desktop in front of him.

Not a second later, the door opened again, and in walked a tall man round 50years of age. "You are Marshal Traven?" the large man said in more of a statement than a question.

"Yes sir. I am."

"I am Micajah Ezzard. I am a tinsmith. I arrived three day ago and plan to erect a shop here in Copperopolis."

"Yes sir. How can I help?"

"Well, last night several cowmen harassed my wife and oldest child. I want something done, right away."

"Come in Mr. Ezzard, and tell me a little more about it," the Marshal said rising from behind his desk and reaching for the other chair that was leaning against the back wall.

"What is there to tell? They come and make vulgar talk to my women. I want them arrested."

"Well, here, sit down sir, and tell me, how do you know they were cowboys?"

"They ride horses and have big lariat ropes, and they say vulgar invitation for my wife and child to come back to their ranch house!" the older man said in a strong and angry voice. "A, a Bar J something ranch."

Immediately Elon knew the ranch he was referring to. There were only three ranches within fifty miles, and *The Little Judith Ranch* used the Lazy R-J brand, besides they were the only one that had hands in town within the last week. Unfortunately, the owner of the Lazy R-J was a close personal friend of the Mayor, and he had already been told to ride a loose rein on them.

Even though it went against his grain, he was about to promise this man he would do something about his complaint, knowing full well there was little that could be done. At that moment, the door opened, and a large woman entered, followed by a shorter boy. Both were light complexioned with blonde hair, even though the woman did show streaks of white here and there in hers. "Here, here are my wife and daughter," Ezzard said. "They will tell you."

'*Daughter?*' Traven thought, looking more closely at the smaller person. When she looked at him and he saw her face, he almost kicked himself for his mistake. '*She is beautiful; only why is she wearing those britches?*' he questioned.

"Ma'am," he said to the older woman, not taking his eyes from her daughter.

"Here Momma, you tell the Sheriff what happened," Micajah said to his wife.

"Marshal," Traven corrected, still looking at the girl.

"Yes, yes you tell the Marshal what they did."

"I surely will," the woman said back in a loud and forceful tone. "These ruffians came upon us as we walked from Mr. McGinnis' drug store, and they grabbed me in a most unpleasant way, and they tried to kiss my daughter. They would have too, had I not had my umbrella to ward off their attack."

Elon could picture a couple of skinny cowboys out on a bender, trying to defend themselves from this large-boned woman who was beating away at their heads with an umbrella. He almost smiled but knowing better, kept his serious poise.

Finally, still looking at the smaller woman he asked, "Did they hurt you Miss Ezzard?"

"Dean," she corrected. "My name is Cimarron Dean."

His expression showed he was balled up. "Dean?"

"Yes, my daughter's married name is Dean."

It was not hard to see the disappointment swiftly sweep across his wind-wrinkled face. Still, he touched the brim of his hat before saying, "Mrs. Dean."

The short blonde woman smiled at him, and he looked at the brightness in her blue eyes and felt a tingle in his chest.

After listening to the complaint of the Ezzards, he watched them cross the dusty street as he rolled a quirley. Elon was fully aware he was headed down a rocky road. Everyone knew John Pell was the Big Bug of the Lazy R-J outfit, and it too was no secret he was a close personal friend of the Mayor. Traven wanted no trouble with Pell or the Mayor, but he too did not want the Ezzard family to think he was not a man one could tie to, especially Mrs. Dean.

'And also, I have to do something about those two dead miners over to Gideon Merewether's,' he thought, still watching the short woman until she disappeared from his sight behind a prairie schooner that was stopped in front of Crouch's place.

A week passed while Cliff and his companions helped the James family rebuild a living structure within a few yards of what was left of their old soddy. They used their wagon and some dry timber they had gathered along the creek bank to start the makings of their new home.

Latched canvas and rawhide kept the sun from burning their skin during the day and kept what warmth could be captured in at night. It was not much, but this land was their home, and they had no intention of being run off. Finally, when he thought Ginny and the boy could make do on their own, Blackcat suggested he head south to Coulson.

"I think you are right, but I don't think you should go it alone. If you are to talk a United States Marshal into riding morn' a hundred miles one way, you might need a witness or two," Cliff suggested.

"Your point is well-taken, but I wus kind a' hoping you would be staying here to watch over Ginny and Otie while I was gone," Blackcat replied, as he looked down to the yellow earth and kicked a small hole in the hard ground with the toe of his boot.

Cliff looked out at the two boys who were walking back from the creek. They were picking up twigs or small stones and throwing them far off in the distance, each trying to out-throw the other. They were neither hay nor grass; no longer boys, mainly because of the tragedies rained upon their young lives but neither were they men. A happy time in one's life, a time Clifford Brown wished he could recapture from his own life, but of course, he knew that was not possible. Nonetheless, he envied the youngsters.

"I will leave Black Band here to watch over them, and Laramie to help Otie with the chores."

"Can the Indian be trusted?" Blackcat asked, almost embarrassed at the question.

Cliff turned and looked into the eyes of the man standing next to him and swallowed before speaking, "I trust him."

Blackcat reached over and picked up a small stone he had unearthed with his diggings and rolled it around in his hand a few seconds, clearing all of the clinging clay away. "Then, I reckon we should get started come first light," he said a moment before he tossed the little pebble far off to his right, just as the boys had been doing.

"First light," Cliff agreed.

That night the boy watched Reb ease up onto the ridge, where the Indian made his bed. He stayed there a long time talking with the old Crow. Laramie had not been invited, and he was a little hurt. Finally, sometime after dark he saw the faint glow that came from the man's quirley when he drew the smoke deep into his lungs, and he knew Reb was returning.

"Laramie," was all he said, as he passed the boy and walked beyond the make-shift James home, into the darkness of the pre-moon night.

The boy followed a short distance behind.

Somewhere off in the distance, the ghostly cry of a lone dog broke the other more common but less noticeable noises that fill the night air. When he approached the spot where his leader had stopped, he took notice the man was looking in the direction of the cry.

Without turning, the man spoke aloud, "He cries for his mate."

Laramie nodded his head in agreement, even though the man could not see him.

"She doesn't answer," Cliff added after a short pause. "Mee'be she is dead, and he misses her deeply."

Even at his tender age, Laramie could read in the man's voice he was speaking more of himself than of the coyote.

Silence remained between them for nearly a full minute; finally he spoke, "Laramie."

"Oui," the boy answered.

"Tomorrow I will be going down to Coulson with Mr. James. I want you to stay here and help Mrs. James."

"But I want to ___."

"There will be plenty of time to learn more about your mother. You are needed here to help protect the woman."

"Black Band?"

"He will stay also but out of sight. I have told him not to come near the homestead. It will be your responsibility to take him food and water every night. Now don't forget, there is no place he can get water up there, and a body can do without food for two or three weeks, but without water in two or three days he will be dead."

Laramie wanted to say he knew that but decided not to, and instead simply replied, "Oui."

He was feeling somewhat proud of his importance but still disappointed he would miss a chance to go back to Coulson where news of his mother might be found. "Me and Otie can carry___,"

"No. Not Otie," Cliff broke in. "Never is Mrs. James to be left alone. Just you will go to him."

This even more emphasized the importance for him to be left behind, and it again made him feel proud the man thought he could be so trusted.

"Oui, I understand."

Cliff turned and placed his arm over the boy's shoulder, and turning him back towards the small campfire near the wagon, which was now beginning to flicker, he added, "I knew I could count on you, son."

The next morning, as the sun rose on their left, the two riders and the lone pack animal that trailed behind them were a sizable distance from the James spread.

Ola kept moving ahead of Julian, and more than once Cliff had to draw back on the reins to keep him beside the mule.

"That stud of yours is sure bustling about this morning," Blackcat said.

"I think he is embarrassed to pair alongside half an ass," Cliff replied, kidding his friend.

"He might be more embarrassed if we get in a long pull, and this half an ass walks off and leaves him gasping for air," Blackcat snapped back.

Julian had been broke to a saddle before he was teamed to Marion. Marion on the other hand, never did take kindly to being ridden, but she pulled hard when asked to do other, much harder, chores. Not that it was impossible to ride her, but she had a mind of her own and saw no need to carry a man around on her back. She often let the rider know of her feeling on the matter. In this case, she showed no ill signs trailing as the pack animal behind the other two.

Ola was larger than the average Appaloosa. He carried the compact hardiness of the breed but stood a full hand higher than most and was overall a bigger animal. In fact, he was almost as tall as the leaner Jack, Blackcat was riding, and each eyed the other as they progressed towards Copperopolis.

The two riders stopped by Traven's office and picked up an introductory note he wrote to Marshal Slade in Coulson. "I met Slade down at Fort Mack a few years back, when I was working along the Big Red." Handing the folded paper to James he added, shaking his prematurely balding head, "I hope this will be of help. I'm not sure if he will recollect me or not."

"Oh, I'm sure he will. I know I will never forget you," Cliff said, in just such a straight tone, the lawman was not sure if he had just been insulted or complimented.

Standing in the open door of his small office, he watched the two mount and ride south leading a molly[36] behind them.

Blackcat didn't like the idea of leaving Ginny and Otie without an animal, should the need to flee come. *'At least the kid Laramie and*

---

36 Molly: A female mule in theory can carry a fetus and is called a Molly. A male which has no opportunity to produce off spring is called a Jack.

the Indian are there, and each are well-mounted. I reckon it's best; we certainly need a pack animal for such a long trip as this.'

Late in the afternoon, just as they were topping a small hummock, Cliff noticed dust to the east. Immediately, they both dismounted and led the animals back a few yards where they would be hidden from view by the rise. Drop reining Ola, Cliff slipped up the acclivity on hands and knees, a moment later his friend was beside him.

Cliff was trying to focus the small field glasses he had taken from his saddlebags on who or what was stirring up the line of dust.

"Can you tell?" James asked.

"Indians," was all Cliff said in reply.

"How many?" This time Blackcat's voice was a little more concerned than a moment before when he hoped they had come on a small herd of buff, and fresh hump steaks would be in order for the evening meal.

Cliff waited for near a minute before answering, turning and returning the little glasses trying to make them give him a better view of the distant riders. "Half a dozen, I reckon mee'be more. Hard to tell. They are a mite far off, and these ain't no ace-high glasses."

They waited a long time while the line of distant riders moved past them towards the north. Finally, Cliff sat up and wiped his brow with the red rag he wore around his neck. He looked back, making sure the animals had not strayed. Satisfied, he turned and gazed one last time to the spot where he had last seen the Indians. "I think we would be ahead to back down and cut a trail west a' here, before we veer back south. I ain't in no mood to dicker some lead with a passel of Indians who consider us as invaders."

"I thought we were rid a' them in these parts," James added as he too sat up.

"Well, I don't know much about them here about's, but we ain't too far from Canada, and Black Band said most of the Sioux that the Yankee Army claims is dead, just high-tailed it up there."

"You tell who they were?"

"Naw, but there weren't no travois in the bunch, so I reckon there ain't no women or children neither. I'd say a hunting party or ___," he paused and wet his lips before finishing his statement, "a raiding party."

That evening they faced the dying sun for at least an hour before stopping in a shallow arroyo. There they made a small fire to boil some coffee and fry a couple strips of salted pork belly. Then they moved on another mile and made a cold camp for the night.

The next morning, not long after starting out, they came across a trail made the day before by many Indians. Cliff could count seven ponies and maybe another. "I sure wish Black Band was here," he said picking up some of the disturbed dirt and rubbing it around in his hands, before tossing it away, and standing.

James watched as the man rubbed the dirt from his hand, on the backside of his trouser leg. "Can you tell what kind they were?"

"Naw. I'm just not good enough," he replied, slapping his hands once more against his legs. Then as a last minute comment, he added, "They ain't Creek[37], I can tell you that."

James smiled at his friend's last comment but offered nothing in reply.

Cliff turned and looked off in the direction they had last seen the Indians, "I don't think these will be back soon, but I just wonder if that was all of them."

"That's good. Good and sobering for such a early morning thought," Blackcat said looking around behind him.

They continued south another ten miles before crossing a dry creek, and soon after, they came upon a well-used wagon road that led east to west.

"I reckon this might be the stage road from Bozeman to Coulson[38]."

"I would say so."

An hour after darkness fell, and just moments before Cliff was about to say they should camp, James called out suddenly, "What's that?"

Cliff looked up and strained his eyes. Definitely, there off to the east was a light. Not a big light, but still it was a light.

"Let's get closer," Cliff suggested.

On they traveled for another hour, losing sight of the light as the road twisted around one little hill after another. However, each time when it became visible again, it seemed to be larger. Finally, as they stopped atop a hill to rest the animals, it came to both of them at almost the same time, but it was James who spoke, "Lights on the prairie means a town ahead."

---

37 Creek: Georgia Indians.

38 **Coulson: Originally the largest town along the Yellowstone. However, when the railroad arrived it came on the other side of the river, and the Northern Pacific started the town of Billings opposite the thriving Coulson. Today Coulson is considered a part of Billings.**

"Yep. I think you're right, Sodbuster," Cliff replied.

"I ain't no sodbuster, I'm a rancher. Small rancher I give ya but no sodbuster."

Cliff smiled back at his friend's defense, fully aware Blackcat could not see his expression in the darkness.

They rode south on what appeared to be the main street, passing *The Bison Hotel,* a two-story affair with a small restaurant downstairs. Blackcat took notice *Whiskey George's Saloon* was next door. "Last time I heard a' him he was a bullwhacker," Blackcat said. Cliff made no comment, as he had never heard of Whiskey George before.

"What day you reckon it is?" The Georgian asked.

"I don't know. September something, I reckon. Why?"

"Just wondering. You know snow comes early this far north," Cliff replied raising his shoulders as recourse to the chilly wind they were facing.

'Coulson is not a large town by the standards of some folks,' Cliff thought as they slow-walked the animals down the dusty street, *'but it is the biggest collection of businesses between Bozeman and Miles City.'*

"There, yonder is a livery," Blackcat said, pointing to the tall log structure ahead at the intersection of a road or street, he couldn't tell which in the darkness of that part of town. However, he could make out *Flynn's Livery,* on the shingle over the closed doors.

The hostler was conked out in the back of the barn, but the noise of them stalling their animals awakened him, and he came out rubbing the sleep from his face. "Where did you come from?"

"Up to Copperopolis."

"Up on the Musselshell?"

"Yeah, there abouts."

"When you come down?"

"Started out yesterdee' morning," Blackcat said back, frowning in the dim light at the strange questions.

"No way," the bent old man replied.

"Why, we shore did," Blackcat shot back having his neck bowed up at his truthfulness being questioned.

"Why do you ask?" Cliff questioned the hostler.

The old man looked queerly at him and then said, "You'll find out." Then he added, "It'll be a dollar-a-day per animal."

"That's a mite high fer mules."

"Including today," the old man then added sternly.

"Come on Reb, we can find another place to board these animals."

"No, you can't," the old man said and snickered a little. "This here is the only'st one this side a' Miles Town."

"Come on, we'll pay when we leave," Cliff said to his friend. Then turning to the hostler he asked, "Where can we get a room and a bite to eat?"

"You can try Bud McAdow's," the old man said. "But if you tell that fool tale there, we won't be worrying about you coming back and paying fer these mounts."

They both looked strangely at him, but since he had offered nothing positive thus far, neither bothered saying more to him.

Perry W. (Bud) McAdow had the first trading post in Coulson, and in less than a year, he had expanded it to include a saloon on the north side with a connecting entrance through the separating wall. They had no trouble finding McAdow's, it was the only building along the dark street where light could be seen, and human noise could be heard rumbling from its bowels and spilling into the street. It was the saloon side that was lighted when the two weary men walked up the three steps to the boardwalk.

Cliff had removed his sheep-lined buckskin coat from his bedroll before leaving Flynn's and was glad he had, as the cold wind funneled itself up the valley between the two rows of buildings.

The outer doors were closed to ford against the wind and when opened, a loud voice complained from the group of men who were gathered around the potbelly stove near the center of the room. Otherwise, there was no recognition of their existence from this gathering.

Before moving further into the building, Cliff stopped and gave the entire room a good onceover. There was a long bar along the north wall and three round tables with chairs scattered about the plank floor. A wide cut in the south wall was barred by a windowless double door.

A lone man sat at the only non-round table along the back wall. One man was behind the bar, leaning his elbows on the rough-hewn timbers that made up the counter. This barkeep was coatless, but the man at the back table was dressed in a long black duster that did a fair job of hiding his body from assessment. Cliff also took notice that the man in the black ulsterette was the only one in the room who looked their way.

The theme of the conversation, which had so captured the minds of those at the round table, was soon revealed when someone yelled, "I tell ya', 'em Injuns aim to kill every Christian body in Montana."

"Not if we get together and massakee' them first."

"Hell fire, Hiram. They done whipped all that's left of the Seventh Calvary," the loudest mouth of the bunch cut into his friend. "And several dozen a' civilians too."

"Women and children too, I 'spect," came another voice.

The strangers approached the bar, near where the man was leaning on his forearms. "Could we get a whiskey?" James asked.

The barkeep looked over at his customers as if terribly irritated at the interruption before he stood and sharply replied with a voice that some would have called sissy, "Rye or shine?"

"Rye," Cliff replied, realizing it would cost more but not trusting the quality of unknown homebrew.

"Glass or bottle?" the squeaky voice asked.

"Two glasses will do," Cliff replied, with his back to the man.

"Be four bits."

Blackcat dropped a fifty-cent coin on the bar and reached for one of the half- filled glasses of dark drink. His friend did not turn back for the other. Cliff's attention was on the man in the duster, a man who had not looked away from them since they arrived at the bar. Their eyes locked, and each could tell the other appeared to be an adversary.

This confrontation was only interrupted by a man coming out of one of the rooms upstairs and yelling to the barkeep, "Oscar, stoke up that stove a little, it's getting cold in here."

Bud McAdow was a large man, not only over six-feet in height, but it looked as if his shoulders were rubbing both the handrail and the wall, as he descended the stairs. His long stringy hair blended into an equally wooly looking beard. It was obvious at one time, the color had changed, as now the red only tinted the otherwise gray hair. The big man crossed the floor, skirting the group who were still deep in conversation about those savage heathens, and stopping only when he was behind the bar.

"You boys are new in town," he said reaching for the bottle, filling Cliff's glass and refilling the one Blackcat had just emptied. "I've told you Oscar, not to cheat paying customers," he said as he poured.

Cliff had turned when the man rounded the end of the bar and now reached for the full glass, "Obliged."

He lifted the drink and took a sniff of the liquid. Satisfied, he swallowed the whiskey in one long gulp.

"We are from Copperopolis," Blackcat replied to the man.

"You just come in?" the big man asked, as if with great interest.

"Just got here, mee'be an hour now."

"And you didn't run into Injuns?"

Cliff looked up at him and frowned. "That surprise you?"

"Well, we've been told the Nez Perce are roaming the whole territory, killing every white they find."

"Huh?" was Cliff's only reply.

"That's what the army has told us," the big man replied.

"Hey, these two claim they just rode through the whole bunch a' Nez Perce killers and never got a scratch," the squeaky voice called out.

A sudden quietness seemed to descend upon the room as his comment was digested by the group. Suddenly the attention of the crowd turned to the strangers standing at the long bar.

"'s that right?" the loudmouth suddenly questioned.

"We came down from Copperopolis. Don't know anything about no Nez Perce," Blackcat said back.

"Well now, ain't that something. We got friends dead over to the back a' Woolly's newspaper office, and the whole of Colonel Sturgis' troops are licking their wounds. Now you two claim you done marched through the very nest of the savages, like Sherman did Georgia."

Immediately the hair on Cliff's neck bristled. He bowed up like a bobcat which had just been treed by a passel of blue-ticks.

"Naw Sur," he shot back, with resurrected bitterness that had suffered itself to be buried for several years. "Not like Sherman in Georgia, we didn't leave no fires behind us burning out the home folks' farms as we passed today. No raped defenseless women. No shot dead children."

His sudden and forceful reaction caused the loudmouth to stop his assault and immediately become as silent as the old brown dog that was lying on the backside of the stove.

"Easy now, Mister," came a voice beside the Georgian.

Cliff turned and looked at the man in the black duster who was now standing beside and slightly behind him. Immediately, his hand moved towards the well-worn walnut grip of his converted Colt. Not as in a rush to draw the weapon from its leather pocket, rather a quick but smooth move that placed his hand nearer, should the need be. Only two noticed his hand move, the man who had caused the reaction and the man who was about to speak to him.

Cliff was madder than a wet hen. First at the comments made by the loudmouth inferring their story was not truthful. Even more so of the casual comment about the terrible carnage the union troops had done to the civilian populous of his home state. However, what angered him the greatest was the black duster had moved to his flank, without him realizing it.

"Have you met Marshal Slade?" McAdow asked Cliff.

Looking at the man who had given him such concern, a load seemed to lift from his shoulders. "No. No I haven't," he said, still with his eyes locked with the lawman.

"Marshal Slade?" Blackcat injected. "You are who we come to see," and shot forth his hand.

Both Cliff and McAdow saw the stress appear in the eyes of the man. Finally, he decided to shake with the stranger and eventually also reached forward with his hand.

"I'm James, Otis James, but my friends call me Blackcat."

"Slade, Jim Slade," the man replied, still looking at Cliff even though he was shaking hands with the other stranger. "I don't have any friends, anymore."

"Oh, I don't know about that; it wus one of your friends that sent us to you," Blackcat replied.

By this time, the crowd had moved from the potbelly nearer to the men who were standing by the bar, and the loudmouth, missing being the center of attention, again began his assault on the new men in town. "Well now, perhaps you can tell us just how you achieved this trip unharmed?"

"We didn't see no Indians at all today," Blackcat replied. "Saw a small bunch yesterdee south of the Musselshell some but not more than half a dozen."

"Half a dozen," he restated loudly. "These here men must have been near blind," and then he laughed loudly, which was contagious with most of the crowd.

"Well, it's the truth," Blackcat said back, himself becoming angered at the man.

"You just rode through a hundred Crow and nigh on a thousand Nez Perce and only seen a half a dozen?"

"You, or maybe them savages, must be near invisible," another said catching on to the loudmouth's steam. This, once again, was followed by a round of laughter from the crowd.

"Listen Mister," Blackcat said, looking straight in the face of the man who had just questioned his statement, "I don't take kindly to being called a liar."

"Then don't come in here telling some wild tale everybody knows can't possibly have no truth in it," the man replied and turned his body to his friends and smiled. When he turned back around, he met the fist of Blackcat James squarely on his nose.

The suddenness of the unexpected blow sent him to the floor with blood flying not only over his face but onto the shirts of others who stood nearby.

There was a moment of silence as the group digested what had just happened, and then a roar erupted condemning the battery.

Slade stepped forward between the locals and the strangers. Even though he was half-a-foot shorter than Cliff, he moved with the determination of a man who knew what he was doing and with the confidence he could get the job done. "Just let's all settle down."

"Why, he had no cause to bust my nose," Lucas Warren shot back, though his words were muffled by the neckerchief he was tightly holding to his nose.

"Best you shet' up Lucas. Had you been questioning my honesty like you did him, I'd a pistol whipped ya," the Marshal replied looking at the injured man, eye to eye.

With the intrusion of the Marshal, the strength of the argument seemed to lose heart, and the others turned and moved away leaving only the man with the bloody nose and the loudmouth. After a few moments of realizing they had lost their audience, they too finally turned and walked over to a table, carrying a bottle of clear liquid with them.

Jim Slade watched the two for half a minute and then looked over at the gun hand of the taller man beside him.

Cliff saw the direction of his stare, and let his right hand drop from where he had been keeping it, close by his Colt.

Slade nodded his head slightly as a gesture of thanks and then without further comment on that subject asked, "You said you were sent here by a friend of mine?"

"Right friendly town you have here, Marshal," Cliff replied as he reached into the upper pocket of his vest where he had Traven's note.

"Oh, they are a good lot, for the most part. Whiskey and this Indian business has everybody on edge."

Blackcat looked around at the other men who were now in small bunches talking among their own group. "What about this Indian business. I never heard of no Nez Perce before."

"That's cause they have not been troublemakers before. Come from over in Oregon Territory where the Army got 'em stirred up and run 'em out of their homelands. The way I got it figured they planned to link up with their friends the Crow, but the Crow was already allied with the Army, and they too turned on 'em. Pretty big fight occurred north a' here, the day before yesterday. A dozen or more soldiers got shot up pretty bad, and three or four civilians were killed. However, it were the Crows that took most a' the causalities though, from what I hear. Anyways, they are moving north, to Canada I reckon," he replied as he opened the letter.

After reading it, he removed his round specs and replaced them in his vest. "I recollect Traven. He were a good hand, stubborn as a mule, even when he knew he was wrong, but I liked him. Honest man, one a fellow felt he could ride the river with. Glad to see he's behind the badge."

"We would like to talk to you about our problem if you have time," Blackcat said.

The man took a deep breath and let it out before he replied, "Yeah, sure, come on over to my office, and I'll boil some java."

They followed the shorter man out into the windy street and up the boardwalk. Passing three other closed businesses, they came to a one-window, one door cut, in the otherwise continuous flow of bat and board structures, which lined the north side of Main Street. There was no shingle or other sign to show a stranger this was a Lawman's office, but it was here Slade stopped and opened the door.

A coal oil lantern hung just inside, and with a sharp rub on his canvas trousers, Slade struck a Lucifer and was lighting the wick in what seemed like a single motion.

The one-room office consisted of a desk, one chair, a bunk and the stove. On the stove was an old Birdseye porcelain pot, which had a fair size round chip marring its finish.

After stirring around in the embers until a deep glow appeared, he dropped in a rolled up piece of paper, followed immediately by a splintered piece of cottonwood. "Shouldn't take long, it were hot when I left an hour ago," their host said before turning and dusting off his hands. "Now, what is it I can do for you fellows?"

Blackcat explained the occurrences that had brought about their coming to see him. He finished with, "We wus a hoping you would come up and give us a hand, since Traven ain't got no authority outside a' town."

Slade raised his eyebrows at the request. "Well, I'm not the U. S. Marshal for the Territory, that's Willy Wheeler. He's in Helena. I'm only a Deputy Marshal."

"Does that mean you won't help us?" Blackcat asked harshly.

"It means I can't help ya'. I'm assigned here, and I can't just go anywhere I want."

"Oh, sounds like I've heard that tune before," Blackcat replied, turning to Cliff with a pretty disappointed look on his face.

"Besides," Slade continued, "what you are askin' me to do is local. Running down Night Hawkers or possibly becoming involved in a range war is not Federal. I enforce Federal warrants and arrest for Federal offenses."

For the first time Cliff spoke, "This Homestead Law, that's Federal Law ain't it?" Before Slade could answer he added, "Seems to me if someone runs off a family that is living on the land the Federal Government has done said was his, ____," he paused then added, "that ought a' be a Federal offense."

Slade again took a deep breath. He was not sure if Brown was right or not, but he did have a point. The last thing he wanted was to get involved in a range war. Especially when the bad guys might be well-connected politically. In turn, he knew his job could require just such, and if so, like it or not, he would do it. "I can't rightly answer you on that. Maybe it is, maybe it ain't, that's something Marshal Wheeler will have to answer."

The sound of the liquid boiling soon became obvious, so he walked over, and taking a white towel from a peg on the wall, lifted the hot pot and poured three cups nearly full of the black water. After setting the pot back on the stove and replacing the towel on its peg, he looked through the curtainless window at the dark street, cleared his throat and then said, "Come morning, if the lines ain't down, I'll wire Wheeler."

"Thank you Sur," Blackcat said. "Somebody's got 'a pay fer murdering my little girl."

"Don't get your hopes up yet. The Nez Perce cut the telegraph lines between here and Big Horn Barracks[39] when they come through, maybe to the west too."

Riding north, they encountered a drastic change in the weather. September 30 had turned off hot and dry with the temperature passing the eighty-degree line on the thermometer out front of *McGinnis' Drug Store*. The southwest wind had burned their necks, as they rode the last few miles.

When the two weary travelers finally reached town they stopped in front of the brilliantly lit *White Castle Saloon*.

"Well, it's finally open," Cliff said, looking at the now largest building in Copperopolis.

The new saloon not only had the usual false wall, which had been whitewashed several times, it sported a tall turret on each side, giving it a castle appearance, at least as much as could be expected on the plains of Montana.

John had decided, on Bea's suggestion, to simply call it *The White Castle* and drop the Mountain. At first, he had not liked it but finally agreed it did flow better.

The letters *The White Castle* were painted in gold, as was all the trim. There was no doubt but what this was the finest saloon within a hundred miles, and every miner and puncher wanted to be there on her opening night.

"Well, should we?" Blackcat said to his friend.

"I don't know about you, but I aim to," Cliff replied as he dismounted moments before tying Ola's reins to the hitching post in front, and then loosening the cinch.

Blackcat looked at the inviting swinging doors and then at his molly and shook his head. "I'll go down and stall these mules fer the night and come on back, we need to find Traven."

"My guess we'll find him right in there," Cliff answered then walked up the three steps.

"You want me to take your horse too?"

"Naw, I'll do it later," he said without explaining that long ago he had learned to make it a practice to have a saddled horse nearby when he entered a saloon.

---

39 Big Horn Barracks:Later the name was changed to Fort Custer.

The interior of *The White Castle* was not very different from a hundred other saloons he had been in, only bigger. Along the north wall was a highly polished counter. Behind this was a beautiful hand carved back-bar, with several mirrors, inlayed here and there. At least ten round tables were scattered about the floor along with a roulette wheel and a faro table, to lift the money from the miners' pockets. A long staircase, carpeted with a deep red cloth, ran up the south wall to a veranda, which overlooked the floor. Even the felt coverings on the tables were of this red, rather than the usual green so often seen in the west. Every other color in the place was either white or gold.

At the very back of the room was a small stage, where a woman dressed in a rather formal and certainly displaced gown was singing Beautiful Dreamer.

Half a dozen other girls were milling around among the crowd.

Cliff also noticed most of the men and girls working there were new to Copperopolis.

'There is no doubt about it,' Cliff thought, *'this is the biggest gold mine in Montana these days.'*

Leaning his left elbow on the high-back piano near the stage, was the lanky figure of Elon Traven. Traven was dressed in a shirt which was loosely tied at the opening with a rawhide strip. A pair of canvas trousers were held up by leather braces. His hat was a butternut, wide-brim Stetson, with a small braided horsehair band. This not only circled the base of the crown but also ran down through eyes cut in the brim, forming an adjustable tie at the back of his neck, to combat the ever-present Montana winds. The only contrasting accouterment to his otherwise all brown outfit was the black gunbelt.

Cliff looked straight at it and knew it had taken some skilled Mexican hours to carve an almost perfect basket-weave pattern on the leather. In a single loop matching holster was a large six-shot Dance Brothers revolver. To the holster was pinned the round badge of a Town Marshal.

Cliff though it strange to see him standing there without a vest. *'Hell, every man in three hundred miles is wearing a vest and Traven isn't. He is even still carrying that old cap & ball,'* he thought shaking his head. *'That ornery rascal sure likes to kick against the pricks.'* Cliff strolled over to him.

Traven spoke without showing a change in his determined expression, "I see the Indians didn't get your hair."

"At least I have all of mine for them to prize," Cliff said back.

Traven took a deep breath, accepting the dig as an equal to his greeting.

"You see Slade?" he asked, still not showing any change in his expression.

"We saw him," Cliff answered, turning and looking back at the busy scene before them.

Elon then nodded his head as he spoke, "See that bloke over there at the faro table, the one with the filthy, wool Irish beanie?"

Cliff looked to his left at the group of men standing in front of the table, "Yeah."

"He's been Bucking the Tiger for an hour and has not won a single hand. Today's payday at the mines, and I reckon he has lost just about his whole month's wages. In about two more minutes he is gon'a want a piece of that dealer's ass, and I'm not sure I want to stop him."

"You think it's a dirty game?"

"I know it's a dirty game, but I haven't been able to figure how he's doing it," he paused and then added strongly, "yet."

Scarcely had the word entered Cliff's ear than the miner screamed loudly, "You caffler, you done stole me rake a' wages, and I ain't gon'a let you get away with it."

Before the man could get the long stiletto out of his boot fully, Traven had the heavy barrel of his revolver tight against his brain stem. "Let it go, O'Brien. It ain't worth a bullet."

"Easy there, Razzer, don't you get waxed. I don't want a go with the shades. If you be pleased, move that shooter from me gregory peck[40]." The man was frozen save his eyes, which seemed to desperately be trying to look backwards at the man with the gun barrel poked in his neck. "I didn't come here to do no river-dance. I'm not no hardchaw, it's just this banjaxed wojus what done hockeyed me quid."

"Just slide that pig sticker back in its jacket," Traven said, still pressing the barrel of his revolver against the man's neck.

"Aye. No problem. I ain't going to loaf with no peeler."

40 Gregory peck: Irish slang for neck, especially a chicken's neck.

"Just see that you don't," Traven said, and when satisfied the knife was back in the man's boot, he reached up, took hold of his shoulder and turned the miner towards the front door.

The singer had stopped her tune, and the noise of the crowd had gone silent, as every eye in the place waited to see the scene play out. It was the first time their new Marshal had really been called upon to show them what he was made of, and all wanted to know.

"You have had enough for tonight, O'Brien. Best you head back to the barracks and sleep it off."

"Aye. I'll be leaving this Gammy Fleadh," the Irishman replied, and started a slow stroll towards the swinging doors.

Cliff was surprised to see the miner give up his fight so easily, but it did appear Traven had done his job and without bloodshed. He nodded his head in a private approval of the actions. However, his appraisal of the situation was premature, for the moment O'Brien saw, in one of the mirrors over the bar, that the lawman had returned his revolver to its holster, he smiled. Then he whirled, and in a movement almost as fast as a blink of the eye, had his stiletto back in his hand and was drawing a bead on the Faro dealer.

Just as quick was the drawing of his revolver by the lawman, but the sickening pop of the percussion cap without a following bang was heard as loud as thunder in the big room by everyone, including O'Brien.

Now the man turned his attention from the gambler to the Marshal. Adrian O'Brien had intended to kill the Faro dealer, fully realizing he would be shot for his deed moments later, but the affront was great enough for him to accept this fate. Suddenly the situation had changed. *'I can kill the razzer first, and then the cheater, and since the room is filled mostly with me fellow miners, I don't think a soul will stop me.'*

Traven did not fail to see O'Brien's expression change from determined to satisfaction, and in a split-second, he cocked and fired again. Once more, the pop of only the cap with no powder discharge was heard, and a smile came across the lips of O'Brien.

Elon watched as the man seemed to suddenly go into some sort of slow motion, he cocked his wrist for the flinging of the knife, and Traven knew there was no time to move to cover. Suddenly the thought of the green hills of North Carolina, where he had played as a boy, appeared in his mind. He saw a fair-haired young girl running and jumping, almost bouncing, through the tall grass of late spring and the sight pleased him.

His thoughts were interrupted by the thunder of a Henry round going off fairly near his head, and he flinched at the sudden pain in his ear. A split-second later, when he opened his eyes, he saw a pinkish cloud spewing from the back of O'Brien's head. The Irishman fell with the blade of his knife still clutched tightly between his thumb and forefinger.

Regaining his composure, Elon Traven turned to the other miners who were sure to be angered at the killing of their friend, and he said, "Alright, everybody stand easy." Satisfied they were doing as he had ordered, he looked over at the man who had caused all of this and said, "Alright Alfano, you carry him out."

"Me, why me?" the dealer asked, in a protesting manner.

"Because I said so, and besides I'm closing your table for the night."

"You can't do that you___,"

"Stop your bitching and do like you are told," came a strong but very feminine voice.

Traven looked over at the large woman who had been singing. Then back at the dealer.

"Go on Alfano, your table is closed for the night," Windy Willows added, this time as a command no one could misinterpret.

The dealer didn't like it but also knew she was the boss, and if he didn't want his first night to be his last, he had better do like he had been told.

"Where do you want me to take him?"

"Merewether's," was all Traven said in reply.

"Jones, give him a hand," she said, and then as soon as the two had the dead man lifted and were headed for the door, she turned to the crowd and shouted, "Drinks on the house everybody."

Soon the noise began to return to the room, with the men beginning to talk to one another as they moved towards the bar.

"That was a close one," Cliff said standing beside Traven.

"Yeah," was the only reply he received.

Seeing the Marshal was not in a mood for conversation Cliff said, "I think I'll take the lady up on her offer."

"Yeah," again came the reply from the man who also headed towards the end of the bar.

Later in his office, he sat behind his desk cleaning his revolver. He was indebted to Brown, and he knew it, and it did not set well with him. He hated owing anyone anything, especially something that would be so hard to pay off.

"You need to get rid of that old junker," Cliff said, nodding to the percussion revolver.

"Weren't its fault. Mine. I should have cleaned and reloaded it today. Fog wus heavy last night, and I didn't clean it."

"Get you a cartridge gun, and you won't have to reload it every-day," Cliff said back at the man's stubborn attitude.

"This ol' girl will be spitting lead years after that puny cartridge Colt you carry has wore out," he said defiantly. "Besides, I got me a cartridge gun." With that, he pulled a small 30 caliber five-shot Marlin pocket revolver from his boot.

Cliff just shook his head and smiled slightly.

"Well, what's so important that we have to be alone, for you to tell me?" Traven asked without looking up from his chore of wash-ing the big revolver in the pan of hot water.

Blackcat stepped forward and handed him the folded paper.

Traven wiped his hands dry on his pants leg, before turning up the wick on the lamp. Then he began reading the telegram:

MARSHAL SLADE
STOP

I AGREE WITH YOUR RECOMMENDATION
STOP
ELON TRAVEN IS APPOINTED DEPUTY U.S. MARSHAL COVERING THE WHITE DIAMOND CITY SULPHUR SPRINGS COPPEROPOLIS AREA
STOP

HIS BADGE WILL BE SENT BY MAIL ON NEXT STAGE
END

SIGNED WILLIAM WHEELER UNITED STATES MARSHAL MON-TANA TERRITORY

"What the ___?" Traven stammered.

"That's right. You are now a Deputy U.S. Marshal," Otis said smiling.

"Hell. I don't want no part of it."

"You don't have a choice, you already been appointed," Blackcat said back still smiling.

"I won't take it," Traven said flatly.

"Yes you will," Cliff declared just as strongly.

'Damn,' Elon thought. *'That Bastard has me over a barrel, and he knows it.'*

"Shit. I'll starve to death on a U.S. Marshal's pay here. You know they only get paid for arrests. They don't get no salary."

"You can keep your salary job with the town," Blackcat pointed out. "Nothing has changed."

"Only, you can't hide out inside the town limits no more," Cliff said, knowing it would hit hard.

Traven shot a dangerous stare at the Georgian. It seemed to be fired from a gun filled with explosive hate. Then he took a deep breath and let it out, "I'll think on it."

"Good, that's all we are askin'," Blackcat said, with the smile still on his face.

"Now get out a' here. I got work to do."

"Come on, Blackcat, let's see if it's a little more peaceful over to the Musselshell," Cliff said, turning for the door.

He had to duck his head to keep the low door casing from knocking off his hat, and still, just as he exited he said, "See ya, Marshal," without looking back. The emphasis had been placed heavily on the word Marshal, and Elon knew, although the words United States had not been used, they were implied. Immediately he threw the cleaning rag hard on the desk and too low for anyone to hear, uttered, "Bastard!"

There was not a single soul in *The Musselshell Saloon,* save the Mexican Sally Mustang had hired and herself.

"Hey, now this is the place to be tonight," Blackcat remarked.

"You think," the good-looking woman replied, almost in an attacking voice.

"Hey, don't get sore with us, we come to support you, Sally," Blackcat said back.

"You want whiskey, tequila, what?" she asked, still not in a friendly voice.

"Whiskey will do fine," Cliff replied looking at her.

He had been in here several times before but had never really given her much attention. This night she was fiery as a banshee, and it accented her beauty, '*I would do her,*' he thought.

They drank slowly while they talked about the events that had occurred in the last week. "You think he will do it?"

"Yeah, he owes me," Cliff said, pausing and looking at the nearly empty glass, "and he's not one to like it, but he will do what we want. At least until he finds a way to clear the debt."

It was then he overheard, or thought he overheard, the woman say to the Mexican, "I will get even with Jean. He promised me *The White Castle,* and now he gives it to that fat bitch."

Cliff rose from his table and walked over to where she was leaning against the bar. There he sat his glass down and nodded for her to refill it. While she was doing so he asked, "Did I hear you say Jean owned *The White Castle?*"

She looked up at him surprised and studied his face for a few monuments before answering, "No. I said nothing about anyone named Jean."

Cliff nodded his head, "My mistake," he said back, before touching the brim of his Stetson. He then returned to the table where Blackcat sat. Truthfully, he wanted to stay around to see if he could overhear anymore of their conversation, but Alfano walked in, and upon seeing Cliff, he headed over to their table. "I sure am obliged to you. That crazy Irishman would have killed me, and that stupid Marshal was gon'a let him."

"You are a lucky man," Blackcat said looking up at the intruder.

"I want to buy you a drink," he said. Then turning to Sally he called out, "Bring a bottle."

"No," Cliff said.

"But, I owe you."

"No," Cliff said again. Rising from his chair he finished his drink, looked over to the dark-skinned woman, and after setting his glass gently on the table, he touched the front brim of his hat in a salute to her once again and said, "Ma'am." Then he turned and walked past the faro dealer and out into the night.

"I just wanted to thank him."

"You best leave it alone," Blackcat said before following his friend out.

"I'm going to put up Ola. Will you get us a couple a' cots over at *The Bunkhouse*?"

"Sure," Blackcat said and then stood there for almost a full minute watching the lanky man ride the big horse toward the livery at the far end of town.

A few minutes after midnight Cliff stepped on the boardwalk in front of *The Bunkhouse* and moved to the front door. Suddenly he noticed Orr had nailed an alcohol thermometer to the wall next to the door. On this first of October, 1877 it was showing 47 degrees, and with the winds coming out of the southwest, at around ten miles an hour, he felt a chill. *'Hellfire, it were nigh on 80 in the heat of the day and now it's down near half that. No wonder a man can catch his death in such weather.'*

Entering, he felt suddenly warmer, as the thick walls stole the bite from the wind. Both heating stoves contained small fires, and he immediately felt much better.

The Bunkhouse was laid out with two rows of cots, each along the walls. A fat potbelly was located at each end in the center isle, which ran between the cots.

Blackcat was lying on a bunk near the far end and upon seeing Cliff enter, motioned him over. "What took you so long?"

"I had to clean the burned powder from my barrel," Cliff replied without saying more. He didn't want anyone to overhear that after cleaning his gun, he had returned near *The Musselshell Saloon* where he could watch. Unfortunately, after Alfano left, the lights went out, and Sally Mustang gave it up for the night; so he did too.

"Oh," was his friend's reply. He looked up at Cliff as if he wasn't sure whether to believe him or not. Finally, Blackcat figured it best to let it lay, and he nodded across the row of beds to an undisturbed cot, "That's yours yonder."

The next morning the sun was breaking on their right, as they reached the Musselshell River, a mile northwest of town.

Ginny was very anxious to find out what they had accomplished, as were Laramie and Otie. Black Band showed no emotion upon seeing them, but Cliff knew he was glad they were back as well.

The snow had been hard on Ginny, but it had not stayed long. The winds soon had blown it far away, and now, other than a noticeable drop in the noonday temperature, the little homestead was no different than when they had left it over a week before.

After making sure all was well at the James', Cliff planned to move forward with his next self-imposed chore. He learned a man named Henry Cain had built a sawmill along Indian Creek, near Placerville.

Cain had worked for Andy Sharp, when he began his ranch not far away. Being an industrious man, he soon saw the need for cut timber. By saving his wages for over a year, he sent east for a saw blade big enough to cut the ponderosa which grew abundantly in the nearby mountains.

With the Big Belt Range to the east, and The Elk Horns to the west, Cain located in a perfect spot for his new enterprise. At first, he used the energy of the river water to power his mill, but after the Indians had mostly been cleared out, the cattle industry in Montana enjoyed rapid growth. With this, his business flourished. Once again, the forward-thinking man envisioned a better means of production and bought a steam engine to power the mill. However, this was no small undertaking in itself.

The riverboat Big Muddy, had been caught on a sandbar during the late fall of '76. Before the spring thaw had caused the water level to rise enough to float her out, the ice had crushed her hull, and she was little more than an obstruction to the highway.

Her wood became fuel for other, luckier Captains, and her engine was sold to Cain. He had it disassembled and hauled by bull train to his mill. He then sent east for a steam engineer, to come and direct the reassembly of the big engine.

This engineer was known as Railman Rover. He earned this title because he moved all over the country aiding in the reconstruction of wrecked steam engines, usually steam locomotive engines.

Railman had Cain's engine puffing away before the first snows arrived in 1877.

The winter of 1877 was the mildest of the decade thus far, and with its warm days and cool nights, Copperopolis had grown considerably. The addition of such a sawmill, only some fifty miles distant, was God sent to the heart of Copperopolis. Soon dozens of new buildings sprang up. At least half were buildings intended to be of a business enterprise.

Ola needed some rest, and a week of grazing before another long trip. However, as soon as he felt it would not hurt his horse,

Cliff prepared to leave, and it would be Cain's new enterprise he planned to investigate.

"I would like to borrow Julian for a few days, if you will allow me."

"Borrow Julian?" Blackcat repeated. "Whatever fer?"

"I want to go to White Sulphur Springs, and I will need a pack animal," Cliff replied.

"Sure, I reckon so. White Sulphur Springs?"

"Yep," was all Cliff said back.

"Sure, you can have anything I have, except my wife."

"Won't need her," Cliff said back and winked.

"When you leaving?"

"Come morning. I'll take Laramie but leave Black Band."

"Alright," was all Blackcat could think to say.

They were gone a week. During which time, while passing through White Sulphur Springs, Cliff wired Sam Brooks to send him a few things, along with some of the money he had left back at Estherbrook. Next, as this little burg had temporarily been made the county seat, after Diamond City had pretty much failed, he made a stop at the Land Office. There, he and Laramie both filed for homesteads, next to Otis' land.

The land agent questioned Laramie about his age, but he assured the man he was twenty-one years old, and Cliff swore that he was the lad's brother and knew it to be a fact. Cliff also lied about never having taken up arms against the Government, as did all former Confederate Soldiers at the time.

Before leaving, Cliff bought a large farm wagon and another Jack to help Julian pull the heavy-loaded wagon back to Blackcat Creek. It was the name, he told the Land Agent, the little stream, where their land was located was locally known by. The agent then noted the name change in the official records.

It was the first day of November when they returned to Blackcat Creek.

The James family was working on repairing the canvas roof, which the winds had torn away the night before. Ginny looked up and seeing a wagon approaching said, "Wonder who that could be, Otis?" She lifted her open hand to shade her eyes from the late afternoon sun.

"Beats me."

When Cliff and Laramie pulled up and stopped in front of the group, everyone looked as surprised as if a herd of wild horses had just run through the yard.

"What on earth?"

Otie and Laramie immediately began wrestling around, like two little kids, and Cliff saw the sign of relief in the eyes of Black Band.

"What have you done?" Blackcat asked walking around the wagon and looking at the stacks of cut lumber in its bed.

"Brung you some wood for your new house," Cliff said, as he untied the lead rope of the four horses that trailed behind the Studebaker.

"My new house?"

"That's right. There is no way your family will survive the winter here in that lean-to you have there." Cliff never stopped walking as he moved around removing this and that. Blackcat never stopped following him as he did, continuously talking.

"Look, I'm obliged to you, but I can't pay fer this stuff. It could be years before I will make enough money to pay you back."

"I can wait years," Cliff said. "Now are you going to keep talking or are you going to help me. These animals need water."

"Well, hell. I don't know what to say."

Cliff looked over at Ginny seeing the tears building in her eyes, and he looked away quickly so as not to embarrass her and said to his friend, "Well, don't say nothing; just lead your horses over to the creek and give 'em some drink."

"My horses?"

"Yeah, those two yonder come with the package, as does that other mule. The other two still belong to me and Laramie."

That night after supper, Cliff opened a well-oiled leather case and removed some papers. "I want you all to see these," he said motioning them to surround him by the small fire.

"What is it?" Otie asked anxiously.

Cliff waited until Otis and Ginny were near and then he handed them one of the papers. "These are the Homestead papers Laramie and I filed on. Quarter sections here. Mine next to yours," he said to Otis, "and Laramie's across Blackcat Creek next to Otie's."

"Blackcat Creek?" Otis said enthusiastically.

"Yep, th' name's been officially recorded."

"I thought it was Yadkin Creek," Otie spurted out.

"Not no more. Blackcat Creek now," Cliff replied, handing over the papers for them to examine.

Finally, Otis said, "I never figured you fer a man who'd settle down."

"Well, someday mee'be but not just yet. These here papers are also for you," he said handing them over to his friend. "If you will notice they are dated November 1, 1883, and they are legal transfers of the ownership of our land to you. That is, they will be legal providing no one sees them before then. Now I don't plan to make improvements on this, so if you want it, that will be up to you to fulfill the legal requirements. You will also take notice that Laramie is now twenty-one years old."

With that, they all laughed out loud.

"I would suggest you take Ginny in, and have her file on a connecting quarter section, as soon as you can," Cliff added.

"Didn't know women could own land," Ginny said.

"Well, it seems when the Yankee Government passed this act, they planned to use it to steal as much of our land as they could and give it to the Darkeys. So they put in it a provision where women could file, just like a man."

"Really?" she replied with a pleased expression.

"They didn't tell us that when we filed for this here land," Blackcat added.

"No, I 'spect not. I didn't know it either, but when I was in the land office, there in White Sulphur Springs, I read the whole Homestead Act signed by ol' Abe Lucifer himself back in '62, and it is there."

"I be dogged," Blackcat said looking over at his wife.

"If Ginny does, and you do as I suggest here, you will have morn' a full section of deeded land, plus all the surrounding free grazing land butting up to you. That ain't a small hand a' change. Shucks, folks here abouts will be calling you a rancher, instead of a squatter. Hell, by then you may be a premature cattle baron."

That statement really caused laughter to erupt from the five excited people sitting around the small fire on that moonless night.

Two sets of inquiring eyes watched this little gathering from a distance: those of Black Band, from his dry camp on the ridge and a lone wolf who had ventured up the creek bed. He was now hidden in the willows, waiting the retirement of the humans, so he could scrounge for scraps fallen from their table.

Just before she turned in, Ginny came over, kissed Cliff on the cheek, and said, "God will reward you someday, Reb Brown."

"I don't know about that," he replied.

"I do," she said with great conviction.

Later that night, Cliff took Laramie aside and gave him a small leather pouch. "I want you to take this up there where Otie shot those two bandits. Hide it in a place where Otie will find it and make sure he does."

"What is it?"

"Just a little money to help them get by until they make a go of it here."

"Why don't you just give it to them?" the boy asked.

"Some men are too proud to accept such. I think Blackcat is one of those men. Now do as I say and be sure he finds it. Don't you find it; he must. But Laramie," Cliff said. Standing close he placed both hands on the youngster's shoulders and added, "give me your word, as long as you live you will never tell anyone that you put it there."

"Oui. I give you my word," the boy replied, feeling quite grown up having such responsibility placed in his hands.

Sometime after noon, Otie came rushing down to where they were working yelling, "Ma, Pa, look! Look, look what I found," holding out in front of him the small pouch.

Laramie followed a short distance behind. He looked over at Cliff and smiled, but when the older man frowned, he erased the smile from his face.

Upon emptying the gold coins from the leather bag, Otis began to count. Finally, he finished at thirty-two. Then looking up he said, "Why, there's more than six hundred dollars here."

"Oh, Lord!" Ginny exclaimed.

"Otie, where did you get this?" his father questioned, as he placed his hands on his son's shoulders, not unlike what had happened to Laramie the night before. Seeing this, Laramie felt warm, felt like he had a second father.

"I found it yonder," Otie said, pointing back up the hill. "Where the men were. You know, the ones I had to shoot."

"You think it fell from one of their pockets?" Blackcat questioned, looking around at the others.

"I can't see it any other way," Cliff replied. Then he added, "Looks like come spring, you'll have the money to buy some fine beeves and get this ranch producing, Mr. Cattle Baron."

"Oh, Lord!" Ginny repeated.

When he left for Copperopolis the next day, Cliff had Laramie and Black Band stay behind, as added protection.

Hank Groll's first edition went out on November 1st 1877. The headlines were:

I WILL FIGHT NO MORE FOREVER

Below this was a long account of the flight and surrender of the Nez Perce. There was also a paragraph about a man being shot in *The White Castle* on its opening night, but no names were printed. Groll named the paper, *The Blackheart Gazette*, which no one, save the author, understood.

When Cliff got to town, the first place he went was to the Marshal's Office.

"Come to antagonize me some more?"

"No. Come fer information."

"Yeah, what?"

"Who owns *The Musselshell Saloon*?" Cliff asked, reaching for the coffee pot.

"Sally Mustang."

"I know she runs it, but who owns it?"

"I don't know, if she doesn't," Traven admitted.

"Well, she don't," Cliff said back. "That much I'm sure of."

"Why do you need to know?" Traven asked, as he looked out his window at Mrs. Dean walking down the opposite side of the wide street.

"Personal," Cliff replied.

"I'll look into it," Traven said back, reaching for his hat. "Wash up the cup when you're finished." Then he left.

Next, Cliff went to see just how honest the new newspaperman really was.

"I see," Hank said, after listening to Cliff's story, "and how can I verify all this?"

"See Marshal Traven. He is fully aware of it all. By the way, I know it's supposed to be kind a' on the quiet, but did you know he's been appointed Deputy U. S. Marshal for this district?"

"No. I didn't know that," Hank Groll said with great interest.

"You know he's a modest man. He probably hasn't let everyone know fer fear they would think he was a bragger."

"Yes. I can see that," the reporter agreed, as he penciled notes on a yellow pad.

The second edition of *The Blackheart Gazette* carried a story about Night Hawkers attacking a family of new settlers to the valley, burning their home and murdering their daughter, but this was the secondary story. The headlines were:

COPPEROPOLIS GETS ITS OWN
UNITED STATES MARSHAL

"Look at this," John Pell shouted as he threw the paper on Glaze's desk. "Hell, that damn newspaper has the whole blame country feeling sorry for these damn squatters." He turned, and placing his hands on the desk and staring straight into the banker's eyes, he added, "And your lawman has gone and got himself appointed Deputy U.S. Marshal, the last thing we need."

Glaze could not help but shiver when he saw the anger in his partner's eyes. "I had no knowledge of this until today," he said in his defense.

"Oh, that we can be sure of," John snapped back.

"Well, I'll just have him dismissed as Town Marshal, he can't survive on government pay."

"No. That will just rile the whole town. Besides, if he needs money he will start looking for Federal cases he can make arrests on."

"We have done nothing wrong. We have broken no Federal laws," Glaze said.

"What do you call running off those squatters from land the damn Federal Government gave them?"

"I had nothing to do with that," Glaze replied sharply. "That was strictly your doings," he added as the beads of sweat broke out on his forehead.

"The hell you didn't! You knew damn well what I was doing, and you changed the bank's policy on loans. You are a part of everything I do in this area. If you try and squirm out of anything, I will skin you alive."

Turning and walking over to the window, John took a deep breath, regaining his composure. "Now, how much money has Windy Willows placed in *The White Castle*'s account so far?"

That night Cliff entered *The Musselshell Saloon* sometime after eleven. The next morning, just after first light, he dressed and eased out without awakening the dark-skinned beauty who had so enjoyed his company only a few hours before.

By the time the James family sat down for Christmas viand[41], they did so in a well-built bat and board house with two rooms and a cellar. Both the sides and back of the cabin were piled high with rocks to help stave off the cold, as well as for protection, should an arsonist try and fire their new home.

Blackcat had added one thing more, which was pretty strange for a ranch to have. He had constructed an eight by eight bastion[42] on the roof of his house at the opposite end from the chimney. It was constructed of large ponderosa pine he and Otie had taken in the Big Belt Mountains on their way back from a trip to Diamond City. It could only be accessed from inside. The timbers were thick enough no bullet could penetrate them, and it gave a commanding view of the area within range of any Winchester. They had reinforced the roof with a layer of earth, to stop any fire someone might attempt there.

The only way one could assault this new house was from the front and that would be met with murderous gunfire from the tower citadel, as well as the gun-ports cut into each of the forward facing windows.

Cliff was pleased to see the thought in its design, as well as the obvious hard work that had been put forth to have it ready for Christmas.

A few days before, Otie and Laramie had been gathering deadwood from along the creek near where it branched off the Musselshell. Suddenly they spotted a dry cow elk, browsing bark from some large cottonwoods.

Otie placed a well-aimed 45 government slug in the cow's neck, and she dropped in her tracks. This good fortune had brought needed meat for the winter, as well as elk roast for Christmas supper.

---

41 Viand: A collection of food, especially the food that makes up a large meal or feast.

42 Bastion: Rook, Bulwark, Citadel, or Castle Tower.

Cliff had found some sweet potatoes in Coker's store, and Black Band had cleanly taken the heads off three prairie chickens with his skillful throwing of sharp stones, a trick he had learned as a boy along the Elk River, known to the white man as the Big Horn.

The day had been unusually warm for late December, as had pretty much been the case for the whole winter thus far. Therefore, Ginny asked that they take the table outside, where they could not only relish God's blessing for their stomachs but also see his beautiful country and sky.

As the coolness of evening came on, the boys built a large fire nearby so when a body had stood all the Montana wind they wanted for a while, they could stand close and warm themselves without having to go inside.

This was the only day after the raid that not at least one of them stood watch on the distant ridge. However, unknown to them, a watch from there was in progress. Two Bucks and Lobo had eased up to the ridge on their bellies and peered over at the scene taking place some four hundred yards away.

"Why they eat outside, they have a warm house?" the Mexican questioned.

"Some whites do not have all the brains they are born with," replied Two Bucks.

They had not been in this part of the Territory for some time and were surprised to see the new house built there.

"We take those mules," Lobo said, pointing to the animals grazing across the creek.

Two Bucks watched for a long time, but he didn't like the looks of the tower. *'These whites savvy trouble,'* he considered and then quickly gave his head two small shakes. "No."

"No?" Lobo questioned, looking at the bred, "Why no?"

"No need take chance for mules when mucho caballo can be had with leetle chance."

"I say you loco. Not too much chance here. White family, no more. No federales, no posse. I think you scared."

Before the words were lost in the wind, he felt the cold steel of Two Bucks knife on his neck. "I no scared of Lobo," Two Bucks replied and let just a tiny slice of flesh be cut before he lowered his knife.

The others, who had stayed back with the horses, saw the confrontation, but were too far away to hear what had been said. Nonetheless, it was well understood Lobo had in someway challenged Two Bucks' authority, a gesture none of them thought wise.

That night, Two Bucks and his band, stole forty horses from *The Little Judith Ranch* and headed north to sell them in Canada.

Although he had taken a room at the newly built *Montana House*, Cliff enjoyed his newfound relationship with the whore and encouraged her to hire another girl to do most of the back work.

John Pell had not been to town for over a month, due to the constant problems of building his cattle enterprise and the struggle with the raiders who seemed to constantly steal his stock.

Just after the first of the year, the herd John had contracted to be delivered to him arrived. A drive that started out with five thousand head the previous April in south Texas. Some had been sold to a buyer in Wyoming when funds ran out, and some were lost along the long trip, as is always expected. Still, slightly over three thousand longhorns soon were feeling the burn of the Lazy R-J brand.

Accompanying the beeves were a dozen cowboys, well-educated in handling bovines. Of the twelve, John Pell enticed nine to stay and become hands on his now huge ranch.

The arrival of the herd at last, along with the additional men, gave him a sense of relief and a need to let off some of the stress all this had brought to his strong shoulders. He needed time with a woman and also needed to tend to his businesses in town. *'And there is also the key. I must not let Moreton's key venture far from my thoughts daily.'* John always carried this key in the inner pocket of his vest. *'I must soon find the time to go to Omaha and use this,'* he thought as he rubbed it between his forefinger and thumb, without removing it from his pocket. *'Perhaps soon I will go. Maybe take Brigitte with me. She would like that.'*

The first place his black buggy stopped was at the bank. After a long discussion with Glaze, he headed to *The White Castle,* mainly to congratulate Bea on her handling of the profits. He was just entering the front doors when Sally Mustang came out of the new dress shop Miss Beverly Moore had begun. She started to call out to him but decided against it. She knew he would be to see her soon, and she headed back to pretty up for him.

As she put on the new dress she had just purchased, she suddenly thought of Reb. *'What if he should come here tonight?'* she twisted her head and bit at her lip. She was far too much a woman of the world to allow herself to fall for any man, but she had to admit every time that tall lean man with the big hat came in, she felt a stirring in her lions. Furthermore, when he spoke that smooth Georgian tongue, she felt warm inside. It was not the tongue of her Louisiana, but it was southern, and that made her feel he was homefolk.

'Still, he is just another man,' she convinced herself. *'A toy to amuse myself with when Jean is not around. It is Jean who has the money, not Reb, and it is money that I need, not a man.'*

Her luck was both good and bad that day. Cliff was over in White Sulphur Springs and was not going to be by, but John stayed with Bea Desmond that night. He had not planned to do so, but he did enjoy the atmosphere of *The White Castle*, and before midnight he was seduced by his own vices, and had almost dragged Bea upstairs to her bedroom.

Sally sat up all night waiting on him, and when he never arrived, she took a knife and shredded her new dress to pieces. John Pell had no idea the fury that awaited him in his other saloon.

Cliff was just returning and had decided to stop by and ask Sally to have a noon lunch with him at *The Alamo*, a restaurant newly opened by a short, round fellow who went by the handle, Texas Jess.

Jess claimed he had an uncle who had been one of the defenders of the famous mission, but no one really knew him to be truthful or really cared. Still he never let a new customer leave without telling them of his dead uncle, The Hero of San Antonio.

When Cliff asked Sally to have lunch with him, she suddenly became more angered, not at him but at herself, for destroying her new dress. "I will, but I must find another dress to wear."

"Oh bull hockey, you look great. Come on."

"No. I will change first," she said sternly.

He waited.

When she came out, she was dressed in a long black skirt with a bustle in the saddle, her blouse was also black. However, it was made of Chantilly lace that almost, but not quite, hid her breasts.It wasn't until they were outside in the light of the sun, did he realize just how little they were hid. He almost turned her around, but just then, he saw Elon Traven and Mrs. Dean enter *The Alamo*. She was wearing a striking sky-blue prairie dress. Suddenly Cliff had no intention of the Marshal escorting the only stunning woman in the restaurant.

Although they did not share the same table, the two couples sat close enough for them to pay their respects. This nearness also afforded a good view of each other. The men were proud of their lady's beauty, and the girls checked out the competition.

John Pell was just leaving *The White Castle* when Sally stepped out on the boardwalk across the street with a tall lanky man.

Immediately he moved back so the doorframe would hide him. There was no doubt within his mind who she was with. *'How did he find me?'* he wondered as he stood hidden. He watched them return to *The Musselshell Saloon* at the far end of the street, and then he went back inside *The White Castle*. A cloud had surrounded his world, and Bea immediately recognized it, although she did not understand it.

She had hired a young boy who spoke little but Spanish. His English was so broken very few could understand him. He was perhaps ten years old but not much larger than a boy six or seven. No one really knew much about him, other than his forehead indicated he was living with the Flathead Indians at birth. He seemed quite mature for ten, especially when he looked at the working girls who plied their trade upstairs. At times, he was found hiding in their rooms when they were entertaining or bathing. However, since he was not very bright and Bea liked him, they put up with his peeping. His one great attribute was he was extremely loyal and grateful for the job as well as the shelter from the elements. Bea called him Felipe because he reminded her of her sister's child, Philip.

That day, John Pell called Felipe aside and asked, "Do you know the man who rides a spotted horse?"

The boy answered, "Si Señor."

"Where do you know him from?"

"He sleeps at *The Bunkhouse*. He horse sleeps at the stable."

"Have you seen him in here?"

"Si Señor, som'times."

"Where else have you seen him?"

"He sleeps at the dirty saloon, som'times."

"Dirty Saloon!" John Pell repeated, somewhat angered at such a word being expressed concerning one on his businesses.

"Si, 'ees what the Señora calls the little cantina far down de street."

"I see." John nodded, understanding who Felipe had heard call *The Musselshell Saloon* dirty.

"Do you want to earn this?" he asked, holding a silver dollar between his fingers.

"Si Señor," the boy replied enthusiastically.

"Good. I want you to go and watch the man who owns the spotted horse. He is in *The Musselshell Saloon* right now," John Pell told him, pointing in that direction. "You are not to leave until he leaves, and then you follow him. If he leaves town, come back and tell me. Do you understand?"

Before he answered, he looked over at the lady of the house and only after she nodded her head did he reply, "Si, Señor, I weell do as you say."

Cliff stayed overnight with Sally, and it wasn't until the sun was high in the sky, did he exit the saloon.

The night had been cold, and a strong wind was blowing from the northwest. Nonetheless, Felipe stayed in the little alley between *Cotter's Dry Goods Store* and the new Tinsmith's shop. From there, he could see both the front and rear doors of the saloon. Only when he watched Cliff ride out of the livery barn, did he return to *The White Castle*.

"Where have you been?" she scolded him, "I have been so worried."

"I have been earning my silver dinero," he replied, not understanding her concern.

"All night?"

"Si Señora, all night," he replied quite proud of his endurance.

"Never do that again," she said sternly.

"Si Señora," he replied, totally confused. *'She was there when de Señor told me to stay until de man who rides the spotted horse leaves. She nodded for me to do dis t'ing. Now she ees sore that I do as she say?'*

"Alright go upstairs and get your silver dollar. Mr. Pell is in my room," she said and gave him a little push in that direction.

Bea Desmond had no idea what John Pell feared in the man who rode the spotted horse, but she had seen a change come over him, a change she never thought would or even could happen. It was as if he had been pierced with a sword honed sharp with pure panic. His nerves were on edge, and he drank endlessly of the brandy she kept for herself.

Ten minutes after Felipe went up stairs to give his report, John Pell came down. His demeanor had completely changed. The small, frightened man who had spent the night in her room, afraid to show himself on the floor of his own saloon was gone. The old, strong, stalwart Jean Mouton, she had met in Saint Louis was descending the stairs, displaying an air of total confidence in his abilities. She was now totally confused.

He walked out the front doors as if yesterday had never happened and marched straight to *The Musselshell Saloon*.

When he entered, there were three men inside besides Felix; of these, he paid little notice, he knew if she was not to be seen, she had to be in the backroom. *'It is there I will find her,'* he thought. Without saying a word to any one, he went straight back and closed the door.

She indeed was there, doing the paperwork Mr. Glaze required before he would take her daily deposit.

Everyone heard first the slap, followed by her scream.

Felix said, "Chihuahua," quietly as he rubbed the palms of his hands down the full length of his face.

The others looked questioningly at each other and then at the Mexican behind the bar. He slowly shook his head and looked downward.

"I think we had better go," one of the miners said to the other. He nodded his head and swallowed the remainder of his clear drink before turning towards the door. However, the third man stood straight and stopped them.

"You gon'a walk out a' here and let that gunsel[43] beat a woman?"

"Ain't none a' my business, cowboy," one of them said.

"When a man beats on a woman, it's everybody's business."

"Look, I can't afford to get mixed up in something that might bring down the law. I'll just be moving on now," the other miner told the tall teenager who worked on *The Albermarle Ranch*, a big spread who ran its brand north of the Musselshell, between White Sulphur Springs and Copperopolis.

The Albermarle Ranch was owned by a man from Virginia named Jefferson, who forbade his hands to frequent Copperopolis. This was because of his holdings in her sister town, White Sulphur Springs.

Tommy Randolph had just enough old south upbringings in him to be unable to stand by while a woman was being beaten by someone other than her husband, and it would be his downfall.

---

43 Gunsel: Western slang for Dude or Easterner.

"Who is this man?" John screamed, as he held her upper arm.

"What man?" she screamed back, trying to wipe away the stream of blood that was flowing from her nose.

Bam! He slapped her again harder than before, and once more she screamed.

"You know damn well what man; that son-of a-bitch who stayed here all night!"

She was now on her knees and knew she could not fight his rage. Looking off at the still messed bed, she said, "His name is Reb."

"Reb Brown?" he yelled back.

"Oui, Reb Brown," she agreed, as the tears rolled down her cheeks.

"Has he ever asked about me?"

"No," she replied.

"Are you sure?"

"Oui," she yelled back. Her manner of reply angered him, and once again, John slapped her hard.

This was all Tommy Randolph could stand, and he burst through the door and drove his fist hard against the astonished face of John Pell. The surprise blow caught the older man off balance, and he fell to his side. Tommy mistakenly took this as him being knocked out.

The boy reached forth his hand to assist her in regaining her feet, but their fingers never touched. The blast of Pell's revolver was deafening in the small quarters. The pistol ball struck the boy in his right side, where his arm would have been had he not been trying to help the woman. It passed straight through his heart and was stopped inside the skin of his left breast, after breaking a rib bone.

'He looks so strange,' she thought during the long second he stood there before he fell dead at her feet.

The closeness of the pistol shot had caused the cowboy's shirt to catch fire, and it was still smoking when she rushed from the room into the arms of Felix.

When the Mexican saw John Pell follow her through the door a few seconds later, he became so frightened he lost his bladder, but his panic had been in vain. The killing of the wrangler had quenched the anger in the man, and he no longer wanted to hurt anyone.

John Pell walked over to the bar and stopped. He reached for the bottle left there by the miners and took a deep swallow. *'My how I dislike mescal,'* he thought, but what he said was, "Close the doors and lock up."

"Si, Señor," Felix replied, and he quickly removed her arms from around him and moved over to the entrance.

Immediately she witnessed Jean's expression change, as his old companion rushed into his conscious mind. Frightened, she dared not deny him as he grabbed her arm, before guiding her towards the bed in the backroom.

Later that night, following her orders, the old Mexican took the body of Tommy Randolph east of town. However, after sliding it off into a brushy arroyo, he continued on, never to return to Copperopolis.

While Felix was traveling hard towards the Missouri River, Sally Mustang was once again being savagely pounded. Unlike the pounding she had received earlier, the man now was determined to leave her feeling she had been better taken care of, than she had been the night before. The near rape had the exact opposite effect.

She did not know why Jean Mouton hated Reb Brown. She didn't even care. She just knew she hated Jean Mouton or at least what had become of him.

While she lay there, with him having his way with her body, she thought about a lot of things. It was during this time she remembered the first occasion she had ever seen Reb Brown. He had indeed asked about a man named Jean. It was such a small thing, and he had never asked again; she had forgotten it. She decided she would tell Reb when she saw him again; however later she thought better of it.

Pleasure was not found by her that night, and as she lay there staring at the black air above her bed, she also considered perchance there was another cause of his assault on her. *'Jean had just come from The White Castle. He had said something about seeing Reb from, or was it at, The White Castle? Could it be that his anger was caused by the Yankee woman?'*

Brigitte had never forgiven Windy Willows for taking over *The White Castle. 'Jean had promised it to me as soon as it was finished. Then this woman comes here, and he gave it to her. Could it be she is trying to split up the relationship Jean and I have?'*

On and on he pounded his manhood into her.

'I would not be surprised if she is not the one who told Jean about Reb Brown enjoying my bed when he is out of town.'

There was no question that Sally had found herself having strong feelings for the Georgian, nonetheless her thoughts were, *'I know only too well his talent rests solely in the bed. He has little money and no future. My future is here with me now.'* She decided as she felt Jean spew his seed deep inside her loins, she would never let anyone come between them again.

Later, when she was getting the bottle of *Madame Restell's Preventive Powder*[44] from her small chest of drawers, she said a silent prayer asking God to never let her fail again.

Cliff spent the remainder of the week with the James family and only returned to his room on Saturday. There he bathed and dressed in fresh duds, before heading to Traven's office.

The Marshal was sitting behind his desk, writing a letter to Jefferson concerning Tommy Randolph's disappearance.

"Well, I see you can write. You must be an educated man," Cliff said hoping he could get a rise out of Traven.

"Yes. I can write. I even can read," the man said back, not looking up at Brown.

"Well, I was wondering if you would buy me a drink. I have a powerful thirst on."

"No."

"Pray may I ask why?"

"It's none of your business why."

"Everything that concerns a Deputy United States Marshal is the business of the citizens what helped him get promoted," Cliff said back knowing that would be more than Traven could stand.

"Look you long-legged bag a' wind, I ain't been promoted. This here United States shit damn near got me fired. The mayor done eat me out about spending my time outside of the town limits while the town is paying for my services, and that brings up another subject. Just who let the cat out of the bag about this here appointment anyway?"

"What are you talking about?" Cliff asked.

"You know blame well what I'm talking about. I wasn't sure I was going to accept this government shit, and then I read in the papers ___, actually, Mrs. Dean read me from *The Blackheart Gazette*, where I had been appointed." He threw the paper he had been writing on down hard enough that it slid right off the front of his desk.

---

44 Madame Restell's Preventive Powder: A nineteenth Century form of birth control.

"How is Mrs. Dean? Mighty fine-looking woman if I do say so myself," Cliff said.

"None of your damn business, and you stay away from her."

Cliff brought his hands back at his chest in a gesture indicating, "Me?"

"Don't give me that innocent look. You got no business even speaking her name. Anyone who would bring a whore in a' establishment where decent women were, should be ashamed."

"Whore? Who are you calling a whore?"

"You know damn well who. You and that damn whore come strutting right in *The Alamo* after you seen us go in there, and her in that sleeping gown so thin, a bald eagle could have seen her tits from a mile in the sky."

"You must a looked at them, or you wouldn't know to criticize."

"Hell yes, I looked at them, and it were damn embarrassing too. Here I wus with a respectable lady like Mrs. Dean, and you bring in a whore and sit down mightn' near next to us."

"First off, she ain't no whore."

"The hell she ain't!"

"Well, mee'be you have paid her. I can't say about that, but she never charged me."

"I never boned her, free or otherwise."

"Then you don't know fer sure she's a whore. A Wheeligo Girl maybe but not a whore."

"A what?"

"A Wheeligo Girl. Surely a body that stayed down in Texas as much as you claimed to have, knows what a Wheeligo Girl is."

"Never heard the expression before."

"Well, a Wheeligo Girl is one that is free with her resources, where a whore is one what charges for hers. Now don't tell me you never been with no Wheeligo Girl."

"Never heard that before."

"By the way, you never did tell me how Mrs. Dean is. Did they ever find where her husband has gone off to?"

"I told you before, you never-mind about her. She's a respectable lady. Now get out of here and let me finish my letter," he said looking around for the paper.

"This what you are looking for?" Cliff asked, picking up the paper from where it landed after flying off the desk.

In doing so he saw the words Musselshell Saloon and stopped his motion, then started to read what Traven had written.

The Marshal grabbed the paper from his hand and said, "This too ain't none of your business, neither."

"I just saw you had mentioned *The Musselshell Saloon* and was wondering if you were now using your Federal influence to advertise for Miss Mustang."

"Just for your information, this here cowboy was last seen in your whore's saloon. Now he's disappeared."

"Speaking of that, did you find out who owns *The Musselshell Saloon?*"

"No," he replied in a totally different tone. "I run into a brick wall when I tried to find out. Even the mayor seemed queer when I asked."

"Queer?"

"Yeah, like he suddenly became nervous," Elon replied, uncertain himself.

"Mee'be he owns it," Cliff suggested.

"Me'bee he does."

"No, it's owned by a Frenchman with the first name of Jean," Cliff corrected.

"Where did you find that out?"

Cliff just smiled.

"Oh yeah, your whore. I should have known."

"Wheeligo Girl," Cliff corrected again.

"Wheeligo Girl," Traven repeated and started again writing on his letter.

Being especially curious about Mr. Glaze becoming nervous when asked about the ownership of the saloon, Cliff headed towards the bank from the Marshal's Office.

Entering, he was surprised to see there were now two tellers working behind the wrought iron bars. A man facing forward and a woman who was bent over placing something in the bottom drawer of a tall cabinet. Cliff could tell she was a woman because of the dress but otherwise could not see who she was.

"Can I help you?" Kohrs asked.

Cliff shook his head and motioned towards the woman, "I need to speak to her."

"Oh," the teller replied, obviously annoyed.

Upon hearing this exchange, she turned around, and seeing him, smiled.

"Why blow me down, if it ain't Mrs. Dean."

"Mr. Brown, how nice to see you."

"I didn't know you worked here," he said thinking, '*She sure is a comely little thing.*'

"I have been here a whole week now, and Mr. Glaze hasn't run me off yet."

"I can't imagine anyone running you off."

"Oh, it's been done before."

"Not by a gentleman, surely."

"Thinking back, I do believe you have me there, Mr. Brown. Now what can I do for you?"

"Well, I heard *The Musselshell Saloon* was being put up fer sale and I wanted to inquire about just how well it's doing. I mean would it be a good investment?"

"That is something you will have to discuss with Mr. Glaze. I'm not sure it's even open information," she said, knowing Kohrs was listening.

"Is he busy?" Cliff asked.

"As a matter of fact he is. There is a Gentleman in with him right now."

"I'll wait," Cliff said and smiled.

After several minutes, she began closing her drawer and speaking to the other teller, then she came from around the counter.

Cliff stood and asked, "Are you leaving?"

"Yes. I have a lunch engagement with Mr. Traven."

"Well, would you permit me to escort you to the Marshal's Office?"

"I thought you wanted to speak to Mr. Glaze?"

"Not as much as I want to walk with you."

"Well, in that case, let us be off," she said and smiled at him.

They had walked a short distance speaking of first one trivial thing and then another until he finally said, "Back there I had the feeling you wanted to tell me something about *The Musselshell Saloon*."

"Well, I don't know if I should or not, but I can say, I suppose, that Miss Mustang makes a deposit everyday."

"Much?"

"I really don't know, she always goes straight into Mr. Glaze's office to conduct her business. Besides, I would think you could find out these things from Miss Mustang yourself, you two certainly seem to be good friends."

"Friends. Just friends nothing more and certainly not business acquaintances," he assured her.

"Oh," she replied, knowing full well he was lying.

"That is strange, though," he said frowning.

"What is strange?"

"That she only does her banking behind closed doors."

"Not really, Miss Willows does the same thing," she pointed out.

They walked on a few more paces without saying anything, and then he began, "You know, I've been all over the west, and I haven't seen half a dozen saloons owned by women, and here we are in a booming town like Copperopolis, and the only saloons here are both owned by women," he paused and then added, "supposedly."

"You are right. I never thought of that," she said back.

"Unless ___. Oh that couldn't be."

"What?" she asked.

"Unless they are both owned by the same person, and the ladies are just fronting for him."

"You mean like a silent partner?"

"Yes, something like that," he agreed. "Well, here we are Mrs. Dean. I do hope you and the Marshal have a nice lunch, and I hope he is feeling better."

"Is he sick?" she questioned obviously concerned.

"Not really, it's just, I was in earlier, and he seemed to have a bad case of ___," he removed his hat momentarily and then said, "if you will pardon my boldness, heartburn."

Looking through the window, he saw Traven was still busy with paperwork so he didn't interrupt him, rather left her to her date. "Good day, Mrs. Dean, it's been a pleasure," he said again saluting her with his hat.

"Good day, Mr. Brown."

Walking away he pondered, *'I'm sure it won't be long before she asks the good Marshal how he is feeling. Then she will have to tell him about our walk together from the bank, and then he will really get a case of heartburn. 'Mee'be even spoil his lunch.'* This latter thought made Cliff chuckle to the point his shoulders began to bounce up and down slightly.

John Pell had no doubts but that Reb Brown was there in search of him. Suddenly his inner feelings of confidence began to flee, and he felt himself quiver for a moment. Then his eyes narrowed, and he stopped his fears cold with a strong determination.

Remembering who he was and how he had become the man he was, John Tidwell's thoughts raced back, *'Jacob Hood and Frank Coleman and that miserable old man Cap' Burgess. The boy, Diane's son. What was his name? Mitchell, no Michael. Yes Michael Coleman, and Ch'ing Hung in China, and that idiot Major Scott. And the stupid news-paperwoman in South Georgia. Kimball's idiot nephew. I can not forget that dumb Chad Cheltenham in Dodge, and that stupid Ute Warrior in Colorado. And poor dumb Allen Moreton. But most of all, Will Hickey.'* Suddenly recalling these men he had killed over the years remind-ed himself of why he was in Montana at all, and of his determina-tion to fulfill the dream of reaping the riches of a cattle empire, an empire which was so close in becoming a reality.

'I can not just leave it now. Not now. Not when I have found a means to secure Hickey's fortune, as well as Moreton's pound notes, now that finally the army has, for the most part, settled the Indian problem.'

His breathing became stronger, his chest grew slightly, and he felt his body straighten. *'Only that Bastard Copperhead has eluded me, my one and only failure. No, I will never run from that ignorant back-woods cracker again,'* he thought as his shrewdness grew.

As he drove the buggy back to the *The Little Judith Ranch,* he de-liberated deeply. *'Perhaps, I have underestimated Reb Brown in the past, but this time I will not. He is not an easy man to kill, but it can be done. I will just have to plan a little better than I have in the past. Now let me think, he knows York, at least he may know York from the incident in Colorado. I can't let those two cross paths. If he doesn't know for sure I am here, that would convince him most assuredly so. No, I must keep those two apart.'*

When he arrived home, a young wrangler, whose name he had not learned, caught the lines of his horse and stopped him. "Good afternoon, Mr. Pell."

John studied him for a few moments before replying, "You are one of the men who came with the last herd, aren't you?"

"Yas, Sur. I'm Jep Wesley. I come hyar with Mr. Waco. I been with th' ootfit all the way from south Texas," the lad responded proudly.

"Where is Waco now?"

"I don't rightly know. He just tol' me to stay here and bust some of these broncs. I'm a good peeler[45]."

"I'm sure you are. How are they coming?" John asked showing an interest.

"Oh, they's coming along right fine. A couple a' them 'aire actin' like they got minds a' thar own, but they will be the best ones when we teach 'um who's really the boss. I jest as lief ride 'em as look at 'em," the boy replied turning his eyes to a mean-looking dapple gray stud, which had just cleaned his back of rider, saddle and all.

"When Waco gets back, tell him I want to see him," Pell said, then turned and walked toward the house without waiting for an answer.

"Yas, Sur," the boy replied anyway.

Waco was coming on forty and really too old for bossing such a long drive as he just completed, and he well knew it. His wife and two boys had been lost to Scarlet Fever two years past while he was away. Agreeing to do this one last drive was needed therapy. He simply could not stay there on the place, where they had shared so much joy and so many dreams. When the opportunity to head up the drive all the way to Montana came along, he jumped at the chance.

He knew he would have gone along as a hand, had he not gotten the job as trail boss. Then when it was over, and Mr. Pell offered them a chance to stay on, it just seemed like the right thing to do.

This afternoon, when Little Jep told him the boss had sent for him, he wondered if it had all been for nothing. *'I can't think of a blame thing I done wrong. But when a boss sends for a man rather than the foreman, it usually means only one thing, a firing. Only I just can't for the life of me, figure out what brung it on.'*

Waco looked all around, hoping to see York to find out what was up, but he was nowhere to be found. *'Me'bee he's inside with Mr. Pell,'* he thought, as he walked up the steps to the wide porch. He took the time for one last look around, then before knocking on the door, he slapped the dust from his chaps with his Stetson. Entering without a beckoning after the knock, he found no one immediately inside. He had been in there only once before, and that was his first day on the ranch when Mr. Pell paid him off for delivering the herd. On that occasion, York had taken him in, and their business was conducted in the dining room, where Mr. Pell was having a

45 Peeler: Bronc buster.

late breakfast. It was the time when the offer, for as many of his trail hands as wanted a job, could remain with the Lazy R-J brand. He had gladly taken the opportunity along with the others who wanted to stay.

The sound of someone approaching could be heard coming from the back, and he waited with hat in hand. Finally, a very short, round Chinese appeared and asked, "You wait see Mistla Pell? You sabbee?"

Waco just nodded his head. He wasn't sure just how to communicate with a Chinaman and wasn't sure he wanted to know.

The little man looked at him a few moments as if he was trying to make up his mind on something, then he said, "You come, Sing Lee." Then he turned and pattered away through the door to their left. Waco followed.

The room they entered was quite large for any ranch house in the west. It took up almost half of the building, and Waco had never dreamed it to be so big. There were several pieces of leather-covered furniture and a huge set of longhorns hanging over the fireplace mantle. A liquor decanter and two glasses, etched to match the bottle, were sitting on a beautifully finished table.

Once Waco had ingested the magnitude of the room, he realized the Chinaman was no longer there. Now, he really did not know what to do, as he stood there all alone.

He was looking out of the window at the men working in the corral when he detected the odor of a cigar, and shortly there after, a door he had not even realized was there, opened and John Pell entered the room.

Although Waco knew he was younger than his boss, he had to think on the difference questioningly. The man had a few wrinkles about the face, and his dark hair was streaked with lines of silver here and there, especially around his temples. Nonetheless, he was quite fit and could have been anywhere between forty and sixty. Waco truly couldn't determine where his age would fall. It was obvious though, he was a man who was in charge and knew just what he wanted in life, a man Waco could admire, given the chance to know him better.

"Mr. Waco."

"Just Waco I reckon. It's only a name my boys give me 'cause that's where I hail from."

"Very well, Waco. First I want to know what you think of *The Little Judith Ranch*?"

"Ahh, Mr. Pell, she's a wonderful spread. A place a common cowman only dreams of."

"Yes. I hold those same sentiments," the older man replied. "So you are satisfied with your job here?"

"Yas Sur. I am, truly am."

"I hate to hear when a man of talent is satisfied with a position below himself."

Waco, with narrowing eyes, was not sure what to make of that statement or how to reply. Finally, he simply said, "I'm not shore what place ya think I should have around hyar, Sur."

"I would think you would desire a position of authority, you certainly proved you could handle men, or you would have never been able to deliver my herd over such a long and arduous journey as you did."

"Mr. Pell, even a spread this size can't tolerate mor'n one foreman, and Mr. York is doing a splendid job."

"Yes he is, but I have been thinking of perhaps sending Mr. York to head up my other ranch, over in the Dakotas," John said relighting his tobacco.

"Oh, I didn't realize___."

"No. I suspect you didn't. Anyway, if I do decide to replace York here, would you be interested in the position?"

"Yas Sur. I'd be powerful keen on it," the cowman replied anxiously.

"I would require absolute and total loyalty."

"Yas Sur," Waco replied, almost before he realized what he was promising.

"Alright. If I decide to make the move with York, I may call on you. No promise but maybe." He stopped while he drew a breath of the foul-smelling smoke deep in his lungs and then added, "And Waco, until then, this meeting will remain strictly between the two of us."

"Yas Sur."

With that, Pell turned and left the room through the same door by which he had entered.

Waco shook his head to make sure he was not dreaming. *'I come in here thinking I wus about to be fired, and now I'm walking away as the foreman. Well, almost the foreman. I jus' hope I ain't promised my soul to John Pell.'*

Cliff was eating breakfast at *The Alamo* when he saw Traven come in. The Marshal headed straight for his table and drawing a chair, sat down uninvited.

"Well, to what do I owe the pleasure?"

"I've been waiting for you to come back to town."

"How did you know I was back in town?" Cliff asked, lifting his tin cup and sipping the dark liquid.

"I left word at *The Montana House* for them to let me know anytime a no good, ornery-looking, hombre came into town, especially one from Georgia."

"Didn't know you cared," Cliff said back enjoying the verbal tussle they seemed to always have.

"You got some nerve taking my gal for a walk," Traven said back, ignoring Cliff's comment.

"Your Gal? Now who would that be?"

"You know damn well who that would be."

"Surely not Mrs. Dean. Why she is a married lady."

"Me'bee, me'bee not. Her old man ain't been heard from for ages. He's daid by now."

Cliff smiled and replied, "Mee'be, mee'be not."

"Another thing, I don't appreciate you askin' her to check up on people's banking business. That sort of thing could get her fired."

"I didn't tell her to check on anything that wasn't open to the public," Cliff protested.

"Well, I don't like it no way. If there is any detective work to be done around here, I'll be the one to do it."

"Great, when are you going to start?" Cliff shot back.

"For your information, I already have."

"Want to share it?"

Traven shook his head, "Not in hyar." Then he added, "Come on back to the office. I have something there fer you anyway."

This really surprised Cliff, so he took a long last gulp of the hot Java and standing, dropped a fifty cent piece on the table, just before he retrieved his hat from the chair beside him.

In the corner of the small office were two boxes, one about four feet long and a foot wide, and another almost square and about the size of a Wells Fargo cash box.

"A feller what calls himself Red Mesa dropped these off here the other day when he passed through. It's obvious the long box contains a gun, and since its already got a fair size crack in the top there, he thought it best not to leave it over to the depot, fer fear it might get tampered with."

"I'll have to thank him next time I see him," Cliff said back, looked closely at the long box. It did have a large chunk out of the top, and some of the pegs were busted where it had been dropped or tossed in its long journey. However, it didn't seem the worse for wear, considering.

"Whoever made them boxes ain't no shorthorn," Traven mentioned, nodding at the workmanship.

"Yep, he is a true friend."

Cliff turned around looking for something he could use as a pry tool for opening the box but saw nothing.

Elon seeing his predicament said, "Wait a minute. I got a hammer hyar som'ers."

Cliff soon saw Sam had removed the stock and wrapped it separately and tied it between two leather covered Blakeslee boxes. The rifle's metal was completely covered in a heavy coat of axle grease to protect it from the changing elements it would go through during the two months it took for the packages to travel from Florida to Montana. As soon as he found the stock screws, Cliff twisted them in with his fingers as far as he could and began rubbing the grease off with the heavy linen sock he was sure Esther had made for the rifle's long trip.

"What's so special about that Henry? Hell, a body could have bought one fer less than it took to build that box, to say nothin' of the cost to post it here."

"No, this Henry has personal feelings. It's like one of the family," Cliff said, as he lovingly rubbed the old gun.

"Well, what's in the 'tuther box?"

"Cartridges," Cliff replied.

"Now I know you're crazy. You done had a case of cartridges shipped in when Coker has a' ton a them right yonder, in his store."

"Mee'be I didn't want everybody in the county knowing I have this many rounds."

"Still, it's plum crazy," Traven replied but thinking on what Brown had said, saw the merit in it.

"Now, are you going to share with me what your gal done told you about who owns *The Musselshell Saloon?*"

"Who said it were her what told me?"

"Alright, let's just say, are you going to tell me what information fell into your hands?"

"Not much really," Traven said, removing his hat and rubbing his palm over the top of his head. "It does seem there is a silent partner in with Sally Mustang and me'bee in *The White Castle* as well."

"Yeah, I figured that. I also think it's the same silent partner."

"Yeah, Cimarron thinks so too. She thinks it's Mr. Glaze."

"Mee'be, but I'm thinking of someone else."

"Who'd that be?" Traven asked, squinting his eyes at the statement.

"You hear of any Frenchmen in the area?"

"Naw, not that I recollect."

"Someone named Jean?"

Traven shook his head, "Naw."

"Well, the first time I was in *The Musselshell Saloon*, I heard Sally say something about Jean, and when I asked her about it she clamed up and denied it."

"What's this Jean have to do with anything?"

Cliff told him the whole story.

"So you think this Jean she was talking about, is the same John Tidwell that murdered your wife?"

"Could be. I know he came to Montana a year or so ago. He was in Helena and mee'be Virginia City."

"That's a far reach, Reb."

"Mee'be," Cliff admitted, "but it's possible, and there's something else, I know his side-kick in Colorado was called York. The foreman of *The Little Judith Ranch* is also named York, and that's the outfit what murdered the little James girl and burned them out."

"Just how did you come up with that?"

Cliff reached in his vest pocket and dug around until he got his fingers on the spent shell. Handing it to Traven he added, "I found this the day of the attack on James' place. Mr. Coker says the only one around here that buys them 45-75's is York, the foreman of the Lazy R-J outfit."

"You have been digging, ain't you?" Traven said, rubbing his fingers and thumb over the spent round.

"For years," Cliff replied and reached for the shell back.

"You know none a' this proves nothing," Traven pointed out.

"Does make a body wonder though, don't it?"

Traven didn't answer. He was trying to digest all he had been told during the last hour.

Late in March, Two Bucks watched as the six wranglers moved a remuda of twenty horses north. They were at the far reaches of the land claimed by the Lazy R-J brand. "It looks like dey are driving dem to Camp Lewis. Me'bee to sell to the army, or to Benton for trade," he said to Lobo.

They watched as the men camped in a canyon for the night. The wranglers made a makeshift corral of some dead wood and rope, but it would serve well, as there was a small spring there and enough grass for the broncs to be content for the night.

"They find so good a place to camp for the cayuse," he said to Lobo, "and so miserable a place for dem'selves."

It was true, this was the last place York, or any one of his men, would have chosen to camp. The walls were high and almost impossible to climb from the floor of the canyon but easily descended to well within rifle range from above. A body of Indians could ambush them, and there would be very little they could do to fight back, except run. The canyon was so crooked that a blockage could be set in place ahead, or behind, without them even knowing, until they busted head long into it.

York just couldn't figure out why Jean had been so headstrong about having the other men meet them here.

A week before, while York was moving beeves from south of the Musselshell to the north pasture, Waco reported to John Pell he found several of their freshly broke broncs had been moved into an arroyo and boxed there. "There were also tracks of unshod ponies mixed in with theirs. However, among 'em also 'aire boot tracks as well as moccasin, indicating thet perhaps Indians were stealing 'em and selling 'em to some white man, possibly a trader."

"Have you told Mr. York about this?"

"Naw, I intended to, but he is gone, and I'm not sure when he will be back. I felt bound to speak to you though, thought you needed to be appraised aboot this before they are moved oot and sold off, me'bee up Canada way whar our brand don't mean much."

"You did right. In fact, I don't want you to tell anyone about it. The culprits just may be some of our own men," Pell said.

"I can't rightly believe that," Waco said back.

"Oh, I can. You know your boys, but I have had to hire a lot of men that I know very little about. Some men just have greed in their hearts."

"You could be right, Sur," Waco agreed. "I won't say nothing to no one, and I'll tell the others, what were with me, to keep it under thar sombreros as well."

"Good."

John was sure the white men involved were not any of his men. He knew them far better than he let on to Waco. He was convinced the rustlers were squatters, and what he had just been told ignited an idea of how he could take care of a couple of thorns in his side.

When he ordered York to take the horses north he had given him specific instructions as to who to take along on the drive, and none of them were from Waco's bunch. The Texicans would ride with him a few hours behind York and his men.

Everything had gone well. The half-bred, Charlie Lone Wolf, who had been recommended by Waco as a top tracker, reported that the men had camped where they were supposed to. He also reported of several others, who had followed the remuda from shortly after they left the Musselshell.

Pell had his bunch wait, making a cold camp, until the moon was high enough to let them travel again. Then the ten men moved out as quietly as possible, with Charlie Lone Wolf a half mile ahead.

It was near two in the morning when Charlie was found waiting for them.

"The trail goes there," he said pointing at the canyon ahead. "Men camp, one mile yonder." Then he pointed to a dim but fresh trail left by several horses. "Riders go up there," he said pointing up the ridge that would overlook the canyon. "I t'ink 'dey leave hoss' and go down side to make de ambush."

"Can we get above them?" Pell asked.

"Come," was his only answer.

Pell wanted to catch the squatters after they had attacked his men in the canyon, not be caught by them himself, and he cautioned the riders with him by the merest whisper, "Now even more than before, move ever so slowly, keeping any sign of our approach hidden."

It was near the four o'clock hour when Charlie stopped them. "Men go down there. They attack with sun."

John placed his hand on the breed's shoulder and gave him a soft pat, showing his gratitude for a job well done. *'Now it is simply a matter of waiting until first light.'*

The sun's rays were moving high in the sky long before they began to reach to the floor of the canyon. Though it was day on the heights, it was still predawn in the valley, and what light there was up there, only the western wall

was getting the benefit. The canyon wall where the ambushers waited in secret was as dark as midnight.

York looked nervously up at the precipices looming above, trying desperately to identify anything that was amiss. However, he could see nothing in the darkness save the outlines of several large boulders. He didn't like it one bit. Far too many times had he used just such a setup to ambush trains being led by inexperienced wagon masters or scouts. He knew the danger that could be waiting behind any one of those boulders. He also was still bumfuzzeled as to why Jean had been so stern about them waiting here for the rendezvous.

"If it wasn't his own horses that would be lost, I would think he meant for us to be hit," he said to himself.

The others with him were also restless at the camps location and wanted to move on before the sun exposed them anymore. Billy Nelson spoke what was on each of their minds, "Come on York, we need to be out a' here before the full light of day hits this canyon floor. That ridge up thar is a perfect place fer ambushers to be hid."

York knew he was right, but he also knew the wrath Jean Mouton could unleash when his orders were not followed, so he said no to their request. "We'll wait here for the others, like we were told."

"I don't like it none; it don't make no sense when we can move on two miles and be out a' here."

"I don't like it none neither, but I follow orders, and unless you want to draw your wages, you'll do the same," he said back to the unhappy wrangler.

The words had scarcely left his mouth when Nelson's head exploded, spewing blood and brain parts all over York.

In a matter of seconds, the hillside to the east was echoing with the thunder of bursting powder. Though they tried to return fire, the only targets they could see in the darkness of that side of the canyon wall, were flashes from the muzzles of half a dozen rifles.

From the moment Nelson's head exploded, until the bullet struck him hard in the left breast, seemed like a lifetime to York, in reality it was only seconds.

"Wal' aren't we going to help 'em?" the boy standing beside Waco ejaculated.

Waco looked over at the boss and saw he was making no move to fire at the ambushers and he said, rather disgustedly, "We wait for Mr. Pell's order."

Finally, when everyone on the red wash of the canyon floor lay dead or hit and down, Two Bears raised his arm and called out for his men to stop firing.

John Pell watched them slowly stand and begin laughing and calling out to one another, and only then did he realize they were not the squatters he had expected. His first thought was to leave, but he knew the men with him would want revenge, so he motioned for them to stay out of sight.

'There is no way anyone can get to the bottom of that canyon from the wall by climbing down. They will have to come back up to the top and then go around and enter as York had done,' John thought, but what he said was, "Easy men, stay down and stay quiet. It is here we will wait for them."

The seven renegades slowly, and quite noisily, climbed back up to the ridgetop laughing and yelling as they came. Two Bucks and Lobo were ahead of the others, but just as they reached the top of the ridge, Two Bucks dropped to one knee and began reloading his Winchester. Lobo moved on past him, followed by the others.

John waited until they were all on top before he fired his own Winchester. The lead struck Lobo full in the chest, and he fell backward off the side, without even a scream erupting from his lips. Two Bucks jumped up and immediately jacked a round into his chamber and got off a quick shot at the muzzle flash, but it was high. Waco immediately had a sight picture on him and fired before the breed could chamber another round. The other raiders were not so lucky. Each was hit several times by the murderous fire of the angered cowboys.

Waco's shot had hit the leader, but not realizing the shortness of his target he failed to aim low enough, and the round only grazed Two Bucks' forehead. However, it did knock him unconscious, and he fell backward as his rifle flew high and away.When there were no more targets for them to shoot at, Pell stood and looked over at Waco and said, "Well, I guess you have become foreman sooner than either of us expected."

The Texan suddenly realized the loss of the men on the canyon floor was as much a part of this boss' plan as killing the rustlers, and he felt sick about it.

Turning to his men, Pell spoke loudly, "I'm afraid Mr. York may have been hit down there, if so, from now on Mr. Waco will be foreman of *The Little Judith Ranch*. I expect you all to follow his orders." Then turning to Waco he added, "Go get my remuda and wagon." He then started off to where their horses were tied.

"Yas Sur," Waco replied, but in his mind he added, '*And bury our daid.*'

It was nearly an hour before Two Bucks awoke. Slowly he tried to move, but intense pain shot through his right leg. It was only then he realized, from the knee down, the limb was twisted out at a seventy-degree angle from his thigh, and the pain was poignant. "She-eit!" he exclaimed.

Gradually he was able to crawl over and look below, just in time to observe two wranglers moving out behind the last of the horses. Instinctively he ducked back, using the crag to hide him from any eyes below. After a few minutes, he again chanced a look and saw nothing, save the red wash that bisected the canyon, and a shadow slowly circling below.

"Good, da hav' gone," he said, with no one to hear. Once more he raised his head and looked at his twisted leg, "She-eit," he said, long and slowly followed by, "She-eit, she-eit, she-eit!" very rapidly and then took a deep breath.

His sombrero was between his back and the rock floor of the little outcropping that had stopped his fall. Gradually, with great pain, he managed to wiggle and twist until he had the old sugarloaf free of his weight. Using a balled fist he punched its crown out where he could use it to shade the sun from his eyes as well as his head. The effort had used all his immediate strength, and he fell back, succumbing to his pain and exhaustion.

When he again awoke, he did so with a fright, and quickly looking about, he gradually remembered where he was and how he had come to be there. Now he was thirsty, and he reached for the skin he had filled just the night before, as they were leaving for this raid. Unfortunately, when he located it, still tied by the rawhide stringers he used to carry it over his shoulder; he found the bottle was flat and dry. "She-eit," he said and tried to wet his lips with his tongue but it too was dry. Even though the urge to swallow was great, he found he could not accomplish the task, and once more, he fell back.

His thoughts came at length and finally the realization was upon him. *'If I am to survive, I will need help.'* Suddenly, once again he shot a gaze to the canyon floor. *'Da men, da hav' all gone. But I need dem.'* "Hey, come back," he shouted, but there was no one close enough to hear his cries. It was then, he once more, saw the shadows circling. *'Now dar are tres or ees et cuatro. Why do I not see dem. I see dey shadows, but I can no see dem.'*

It was then the realization struck him, and he whirled back. Then shading the sun with his big hat, he spotted the large black birds flying in an ever-tightening circle above.

Eventually, one of then dipped and landed on another body some fifty feet from him, a body he had not noticed before. He couldn't tell who it was as the man had come to rest face down. Nonetheless, he was there, and the scavenger was suddenly atop his back and with a horrible looking beak, pecking short strings of flesh from his broken body.

Two Bucks franticly grabbed for the Adams[46] in his belt holster and quickly blasted three balls at the bird. The noise startled the buzzard and with huge wings lifted his body up and away from the danger momentarily but quickly caught a thermal rising from the canyon floor and began a wide but definite circle that would bring him back to where he had just launched from. Only, when he lit again on the food source, he had to share it with a companion.

Twice more Two Bucks fired at them, and as before, they vacated the spot momentarily. This exhausted his strength, and once again, he passed out.

He had no idea how long he had been unconscious, but when he awoke, he saw three of the huge birds squatted on the sharp shale only ten feet above his bed. Immediately he brought up his revolver and pulled the trigger, but there was no report, only the sickening sound of hammer striking spent caps. Realizing he was empty, he gazed into the eyes of the nearest bird, and with tongue cleaving to the roof of his mouth, he was sorely afraid, for his fate was sealed.

---

46 Adams: A five shot double action revolver issued to Union Troops during the war.

Traven saw Brown enter *The White Castle* and followed him. The tall Georgian was standing at the long bar, waiting on the barkeep to bring his schooner[47], when he walked in.

In one of the mirrors on the back bar, Cliff saw him approaching, but didn't turn around.

"What'll you have, Marshal?" the barkeep asked, as he sat the cool beer in front of Brown.

"The same," Traven said. Then he reached into his trouser pocket for a coin.

"Keep your money, I'll buy," Cliff said, and then after taking a sip he added, "I wouldn't want you to have to go out and serve a federal warrant to get the money to buy a beer."

"I can buy my own," Traven said, laying the dime on the hardwood bar. "Besides I don't plan to be obligated to you fer nothing."

"Well, I don't mind being obligated to you, so why don't you buy the next round?"

"Ain't gon'a be no next round," he spat back. Then looking at the empty table near the wall said, "Come on, I want to talk to you."

Cliff watched him head for the table. Then he gave the barkeep another coin, speaking something too low for the Marshal to hear as he walked away.

"I went out to *The Little Judith Ranch* to talk to York," Elon said, removing his hat and dropping it on the table.

"And?"

"He's daid."

"What? How?"

"Mr. Pell, the owner, said he was ambushed by some squatters," Traven replied. Then seeing the frustration spread across Brown's face, he added, "Said these squatters killed six of his men and stole several horses."

"You believe him?"

"I believe York is daid. Too many others confirmed that."

"Killed by squatters?"

"No, they didn't seem to know who killed him. Only Pell knew that," he replied, not looking at Brown.

"Strange ain't it?"

"Me'bee, me'bee not," Traven said back. Then he asked, "Strange to see you in this high class joint. I thought the Musselshell was more to your liking."

---

47 Schooner: Mug.

"Mee'be, mee'be not," Cliff mocked him.

"Well, there is one thing I got 'a say," he took a long pull from the mug. After swallowing it, he still hesitated a few seconds, then finally spoke, "I was wrong to call your woman a whore."

"She ain't my woman. In fact, she has given her new barkeep orders for me to stay out of her saloon."

"What brought that on?"

"Beats me, but I shor was told to get. On her orders."

"You all have a fight?"

"Nu-pe."

"What then?"

"Beats me," Cliff said slipping his drink. "But there is one thing."

"What's that?"

"She is a whore, but she never charged me. It don't make no difference though, I like whores. The most beautiful woman I ever knew was a whore before I married her, and I loved her deeply," he said and then looked away, and Traven knew he was looking into another place and another time, a place he realized he was not welcome, so he said nothing.

Finally, Cliff dropped his stare back to the table and finished with, "I still do."

Traven didn't know what to say and thought it best to continue saying nothing.

Brown broke the silence by asking, "What does Pell look like?"

"He's me'bee forty-five, around six-feet. Good shape for his age."

"Mee'be fifty-five, black hair with streaks of gray," Cliff suggested.

"Could be," Traven admitted. "But I don't think he's that old."

Cliff just stared off at the front doors without replying.

"You think he's your Frenchman, don't you?"

"He's somewhere in these parts," Cliff replied, still staring at the door.

"You don't know that. It's been morn' a year since you had any such knowledge."

"He's here and not far away. I can feel him," Cliff said back bitterly. "Who's running the ranch for him now?"

"The new foreman, a fellow by the name of Waco."

"Came up from Texas with that last big herd," Cliff suggested.

"Yeah, that's the one," Elon agreed. "Seemed like a good enough fellow."

"Did he say it were squatters what killed York?"

Traven thought back, and then wetting his throat with saliva he replied, "No. As I recollect he never said nothing on the subject."

"Well, mee'be he ain't the liar his boss is," Cliff suggested.

"You could be wrong, Brown."

"Mee'be," Cliff said just before standing and downing the last of his beer. He sat the mug back on the table and then again looking off in the direction of the doors he said, "I'm obliged," before he walked out.

Traven remained there for some time, wanting the man to be out of sight when he left. After a couple of minutes, the barkeep came over with another mug of beer.

"I didn't order that," the Marshal said when he set it down.

"The other gentleman paid fer it when he paid fer his," the big man replied.

"Damn him," Traven said just above a whisper. "Well, I don't want it. You drink it," he said, and then he too got up and walked out.

Cliff had taken the Henry rifle Sam Brooks had sent him out to the James spread. He also left the large wooden box of cartridges with them, cautioning them to always remain on alert. He was convinced the same bunch that attacked them before would return. He was also convinced it was men from the Lazy R-J spread. Now, since this Pell was claiming the killers of his foreman were small ranchers, Cliff was even more concerned.

No one would argue that by December of 1877, there were a dozen small spreads within fifty miles of Copperopolis. The farmers were settling along the riverbanks, where they could get irrigation during the dry months, and that was most months. However, like James, there were also a few small ranches. Cliff doubted it, but he had to admit, it could have been one of these that killed York and rustled his horses.

He still had the hunch tickling in the back of his mind, *The Little Judith Ranch* would blame it on the Blackcat Creek outfit, mainly because they were the first to make a challenge in the area.

An hour before dark found him leading a mule, carrying a heavy load of supplies north towards his friends.

Just as the ruddy rays of the sunset were bathing the western hills, Mrs. Dean came in the Marshal's office. "Elon, I am worried about Mr. Brown," she said with a true expression of concern on her pretty face.

"What is it?" he questioned, equally concerned about her.

"I, I don't know if it means anything or not, but Mr. Pell was in speaking with Mr. Glaze, and I could hear them arguing."

"What is so strange about them jawboning?"

"Nothing, they do often, but suddenly Mr. Pell came out and hurried to the door. When he opened it, I saw there were two or maybe three of his hands waiting there for him, and he pointed at Cliff Brown, who had just ridden past. I had seen him through the window, and I suspect Mr. Pell had done the same from the window in Mr. Glaze's office," she said, finally stopping and taking a breath. "Well, like I said, it may be nothing, but I saw one of the men check to see if his revolver was fully loaded and finding it not, he inserted a bullet. Then they all mounted and rode off following Mr. Brown."

"Does seem strange," Traven agreed. "What did Pell do then?"

"He went back in Mr. Glaze's office and slammed the door. They began to shout at one another again, only Mr. Glaze was even louder than before."

"What were they shouting?"

"I don't know. You can't really hear the words, but you sure can hear the shouts," she said. Then looking innocently, she added, "I'm scared. I think they are planning to harm Reb."

"Why are you so worried about him?" Traven asked her. "He could stand takin' down a notch or two."

"He doesn't need to be killed. Besides, he is your friend, whether you will admit it or not, and he is a good man," she said.

Traven knew she was right and finally nodded his head, "Alright, I'll follow after them just to make sure."

"Thank you," she said and let out a deep breath before turning towards the door.

"Cimarron," he said softly, stopping her.

"Yes?" she replied without turning back to him.

"I love you."

A warm feeling swept over her bosom, and she suddenly felt like she was light enough to fly like a bird, and she said back to him, "I love you too, Elon." Then she left the office without ever turning to look at him. She realized she couldn't look at him. If she did, she would not be able to let him go right then, and she knew his leaving was most urgent.

Walking away, she still felt like she was floating on air. It was the first time she had said that to him, or he to her, and it was so special that he had said it first.

Traven hurried to the livery to get his horse and soon was on the road that headed north towards Fort Logan, the trail that would take him past Blackcat Creek.

Night comes early in late fall, and before the Marshal overtook anyone, darkness was upon him, but he continued on. Once, off in the distance, he thought he could see riders ahead, and he reined up. However, the moon had not yet risen, and there was only the light of ten thousand twinkling stars shining down through the cool thin air to light the road and then only enough for him not to wander afar.

"Hal-low the house," Cliff called out when he stopped Ola about fifty yards south of the James home. The moon was just creeping up on his right, and he soon saw a figure appear between the wide slits of the bastion.

"Who calls?" Blackcat's voice questioned.

"A wayward Georgia boy, lost in this treeless wilderness," Cliff called back.

"Well, wayward Georgia Boy, come on in," his friend called back.

"Who is it, Otis?" Ginny yelled up to her husband.

"It's Reb. Open the door fer him."

Suddenly both Otie and Laramie lunged for the door at the same time, and it was anybody's guess who actually lifted the heavy plank that secured it so well.

An hour later, the same call was once again heard.

"Who could that be?" Ginny asked.

Cliff knew the voice sounded familiar but could not put a face with it.

Again, Blackcat hurried up the ladder and through the trapdoor in the tower floor, followed closely by his friend.

Once more he asked, "Who calls there?"

"Marshal Traven," came the reply.

"What would he be doing out here?" Blackcat questioned.

"Doe-no," Cliff replied then added, "but it's him, sure enough. I know that voice."

"Come on in, Marshal," Blackcat yelled back.

Cliff was down the ladder first, and everyone downstairs looked at him with anticipation.

"Go head boys, open the door," he said to the two teenagers.

When Elon entered, a big smile crossed Ginny's face. "Why, it is the Marshal."

"Howdy Ma'am," he replied, removing his hat.

"What on earth brung you way out here?"

"Well, Ma'am, I need to talk to Mr. Brown," he replied, not wanting to give unnecessary concern to the others.

"Alright, let's go back outside," Cliff suggested, realizing Elon didn't want to talk in front of the others.

They stepped out by Traven's horse and each rolled a quirley.

Elon explained to Cliff what Cimarron had told him and that she had been truly concerned about his welfare.

"I'm a mite balled up about that provokin' you to ride all this way, just to warn me."

"Well, that still is why I'm here," Traven said back, looking off to the ridge north of them. Suddenly he stopped and placed a hand on Cliff's shoulder. "I just seen something move up yonder on that ridge."

"Probably Black Band," Cliff said. "He stays up there until midnight and then one of us relieves him."

"Every night?"

"Most," Cliff returned. Then also looking up at the dark hill he asked, "You figure those three are planning on dry gulchin' me, eh'?"

"Me'bee, me'bee not."

"If not, you shor took a long ride fer nothing."

"Well," he started, "Cimarron was concerned, and I figured I'd do my part."

"I do appreciate that, but if they try something here, we'll give them a fandango they won't soon forget."

"I see this place is built better than most forts. Who came up with the idea of the turret?"

"The boy, Otie."

"Good idea."

"Yeah, it can only be gotten to up a ladder from inside, and the trap door can only be opened from inside as well. From there, a fellow good with a Winchester can cover most of the ground all around fer a far piece."

"Or a Henry."

"Or a Henry," Cliff said back, seeing Traven had deducted his reason for sending for the rifle and ammunition.

Traven nodded his head, liking what he saw. "Well, I reckon I'd best be moseying on back."

"I reckon you had best be moseying inside, unless you want Ginny James for an enemy."

"Yeah," Traven replied, realizing the affront he would leave rushing off so soon.

"I 'spect right about now she's warming you some of that fine elk stew she fixed fer supper," Cliff said, and then taking the reins of Elon's horse he added, "I'll take him over to the corral and get him some grain. I 'spect he's as hungry as you."

"Obliged," was all the Marshal said.

Cliff pushed on the rump of the big bay, moving him around and then looking back at Traven in the moonlight he said, "When are you gon'a stop beating the devil around the stump and ask that girl to marry you?"

"That's none a' your business," Traven snapped back and hurried inside before he had to talk more on the subject.

When they saw him cut off the road and head for the squatter's cabin, they split up. Two followed him on, but Jeptha Wesley was sent back to deliver the note Mr. Pell had given them, with orders to take it to Waco at the ranch as soon as they knew where Reb Brown was headed.

Wesley rode all night, stopping only long enough to give his pony a drink, arriving at the west line camp just as someone inside was stoking the stove to bring the left over coffee to a boil.

The temperature had dropped to a little below freezing a half hour before, and his toes were starting to go numb.

Jeptha was only a boy himself, not quite a year older than Laramie and Otie. Yet, he had endured the hardship of the long drive northward and was more than appreciative when Waco had recommended him to be one of the hands to stay on.

He had been born and raised near Graza, Texas and had never had a job other than chores before leaving on the trail drive. His devotion to Mr. Waco, as only he called him, was unconditional.

Needing a fresh mount and to thaw out some, he stopped at the line shack. While sipping on a cup of hot brew, he explained his charge and showed the note to Zeb Grandville, another of the Texas boys who was now working the Lazy R-J brand.

The difference between the two was Zeb was totally loyal to only himself. Anytime he saw the opportunity to advance, he usually seized it and ran. In his eyes, this was just such an opportunity. As soon as Jeptha was again moving west, he suggested to the others that they go ahead and be the ones to rid the range of this vermin, building shacks on land belonging to *The Little Judith Ranch.*

None of these hands had been on either the raid on James' home previously, or in on the dry gulching of Two Bucks' clan, so they were riding in total ignorance of the ramifications that their reckless folly was about to bring on their boss.

It was near noon when Jeptha finally arrived at the ranch plaza and found Waco.

The note he handed the foreman simply said:

> The man who led the raid on us before and has threatened my life is being followed by Maxwell, Merrill & Wesley. As soon as they see where he's headed I want you to take as many men as necessary and rid us of him and any of his confederates.
>
> J Pell

"Where is he?" was all Waco asked.

"He cut off to that squatter's shack on what they call Blackcat Crick."

Waco didn't like any of it, but he did like working for *The Little Judith Ranch* and especially the sixty a month and found his new position offered. Gritting his teeth, he slapped his gloves in the palm of his hand and said, "Alright, ten of you boys get your rifles and your overnight gear, and let's be moving out in fifteen minutes."

Turning again to Jeptha he asked, "All six of the boys were in the west line camp when you come by?"

"Yep. Zeb and Tim Levi were up, and the others were still in thar bunks, but I seed them all."

"Alright, get you a new mount and head back thar and tell them of our plans. Tell 'em to wait for me at Garrett's crossing. We'll all hit 'em at the same time."

"Yas Sur," the boy said. Turning, he started to run to fulfill his new orders.

"Wait. Also fetch some coal oil."

"Coal oil?" the boy asked, not understanding the reasoning.

"Yeah. Thar's a two gallon can in the barn, fill it with coal oil and bring it along."

"Yas Sur," he repeated, before he started off headed for the tack-shop.

By the time Elon had eaten, he saw the folly of returning during the night and decided to wait and ride back with Cliff in the morning. However, that too began to drag on as one thing after another caused a delay in their departure. He was anxious to get back and keep an eye on Pell, but just as they started to saddle up, he discovered his horse had thrown a shoe sometime in the night. Unfortunately, they didn't have one that fit, so this delayed their departure until a fire was brought up enough to form fit the hoof.

"Must 'a been just as I was getting here, or she would a' gone lame," Traven said, looking back down the trail as if he expected to see the U shaped piece of iron laying there in plain sight.

It was nigh on eleven when they finally got saddled up and were about to mount. Suddenly a single shot rang out, breaking the morning sounds of the cool clear air.

Cliff immediately looked to the north ridge where Black Band was signaling. He knew the Crow had seen something that he determined was trouble, or he would have simply signaled with his mirror or sent word back when he had relieved Laramie a few minutes before.

Pulling his rifle from its scabbard Cliff said, "Let's get inside until we find out what this is all about."

Traven followed the others only as far as the edge of the barn. There he waited, not sure if all the concern was justified.

Zeb Grandville and his boys had also heard the shot. Pulling up, Tim Levi asked, "Yu hyar thet? What wus it?"

"A shot," Zeb replied.

"Where you reckon it come from?"

"Doe no, but it were a long ways off. Probably some'un downing a prairie chicken fer noon chuck. Come on we got ourselves a nester to run off," Zeb said heeling his horse.

Topping a slight hummock, suddenly they spotted the house, and they reined up sharply, not expecting to see a bulwark tower on its side.

"What the hell is thet?"

"Hellfire, aire yu a bunch a gurls or what, it's still only some fool nesters. They ain't no match fer seasoned Texicans like us," Zeb said to the others and started down the hill towards the cabin.

Elon saw them coming and stepped out from the barn with full intention of his authority stopping them, but they didn't wait until they were close enough to see who it was and started shooting as soon as they saw him.

"Yonder's one of 'em!" Zeb yelled and discharged his big Colt at the man on foot while his horse was in full gallop.

The ball struck the ground a few yards in front of Elon, and it cleared up any idea that this was going to be settled by talking. Traven immediately turned and took to the cover of the barn once again.

A moment later, Cliff put a 44 slug in the brain of the horse Zeb was riding, and it tumbled tail over head down the slope, with rider still attached.

The others were too committed to stop and continued on towards the cabin at full speed. When they were close enough, Cliff and Blackcat opened up with well-aimed shots from their repeaters dropping each of the attackers from their saddles before they reached the east fence line.

When the dust began to clear and they were reasonably sure no more were coming, Cliff came down, leaving his friend up there just in case.

The Marshal had caught one of the riderless horses that had come running into the yard and was examining it when Cliff came out of the house.

The first thing he did was to look up at the north ridge and see the Indian waving. He then walked over to where Traven held the roan.

"He sports a Lazy R-J brand," Cliff pointed out.

"Yeah, I seed thet," the lawman said. "I guess I had better go have another talk with Pell."

"Come on, let's see if any of them are still alive."

The boys who had been shot were dead, save Tim Levi, and he was so far gone he was unconscious from the loss of blood spewing from a chest wound. However, the boy who had been thrown was laying there flat of his back staring at the blue sky.

"Are you hit, boy?" Cliff inquired.

"No. I don't think so," Zeb replied, turning his eyes toward the two men who stood over him. It was then he saw the round badge pinned to Elon's holster. "You the law?"

"I am."

"I'm Zebulon Grandville, and I ride for The Lazy R-J brand," he gasped. Then taking a breath, he began again, "We come hyar to clear out some bushwhackers, what killed several of our men a few days ago."

"There are no bushwhackers here, boy," the Marshal said back to him.

"Oh, yes thar 'aire. Mr. Pell sent a note to come here and wipe 'em oot. They is being lead by a bad cuss. Goes by Brown," he said, and then blinking his eyes several times he added, "Sheriff, you got to help us get him."

"Where is this note?" Elon asked, knowing it would be the kind of evidence to get him the federal warrants to arrest Pell.

"Jep, Jep Wesley took it on to Waco. They be coming soon and'll help you, Sheriff."

"Son, there ain't no bushwhackers hyar. These are just folks trying to etch out a living. Most likely, like your folks."

"Can't be. Mr. Pell's note said they wus bushwhackers."

"Come on, let's try and get him inside. Me'bee Mrs. James can help him some."

It was a big mistake on their part. The moment they moved him, his broken neck fell backward and snapped out his life.

"Hell, not one of them is mor'n twenty years old," Traven said, as he walked back past the dead bodies towards the cabin.

Simon Maxwell and Seth Merrill had hid themselves among the willows along the creek, long before daybreak. They were awaiting the arrival of the force they expected to come. When only a handful of boys came charging down the hill firing their revolvers wildly, both of them hugged the creek bank for fear of being hit by a stray round. From there, they witnessed the whole affair.

Black Band spotted a dust cloud approaching from the east, and studied it carefully for a long time, trying to make out if it was being caused by more riders or just a herd of antelope. It was during this time, Maxwell and Merrill slipped off to where they had cached their mounts and were riding away in a fast trot when he finally turned back and spotted them.

The Crow fired off a round to signal Clifford. Unfortunately, by the time he realized what Black Band was excited about, the two were half a mile away, making tracks for Copperopolis.

That afternoon, another six graves were added to the Bone Orchard behind James' cabin.

"I'm headed back to town to see if Pell is still there. I'd rather tangle with him on my turf than at his ranch, where all his hands are there to back him up. So I got 'a get a wiggle on."

Cliff nodded his head, "That's a good idea, but I'll tell ya', John Tidwell is a Curley Wolf and won't be taken easy."

"You still think he's the same man?"

"I'm more convinced now than ever, and the only thing that keeps me from going after him right this minute is what that boy said about more riders coming to wipe out this good family. That just mee'be is what Black Band saw, yonder to the east."

"Luck to you, Brown."

"The same," Cliff replied and stretched forth his hand in hopes this was not the last time he would get to have a shake with this man.

The dust trail was indeed riders, however Waco had held up some six miles east of Blackcat Creek at a little ford called Garrett's Crossing. There was never any water in the stream, except during the spring runoff, and this year the winter had been so mild there wasn't enough snow to fill the cut, and she was as dry as a sidewinders belly.

It was closing in on four o'clock when Jep finally arrived alone, only to tell Waco that the boys from the line camp were no where to be found.

"Shit!" the foreman said. "None of the six?"

"Naw, nary a soul."

Looking around at the worn out men on over-taxed mounts, and considering the lateness of the hour, he finally said, "We'll camp here for the night and hit them come first light."

The news came as a welcome song to his men. They had started out full of piss and vinegar, but the long hard ride had taken most of the enthusiasm out of them. Now no one really relished attacking that afternoon.

During the night, Cliff showed the boys how to load from a Blakeslee Box. He took one of them up to the bastion, but left the other downstairs where the Henry, covering the front of the house, could be reloaded rapidly as well.

Black Band took the Government Carbine to his hiding place on the ridge, where he could take advantage of its long-range capabilities.

Traven checked *The Montana Hotel, The Musselshell Saloon, The White Castle*, and finally was at the bank when Cimarron told him that Pell had not been in that day. Just as he was about to leave, Windy Willows came out of the back office after making her deposits from the previous evening's take. As she passed the couple, she overheard the Marshal asking the clerk about Pell. Then when he asked to see the bank president, she lingered.

Cimarron escorted him back but did not fully close the office door, and Bea could just make out that indeed, he was looking for John Pell, and the words Federal Warrants were clear, although she did not hear the charges. This concerned her, but the fact that she had heard the voice of the Marshal say the name Jean Mouton was what really concerned her.

John Pell was at that very moment asleep in her bed at *The White Castle*, and as she hurried back to awaken him, she began to feel the emotion of panic sweeping over her. *'If he is arrested on some federal charge, Ace Spade just might find out where he is, and since I have eluded Spade, I will most surely be wanted also by the detective agency.'*

"Get up! You have to get out of here."

"What are you talking about?"

"I was just down at the bank, and Marshal Traven was there looking for you. He has Federal Warrants to arrest you."

"What! Whatever for?" the man asked, shaking the sleep from his head.

It had not been a good night. He had spent the early hours with Brigitte, but she and he had ended up in a huge argument over who was to run *The White Castle*. He had slapped her hard and left for the comfort of Bea and her bed. His head hurt from too much indulgence in the cheap brandy she kept in her room, and his stomach was crying for the food it did not get the night before.

"Give me some money."

"I haven't got any. I just came from the bank," she said back, as she watched the anger build in him.

Slipping on his dark trousers, he reached for the blouse that yesterday had been freshly boiled but now was stained by the dark wine that had dribbled from his chin after too much indulgence and wrinkled from its night on Bea's floor.

"Well, get me some from the cash box," he ordered, looking to make sure his revolver was fully loaded. "I can't go to the bank right now. Now can I?" he pointed out. Then in a demanding tone added, "And I need some money to get away for a few days."

"No. There is only enough there to get the games rolling. Here I have some of my own," she replied and gave him two twenty-dollar red-backs from her handbag.

"Shit!" he said disgustedly and then thought that even though it was past noon, most likely Brigitte had not made her daily deposit. *'She has so much trouble with the figures. Glaze is always complaining about her being late and him having to wait on her.'*

Finally, Jean buckled on his gunbelt and lastly, covered it all with a frock coat which matched his pants. "I'll be back in a couple of days, have me a couple of thousand in folding money put away, in case I need to go somewhere until this silly mess can be cleared up."

"Now where will I get a couple thousand dollars?" she spat at him.

He looked hard at her, and as he did, his lids narrowed over those cold blue eyes, and a moment of terror shot through her veins. Bea however was a strong woman, and before her fear showed, she had control of it.

"Don't make a deposit for the next two days," he shot at her and instead of shivering in fright, she sternly returned his stare as she nodded her head in agreement.

Jean slammed her door as he left and heading down the back stairs. He had resolved he would take Sally's deposit and head for the ranch where his men would cover for him.

This might have worked, only on this day, Sally Mustang had gotten her deposit made up early. In fact, she had done it late in the night. Being so angry over their quarrel, she had not gone to sleep at all, and doing her figures was one way she tried to erase the ugly mood she was in but to no avail. The longer she worked on the figures the more mistakes she made and the more her anger grew and festered. By the time she had everything tallying, she was in a near state of rage, and Windy Willows was the center of this rage, followed very closely by Jean Mouton.

He was just leaving, by way of the back entrance, when she passed by on North Street. Seeing her, he called out, "Brigitte."

She stopped. *'It has to be him. No one else here knows me by that name.'* Looking around, she spotted Jean in the alleyway, beckoning her to come to him. As she crossed the street, she thought it strange, until she realized where he had to have come from.

"You been with the fat one," she spat, looking up at the rear window that was Bea's bedroom.

"Have you made your deposit yet?"

"No. I go there now," she said, holding up her purse.

"Give it to me."

"Why?" she questioned.

"Because I said so."

"No. You get money from the one whose bed you sleep," she growled, and then she spit at the wall of *The White Castle*.

"I said give it to me," he demanded, almost in a shout.

She realized the desperation in his voice. "Here take it. Take it all. I hate the sight of you," she yelled. Then she spit once more, this time at him.

Suddenly he realized true fear had swept through his mind upon hearing that the Marshal was looking to arrest him. He was all too aware that being incarcerated could, and likely would, lead to an investigation of his past, and no one knew what past crimes might turn up. Being arrested was unacceptable.

However, the gesture of being spat upon had instantly quenched his panic. Now he only felt anger, anger at being pushed into such a situation and anger at himself for falling prey to panic but mostly at the audacity of a woman spitting in his face. He reached forward to take her handbag, and in doing so, he grabbed firmly to her wrist, pulling her forward and twisting her arm behind her. "My dear Cajun whore, you should have not done that," he said, as he used his free hand to wipe her spit from his face.

She could now see the depth of his fury, and suddenly she felt extremely fearful. She wanted to scream out. There were people passing by on the boardwalk in front of the line of buildings only a few yards away. Maybe one of them would hear her and come to her rescue, but something inside her would not let her screams come out. Her eyes, now full of terror, widened when she saw him wipe away her spit on his trousers. Once cleaned, he reached for the ivory handle of the dirk he always carried.

Her head was back and twisted as she strained to see his left hand, which was surely grasping the knife, while his other held her fast by the wrist.

The swiftness with which he slipped the thin blade in her side was amazing to her. In one blink, his hand was on the knife at the back of his neck, and then the steel was deep in her side. It was not painful, not like she would have imagined. Instead it was more like a bite from an insect or a sting of a summer bee and that only just for a moment, then she felt no more pain.

In that instant she had cried out once, but no more. Now she just watched the cruelty of his expression and thought, '*I am dealing with the devil himself.*'

However, her small cry had not gone unnoticed. Hank and Marsha Groll were passing at that very moment, and the high-pitched squeal did not fail to attract their attention. Turning, they entered the alley and saw the man holding the woman, obviously against her will. "Here you. Let her go," Hank bravely called out.

John looked at the couple, and although he did not recognize them, he recognized the predicament they put him in, and returning the Arkansas Toothpick to its small scabbard behind his neck, he pulled the Navy Colt from his gunbelt before advancing towards them.

"Go get help," Hank said, pushing his wife behind him.

The newspaperman was not carrying a weapon, save a strong hickory walking stick which had become a constant companion ever since his slight stroke three years before. It was with this raised at port arms, he moved towards the man who now held a Colt revolver.

John did not understand this man. He had no chance of survival except to flee and instead he was advancing.

"Let the woman go," the man demanded.

John looked into the man's eyes and saw no fear, only determination. He also could hear the screams of the wife calling for help on the street and the sounds of people responding to her pleas. To kill this man would have been a pleasure. To kill anyone who so defied him always gave him pleasure, but he realized also, at this time it would be very unwise.

"There. There, stop him. He's hurting a woman," Marsha cried and pointed down the alley. Two men dressed in cowboy attire appeared and looked where her out-stretched arm pointed.

John knew those idiots would come to the defense of this stupid man, so he lowered the hammer on his revolver. "There will be another day for you to grieve not minding your own business, Monsieur," he said coldly, before pushing Brigitte against the side of the saloon. Turning, he fled up the back street towards the livery, carrying her handbag.

"Minding my own business, is not my business, Monsieur John Pell," Hank growled back at the man, now running away. "And there will be many days, for you to grieve this day."

The two men who came rushing down the alley to assist stopped when they saw the bloodstain smear on the white building and immediately turned their attention to assisting the pretty woman rather than giving chase to her attacker.

Traven was soon called to Doctor Cavenaugh's office, where the young surgeon was gathering several bandages he hoped would stop the bleeding from Sally's side.

"Can I talk to her?"

"If you stay out of my way," the doctor replied, hurrying back into the room where she lay. "I don't think you will get much. I gave her laudanum to ease her pain."

"Sally, it's Elon Traven. Can you hear me?"

"I hear you, lawman."

"I need you to tell me who stabbed you," he said leaning over her.

She looked up at him and through gritted teeth said, "Windy Willows, the fat bitch."

"Now Sally, Hank Groll and his wife both have said it was John Pell. I just need you to confirm it."

"I say it was the fat bitch," she replied and then turned her head away.

"That's enough for now, she is out of her head from the laudanum," the doctor said, moving between his patient and the Marshal.

He didn't know what Sally had against Miss Willows. It must be something very strong to cause her to make a false accusation on such a serious charge, but it didn't really matter to him. Too many people had identified the assailant as John Pell, and he knew his duty. It didn't take Elon long to find out where Pell had gone after fleeing the scene, and he too was soon mounted.

He stopped by the bank to tell Cimarron where he was headed.

"But shouldn't you get a posse?"

"No time. If Pell is as elusive as Reb Brown says, he may clean out his safe there and disappear into the wilderness, where I will never find him."

"You look pale, are you feeling alright?" she asked, placing her palm on his cheek.

"I got a little case of the Colorado Quick Step, but I can't let that stop me."

"I think you should not try this alone," she again said, almost in a plea.

"I have to. Reb was so sure, and I wouldn't listen to him. If I let this man get away, and he is the one who killed his wife___." He let the idea finish his statement.

"Well, take Reb with you."

"I can't, he's still out at James' on Blackcat Crick. No, I have to go it alone. See you soon," he replied mounting.

"I love you, Elon Traven," she said, knowing further words to stop him would be in vain.

"I'll be back," and with that he heeled his horse and rode off towards the northeast and *The Little Judith Ranch.*

Hours before Bea Desmond had departed *The White Castle* to take her daily deposit to the bank, Clifford Brown had missed the bottom rung of the ladder, while descending and had fallen to the plank floor of Blackcat's cabin. The fall embarrassed him more than it caused injury, but he did twist his left ankle, which soon began to swell.

First light found him in the tower along with Laramie. They had been watching the dark figures move among the scattered sage ever since they heard the unquestionable report of Black Band's heavy gun.

Waco also had heard the signal and spotted the muzzle flash in the darkness. He sent two of his riders around the north side of the ridge, where a sentry obviously was posted. Then he had half of his men dismount and slip in as close to the nester's cabin as they could get before sunrise, while he and the others waited with the horses.

"Keep a track on where they are," Cliff said to his young companion.

"Exactly what I'm doing," Laramie replied proudly as he peered into the dimly lit side of the east slope, the very same slope from which the other young lad had led his boys to their death, only the day before. Now the people in the cabin were hoping the results of this attack that would surely occur, would turn out as good as that one had.

However, Wallace Evans, known to those who now rode with him as Waco, was not the novice Zeb Grandville had been. Captain Evans had led a company of Hood's Texas Cavalry into the jaws of death at Franklin, Tennessee, eleven years before. He was not about to be caught off-guard as Grandville had been.

This was also the first time Waco had seen the James homestead. Now the gray light of pre-dawn revealed the citadel on the side of the cabin, and he fully understood its ramifications.

His plan was to split his mounted forces and charge the cabin from both the north and east sides. At the same time the men on foot, who he had sent to occupy the barn, could keep the man in the bastion pinned down. He surmised the rocks that had been piled along the sides to prevent firing the structure only provided a strong-willed man an opportunity to ascend to the roof and then enter the cabin from the tower.

The sun would be at their backs when they began the charge down the slope, and he was strong in his belief the whole affair would be over in a matter of minutes.

Just as the first rays began to twitch on the eastern horizon, he tied a white neckerchief to the barrel of the Winchester, which had once belonged to York, and rode slowly down the slope.

If he could get them to surrender, it would save lives, even though he had no doubts but to the success of his men; there still was the likelihood that some of them would be hurt, and possibly killed. He surely wanted no unnecessary killing.

He also surmised, *'With me riding out in the open, the eyes of our enemy will be on me, and the men on foot will be less likely spotted as they close on the barn.'*

Cliff saw him the minute he started down the long grade. Taking a fine bead on his chest, he waited on the squeeze of the trigger.

"Stay low and keep your eyes on the sneakers. I'll stay on the rider," he said to the boy beside him.

He knew the cover of the roof over the tower would shade them in darkness for some time after the cabin was lit. Only the background of the distant sky behind them would reveal where, and how many men were in the bastion.

When Waco was a little less than a hundred yards away, Cliff hailed him, "That's far enough."

Waco didn't like being halted so soon, and he stopped for a few moments to reply, "I want to parlay," then nudged his mount forward again.

"Speak your piece," Cliff replied.

"No need for blood to be shed."

"If you don't stop that hawse, yours will be the first shed," Cliff called back. Then he reached down, removed the hat from Laramie's head and dropped it to the floor before saying to the boy, "Stay down. I don't want him to know there is more than one a' us up here."

Waco held up his horse realizing he had better not proceed closer. He could just make out the dark image of a man's head in the citadel. He realized taking him would not be easy unless the man stood higher to shoot, and then he hoped one of his men from the barn could drop him.

"Look friend, I don't want to kill you, but you are on Lazy R-J range, and you have to go."

"This is homesteaded land. Legal and proper. You are the one who's trespassing, and the Federal Marshal will see you are put in Leavenworth, if you don't leave now," Cliff replied. A moment later he added, "That is, the ones of you that are still alive."

"And your family. How many of them will still be alive?"

Cliff nodded his head in satisfaction. The man thought he was Blackcat and that was good. "We made out alright against that bunch of bushwhackers you sent yesterday to try and take us," he called out to the rider.

"I sent no one to bother you yesterdee," Waco said back truthfully.

"They were all riding Lazy R-J stock," Cliff replied.

"I know nothing of this," Waco yelled back, "Who were they?"

"Never got introduced, but if you will look over to your left you will see six new crosses in that bone-yard yonder."

Of course, Waco couldn't see them from where he was, but the statement had the same effect. He now knew why the boys from the line camp had not made the rendezvous.

"I say again, let there be no more blood spilt over so small a piece of land."

"You in the war?" Cliff implored.

"I was."

"Which side?"

"From the sound of your drawl, I would say the same as you."

"Well then, why are you trying to hurt good southern folk?"

Waco thought hard on what the man had said and then replied, "Sorry brother, I ride for the brand."

"Even when the owner of the brand is one of the very ones who represented those who bulldozed our families after the fighting was done? A' ace high carpetbagger. A Yankee who murdered women and children. Murdered Southern families, for greed?"

There was a long silence before the man spoke again, and when he did, Waco only called back, "I ride for the brand."

"That's powerful interesting, but I have two things to say to you. I hope you are wearing your best bib and tucker, because you are going to be buried in 'em," Cliff said and waited to see if his statement had any effect on the invader.

Waco then spotted one of his men running low and fast from the last of the rabbit-brush towards the barn. He wanted to keep the nester's attention long enough for Brazos to make it, so he yelled back, "And what's your second point?"

"How are you going to get back up that hill?" Cliff yelled, as he squeezed the trigger of his Yellowboy.

In the brief moment between hearing the statement, realizing its meaning, and the bullet sticking him full in the breadbasket, Waco thought *'I have a good plan here. I just have to be able to give the orders, or with these kids the whole thing will fly apart.'*

Before he could give the first order though, the heavy slug knocked him from his saddle, and he fell backwards on the rocky ground.

It was a good plan too, and possibly would have worked, had not Blackcat the night before used his mules to drag in more wood from the creek, building a near impregnable, breast high, triangular rampart, on the southwest corner of the barn. From there he had a commanding view of both the yard and the creek bank, and it was there he waited on one knee.

From the direction Waco had come, the barn hid the breastworks from his view, and the darkness of the morning had not revealed it to the men descending on foot either.

Otis had listened to Reb's side of the conversation with someone, he knew not who, but when he heard the report of the rifle come from the tower, he realized the time had arrived. He then rose, readying himself for what was to come.

Buckie Brazos was the first to cross the short opening from the sage to the barn, and Blackcat let him get almost to the log structure before he dropped him with a shot to the chest. The next three boys seemed not to understand the death that lay ahead and followed him one by one to their reward. Two more, who looked at the lifeless bodies on the ground between them and the barn, suddenly realized their peril and stopped. Unfortunately for them, this too was a mistake, for Laramie had them in his sights and dropped them with two quick shots from Cliff's Henry.

By then the riders were charging down the hill and coming at the cabin from both directions. Cliff turned his attention to them and began to pour a murderous rain of lead on these attackers.

The whole affair lasted less than five minutes, and then there was nothing but the smell of burned sulfur and the cries of the wounded.

Slowly, the defenders began to realize it was over, gradually they began to come from their respective positions, and the count of the dead started.

Otie had dropped three at short range as they tried to bust in the front door. There were another five bodies on the east side of the house, who had mistakenly tried to ascend to the roof. On the slope where Waco had fallen, were another six dead men and three more in the sage, where Laramie had spotted them.

Only Waco and two other wounded were still alive, save one lone lad, who had wisely thrown away his rifle and lifted both arms high in the air, as he saw his friends falling like rotten apples in the wind.

Cliff walked cautiously up to the man he had talked to before, and looking down at him he said, "You sure rode for the wrong brand."

"How many of my men are dead?"

"All, except three. Two of them might not make it," Cliff said back.

Waco shook his head and fought back the tears. "This is worse than Franklin."

Cliff looked down at him and suddenly a camaraderie bonded the two enemies, and he inquired, "You at Murfreesboro?"

Waco shook his head again, "No. I was captured south of Nashville, spent the last year in Point Lookout."

"Ain't life funny, so was I, but I can tell ya, it ain't worse than Murfreesboro. There the Stones River ran red for two days," Cliff said, before reaching over and removing the revolver from Waco's sash. Then he turned and walked away leaving the man to bleed on the cold Montana ground.

"You gon'a just leave me here?"

"Naw, we'll land ya' in a shallow grave later with the others."

"You are a hard man," Blackcat said to him as he approached, after listening to the exchange between the two.

"He didn't come 'ere for no picnic, and I ain't about to provide 'im one."

After some time, when there was no show from Black Band, Cliff sent Laramie and Otie up the ridge to tell him to come on down.

They had just reached the top when Cliff heard a rifle report, and looking that way, he saw Laramie waving his rifle over his head and he knew something was wrong.

Cliff jumped on the back of Ola, without waiting for the benefit of a saddle and raced towards the distant ridge.

There he found the boys standing over the body of Black Band. Ishté Shipite had received a direct blast from a shotgun in the back. It appeared he had been shot twice, once from a distance that surely knocked him down and then once more at close range. His trap-door carbine was gone, but there were two spent 45 government casings on the ground near where he fell. Otie just stood there looking at the large wound in the man's back, but Laramie was crying loudly. Cliff felt like joining him.

He thought it would be best to load the body on Ola's back, but before they had this accomplished, there was a shot from below. They all looked down the four hundred yards to where a rider was sitting in the front of the cabin.

Cliff also spotted Blackcat waving for them to come down.

"I'm going on back with Otie, you stay here. And keep a sharp look see on your back," he said to Laramie.

The boy nodded and sat beside his old friend, but he thought not of covering his back. He just had too much grieving to do.

"When we get there, I'll send Otie back with another animal to bring him down on."

Again, Laramie nodded but said nothing.

Upon arriving at the cabin, Cliff saw Barry Beal. "What's the trouble?"

"Miss Cimarron sent me to fetch you," the solidly built man said, and then he told of what had transpired since Cliff had left town.

Cliff immediately saddled one of the horses he had bought for the ranch, when he brought back the wagonload of lumber. Next, he gathered up a box of cartridges from inside and two grain sacks from the barn. Climbing on the sorrel, he turned to Barry and said, "I consider myself obliged for your hard ride out here."

"Want me to go with ya?"

"No. You have done enough riding for one day."

"Don't you want any of us to come with you?" Blackcat asked.

"I reckon not. You have too much to do here with the burying and all." Then he looked up to the ridge where his young friend was waiting, and he added, "Tell Laramie I'll be back as soon as I can."

Then he touched the front brim of his gray hat moments before he spurred the red horse and left northbound with Ola following on a long lead.

"I sure hope he knows what he's doing," Barry said.

"Yes, as do I."

Dark clouds were racing by overhead, and the wind had picked up considerably by the time Traven arrived in view of the cluster of buildings that made up *The Little Judith Ranch's* plaza.

'*There's promise of snow in this storm,*' he thought, as a chill ran across his broad shoulders, and he raised them to shake it off.

Stopping atop the western hill, his eyes keenly surveyed what appeared to be a deserted ranch. Seeing no one around the corral, or any activity anywhere except a thin trail of smoke rising high from the cook's chimney, he decided to circle completely around the main house, from a distance of two hundred yards.

Upon being satisfied that the only tracks made within the last several hours were left by a lone horse entering and not leaving, he smiled. Next, he studied the wide trail made by many horses headed west, but he was content they had been made hours before, perhaps even a day or two.

"Well, they are all gone, or they are all down there laying in ambush for a target to ride in," he said to his horse.

Taking a deep breath, he let it out slowly before gently touching the heel of his boot to the animal's side, and they moved slowly towards the buildings.

He headed for the corral fence, keeping the barn between him and the ranch house. This exposed him to the bunkhouse, but he figured that his greatest danger would be from Pell himself, and that he figured would come from the large château, which seemed out of place in these rolling hills of the Montana prairie.

Tying his reins to one of the peeled poles on the back side of the corral, he slipped around to the rear door of the big barn. Once inside, he saw there were only three horses there. One quite lathered up and another saddled but the third appeared to be favoring a front foot.

Smiling, he looked around until he found the tools he wanted, and then he went to each of the animals there. Satisfied with his labor, he looked one last time at the big house, and then he went back to his horse and rode up the hill in the direction he had come.

They almost made it to the top, when he was suddenly knocked from his saddle. It was perhaps a half-second before the report of the Sharps was heard thundering up the valley. The big slug had entered his right thigh, breaking the bone as it passed through and grazing the rib cage of his cayuse without stopping. The animal sunfished and then took off, leaving him flat of his back and almost unconscious.

An unspecified period of time passed in his mind before he became aware someone was approaching and presently not too far away. Traven tried to twist around to see who it was, and at the same time, he reached for the big revolver on his hip. However Pell was too swift for him, and he kicked the Marshal on the injured leg only inches from where the blood was seeping. The pain was so intense Elon passed out.

When he awoke, he could see the dark-haired man walking away. He reached again for the revolver but found only an empty holster. His blood was flowing even more so than before the last assault and he was sure that if it wasn't slowed soon, he would blackout again, and that time he might not wake up.

However, right at that moment there was one thing he desired more than living and that was killing the man who had perhaps killed him. With this conviction, he moved with great difficulty until he could touch his recent purchase, a Smith and Wesson Model Two, which had been overlooked by his assailant. Pulling the small flat-barreled revolver, he dropped it twice from his blood-covered hands. Then, holding it with his left and wiping his right hand as dry as he could on his duster, he cursed. Realizing he could do no better, he again took it in his gun hand and cocked it before taking a bead on the man's back, who was now thirty yards distant.

Traven held his breath and took as sharp an aim as he could, but his hand was shaking so badly he dared not fire, for surely if he missed, the man would kill him on the spot. Again, he wiped his hand on the duster, and taking the little silver revolver; he once more cut another fine bead on the back of his target's head and squeezed the trigger.

The little 32 caliber, rim fire cartridge barked more than it boomed, allowing him not to lose sight of his victim.

A puff of dust bounced off the man's back a little left of center, about shoulder blade height. It was a solid hit, and he knew it. A moment later the long rifle fell from the man's hand, and he slowly turned around dropping his left arm.

Pell picked up the heavy Buffalo gun but was unable to aim it one-handed, and thus he tossed it aside pulling instead Traven's Dance Brothers revolver from where he had placed it in the waistband of his trousers.

'Son-of-a-bitch! I'm about to be put under with my own gun,' Traven thought. He then was staring at the huge dark opening of the revolver's muzzle, as Pell pulled the trigger. Both men displayed surprise when the only sound they heard was the hammer snap loudly on a dry nipple.

When he had fallen from his horse, several percussion caps had come loose, and some of them departed the revolver, however one had landed in the small opening at the base of the cylinder. As Pell tried to recock the gun for a second attempt at firing it into the downed Marshal, the cap became lodged between the cylinder and the frame of the gun, jamming it tightly.

At this point, Traven fired a second time, and even though he missed, Pell suddenly decided it was in his best interest to let the man bleed to death where he lay; thus, he turned and ran down the hill.

Elon watched as the slight rise between where he lay and Pell's residence temporarily hid his quarry, but he thought, *'I might just get in a lucky shot as he makes it to the house.'* However, almost as if some unknown force once more protected Tidwell, large flakes began falling as if dumped from the tailgate of a huge wagon in the sky, and any such chance was lost.

Once inside the house, John had Sing Lee apply a bandage to his back. In less than an hour, he was riding east towards Martinsdale, where he could get a stage to Miles City. From there he could transfer over at the new *Northern Pacific Railroad* and be in Bismarck in a couple of days.

It was an hour after sunrise the next day; he awoke shivering and feeling generally quite cold. Tossing his head back and forth, he realized he was lying on a large table in the biggest room he had ever seen. A Chinaman was spooning soup to his lips, and his leg felt like someone was twisting it off.

"Shit!" he exclaimed, and it startled the Chinaman so, he spilled the broth on Traven's bare chest. "Damn that's hot!" he yelled, brushing the yellow liquid away and giving the funny-looking little man a hard glare.

"Glad to see you're back among the living," he heard a familiar voice say.

"What took you so long?" Elon replied, without looking back to where the voice had come from.

"Had some business of my own to take care of," Cliff replied.

Traven looked over at the large clock attached to the wall and squinted his eyes, "What day is this?"

"Thursday. The forth Thursday of November," came the reply.

Satisfied he had not been out more than a day, he then looked straight into Cliff's eyes and asked, "Did you get him?"

"Not yet. Probably would have had I not stopped to save your life, though."

"There you go again, making me feel like I owe you something."

"I don't mind," Cliff said back.

"Well, I do," Traven shot at him.

"I see your old Dance Brothers let you down again," Cliff teased.

"Not at all. It saved my life," Elon said smiling, knowing that would confuse his friend.

"Looked jammed to me," Cliff said, picking up the heavy revolver, looking at it and then laying it back on the table alongside the Sharps, where it had been ever since he had cleared the jam and reloaded the cylinders.

"That's alright. It still saved my life, and so did this," he said reaching for the little S&W he had in his pocket and holding it up for Brown to see.

"Well, I'd like to stay and chew the fat, but I have a job to finish. A job I've been laboring at fer nigh on five years, and I don't want to lose a hot trail; snows building."

"You won't," Traven said.

"You seem awful confident with my abilities."

"No. Just confident with my work," Traven said back, and a slight smile crossed his face.

"I don't follow you, but neither do I have time to wait around to pull and tuck with you right now."

"You'll catch him this time."

"You're sure?"

"I am," the Marshal replied, still smiling.

"I'll send a wire back to Mrs. Dean when I get to the Martinsdale station. Let her know where you are."

"You are so kind," he replied. Then said, "Now if you don't mind, get on with it, so I can get some sleep."

Traven took notice Cliff was favoring his right leg as he headed away, and in a last gesture of defiance he called out, "You look like an old man the way you are limping."

Cliff was placing his hat on his head when he replied, "At least I'm walking," and then he disappeared through the front door.

Leaving the sorrel in the barn, he saddled Ola and moved away, circling the ranch much as Traven had done more than a day before. Eventually he found the trail left by a single rider, some sixteen hours before. They were the only tracks leaving the place made in the last two days, save those made by Traven's horse and he found it dead up on the west ridge only a couple hundred yards from where he had found his wounded friend.

Nodding, he was satisfied with his find. *'Admittedly this here lead is cold but not near as cold as many I have followed during the long trail that has brought me from the Withlacoochee to these high rolling lands of central Montana.'*

Less than an hour later, he rode out of the storm, and although he knew it was closing in behind him for the time being, what lay ahead was brown grass scarred with a single set of tracks.

Five miles later he came upon the remains of a small campfire and other evidence his old enemy had stopped here for the night. Cliff smiled knowing he was closing on him.

On he rode for another hour until he came upon a small bone-yard where it was obvious a little burg had been some time in the past. Now all was gone from there, save a few grave markers made of wood. There beside one of these, he spotted something that just did not fit the scene. Dismounting, he pulled his Winchester from the saddle sheaf and looked carefully around. *'It would be just like that bastard to leave something to distract me while he took a fine bead on my head,'* Cliff thought. However, seeing no movement and realizing it was a far piece to any cover, he relaxed some before walking to the tombstone.

There he stooped and picked up the iron shoe lying against the marker. *'Looks as if someone has thrown it there playing horseshoes, only no one would have been playing here. In fact there is no sign of anyone having been here in a long time, save that lone rider whose trail brought me here.'*

Buffalo grazing on a hill side just north of the Musselshell River

Cliff again looked all around before placing the horseshoe in his saddlebags. While in them, he removed the long sausage of pemmican Black Band had given him a week before and took a large bite from it. Replacing his carbine, he once more mounted and started out, following Tidwell's tracks.

The trail turned slightly south for a while, until it passed some tall, red bluffs, where at one time, the Musselshell had obviously been far out of its banks, and moving at such speed, it had cut the river bed quite wide at this location. Only at this place the hardness of the red clay or the embedded rocks had stopped it from spreading farther north, and its force had cut an almost straight wall there on the prairie.

Evidence showed Tidwell had turned straight south here and headed to the river a hundred yards distant, there allowing his horse to drink, alongside him. Cliff easily spotted the indentations mashed into the soft shoreline where his enemy's knees had been as he drank.

'Those aren't an hour old,' he thought as he forked Ola. "Come on ol' boy, we're closing in on him."

After passing the length of the red bluffs, the tracks once again gradually eased back a little farther north of the river, then once again wandering back, and Cliff wondered if his prey was in full control of his mental facilities. 'Although I ain't seen such, it may be he's losing enough blood to keep from thinking straight. Elon did say he put a slug in him and even that little chunk of lead could cause such.'

After he had stolen on a little further, Cliff spotted a horse standing alone holding one of his front legs high off the ground. He approached the animal cautiously but trusted the alertness of Ola to warn him of the presence of any other living creatures. Finally, he stopped, dismounted and examined the horse's leg. Finding it to be badly swollen, Cliff thought, 'He is surely lame.'

Retrieving the shoe from his saddlebags, he checked and found it to fit the horse's hoof perfectly. He then removed the saddle and bridle from the bay, and patted him on the neck. "If you're still alive when I've finished with business, I'll try and get you back to the barn," he said, turning and looking at the boot prints that led eastward. It was then a knowing smile came to his face, as his resolve was within him.

Thirty minutes later, while skirting a hillside where a small herd of buffalo were grazing among scattered pines, he spotted distinctly in the mud on the north side of the Musselshell, the same boot prints, 'He stopped here and drank again,' Cliff thought, but what he said aloud was, "Must be wearing out, you old bastard."

John had not even realized it when his bay threw the shoe. He was moving as fast as he dared, and it wasn't until the animal began to limp badly did he recognize something was wrong.

Tidwell took the carpetbag that contained all of the folding money that was in his safe, the saddlebags he had stuffed with the gold coins and started off on foot. He thought of shooting the horse to keep it from becoming the prey of wolves or a lion. However, he realized he had failed to bring additional cartridges, and he left the animal to deal with his own problems, as he himself was having to do.

He also realized the wound in his back, even though it was quite painful especially when he tried to carry the heavy saddlebags over that shoulder, was not serious, as long as he could get to a doctor and have the lead removed before a fever set in.

Shortly before noon, Cliff saw the bags laying on the trail. There was some blood on them but not a great deal. They were still nearly filled with the gold. Carrying them back to Ola he said, "Well ol' boy, I think he's pert-near tuckered out. It won't be long now."

It wouldn't have been either, had he not heard a revolver shot just over the next rise. Cliff hurriedly mounted and took off in the direction of the sound.

Less than half-a-mile away, he found a man lying on his back with a small hole in his chest. The blood was still squirting from the wound every time his heart beat, and it was quite obvious to them both, he had minutes to live.

"What happened to you?" Cliff questioned.

"Dumb fool thing I did," he man gulped, coughing as he spoke. "Saw this fellow here laying facedown, and when I went to turn him over, he just up and bored me. Then the bastard stole my mule."

Looking around Cliff asked, "Where's your gun?"

"Never carry one, just my tomahawk and my knife," the man said, and then looking up through cloudy eyes, he inquired, "You the law?"

"No."

"Too bad, it would relieve me to know you'd get him fer me."

"That's one thing you can count on, and I'd like to stay and do some range gossipin', but it ain't the time. I'm sorry, I feel obliged to stay with you but,____." Cliff dropped off his statement.

"No obligation here boy. I'll be fine. 'Sides he who fears death lives poorly, and no jasper can say that about Josephus Harrison."

Cliff nodded, appreciating the courage of the old timer, and then he laid him down, mounted Ola and started off at a gallop.

"Luck to you Mister," Harrison called out with a dry raspy voice, the last words he uttered on this earth.

Cliff knew if he didn't overtake him presently, the mule would out-distance his horse, and that was something he desperately wanted to avoid.

Ola was emitting a cloud of fog with each breath of the below-freezing air, and he knew his faithful steed was giving him all he had. So after a full mile of hard running, Cliff slowed him some to let him get a little wind. Finally, after another mile, he glimpsed them only moments before they disappeared over a slight rise, and no tongue could express nor mind imagine the elation that filled him at that sight.

Cliff slowed Ola even more and soon was just walking him. When he got to the top of the hill, he saw man and beast below some four hundred yards away, at a little running creek.

Tidwell was allowing the animal to drink his fill, while he used the cold water to bathe the ever-increasing fire in his shoulder.

Cliff waited while Ola rested, and only when he saw his quarry mount, did he do the same.

"This time luck is smiling on us Ola," he said, seeing the rising ground leading away from the creek was long and considerably steeper than the deviation leading to it. He then kicked his faithful horse hard with his heel, and Ola gave him a fast run down the slope. Even though he was big for an Appaloosa, Ola was not as long-legged as Red had been, yet somehow the animal seemed to realize the importance of this moment, and he charged down the declivity with a speed greater than Cliff had imagined was in him.

He didn't know why. He had not heard anything, but some unknown sense caused John to look behind him, and there, coming like a thunderbolt from hell, was a rider.

The distance was too great for him to see who it was, but he knew, as sure as the sun rises in the east, it was Reb Brown. He spurred the mule mercilessly until the big Jack started off on a hard run up the steep rise.

When Cliff reached the eddy, he pulled Ola up sharply and jumped from the saddle. Unfortunately, he landed on the swollen ankle heavily causing a streak of pain to shoot forth, and for a moment, it blinded him, but his determination was greater than his pain and he cleared his eyes and took careful aim. *'Why does everything have to be so difficult?'* he questioned.

It would be a long shot at a moving target, but he knew his rifle and the rainbow of its trajectory, and he squeezed the trigger.

The bullet grazed the mule on the right hip, just under the britchin[48], and he began bucking like a sunfisher. In seconds, John Mouton Tidwell was flat of his back on the hard ground.

Suddenly an expression swept over Cliff's face that had not been seen in years. "You are mine at last," he said aloud.

Taking his time, he remounted Ola, and began slow-walking the stout horse up the hill.

Struggling to his feet, Tidwell fired twice at him, but the little 38's fell far short of his target.

Finally, when the man was less than fifty yards away, he aimed and fired again. Once more, he missed, but he did not miss the sight of his old enemy raising the rifle to his shoulder. Neither did he miss watching helplessly as the puff of blue smoke burst from the muzzle of the gun.

The Musselshell Valley Looking Towards The Little Belt Mountains Where Tidwell Died

The 44 slug struck him in the left leg, and he dropped on his face, but gathering the Colt from where it lay only a foot away, again he aimed and fired.

---

48 Britchin: Leather strap arrangement fitting over a mule's hind quarters to keep a saddle from slipping forward.

Cliff heard the whistle of the lead as it passed near his head, and he again fired at the man.

This time the Colt flew from his hand and landed several feet away, and John Tidwell began to crawl towards it. With only inches before reaching its stock, he saw an old, well-worn, brown cavalry boot step between his hand and the revolver. He turned over and looked up. With tongue cleaving to the roof of his mouth he pleaded, "No, no, don't kill me."

Cliff looked at the pitiful, whining creature laying on the ground and spit. Raising his left eyebrow slightly, he lifted the Yellowboy where Tidwell could see it before he spoke to his old enemy, "You see this carbine?"

Tidwell's face was twisted with a combination of pain and fear, and with narrowing eyes he wondered why such a question would be asked but gave no reply.

"It belonged to the woman you murdered in Georgia."

A frown swept Tidwell's forehead as he thought back, and then it suddenly came to him and he replied, "The newspaperwoman?"

Cliff slowly shook his head, wondering why Tidwell would say that when they both knew Mrs. Gillie had not been murdered. However, the thought did not dig deep enough into the channels of his mind to distract him from completing his long ago promise, and with determination and bitterness he replied, "No. My wife."

Suddenly the New Englander realized why this man had dogged his trail so hard and so long, and an emotion he had not felt in more years than he could remember, if he ever had, grabbed tight to his very mind, and true terror rushed into his eyes.

Cliff raised the Winchester, and taking deliberate aim at Tidwell's body, he began squeezing the trigger.

John Mouton Tidwell watched as the man's finger began to gradually move back, and he knew his fate was moments away and panic swept throughout his body.

The instant the bright flash appeared in the muzzle of the rifle, he remembered the same flash appearing in the muzzle of Frank Coleman's musket, so many years before[49].

Cliff's well-aimed round twisted its way through the black vest and boiled shirt into Tidwell's chest.

---

49 Bright flash appeared in the muzzle: See 'The Withlacoochee Renegades' Chapter Fourteen.

Ejecting the spent round, he levered another into the chamber and fired again. Then he continued doing so until the hammer was striking on an empty chamber. Still, he worked the lever and squeezed the trigger, but there was the same dull sound of metal against metal, not followed by anything else.

John Tidwell had nine holes in him, most in the chest, but two Cliff had directed at his twisted face. Now looking at the bloody mixture of bone and flesh, which had been the source of his reason for living for so long, he smiled slightly at a new thought, before he spoke, "Well Tidwell, tonight the wolves will eat well." Then he reached for the large bundle of folded bills that could be seen protruding from an inner coat pocket, and he said one last thing to the dead man, "I do believe these belong to Mrs. Hickey."

Upon reaching Ola he stuffed the greenbacks in his saddlebags along with the gold. When finished, with a long sigh he felt some relief of the weight that had so long tugged at his shoulders. His insides suddenly felt strange, they were filled neither with fear nor sickness, rather with the lack of gall and adrenalin which he had endured for so long.

He wet the insides of his lower lip with his tongue before swallowing, and nodding his head in satisfaction. Next he reloaded his Yellowboy and slid it home in its scabbard.

Raising his head, he looked out over the seat of his saddle at the big open of the rolling Montana prairie and low clouds above the snow-capped mountains to the north, and suddenly he started crying. Not sobbing, but the tears burst forth uncontrollably and began flowing from his eyes, and he spoke aloud, "Nadine, Nadine."

It was then Ola reared, obviously startled by something, and this caused Cliff to have to step back. Looking up, he saw the horse's ears shoot forward almost touching at their tips, and an expression of near panic was seen in the great stallion's eyes. Cliff did not know what could be behind him, causing such a fright in Ola. He knew it could not be Tidwell, but something was there, something fearful, and his rifle was on the other side of his horse.

Slowly he lowered his hand to the revolver stock, and then with all the speed he had in him, he whirled and drew the long barreled Colt, but what he gazed upon did not frighten him as it had his horse, rather it caused confusion.

There before him, from as far as he could see to the north and back to the south, was a new scene. Gone were the rolling hills and the Little Belt Mountains, gone was the sage and the brown grass, gone were the splattered patches of dirty white where the last remnants of a passing storm had clung to the short bushes, and gone was the blue sky of Montana. Instead, he gazed upon a green forest, split by a black water stream. Some of the maples along its banks had begun to turn yellow and orange, as they do this time of year, and suddenly he realized he was seeing the Withlacoochee River, as if he was standing on Bass' Ferry looking towards Sam's Tree. It was then he saw the ripples in the water, and the lone swimmer headed towards the west side of the river. When she ascended the bank, he realized it was Nadine. She stopped just before entering the forest, turned to him and smiled, before walking forward and disappearing behind a giant sweet gum tree, whence came the sound of a mockingbird making melody.

The whole scene was more than he could comprehend, "Nadine, Nadine wait," he called out, but it was no use. She was gone, and suddenly he realized, straight ahead through the hammock where she had gone, less than a mile, was the cemetery at Estherbrook.

Again, Ola reared, and Cliff turned and pulled hard on his reins before quickly whirling back, hoping desperately for another glimpse of her, but now it was all gone. Once more, he saw the rolling hills and the sage, and there in a twisted clump was the body of the demon who had harmed his life for so many years. Now, he did not cry openly, however his eyes did fill once more with tears, when he realized she had come to him this one last time showing her approval of him finishing his promise.

Cliff buried the old sourdough with a covering of small rocks and gave him a salute before saying, "I fulfilled my promise to you, if you don't already know that."

Moving on he came upon Tidwell's horse and he pulled the other three shoes from the bay. Taking his one soiled shirt from his saddlebags, he managed to bind the leg on the lame horse, and then he led the mule and the bay slowly back to *The Little Judith Ranch*. There, he put the mule and the lame gelding in the barn, before he slow-walked into the ranch house to wait out the storm.

The mild winter Montana had enjoyed thus far, became little more than a remembrance. That night, after the sun moved beyond the western mountains, the temperature began plummeting south. Before daybreak, it was eight below with little promise of a high above freezing.

'I could wait. Be smart to wait, but Miss Cimarron and the James' will be worrying. Better get on with it.'

Cliff finished the cup of hot tea Sing Lee had brewed and then slipped into his fleece-lined buckskin before placing his old hat on his head, "Be back soon. Be ready to travel when I do," he said to the little man and was rewarded with a strong nod of the head and the patter of soft shoed feet moving quickly away.

He hitched the sorrel he had ridden from Blackcat Creek, alongside the horse Tidwell had ridden from town to a hay-wagon found in the barn. He was not sure they would pull together, but he had little other choice. Next, he made a bed of horse blankets for Elon to ride on. Sing Lee would drive the team.

After being carried to the wagon and gently laid on the blankets, Elon asked, "You fix the shoe on that nag?"

Cliff looked over at the gelding and answered, "I pulled all of them, that's him yonder in the corral."

"No, I mean on this nag."

Cliff looked at him and then at the hitched horse, with a questioning expression.

"I pulled all, save one, a' the nails out of at least one shoe on all the animals in the barn. That way, if he was to get by me, he wouldn't get too far, too fast."

Cliff smiled and then walked up to the black and lifted his left front leg. Sure enough, there was only one nail holding the shoe in place. Turning back to Traven he asked, "This the only one?"

Traven nodded his head, "One loose shoe per horse."

"Pretty clever, these Travens," Cliff said to Sing Lee and winked. The Chinaman smiled broadly before winking back.

Bea Desmond, upon hearing what had happened between John and Sally Mustang, immediately went to Coker's store where the post office was. She knew a telegraph office had recently been installed in a portion of it, set aside for that purpose. There she wired *The Saint Louis Detective Agency* concerning her discovery of the whereabouts of Jean Mouton.

Later she explained that during the entire time she had been in Copperopolis, she had been working undercover, gathering evidence on Mouton and Ephraim Glaze. She informed them of the illegal transfers of Will Hickey's money into joint accounts of their own, here in the *Big Sky Bank,* as well as other locations.

Although Ace Spade did not believe a word of her tale, when she pointed out to the officials it had really been his idea for her to go undercover, thereby effecting the discovery of the conspiracy; the agency heaped praise on him, and he kept his mouth shut about her lies.

Cliff had planned to leave sooner, but when she implored, he could not refuse and stayed until she was pronounced a wife in the spring. Now he was packed and ready to depart, he turned to his friends. He kissed Ginny on the cheek when she gave him a red plaid bandana filled with food goods she had prepared for his trip. He shook hands with first Otie, then with Blackcat, and when he turned to Laramie he took the boy and held him close.

When they separated, Laramie removed his hat and holding it between his thumbs and forefingers, he spoke, "There is something I need ____. I, I must ask you."

Cliff nodded his head.

"Before he died, did he say anything about Me-Ma?"

Cliff looked into the pleading eyes of the lad, then he nodded his head and lied to him, "Yes. I didn't want to tell you, but he said she is dead. Killed accidentally in a fall from her hawse when they were fleeing them Arapaho. You know, when they left the stage. Broke her neck," he said tenderly. "She died instantly."

Suddenly a huge yoke lifted from his young shoulders and he smiled. "Thanks for telling me. It relieves me, knowing she is not being mistreated."

Cliff nodded his head again, and then he turned to the recent bride and hugged her tightly before he said, "You gon'a have your hands full keeping him out of trouble, you know."

"Yes, I know," Cimarron replied smiling. There was moisture in her eyes but gladness in her expression.

"Good bye, Mrs. Traven."

"Good bye, Mr. Brown."

Lastly, he turned to the tall man leaning on a single crutch. "Well, it's been a pleasure." Then he walked around to his saddlebags and took one of the opentop 1871 Colts he had bought from Captain Inglis. He rubbed it affectionately, remembering the many days and nights he had carried it in his pommel holsters. He had strong feelings for the assembly of those finely machined metal parts. It was something special to him, something from a better time in his life. Nonetheless, he felt the call to part with it, and moving back he handed it to the Marshal. "Here, I can't leave Montana thinking you are going to try and keep the peace with that old cap buster."

Elon started to put up an argument but considered better of it. Instead, he said, "Where are you going?"

"Oh, back to the old states I reckon. I've been on the owl hoot trail ever since ol' nigger Polk was shot."

"When did you shoot him?" Traven implored.

"I didn't," he replied, then taking a long breath and giving his head a couple of short nods, he added, "but it were back in sixty-six."

"Oh Reb, that is such a long time," Cimarron said tenderly to him.

"Yeah, I figured you'd be headed back to Georgia a'for long," her husband added.

Cliff looked towards where Dixie lay for a few long seconds, then spoke without changing the direction of his gaze, "I have no one left in Georgia anymore. Everyone I loved there is dead," he paused. "I reckon I'll just stop off in Missouri and see what develops."

Mounting, the tall, lean man then touched his boot heels to Ola's sides and the big stud moved south, towards the docks at the river port of Coulson.

As they watched the lone rider move away, leading a tall pack mule, Cimarron spoke, "I wonder what he meant by that."

"Hell, thar's no telling. A great deal of what he says makes no sense to me," her husband replied, slowly shaking his head.

Today some 130 plus years later, were one to feel the need to go to Copperopolis, they, like me, would be somewhat disappointed. White Sulphur Springs is easy to locate. I found several good and friendly people there. I enjoyed my stay, although it is not the thriving metropolis it once was.

Also Martinsdale is still there, at least some of the old weathered buildings are, and a few folk who call it home but not many.

However, when you look for Copperopolis, you will find gone are the great copper mines bored into the southern slope of the Castle Mountains, just south of the North Fork of the Musselshell River, all 21 claims, which made this region so famous in the late nineteenth century.

Gone as well is *The White Castle* saloon, and Hank Groll's newspaper, even the *Big Sky Bank*. Any modern-day seekers would be unable to locate Marshal Traven's office or even Sally Mustang's grave. In fact, they would be able to find almost nothing of this once growing community. For today, it is only a ghost of a town; there is not even a historical marker along Highway 12 in the beautiful mountains where it once stood.

Locals there refer to it simply as 'Copper', and a few will point out some shale dumps from one of the mines, but that is about all. It is but a memory in the minds of far too few who bother with such, and after the state paved the Carroll Stage Road in these parts, even some of them don't agree exactly where the town stood.

Nonetheless, it is a record in the history of Montana but only a small piece of that history and one not very many people care about, simply lost in the turning of the earth to most but not to descendants of Clifford James Brown.

The trail of Clifford James, 'Reb' Brown ends here, unless one was to go back and read the last paragraph in The Withlacoochee Renegades, Book Two of The Owl Hoot Trail trilogy.

However, it is not the last word on all of those who rode with Reb Brown.

To learn more about the life of Buckshot Gunter and Jacque Louis Laramie Patay, read the book, The Big Open, also by T.H. Bear.

Chronicles of The Long Trail

I received requests from my readers for a listing of the main characters. Some names of people and places the reader will find more than once. There are others in the story, but the need to remember them is not important. Below is such a list:

Georgia

Clifford James Brown:	aka Reb
Nadine Brown:	aka Nadine Maynard, Nadine Tipper, Reb's wife
John M. Tidwell:	Murderer of Cliff's wife, aka Jean Mouton
Sam Brooks:	Ran the Stage Stop at Estherbrook Florida
Esther Brooks:	Sam's wife
Ola:	Cliff's Appaloosa named for the great chief Osceola
Rufus Bullock:	Governor of Georgia
Hannibal Kimball:	Richest man in Georgia at the time
Connie Cabela:	Hannibal's niece
Charles Cabela:	Connie's husband
Iris Damon:	Charles' lover

Missouri

At Poplar Bluff

Bill Percival:	Sheriff of Butler County
Nora Percival:	The Sheriff's wife
The Black River:	A dark water stream running through Poplar Bluff
The Black River:	A Hotel near the river
The Poplar Bluff:	Hotel in Poplar Bluff
Miss Thelma:	Transplanted Tennessean who owned a dress shop

At Kent

William Telfair Hickey::	aka Will, owner of Kent
Lesley Hickey:	Will's wife, aka Honey Brodel, former singer in Detroit
Troy Meyers:	Horse Whisperer at Kent
Wanda Meyers:	Troy's wife
George:	Black house servant
Hanna Mae:	George's woman
Chesterfield:	Mrs. Hickey's favorite horse
Gray Wind:	A dapple gray stallion at Kent

Kent Riders

Lance Spain:	Foreman at Kent
Charlie Nash:	Former Kent hand
John Striker:	Kent Rider
Dusty Agar:	Kent Rider
Jeremiah Star:	Kent Rider
Tyrone Dunn:	Kent Rider
Fuzzy Karn:	Kent Rider
Windy Burr:	Kent Rider
Eddie Ford:	Kent rider who shot Granny Vernell

Ozark People

Granny Vernell:	Old woman who helped nurse Lesley
Horace Fleetwing:	Ad's brother

Adam Fleetwing: aka Ad, Horace's brother
Fleetwing's and Alsop's: Feuding mountain families

Kansas

J.D. Mather: One of John Tidwell's alias'
Sydney Coey: aka Muley
Steve Boron: Partners with Muley and J.D. Mather
John Fisher: aka King Fisher built The Border Outpost

In Dodge City

Charles Basset: Sheriff of Ford County
Chester Yates: Hostler
Chad Cheltenham: Cattleman from NM
Charles Rath: Store owner and city official
J. G. McDonald: Store owner and city official
James Hanrahan: City official
Chalk Beeson: Owner of the Long Branch
Cornelia: Whore at the Long Branch
Asa Nixon: Town marshal and later JP

Texas

John Rumans: Texas cattleman
Tom Smith: Texas cowboy
Tyrell Johnson: Married Tom's older sister Josie
Josie Smith: Sister Tom's younger sister
April Smith: Sister
Mary Smith: Tom's Mother

Reb's chosen few who rode with Rumans' herd

Billie Ellis:	Lost his right eye at Shiloh
Johnny McGee:	Billie's buddy
Pete MacSlade:	Lost his left arm at Fredericksburg
J. J. Carlson:	Rode with Colonel Herbert's **Battalion from Tucson**
Tommy Walker:	Rode with Jeb Stuart during the war
Ethan Adams:	Sharpshooter in the war
Shep Adams:	Ethan's twin brother
Nathan Denver:	Rode with The Beaver Creek Rifles during the war
Billy Anderson:	A Sergeant in The Red River Dragoon's during the war
Tom Dawson:	Rode with The Red River Dragoon's during the war
Jubal Currie:	Rode with The Red River Dragoon's
Cyrus Cox:	Rode with The Red River Dragoon's
Nathan Denver:	Rode with The Red River Dragoon's
Jubal Currie:	Rode with The Red River Dragoon's
Jimmy Langworthy:	aka Dancer Rumans outfit's Little Mary
Cookey:	Typical nickname for a Chuckwagon cook

In Colorado

York:	Jean's partner
Tennessee Lobell:	aka Porsche
Lola Rodgers:	Owner of Miss Lola's Parlor House
Sir Jonathan Wesley Brooke:	Piano player at Miss Lola's
Quai Toi:	Chinese cook, aka Toy
Little Toy:	Half American- half Chinese boy used as a gopher
Jewell Allen:	Ran a Parlor House in Cheyenne.

The Table Mountain Boys

Loomis:	Leader of the bandits
Pike:	One of the bandits
Rome:	One of the bandits
Fargo:	One of the bandits
Bud Casin:	One of the bandits
Oiley Wick:	One of the bandits
Micah:	One of the bandits

At The Dale

Joseph A. Slade:	Built the Virginia Dale Stage Station
Virginia Slade:	Jack's wife
Spuds Lords:	Owner of The Virginia Dale during the siege
Sarah:	Spuds' wife
Sissy:	Spuds' daughter
Old Woman:	Sarah's mother
Alex Culpepper:	Former Union sharpshooter
Yazoo:	Stage Driver
Chigger Morgan:	Blacksmith & Wheelwright
Eve:	One of Lola Rodgers' loaned out girls
Faye:	One of Lola Rodgers' loaned out girls
Frenchy:	One of Lola Rodgers' loaned out girls
Sky Warrior:	Ute chief
Lone Fox:	Ute warrior who kidnapped Porsche

In Wyoming

Celeste Patay:	French Canadian wife of Jacques, mother of Laramie
Jacques Patay:	French Canadian trapper & owner of sutler's store at Fort Laramie
Jacque Louis Laramie Patay:	Son of Celeste & Jacques

Circle Rocking AR Ranch

James Donald Moore:	aka Jimmy Don owner of Circle Rocking AR Ranch
Elaine Dumas:	Moore's wife
Gilberto Rodriguez:	Foreman of Circle Rocking AR Ranch
Arturo Mendoza:	Elaine's rider
Ellie:	aka Ethel, Elaine's sister
Carlos Rodriguez:	One of Gil's sons shot at Don's hanging
Pedro:	Gil's youngest son
Juan:	Vaquero
Juanita Gaztambide:	Gil's sister
Absalom Gaztambide:	Juanita's son
Ishté Shipite:	aka Black Band, Crow brave

Reb's Texas Boys

Ethan Adams:	Shep's brother the Sharpshooter
Shep Adams:	One of Reb's Texas boys
Billy Ellis:	One of Reb's Texas boys
J. J. Carlson:	One of Reb's Texas boys
Tommy Walker:	One of Reb's Texas boys
Nathan:	One of Reb's Texas boys
Tyrell:	One of Reb's Texas boys
Ron:	One of Reb's Texas boys
Howard:	One of Reb's Texas boys
Tommy:	One of Reb's Texas boys

In Cheyenne

Mr. Walcott:	Prominent cattleman in early Wyoming
Big Ed:	Owner of Frenchy's Saloon in Cheyenne
Deputy Stillwell:	Cheyenne jailer
The Dyers House:	Hotel in Cheyenne where Reb stayed
The Inter Ocean Hotel:`	Cheyenne's finest
Ames Boarding House:	A cheap rooming house where cow boys often stayed when their money began to run low

The Wolf Creek Outfit

The Wolf Creek Ranch:	Owned by The Birmingham Social Society
Allen Moreton:	Nephew of Sir Frances Moreton American and representative of The Birmingham Social Society
Major John Brown:	aka John Tidwell- Jean' Mouton- The Wolf Creek Ranch superintendent
P. C. Defray:	Foreman of The Wolf Creek Ranch
Slim Carver:	Wolf Creek rider
Gab Easterman:	Wolf Creek rider
Omaha:	Wolf Creek rider
Bullbat Drew:	Wolf Creek rider
Russo:	Wolf Creek rider
Snake Canyon:	Wolf Creek rider
Bun White:	Wolf Creek rider
Billy Dees:	The first to fall to the Whitworths

In Laramie City

Pike Pepper:	Sheriff of Albany County
Dennis King:	Attorney
Jesse Owens:	Laramie Undertaker
Doc Lathrop:	Doctor in Laramie

Montana

John Tidwell:	aka Louis de la Motte, who seduced the Queen Marie Antoinette in France
Russell Thorp:	Owner of The Rawhide Ranch
Jake Stoner:	Rawhide Ranch hand
Jack Gilmore:	Stage driver
Bill Mansfield:	Stage shotgun
Emmett Parkhurst:	Gambler on the stage
Dale Yukon:	A wolfer on the stage
Ben Maynard:	Gambler and Miner
Stony Silverton:	Gambler who was shot
James McAndow:	Owner of a Bozeman to Bismarck Stage Stop

Luther Kelly:	Yellowstone Kelly, a scout for the army
Muggins Taylor:	The dispatch rider that carried the news of the Custer massacre
Horace Countryman:	Owner of the Stillwater Stage Station
Frank Quinn:	Ranch owner
Jim Fesslor:	aka Bearpaw, stage driver
Augustus Spade:	aka Ace, detective for the St. Louis Detective Agency
Henry Cain:	Owner of a saw mill on Indian Creek near Placerville
Andy Sharp:	Owner of a ranch near Placerville
Jim Slade::	Deputy U. S. Marshal in Coulson
Perry McAdow:	aka Bud, owner of a saloon in Coulson
George B. Hulme:	Owner of saloon and hotel in Coulson
Tommy Randolph:	Cowboy at the Albermarle Ranch
T. J. Jefferson:	Owned the Albermarle Ranch

Bandit Renegades

Two Bucks:	Leader of the Bandit renegade
Lobo:	One of the Bandit renegades
Lefty:	One of the Bandit renegades
Ben Curry:	One of the Bandit renegades

In Copperopolis

John Pell:	aka Tidwell used in Copperopolis
Bea Desmond:	aka Windy Willows ran White **Castle Saloon**
Brigitte Daiquiris:	aka Sally Mustang ran the Musselshell Saloon,
Noel Coker:	Owner of the General Store
Bragg Crouch:	Owner of the Blacksmith shop
Fannie Sharpshire:	A widow, owned a restaurant and boarding house
Rufus Orr:	Owner of The Bunkhouse
Sophie Orr:	Rufus' wife
Gentry Beck:	Sophie's brother
Jack McGinnis:	Owner of the Drug Store
Ephraim Glaze:	Copperopolis' Bank President

Tuff Kohrs: Bank clerk
Gideon Merewether: Undertaker
Crouch: Store Owner
Texas Jess.:   Owner of The Alamo restaurant
Miss Beverly Moore: Owner of a dress shop
Elon Traven: Copper's town marshal
George Saddler: A bullwhacker aka Whisky George
Henry Groll: Newspaper man in Copperopolis
Marsha: Hank Groll's wife
Micajah Ezzard: A tinsmith
Jewell Ezzard: Micajah's wife
Kyle Ezzard: Micajah's son
Alida and Alvah Ezzard: 10 year old daughters
Cimarron Dean: Ezzard's oldest daughter
Doctor Cavenaugh: Copperopolis surgeon
Barry Beal: Telegrapher

At The Blackcat Ranch

Otis James: aka Blackcat, Owner of The Blackcat Ranch
Ginny: Blackcat's wife
Otie: Blackcat's son
Ginger: Blackcat's daughter

At The Judith Ranch

York: Ranch Foreman
Loco: Ranch Hand
Mesquite: Ranch Hand
Billy Nelson: Ranch Hand
Gila: Ranch Hand
Bitterroot: Ranch Hand
The Deacon: Ranch Hand
Simon Maxwell: Ranch Hand
Seth Merrill: Ranch Hand
Tim Levi: Ranch Hand
Sing Lee: Ranch's Chinese Cook

Waco's Texicans who worked for The Judith Ranch

Captain Wallace Evens: aka Waco
Jeptha Wesley: aka Jep
Zebulon Grandville: aka Zeb
Buckie Brazos: Wrangler
Charlie Lone Wolf: Half-bred Kickapoo Scout

Timeline

1800 — Jonathan Erick Hickey Senior, Will's grandfather born in Kent England.

1814 — Louis Brown was born in Grayson County Kentucky. Esther Hobart Morris born in a Tioga County, New York.

1817 — John Morris born in Illinois.

1825 — Jonah was born.
John Tidwell, aka Jean Mouton was born October 10.

1826 — Ishté Shipite born in the Valley of the Greasy Grass.

1827 — Titus born.

1829 — Schultheiss family fled Salzburg Austria.
Jacques Patay born.

1830 — William Telfair Hickey born in Folkestone, Kent, in southeast England.
Pebbles Stone was born Madison County Florida.

1833 — Sholtz family arrived in NYC.
Arthur Langford Houghton was born.

1835 — Erick Hickey Jr. & brother Bartholomew arrive in Quebec, Canada.

1836 — Ernie Teachman was born.

1838 — Marline Yates Teachman was born.
Two Bucks was born.

1839 — Louis Brown married Addie.
June 1 Celeste Patay, a beautiful blonde girl, was born southeastern Quebec.

1841 — Jonah married Vashti Jude.
Samuel Brown was born.

1843 — Cliff was born with steel gray eyes.

1844 — Rob Scogins was born in Missouri.

1845 — Carol Steele was born in Shelby County, Missouri.

1846 — Nadine Maynard was born in Clay County, Missouri.
Johnny Brown was born.
Elaine Dumas was born in Texas.
Leslie Brodel was born in Michigan.

1848 — Charles Scoggins was born in Missouri.

1849 — Titus runs over the Mullier brothers.
Brigitte Le Petit Daiquiris, was born near New Iberia La.

1850 — Titus and Jonah were in NYC.
Connie Steele was born in Missouri.
Ash Scoggins was born in Lafayette County, Missouri.

1852 — Phil was born to Titus and Monia Lissia Sholtz.

1855 — Titus killed Peter Saltsman, changed his name to Edward fled with Reata Nylen.

1856—Tennessee Lobell aka Porsche was born near Jennings, Louisiana.

1858— October 29, the first store opens in a small frontier town in Colorado Territory that would soon be called Denver.
Two Bucks, a twenty-year-old warrior, raided with the Comanche.

1859—June 1 the Patay's left the Illinois River and entered the Mississippi.

1860—September 1 Jacque Louis Laramie Patay was born at Ft. Laramie.

1862—Titus killed Reata in Tennessee.
Reb took the Colt from John Morris in Lebanon Tenn.

1863—Tom Smith's father and two brothers rode off with The Red River Dragoons.

1864—Cliff first saw a Henry Rifle.
Oct 30, Helena, Montana, was founded after miners discover gold.

1865—Cliff was released from Point Lookout Prison in Maryland.
Lt. Caspar Collins was killed near at Platte Bridge Station in July.

1866— John M. Tidwell was appointed commissioner of the Division of Freedman's Bureau.
Cliff fled Georgia, to ride The Owl Hoot Trail.
Ben Holliday sold his vast stage holdings to the California firm of Wells, Fargo and Company.

1867— November 19, The Denver Pacific Railway and Telegraph Company was incorporated, linking Denver with the UP at Cheyenne.

1869— Rob Scoggins was murdered.

1870—Wild Bill Hickman kills Ed Sholtz.

Cliff and Nadine marry.
The first all woman jury was sworn in March 7, 1870 in Laramie.

1871 — Tillie was murdered.
Addie Brown died.

1872 — September 16 Reb finds Leslie injured from a fall from her horse.

1873 — January 30 Bill Percival killed Lance Spain.
In April the town's name was changed from Buffalo City to Dodge City.

1874 — Mouton, York and Brown arrive in Denver.

1875 — The second week of December, Laramie asked Black Band to help him find his mother.

1876 — June 25 Custer is killed.
June 28 Celeste is captured by Arapaho.

1877 — Hank Groll's first edition went out on November the 1[st.]
In the winter Henry Cain built a saw mill along Indian Creek near Placerville.
April Fools Day found John Pell the new owner of *The Little Judith Ranch*, carrying the Lazy R-J brand.
September 26 *The White Castle* saloon opened.

1878 — By the spring there were a dozen small spreads within fifty miles of Copperopolis.
November 27, Reb Brown encountered Tidwell for the last time.

1883 — November 1, Blackcat's land was officially recorded.

The photo on the back cover reveals the ridge near where Copperopolis once stood. About a mile from the mines.

www.ingramcontent.com/pod-product-compliance
Lightning Source LLC
Chambersburg PA
CBHW032250020726
47495CB00001B/39